Flying

THE PERSONAL HISTORY,
ADVENTURES, EXPERIENCES
& OBSERVATIONS
OF PETER LEROY

BY ERIC KRAFT

(SO FAR)

Flying

ERIC KRAFT

PICADOR · NEW YORK

Author's notes: The illustrations on pages 43 and 159 are adaptations of an illustration by Stewart Rouse that first appeared on the cover of the August 1931 issue of *Modern Mechanics and Inventions*. The boy at the controls of the aerocycle doesn't particularly resemble Peter Leroy—except, perhaps, for the smile. The passage from *Antique Scandals* on page 37 is a fabrication; as far as I know, no such book exists. The photograph on page 39 is from *Elements of Aeronautics*, by Francis Pope and Arthur S. Otis, copyright © 1941 by the World Book Company, Yonkers-on-Hudson, New York. The page from *Impractical Craftsman* on page 44 is an adaptation of a page from the August 1931 issue of *Modern Mechanics and Inventions*. The advertisement for Dædalus Welding on page 68 is based on an advertisement for Hohner Harmonicas that appeared in the September 1937 issue of *Modern Mechanix*. "Build a Power Saw from Scrap Parts" on page 88 is based on an article in the May 1936 issue of *Modern Mechanix & Inventions*. The frontispiece from *Elements of Aeronautics* reproduced on page 114 is, in fact, the frontispiece from *Elements of Aeronautics*. Peter's conversation with the neighborhood character known as Baudelaire on pages 163 and 164 is based on a passage in Baudelaire's *The Painter of Modern Life*, translated by Jonathan Mayne, and the photograph of the neighborhood character is in fact Nadar's 1863 portrait of Baudelaire. The part of the Electro-Flyer on page 190 is played by the Starlite Electric Runabout, a prototype conceived by the Nu-Klea Automobile Corp. of Lansing, Michigan, in 1960, but never manufactured; the image is reproduced from an advertising postcard in the author's collection. The passage on aerodynamic lift on page 199, and the accompanying illustration, are from pages 104, 105, 112, and 113 of *Elements of Aeronautics*, by Francis Pope and Arthur S. Otis, copyright © 1941 by the World Book Company, Yonkers-on-Hudson, New York. The photograph of the helicopter in the poster on page 404 was taken by Douglas Bailey for the U.S. Army Corps of Engineers and is in the public domain. The mathematics problem on page 465 originally appeared in *Elementary Differential Equations* by Lyman M. Kells (copyright © 1954 by the McGraw-Hill Book Company, Inc.), which I purchased in the bookstore at the New Mexico Institute of Mining and Technology in the summer of 1960, when I was a student in a summer institute for high school students sponsored by the National Science Foundation. The answer is $xy^{-2} + x^5 = c$. The second of the two circuit diagrams on page 486 is adapted from a diagram in the June 1966 issue of *Popular Electronics*. Except for those credited above, all illustrations and photographs are the author's.

www.picadorusa.com
www.erickraft.com

Picador® is a U.S. registered trademark and is used by St. Martin's Press under license from Pan Books Limited.

For information on Picador Reading Group Guides, please contact Picador.
E-mail: readinggroupguides@picadorusa.com

Library of Congress Cataloging-in-Publication Data

Kraft, Eric.
    Flying / Eric Kraft.—1st ed.
        p. cm.
    ISBN-13: 978-0-312-42872-3
    ISBN-10: 0-312-42872-3
    1. Flying-machines—Fiction.   2. Hoaxes—Fiction.   I. Kraft, Eric. Taking Off.   II. Kraft, Eric. On the Wing.   III. Kraft, Eric. Flying Home.   IV. Title.
    PS3561.R22F69 2009
    813'.54—dc22

Parts of this book first appeared in *Taking Off* (St. Martin's Press, 2006) and *On the Wing* (St. Martin's Press, 2007).

APR 2 3 2009

10 9 8 7 6 5 4 3 2

FOR MAD

Part One

....

TAKING OFF

I'd often dreamed of going
West to see the country,
always vaguely planning and
never taking off.

—JACK KEROUAC,
On the Road

LETS AND HINDRANCES, VIEWS
AND PROSPECTS

• •

When a man sits down to write a history,—tho' it be but the history of
Jack Hickathrift or Tom Thumb, he knows no more than his heels what
lets and confounded hindrances he is to meet with in his way,—or what
a dance he may be led, by one excursion or another, before all is
over. . . . For, if he is a man of the least spirit, he will have fifty deviations
from a straight line to make with this or that party as he goes along,
which he can no ways avoid. He will have views and prospects to himself perpetually soliciting his eye, which he can no more help standing
still to look at than he can fly. . . .

—Laurence Sterne, *Tristram Shandy*

WHEN I WAS fifteen, I made a solo flight from Babbington, New
York, on the South Shore of Long Island, to Corosso, New
Mexico, in the foothills of the San Mateo Mountains, on the banks of
the Rio Grande, in a single-seat airplane that I had built in the family
garage. Because I was still a boy, a teenager, the feat was breathlessly re-
counted in the Babbington newspaper, the *Reporter*, and in the regional
press as well. There were errors in those reports, and the errors have
been repeated in anniversary recaps at intervals since then. The errors
have now been so fully sanctioned by repetition that they have the ring
of truth. From time to time my day is interrupted by phone calls from
eager interviewers who want me to tell the story again. Without exception, they want me to retell the story as it has already been reported. I
have tried, during some of those telephone interviews, to correct a few
errors of fact and interpretation, but my efforts have been dismissed
with the condescending politeness that we employ with those whom
we regard as having had their wits enfeebled by time.

Because I have consistently failed to set the record straight by
phone, I have for some time intended to prepare a full and accurate
written account that would do the job without my having to pause in
the telling to endure the protests of reporters who accuse me of being
"modest" when I am only trying to be, at long last, honest. When I fi-

nally began writing that account—at some point during the writing of the first part of it, which chronicles my preparations for the trip—I stepped back from it, paused, and read what I had written. I found, to my surprise, that it *was* full and accurate, and that I had set a standard of completeness and accuracy that I was going to have to strive to maintain in the parts of the tale that were still to be written.

In the spirit of completeness and accuracy, I will confess to you here that the account that I have found myself writing is not quite the account that I had intended to provide. I'll be frank: I had not intended to set the record quite so straight as I have done. I had intended to allow some of the old errors to stand—the ones that conveyed an impression of me as more capable and my trip as more successful than either actually was—and I had intended to perpetuate the myth of myself as a daring flyboy, the "Birdboy of Babbington," the epitome of American ingenuity and pluck, teen division. My intentions altered after I revisited Babbington, the start and finish of that famous flight.

As you will soon see, I revisited the town because I received a note from a former schoolmate urging me to see what had become of the place during my absence.

Following that visit, upon my return to Manhattan, I sat down to write, full of good intentions, determined, focused, a man with a mission. Almost at once I began to meet with lets and confounded hindrances, difficulties and disappointments, and even a personal disaster—an injury to my beloved Albertine—that delayed my work, stretching it out over a far longer time than I had intended to give it. This unexpected extension of the time given to thinking about what I wanted to say led me to compose a more complete account than I had intended. For me, you see, the lets and hindrances abetted my love for a full account, because they gave me time, and, given time, I tend to wander, and when I wander the byways of memory, surprising views and prospects solicit my eye. I pause. I look. I enjoy the view. I explore the prospects. I add the view or prospect to my account. I can't help myself. I am by nature digressive, within limits.

My friend Mark Dorset, an unaffiliated academic who specializes in human motivation, has written at some length on digression, and some of what he has said applies to me:

Digression is antithetical to, but dependent on, the intention to progress along the straight and narrow way. In order to digress, one must first be progressing. One cannot be sidetracked unless one is first on track. One cannot stray unless one is first on the right path. One cannot turn aside unless one is first moving straight ahead. Proust famously pointed out that we cannot remember what has not occurred; he might just as well have pointed out that we cannot digress from a route that we had not intended to take.

If one's honest answer to the question "Where are you trying to go?" is "I don't know," then one cannot digress.

To digress, then, you must begin by traveling a route that will get you where you intend to go. You must have a goal and a plan for achieving it in order to depart from it. You cannot digress from the right path unless you are already on it.

The easiest path to digress from is the straight and narrow, the straight and strait, rather than the broad way that rambles on its own. The slightest deviation from the straight and narrow is a digression, but the broad way allows a lot of wandering within it, so that one may amble a meandering course and still be within its limits, not really digressing at all.

The digressive thinker is by nature an explorer rather than a point-

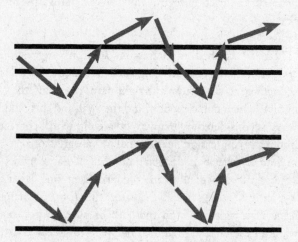

The slightest deviation from the straight and narrow is a digression [top], but the broad way allows a lot of wandering within it [bottom], so that one may amble a meandering course and still be within its limits, not really digressing at all.

A-to-point-B traveler. What is the opposite of a digressive thinker? Someone like Phileas Fogg as Jules Verne portrayed him in *Around the World in Eighty Days*:

> He gave the idea of being perfectly well-balanced, as exactly regulated as a Leroy chronometer. . . .
>
> He was so exact that he was never in a hurry, was always ready, and was economical alike of his steps and his motions. He never took one step too many, and always went to his destination by the shortest cut; he made no superfluous gestures, and was never seen to be moved or agitated. He was the most deliberate person in the world, yet always reached his destination at the exact moment.
>
> He lived alone, and, so to speak, outside of every social relation; and as he knew that in this world account must be taken of friction, and that friction retards, he never rubbed against anybody.

That is certainly not me. I am no Phileas Fogg. I rub against everybody—and against every memory—and against everybody in every memory. The friction retards my progress but warms my heart. Mark continues:

> There is attached to digression a strong suggestion of weakness of character in the digresser. The digresser is digressive, inclined to stray from the right path, the point, the main subject, the intended direction, and the goal, and this tendency to stray is considered by many to be a fault, which characterization makes digression nearly equal to transgression. Progression, on the other hand, is generally regarded as a virtue. The progresser, if you will allow me the term, is progressive (not in the political sense, usually, but in the forward-marching sense), never straying from the path or plan, always moving toward an established goal step by step. To go off course by choice, or to be lured from the right path by a seductive roadside attraction, is regarded as a fault, but to be forced off course is not. The sailor blown off course by mighty Aeolus is

guiltless, a victim, but the sailor drawn off course by the Sirens' song is a fool who ought to have stopped his ears with wax and stayed the course.

I was, as I hope you will agree after reading the pages that follow, blown off course by the accident of Albertine's injury as much as I was lured off course by the siren call of unsolicited recollection. The first was no fault of mine, an accident. The second I count a virtue, since it served the cause of completeness and accuracy. As a result, however, the short book that I had intended to write about my exploit has become a long book in three parts: *Taking Off* (in which I make my plans and depart), *On the Wing* (in which I meander from Babbington to New Mexico), and *Flying Home* (in which I return to Babbington, somewhat older and, perhaps, somewhat the wiser).

Allow me a couple of thank-yous and a couple of apologies, and then we can begin the show.

To the members of the Faustroll Institute: Thank you for preserving my secret throughout my stay at the Summer Institute in Mathematics, Physics, and Weaponry. Among the things that I should have learned at SIMPaW is the fact that fame, celebrity, and notoriety are equally dangerous. If I had learned the lesson well enough I would have applied it when I arrived back home in Babbington; I would have refused a fame that I didn't deserve, and I never would have had to confess that my storied flight was something less than I allowed everyone to believe. Confronting my failure to learn that lesson, I am astonished that I didn't learn it, because so many of my experiences at SIMPaW gave me opportunities to learn it. Among them was my status as an interloper who had to make himself as close to invisible as he could manage. However, the experience that should have taught the lesson most powerfully was the fame achieved by Nick's picture of the girl in the window—and the danger that its fame unleashed—as you will see. Reflecting on the danger of fame and the fragility of a secret has made me appreciate your loyalty. How difficult it must have been for you to keep my secret, and how unselfish you were in keeping it. You must have been tempted many times to barter the secret for some advantage, yet none of you betrayed me, not even the one of you whom I have represented as calling himself Count Übermensch.

To Matthew Barber: Thank you for the many, many pages of "corrections" that you sent me, unsolicited, after I yielded to your repeated requests that I allow you to read the manuscript before publication. You will find that I have made some of the changes you suggested, but I'm sure you will think that I haven't made nearly so many as I should have. Your memory of that summer when we were in New Mexico differs from mine on so many points, Matthew, that if I had made all the changes you wanted the story would have become much less mine and much more yours. We don't even agree on the name of the organization that sponsored the Summer Institute; you remember it as the National Science Foundation, I as the Preparedness Foundation. You also insist that the New Mexico Institute of Mining, Technology, and Pharmacy was simply the New Mexico Institute of Mining and Technology. This book tells my story, and in order to be able to say that it is mine, even in its errors, I have had to ignore most of your "corrections."

To *Spirit of Babbington*: Thank you for carrying me all those miles, and thank you for being my traveling companion as well as my conveyance. I don't know what has become of you, but I hope you don't think that I abandoned you. What happened really wasn't my fault. After we got home and I parked you in the family garage, your "hangar," I supposed that you and I would be seeing each other often. I thought that I would be piloting you on short jaunts here and there in the vicinity of Babbington, making together the little local trips that the editors of *Impractical Craftsman* had expected an aerocycle to make. At some point, though, I began to realize that if we made those jaunts the people of Babbington would eventually notice that you and I never left the ground. So I left you in the garage. Time passed. I graduated from Babbington High and went off to college, and my mother bought a second-hand car. For a while, she parked her car in the driveway in front of the garage bay where you were stored, and you still had your "hangar" to yourself, but when winter approached my mother reasonably decided that her car ought to have the shelter of the garage. She persuaded my father to move you from the garage to a place behind the garage, where he covered you with a tarpaulin. There you sat in all weathers, until time had taken its toll enough to make it unlikely that you would ever again go anywhere under your own power. My mother asked me to get rid of you. My friend Raskol and I loaded you onto the Lodkochnikov family pickup and carted you to Majestic Salvage and Wrecking. I like to think that the doctrine of perpetual utility to which Majestic's customers subscribed didn't fail you, and that pieces of you found their way into many useful and intriguing gadgets.

To Albertine: I know that I have been insufferable at times during my work on this book, and yet you have suffered me, as you always have, my beautiful dark-haired long-suffering wife. Thank you. The next book will be easier, I promise. It will involve no soul-searching, no confessions, and no hand-wringing. It will be the story of our meeting, that day when our paths intersected.

Peter Leroy
New York City
February 29, 2008

BABBINGTON NEEDS ME

I **WAS BORN** and raised in Babbington, a small town situated on the South Shore of Long Island, lying between the eastern border of Nassau County and the western border of Suffolk County. (Actually, I was born in the hospital in neighboring South Hargrove, since there was no hospital in Babbington, but that made mine a birth so close to being born in Babbington as not to matter.) My roots in the town reach several generations down into its sandy soil, deep roots for an American family. Babbington formed me: I was a Babbington boy. I enjoyed my childhood there, but, like many other small-town boys, I began to want to leave the place in my adolescence. During junior year in high school, a friend of mine, Matthew Barber, had the good fortune to win a scholarship to a summer institute sponsored by the National Prepared-ness Foundation. It was to be held at the New Mexico Institute of Mining, Technology, and Pharmacy, in Corosso. Matthew's winning the scholarship inspired in me a fierce envy and an even fiercer deter-mination to get to Corosso myself. By giving me a destination, Matthew's acceptance at the summer institute justified my building an airplane, an undertaking that my father might otherwise not have been willing to allow—certainly not in the family garage—and by taking me such a distance from home, my trip to Corosso gave me the taste of a wider world that I had come to crave.

While sampling that wider world, I was surprised to find how much I missed Babbington and how much I measured the rest of the world by the standards and peculiarities of my home town. Later in life, in college, and later still, during my brief experience of conven-tional work, the larger world made a further impression on me, but I persisted in interpreting it by translating it into the familiar terms of the small world of Babbington and my childhood experiences there. Late in my twenties, I returned to Babbington, with the intention of staying. My wife, Albertine, and I worked at one job and another to accumulate enough for a down payment on Small's Hotel, and when a surprise bequest from the estate of an old bayman, "Cap'n" Andrew Leech, gave us the last bit that we lacked, we put our money down and bought it. For the next couple of decades we tried to make a suc-cess of Small's, but in the end the sum of our success was that we were able to sell it, pay our debts, and escape with a small amount of equity. We moved to Manhattan, where we live now, with the inten-tion that we would return to Babbington often. Albertine has rela-tives living in the neighboring towns, and for me the place has the draw of a spiritual home, the place where the heart lies. I fully ex-pected that in Manhattan I would be homesick for Babbington, as I had been so often during my trip to New Mexico, but I was not. I kept intending to return, but my intention was inspired more by feelings of obligation than by desire. I felt that I ought to visit certain old friends and acquaintances, ought to see how the hotel was faring under the management of its new owners, ought to go clamming, just to keep my hand in, and yet, however much I felt that I *ought* to go, I never quite managed to get around to going.

Years passed. The Long Island Rail Road continued to run trains to Babbington at convenient hours daily, but I never took one, never attempted to go home again. In a very short time, Manhattan became my home, my playground, my seat of operations. I had been a Babbington boy, but I had become a man of Manhattan, a part of the great urban crowd.

Then, not long ago, I received a postcard from a woman who had lived in Babbington throughout her childhood and youth, as I had, a coeval named Cynthia, who had been called Cyn or Sin or even Sinful

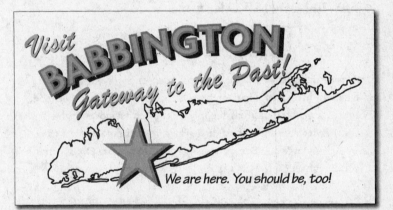

Then, not long ago, I received a postcard . . .

when she and I were classmates in elementary school and high school. During the critical formative years of our lives, we had been suckled on the culture of Babbington, in circumstances that were nearly identical. However, Cyn had remained in Babbington after high school, had married a Babbington boy, was still living in Babbington, and had no intention of leaving.

Her message was brief but unsettling.

Peter,

    I wish you would return to Babbington and see what they are doing to our town. It's enough to make your flesh crawl. If you can possibly get here on Friday the 29th, at around five, I'll meet you at the bar at Legends restaurant in the "Historic Downtown Plaza." Please come. Babbington needs you.

Cynthia

Her words dealt me a stab of guilt, for they inspired within me the feeling that I had betrayed the town by leaving it. I would have to return. I would have to see what "they" were doing to the place. I would have to see what I could do to make things right.

IN THE HISTORIC DOWNTOWN PLAZA

· ·

Already the teaching of Tlön's harmonious history (filled with moving episodes) has obliterated the history that governed my own childhood; already a fictitious past has supplanted in men's memories that other past, of which we now know nothing certain—not even that it is false.

    —Jorge Luis Borges, postscript to "Tlön, Uqbar, Orbis Tertius"

THUS IT WAS that, late in the afternoon of the Friday following my receipt of Cyn's note, Albertine and I found ourselves seated side by side aboard a Long Island Rail Road train bound for Babbington, where, for me, it had all begun. Albertine was with me because she and I are together whenever it is possible for us to be together. We discovered long ago that the point of our lives is to be together, so we try to avoid all individual experience, within the limits of practicality and gracious living. This practice has brought us as close as any two people can be, I think. It also allows her to keep an eye on me.

    "I have no idea what the 'Historic Downtown Plaza' might be," said Albertine, who knows the town as well as I do.

"I picked up this brochure in the station," I said, handing the brochure to Albertine. "It promotes excursions to Babbington. The writer attempts to explain the Historic Downtown Plaza, but the explanation doesn't succeed in clarifying it."

The brochure was titled "Babbington: Gateway to the Past." It bore the logo of the Babbington Redefinition Authority, and it described my home town in the following manner:

> The delightful town of Babbington is the Central South Shore's nostalgia center—or, if not precisely its center, not far off the mark. Babbington offers fine accommodations, restaurants, its own historic charm, and many fascinating attractions and diversions.
>
> The Historic Downtown Plaza, a pedestrian mall lined with buildings dating from the 1950s and even earlier, serves as one of the major "destinations" for Babbingtonians and "out-of-towners" alike.
>
> Downtown employees and shoppers frequent the Plaza to have lunch or stroll through the variety of shops, to slip out of the drudgery of everyday life in the early twenty-first century and back into the blissful middle of the twentieth. The beautifully landscaped Plaza provides a setting for town festivals such as the Clam Fest, traditionally held on the first weekend of May. Highlight of the weeklong extravaganza is the crowning of Miss Clam Fest. Despite the controversy that has plagued the Fest for the last several years, it still draws an enthusiastic crowd. The clam-fritter-eating contest is always exciting and tense. Deaths have occurred.
>
> The Babbington Redefinition Authority is hard at work to make Babbington everything it might once have been. In Babbington you will find the perfect starting point for your passport to the past, the perfect place to start or end your day.

" 'The perfect starting point for your passport to the past'?" said Albertine. "What on earth does that mean?"

"Oh, it's just somebody's attempt to squirt a little of the flavor of foreign travel onto a visit to Babbington," I said.

"That somebody has confused *passport* and *passage,* I think."

"Probably a fellow graduate of Babbington High," I muttered, rescuing the poor pamphlet from her before she picked any other little nits of illiteracy from it.

"Sorry," she said. "I forgot how touchy you are about—"

"Here we are," I said. "Let's find out why my town needs me."

Albertine and I found the Historic Downtown Plaza easily enough. It was a T-shaped stretch of Upper Bolotomy Road and Main Street at the center of town. Two blocks of Upper Bolotomy and four blocks of Main (two to the east of the intersection and two to the west) had been closed to vehicular traffic, though there were cars parked at the curb. I admired some of these as I walked along, because they were handsome examples of the cars that had been the objects of my adolescent carlust when I was in high school.

"Wow," I said in exactly the tone of awestruck reverence I would have used when I was too young to drive.

"Watch where you're going," Al cautioned me, taking hold of my arm and steering me away from a collision with a vintage lamppost.

"Did you see that car we just passed?" I asked. "A 1956 Golden Hawk. Two-hundred-seventy-five horsepower and Ultramatic Drive."

"But not much of a back seat," she said with a wink and a leer. With a sigh for days gone by, we went in search of the restaurant called Legends.

It would have been hard to miss. It announced itself with a large neon sign that bore its name and the slogan "Portal to the Plaza." A smaller sign beside the door offered "Our Incomparable Happy Hour" Monday through Friday, 4:30 P.M. to 6:30 P.M., featuring free hors d'oeuvres and "special drink prices."

The restaurant was just at the northern limit of the plaza in a space that had been filled by a large grocery store when Al and I were kids. The interior had been turned into a miniature shopping mall, with skylights overhead, giving it some of the feeling of a suburban shopping mall, but on a compact scale. Legends occupied the center, and the surrounding area was filled with shops, kiosks, and pushcarts stocked with souvenirs, gewgaws, and "antiques" from approximately the time when Albertine and I were spending Saturday nights in the back seat of her parents' Lark sedan, parked among the concealing rushes at the edge of Bolotomy Bay.

A small group had gathered at the circular bar for the incomparable happy hour. They all seemed to be regulars. They sat and drank. Now and then they spoke to one another. One of their number was addressed by the others as "Judge." The free hors d'oeuvres on this evening were potato chips and a bowl of clam dip.

"Amazing," I said after sampling the dip. "This could have been made from my mother's recipe."

A younger woman came in, apparently stopping by after work, climbed onto a barstool, crossed her eye-catching legs, and ordered a Tom Collins.

"A Tom Collins," I whispered to Al. "When was the last time you heard anybody order a Tom Collins?"

"Nineteen sixty-one," said Albertine, "in the summer, the night we crashed that party in—"

"Shhh," I said with a finger to my lips, and we settled into the poses we assume when indulging in silent eavesdropping.

The happy-hour drinkers were talking of an approaching storm, Hurricane Felicity. Thousands had been evacuated from the New Jersey Shore, one of them noted. Tens of thousands more were without power in that area, according to another. Weekend plans were off, announced the woman with the Tom Collins.

"Hurricane Felicity," I whispered to Al. "There was a Hurricane Felicity when we were in high school, wasn't there?"

"There was," she said.

"Al," I said, "this place is—"

THE BIRDBOY OF BABBINGTON

· ·

JUST THEN, CYNTHIA arrived. She seemed to be wearing a disguise, having gotten herself up as a woman of a certain age. "Hey, there," she said, in the breathy come-hither-big-boy voice that had inspired her teenage nicknames, "if it isn't the Birdbrain of Babbington in the flesh."

"That's Birdboy, Sinful."

"It may have been Birdboy to your face, but it was always Birdbrain behind your back."

"It was?" I asked. "Are you serious? Or are you just making that up? I never knew that anyone—"

"My goodness!" she exclaimed. "Albertine! Look at you, girl. You're gorgeous! *Still* gorgeous, I should say. What did you do, make a pact with the devil?"

"How sweet of you—"

"Come here," said Cynthia, taking our drinks and leading us away from the bar to the table farthest from it. When she had us arranged as she wanted us, she leaned toward the center of the table, dropped her voice to a hoarse whisper, and said, "Let's get to the point." She glanced from side to side to see if anyone was listening. "They're turning this town into a theme park," she said. "It's enough to gag a maggot."

"They?" I asked.

"The BRA."

"The Babbington Redefinition Authority," I said.

"You've done your homework. Good. You see those people at the bar? They're actors. Playing the part of residents. Paid by the BRA."

"Are you saying that they're actors?" I asked.

"Birdbrain—"

"I mean, are they professionals?"

"I was speaking in the broadest sense," she said, rolling her eyes.

"Of course," I said. "Forgive me. From time to time, my keen and hard-won adult acumen is replaced by the naïveté of a boy who lives somewhere within me, a child, or the remnants of a child, who yearns for things to be simpler than they are, and I forget that people rarely mean quite what they say."

She gave me a very odd look. Then she went on. "They are actual residents of the town—when they're offstage, so to speak—but right now they're actors, *playing* residents of the town," she said.

"I see," I said. "Of course. You were speaking in the broadest sense, figuratively, not literally." I paused. Then I said, "I don't have any idea what you're talking about."

"Did you walk through the 'Historic Downtown Plaza'?"

"A bit."

"What did you think?"

"It looks—the way I remember it—pretty much the way it was when we were kids here."

"Peter," she said, shaking her head at my denseness, "it's *exactly* the way it was when we were kids here, when we were in high school."

"Exactly?"

"As close as they could make it."

"Well, they seem to have done a good job—"

"They chose one day, the most fully documented day in the history of mid-twentieth-century Babbington, the one with the most available snapshots, news clippings, and anecdotes. In the Historic Downtown Plaza, they relive that day every day. Over and over. Ad nauseam."

"What day is that?"

"It's the day you flew back into town in that little airplane you built."

"It is?" Unbidden, a feeling of pride began to spread through me, and I think I may have blushed.

"That's what I said."

"So it's a form of historical drama that they're staging," I said, off-handedly, as if nothing I had ever done were involved in any way. "It seems harmless enough to me."

"You don't understand," she said, and she was almost pleading now. "It's spreading. It's spreading beyond the Historic Downtown Plaza, infecting the entire town, and all the residents in it. The BRA's efforts to make the town a more marketable version of itself have not been lost on residents outside the district of the re-enactment. They see the way the town is going, and they're eager to get in on the act. Babbington is not going to remain just-plain-Babbington. It's already well on the way to becoming Babbington™, Gateway to the Past®."

"What happened to 'Clam Capital of America'?" asked Albertine.

"It was officially declared 'unattractive.' I wish you could have been at the town meeting. I was eloquent. I invoked the Bolotomy tribe, shell mounds, wampum—"

"To no avail, I take it," I said.

She shook her head sadly, and turned a thumb down.

"They could have replaced it with 'Cradle of Teenage Solo Flight,'" I suggested.

Cynthia didn't laugh. With her eyes, she appealed to Albertine for support, and Al frowned at me.

Cyn rubbed her brow as if her head ached and said, "People all over town are coming to feel that in such a place as Babbington—that is, such a place as Babbington is becoming—it is not enough to be Jack Sprat, the local butcher; one must be Jack Sprat, Garrulous Butcher of Bygone Babbington, Gateway to the Past."

"I see," I said, wondering how she would describe herself in the list of town characters, what epithet she would attach to herself. "You said 'paid by the BRA,'" I reminded her.

"That, too, I meant in the broadest sense."

"Of course."

"The BRA is seeing to it that the only real business left in this town will be the business of being itself, though not really itself but an image of itself as it never was. To their credit, they have chosen a Babbington that's more like the earthy images of Brueghel the Elder than the kitsch of Norman Rockwell or Thomas Kinkade, but still they are turning the town into a simulation, and because that simulation is to be the engine of the town's economic recovery, everyone who agrees to participate in it is, in the broadest sense, on the payroll of the BRA."

"I see," I said again, thoughtfully, "and you say that all this is centered on my solo flight, my triumphant return, the parade—"

"Don't go feeling proud of yourself," she said. "You ought to be ashamed."

"You're right," I said. "I am." Still, in my silent thoughts I couldn't help wondering if it might not be possible to return to Babbington, become an actor in the BRA pageant, and play once again the part of Peter Leroy, Daring Flyboy. No. Of course not. Whoever played the Daring Flyboy would have to be considerably younger. A boy.

"Look," Cyn said suddenly, gathering her things, "I've got to go. There's a meeting of the Friends of the Bay that I've got to attend. But do me a favor. Take a walk around and look at the walls."

"The walls?"

"Haven't you noticed the walls here?"

"Here in the restaurant?"

"No, all over town. Of course I mean here in the restaurant. What's happened to your mind, Birdbrain?"

"He's often distracted," said Albertine. She may have been speaking in my defense.

"He's always been like that," said Cyn.

"And always will be," Albertine predicted.

"Drag him around the place to look at the walls, okay?"

"Okay."

"Promise?"

"Promise," said Albertine, woman to woman.

Cyn left in a rush. Before Albertine and I left Legends, we did as Al had promised we would do. We took a walk around the place and looked at the walls. They were covered, and that is nearly the truth, with caricatures of people who had been designated by the management of Legends as legendary figures in Babbington's past. I recognized many of them, and among them I recognized myself. Actually, Albertine recognized me first.

"Oh, no!" she squealed. "It's the Birdboy of Babbington."

There I was, celebrated and exaggerated, and there I stood, exhilarated and exasperated.

Albertine linked her arm with mine and hugged herself to me.

"Oh, that takes me back," she said warmly.

"Yes," I said, with considerably less enthusiasm. "It takes me back, too."

STRAIGHT

· ·

MY SOLO FLIGHT. I have quite a mental scrapbook devoted to that flight. To be truthful, *flight* isn't quite the right word; *flights* would be more accurate, because it was not one continuous flight, though in the minds of most of those who remember it, or think that they remember it, it has come to be a continuous flight. I even think of it that way myself sometimes, as a nonstop flight from Babbington out to Corosso and another nonstop flight back. When I was interviewed upon my return, I tried to be honest about what I had accomplished and what I had not, but the interviewers had their own ideas about what the story ought to be, and nothing that I told them was going to change those ideas, so I began to go along with what they wanted. The account published in the *Reporter* was typical, an account that made the flight seem more than it actually was.

BABBINGTON BOY COMPLETES SOLO FLIGHT
Flies Cross-Country on His Own
HOME-BUILT PLANE FUNCTIONS FLAWLESSLY

Babbington — Peter Leroy will sleep in his own bed in Babbington Heights tonight, for the first time in more than two months, but you can bet that he'll have dreams of flying, as he has for as long as he can remember. We all have those dreams, said by some to be the remnants of our species' memory of swinging through the trees when we were apes, but most of us remain earthbound. Our flying is confined to our dreams. Not so for young Peter Leroy. This is a lad who makes his dreams come true.

"I found some plans for a plane in a magazine," he says, with disarming simplicity, "and I thought it would be fun to build it and fly it across the country."

The modesty of Babbington's aeronautical pioneer is charming. (Local politicians, please take note.) When asked by C. Nelson Dillwell, publisher of the *Reporter*, how he got to Corosso, New Mexico, some 1,800 miles from home, he responds, "Well, I flew," with a shrug, as if the feat were really nothing much more than a bike ride to the corner store to pick up a quart of milk for his mother. And how did you get back? "Flew," he says, with another shrug. When it is proposed to him that flying nearly 4,000 miles in a plane that he built in the garage of the modest Leroy family home is a significant feat, he grins the grin that has already won the hearts of all the secretaries at the *Reporter*'s spacious new downtown offices and says, "Well, I didn't fly all the way." What? You didn't fly all the way? "No," he says, shaking his head, apparently all seriousness. "I did some taxiing, before takeoffs, and

BABBINGTON TO COROSSO = ✦

COROSSO TO BABBINGTON = ➚

then after landing, when I rolled along the ground for a way before coming to a stop." Ah, yes, let's set the record straight. Young Leroy did not fly all the way to New Mexico and back. He did some taxiing and rolled along the runways a bit on landing. Noted.

Yes, let's set the record straight. During my return trip, from Corosso to Babbington, I thought a lot about what I was going to say when I got home, and about the impression that my story would make, and I decided, quite deliberately, that I would be honest but not accurate. I would be honest overall but vague about the details. I intended to say that I had flown part of the way but not all the way. I don't recall when, in rehearsing my remarks, I began to refer to the earthbound portions of the trip as taxiing, but it was well before I came within sight of Babbington.

When I reached Babbington, I rolled into town along Main Street, coming from the west. There are people in Babbington to this day who will tell you that they saw me *fly* in from the west, make a lazy circle in the sky over the area now occupied by the Historic Downtown Plaza, and touch down near the park before rolling to a stop at the intersection of Bolotomy and Main, where the reviewing stand had been set up. Some of them honestly believe that they saw that landing, just as some people honestly believe that they have seen the ghost of a beloved aunt climbing the back staircase at midnight and others think that they have seen the silver spaceships of interstellar travelers flash in eerie swift silence across the night sky.

I was paraded up and down Main Street in the back seat of a convertible, with the mayor at the wheel and Miss Clam Fest at my side. People screamed my name as I passed. They threw streamers and confetti. I was given the key to the city. The high school band played "For He's a Jolly Good Fellow" again and again. Feeling like a jolly good fellow indeed, I went where I was led, into the building where the *Reporter* had its office, and found myself the subject of a press conference. All of the Babbington media were represented: the *Reporter*, of course; and the radio station, WCLM; as well as the Babbington high school paper, the *Esculent Mollusk*. All eyes were on me. My audience hung on my every word. I was the boy of the hour. I was completely intoxicated, drunk on fame, besotted with adulation.

The first question directed to me wasn't really a question at all. The publisher of the *Reporter*, who assumed control of the proceedings, said, as a preliminary to taking questions from the floor, "Peter, it is an honor for the *Reporter* to have you here today, and we all want to hear how you got from Babbington to New Mexico."

He paused, and I took his pause as my cue. Feeling even more full of myself than I ordinarily did, I said, "Well, I flew—"

I meant to add "part of the way." I really did.

However, when I said, "Well, I flew—" the response was immediate and overwhelming. People laughed. Then they applauded. Miss Clam Fest blew me a kiss from her seat in the front row. I added nothing to what I had said. I just shrugged. They loved it. They loved me. Miss Clam Fest in particular seemed to love me, even though she must have been a mature woman of twenty-two. I wasn't going to let the truth come between us. I told a version of the truth, as I had intended to, but it became a version that allowed people to believe what they so clearly wanted to believe, and what they wanted to believe was far from the version of the truth that I had planned to tell them.

I flew part of the way. That's true. As I carefully said later in the press conference, I also taxied part of the way, before taking off and upon landing. I would say now, years beyond the influence of Miss Clam Fest's strapless gown, based on the sober calculations of an essentially honest man, that I flew a total of about 180 to 200 feet on the way out to New Mexico. My longest sustained period of flight might have covered six feet. For the rest of the outbound trip, I was on the ground, "taxiing." On the way back, I flew nearly 1,800 miles, but I was a passenger in a Lockheed Constellation, and *Spirit of Babbington* was in the luggage compartment, disassembled, in crates. There. The record is straight.

OH, THE SQUALOR

THE TRAIN ROLLED on, carrying Albertine and me from Babbington to Manhattan, away from my past and toward our future. I noticed with a mixture of surprise and sadness how squalid the buildings beside the tracks were. All the businesses that the commercial buildings housed seemed to be involved in some sort of salvage, and the dwellings looked as if the passage of the trains so near had weakened them, made them list and tilt. Human life and all of its impedimenta began to seem senseless, fragile and impermanent, poorly made, like my life, like the story of my life, my rickety story.

"You're being quiet," said Albertine. "Is something bothering you?"

"Oh, no," I said. "Nothing."

"What is it?" she asked.

"You always know, don't you?"

"Always."

"I've been watching the scenery roll by, thinking about the squalor of it all, the way people mar the landscape, littering it with their junk, and I've been drawing the inevitable analogy between this landscape that we're passing through and the history of Babbington, the way I passed through that history, and the way I've littered it with my junk—"

"What junk would that be, exactly?"

"You know what I mean."

"Come on, Birdboy, speak your mind."

"The story of my solo flight to Corosso—"

"Are you calling that junk?"

"It's like one of those shacks along the tracks: rickety, jerry-built, cobbled together out of bits and pieces, not at all sturdy enough to—"

I didn't want to say it.

"Stand up under close scrutiny?" she suggested.

"Right," I said with a sigh.

"I see," she said. "And with the controversy that's developing over the redefinition of the town, some bright young reporter is going to start investigating the central and essential legend—"

"—the Legend of the Birdboy of Babbington—"

"—and discover that the legendary birdboy has wings of clay."

"That's it."

"Then you'd better get to work."

"On a cover-up?"

"A full and frank disclosure, I think."

DREAMS OF FLYING

．．

I HAD DREAMS in which I flew, of course. I still do. The manner of my flying in those dreams, and the style of my flying, has not changed with the passage of time. In my dreams, as a man, I fly as I flew as a boy. Essentially, I drift. Most often I jump from a height—a cliff, a balcony, a bridge—and I drift slowly toward the ground. I am able to will myself forward, but I remain upright, or nearly upright, in the position I would expect to land in, prepared to plant my feet on the ground. I seem always about to land, to come to earth, though I may keep drifting forward, or gliding forward, for a long time, covering quite a bit of distance. I never seem to begin a flight with the intention of going forward, or going in any horizontal direction at all. I seem to intend only to let myself drop slowly, safely, gifted as I am with the power of flight, from a high place to a lower place. Traveling, getting somewhere in some direction, seems to come along as an afterthought, almost as if, once dropping slowly in my controlled fashion, I let myself be carried by a breeze, or by an inclination. Part of the pleasure of these dreams seems to come from this accidental aspect of flight, the notion that it seems to free me not only from the weight imposed by gravity but from the purposefulness imposed by a destination. I do not fly to get anywhere, but only to be a flier, or—simpler still—I fly because I am a flier.

I also had *daydreams* of flying, waking dreams, wishes and fantasies, but they were quite different from my sleeping dreams of flying. My daydreams were about getting somewhere, or about getting away from where I was and flying to somewhere else. They were about escape and exploration, and they were deliberate. I launched my daydreams as I might have launched a flying machine. I got into the dream and took off. Often I launched one of these daydreams on a Sunday, when I was in the back seat of the family car, and my family was out for a Sunday drive.

There were parkways on Long Island, highways built to resemble country roads, with bridges faced with rustic-cut stone, wooden railings and wooden dividers between the opposite lanes, light poles of wood, and landscaping that was designed to look as if the hand of man had not been involved in it. Parkways were ideal for a Sunday drive, the next best thing to a country road. These parkways still exist, but the density of the traffic has made them less attractive for a Sunday drive. The density of traffic has made the whole concept of the Sunday drive less attractive.

On either side of the parkway's roadway, running alongside it, there was a pathway. I think that I am right in saying that I never saw anyone walking along one of those pathways, and it occurs to me now that the paths may have been provided more as an element of landscaping than as a way that was intended for actual use by hikers or bicyclists. They were, perhaps, intended to heighten or strengthen the impression of driving along a country road by evoking the notion of a footpath that one might walk or hike with rucksack and alpenstock, or to provide the expectation that one might while driving see someone else doing the hiking, a generous someone who thus completed the country-road impression while allowing the driver and passengers to remain comfortably seated in the family car.

For the boy sitting in the back seat of *my* family's car, the pathway was more interesting than the roadway. It wandered a bit, for one thing. The road may have been made to resemble a country road, but its route had been laid out to eliminate as far as possible anything that stood in the driver's way, including the hills and turns that make a country road a pleasant meander. The land beside the roadway had not been flattened as the roadway had. In fact, I think that if I were to take the trouble to do the research, I would find that it had been deliberately contoured to give the illusion of land in a natural state, uneven, untamed, and that when the little pathway had been built the landscapers had made it meander, within limits, like a miniature of the country road that the parkway was intended to suggest. The path had its ups and downs, its meanders and rambles and digressions. It had stretches that seemed a bit off course. Now and then it would disappear from view behind a clump of trees, becoming all the more attractive for having disappeared.

As we rolled along the parkway, I followed the pathway with my eyes, and in my daydreams I imagined moving along the pathway in a kind of hovercraft. It rose no more than a couple of feet above the surface, but it flew, though I have no idea how. As it flew, it was utterly silent, since it was powered by wishful thinking, by my powerfully propulsive wish to be out of the back seat of the family car.

ON INTENTION AND TRAVEL

....

ALBERTINE AND I rolled on, in the stutter step of a Long Island Rail Road commuter train, making all the stops. I sat beside the window, looking out, daydreaming. There was no rambling path beside us, but my daydreams no longer need the stimulus of a rambling path. These days, I ramble most of the time, though I rarely go anywhere.

"I wish we could go somewhere now," I said to Al suddenly. "Right now, this minute."

"Where do you want to go?" she asked lazily. She was curled on her side with her head on my shoulder, trying to doze.

"Nowhere," I said truthfully, "or anywhere. I am convinced that the best travel is travel undertaken without a destination, just wandering. I am not the first to say that the slower the traveler goes, the more he sees. If I could, I would set out now and walk, hither and yon, following a course like that of the river Mæander."

"Why don't we?"

"Because we're tethered here."

"Can't we loose the surly bonds?"

"Not until we've paid our debts and put enough aside to finance a ramble and the time that it would take."

"But we'll have that goal?"

"Yes. The goal of traveling without a goal."

"It's our intention. Shall we put this in writing and ink the pact?"

"Let's just say it out loud and shake on it. Or make love on it."

"It is our intention to work very, very hard to pay off our debts and put some money aside and then to walk out our door on the way to nowhere."

"Without a map, without a destination."

"But every night we'll stop somewhere to have a hot shower, a fabulous meal, and a dreamy sleep in a comfy bed."

"If possible."

"I'm going to insist on that."

"But that means that we would have a destination—actually, a series of destinations—a destination for every night."

"Even the river Mæander winds somewhere safe to sea."

ONE IN A LINE OF IMPRACTICAL CRAFTSMEN

THE LOW-FLYING VEHICLE of my daydreams, strong, swift, and silent, was derived from an article in *Impractical Craftsman* magazine. I was a faithful reader of this magazine. So was my father. Both of my grandfathers were subscribers, and they had made many projects from plans published in its pages or ordered from its Projects

Department. I had made a couple of things from *Impractical Crafts-man* plans myself. They gave me satisfaction, not only the satisfaction of having completed a job, made a thing, but also the satisfaction of taking my place in the family line of impractical craftsmen. Dædalus was the household god of *Impractical Craftsman*. The masthead of each issue included a small drawing of him (with his disobedient son beside him), and the best of the projects in the magazine were truly daedal: ingenious, cleverly intricate, and diversified.

My father had also made things from plans in *IC,* as its devotees called it, but he tended to prefer the plans in other, less visionary, magazines for backyard builders, and he would usually build useful, boring things like bedside tables and chests of drawers rather than the marginally useful but intriguingly complicated mechanical, electromechanical, and electronic gadgets that my grandfathers and I favored.

I am wronging my father somewhat by suggesting that some short-coming made him the sort of person who lacked the daring to venture beyond making simple pine tables and chests. Certainly he fell short of my grandfathers, and even of me, in his willingness to undertake a project that promised long periods of baffling, exacting work and little chance of success, but he wasn't entirely immune to the desire to stretch himself out into the realm of the unbuildable. I recall that he became excited about an *IC* project that, if it had been completed successfully, would have resulted in an early form of wireless television remote con-trol. He never succeeded in getting the device to work, and it "plagued" him, as my mother moaned when he sank into a blue funk over his fail-ure. As I recall the gadget, it wasn't going to do anything more than turn the television set on and off and raise or lower the volume. Before my father began this project, I had already built, from a kit advertised in the back pages of *IC,* an "electric eye" that would have done the job of turning the set on and off and could have been triggered by a flash-light from my father's chair, which would have qualified it as a wireless remote control, so it seemed to me that I could have solved half of his problem without really trying, and I felt a brief superiority until I be-gan to try to figure out how the electric eye could be modified to con-trol the volume and saw how much more difficult that was. My father dismantled the device that he had built and reassembled it several times, checking off the steps in the article systematically each time, but never could make it work. He banished it to a spot on the bottom shelf of his huge, cluttered workbench in the basement, but the anticipation of reaching a goal, a destination, had infected him with determination, and now he could not stop thinking about the idea of remote control for the television set. He would sit in his favorite chair, watching television, dreaming of a way to control it from where he sat, chewing the bitter cud of failure.

My father must have been one of the country's greatest television enthusiasts in those early days. His chair sagged nearly to the floor from the thousands of hours he had spent in it, pursuing his hobby. If the industry had known about his devotion to the medium, its captains would probably have rewarded him somehow. They might have given him a dinner. They might have given him a remote control, if they had one that worked.

One evening, while he sat there watching and brooding, the thought dawned on my father that he could achieve remote control if he simply removed the essential controls from the cabinet that held the television set, extended the wires that connected them to the rest of the circuitry, and placed them beside his favorite chair, where he could twiddle the dials at a distance from the set itself, remotely. Making the modifications was a tedious task, but not a difficult one, and he accomplished it in a few evenings. He drilled a hole in the floor under the place where the set was positioned and ran the wires through that hole. In the basement, he ran them along the rafters to another hole under the position of his chair and up through that hole to the living room, where he connected them to the controls. To house the controls, he built a handsome pine box that he kept at his side on the table between his chair and my mother's. He was a contented man.

What my father did not realize, and I did not realize, either, was that some of the projects in *IC* were impossible to build. Though the magazine emphasized projects that one could, presumably, actually build, it also featured in every issue visionary articles about things that were not buildable yet but might be buildable someday. There was a tension between the here-and-now projects, which had a crudeness about them that made them achievable by the craftsman or hobbyist working in the basement or garage or back yard, and the sleek, seamless devices that were forever just on the horizon, someday to be ours in our bright future of swift transportation, gleaming gadgetry, and easy communication. The visionary articles carried with them an inherent frustration. Always there was at some point, toward the end, after the reader had become convinced that the holographic teleportation device described in the article would probably require no more than an afternoon's work, the almost casual mention of technical lets and hindrances to its realization, mere details that would "doubtless soon be solved" but stood in the way of attaining the vision now. "In other words, Faithful Reader," the article quietly cautioned between its lines, "don't bother trying to build one of these holographic teleportation devices in your garage, because it won't work. You'll run up against a wall of ignorance. We couldn't even do it here at *IC,* in our world-famous Projects Development and Testing Laboratory." In another magazine, articles of this you-couldn't-build-it-in-a-million-years-sucker sort would not have included cutaway drawings, wiring diagrams, and accounts of the assembly of the device that could not be built, but in *IC* they did. I now think that the zest for building, for making manifest what the imagination had conjured in the mind, was so strong at *IC* that the illustrators, writers, and editors who worked there found that they could not prevent themselves from drawing pictures of the device and writing about its construction as if it had been built. They had, I suspect now, in an example of mass delusion, already convinced themselves that the thing *had* been built, that they had built it. This device that they had imagined *ought* to work surely *would* work someday, and if that was so, as they believed it surely was, then one ought to be able to build it this way: Step 1 . . .

I suppose that most readers of *Impractical Craftsman* were adept at distinguishing between the two types of article. My father was not. Neither was I.

My friend Rodney Lodkochnikov, known as Raskolnikov or Raskol, was, in marked contrast, very good at distinguishing between the practicable, the doable, and the visionary, the as-yet undoable. When I showed him the article about the personal hovercraft and confessed to him that it was the flying machine of my daydreams, he took the magazine, glanced at the article and the accompanying drawings, and said, "This is great, but it's not the sort of thing you could build."

"I wasn't thinking of—" I began to protest.

"Yes, you were," he said, accurately.

THE EXAMPLE OF DÆDALUS AND ICARUS

THE THINKING AT *Impractical Craftsman* was exactly the sort of thinking that got Dædalus and Icarus off the ground and into trouble.

In the words of Charles Mills Gayley, Dædalus was "a famous artificer." Gayley's *Classic Myths*, first published in 1893, was, along with *Ancient Myths for Modern Youth*, required reading in Mrs. Fendreffer's class, a class that was a rite of passage for all freshmen at Babbington High during my years there. Both texts sit on the bookshelf above my desk today.

The story of Dædalus's life is full of curiosities. This is how that story appeared in *Ancient Myths for Modern Youth*:

> We may as well acknowledge from the start that none of the characters in this drama is particularly admirable. The major players are King Minos of Crete; his queen, Pasiphaë; the god Neptune; Dædalus, a craftsman, tinkerer, putterer, and inventor, the original of the type; and a beautiful bull.
>
> The bull was bullish. King Minos was boastful, vain, and cruel. Pasiphaë was disrespectful of the gods and apparently driven by lustful thoughts. Neptune was, like the other gods, exceedingly jealous and apt to be vengeful. Dædalus, though he was a clever artificer, was also a murderer; he was so envious of rival artificers that when his nephew, Perdix, invented a saw—modeling it on the shape of a fish skeleton—Dædalus pushed him off a tower to his death.

King Minos often boasted that he was a favorite of the gods, that they listened with particular favor to his prayers, and that, therefore, he could obtain virtually anything he wanted by petitioning the appropriate god. Perhaps, down the long corridor of time, you seem to hear the snorts and snickers of skeptics in the king's audience when he made these assertions; apparently, Minos heard them, too. To silence them, Minos went into his act, calling upon Neptune in his prayers, beseeching the god to send him a bull, which he promised to sacrifice to Neptune as soon as the Cretan skeptics had been silenced.

Neptune delivered; the bull appeared. However, because the gods like to work in mysterious ways, it was no ordinary bull. It was an extraordinarily beautiful bull. (We may find the notion that a bull might be "extraordinarily beautiful" a bit hard to swallow in our enlightened times, but the Cretans seem to have had no trouble with it.) Minos was dumbstruck by the bull's beauty; so was Pasiphaë, as we shall see. Under the influence of the bull's beauty, Minos reneged on his deal with Neptune; he refused to sacrifice the animal. Neptune was not happy with this turn of events. Gods, as a rule, like obedience. They go for groveling and abasement. When promised a sacrifice, they expect a sacrifice. Minos's impudence did not sit well with Neptune, who determined to make Minos pay dearly for it. With a god's ingenuity, he infected the beautiful bull with a kind of madness, inducing in it a violent fury that made it intractable and unpredictable, like the crazy people one encounters in small towns, characters who may be quaint in their way but are subject to irrational outbursts of violence and are best avoided.

The bull was not the only earthly agent of Neptune's wrath. He infected Pasiphaë with a kind of madness, too, but a madness different from the bull's; in her case, it was an irresistible passion for the bull. We shall have more to say about this later.

Minos needed help. He called on Hercules, the ubiquitous hero of ancient myth, archetype of all the heroes you find in your comic books. Hercules caught the rampaging bull, subdued it, and took it away to Greece, riding it there, the myth tells us, through the waves. (That bit about riding the bull through the waves is a detail that, like so many of the details, large and small, we are asked to accept in these old myths, doesn't seem likely.)

However, Hercules's ridding Crete of the rampaging bull did not end Minos's troubles. During its time in Crete, the bull had managed to sire a child, and now that child, the Minotaur (that is, "Minos's bull"), was causing no end of trouble. The Minotaur was a monster with the head of a bull and the body of a man. It went about terrorizing the people of Crete as its father had, but did an even better job of it.

Again, Minos needed help. He turned to Dædalus, that famous artificer. Minos had long admired Dædalus's skills, but he had become less than fond of the man after Dædalus had abetted the love of Pasiphaë for the Minotaur's father, that extraordinarily beautiful bull that Neptune had sent in devious fulfillment of Minos's imprecations. In his hour of need, Minos seemed to set aside his animosity toward Dædalus, and the great artificer constructed for him a labyrinth, with passages and turnings winding in and about like the river Mæander. In this labyrinth he enclosed the Minotaur, which could not find its way out. Minos found that the labyrinth was also a fine place to imprison miscreants and foes, who became feed for the Minotaur that roamed the twisting passageways. In addition, after Dædalus had completed the labyrinth, Minos imprisoned Dædalus and his son, Icarus, there, for Minos's animosity toward Dædalus had never really waned and he hoped that imprisonment in the labyrinth would mean the end of Dædalus and his issue.

However, crafty Dædalus fashioned wings from feathers and wax so that he and Icarus could fly out of the labyrinth. Before they took to the air, Dædalus instructed Icarus in the use of the wings and the safety rules of the art of human flight as they were then understood. "Fly neither too high nor too low," he counseled his son, "but keep to the middle way." Well, you know how youngsters are: headstrong. Icarus took off, and in the manner of daredevil youth since time immemorial he soon scoffed at his father's advice, flouted his warnings, and stretched his wings. He flew too high, too near the sun, and the heat melted the wax that held the feathers in place. Without feathers, he was no longer a flyboy, merely a boy, and boys cannot stay airborne for long. Icarus fell into the sea and drowned. Let this be a lesson to you.

Something seemed to be missing from this story. The bull's child, the Minotaur, seemed to pop into it from nowhere, sired but unborn. The bull was the father, clearly, but who was the Minotaur's mother? The hints pointed to Pasiphaë. Could that be? Just imagine the storms raging in the teenage brains of Mrs. Fendreffer's charges upon hearing the phrase "abetted the love of Pasiphaë" for the extraordinarily beautiful bull. What on earth did that mean? We were young people eager for knowledge—or at least we were eager for knowledge in certain areas. Could a woman fall in love with a bull? Could a woman—ah—make love with a bull? How, precisely, would one abet such a love?

"Wait a minute, Mrs. Fendreffer."

"Yes, Bill?"

"You mean Pasi-whosis was in love with a bull?"

"Yes," Mrs. Fendreffer sighed, recognizing the opening wedge in a line of inquiry that she had endured every year for all of the thirty-nine that she had been teaching.

"Isn't that a little—" Bill, ordinarily forthcoming, hesitated and even seemed embarrassed.

"Yes?" prompted Mrs. Fendreffer.

"Perverted?" suggested Bill.

"Today I suppose we would call it a kind of bestiality," Mrs. Fendreffer conceded, "but the ancients had standards different from ours."

"Is that why you call it the golden age, because they were fornicating with bulls?" asked Rose O'Grady, known as Spike.

"I don't want to hear any language like that in my classroom."

"Hey, I don't want to hear any stories about women—and married women at that—consorting with bulls—or any other animals for that matter—behind their husbands' backs," said Bill.

"You don't object to their consorting with bulls if their husbands consent?" asked Spike.

"Even that would be pretty sick."

"Mrs. Fendreffer, may I ask a serious question?" said Spike in a serious tone of voice.

"Please."

"It says in the book that Dædalus 'abetted the love of Pasiphaë for the Minotaur's father, that extraordinarily beautiful bull.'"

"'Abetted the love of Pasiphaë for the Minotaur's father, that extraordinarily beautiful bull.' That is correct."

"How?"

"What?"

"How did he abet the love of Pasiphaë for the bull?"

"That I do not know," Mrs. Fendreffer claimed. "I have been teaching these myths for many years now, and I have consulted many sources for elucidation of their mysteries, but I have never found any commentator who explains just what we are to take *abet* to mean in this case."

None of us knew, then, that Mrs. Fendreffer's ignorance was feigned, that it was a part of her teaching technique. For thirty-nine years she had been claiming not to know how Dædalus might have abetted the love of Pasiphaë for the Cretan bull and, thereby, she had been inspiring her students to go beyond the pages of *Ancient Myths for Modern Youth* and try to find the answer on their own.

Several of us did, that very afternoon. In a group, with Spike in the lead, we trooped to the school library. There, after half an hour's work, we found some additional information, but not enough. We walked to the Babbington Public Library, where, after another half hour's work, we found a bit more information, but still not enough. It was Spike who voiced our common frustration and suspicions to the librarian: "Hey," she said to the woman behind the reference desk.

"Yes?"

"We're trying to answer a question about one of the Greek myths, and all the books we check don't give us the real inside dope."

"Mm," said the librarian.

"Are you hiding the good stuff somewhere?"

The librarian looked up from her work and over her glasses and down her nose at Spike. Slowly a smile formed on her face.

"Are you in Mrs. Fendreffer's class?" she asked.

"Yeah," said Spike. She seemed as surprised by the question as the rest of us were. "How did you know?"

"This happens every year," the librarian said, and then a look of concern crossed her face. "Usually it's a little earlier in the school year, though," she said. "Poor Mrs. Fendreffer must be slowing down." With a sigh and a shake of her head she led us to a locked bookcase.

In that case was a book called *Antique Scandals: The Mischief Behind the Myths.* We took it to a table nearby and, huddled around it, sought what we wanted to know. We found it, some of it, and in the bargain learned a lesson about making inferences from an incomplete text, since some of the essential words had been hidden under thick black ink, there but obscured, the way the precise answer to a calculation on a slide rule is hidden by the very cursor that marks its location. Perhaps creating the opportunity to learn the lesson of inference was the point of blacking out the revelatory words, or perhaps Mrs. Fendreffer and her collaborators in the library merely wanted to conceal from us what they thought we were too young to know. Over the years I have decided to prefer to believe that they wanted us to learn something, not that they wanted us not to learn something.

We studied the passage in silence, making our individual decisions about what was missing.

"Oh," said Spike after a while. "So that's it."

"Just what I thought," said Marvin.

The rest of us made similar assertions to the effect that our suspicions were now affirmed, but I, because I have never known when to keep my mouth shut, said, in a tone that hid none of the disappointment I felt, "I was hoping there would be diagrams." The others burst out laughing, the librarian shushed us in the time-honored manner, and my reputation as a humorist grew considerably.

• • • • • • • • •

I had expected diagrams because I knew that if the tale of Dædalus's abetting Pasiphaë's love for the bull had appeared in *Impractical Craftsman,* there would have been diagrams. Many a reader would have attempted to build a replica of the false cow that Dædalus built, the essential equipment for abetting the love of a queen for a bull. I have no doubt about that at all. My grandfathers probably would have made the attempt. If I'd thought I had the skill, I probably would have tried it myself. Of course I would have.

ANTIQUE SCANDALS: THE MISCHIEF BEHIND THE MYTHS   51

boasting of his special relationship with the gods annoyed Queen Pasiphäe, because she did not believe in gods. Of all the gods that she did not believe in, she particularly refused to believe in the goddess Aphrodite. There was something about Aphrodite or perhaps about the idea of Aphrodite that really rubbed her the wrong way. Let us be frank about this. In all probability, Pasiphäe envied Aphrodite. She wanted to be worshipped and feared as Aphrodite was.

Pasiphäe declined to make offerings to Aphrodite; years passed without her suffering any apparent ill effect from this neglect, so she scoffed at the idea that such a "goddess" as Aphrodite even existed. Dædalus, who was a special friend of Pasiphäe's, warned her that such loose talk might reach the ears of Aphrodite, but it was too late. Aphrodite had heard Queen Pasiphäe's blasphemous words and she planned revenge.

Now it was the case that, for reasons unknown, King Minos admired white bulls. You have to accept this as a given, or the rest of the story makes no sense at all. Minos demanded that the world's most magnificent white bull be brought to him. Lo and behold, the bull was delivered. However, the bull had been sent by Aphrodite, as part of her plot for revenge. No sooner had the bull arrived than Queen Pasiphäe fell passionately in love with it. She confessed her love to her dear friend Dædalus, and Dædalus felt deep sympathy for the beautiful queen, so he abetted her passion by making a remarkably realistic wooden cow, just big enough for Pasiphäe to fit in, arranging her body in such a way that the bull would be able to ████ her and thrust its ████████ into Pasiphäe's ████████ ████████ Dædalus was a thoroughgoing, exacting craftsman, so he finished the job by killing and skinning a cow and sewing its skin around the wooden form as a covering. Pasiphäe climbed inside the false cow, and Dædalus wheeled it to the field where the bull was wont to graze. When the bull arived at the field it seemed to see a beautiful cow already there. Smitten and ████████ the bull trotted to the wooden form, ████████ it, and, thanks to Dædalus's cunning artifice, ████████ with the eager Pasiphäe. After the usual nine months, Queen Pasiphäe gave birth to the creature that became known as the Minotaur, since it had the head of a bull.

. . . some of the essential words had been hidden under thick black ink . . .

A SOURCE OF MOTIVATION

....

STRETCHED OUT ALONG the bulkhead beside the estuarial reach of the Bolotomy River one morning, Raskol and I were daydreaming in tandem, trading ideas about the things we might be doing if the day were not the sort of lazy summer day that invites a boy to do nothing but loaf and daydream, when the subject of flying arose.

"The subject of flying arose." That isn't accurate. I realize, upon reflection, that it suggests a chance provocation, the possibility that a light plane buzzed overhead, introducing the subject, or perhaps some other provocation no less apt but less direct, like a bumblebee buzzing by, or a provocative something even less obvious, like the leisurely ascension of the morning mist from the slack surface of the river. To be truthful, as I am struggling to be in this full and frank disclosure, the subject did not simply arise: I injected it into the meandering conversation by recalling my ride in a floatplane.

On a day several summers earlier, I had flown in what was then called a "seaplane" and is now called a "floatplane" while on vacation with my parents and maternal grandparents in the mountains of New Hampshire. After I had made the flight, my first in a plane of any kind, I couldn't stop talking about it.

Allow me a moment here to explore my motives for wanting to talk about it, for wanting to tell others about the experience I had had, because I think I see in those motives the prototypes of my motives for writing my memoirs. In part I was trying to re-create the experience for myself in the telling; in part I was trying to "share the experience," to allow my listener the vicarious experience of it; in part I was trying to preserve the experience, enclose it in a protective layer of words, within which it would not fade or dim; and in part I was just bragging. None of my friends had flown, and I was, I understood, displaying my distinction every time I brought the subject up, every time I tried to describe for them the sensation of sitting in a light plane (actually, squatting, in a tight space without a seat behind the two seats where the pilot and my father sat), skimming across the water, and then rising slowly into the air.

I injected the subject of flying with this preamble: "It would be neat if we could see Babbington from the air, the way I saw Osopuco Lake and the town of West Burke when I—"

"When you rode in that seaplane," said Raskol with a stage yawn and a tone that indicated more than clearly that he had heard the seaplane story more often than he had wanted to hear it.

"Yeah," I said. I wasn't going to force the story on him. He and I were friends. I might have forced the story on a stranger, or on an acquaintance whose goodwill I would have been willing to risk for the satisfaction of reliving the adventure in the telling, but I wouldn't force it on a friend. I fell silent, waiting. Maybe a stranger or an expendable acquaintance would come by.

After a while, Raskol said, with the generosity of friendship, "That must have been a great ride."

"Yeah," I said, but without much enthusiasm, since I evidently wasn't going to get to tell him about it all over again.

He put his hands behind his head, with his fingers interlaced, closed his eyes, and said the kindest words a friend can say: "Tell me all about it."

I began slowly, as if I were struggling to recover the memory for his benefit. "There weren't many planes up there," I said. "It's pretty far away from things, and it's not on the way to anywhere, so you don't see many planes in the sky, but a couple of times a day I'd hear a buzzing above me and I'd look up and find it there, turning in a wide arc before coming in for a landing. Or sometimes I'd happen to be looking out across the lake, just enjoying the view, and I'd see it taking off. Of

FIG. 155. A seaplane with two floats. This is the most common type of seaplane.

Luscombe Airplane Corporation

I had flown in what was then called a "seaplane" . . .

course, I wanted to be in it. I wanted to take off in it, fly around in it, land in it. Some people said that the pilot took hunters deep into the woods. Others said that he flew sick people to hospitals miles away. When I heard them say those things, I'd smile to myself, because they were the things that adults would say, and even think. They would think that a person had to have a reason for owning and flying a plane with pontoons."

"Fun would be enough of a reason, wouldn't it?"

"That's what I thought. Exactly what I thought."

"I guess that's where I got it. I must have heard you say it sometime."

"There was a tavern of some kind in the little town. I never saw it, but my parents and grandparents used to go there in the evenings to have a beer. I think the parents who were vacationing used it as a way of getting away from their kids."

"In a way, you could say that the kids used it as a way of getting the parents out of their hair," he interrupted.

"What?" I said, rattled by the interruption.

"Nothing. Sorry. Go on."

"Where was I?"

"In the tavern, where your parents met the pilot and persuaded him to take you for a ride in the seaplane."

"I told you that already?"

"Many times, but please tell it again. I keep forgetting the details."

"Well, they were having a beer at the tavern one night, and the bartender said something to the guy sitting next to them that made them think that he must be the guy who flew the seaplane, so they asked him if he was, and he said yes."

"Oh, yeah. That's it."

"They got to talking, and my father bought him a beer and told him that his son watched the plane with obvious longing whenever it flew overhead."

"Is that what your father said, 'obvious longing'?"

"That's what he said he said."

"He's smarter than he looks, your father."

"Maybe."

"No offense intended."

"None taken."

IN SEARCH OF SOME BITS
OF MEMORY

PAUSED IN my reading, because I had come to the point in my account of the flight in the floatplane beyond which I was going to begin making things up. Albertine, because she is as much friend as lover, said, "Don't stop. Tell me all about it."

"I hardly remember it," I said truthfully.

"I hear the sadness in that."

"And I feel it. These memories fade, no matter how much we wish to hang on to them."

"Can't you poke and probe and bring it back?"

"I can poke and probe and bring something back, and then I can add to that whatever else comes drifting in on the wind, and out of what I actually remember and what comes drifting in I can make something that resembles a memory."

"Go ahead. I'd like to hear it."

"I don't think that it would belong in a full and frank disclosure."

"Excluding what comes drifting in would be hiding something, wouldn't it?"

"Are we going to chop a little logic here for my sake?"

"I think I'm going to argue that for you a remembered experience now consists not only of the memory but of the associations that cling to the memory—"

"Like the bits of cat fur that clung to my zwieback when I dropped it on my grandmother's kitchen floor."

"When you were an itty-bitty baby boy."

"Yes."

"Exactly what I mean, I think."

"I can't recall zwieback now without recalling the bits of cat fur stuck to it, and the cat, and the way the cat curled up beside my grandmother on her scratchy scarlet sofa, and the sofa itself, and on and on."

"'The memories of childhood have no order, and no end.'"

"Yes, and I've come to think that the reason they have no end is that the man recalling the boy has a boundless capacity for invention."

"Try to curb that tendency, climb into that floatplane, and tell me what went on."

"Let's see. I remember a lot of aluminum, aluminum sheets, the panels of the doors, the floor. I remember being squeezed into the plane, behind the seats, but I don't really remember my squeezing in, the act of getting into the plane, or getting into place behind the seats. That memory is already confused with others, and with an image of a floatplane bobbing beside a dock from some movie or other. I think it's a movie called *Day of the Painter*. I do remember being behind the seats, in a tight space—"

"It wasn't a four-seater?"

"What?"

"It sounds as if you were squeezed in behind the pilot and your father."

"I was—I think."

"If the pilot flew hunters into the woods, I would think he'd have a plane with three seats available for passengers rather than just one."

"You're right! I was behind the second row of seats."

"Who was sitting in the second row?"

"My grandfather was on the left."

"And?"

"My grandmother was on the right."

"And your mother?"

"She didn't come along. She didn't want to. I'd forgotten that."

I SEEK A LITTLE HELP FROM MY FRIENDS

....

IN ONE OF my grandfather's old, yellowing issues of *Impractical Craftsman*, I came upon an article titled "Motorcycles of the Air." I read it with mounting excitement. This was no visionary, might-be, could-be, someday-in-the-distant-future article. The flying motorcycle, or aerocycle, that it described was built entirely out of things that I knew existed. All I needed was a motorcycle, fabric, tubing, and a few other things that an enterprising guy like me could find almost anywhere. This little airplane could be built. According to the article, it could be built in the family garage in a few weekends. "Could be built

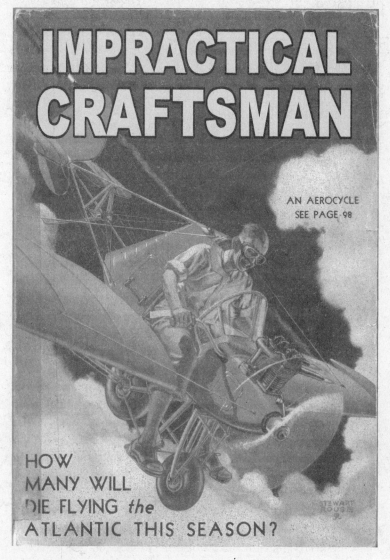

In one of my grandfather's old, yellowing issues of *Impractical Craftsman* . . .

Motorcycles of the Air

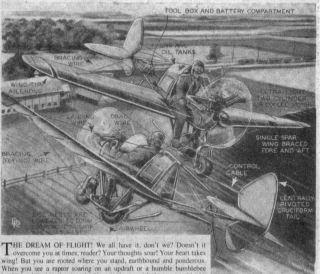

TOOL BOX AND BATTERY COMPARTMENT

GAS AND OIL TANKS

BRACING WIRE

WING-TIP AILERONS

ULTRA LIGHT TWO CYLINDER AIR COOLED MOTOR

LANDING WIRE

DRAG WIRE

SINGLE SPAR WING BRACED FORE AND AFT

BRACING (FLYING) WIRE

CONTROL CABLE

CENTRALLY PIVOTED CRUCIFORM TAIL

AIRWHEEL

THE DREAM OF FLIGHT! We all have it, don't we? Doesn't it overcome you at times, reader? Your thoughts soar! Your heart takes wing! But you are rooted where you stand, earthbound and ponderous. When you see a raptor soaring on an updraft or a humble bumblebee lumbering by with a burden of pollen, don't you wish that you could take wing, too, and soar above the cares and woes that soak the dank earth in this vale of tears? All of us here at *IC* do—particularly around the end of the month, when your letters about the current issue begin drifting in, and we have to spend a sorry couple of days writing corrections and retractions and conferring with our attorneys. After that, some of us try to achieve the trick of levitation by imbibing copious quantities of "aviation fuel."

Many of you objected, some of you in terms that should not be employed between people who feel for one another a great mutual respect, and certainly not in letters sent through the U. S. Mail, that our visionary article on the anti-gravity Hovermobile was "unbuildable" and even "impossible to realize within our lifetime." Well, yes, but we here at *IC* think that some of you out there in Readerland were missing the point. That article was meant as inspiration, not as a blueprint for backyard home-garage builders. If we have inspired one young genius to begin the fundamental research into gravitation and motivation that will eventually lead him (or her!) to transform the Hovermobile from impossible to inevitable, then our article will have done its job.

Nonetheless, we do recognize that many of you were frustrated in your attempts to build Hovermobiles, and that some of you, if your letters are to be believed, spent many exhausting hours and expended considerable sums in the attempt.

Reader, our sole goal, desire, and ambition is to make your dreams come true. To that end, we present you with this exciting new project: the AEROCYCLE!

The above drawing shows details of an aerocycle plane as conceived and drawn by Douglas Rolfe, airplane expert. Ships of this type, though not yet commercially produced, have been made possible by recent development of new materials such as extremely strong but light metal alloys and light weight motors. "Flying scooters" like the one illustrated on this month's cover would not be practical for long-distance flying, but would be ideal for sports use. With the cost at a moderate figure, these aerocycles would very likely displace gliders in popularity. There are no novel departures from accepted airplane practice in these designs.

Impractical Craftsman

...I came upon an article titled "Motorcycles of the Air."

in the family garage in a few weekends": I still use that claim as a joke in my internal running commentary on the world. At that time, to me, a few weekends seemed a reasonable time for building a small plane. I calculated how many hours that might be. "A few," I reasoned, might mean four or five, six at the most. The amateur handyman couldn't be expected to put in more than eight hours a day on a weekend, after a week full of work or school, so the entire project ought to take less than a hundred hours to complete. If I got a friend to help me, we could do the job in fifty hours—not much more than one working week—and I had several friends who would be willing to help me with a project like this, not just one. With so many cooks in the family garage, I might be flying in a couple of days!

Impractical Craftsman offered a complete set of plans, full-scale. "Just roll them out on the garage floor, and you can assemble the aerocycle right on top of the drawings, ensuring that everything fits as it should—and ensuring that you don't leave anything out!" I could understand that working in that way was a good idea, but our garage didn't have a floor at that time, just a layer of sand, and the cost of the plans was not only more than I had to spend but more than I would have been willing to spend if I'd had it. Frankly, I scoffed at the idea that it was necessary to have the full-scale plans in order to complete the project successfully. They might be necessary for the plodding, literal-minded sort of builder who had to be told which way to turn each screw, but not for a clever kid with a good imagination. The pictures in the article ought to be enough for a start, and when in the course of building the aerocycle I got down to a detail that wasn't visible in the pictures, I could pause, think about it, and make a few drawings of my own to work it out before building it. The technique had worked for Leonardo. It ought to work for me.

I asked Margot and Martha Glynn to help, not so much because they were mechanically adept or interested in aviation but because they had listened tolerantly and often to my story of the seaplane ride and because it would be a treat to have them on the crew, a pleasure to watch them working in the tiny short-shorts they were wearing that year.

"Hmmm," said Margot. "This is not quite the sort of thing we enjoy doing, Peter."

"We're likely to get dirty doing this," said Martha.

"Yes," I said, "but you would look so good doing it."

"He has a point," said Martha.

"He does," said Margot, "but then we look good at almost everything we do, and this is just not for us. Sorry, Peter."

I asked Spike.

"Wow," she said, looking at the article. "You're going to have to learn welding."

"I am?" I said. I hadn't counted on that.

"Sure," she said, giving me a friendly punch on the shoulder. "How else are you going to get all these steel tubes that form the support framework for the engine to stay together—wishful thinking?"

"Well—" I said noncommittally. (I had thought, if I could be said to have thought about it at all, that glue might work pretty well.)

A wistful expression came over Spike's face, a distant look into her eyes. "I always wanted to learn welding," she said.

"Now's your chance," I said.

"Yeah. Count me in." She gave me another punch. "Thanks, Pete."

I asked Marvin Jones.

He looked at the drawings and diagrams that accompanied the article. He looked at the drawings and diagrams that I had made. He brought his eyebrows together, furrowing the skin between them, and frowned.

"Anything the matter?" I asked.

"Was this designed by a trained aeronautical engineer?" he asked.

"Um—I don't know."

"And these pencil drawings, who did these?"

"I did," I said with what I thought was justified pride.

"I don't know much about aeronautics myself," he said, "but I think I know enough to say that this is not likely to get off the ground. If it does, it's going to be almost impossible to handle."

"Oh."

"You need a bigger tail surface, for one thing." He began reworking my sketch. "With a larger rudder—and ailerons—"

"So you'll help?" I said.

"Somebody's got to try to keep you from going down in flames," he said. "It might as well be me."

I asked Matthew Barber.

"Um—well—" he said. He fidgeted. He thrust his hands in his pockets. He frowned. He seemed to be stalling. He seemed embarrassed.

"Is there anything wrong?" I asked.

"Wrong? Of course not. What makes you ask that?"

"You're not answering me. You're stalling. You seem embarrassed."

"I—it's just that—I—"

"You don't want to help."

"I'll help."

"What is it, then?"

"Oh—it's just that—there's something I have to tell you. The guidance counselor—Mrs. Kippwagen—told me about a summer institute in math and physics—out in New Mexico—and she gave me a brochure about it—and I read through it and I said to myself, 'Peter would really enjoy this'—but I never told you about it—and I applied for it—and I got in—so I'm going to be going to New Mexico and studying advanced math and physics under the blazing sun—but I'm feeling completely miserable about it because I should have told you—"

"Hey, forget it," I said chivalrously. "I'll go see Mrs. Kippwagen and get an application—"

"It's too late," he said, and to his credit he hung his head in shame when he said it. "The deadline's passed."

THE QT-909, FROM QT FLYING MACHINES

IT'S AN AMAZING thing to say, an amazing thing to realize, but all of this makes me feel an almost overwhelming nostalgia—"

"You're sure you mean nostalgia?"

"I think so. I mean a yearning to return to an earlier experience, to experience again the sensations that I felt then, the springtime fervor and confidence I felt when I decided to build that plane, to see and hear again the responses of my friends, to stand once more on the sand floor in the family garage, even to listen again to Matthew's spluttering admission of his treachery—all of it."

"Nostalgia, you know, was originally perceived as a disease."

"I knew that."

"Of course you did."

"Wasn't it a disease of Belgian conscripts who were posted far from home and so fervently yearned to be back that they languished and died?"

"Something like that. It was originally identified by a Swiss physician, late in the seventeenth century."

"I bet you know who that Swiss physician was, don't you?"

"I'm afraid I do."

"Give, my sweet."

"He was Johannes Hofer, and he found evidence of the disease in Swiss living abroad who would rather not have been living abroad—young girls sent away to serve as domestics, for example, or soldiers fighting in foreign lands. They all felt the pain that accompanies intense and prolonged homesickness, a painful and debilitating desire to be back home again, and that is what Hofer called nostalgia, coining the term by combining the Greek *nostos,* meaning 'a return home,' and *algos,* meaning 'pain.'"

"You've got to cut back on those crossword puzzles."

"I'm thoroughly addicted. It's gone too far. There's nothing I can do about it now. So. Are you sure you're feeling nostalgic?"

"Maybe not, but I am feeling earthbound and ponderous. I'd like to take off."

"Shall we play hooky for the day?"

"It's more than that," I said, pouring coffee for me and tea for her. "This morning I am facing a workday full of annoying tasks that won't bring me any reward at all, not even the reward of feeling that I've done a job, because the job won't be done when the day is done. I'm going to have to work right through the weekend, and when the job is eventually done, in the small hours of Monday morning, I will not be satisfied with what I have done. All I will be is tired."

"I'm sorry for you," she said loyally.

"I know you are, and I am sorry for myself, very sorry for myself, and I know that that is immature and ignoble, but—"

"Yes?"

"Al, I really would like to have that aerocycle. My thoughts soar, but I am rooted here, earthbound and ponderous. You and I would get aboard, and we would fly away. We'd need an aerocycle built for two, of course."

"I should hope so."

"Al! Why don't we go? We could retrace my route to New Mexico."

"Well, (a) we don't have an aerocycle—"

"I could build one. Another one."

"Wait a minute. Are you serious?"

"I've been looking around the Web. Quite a few companies offer airplane kits for the home builder."

"Am I dreaming?"

"Just consider this one," I said, producing a printout that I had earlier kept concealed in the folds of the newspaper. "The QT-909."

"It looks like a coffin," she said. After a moment's further inspection, she added, "With wings," but not with the eagerness of one who hopes to climb aboard and soar above the quotidian cares of the workaday world.

"According to the people at QT Flying Machines, the kit is so complete and the directions are so clear that even a rank novice can assemble a 909 with ease—and I'm not a rank novice."

"How much does it cost?"

"The average QT-909 builder can be flying in less than two hundred eighty hours."

" 'Can be.' How much does it cost?"

"The kit includes virtually everything one needs to build a 909."

" 'Virtually.' "

"Well, everything except a few parts that you can find in almost any hardware store."

" 'Almost.' "

"One of the remarkable things about the 909 is the fact that you can hitch it behind a car and tow it to the airport."

"Currently, the budget will not support the purchase of a car."

"The wings fold back against the sides of the fuselage—"

"Not while you're in the air, right?"

"Rarely, I'm sure."

"Why am I reminded of something made out of feathers and wax?"

"Mostly plywood, actually. Glued together with epoxy."

"You want to take your honey into the clouds in a plywood plane?"

"The 909 needs barely a hundred feet of takeoff roll before she slips the surly bonds."

"Impressive. How much does this plywood kit cost?"

"No more than that used roadster with the FOR SALE sign that you sigh over when you walk past it every morning."

"I suggest that you confine your flying to the realm of the science of imaginary solutions."

Balzac was a master of the science of imaginary solutions. In *Louis Lambert,* he wrote, "Whenever I like, I can draw a veil over my eyes. Suddenly I go back into myself, and there I find a dark room, a *camera obscura,* in which all the accidents of nature reproduce themselves in a form far purer than the form in which they appeared to my external senses."

I sometimes draw that veil. I am not so adept that I can draw it whenever I like, but I can draw it at times. The place where I find the pure reproductions of the accidents of nature, my equivalent of Balzac's "dark room," is memory, of course, and even a painful memory is a refuge from a painful present. Perhaps, reader, you feel, as I do, that much of the present is not what you wish it were, not only your personal present but the present of our contentious, bullying species. Sometimes, I just want to fly away, to take flight, take off, make my getaway.

Flight! The word itself makes my thoughts soar, and saying it, softly, to myself, in a time of troubles, makes me feel a bit of its lift. Balzac has the young Louis Lambert say,

> Often have I made the most delightful voyage, floating on a word down the abyss of the past, like an insect embarked on a blade of grass tossing on the ripples of a stream. . . . What a fine book might be written of the life and adventures of a word! It has, of course, received various stamps from the occasions on which it has served its purpose; it has conveyed different ideas in different places; but is it not still grander to think of it under the three aspects of soul, body, and motion? Merely to regard it in the abstract, apart from its functions, its effects, and its influence, is enough to cast one into an ocean of meditations. Are not most words colored by the idea they represent? Then, to whose genius are they due?

. . . Is it to this time-honored spirit that we owe the mysteries lying buried in every human word? In the word *true* do we not discern a certain imaginary rectitude? Does not the compact brevity of its sound suggest a vague image of chaste nudity and the simplicity of truth in all things? The syllable seems to me singularly crisp and fresh.

. . . I chose the formula of an abstract idea on purpose, not wishing to illustrate the case by a word which should make it too obvious to the apprehension, as the word *flight* for instance, which is a direct appeal to the senses.

Perhaps you sometimes have, as I do, so strong a desire for flight, so strong a yearning to leave your present circumstances, that you are willing to trust your fate to feathers and wax. At such times, if I am able to, I draw a veil.

NO LAUGHING MATTER

. . . .

I **AM ASTONISHED** to realize how deeply I felt the sting of Matthew's treachery, and how deeply I feel it even now, so many years after the first stab. At the time it was like a sudden cramp, or the deep, sharp pain of a broken tooth, or a broken bone. Matthew was right in thinking that I would have wanted to go to the summer institute in math and physics. I wanted to go even after he had told me that going was impossible. Perhaps because I wasn't quite convinced that the deadline had passed, or perhaps because some perverse impulse to increase the pain of missing out compelled me, I visited Mrs. Kippwagen and asked to see the brochure that had lured Matthew to the program.

"I'm afraid it's too late to apply," she said.

"I know," I said. "Matthew told me, but I just want to see what I'm missing. Something in me won't be able to rest until I know what might have been."

She gave me the brochure, and then she added to it a useless application form. I stared at her, searching her face for any evidence of a smile.

"Mrs. Kippwagen," I said slowly, not quite sure whether I would actually ask her what I wanted to ask her.

"Yes?" she said, a bit warily.

"Why didn't you let me know about this in time to apply? I would have liked to go. I probably could have gotten in, if Matthew got in. My grades are better than his, especially in math and science, and I—"

"The feeling here," she said, tapping the eraser of her pencil on the blotter that covered most of the surface of her desk, "within the administration of the Babbington Public School System, was that only one student was likely to be chosen from any one town, and we wanted that student to be the best representative of the system we could put forth."

"That's Matthew?" I asked.

"We decided that it was Matthew," she said. The rhythm of the tapping pencil never altered.

I asked the classic question: "What's he got that I haven't got?"

"The right attitude," she said without half a moment's hesitation. "Matthew is a boy who exudes seriousness of purpose. People look at him and say to themselves, 'This is a sober boy, a boy who has put aside childish things, a boy who probably reads the world news every day and clucks his tongue over that chronicle of human misery—'"

"Mrs. Kippwagen," I asked, "are there any other summer institutes like this—maybe some that I could still apply for?"

"I've never heard of anything like this before," she said. "This is a new idea. It's a response to a national crisis. It's no laughing matter."

The brochure led off with these words:

YOUTH OF AMERICA! UNCLE SAM NEEDS YOU!

This is what followed:

Enemy Powers are training their youth to build rockets, satellites, and fearsome weapons.

Our intelligence tells us that their youth are far ahead of our youth. This means you!

We need a new generation of whiz kids who can build rockets, satellites, and fearsome weapons for us!

That's why Your Government, working through the privately funded Preparedness Foundation, is sponsoring the Summer Institute in Math, Physics, and Weaponry (SIMPaW) for promising high school students.

The Summer Institute is a six-week residential program for bright, serious high school students. (NOTE: For purposes of security and secrecy, the Institute is held on the campus of the New Mexico Institute of Mining, Technology, and Pharmacy, and accepted students should refer to themselves as "future pharmacologists of America.")

As a student at the Summer Institute, you will pursue a challenging curriculum that will prepare you for the struggle that lies ahead.

Don't think that you'll be sitting in dusty classrooms studying empty theory! Oh, no! You'll get useful, practical experience in calculating missile trajectories and weapons yields.

Should You Apply?

The Summer Institute is not for everyone. We're not looking for sluggards, laggards, or dullards. If that's you, pass us by. No comedians, either, thank you. We're looking for boys (and girls) with *promise,* the ones who stand at, or near, the top of their class, do their homework, and take out the garbage. If that's you, Uncle Sam says, "I want you to fill out the application form."

You must submit the application, school transcript, signed loyalty oath, and letters of recommendation in triplicate by April 15. No application received after that date will be considered for any reason under any circumstances. (And don't try to blame a late application on the U.S. Mail. Nothing stays those loyal couriers from their appointed rounds, and we will look with double disfavor on the application of anyone who claims that something does.)

Despite the clear statement that no applications would be entertained after the deadline, I decided to make the effort anyway, in the never-say-die spirit of Dædalus. I completed the application. I arranged to have my transcript sent to the institute. I noticed that the application did not include the loyalty oath that was mentioned in the list of required documents; I considered this the application's equivalent of an exam's trick question and devised a loyalty oath of my own. I lined up letters of recommendation, and I wrote a heartfelt cover letter explaining why my application was late and all but begging to be considered after the deadline.

> *Dear Admissions Committee:*
>
> *I am submitting an application for admission to the Summer Institute. I realize that this application will reach you after the official deadline for submission of applications, through no fault of the U.S. Mail. I trust that you will consider my application, despite its lateness, on the grounds that I have a good excuse for being late. Here it is: until now, no one had ever told me that there was such a thing as the Summer Institute.*
>
> *I am convinced that attending the Institute is the very thing I need to advance me in my goal of becoming a pharmacologist, if you know what I mean. I have been serious about this goal since I was a young boy, and I have always done my homework on time. (Well, almost always. Nearly on time.) I have enclosed a signed loyalty oath. (None was supplied, so I wrote my own, which I sincerely hope will be acceptable.)*
>
> *You should receive, under separate cover, my school transcript and letters of recommendation from my math and physics teachers and from a pharmacist in my home town of Babbington, New York.*
>
> *I implore and beseech you to give my application full consideration despite its lateness. If, on a winter's night, a traveler arrived at your door late, when dinner was done and the lights were out, seeking shelter and the warmth of human companionship, would you turn him away? Of course not. Though he arrived late, you would throw your door open wide and welcome the weary applicant with*

*hot soup, a warm fire, and a soft bed, wouldn't you? Isn't that the
American way?*
Sincerely yours,
Peter Leroy

Loyalty Oath
 *I hold these truths to be self-evident, that all men are created
equal, that they are endowed by their creator with certain unalien-
able rights, that among these are life, liberty, and the pursuit of
happiness—that to secure these rights, governments are instituted
among men, deriving their just powers from the consent of the governed, that whenever any form of government becomes destructive
of these ends, it is the right of the people to alter or abolish it, and to
institute new government, laying its foundation on such principles,
and organizing its powers in such form, as to them shall seem most
likely to effect their safety and happiness.*
 Peter Leroy

It didn't work. The admissions committee was not amused, and my
application was not entertained. I received a small slip of paper printed
with the following rejection notice:

*Thank you for your interest in the Summer Institute. Your applica-
tion was received after the Institute's deadline for receipt of applications had passed. Therefore, it cannot be considered. The Institute
wishes you the best of luck in your future endeavors.*

ON REJECTION'S GRAY GLOOM

ALBERTINE CROSSED THE room, rumpled my hair, sat beside
me, and gave me a hug, responding as much to the sigh that I
appended to my reading of the preceding chapter as to its text, I think.
"Were you horribly disappointed, my darling?" she asked.

"Yes, I was," I admitted. "I had forgotten this sad section of the tale, or perhaps I had chosen not to remember it. When that letter arrived, I fell into rejection's gray gloom."

"But you hadn't actually been rejected. Your application was late. It was never considered, not rejected."

"Try to tell an adolescent boy that there is a difference. Do you suppose that if he calls a girl and asks her to go with him to the first dance of the school year and hears her tell him that she already has a date, he allows himself to feel that he hasn't actually been rejected because his application was late and therefore could not be considered?"

"I see what you mean."

"Of course you do."

"He sinks into that gray gloom you mentioned just a moment ago."

"His estimation of his own self-worth slips lower and lower—"

"He asks himself why she couldn't invent some excuse to rid herself of the earlier bird and put him, the late applicant, in the place held by the earlier applicant and, ultimately, in the arms of the girl herself."

"Yes, I guess he does—"

"He tells himself that if she cared for him, she certainly would do that."

"Right—"

"He tells himself that if she *really* cared for him, she would never have accepted the invitation of any other applicant no matter how early the application was made."

"Yes, that too."

"He begins to wonder whether he shouldn't have done something to distinguish himself, to move himself to the head of the line of suitors, so that the timing of his invitation would not have been a factor in the girl's decision."

"I don't know about that—"

"He curses himself for not having offered to fly her to the dance in an airplane of his own construction."

"What?"

"That would have made her change the rules and accept him in place of the earlier applicant."

"Hey—"

"But no, no. Such thoughts would bring the fault too near himself, and the gray gloom of rejection is better than the bitter tea of inadequacy or incompetence or ineptitude, so he allows himself to slip a little lower, and a little lower, until he is sure that the girl wouldn't go to a dance with him if he were the last young aviator on earth, covered in glory, and he suspects that she would stay at home on the night of the dance, watching her parents play mah-jongg, rather than be seen in public on his arm."

"I think I'll move on to the next chapter."

"Oh, goody."

MR. MACPHERSON RAISES A QUESTION

....

MY FRENCH TEACHER, Angus MacPherson, must have noticed the downcast look that I wore throughout his class—a particularly knotty one on the uses of the subjunctive—because he stopped me on my way out the door and said, with a look of concern, "Peter, you seem a bit—how do you put it—down in the dump."

"Dumps," I said.

"Yes, that's it, the dumps, 'down in the dumps.' But why should it be so? Here in Babbington there is but one dump, unless they are hiding another from me. Are they? Is there a dump known only to initiates in a secret society of refuse and rubbish?"

"Um, no," I said. "I don't think so."

"Then one must be down in the dump, not the dumps, and that is where you seem to be. Why is that, Peter?"

"I've been rejected," I said.

"Ah! An affair of the heart! Of such sweet pain the teenage years are full to overflowing, I am afraid. Doubtless you will experience rejection many times. 'Learn young, learn fair; learn auld, learn mair.' In my own case—"

"It was more like being rejected by a college."

"How time flies! 'There's nae birds this year in last year's nest.' Are you after leaving us for college already?"

"No. Not yet. But I was hoping to spend the summer in New Mexico at a summer institute for promising high school students."

"Ah. That's a lot to parse all at once. An institute, you say?"

"Yes."

"What would that be? Not an institution, certainly? Not a house for the mad, I hope?"

"No, no. It's just—I guess it's—well—I don't exactly know what it is. A kind of summer school."

"Glorified by the name of Institute. I see. For promising high school students, you said?"

"Yes."

"I'm fully familiar with high school students, after trying to teach them to conjugate irregular verbs these past eight and twenty years, but I'm a bit less certain about what *promising* might mean."

"I think it means students who show promise."

"Students who show promise? What do they promise, pray?"

So far as I know, the Socratic dialogue had not yet become a Method of Instruction in the pedagogical armamentarium of American education, as it was to become not many years later, but Mr. MacPherson was already a practitioner of it, a pioneer in his way.

"I guess they promise to get better—improve—do remarkable things."

"Do you consider yourself a promising student?"

"Yeah. I think I've got promise."

"You think that you are likely to do remarkable things?"

"Well—I hope so."

"'Him that lives on hope has a slim diet.' What do you hope to do that's in the remarkable class?"

"I—um—I don't know—I—"

"Not a promising beginning," he said.

"I'm going to build an airplane out of parts of old motorcycles," I asserted suddenly.

"Now that is a promise! I see that you are a promising lad after all. So, with your being such a promising lad, why did the Institute for Promising Lads not accept ye?"

"Oh—my application was late—and I didn't mention anything about building the airplane."

"Hmmm. I see. Well, 'nae great loss but there's some smaa 'vantage.' With the loss their having passed you over, the advantage is that you are, I suppose, available if other institutes come looking for recruits?"

"Sure—but—"

"Yes?"

"I'd like to go to one that's held in New Mexico. I've kind of got my heart set on going to New Mexico now."

"And 'where the heart yearns to go, we mun go or die in the attempt,'" he murmured, mostly to himself, while he began rummaging through some papers on his desk. "Let's see—I've got a notice from the Institute for Future Œnophiles—but that's in Paris—and there's the Institute for the Study of Callipygian Women—but that's on the island of Martinique—and—ah!—here's the Faustroll Institute of 'Pataphysics—in New Mexico."

"What?" I blurted hopefully.

He held a clutch of papers toward me. I snatched them from him and examined them. There was a notice from the administration about scheduling final exams, a list of lunch menus for the remainder of the school year, and a memo from the vice principal reminding faculty members that only he was permitted to park in the space beside the space allocated to the principal himself.

"Oh," I said, managing a smile. "It was a joke."

"Something to lift you out of the dump."

"You really had me going there."

"'Nane can play the fool sae well as a wise man.'"

"I guess so," I said on my way out the door.

"Peter," he said to my back, "ask yourself something."

"Yeah?"

"Does it really require an institute to get you to New Mexico?"

ANTINOSTALGIA

···

THE ANSWER TO Mr. MacPherson's question was, I decided while thinking about it on the way home, yes. Something as solid and convincing and worthy as the Summer Institute that Matthew would be attending would be required to justify my going to New Mexico—to justify it to my father, who retained full veto power over any travel that might take me farther than the next town. A trip to New Mexico was likely to cost some money, and if I was going to ask my father to contribute to the expenses—which was what I had in mind—I was going to have to be prepared to convince him that I was going in pursuit of something that he would approve, like an education at an institute sponsored by an agency of the United States government.

New Mexico. "Land of Enchantment." The slogan stared at me from a poster that I had tacked to the wall beside my bed. I had written to the Department of Tourism of the State of New Mexico and requested everything that they could send me. I'd received a large, fat envelope stuffed with maps, posters, guidebooks, and brochures. Any of it that was suitable for framing I had thumbtacked to the walls of my room, in the gaps between my maps. I was surrounded by New Mexico and potential routes to New Mexico, but I was stuck in Babbington; my mind was in the Land of Enchantment, but my physical self was in the Land of Disappointment. I had to find a way to get there—but how?

I summoned a council of friends. We met in a booth at Kap'n Klam, Porky White's clam bar.

"If only there were some other institute that I could get into," I said, concluding my opening remarks, "I'm sure my father would let me go. In fact, it's the kind of thing he'd be eager to have me do. But if I just told him that I wanted to build the aerocycle and fly to New Mexico for the hell of it, he'd never let me do it in a million years."

They sat in glum silence. They all lived in similar circumstances. I wonder how many dreams of going elsewhere were entertained in the adolescent heads hanging over root beer and Coffee-Toffee soda that afternoon. We all wanted to go somewhere, anywhere, anywhere beyond Babbington. We wanted to be broadened by travel. Broadening was what we expected from travel, an enlargement of experience, an inflation of our essential selves.

Our teachers were to blame for this expectation and our collective wanderlust. They couldn't stop talking about the broadening effect of travel. Each of them had been somewhere and could prove it. They had slides. They had snapshots and postcards. They had souvenirs. Whenever one of those school days arrived with something in the air that made sitting in a classroom almost unbearable, we could mitigate the annoyance of our having to remain in school simply by asking about their travels.

Take, for example, Mrs. Bond. "Mrs. Bond, when you were in Minnesota, Land of 10,000 Lakes, did you find that—" one might begin, and following that prelude anything at all might be appended, and whatever it was it would induce in Mrs. Bond—who is serving here as a representative of all her colleagues, you understand—a reflective pause, bringing a recollective distance into her eyes, and sending her into what might be called a state of antinostalgia, the pain not of a yearning to return home but of a yearning to get away from home, or to return to a place other than home where one had felt for a while more keenly alive than one did at home, which, for Mrs. Bond, was more specifically the disease of Minnesotalgia, the yearning to be back in the Land of 10,000 Lakes rather than suffering the daily durance vile of teaching the history of New York State to some of its denser young citizens and spending her evenings in the smothering presence of Mr. Bond, who liked to think of himself as a humorist, the Man of 10,000 Jokes.

"Apply to the Faustroll Institute," said Matthew quietly.

"There isn't any Faustroll Institute," I said. "I told you—"

"Your father doesn't know that," he said, just as quietly.

Reader, I wish you had been there. I wish you could have seen those young heads rise, buoyed by the possibilities that Matthew had placed before us.

"Oh, this is going to be good," said Spike. She had a luminous smile, and she gave it to us now, allowing it to emerge slowly, to warm us, to drive away the chill drizzle of disappointment. "Very, very good."

"We'll need a brochure—" I said.

"It could just be an announcement," said Raskol. "If it's on official stationery, it wouldn't have to be a brochure."

"Then we'll need official stationery."

"I can do that," said Marvin. "I can make a linocut based on the seal at the top of the letter Matthew got, set some type, and run off a few sheets in the print shop."

"We'll need an application form—"

"We'll copy the one for SIMPaW," said Matthew.

"Don't forget to change the due date," Marvin cautioned him.

"And I'm going to have to get Mr. MacPherson to tell me what the Faustroll Institute of 'Pataphysics is supposed to be," I said.

I AM CHALLENGED

···

ALBERTINE FROWNED. SHE rarely frowns. When she does, my world churns.

"Don't you think that perhaps you're being too hard on him?" she asked softly.

"Mr. MacPherson?"

"No. Your father."

"Too hard on him?"

"You're making him into the grand naysayer, the crusher of all dreams, a comic-book villain. It seems a bit much to me."

"Have I never told you about the time when I was given the opportunity to see a play, in New York, a professional production, in a real theater, for the first time in my little life?"

"You have."

"I'll tell you again. These memories are so sweet. I love revisiting them. My father, the Grand Naysayer himself—"

"That's enough. I know the story. He wouldn't let you go. He made you paint the garage."

"Right."

"You've resented it ever since."

"Right."

"I just wonder sometimes if you have done the difficult work of getting inside his mind to find out what he wanted out of life, out of his life, what he might have yearned for."

I said nothing for a while. I went to the living room window and looked out over East 89th Street. Across the way, on the roof of a town house, one of our neighbors had set up a telescope and invited friends to view Mars during its extraordinary perihelic opposition. Host and friends were behaving in the cocktail-party manner, drinking drinks, eating snacks, and chatting, but one by one each of them would bend to the eyepiece of the telescope and peer through it, and I found that I could easily imagine that for some of them, the ones whose expressions altered while they were looking at the planet that had drawn so near but was still so far, the experience was broadening. They came away from the telescope silent and distant. They had been away for a while. They weren't quite back.

"It's not nostalgia that sends me back to where I've been," I said, turning toward Albertine, who had been reading while she waited for me to return. "It's curiosity. I want to notice what I didn't notice."

"Well, then, in that case—"

"Yes. In that case, you're right. Completely right. I ought to spend some time in my father's mind."

"I agree, but I think I'm going to be sorry that I brought it up."

I began to wonder. I began to wonder whether my father might have wanted many of the things that I had wanted myself. I began to employ the techniques that I learned during that summer I spent at the Faustroll Institute, the methods of the science of imaginary investigations, and some of my discoveries have found their way into the pages that follow.

A BAEDEKER FOR A WILD GOOSE

....

I **WAITED UNTIL** Mr. MacPherson was alone. I stood outside his classroom, watching through the narrow window beside the door. He was conjugating some esoteric verbs for half a dozen students, who were wearing the black berets and ribbons that identified them as members of the French Club, the *Coterie Française*. When they filed out at last, I knocked on the open door.

"*Oui?*" he said, still in the *Coterie* frame of mind.

"Mr. MacPherson, I have a question for you."

"Yes?" he asked, since it was only me.

"When you were trying to lift me out of the dump, with that joke about the Faustroll Institute—"

"The Faustroll Institute of 'Pataphysics."

"Right."

"Yes?"

"What made you pick that?"

"Pick that? What do you mean by 'Pick that'?"

"I mean, why did you make that up? The Faustroll Institute. Did you just pull that out of thin air, or is there something like it? Is it—by any chance—based on something real?"

"Ah. I see what you are asking. You are wondering, where do we get our ideas? When we have a burst of creative inspiration, where does it come from? Is it stimulated by something real—that is, as you put it, 'based on something real'—or does it come from 'nowhere,' so to speak? Is there a place within the mind called the imagination where nothing real resides, a place that holds only things that are imaginary, or is the relationship between the real and the imaginary a more intimate one, with a great deal of easy travel between the realm of the real and the realm of the imaginary, no passport required, no entry or exit visa demanded, come and go as you will—"

"I just want to know if there is anything like the Faustroll Institute; if not, I'm going to have to make the whole thing up from scratch."

"'From scratch.' Why do we say that?"

"I don't know," I said. "It means 'from nothing'—"

"Not quite, I think. More likely it means 'from raw ingredients,' like 'from whole cloth.'"

"I guess—"

"Perhaps you'll inquire about that at the Faustroll Institute."

"The Faustroll Institute, that's what I—"

"If they set you the task of writing a dissertation, perhaps you'll choose to do it on the question of whether an imaginary solution can be built from scratch, from whole cloth, or must needs be built from a kit, a set of precut pieces—pieces that we cut as we live, without even noticing that we're doing the work, and stack away in a cabinet, where perhaps they grow dry and dusty with time, until the day when we find that we need them, take them out, and assemble them to make a flying machine or the underpinnings for a château in the Pyrenees."

"Sure. Okay. I don't know what you're talking about, but I'll do it if I'm given the chance. What I need to know now is—"

"You need to know that 'pataphysics is the science of imaginary solutions, which symbolically attributes the properties of objects, described by their virtuality, to their lineaments."

"Oh."

"Do you see what I'm saying, lad?"

"No."

"It's all in here." He opened a drawer of his desk, the top right-hand drawer, which, for a right-handed person, is the drawer in which are kept the things that are most frequently used—like a stapler—or the things that one wants near at hand in a crisis—like a revolver. From the drawer he took a small book. He handed it to me. It was *Gestes et Opinions du Docteur Faustroll,* as by Alfred Jarry, described in its subtitle as a "*roman néo-scientifique.*"

"It's in French," I said.

"Sharp lad. If you want me to write you a recommendation for the Faustroll Institute, I'll need to see a translation of the first chapter."

"Oh."

"Shall we say tomorrow?"

"I guess."

"If you bring me a complete translation at the end of the summer, or at the start of the school year, I'll move you up to French IV."

"I'll try," I said, flipping through it.

"And if you bring me several translations, each different from the others, I'll put you in the advanced-placement class."

"But what about the Faustroll Institute?" I asked, almost pleading, almost whining.

"If you set out from here and go looking for it, with this book as your Baedeker and *vade mecum,* I'm sure that you will find the Faustroll Institute and perhaps even get to know the great Dr. Faustroll himself."

"You make it sound like Neverland, or Oz," I said, with the growing suspicion that he was having more fun with me than I ought to allow.

"Go to New Mexico. Take the book with you. Translate it as you go. See what you find."

"But I don't even really know what I'm looking for."

"'Seek till ye find, and ye'll never loss yer labour.'"

"Well—if it gets me to the Land of Enchantment—I'll do it—but it feels like a wild-goose chase."

"Now why in the world do we use that expression, apparently attributing to wild geese an aimlessness that surely isn't evident from their methodical migrations?"

A FATHER-AND-SON CONSPIRACY

MY MOTHER WAS easy to please; that is, I could please her easily. All I had to do was do something—and almost anything would do. She was ready to approve very nearly anything I did. She always expected the result to be something that would enhance my reputation and my résumé and make the world see my merits at last, which put her in marked contrast to my father, who, it seemed to me, expected most of my undertakings to turn into the sort of black mark that one did not want on one's permanent record.

"Peter's going to learn welding," my mother announced at dinner, flushed with the rosy prospects that this presented.

"Is that right?" said my father.

"I've already started," I said. "I got a free welding instruction book. I've been reading it."

"I always wanted to learn welding," my father said, and as he said it a wistfulness came into his voice that, to the best of my recollection, I had never heard before.

"Really?"

"Yeah. In my day, a guy who could weld, really weld, was sure to be popular."

"Is that true, Mom?"

"Oh, yes," she said. "I remember one boy in particular, Darren—"

"Darren," growled my father, evidently feeling the pain of an old wound. "What kind of guy is named Darren?"

"A guy who could weld," said my mother with a directness that made my father grunt and bend to his American chop suey. "Darren Smith. He had the most amazing hands," she recalled, extending her own and examining them. "They were large and sinewy."

"Darren Smith, 'a mighty man was he, with large and sinewy hands,'" I quoted.

"That's right," she said. "How did you know?"

"Just a guess," I said.

"His hands were so strong—and yet so fine—and in a way delicate—like the hands of a pianist."

I risked a sidelong glance at my father. He seemed angry. I might have said to myself that he seemed angry, as usual. I might have taken some cheap pleasure in the discomfiture that my mother's memory of Darren the welder had caused him. However, something—who can say what?—made me see him differently. Instead of anger, I saw disappointment. I saw that he really had wanted to learn welding. He had wanted to be popular. He might have wished, now, that some woman who had once been a girl when he was a boy might be recalling his capable hands.

"I'll lend you the free welding instruction book, if you like," I said. He grunted.

"It's never too late," I added with the wisdom of fifteen.

Having said it, I immediately regretted what I'd said, realized that it

"I always wanted to learn welding," my father said . . . "In my day, a guy who could weld, really weld, was sure to be popular."

was presumptuous of the son to counsel the father, and feared that I'd be belittled for it, but my father began to nod his head, slowly, then turned to me, and, with a smile that would have been invisible beside Spike's but lit our little dining room with unusual fluorescence, said, "You're right. Thanks. I'd like to take a look at it."

Obviously there would never be a better time for me to announce that I'd been accepted at the Faustroll Institute.

"I've got exciting news," I said.

"*More* exciting news?" said my mother.

"Much more exciting," I said. "I've been accepted at the Faustroll Institute for Promising High School Students."

"Oh, my goodness!"

"Promising?" asked my father.

"Yes. Showing promise. Likely to do remarkable things. That's me. I've got promise. It's official. The Faustroll admissions committee has decided that I show promise. I'm in."

I put the forgeries on the table. When I had met with Matthew and Marvin and first seen what they had produced, I had been more than impressed. The package seemed solid enough, full enough, and well enough executed to fool anyone. Now, when it actually had to fool my father, I was suddenly not so sure.

"Oh, Peter. This is wonderful," said my mother. "I can't wait to tell the neighbors."

"It's in New Mexico," I added, by the way, "and I'm thinking of flying out there—"

"Flying!"

"—after I build an aerocycle."

My father, nobody's fool after all, looked at me for a long moment, and then we exchanged two things we had never exchanged before: one wink and one grin.

I PREPARE TO WELD

....

A finite universe is unimaginable, inconceivable. An infinite universe is unimaginable, inconceivable. Doubtless the universe is neither finite nor infinite, since the finite and the infinite are only man's ways of thinking about it; in any case, that finiteness and infiniteness should only be ways of thinking and speaking is also something inconceivable, unimaginable. We cannot take a single step beyond our own impotence; outside those walls, I feel sick and giddy. If the wall is no longer there, the gulf opens at my feet and I am seized with dizziness.

—Eugene Ionesco, *Fragments of a Journal*

THE FREE WELDING instruction book was actually something less than a book, barely a booklet, but in the space of its few pages it managed to be extremely discouraging. Welding, I discovered as I read, could not be accomplished with the tools and equipment I already had or with supplies I might find around the house. Knowledge, skill, and large, sinewy hands were not sufficient to the craft of welding—not that I had large, sinewy hands, but had I had them, they would not have been enough. Equipment was required: tanks, torches, an eye-shield, gases, gloves, and a cart to lug all the gear from place to place. All of this equipment, the book announced every time a piece of it was mentioned, could be purchased from Dædalus Welding, and there was a handy order form in the back of the book.

I couldn't afford any of the equipment or supplies, and I doubted that my father could afford any of it, either, so I began to fear for my prospects as a welder and, welding being apparently prerequisite to the construction of an aerocycle, my prospects as an aviator, a sojourner in the Land of Enchantment, and student of the Faustroll Institute. However, hope has always come as easily to me as despair, so, by reading the book carefully and thoroughly and by performing the welding exercises in my mind, as thought experiments, I prepared myself for the unlikely but not impossible event of my coming into some welding equipment through the agency of some sponsor, mentor, or angel as yet unmet.

Permit me an aside on thought experiments.

According to the *Stanford Encyclopedia of Philosophy*, thought experiments are "devices of the imagination," employed when "a real experiment . . . is impossible for physical, technological, or just plain practical reasons." The author of the encyclopedia article, James R. Brown of the Department of Philosophy at the University of Toronto, asserts that the "main point" of interest about thought experiments for a philosopher "is that we seem able to get a grip on nature just by thinking. . . . We visualize some situation; we carry out an operation; we see what happens."

Among the famous thought experiments that he cites are Maxwell's demon, Schrödinger's cat, and, "one of the most beautiful early examples," Lucretius's lance. My copy of Lucretius's *De Rerum Natura*, in W. H. D. Rouse's translation, being ready to hand, I am able to insert here the relevant passage:

> The universe then is not limited along any of its paths; for if so it ought to have an extremity. Again, clearly nothing can have an extremity unless there be something beyond to bound it, so that something can be seen, beyond which our sense can follow the object no further. Now since we must confess that there is nothing beyond the sum of things, it has no extremity, and therefore it is without end or limit. Nor does it matter in which of its quarters you stand: so true is it that, whatever place anyone occupies, he leaves the whole equally infinite in every direction.
>
> Besides, if all the existing space be granted for the moment to be finite, suppose someone proceeded to the very extremest edge and cast a flying lance, do you prefer that the lance forcibly thrown goes whither it was sent and flies afar, or do you think that anything can hinder and obstruct it? For you must confess

and accept one of the two; but each of them shuts you off from all escape, and compels you to own that the universe stretches without end. For whether there is something to hinder and keep it from going whither it is sent and from fixing itself at its mark, or whether it passes out, that was no boundary whence it was sped. In this way I shall go after you, and wherever you place your extremest edge, I shall ask what at last happens to the lance. The effect will be that no boundary can exist anywhere and the possibility of flight will ever put off escape.

Among the many fascinating things about that passage is the image at the end of it of Lucretius harrassing his reader, his opponent in the argument over whether the universe has a limit, driving him to the extremity, that is to say, to whatever, wherever, the reader has presumed the extremity to be, and annoying him so persistently with his badgering and yammering that the reader is urged or forced to flee ever farther, and the fact that the reader can keep fleeing Lucretius is the refutation of the reader's argument that there is a boundary beyond which he cannot go, the border of a land that none of us may ever enter. Is it only me, or do you also hear a plaintive moan under the triumphant tone of that ending sentence? "I'm right! Fly, fly, fly as far as you can possibly fly, but you can never escape. There is no way out of here, reader, none. I wish there were, but there is not. There is no escape."

Lucretius's thought experiment was popular in my set when I was a boy. I don't mean to suggest that any of us had read Lucretius or had the slightest idea who Lucretius was or that any of us had ever thought his way to the distant reaches of space with an argumentative companion and watched while the unnamed someone who had accompanied him cast a flying lance; I mean only that we rode third-class on the same train of thought. On nights when we lay in someone's back yard looking at the stars and exploring the limits of our little minds, we asked ourselves and one another, again and again, what was at the end of the universe. Every time we asked we concluded, as Lucretius had when he was out in his back yard with the argumentative lancer, that there was no end.

"You ever ask yourself what's at the end of the universe?" someone would ask, even if the question had been asked not so long ago, on another night.

"Yeah."

"I mean, what could be there? A brick wall?"

"Search me."

"Because if there's a brick wall, then what's on the other side of the wall? You know what I mean?"

"Yeah."

We would continue in this manner until we were at our wits' end, though we never reached the universe's. The little philosopher in these exchanges may not have been doing a very good job of playing Lucretius, but I suspect that the respondent was a lot like the lance-caster, and together they were working their way toward the age of reason.

> It is not difficult to gain some faint idea of the immensity of space in which this and all the other worlds are suspended, if we follow a progression of ideas. When we think of the size or dimensions of a room, our ideas limit themselves to the walls, and there they stop. But when our eye, or our imagination, darts into space, that is, when it looks upward into what we call the open air, we cannot conceive any walls or boundaries it can have; and if for the sake of resting our ideas, we suppose a boundary, the question immediately renews itself, and asks, what is beyond that next boundary? and in the same manner, what is beyond the next boundary? and so on, till the fatigued imagination returns and says, there is no end.
>
> —Thomas Paine, *The Age of Reason, Part One*

TO HELL WITH WELDING

WELDING SEEMED TO stand in my way like a schoolyard bully blocking the water fountain, and I will admit that for a time I thought of abandoning the entire project and resigning myself to spending the summer in Babbington, but my friend Raskol salvaged my hopes and dreams by making welding not only unnecessary but useless.

One day he found me studying *Impractical Craftsman* during study hall (engaged, I thought then and think now, in an activity entirely appropriate for study hall, but one that was forbidden, since *study* was constrained to mean "doing work assigned in a course taught at Babbington High School," and if one was found to be engaged in any other pursuit—writing a love letter, reading a magazine, trying to calculate the size of the universe, or making mechanical drawings of a single-seat airplane—then the product and any attendant supplies or materials were subject to confiscation and, theoretically at least, destruction). I was studying the drawings of the aerocycle and sketching its structural skeleton. I had known that this sketching would be necessary, since the article did not include a plan for the skeleton, and I had expected it to be tedious and annoying, but it was turning out to be fascinating and puzzling. From the pictures in the article, I was trying to make working plans, translating the pictures, none of which showed the craft with its skin off, into the type of three-view drawing we had been taught to make in shop class, where our drawings were limited to much simpler projects, such as, in my case, a wrought-iron armature to hold a plaque that read LEROY, which when it was finished I nailed with pride to one of the pillars that supported the roof over the front porch of the family home, and a wooden box that held and hid the cardboard box that Sneezles tissues were packed in, still allowing them to pop up one at a time when the projecting tissue was tugged, which my mother had installed in the bathroom, on the back of the toilet, on top of the tank.

"Are these the plans for the aerocycle?" Raskol asked.

At the time, I assumed that he must have mistaken my handmade, pencil-drawn plans for a commercial product, an assumption that, I realize now, may have been wrong.

"Yes," I said, "but not the plans that *Impractical Craftsman* sells. I haven't ordered those. They're too expensive. I'm trying to make my own plans based on the pictures in the article."

He bent over the plans and studied them closely. "Is this why you're going to learn how to weld?" he asked.

"That's right," I said, though my learning to weld was becoming less and less likely.

"Are you nuts?"

"Why do you ask that?"

"If you make this thing out of welded steel, it's not going to get off the ground. Never. Not a chance. It's going to be much too heavy."

"You're sure?" I asked hopefully.

"Sure. You've got to make this out of aluminum."

"Oh."

"It's light but strong."

"Sure."

"But you can't weld aluminum."

"Oh?" I asked, brightening.

"Well, I guess, theoretically, somebody could weld aluminum, but it would be a real bitch, what with aluminum's high thermal conductivity and low melting point. I wouldn't bother trying if I were you."

"What should I—"

"You've got to rivet it together."

"Oh." I was going to have to learn riveting. Did I sigh? Probably. Did I frown? Almost certainly. Riveting sounded as arcane, difficult, and expensive as welding. I think I recall that I began to consider flying to New Mexico on a commercial airliner, as Matthew would be doing. His expenses would be paid by the Preparedness Foundation, and he would enjoy tasty meals served by smiling stewardesses, whose attentions were, among my friends, none of whom had ever flown, legendary.

"Or—" said Raskol, with the impish grin of a person bearing good news, "you can just drill the parts and bolt them together."

Perfect. Not only was drilling already within my repertoire of skills, but my grandfathers owned jars and jars of nuts and bolts. I'd been playing with them since before I could walk. I could drill as well as the next guy, and I could bolt far better than most. To hell with welding.

That afternoon, I began scavenging Babbington for aluminum. I was astonished to find how much aluminum was going to waste in garages and attics: tent poles, flagpoles, folding clothes poles and outdoor drying racks constructed like umbrellas, folding chairs for lawn or beach, the legs and tops of folding tables, the pylons from beach umbrellas, and even window mullions and frames.

I want to take this opportunity to thank the citizens of Babbington for contributing their scrap to my dream. My heart soared when my friends and acquaintances, and even a few of my enemies, endorsed that dream by donating some of the raw materials that would make it a reality. My call for assistance sparked such a remarkable response, an outpouring of aluminum, that it resembled a movement. Its adherents and workers were zealous, some of them wrenching aluminum from the arthritic hands of their reluctant grandparents, and the most fanatical of them resorting to stealing.

I will confess to a heady feeling of power when I saw what I had unleashed—followed by a deflating feeling of impotence when I discovered how difficult is the task of leashing a movement once unleashed. Aluminum scrap kept showing up at our house for years. Eventually the flow dropped to a trickle, but the idea that I needed aluminum was still alive in the world even after I had left Babbington for college, and my mother would often finish her letters to me with a postscript laconically listing the recent deliveries, such as: "P.S. Two folding chairs and a tray today."

PINCH-A-PENNY, THE PEOPLE'S PLANE

ALBERTINE STARTLED ME. I had been lost in thought. (If Mr. MacPherson were here, he would ask me why I use that expression. In this case, I could tell him that I have often marveled at how apt it is as a description of my state when I am thinking in the experimental mode. I begin somewhere, with an idea or a question, and from that starting point I begin to wander. I go where my thoughts take me, and that is why Albertine has decided that I should no longer drive unless she is with me to bring me, when necessary, back from the distant place to which my thoughts have flown into the immediate context through which the car is hurtling. Sometimes she gives me a nudge to bring me back; sometimes she screams.)

She was looking over my shoulder. I was looking at my computer screen.

"What's that?" she asked.

"It's Pinch-a-Penny, the People's Plane," I said.

"Ah. The People's Plane."

"Anyone can fly it. You don't need a license. It democratizes flight."

"Anarchizes flight, you mean. Driving is bad enough, but just imagine 'anyone' getting into one of these things and whizzing around without training, tutelage, examination, or certification."

"Scary," I admitted. "I would like to point out, however, that the frame is made of aluminum tubing."

I pointed to the photograph.

"It looks like a folding table," she said.

"There are remarkable similarities between this plane and the one that I built—the resemblance to a folding table being only one of them."

"Did it really look like this?"

"The frame did—part of it—but by the time I was finished, I had made many original contributions to the design—"

"Improvements?"

"Adaptations inspired by necessity."

"Necessity being defined as the demands of aeronautical engineering and fluid dynamics?"

"Necessity being defined by what I had on hand," I muttered, returning to my study of the Pinch-a-Penny.

"Come on," she urged, with a nudge of her hip. "Tell me about the People's Plane."

"Well, Norton Prysock—"

"Norton Prysock? Who's he?"

"The designer of the Pinch-a-Penny."

"Nort to his intimates, no doubt."

"Well, *I* certainly wouldn't doubt it. Nort says here on his Web site that this plane can be built in about two hundred fifty hours, using only simple hand tools. Anyone can do it, just by following the steps in the construction manual and referring to the detailed plans."

"'Anyone,' says Nort."

"Says Nort."

"An unsupportable claim, I think. 'Anyone'? You would think that 'anyone' could make a decent bagel just by following the steps in the manual and referring to the detailed plans, but experience belies it again and again."

"He makes a point of the fact that no welding is required."

"The bagel analogy holds."

"He says he's sold more than two thousand sets of plans."

"I smell a home business for you there."

"Hundreds of Pinch-a-Pennies are currently under construction," I went on.

"Says Nort."

"Says he."

"I take that to mean that hundreds of Pinch-a-Penny projects are languishing in back yards and garages."

"Seven are flying. Have flown."

"Seven." She leaned toward the screen. "Tell me what you see here," she said.

I looked at the photograph on the Pinch-a-Penny Web site.

"I see a stocky man, whom I take to be Norton Prysock, standing beside what I assume is his own Pinch-a-Penny, at the point in its construction when it was complete except that the fabric that would eventually cover the wings, control surfaces, and, optionally, the fuselage aft of the cockpit had not yet been applied."

"Do we know that he ever did get around to covering the thing?"

"Skeptic," I whined.

"And daughter of a skeptic," she reminded me. "What did my father always say?"

" 'Assume nothing.' "

"Look behind Nort and the Pinch-a-Penny, Peter, and tell me what you see there."

"There's an outbuilding of some kind, a shed or garage, or a shed with a carport attached—"

"—and the siding has never been put on it, just the raw boards that are supposed to underlie the siding."

"Right."

"And the roof has been covered with tar paper but not shingled."

"Right."

"There is a stack of something on the left and a stack of something else on the right, both stacks covered with tarpaulins."

"Maybe he's going to use those tarps as fabric for the wings."

"I wouldn't be surprised. And then whatever is under those tarps will be exposed to the weather, and in time will molder and rot."

"Maybe."

"Nort has a serious personality flaw, Peter. He is not a finisher. He probably abandoned the carport project when the Pinch-a-Penny passion struck."

"I don't know about that. He looks so relaxed and self-confident— the way he's leaning on the plane—" In the photograph, Nort was resting his right elbow on the aluminum just ahead of the cockpit.

"He *appears* to be leaning on it," said Albertine, "but I don't think he actually is."

"You don't?"

"No. There is a tension in his body that makes me think he is holding himself in that position, giving the appearance of the builder at his ease, resting on the plane he has built, but in fact being careful not to put any weight on it."

I looked more closely. I took the magnifying glass from my desk drawer and looked more closely still.

"Well?" she asked.

"You may be right," I said.

SURPLUS MOTORCYCLES? WHY NOT?

THE HEART OF the aerocycle design was a surplus motorcycle. The people at *Impractical Craftsman* asserted that the builder could obtain a surplus motorcycle locally and easily. They passed over the acquisition of a surplus motorcycle so quickly, in so few words, that I got the impression of a vast glut of surplus motorcycles, a buyer's market in surplus motorcycles, and I was amazed that I hadn't ever seen any abandoned by the side of the road, considering that the glut must have made them all but worthless.

I looked in the Yellow Pages under "Motorcycles, Surplus," but there was no entry for "Motorcycles, Surplus." I looked under "Surplus," but the only listing there was for the Babbington Army and Navy Store, and I knew from my frequent visits that although they carried lots of useful gear, they had no motorcycles.

"Where are all the surplus motorcycles?" I asked my friend Raskol, who, I assumed, was likely to know.

"Surplus motorcycles?"

"Yeah. Aren't there a lot of surplus motorcycles going begging?"

"What makes you think that?"

"I got the impression—"

"—the misimpression."

"I don't think so."

"Hey, Ernie!" he called into the house.

"Whaddaya want, shithead?" growled one or the other of his brothers, both of whom were named Ernie, possibly because Raskol's parents were twice as fond of the name as were the average parents of an Ernie, or because they were half as inventive, or because they were much, much more forgetful.

"You know where there are any surplus motorcycles?"

"Surplus?"

"Yeah."

"Motorcycles?"

"Yeah."

"Surplus motorcycles?"

"That's the concept: surplus motorcycles."

"Where the fuck did you get the idea that there are surplus motorcycles?"

"Peter."

Ernie advanced out of the perpetual gloom of the Lodkochnikov interior, astonishment and contempt struggling for dominance in his expression.

"Surplus fucking motorcycles?"

"Well—yeah."

"Hey, Ernie!" he called into the house.

"Whaddaya want, shithead?" growled the other Ernie.

"Is there such a thing as surplus motorcycles?"

"Oh, yeah. Sure."

"Where the fuck are they?"

"Somewhere over the rainbow, beyond the sea, in never-never land, on the unicorn ranch, where virgins ride them when they herd the beasts."

"That's a good one, Ernie," said the Ernie standing in front of us, shaking his head in chortling admiration. "Jesus, that's a good one."

Raskol and I walked down the plank that linked the front porch of their riverside house on stilts with the margin of River Sound Road. When we were well out of earshot of the two Ernies, I said, "I thought they'd know. I thought you'd know."

"Nobody can know something that can't be known," he said. "There aren't any surplus motorcycles, so there isn't any way that anybody could know where to find them." He took note of my crestfallen look and gave me a punch on the shoulder. "However," he said, "there are wrecked motorcycles, quite a few of them, and I know where they are."

"Where?"

"Pretty far. We'll have to drive. I'll pick you up tonight. Midnight."

In defense of the editors of *Impractical Craftsman*, I will say that I have come to think that an assumption underlay their assertion that a surplus motorcycle would be easy to obtain, a collective assumption arising from what today I can recognize as the naïveté of the incurably hopeful. I recognize it now between the lines in those old issues of *Impractical Craftsman* because I recognize it now in myself. You need a motorcycle. You want a motorcycle. You know you can't afford a new one, and you don't want a used one because you've learned, at second hand, from your parents' experience, that used cars break down so often, and you've extrapolated from that the likelihood that used motorcycles would break down just as often. If only there were some surplus ones available, new but unneeded, reliable but cheap. Surplus motorcycles? Well, gee, why not? Sure. Of course. The world must be rich in them, if there's any justice.

A SOP

∙∙∙

RASKOL DID NOT have a New York State driver's license, nor did he have his father's license to drive the family truck. However, occasionally, at night, when the rest of his family was asleep, he would slip outside and cross the street to the weedy lot where the Lodkochnikovs parked the family truck, an old Studebaker C-Cab pickup, put his shoulder to the door frame, and roll the truck away silently, pushing it along the road until he was far enough from the house to start it without being heard, and take it for a ride. I sometimes went with him on these rides. Most of the time, we went wherever fancy took us, inventing ways to let chance determine which turn to make at the next intersection, but now and then we would get the urge to go somewhere in particular, to take a trip with a destination, and when we did, the destination was usually Montauk, at the eastern tip of the south fork of Long Island. I would slip out of my house and wait for him at the corner, three houses south, distant enough so that my parents, who were sometimes wakeful, wouldn't hear the door when I climbed in and pulled it shut.

I was waiting there when Raskol pulled up in the sputtering truck.

"Something wrong with it?" I asked.

"Ahh, my father doesn't take care of this thing," he said, shaking his head. "The engine keeps quitting on me."

It did.

"See what I mean?"

"I do."

"Might be points, plugs, points *and* plugs, the coil. I don't know. You got any money?"

"Some."

"We'll stop at the all-night gas station and see what they can do."

It was the coil. There were no coils for an old C-Cab pickup in stock at the garage. The mechanic suggested that we get one at Majestic Salvage and Wrecking.

"As it happens," muttered Raskol, "that's where we're headed."

"Midnight discount?" asked the mechanic.

"Yeah," said Raskol.

We lurched off in the reluctant truck, Raskol urging it on, alternately threatening and cajoling it. When the engine quit again and we were sitting in the dark, letting it rest before he tried restarting it, he said, "I bet this sends a little shiver down your spine."

"What?"

"The way the engine quits unexpectedly."

"Not particularly—" I began.

"Doesn't it make you wonder what would happen if your engine quit while you were sky-high over St. Louis?"

It hadn't until then.

"A little, I guess," I said, shrugging in the manner of a kid with a lot of nerve. Later, when he had the truck on the road again, I began wringing my hands.

When we neared Majestic Salvage and Wrecking, Raskol turned the headlights off, and then the engine, and we rolled into the parking lot as quietly as one can in an old truck with weak shocks, sagging springs, and a couple of clam rakes in the bed. We settled to a stop in front of a padlocked gate in a chain-link fence. Raskol reached under the seat and pulled out a paper bag.

"Midnight snack?" I asked.

"A sop for Cerberus," he said.

"Huh?" I queried, if I remember correctly.

"There's a dog," he said. "The junkyard dog."

"Ahh," I said. "The junkyard dog. A mythic figure in American life."

"That's right, and his ancestor is Cerberus, the three-headed dog that guarded the entrance to the infernal regions."

"Oh," I said. "Of course. *The Æniad*."

We got out of the truck, closing the doors so carefully and quietly that I would have thought no ear, not even a dog's, could have heard the sound, but no sooner had we done so than something dark, snuffling, and snarling lumbered to the fence near us, on the other side, the inside. Raskol quoted from Dryden's translation of the *Æniad*, whispering:

"'No sooner landed, in his den they found / The triple porter of the Stygian sound . . .'"

"'Grim Cerberus,'" I finished.

"I've been working on this dog for quite a while," he whispered.

"Just in case?"

"Just in case," he said.

"Amazing," I said with deep and sincere admiration.

He called into the dark, hoarsely. "Cerberus. Here, boy."

"His name is actually Cerberus?"

"Are you joking?"

"No."

"How the hell would I know if his name is Cerberus?"

"I don't know. I thought, since you called him Cerberus—"

"It's what I call him. He answers to it."

The dog, a single-headed dog, came bounding over. He didn't bark. He didn't growl. If he had not been so fearsome to look at, I would have said that he was glad to see us. Raskol reached into the bag and brought out a fistful of ground beef. He held it at arm's length like Yorick's skull and soliloquized: "'The prudent Sibyl had before prepar'd / A sop, in honey steep'd, to charm the guard. . . .' In this case, the prudent sibyl was my sister, Ariane. What she put in this, I don't know, but she told me she uses it to get away from guys who want stuff she doesn't want to give—you know what I mean?"

"Yeah," I said, with a knowing chuckle, or, to be honest, a simulation of a knowing chuckle. Raskol tossed the meat over the fence. Cerberus watched it arc and leapt to catch it as it fell. It was my turn to quote: "'He gapes; and straight, / With hunger press'd, devours the pleasing bait. / Long draughts of sleep his monstrous limbs enslave; / He reels, and, falling, fills the spacious cave.'"

AN URGE

· ·

WHEN THE DOG was clearly unconscious, we clambered over the fence and inside the yard," I wrote. During the act of writing, while bringing the fence to mind and recalling our clambering over it, the thought occurred to me that today we probably wouldn't have been able to get beyond that fence. It would have concertina wire strung along the top, wire that bore, at intervals, projections in the shape of trapezoids, the inverted bases of decapitated triangles, razor-sharp, far sharper than the teeth of Cerberus, and a better deterrent to teenage midnight salvage. I got the urge—

As I age, I am continually amazed by the vastness of my ignorance. "I got the urge" is another example of it, an expression that I have taken for granted, and I see now what a limp one it is. Mr. MacPherson, wherever you are, you will, I think, be happy to know that I looked it up. The origin of *urge*, the Latin word *urgere*, "to press, force, or drive," suggests something much more active than the expression does. It suggests that there is a someone or something doing the pressing, forcing, or driving—a god, perhaps. I'll try again—

Urge, the Roman god of curiosity and shopping, powerful and compelling, beloved of Pandora, entered my bedroom through the open window and began pressing me to drive out to Long Island, beyond Babbington, to see what the junkyard might look like now. Did it still exist? Had it been replaced by a gated community of "luxury" condominiums? Something called, say, Majestic Acres? Or Mirabasura? Albertine and I could pack a lunch, drive out, find the junkyard or its replacement, and then picnic on the beach, weather permitting.

"Are you asleep?" I whispered, softly, in Al's direction.

"No. Do you want to read?"

"Actually, I was thinking about going for a drive."

"We don't have a car."

"We could borrow one."

"From whom?"

"Just kidding," I said, as if the whole thing had been the best I could manage in the way of a joke in the middle of the night.

I hadn't really been kidding, though. I think that, inspired by my memories of the midnight discount escapade, I must have been playing with the idea of finding a car that we could appropriate for a couple of hours in the middle of the night, when its owner wouldn't notice that it was gone, someone who would be as unknowingly openhanded with his car as Raskol's father had been with his truck. I astonished myself. Perhaps you think that I was astonished and a bit ashamed to find that I was even thinking of "borrowing" someone else's property. I was, a bit, but I've been living in Manhattan for a while now, and my sense of the rightness of ownership has decayed. I was more astonished to recognize that I did not possess the skills required to borrow a car without license to do so. I didn't even know how to jump the ignition. How could it be that I had gone through an entire youth and young adulthood in the United States of America in the twentieth century without learning such a skill?

"We could rent one," I suggested.

"Or," she said sleepily, "here's an idea—you could build one—"

"Hey."

"—out of the parts of abandoned Pinch-a-Penny projects."

"Ouch."

"Not such a bad idea, really."

"Come on, Al."

"It could be a real city car."

"Is this a joke?"

"It was, but now I'm wondering."

"Wonder on."

"Room for two, and room for shopping bags—"

"Shopping bags, of course."

"—shelter from the rain and snow—"

"This is starting to sound like—"

"That little white plane you were looking at this afternoon."

"How often are you looking over my shoulder?"

"When there's a picture on your screen, it's hard to resist."

"That was the Mistral, that little plane."

"It was attractive, chic, sleek, like a shoe."

"It's French."

"Ah! I should have known."

"It is a sleek little thing."

"Very. And when I saw it, I thought at once that it would make a beautiful little city car, without the wings."

"It's really just one wing."

"It's not as sleek or chic as the rest of the plane."

"You're right."

"It's so big, and so rectangular."

"I was thinking the same thing myself."

"That it would make a good car?"

"No. That the wing looked clumsy compared to the rest of it."

"So, subtract the wing—"

"—and lop off the tail, which sticks out like an afterthought—"

"—something tagging behind—"   •

"—like a trailer—a dog on a leash—"

"—a clerk in a shoe store who hovers when you want to browse the stock at your leisure, raising each shoe, assessing its heft, fingering its heel—"

"Good night again, my darling."

"Good night."

I lay there for a long while, imagining a flight in the sleek Mistral, out to Long Island, for a low overflight of Majestic Salvage and Wrecking. I was pleased to see that it was still there. There was no razor wire. Two kids, the age I once was, were clambering over the fence. They froze when they heard the Mistral humming overhead and ran when I buzzed them. I don't know why I buzzed them. It was just an urge.

MAJESTIC SALVAGE
AND WRECKING

WHEN THE DOG was clearly unconscious, we clambered over the fence and inside the yard. Raskol had a flashlight. He switched it on, then off again at once. "The motorcycles are over in that direction," he said, meaning the direction in which he had shone the beam.

"How do you know?" I asked, not because I doubted him but because I wondered how he knew.

"I come here during the day now and then and buy something. It gives me a chance to browse."

"Wow," I said, in deep admiration of his thoroughness and foresight and, I think I realize now, his daring and his audacity in taking such a step toward an outlaw's life.

The night was dark, but after a few minutes I could see the vague outlines of masses of things, and plenty of them, though I couldn't have said what most of them were. We had to step carefully as we made our way in the direction of the motorcycles. Everywhere in our path lay items awaiting salvage. Junk, one might say, but why demean it by calling it that? What should properly be called junk, I think, is only what is useless, nothing more than trash, but what surrounded us in such looming profusion was useful stuff. That is, it was *potentially* useful. All of it had outlived its original use, but it was waiting here in limbo for a new life, waiting to be salvaged, put to a new use, the way memories that seem to have been forgotten wait in the dark recesses of the majestic salvage and wrecking yard of the mind, patient in that limbo until they are salvaged and put to a new use.

I remember seeing in *Impractical Craftsman* an article that told how to make a power saw out of an engine block and another that featured a potter's wheel made from the guts of a washing machine. Nothing is ever completely useless: that was the *IC* creed. If you looked at things with that *IC* mind-set, there was no such thing as junk. Everything that had lost its original value, that was no longer fit for its original use, had another potential use. It was the philosophy of reincarnation applied to anything too old and worn and broken to do what it was accustomed to do, but not dead yet if someone would come along and recognize the potential within it, recognize that it was not a piece of junk but an object awaiting salvage and re-employment.

One might have been able to establish a religion on the *IC* philosophy, a religion that asserted as doctrine the continuing usefulness of everything, the Doctrine of Perpetual Utility.

Proust might have become a congregant. He wrote, in the Overture to *Swann's Way*, "I feel that there is much to be said for the Celtic belief that the souls of those whom we have lost are held captive in some . . . inanimate object, and so effectively lost to us until the day (which to many never comes) when we happen to . . . obtain possession of the object which forms their prison. Then they start and tremble, they call us by our name, and as soon as we have recognized their voice the spell is broken. We have delivered them: they have overcome death and return to share our life."

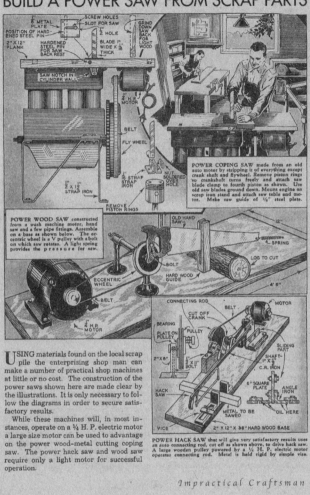

BUILD A POWER SAW FROM SCRAP PARTS

POWER COPING SAW made from an old auto motor by stripping it of everything except crank shaft and flywheel. Remove piston rings so crankshaft turns freely and attach saw blade clamp to fourth piston as shown. Use old saw blades ground down. Mount engine on scrap iron stand and attach saw table as shown. Make saw guide of ⅛" steel plate.

POWER WOOD SAW constructed from a wash machine motor, hand saw and a few pipe fittings. Assemble on a base as shown below. The eccentric wheel is a V pulley with a bolt on which saw rotates. A light spring provides the pressure for saw.

USING materials found on the local scrap pile the enterprising shop man can make a number of practical shop machines at little or no cost. The construction of the power saws shown here are made clear by the illustrations. It is only necessary to follow the diagrams in order to secure satisfactory results.

While these machines will, in most instances, operate on a ¼ H. P. electric motor a large size motor can be used to advantage on the power wood-metal cutting coping saw. The power hack saw and wood saw require only a light motor for successful operation.

POWER HACK SAW that will give very satisfactory results uses an auto connecting rod, cut off as shown above, to drive hack saw. A large wooden pulley powered by a ¼ H. P. electric motor operates connecting rod. Metal is held rigid by simple vise.

Impractical Craftsman

I remember seeing in *Impractical Craftsman* an article that told how to make a power saw out of an engine block...

He had the *IC* spirit, Marcel. All the objects we have ever encountered in life, even simulacra of the objects we have encountered in life, have the potential of enjoying a second life. When we recall them we resurrect their original significance, and when we recount for others our experiences with them we construct a new significance for them, we revivify them. In the weltanschauung of *Impractical Craftsman* and *A la Recherche du Temps Perdu*, and *The Personal History, Adventures, Experiences & Observations of Peter Leroy*, there is no junk.

"What is all this stuff?" I asked in an awestruck gasp. It seemed to me a chaotic profusion of unidentifiable masses, a landscape made of who knew what.

"Cars over there, stacked on top of one another. Trucks there. The bodies, that is. Engines over there. Transmissions behind them. Driveshafts, axles, wheels. Appliances in that section. Stoves, refrigerators, washing machines . . ." He shrugged and did not continue. The enumeration would have been too much and, he suggested in the shrug, unnecessary, because it would have amounted to the enumeration of all the mechanical devices one might have listed as the machinery of human life in the middle of the twentieth century. He left it to me to continue the list on my own if I wished.

"It's like those maps," I said, "the ones in the atlas that show the products for every state, with little cars scattered over Detroit and South Bend and wheels of cheese all over Wisconsin." A map like that had taken shape in my mind, a map of Majestic Salvage and Wrecking that had replaced my original impression of chaos with a neat overhead view, with little wrecked cars in one region, little broken stoves in another.

"We're there," he said. He stopped. I stopped.

We were standing in an area that at first seemed not to be distinguished in any way from any of the other areas, but then, gradually, I began to be able to see that we were surrounded by lean creatures standing frozen like a herd of the metal deer that people bought to decorate their front lawns. I put my hand out and felt the rack of one, the flank of another.

"Motorcycles," I said, with the reverence of a naturalist.

"Motorcycles," Raskol said in confirmation.

We began prowling among them, running our hands over them, bending close to peer at their mechanics, giving them a shake now and then to see what was loose. As I moved among them, I began to feel like a battlefield medic, one of the skinny, ill-trained, well-meaning kids I'd seen in so many war movies at the Babbington Theater. Most of the motorcycles that I examined in the dark felt like hopeless cases, calling into question the precepts of the Doctrine of Perpetual Utility and making me feel that I should call for one of the grizzled, wise, infinitely compassionate battlefield padres I'd seen in the same war movies.

With thoughts of war and death and movies in my mind, I was hardly surprised to hear a deep and rumbling voice from somewhere in the mysterious darkness ask, "How you planning to get one of those 'cross the fence?"

I, SVEN

RASKOL AND I turned toward each other. There was a moment when each of us thought that the other had asked the question, but that error lasted only a moment. The voice still seemed to rumble in the yard, deeper and older than either of us could have managed if we had affected a tone meant to rattle the other.

My first thought was to run, but my legs would not respond to the order. Apparently they did not agree that running was the right strategy. I looked at them, astonished that they should disobey me in such a comical manner, behaving, as they were, like the legs of a frightened boy in an animated cartoon.

To my further astonishment, Raskol answered the question, while swiveling his head to try to find its source. "We're going to fly one out," he said. "Like Icarus and Dædalus."

"That stunt didn't work none too well, as I recall," said the voice. Resurrecting that voice from Majestic Salvage and Wrecking now, I hear in it something that I did not hear then. I hear in its dark depth of sound a measure of concern for our safety, a certain quality that tends toward a plea. It's not a matter of pitch or volume so much as a timbre, a tenseness in the vocal cords, perhaps. A timbre like that came into my mother's voice when she cautioned me about the dangers of snorkeling or dating. At the time, in the salvage yard, I didn't hear it. I heard only the threat of capture, interrogation, trial, sentencing, imprisonment,

durance vile, and physical harm of some kind—unspecified and therefore as horrible as I could imagine. "Icarus crashed, you know," the
voice added, and if I'd known how to hear it, I would have detected
something like regret.

"We're not going to crash," said Raskol. "We've got plans. From a
magazine."

"Hmm," said the voice. "Plans. Let's see 'em."

"I don't think we've got them with us," said Raskol. "Have you got
the plans, Peter?"

My voice had allied itself with my legs in a policy of passive resis-
tance. I wanted to speak—not as much as I wanted to run, but I did
want to speak, since Raskol seemed to be having some success with
speaking as a tactic, if only a delaying tactic. I may have been inhibited
by the formula I had heard so often in cop movies: "Anything you say
may be taken down and used in evidence against you."

"Peter?" Raskol prodded.

"Wahuhih," I said, though I may be misspelling that.

"You Danish?" asked the voice.

"Nuühahnah," I said, approximately.

"Norwegian?" asked the voice.

"Swedish," said Raskol.

"Don't he speak no English?"

"Ooka hap-pa nih ka heppa wah Eng-leesh, Sven?" Raskol asked me
with exaggerated enunciation.

"Heppa wah Eng-leesh," I said, and found that I had regained my
voice. "Are you going to arrest us?" I asked, with an attempt at a
Swedish accent.

The shape in the dark began to rumble good-naturedly. I wouldn't call
it laughing, but there was a jovial quality to it. "That's a good one," the
voice said. "Me on the lam, and you asking if I'm going to arrest you."

"You're on the lam?" I said, more thrilled than I can tell. This was
wonderful news. We were within the limits of the town of Babbington, although we were outside the village of Babbington, so I was quite
specifically right there in my own home town, and I was consorting
with someone who was on the lam. I felt, and I was thrilled to feel, like
one of the innocent people in movies whose humdrum lives were interrupted and enlivened by their being mistaken for crooks or murderers

and driven by mistaken identity into fleeing the cops. It made my town a much richer place than it had been just a few minutes ago. I wondered if he was carrying a gat. "Have you got a gat?" I asked.

"A gat?"

"A rod. A heater."

"You've been watching too many American movies, Sven."

"I take it you're not employed by Majestic Salvage and Wrecking," said Raskol.

"Ain't employed by nobody."

"You're not the night watchman?"

"Not the chief of police, neither. Just a resident."

"A resident?"

"That's right. I live here."

"Here?" I said. "In the junkyard?"

"It may be a junkyard to you, but it's home to me."

"Of course," I said. "I'm sorry. I—"

"I got it made in the shade, Sven. Most of what I need I got right here in the yard. Prowl around this place long enough, you find all the comforts of home. I got a nice little place carved out of a couple of cars at the bottom of the heap over there. Hidden. You'd never find your way to it. Not a chance. Got a nice sofa, coffee table, refrigerator. The only thing I don't find here is my domestic items and consumables. Food and drink. Soap. Linens. Sundry items of that sort. But that stuff's easy to steal outside. I make my little forays over the fence, come back with my provisions. Even the dog don't bother me much. He's got so's he's used to me. Not that we exactly get along. Don't neither of us trust the other much. Sometimes I get the feeling that he's not going to let me back in after one of my shopping sprees. You got him good with that meat you threw him, though. Did you kill him?"

"No," said Raskol. "Just put him to sleep for the night."

"I'd like to have that recipe, if you don't mind."

"It's my sister's secret, but I think I can get you a little bottle of the active ingredient."

"Much obliged. Now about that motorcycle you're after."

"I don't think any one of them is going to do the trick," said Raskol.

"They are in pretty bad shape."

"I think we need the working parts of a few of them," I said.

"Plenty of tools available, and I'm pretty handy. When we got 'em dismantled, we can just heave the pieces over the fence."

"Thanks," I said. "That's a great idea. Let's—"·

"Let's negotiate a price."

"A price?"

"That's what I said."

"But they're not yours," I objected.

The big presence rumbled again. If the rumble was laughter, it was laughter that said that the issue of ownership was no laughing matter.

"How much have you got on you?" Raskol asked in a murmur.

"A couple of dollars," I said.

"Me, too."

"You think he'll go for that?"

"We can ask."

"We've got four dollars," Raskol said in the direction of the presence.

"In all the world?" the presence rumbled.

"Four dollars and the knockout drops," said Raskol.

"I thought you had to get those drops from your sister."

"I do. I'll bring them tomorrow."

"Oh. I see. You'll give me four dollars now, and we'll dismantle the motorcycles, salvage the parts you need, and toss them over the fence. Then you'll make your exit from here, go round the fence, load the parts into that truck with the bad shocks, and drive off, and tomorrow night you'll come back and bring me a little vial of those knockout drops."

"That's the plan," Raskol said hopefully.

"And it sounds like a good plan to me," said the presence, "but—"

He paused. Reflecting on the episode now, reliving it, I recognize the pause for what it was: a deliberate pause, a pause for effect, and it had its intended effect. Raskol and I stood still, waiting for what was to follow, and when, after a while, nothing did, Raskol asked what the presence intended us to ask: "'But' what?"

"You're going to have to leave the Swedish meatball as a hostage."

The word *hostage* had a powerful incantatory effect on my recalcitrant legs. On *hos* I felt energy rush through me, as if the effect of adrenaline were an electric force, and when I heard *tage* the syllable struck me like a jockey's whip. The spell of immobility was broken and I was off, as they say, like a shot.

I ran headlong through the dark, trying to pick my way among the items awaiting salvage, and doing the sort of job you would expect a frightened kid to do in the dark: banging my knees, stumbling, falling, running in blind haste and fear. Raskol was right beside me, so I felt no shame in running, and from the way his breath was coming in bursts and gasps, I felt no shame in being afraid, either. Behind us, we heard the rumbling laughter of the presence, diminishing with distance, and if we had taken a moment to consider what we heard, we would have realized that he wasn't pursuing us and we would probably have concluded that he had been amusing himself at our expense and that he had no intention of putting himself to the trouble of running after us. Instead, we just kept running, stumbling, falling, picking ourselves up, and running again, until we reached the front gate, where Cerberus lay still and sleeping, scrambled over the fence, got into the truck, and drove off, spinning the tires, spraying gravel.

MY CONSCIENCE MAKES AN APPEARANCE

ALBERTINE AND I had given ourselves a brief vacation, a getaway on the weekend of my birthday. We had taken the train to Montauk, at the tip of the south fork of the east end of Long Island, and then the ferry to East Phantom, the largest of the islands in the Phantom Archipelago that stretches from Montauk to Block Island. Autumn offered off-season rates; a night in an inn would be cheap. The sun was weak, but the day was calm. We unfolded our tricky beach chairs and installed their canvas seats. We sat, bundled, enjoying the sun, reading, like inmates at an alpine sanatorium.

In preparation for the writing of this book, I was reading the first volume of my memoirs, *Little Follies*. I hadn't read it in years.

"Is that any good?" Al asked.

"Not as bad as I feared," I said. "I made some mistakes about my schoolmates, especially the one I call Spike—and some about Raskol, too, for that matter—and I seem to have gotten confused about Porky White's age and when he went to high school. Maybe I've never really known his age. Maybe he was chasing the girls at Babbington High at an age when I, the naïve I who wrote this, didn't expect him to be pursuing high school girls, well after he and my mother graduated, even after I was born."

"I wouldn't be surprised," she said.

"Now that I think about it, that's when he was driving a school bus and working at his father's bar at night."

"As I recall, there are lots of high school girls on school buses."

"Sure. That would explain it—well enough."

"You don't sound convinced. Would you like to stop in Babbington on the way back to the city—walk around—make a few discreet inquiries—take some mental notes—get a bowl of chowder—some fried clams?"

"No," I said, "but thanks for suggesting it." Then, after a pause: "Maybe." And then, after another pause: "We'll see."

We went back to our books. After a while I put my finger in the pages of *Little Follies* to mark my place and closed my eyes. I dozed. I had a few minutes of excellent sleep, one of those catnaps that leave me refreshed in a way that an entire night's sleep never does. When I woke, I turned my head toward Albertine, smiling with the pleasure of the sleep I'd had, and found her turning her head toward me, smiling with the pleasure of her own sunny autumn doze.

"We ought to learn to live in the Spanish manner," I said. "We'd be good at it."

"Mmmm," she said, relishing the thought. "A big meal in the afternoon, then sex and a siesta—"

"—then back to work till sometime in the evening—"

"—dinner at eleven and dancing till dawn."

"What time is it now?"

She raised herself on her elbows and looked to the west, where the sun was reddening at the edge of the ocean.

"Cocktail time," she said.

....

At the bar, with a martini in hand, she grinned at me and asked, "Were you really going to steal the parts for the aerocycle?"

"I? Steal? Parts?" I asked. "How can you think that?"

"I was taken in," she said. "Are you shocked?"

"Not shocked exactly."

"Disappointed?"

"Yes. I've certainly never thought of you as someone who thought of me as a thief."

"Sometimes I like to think of you as a lovable rogue."

"Me, too!" I said, arching an eyebrow in the continental manner. "A gentleman bandit, like John Robie?"

She narrowed her eyes and studied me. "No," she said. "I guess not."

I sighed, dismissing with a Gallic shrug another childish fantasy. "The truth is that, at the time, I accepted the idea of the midnight discount."

"Oh, Peter."

"I was a kid with a dream and no money to make it come true."

"And the midnight discount was an accepted thing among your cohort?"

"I guess it was—at least among a certain subset of my cohort."

"I think it was just a little newspeak to mask the fact of theft."

"You were never a teenage boy."

"That's one of my fondest memories of my teen years."

"Let's remind ourselves that I didn't actually steal anything."

"Only because you were run off by the Monster of Majestic Salvage and Wrecking."

"By my conscience, you mean."

"That was the monster?"

"Wasn't it?"

"I don't know. Was it?"

"Maybe," I said mysteriously, in the manner of a raffish rogue.

"Maybe?"

"I think that the truth was something like this: I may have anticipated that if we had gone ahead with the plan to steal the motorcycle parts, then, later, at some unpredictable time, perhaps while I was on the road, making my way westward, on a dark and lonely night, a large and threatening presence would appear to me and suggest that I had better own up to my crime and make some restitution . . . or else."

"I wonder if you are the last man alive with such a fearsome conscience," she said, musing.

A WORTHY CAUSE

· ·

THE NEXT MORNING Raskol and I met at Cap'n Leech's hovel before returning to Majestic Salvage and Wrecking as legitimate customers. Cap'n Leech had once owned a boatyard on the estuarial stretch of the Bolotomy River, not far upstream from the Lodkochnikov house. The boatyard now belonged to his son, Raoul, who had put his father out to pasture in a hovel built from a kit, a temporary shelter that was meant to be a storage shed, a garage for a second car, or a place within which the backyard tinkerer could work in bad weather, but never a home. Because Raoul recognized that he had not provided for his father the comfortable old age that the honored ancestor deserved, Raoul gave the Cap'n some cash now and then. It was conscience money. Raoul may have discovered that from time to time, particularly on dark and lonely nights, a large and threatening presence appeared to him and suggested that he'd better take a few bills to the old man, or else. The Cap'n had no real need for this money. When he gave the boatyard to Raoul, he hadn't expected a pension; he had expected a deep and abiding gratitude for the gift, and for the lifetime of work that had gone into building the boatyard into a business that Raoul could run and enjoy. Specifically, he had expected that he would be given some sinecure there that allowed him a place where he could sit and smoke and spit and shoot the shit with his cronies, happy in the atmosphere of motor oil and bottom paint and varnish that he had known for so long, but without the burden of work. That was what he had wanted, but that was not at all what Raoul had wanted. Raoul had feared that his father, if allowed to remain within the boatyard, would have remained the badgering presence that he had been throughout Raoul's childhood and youth, always demanding, always finding fault, always belittling, but now with the additional expectation of gratitude. So Raoul banished the Cap'n from the boatyard, on pain of anger and ridicule if he should dare to return. In his hovel, the old man smoldered with resentment. He accepted Raoul's conscience money but refused to spend it. Friends brought him what he needed, and Raskol was one of the most loyal of these. The Cap'n stuffed the cash in burlap sacks and used the sacks as seating. He had often said to Raskol, sometimes in my presence, that if Raskol ever needed money "for a worthy cause," they could always dip into his furniture.

"Good morning, Cap'n," Raskol called, standing at the closed door of the hovel.

The door swung open.

"Young Master Lodkochnikov—and young Master Leroy."

"I brought you an egg sandwich and a snapshot of my sister," said Raskol.

"I brought you a Coffee-Toffee," I said.

"What's that?" he asked.

"It's soda."

He examined the bottle as if he had never seen a bottle of Coffee-Toffee before, though that seemed unlikely to me because Coffee-Toffee was the most popular soft drink in that time and place, and there were Coffee-Toffee vending machines all over town.

"Have you no sister?" he asked.

"No, Cap'n," I said. "We've been through that before."

"Oh, yes, yes," he wheezed. "I remember now."

"You were checking on me, weren't you?"

He let slip his reedy, wheezing laugh, "hee-hee-hee," and gave me a playful whack with his cane. "I was!" he said, as if he'd done something extraordinarily clever. "You'd be amazed how many people come here and tell me lies." He drew us toward him, clutched our arms with his bony hands, and leaned inward to ensure that no eavesdropper would hear. "They all want to get the stuffing!" he said, and then released the reedy laugh again.

"That's why we're here," said Raskol.

The Cap'n's eyes popped suddenly and spectacularly, as if Raskol had wrapped him in a bear hug and squeezed. "'Et tu, Brute?'" he gasped.

"You always told me that if I needed money—"

"For a worthy cause!" he cried, swinging the cane in an arc that made us duck. "For a worthy cause! Only for a worthy cause!"

"It is for a worthy cause!" shouted Raskol.

The Cap'n had tired himself. He sank to one of the burlap sacks. He stabbed his finger in the direction of the egg sandwich, and Raskol gave it to him. I gave him the Coffee-Toffee bottle, and he opened it with the beer-can opener that he wore as an amulet on a leather thong around his neck. He refreshed himself with a couple of bites of the sandwich and a long pull at the soda.

"I wasn't expecting any worthy causes until after I was dead," he said, almost tearily. "After that," he added, swiveling his head to survey his domain and ending with his eyes fixed on Raskol's, "all this will be yours." I think my jaw dropped at that revelation; if it is true that people's jaws do drop when they hear startling revelations, then mine must certainly have dropped then; the Cap'n had no mirrors, so I couldn't check, and cannot check in recollection now, since memory refuses to supply the Cap'n with any mirrors, but I think that my jaw dropped, and I gaped. "All yours when I'm gone," he said, "but for now, I'd prefer to keep it myself. I've kind of gotten used to having it around." He squeezed the sack that he was sitting on, and it crinkled internally. "I suppose your mother is in desperate need of a costly operation?"

"No—" said Raskol.

"The bank is threatening to foreclose on the family shack?"

"No—"

"Your sister has to—ah—preserve what's left of her reputation?"

"No," said Raskol. "It's for Peter."

The Cap'n looked at me, studying me, trying to decide why I might need to dip into his furniture. After consideration, he said, "Up to your eyeballs in debt, are you?"

"No," I said, chuckling, little realizing how accurately the Cap'n had predicted the balance sheet for most of the years of my adult life.

"It's for his education," said Raskol. "He's been accepted at the prestigious Faustroll Institute in New Mexico, and he—"

"Pfweh," said the Cap'n dismissively.

"—has to build an airplane to get there."

"What?" the old man said, directing the question at me.

"I'm going to build it out of parts of surplus—I mean wrecked—motorcycles," I said. "I've got plans."

"Damn," he said, and this time he definitely did have a tear in his eye. "Damn."

"What's the matter?" I asked.

Shaking his head slowly, he said, "That is a worthy cause—damn it."

EL PATRÓN'S REVENGE

BECAUSE RASKOL HADN'T yet developed the skill to borrow the family truck in broad daylight, we hitchhiked to Majestic Salvage and Wrecking. While we were standing beside the road with our thumbs out and our pockets stuffed with the crumpled bills we'd extracted from Cap'n Leech's furniture, waiting for an obliging motorist to come by, I said, "Holy mackerel, Raskol, you're going to be rich!" summing up in those few words the surprise and awe that had been inspired within me by the Cap'n's revelation about his intended disposition of those comfy sacks of cash.

I recognized, even as I said it, that I also felt a bit of disappointment. There was the possibility that I wouldn't be around to see Raskol come into his inheritance. Just when I had found a way to get out of Babbington, if only for a summer, the town had begun to reveal depths hitherto unrevealed. Here was my best friend secretly tapped as the inheritor of wads of folding money, wealth beyond anything his family or mine had ever known. He was going to need a pal to help him haul the sacks away when the Cap'n kicked the bucket, and I might not be around to be that pal. I might be in distant New Mexico.

"Rich," he said. "Yeah—but not for long."

"What do you mean?" I asked.

"I know what I'm supposed to do with the money. It comes with an obligation."

This was getting better and better.

"What's the obligation?"

"I'm required to use the money to bring Raoul to his knees. Drive him out of business. Start a small boatyard of my own. Undercut him on every piece of nautical gear and every boatyard service. And when he's on the edge of bankruptcy, deep in debt and desperate for cash, buy him out for a fraction of what the place is worth, make him an offer he can't refuse, a very specific offer."

"What's that?"

"A small annuity and lifetime tenancy in the hovel he built for his father."

"Wow," I said. "You're an agent of justice—more than that—you're an avenging angel!"

"I'm no angel," he said with a practiced sneer.

"This could be a western," I said, thrilled beyond the telling. "Instead of a boatyard, Cap'n Leech—but he wouldn't be a captain, of course, not in a western—instead of a boatyard, he'd have a ranch, a huge ranch—"

A car stopped for us, and we got in.

"Where are you going, boys?" asked the driver. It was Mr. MacPherson.

"Majestic Salvage and Wrecking," I said. "Thanks for picking us up, Mr. MacPherson."

"Glad to be of service," he said. "I can drop you off on the other side of the tracks."

"That's fine," said Raskol. "Thanks."

"The Cap'n," I resumed, "or whatever you call a guy who owns a ranch—"

I paused. I expected Mr. MacPherson to supply the word.

"Hmmm," he said thoughtfully. "I don't think there is a specific word, other than *rancher,* which could loosely be applied to anyone engaged in the business of ranching, whether he was the head of the operation or not, but I suppose that you are looking for something more comparable to *captain* than to *shipping magnate,* so in this case, assuming that the ranch is in the Southwest, you might call him the *patrón,* or even El Patrón."

"Thanks. El Patrón has acres and acres, stretching across the High

Plains, and he has spent the best years of his life turning his ranch into the finest spread west of the Mississippi, with the best beef cattle west of the—um—Mississippi. Years earlier he had graduated from Harvard, with a law degree, but found that the cities of the East were too confining to accommodate the breadth of his dreams and ambitions, so he came out west and settled in Dry Gulch. There he met and fell in love with a young schoolmarm, Miss Clementine, who had come west after graduating from the Baltimore Normal School, her heart afire with a mission to educate and civilize the wild offspring of the other pioneers and homesteaders, bringing with her the beginnings of the finest library west of the—ah—Monongahela. Sadly, after their storybook marriage, she died in childbirth, and the Cap'n—El Patrón—was left with nothing but the dry earth and his cattle and his infant son, Raoul. From the start, Raoul was a problem child. He was stubborn and rebellious and—uhh—pusillanimous."

"Bellicose," said the driver, since he was, after all, Mr. MacPherson.

"Oh, yeah," I said. "Not pusillanimous. Bellicose. He was bellicose, and El Patrón had to rescue him from one scrape after another. Finally, the boy came of age. The old Patrón took him to the porch of the grand house that had grown from the humble shack that he had originally built, put his hand on his boy's shoulder, and said, 'Raoul, today you have become a man, and today you have become a landowner.' Looking out over the vast expanse of Rancho Grande, he said, 'All this is yours, my boy.' He unfurled a deed, a simple document but handsomely engraved and properly signed and sealed, and handed it to his troublesome son. It was a touching ceremony that El Patrón had devised during the long nights when he rode his favorite horse, Thunderclap, through the darkness and into the dawn trying to rid himself of the anger he felt toward his wayward boy and to escape the sorrow he felt over the loss of his darling Clementine, talking to her in the dark as he rode, seeking the advice that would help him tame the wild child. 'Thanks, Dad,' sneered Raoul, and within days he had had his father's personal belongings moved from the ranch house to a tent on the driest and loneliest corner of the domain, where he left the old man to desiccation and despair. Meanwhile, Raoul, as good a rancher as his father and far sharper in his business dealings, grew ever richer at the expense of the other inhabitants of Dry Gulch. He controlled the bank, and he had the mayor and sheriff in his pocket. He bought up mortgages and foreclosed when it suited him to do so, ravishing the virgin daughters of his debtors whenever he got the chance. The whole town lived in fear of him, and it seemed that nothing could be done to rid them of this tyrannical cattle baron until one night, when thunder rocked the plains and lightning lit the sky with angry bolts, a stranger rode into town on a black stallion, seeking shelter from the storm. He found it in the miserable tent where the aged Patrón dwelled, and in the dark, over coffee stretched to tastelessness with chicory, he listened to the old man's tale of woe and filial disrespect. 'The deed I gave him contains a reversion clause,' he told the stranger. 'I put it in there to try to cure him of his pusill—his bellicosity. It states that if Raoul is killed in a gunfight, a showdown, everything reverts to me.' The stranger nodded silently at this, put one strong gloved hand on El Patrón's shoulder, and said—"

"I'm turning here." Mr. MacPherson pulled to the side of the road.

"Thanks for the ride," I said as Raskol and I got out.

"My car's an old and crotchety beast," he said, "certainly no Thunderclap, but then, 'the biggest horse is no aye the best traiveller.'"

Raskol and I walked the rest of the way to the salvage yard, where we bought everything we thought I was going to need. The owner's brother-in-law gave us a ride home, and he heard the story of the epic Gunfight at the Rancho Grande Corral, the reversion of the ranch, and El Patrón's happy sunset years, spent largely on the expansive porch of the ranch house, in the company of his aged cronies, shooting the shit.

THE BEST IN TOWN!

ALBERTINE AND I did stop in Babbington on our way back to the city. We left the train station, a few blocks north of Main Street, and walked southward, along Upper Bolotomy Road, to Main, and then eastward to River Sound Road, where we turned to the south again and followed the estuarial stretch of the Bolotomy River to

Leech's Boatyard. The boatyard was still called Leech's, though discreet lettering below the name read R. LODKOCHNIKOV, PROP.

"Do you want to stop in?" she asked.

"I'm not sure," I said, and I meant it.

I wasn't sure that I wanted to spend the time. Mr. MacPherson would have recognized the full implication of the phrase *spend the time*. "Ken when to spend an when to spare," he might have warned me. There is in the notion of spending time the strong suggestion that time, one's time on earth, is like money, and that one can overspend, run out, be called to account, bankrupt oneself, before one's time ought otherwise to have been up. I had little money, and I was beginning to feel that I had as little time. Having little money, I had the feeling that I should always be at work, turning time into money as well as I could, doing whatever work I could find to try to keep the household afloat. The full version of the Scottish saying that Mr. MacPherson might have quoted to me is "Ken when to spend an when to spare, and ye needna be busy." Ahhh, yes, but if in the early days of your life, when time seemed cheap and plentiful, you did not ken when to spend and when to spare, then in the later years you must needs be busy all the time.

"You're still on vacation," Albertine reminded me.

I checked my watch. Yes, I was still on vacation, but my vacation time was running out. I knew that Raskol would probably be there, at the boatyard, busy, but not so busy that he couldn't spare some time for his old friend, and I would have been glad to see him, but I decided that the time I might have spent shooting the shit with him at the boatyard would be better spent on something else. If I had had more time . . . but I didn't. One has to budget one's time when the days dwindle down to a precious few. (Sorry, Raskol.)

We passed the boatyard and continued to the street where my paternal grandparents had lived, turned onto it, and walked past the house as inconspicuously as we could while examining it, sidelong, for alterations. Only from certain angles was it recognizable as the house I had known as a child. Seen from directly across the street, it was greatly altered, or seemed greatly altered, though the actual changes were neither so many nor so extensive that I couldn't have reversed them if I had had the money to buy the place and have the work done, or if I had had the money to buy the place and the time to do the work myself. I felt a

great weight of remorse and guilt for my never having prospered suffi-
ciently to have had the money to buy the house and preserve it. It
should have been then, that afternoon, just as it had been when I was a
boy and sat with my grandparents on the porch on summer evenings.

"If I had ever made any real money, buckets of it," I said to Al, "we
could have bought this house, and all the others—all the ones that you
and I ever lived in—and preserved them as they were."

"In our permanent design collection," she said.

"Over the course of a year, we could make a progress from house to
house—"

"That would have been folly," she said consolingly, squeezing my
hand, "no matter how much money we had."

We had passed the house, so we thought that we could safely stop
and turn and stare.

The current owners had enclosed the front porch (or perhaps the
owners before them had done it; the house had passed through several
hands since my grandparents had died). They had done it in a clumsy
way that made the entire front of the house look like an awkward addition. They had also painted it.

"What color is that?" I asked in a whisper, as if we might have been
overheard.

"I guess I'd call it saffron," said Al.

"I'd call it aggressive," I said, "an assault on the past, battery of the
memory."

I think that whoever had decided on this bellicose use of color had
meant to make the house appear larger thereby, but to my eyes the
brightness had diminished it. Formerly, it had been a dark gray, and the
quiet dignity of the color had made the small house seem much more
solid and staunch, made it more of a presence, than this saffron did.

We went on our way, made the next right, and headed back up to Main
Street, where we hoped to find a place where I might get some clams,
freshly dug from Bolotomy Bay, full-bellied, fried golden and crunchy. As
we walked along, we noticed a number of small signs in wire frames stuck
into the front lawns of the houses we passed. Some pleaded with the
passersby to support the Andy Whitley Airport, others advanced the
project of a new waterfront park, and some screamed NO CONDOS!

"What do you suppose that's about?" I asked.

"The airport, a park, and condominiums, I'd say," she said. "Chips in play in the game of defining Babbington's future."

"Mmm," I said, in the manner of one aloof from the fray of small-town politics.

We had reached Main Street. Only five years had passed since Albertine and I had left Babbington, but the mix of businesses along the town's throbbing commercial thoroughfare had changed considerably in that time. The diner had become a sushi bar. Many of the shops that had been idiosyncratic and local were now standardized outposts of national retailers. There seemed to be twice as many banks as there had been and three times as many insurance companies. There were five nail salons where formerly there had been none. The post office had become a restaurant called Not the Post Office Anymore.

As we walked along, we noticed a number of small signs . . .

"Clever," said Albertine, and I think she meant it.

We entered and were greeted by a smiling host.

"Do you have fried clams?" I asked peremptorily, even a bit contentiously, prepared to turn on my heels if told that they did not.

"The best in town!" declared the host with trained confidence. "Two for lunch?"

"Umm—" I said, looking around, trying to decide what I thought of the place.

"Yes," said Albertine, and she tugged me along as the host ushered us to a table.

"Stuart will be your waiter, and he'll be right with you," the host claimed. He put menus in front of us and smiled his way off in the direction of his post at the door. Stuart arrived almost at once.

"How are you folks doing today?" he asked in a breezy tone.

"We have fallen under a dark cloud of nostalgia and regret," I said.

"I hate it when that happens," he said, pouting in sympathy. "How about a little drinky?"

"Anderson's Amber," I said. "Two pints."

"And do you know what you'd like to eat?"

"The grilled chicken sandwich," said Albertine, making an assumption, since she had not looked at the menu.

"Best in town," Stuart assured her. "Comes with Whirly-Curly Fries and a side of Super Slaw. Okay?"

"Fine."

"And for you?"

"Fried clams," I said.

"You also get Whirly-Curly Fries and a side of Super Slaw with that," he said, without assuring me that the clams were the best in town. "Okay?"

"Okay."

"Okey-dokey," he said. He swung a tiny mouthpiece into position, said, "Number nine," listened for a second, and then said, "GC platter, FC platter," and he turned to go, but Albertine caught his sleeve.

"Stuart," she said in her most confidential tone, "what can you tell us about the airport-park-condo dispute raging in town?" I think she must have given him the impression that she and I were the vanguard of a television news team and that he had a good shot at an appearance on the six o'clock report, because he leaned toward the table and spilled his guts, figuratively speaking.

"Basically, it's all about the airport and its fate," he confided. "There are three camps. One wants to keep the airport forever and even expand it some. Naturally, the people who have planes are in that group. Another group calls the airport a playground for the rich and wants to bull-doze the whole thing and make a big park out of it. The *Babbington Reporter*—that's the local paper—is behind that. And then a third group supposedly wants the airport land to build a huge development of luxury condominiums. I don't know who's behind that."

"Where do you stand, Stuart?" Albertine asked.

"Off the record," he said with a wink, "I think the condominium plan is a fake, just a scare tactic. I mean, who in his right mind would buy a luxury condominium in Babbington? And as far as a park goes, haven't we got enough parks? Who uses them anyway? Just a lot of stinking bums—excuse me—stinking homeless people. I say keep the airport. It's been a part of this town as long as anybody can remember—and it's historic. I mean, you may not know it, but this is the Birthplace of Teenage Aviation!" A soft beeping sound began to emanate from Stuart. He swung the mouthpiece into position again, said, "Number nine," listened for a second, and then said, "Roger, sir, I copy." To us, he said, in the same confidential tone he had used for the straight poop on the airport dispute, "Your orders are up."

He was gone. He was back. Brisk service was a feature of Not the Post Office Anymore. He put two pints of Anderson's and two large platters of food in front of us.

"What are these?" I asked, regarding the pale beige battered strips on my plate.

"Fried clams!" he said, as if I were an idiot. "Fresh from Ipswich, Massachusetts!"

I PLAY THE LOSING GAME OF TRANSLATION

THE TITLE PAGE of the book that Mr. MacPherson had given me said:

ALFRED JARRY

Gestes et Opinions

du

Docteur Faustroll

Pataphysicien

Roman Néo-Scientifique

I began my translation there. I hesitated at *gestes* and spent some time vacillating between translating it as *jests* or *jokes*. The obvious choice seemed to be *jests,* but it sounded antiquated, even quaint, while *jokes* sounded too casual, too—well—jokey. I was about to settle for *jests* when I recalled Mr. MacPherson's caution against the treachery of *faux-amis,* those pairs of French and English words that resembled each other enough for the student to think that they must be the same, or nearly so, when they were actually so different as to be barely on speaking terms. I turned to my French-English dictionary. It told me that a *geste* was a gesture, a motion or movement, an action, or a wave of the hand. Hmmm. The gestures and opinions of Doctor Faustroll? Not likely. The actions, then. No. Acts. No. Too inactive somehow. Deeds? Accomplishments? Adventures? Adventures. If it were *my* book, I would certainly prefer *adventures* to *acts* or *actions* or even *accomplishments.* Thus:

ALFRED JARRY

Adventures and Opinions

of

Doctor Faustroll

Pataphysician

A Neo-Scientific Novel

I could have stopped there and counted it as a page done, but, flushed with success, I decided to push on. "Livre Premier: Procèdure" I translated as "Book One: Procedure," and the first part of that book I translated as follows:

I

COMMANDMENT

IN ACCORDANCE WITH ARTICLE 819

IN THE YEAR eighteen hundred ninety-eight, on the eighth of February, in accordance with article 819 of the Code of Civil Procedure and at the request of Mr. and Mrs. Bonhomme (Jacques), owners of a house situated in Paris, at 100½ Richer Street, for which residence, abode, house, or premises I am the elected member in my residence, dwelling, or abode and also in the registry office of the Qth or 15th District, I, the undersigned, René-Isidore Panmuphle, bailiff within the civil tribunal of the first instance of the district of the Seine, situated in Paris, residing there, at 37 Pavée Street, have made Commandment in accord with the Law and Justice, to Mr. Faustroll, doctor, tenant or lodger in various premises annexed to the aforementioned house situated in Paris at 100½ Richer Street, where having gone to the aforementioned house, upon which was found equally indicated the number 100, and after having rung the bell, knocked, and called the above-named on different repeated occasions, no one having come to open the door for us, the nearest neighbors declared to us that it was indeed the residence or domicile of the said Mr. Faustroll, but that they were not willing to accept the copy and whereas I did not find at the aforesaid premises either parents or servants, and none of the neighbors was willing to assume the duty of being presented with the copy upon signing my original, I returned immediately to the registry office of the Qth or 15th District, whereupon I returned to the mayor, speaking with him personally, who gave me his initials or signature on my original: within twenty-four hours as a total extension of time, to pay to the plaintiff in my hands for which will be tendered to him good and valuable receipt the sum of three hundred seventy-two thousand francs and twenty-seven centimes, for eleven terms of rent on the above-named premises, due the following January first, without prejudice of those falling due and all other rights, actions, interests, fresh or newly put into execution, declaring to him that failing to satisfy under the present Commandment in the said extension of time, there will be or he will be compelled by all the ways or means of right or law, and notably by the seizure as security or in payment of furnishings, furniture, and personal belongings, furnishing or filling the rented premises. And I have at the domicile or residence as I have said below left the present copy. Cost: eleven francs, thirty centimes, which includes ½ sheet with a special stamp at zero francs, sixty centimes.

PANMUPHLE

Monsieur le Docteur Faustroll in the registry of the Qth or 15th District, Paris.

My translation wasn't all that it might have been. I recognized that. It ran like an engine with dirty plugs, sputtering and stuttering until at last it coughed and died. An engine like that was not fit to pull a plane from Babbington to New Mexico, and a translation like that wasn't going to be enough to endear a matriculating youngster to the faculty of the Faustroll Institute, if such an organization actually existed or could be found, nor was it likely to gain him entry into the prestigious ranks of Advanced French and the racy stuff its privileged students were rumored to read. I decided to sleep on it, give myself a day or so away from it, and then dismantle it and tune it up.

ELEMENTS OF AERONAUTICS

THE *ADVENTURES AND OPINIONS* of *Doctor Faustroll* was not the only text that I studied in preparation for my journey to New Mexico and matriculation at the Faustroll Institute. I had on my own bookshelf, in my bedroom, a text that not only played a part in inspiring me to fly but taught me nearly everything I knew of the art. Years earlier, Dudley Beaker, who lived in a stucco residence or domicile on No Bridge Road beside the stucco dwelling or abode wherein resided my maternal grandparents, Herb and Lorna Piper, had given me a copy of *Elements of Aeronautics* by Francis Pope, B.A., First Lieutenant, United States Army Air Corps Reserve, and Captain (First Pilot) with Transcontinental and Western Air, Inc., and Arthur S. Otis, Ph.D., Private Pilot, Fellow of the American Association for the Advancement of Science and Technical Member of the Institute of the Aeronautical Sciences.

"Study it, Peter," he said. "Study it carefully. I think that the time is coming when air travel will become commonplace, and there will be opportunities for the young man with a prepared mind. I must confess my fear that much of the glamour of the experience of air travel will doubtless be lost when it is available to the great unwashed, but I also realize that its vulgarization will bring opportunities. If you are going to be prepared to seize those opportunities, you ought to have some idea why an airplane is capable of flight."

"And how," I said.

"What?"

"How."

"What?" he asked again, with evident irritation.

"How," I said. "I ought to know *how* it is capable of flight, too. How it flies. How it works. What makes it able to fly."

"Yes," he conceded, "I suppose you should."

Elements of Aeronautics and I were nearly the same age; the book had been published just three years before I was born. This fact struck me when I opened it and began reading it, at the very beginning, in the way that had already become my habit and has never left me. I begin with all the "front matter" that most people skip, so I've been told, often by the very people who do the skipping. There, on the copyright page, was the copyright date, and it put me in mind of my birth date, and the two made me realize in a boy's way that a book cannot do what a boy can: grow and change. In books, as Mrs. Fendreffer so often said, we can find the wisdom of the past, but she did not say that yesterday's wisdom is very often today's nonsense and that books as often turn the foolishness of the past—our myths and bigotries and superstitions—into holy writ, immutable in a changing world.

In a sense, *Elements of Aeronautics* was out-of-date, and my first glance through it showed me that the drawings were done in a style that was almost quaint, not at all the style that a contemporary publication, a new book, would have used. The article about the aerocycle from *Impractical Craftsman* was even older. It had appeared ten years before *Elements of Aeronautics* had, thirteen years before I had. In a way, I felt like the youngest of three brothers. The oldest of us was twenty-eight, a man, seriously pursuing a career in a local bank now and thinking of marriage. His early dreams of teenage aviation, inspired by that issue of *Impractical Craftsman* when it was new and didn't smell at all of mold, had never been anything more than daydreams, daydreams that he never entertained any longer, not even when a little plane came buzzing slowly overhead in the clear sky of a summer day. The middle brother was eighteen, out of school, working the bay. He had no plans for the future at all; he just worked the bay from day to day and chased the girls at night. Life was easy and simple. Why should he complicate it by attempting to learn to fly? The idea had once inspired him, made his heart seem to lift and soar, when he watched small planes taking off from the runway at the Babbington Municipal Airport, but when he had bought and tried to study *Elements of Aeronautics,* he had stumbled when he had reached Part II: Aerodynamics, and he had put the book aside, never to be taken up again. I was the little brother, only fifteen, fascinated by my older brothers and all the things that had once fascinated them, and eager to make a place for myself, a name for myself, in the trio. So I took up the daydream of the aerocycle and the old issue of *Impractical Craftsman* and the abandoned copy of *Elements of Aeronautics* and claimed them as my own. The essential principles of aeronautics had not changed in the eighteen years since the book had been published, and motorcycles hadn't changed much since the article had been published, so their age was not a disqualification; rather, it became a recommendation, like the additional years of experience that lend weight to the pronouncements of older brothers. But, as I said above, the ossified wisdom of an earlier time, codified as writ, can bring trouble to the modern age, to modern youth.

The frontispiece to *Elements of Aeronautics* made me feel important. I memorized it. Phrases from it began to appear in my everyday conversation.

If taking my place in a nation on wings, as the frontispiece assured me I would do, made me feel important, the book's explanation of yaw, "sometimes spoken of technically as rotation about the normal axis," pitch, "sometimes spoken of technically as rotation about the lateral axis," and roll, "technically spoken of as rotation about the longitudinal axis," made me feel queasy. For each of them, I imagined myself astride the aerocycle, executing a maneuver that took each type of rotation to its exaggerated maximum: a circle, a loop, and a spin. Mentally reeling, I set the book aside. However, I knew that, unlike

The frontispiece to *Elements of Aeronautics* made me feel important.

my imaginary older brothers, I would take it up again. I just needed enough time away from it to recover my equilibrium. Inevitably, I suppose, despite the dizziness they induced, the terms began to work their way into my vocabulary. When I rode my bicycle, I would yaw left or right instead of turning, pitch up or down a hill or bump, and now and then roll a bit from the vertical, sometimes spoken of technically as going off-kilter.

ALBERTINE TAKES A TUMBLE

THE CONFINES OF the average garage," I said to Albertine.

"Ahhh, darling," she said with a sigh, "you know how I love that sweet talk."

"The confines of the average garage," I repeated seductively.

"Mmm," she moaned with pleasure.

"Those confines come up again and again in the descriptions of these build-it-yourself planes."

"All the romance has gone from garages, I see," she said, pouting.

"The people selling the kits or plans are always reassuring the prospective builder that the plane can be built 'within the confines of the average garage.'"

"And you suspect them of stretching the truth? Or shrinking the truth?"

"It's not that. It's the word that surprises me."

"*Garage*?"

"No. *Confines*."

"I prefer *garage*. If you say it right, it sounds like a term of endearment. 'Oh, how I lahhhve you, my leettle garrr-azzzh.'"

We were having this conversation on the roadway that winds through Central Park, on a Sunday afternoon. The road is closed on weekends to vehicular traffic but available to runners, walkers, skaters, dogboarders, and bicycle riders. We were on our bicycles. It was a fine day in late fall, the air cool, the sun low but warming, our spirits light.

"It surprises me that they don't just say, 'You can build it in a garage.'"

"Well, Peter, I think they want to make the point that you can build it in the space that would be available in your garage if you have a garage, but that you don't actually have to have a garage."

"Yes, but—"

"Not everyone has a garage. We don't."

"We have no car."

"Exactly. Therefore, no need for a garage. So the people selling the kits or plans may be trying to reassure the prospective builder that a garage is not actually required, just the space that your garage would contain if you had one."

"The space contained by the average garage would easily fit within the confines of our apartment," I pointed out.

She turned to deliver a rejoinder, and I saw the accident occur, the absurd events preceding it, the awful instant of coincidence, and the consequence.

To Albertine's right, a woman was dogboarding, and to her left, another woman was dogboarding. In the space of the five years that Albertine and I had been living in Manhattan, the sport of dogboarding had come from nowhere to attain a status of considerable popularity. I have heard people attempt to explain its sudden rise with the theory that it suited the predilections of many because it was an outdoor activity in which the dog did the work rather than the master, that it required gear expensive enough to give it consumer snob appeal (particularly if you counted the dog), and that it offered a physical and sensual experience that other urban sports did not, combining as it did elements of wake riding, skateboarding, and snowboarding. In addition, though, I think we should not discount the powerful appeal of its giving residents of the Upper East Side something they seem to have craved for a long time: a *reason* for housing a large dog in the confines of a small apartment.

The dogboarder's dog is outfitted with a harness similar in cut to the coats that pampered pets wear in cold weather. It fits over the dog's chest and around its forelegs and back, with reins extending rearward from the sides. Behind the dog, the boarder stands on a platform that resembles a skateboard, with the difference that instead of skate wheels the dogboard has two large wheels, miniatures of the high-tech wheels with composite rims that are used in bicycle racing, one fore and one aft, of a diameter great enough that they rise above the surface of the board, set within slots in the board and turning on axles that run through mounts below it.

I remember wondering, when I glanced at the enormous and powerful dog pulling the woman on Albertine's right, whether it had been bred expressly for dogboarding. The dog pulling the woman on Albertine's left was smaller, but not by much, and it was especially keen. It strained in its harness in a way that the larger dog did not, lunging forward whenever the other moved a bit ahead. I wondered, and I intended to discuss this with Albertine later, after the women had passed by, whether they were longtime rivals, competitors in business and within their social set and now in the dogboarding arena of Central Park. In the manner of superheroes, both were dressed in sleek, form-fitting, iridescent outfits that advertised their fitness and firmness and enhanced the resplendence of their bodies in action. They were running a playful game, crisscrossing, playing their dogs as charioteers would their steeds, tugging lightly at their harnesses to yaw the dogs this way and that. Though neither allowed the other to remain ahead, the race they were running was not a race for position but for prominence in the eye of the beholder, status as the most adept and alluring dogboarder in the city. Their rivalry had infected their dogs; they snarled at each other across the couple of feet that separated them. Later, I told myself that I should have realized that the women and their dogs posed a threat to Albertine, but they were so fluent in their movements, the dogs so good at what they were doing and the women apparently so fully in control of their dogs, that they seemed to be harmless, until the moment when Albertine turned her head, just for an instant, to reply to me, and in that moment the smaller of the dogs did something to offend the larger. What? Nothing that I can see in my mind's eye when I recall the moment. It may have been a look; it may have been something in his tone of voice, a vulgarity in his snarl; it may have been some grosser violation of the code of dogs; it may only have been that he strayed a bit from what the larger dog perceived as the proper confines of his lane. Whatever it was, it made the dog on the right respond suddenly and violently. He lunged at the dog on the left,

to nip at his foreleg, I think, as a warning against persisting in that of-
fensive behavior.

"Al!" I cried.

I saw the look on her face, saw that she was reading the look on my
face. She saw the alarm there, and it made her swing around to face
forward again. The dogboarding woman on the right tugged hard on
the reins, but the dog was determined and resisted her. She yawed involuntarily, she fought to recover, she rolled, and her board shot from
under her directly into Albertine's path. Al saw it. In an instant of peripheral awareness she turned to the left to try to avoid it, but she was
on top of it. Her front wheel struck the board, and Albertine pitched
forward, up and over her handlebars and onto the pavement.

I was off my bike in a moment and at her side.

"Oh, my darling, my darling," I said, kneeling beside her, kissing her,
"my leettle garazh."

She didn't seem to be in pain. She didn't seem to be hurt, only surprised, but, "Something is wrong," she said. "Something is wrong."

FROM THE SYMPHYSIS PUBIS TO THE CREST OF ILIUM

SHE LAY ON a gurney in the hallway of the emergency room at
Carl Schurz Hospital, just down the street from our apartment, just
half a block from home. Hours had passed since the accident. She was
in shock, I suppose, still not quite believing that this had happened to
her. In the park, when she had come to rest on the pavement, she had
worn that look of surprise, but now there was added to it a grimace,
and I could see that she was suffering. She had cried out when the
emergency medical technicians had lifted her onto the stretcher to load
her into the ambulance. Here in the hospital she had been given morphine for the pain, but she could feel it through the morphine.

"Was my skirt up around my waist?" she asked.

"You're wearing shorts," I said.

"I am?"

"You are." I brought her hand to my lips. I had a flash of a memory, one of my earliest. In the memory, I was standing on my maternal grandparents' front lawn, with a kitten in either hand, looking across the lawn to where my grandparents, my parents, Dudley Beaker, and Eliza Foote were gathered for drinks in the summer dusk. Something had happened to disturb my mother, to upset her. I didn't know what it was, and wouldn't have understood it if I had, but I saw that something had upset her, disturbed her equilibrium. When I looked in the direction of the adults, I saw my mother in the act of falling from her lawn chair, and she wore the expression of surprise that I had seen on Albertine. At the time, I thought that my mother was playing, partly because of that expression of surprise. I saw, and understood in my infantile way, that she was exhilarated by crossing the line of equilibrium into a more excited state, and I laughed then, but in the hospital, with Albertine hurting so and worried that the world had seen her underwear, I saw in the mind's eye of memory that my mother had also been shocked at the moment of her tumble, astonished that this should be happening to her, and deeply embarrassed.

"Was I wearing shorts the whole time?"

"Yes, my darling."

"How prudent of me."

"Your dignity was preserved throughout."

"I doubt that," she said. She sighed. "What happened?"

"That woman's dogboard shot in front of you, and you hit it."

"Yes," she said distantly, apparently struggling to regain the memory.

"You had turned backward to say something to me, but I saw what was happening and when I called to you, you turned around, turned forward I mean, and you saw what was about to happen, so you yawed to the left, trying to avoid it. You didn't have time to turn much, not enough to avoid the board, but you did turn enough to avoid going straight over the handlebars and landing on your head."

"Did I execute a full forward somersault?"

"Head over teakettle."

"I think it's cracked."

"Head? Or teakettle?"

"Head, maybe. Teakettle, definitely."

In another couple of hours, after she had been investigated by X-ray and magnetic resonance imaging, we knew that she was right. Her pelvis had been fractured "in three places," according to the surgeon on duty in the emergency room, who later charged an inflated fee but was, in his reading of the film as well as his estimate of what his time was worth, wrong. Her pelvis had actually been fractured along a nearly continuous line from the symphysis pubis to the crest of ilium, making the integrity of the pelvis itself—so essential to supporting the body in its upright human stance and allowing it pedal mobility—tenuous, liable to a painful and perhaps irreparable shift along the fracture if she were to put her weight on her right leg, but we didn't know that until later.

"What did I say?" she asked.

"Say?" I stroked her hand. She was lying on her back. She had been told not to move.

"You told me that I turned around to say something to you. What was it?"

"I don't know. You never got to say it. Do you remember what you were going to say?"

"No. I don't remember," she said. "Something clever, I think. We would have laughed."

Sometime after four in the morning, I came out of the hospital entrance and turned toward home. I doubted that I would be able to sleep if I went home, and it was too early to call Albertine's mother and the boys to tell them what had happened, so when I reached the corner, I turned toward Carl Schurz Park instead. I couldn't stop my mind from replaying the memory of Albertine in the air, flying forward over her handlebars, yawing, pitching, and rolling in her flight, until she landed—crashed, that is—on the unyielding pavement, and then the still way she had lain there, with her legs straight out and that awful look of surprise on her face, and with it, almost superimposed on it, ran the memory of my mother, falling from her lawn chair. For both of them I felt a deep sympathy and, surprising to me, a deeper sadness for the loss of dignity that they had suffered, and I felt, as intensely as if I had fallen myself, how hard it is to hold on to dignity, to attain some scrap of dignity and then hold on to it, and I resented the way that accidents had snatched their dignity from them. I stood at the railing, looking down at the dark water of the East River, feeling useless. I couldn't mitigate Albertine's pain, couldn't alleviate it in any way, and I couldn't imagine how I could restore her dignity. While I stood there, feeling the hollow emptiness of uselessness, I began to feel something else overcome me, a familiar feeling, the overwhelming feeling of being full of my love for her. There were times, and this was one, when the experience of that love was so great that it overpowered all other emotions, rendered me incapable of feeling anything else. This state of being full of love for her was buoying, uplifting, elating, and liberating, and it lifted me, made me feel that if I chose to, I could arise and fly across the river, to Queens.

PLEASE, SIR, I YEARN TO LEARN

FIRST OF ALL," said Rudolph Derringer, Certified Flying Instructor, "I want you to banish from your mind the notion that flying is dangerous." He paused and scanned the room, turning a stern and serious mien on each of his eager students. He wore a leather flying jacket with a silk scarf thrown around his neck, apparently carelessly, and a leather flying helmet with goggles pushed up on his head. "Flying is not dangerous," he said, shaking his head. He stopped. He paused. He raised a finger. And, as if the distinction had just occurred to him, he added, "*Crashing* is dangerous."

After a moment of uncertainty, we allowed ourselves a little nervous laughter. Outside, a storm was blowing through Babbington. (Was it part of the aftermath of Hurricane Felicity? I'm not sure.) Eight of us—seven men and a boy—were sitting on folding chairs in a hangar at the Babbington Municipal Airport, which was still known simply as that, since the supporters of former mayor Andy Whitley had not yet launched their campaign to have it renamed for him. Wind drove the rain against the corrugated metal siding, and we shivered in our seats.

"That's one of the maxims of the aviator," Derringer said, chuckling now. "Flying isn't dangerous; crashing is dangerous." We all chuckled along with him, dutifully, but a joke is never funny the second time around.

"You get what you pay for," muttered the man sitting beside me, dealing me an elbow in the ribs to catch my attention and pointing to the ad in the *Babbington Reporter* that had lured us to the airport.

He let his finger rest beneath the word *nothing*, and he gave me another poke in the ribs to make certain that I hadn't missed the point.

Derringer held up a battered copy of *Elements of Aeronautics*. Momentarily overcome by the desire to stand out in the crowd, court the instructor, get a head start on the competition for teacher's pet, and show that I was not only eager but prepared, I came close to announcing that I owned a copy, but, fortunately for my dignity, Derringer spoke before I had a chance to speak myself.

"You can't learn to fly from a book," he said with a sneer. He turned the cover of the book toward him and read the title as if it were an obscenity. "I sure as hell didn't learn to fly from a book. I learned to fly by the seat of my pants—and that's how I'm going to teach you to fly. You've got to *feel* the plane under you, the way you feel a horse under you when you're in the saddle. Anybody here ride?"

None of us did, and our head-shakings and murmured disavowals seemed to disappoint Derringer so deeply that I thought for a moment of offering my years of bicycle riding as an approximation. Again, Derringer saved me from the guffaws of my fellows by speaking first.

"Well," he said, with evident pity, "it's a shame. If you rode, you'd know what I mean about the seat of your pants. Flying that way—it's something you feel." He stared off into the distance, upward, as if he were looking beyond the ceiling, beyond the storm and the clouds, to the limitless open space above us, his proper realm. "You become one with the plane," he said rapturously, "one airborne entity, a mythical being, a flying man, the way a

"You get what you pay for," muttered the man sitting beside me . . .

rider comes to feel that he and the horse beneath him have become one, have become a mythical creature, a centaur. The seat-of-the-pants rider doesn't put his horse into a gallop; *he* gallops. And when you fly by the seat of your pants, you don't bank the plane, *you* bank. You don't roll the plane or loop the plane, *you* roll, *you* loop. Ultimately, you don't fly the plane—*you* fly."

"Ultimately, you don't crash the plane," muttered the disenchanted guy beside me. "*You* crash."

After a moment of stillness to allow the last note of his lyrical intro-duction to resonate, Derringer began to outline the lessons in the course that he offered, and we began to understand that the lyrical introduction was all that we were going to get for free. His presentation was on the order of what today would be called an infomercial, short on information and long on purchase opportunity. I learned, when Derringer got to the point of closing, that the cost of the course was beyond my boyish means. It may have been beyond the means of the men seated with me as well, because none of them wrote checks when they were invited to. Instead, they filed into the wet night, heads down, disappointed. I followed, adopting much the same attitude.

"It's simply amazing," said the guy who had sat beside me. "In less than a minute, Rudolph Derringer, CFI, managed to become repeti-tious and boring."

"Yeah," growled another guy. He took a drag on a cigarette that he held in his cupped hand to protect it from the rain. "He started out great, too. Full of promise."

"Right," said another. "When we were filing into the hangar and taking our seats, and I saw him standing there, he seemed like a dash-ing adventurer, a living advertisement for the romance of flight."

"He certainly dressed the part."

"That he did."

"I think I'm not alone in saying that when I came into that hangar and saw him standing there, I said to myself, 'This is a guy who can teach me to fly.'"

"With the one mistake of repeating a joke, he became a windbag, nothing but a gag man, and not a good one."

"And we began asking ourselves, 'Am I really going to trust this clown to teach me how to fly? I mean, what if a situation arises in which there's nothing to prevent flying from turning into crashing but what Rudolph Derringer, Certified Fucking Idiot, has taught me?'"

"He crashed."

"One little mistake, and he crashed."

"Let that be a lesson to you, kid."

"Yeah," I said, trying on, to see how well it fit, their snarling rejection of Rudolph Derringer and trying, behind my back, the method of cupping a hand to hold a cigarette and keep it safe from the rain.

"You going to the course at the library next Wednesday?" one of the men asked.

"What course is that?" asked another.

"Cultivation and Propagation of Succulents."

"I don't know. Maybe."

"They make very nice houseplants, I'm told. It's free, and you get to take a cutting home with you."

"I might be there. How about you, kid?"

"I'm not sure," I said. I patted my pockets as if looking for something. "You know, I think I left my—pen—in the hangar. I've got to go back. Maybe I'll see you next week."

I returned to the hangar and found Derringer slumped in a chair, a pint bottle of Don Q rum in his hand and a distant look on his face.

"Mr. Derringer?" I asked.

"Yeah?" he said without looking at me.

"I was wondering if you'd be willing to give me a few lessons for a reduced price. I've got my own plane. Almost. Well, not a plane exactly. An aerocycle—but it's not quite finished. Maybe I could get by with just three lessons—taking off, steering, and landing. Make that four lessons. There's one other thing that I really want to learn—something I yearn to learn."

"Oh, yeah? What do you *yearn* to learn?"

"I yearn to learn the Immelmann turn."

"What's that?" he asked.

"It's—it's—well—"

"Yeah?"

"It's on page eighty-eight," I said, pointing to his copy of *Elements of Aeronautics*.

He flipped the book open and flipped the pages until he came to page eighty-eight. He bent over the book and studied the diagram. "You must be crazy!" he said. "That looks impossible."

Although I had only that one flying lesson, it did teach me something. I think I can see that I took much of what Derringer said about seat-of-the-pants flying to heart. I became a seat-of-the-pants flier when I eventually did build my aerocycle and took off for the Faustroll Institute, and much later in life, I became a seat-of the-pants memoirist. When you are a seat-of-the-pants memoirist you don't write about your life; you live your memoirs. You begin to feel that you and your account of yourself are one, like a mythical beast.

IF ONLY . . .

....

TIPTOED INTO Albertine's hospital room, in case she was asleep. She was. She lay on her back, with the bed cranked up so that her upper body was raised from the horizontal. Her mouth hung slightly open. As she breathed, she snuffled. I wouldn't call it snoring, not quite, but it was a near cousin. I wasn't seeing her at her best. The slack mouth and the snuffling did not become her. I knew that the woman who had worried about exposing her underwear in a dogboarding accident would not want me—or anyone else—to see her this way, so I retreated from the room and returned to the nurses' station down the hall.

"She asleep?" asked a nurse.

"Yeah," I said.

"It's the meds. She'll go in and out. You can wait here if you want, but it would be better if you wait in there with her, so she sees you when she wakes up."

"You think so?"

"She's been asking for you."

"She has?" I said. I shouldn't have been surprised to find that she had been asking for me, but I was. I was so pleased and flattered by the thought of her asking for me, like a wasting heroine in a sentimental movie, that I may have blushed and stammered. In fact, I'm sure I did. I didn't say, "She has?" I said, "Sh-sh-she has?"

The nurse gave me a smile and said, "Of course she has. You know she has." There was something in her manner, and her smile, that made me wonder if she thought that I wasn't really Albertine's husband. "You ought to wait in her room—so that you're there when she wakes up."

"Yes," I said. "I'll do that."

I returned to her room and found her awake.

"Hi," she said shyly, as if we didn't know each other as well as we do.

"Hi," said I, in much the same manner. Perhaps it was the setting that made us feel unfamiliar.

"Did you write about the crash?" she asked, with a bit of vacancy at the end, as if she had omitted *yet*.

"Yes," I said. "I set it in Central Park."

"A much nicer setting," she said. "Much nicer. But why there? Why did you put us there?"

"I had you crash into a dogboarder instead of a construction worker."

"I can't stand those dogboarders."

"I know."

"Did you include the flying EMTs?"

"What?"

"The flying EMTs. When I was in the emergency room, there were EMTs who brought people in by helicopter. They landed on the roof."

"I forgot."

"They were dashing. They had a certain swagger."

"I'll put them in," I promised.

"Thank you," she said, shy again.

"I wish it hadn't happened," I said. "I wish we could take the day back, and choose to do something else instead of riding—"

"—in the park."

"Yeah," I said.

"So do I," she said. "Believe me."

"I'm sure you do," I said.

"Yes," she said, "I suppose so, but that sort of regret can lead you down the dark alleys of If and into the dangerous part of town they call If Only."

RECRUITING THE CREW

. . . .

I KNEW—OR I thought I knew—that I could count on certain people to help me when I actually began to build the aerocycle. I thought that I could count on my friends, and I thought I knew who they were. As I began letting them know that the big day was nearly upon us, however, I began to hear from them a chorus of excuses. Actually, it wasn't a chorus, since their excuses were all highly individual and sometimes quite inventive; it was more like a cacophony of excuses.

Raskol announced that he was spending all his time cramming for the dread-inducing College Competency Exams, the CCEs, though he had often told me that he considered college a waste of time and wanted to go to work on the bay after he finished high school, eventually buy his own boat, and live a life much like his father's. "I'm working with a tutor," he said with apparent pride. "Rudolph Derringer."

"CFI?" I asked.

"Huh?" he said.

"Never mind," I said.

Spike O'Grady claimed to have become a balletomane. "I can't miss any of the performances during the Babbington Festival of the Dance," she said swooningly.

"I didn't even know there was a Babbington Festival of the Dance," I admitted.

With an expression of wonder at my ignorance, she said, "It's an annual affair."

I shrugged.

"All those darling children from Miss Lois's School of Dance and Arlene's Dancing Academy and all the other little dancing schools in the greater Babbington area hold their recitals in one enchanting festival," she said, cracking her knuckles.

Margot and Martha Glynn claimed that they had to spend every waking hour posing for their father, the painter Andy Glynn. "Our father is having a bit of a *crise*," said Margot. "He has not been selling quite so well as he used to."

"And that is putting a pinch on the family finances," said Martha. "Cheaper cuts of meat, domestic wine, the usual cutbacks."

"But he's begun to worry about the future, and he feels the need to put some money by for the wife and daughters, in anticipation of the time when he shuffles off the mortal coil."

"So he's decided to reinvent himself as a painter of frankly erotic studies of beautiful young girls interpreted as nymphs and fairies," said Martha.

"You can see that we are kept quite busy," said Margot with a proud toss of her golden hair.

You may not be surprised, Reader, to learn that I thought then of abandoning the flying project entirely and devoting myself to assisting Andy Glynn, but I was stung by the girls' apparently giving not a thought to the idea of abandoning the erotic painting project and assisting me, so I just said, "Yes, I guess you are," and went to browse in greener pastures.

When I asked Mr. MacPherson what he thought "the mortal coil" was, he said, "The mortal coil is a lot like the madding crowd or the vale of tears. It's where we live, and it's the condition of human life, with its worries and woes, hustle and bustle, turmoil and tumult, which is what *coil* means, as perhaps you did not know, and the certainty of death, which is what *mortal* means, as I suspect you did know. 'Deid men are free men,' my father used to say. They are free of the coil, at least, and far from the madding crowd. Hamlet used the 'mortal coil' phrase in his famous soliloquy, the one that begins with 'To be or not to be: that is the question.' When he's thinking of killing himself, he wonders what death would be like. Like sleep? 'To sleep: perchance to dream,' he says, 'ay, there's the rub; / For in that sleep of death what dreams may come / When we have shuffled off this mortal coil / Must give us pause.'"

"Would you like to help me build a small airplane out of parts of old motorcycles?" I asked.

"Sorry, Peter," he said. "After school hours, I abandon myself to strong drink."

"Really?" I asked, astonished by such an admission from an adult, and particularly from a teacher.

"'It's a dry tale that disna end in a drink,'" he said.

Marvin Jones claimed that he had to entertain visiting relatives. "My aunt Sylvia and uncle Gordon are coming," he said, "and seven of my cousins. There's a lot of cooking to do, housecleaning, turning the basement into a dormitory, that sort of thing."

"Yeah," I said, "but I thought you'd—"

"Family is the most important thing, Peter. As my mother says, 'Friends may be friends for a lifetime, but family is forever.'"

"Yeah," I said. "But remember that 'Freendship canna stand aye on ane side.'"

"Who said that?"

"Mr. MacPherson."

Matthew Barber claimed that he wanted to help but couldn't because his mother had forbidden it, on the grounds that being associated with "Peter and his crazy flying scheme" would make him a pariah at the Summer Institute. Patti Fiorenza was rarely to be seen. She was either off riding in a convertible with a tattooed thug or rehearsing with whatever doo-wop group she happened to be in at the moment. Porky White said that he was so busy with plans to open a second clam bar that he couldn't even think of anything else.

"I know it doesn't seem like such a big deal to open another little restaurant, but I've got a feeling that this is the start of something big," he said. "I see Kap'n Klam Family Restaurants from coast to coast someday, and I want to make sure that I get it right, right from the start. You understand, don't you?"

"Sure," I said. "I feel the same way about my solo flight to New Mexico. I'd like to get it right, right from the start—which is going to be hard if I never get the plane built."

"Mm, yeah," he said distractedly. Then he stopped what he was doing, thought for a moment, and said suddenly, with enthusiasm, "Say, Peter! How about if you trail one of those advertising banners behind you, like the ones you see behind the planes that buzz the beach? 'Kap'n Klam is coming!' It'll get people wondering who the Kap'n is, get them interested in buying a franchise."

"A franchise?"

"Yeah," he said, returning to the papers that were spread across the counter. "It's a brilliant idea. I'll explain it to you later. What do you say about the banner?"

"Okay, I guess, if it's not too heavy."

"How heavy could it be? I'll get to work on it. Sorry I can't help you with the plane."

"Aerocycle."

"Right. Sorry."

My friends, it seemed, had let me down. My father, on the other hand, and to my great surprise, was eager. When I returned home, defeated in my effort to rally recruits to the cause, he was out in the garage, making an inventory of the materials on hand and assigning tasks to personnel we didn't have, pausing now and then to rub his hands in anticipatory glee, looking forward to the start of the work.

"Big day tomorrow!" he said when he noticed me.

"Yeah," I said. "Big day."

I didn't have the heart to tell him that we'd be working alone, or to point out that work without help was likely to be work without glee.

AL AND I, UNSTOPPABLE

ALBERTINE ATTEMPTED TO shift her position, winced, tried to smile as if the pain she felt were not really so bad, then settled back against the pillow and lay there in silence for a while before she spoke, or before she could manage to speak.

"So he did help you," she said.

"No," I said. "I've made him an enthusiastic supporter of my plans so that I could see how things might have gone between us if he had been an enthusiastic supporter of my plans."

"Peter, did he ever actually *prevent* you from doing the things that you thought were important to you, the things that you thought were worth doing?"

"You've forgotten about his not allowing me to see that play?"

"Other than that."

"He told me that I couldn't change my major to molluscan biology."

"But you did."

"He told me that I couldn't marry you."

"So did your mother."

"True."

"And yet you did."

"I was unstoppable. So were you. Your parents offered you Europe to reject me, remember."

"A trip to Europe, not Europe."

"You mean—you had your price—but they wouldn't meet it?"

"Nothing short of all of Europe would have stopped me."

I, PANMUPHLE

TO DISTRACT MYSELF from feelings of bitterness and betrayal, I decided to make another try at my translation of the *Adventures and Opinions of Doctor Faustroll, Pataphysician*. Reading what I had done, I felt that I understood Panmuphle's frustration at being unable even to locate the dilatory tenant of the Bonhommes, felt it at a level deeper than the words on the page. It resembled, I saw on rereading, my frustration at being unable to find a friend when I needed one. I also saw that Monsieur Jarry—as I thought of him in my schoolboy way—intended Panmuphle to be ridiculous. He was officious with regard to the duties of his office, jealous of its perquisites, and vigorous in his efforts to avoid blame. He was a petty bureaucrat, a type of being my father often railed against at the dinner table. I began trying to plod through what I had done, word for word, but the more I worked, the more clearly I could see in my mind's eye the interview between Panmuphle and the mayor of Paris when the bumbling bailiff returned in defeat and began to make his excuses. I found myself straying from the letter of the text to what I took to be the spirit, and I produced this:

The mayor's door stood partly open, as it ordinarily does when he is at work within. I knocked with due deference, employing the modest tap that my dear wife did me the honor of referring to as "the badge of my diplomatism" when I demonstrated it for her. After a moment's pause, during which I detected no response to my knock from Monsieur le Mayor, I peered discreetly around the frame of the door, knocked again, cleared my throat, and said, as a request that he acknowledge and admit me, "Monsieur le Mayor?"

Employing that gruff tone that he affects to hide from others the avuncular affection he feels for me, he asked, "What is it now, Panmuphle?"

"Sir," I said, "today I have—"

"Today?" he said, raising his head from his work and regarding me with querulous eyes. "What day is today?"

"It is the eighth of February, sir." He made no response, but his eyes seemed to grow more querulous. "In the year eighteen hundred ninety-eight," I added.

With an economical gesture of the hand, he indicated that I should proceed.

"Today I have been frustrated in my attempt to do my duty, sir."

"Then today is a day like all days, is it not?" he said, attempting through this drollery to put me at my ease.

"Yes, thank you, sir," I said, with a smile to show that I understood his humorous intent. "The source of my frustration, sir, is my inability to locate a certain Doctor Faustroll."

"Faustroll? Faustroll?" he muttered.

"Yes, sir. He is the tenant, or perhaps the lodger, of Mr. and Mrs. Jacques Bonhomme, owners of a house situated at 100 Richer Street."

"Yes?"

"Yes. They appealed to me, sir, as the elected member for the district."

"Mm."

"Doctor Faustroll—if indeed he has the right to the apellation—owes to the Bonhommes the sum of three hundred seventy-two thousand francs and twenty-seven centimes, for eleven terms of rent on the premises annexed to the Bonhomme house and numbered one hundred bis."

"Mm."

"I made my way to Richer Street, sir, and found the lodgings of Doctor Faustroll."

"You are certain of that?"

"But yes, Monsieur le Mayor. The number one hundred was clearly marked on the house."

"And you were in the correct street?"

"Monsieur—"

"Go on, go on."

"I rang the bell, I knocked, and I called the name of Doctor Faustroll."

"And getting no response, you left, I suppose."

"For lunch, yes, but I returned following my lunch, and again I rang the bell, again I knocked, and again I called the name of Doctor Faustroll. Again and again."

"No one came to the door, I suppose."

"No one."

"Forgive me, Panmuphle, but you are certain that you were knocking at the door of the residence of Doctor Faustroll?"

"I interrogated the neighbors, sir, and they declared to me that it was indeed the residence of Doctor Faustroll."

"Had you prepared a Commandment in accordance with article 819 of the Code of Civil Procedure?"

"Yes, sir. I had, sir." I unrolled the Commandment and displayed it, but he did not look up from the papers on his desk. "I put considerable effort into it, and into the two copies," I said. "Notice the care I've taken with the lettering—"

"Panmuphle," he said with a sigh betraying the weight of his office, "why did you not have some relative or neighbor of Doctor Faustroll sign the original and take a copy to present to Faustroll when he returned?"

"Sir, I could not find anyone who was willing to do that. There were no relatives of Faustroll's there, nor any servants, and none of the neighbors was willing to assume the duty of

signing my original and being presented with the copy." I
paused for a moment. The account of my struggles had left me
a bit breathless. "I was uncertain, sir, what my next action
ought to be, so I returned here immediately to speak with you
personally, seeking your advice and counsel."

"Is the Commandment properly worded?"

"But of course, sir," I said, and, to prove that it was so, I began to read the Commandment to him: " 'I, the undersigned
René-Isidore Panmuphle, *et cetera*, have made Commandment, *et cetera*, to Mr. Faustroll, doctor, *et cetera*, within
twenty-four hours, *et cetera*, to pay to the plaintiff, *et cetera*, the
sum of three hundred seventy-two thousand francs and
twenty-seven centimes, *et cetera*, declaring to him that failing
to satisfy, *et cetera*—' "

"All right, all right, *et cetera*," he growled in his collegial way.
"Let me have it."

I laid the original before him and he signed it with a flourish. "Leave a copy at Faustroll's residence," he said.

"Yes, sir."

"Nail it to the door if you must."

"Certainly."

"And see that the proper stamps are affixed to it."

"Of course, sir," I said, backing out the door. "Thank you, sir."

While I was at work on this version of the very first part of the *Adventures and Opinions of Doctor Faustroll, Pataphysician*, I experienced
the realization—a realization accompanied by a great deal of
pleasure—that I was doing something like flying: I had taken off from
the original and had embarked on a flight of fancy. I could not help but
think about what Mr. MacPherson had said earlier: "If they set you the
task of writing a dissertation, perhaps you'll choose to do it on the
question of whether an imaginary solution can be built from scratch,
from whole cloth, or must needs be built from a kit, a set of precut
pieces that we cut as we live, without even noticing that we're doing the
work." I was working from a kit, a set of precut pieces, and I was
acutely aware of my having done the work of making the pieces over all
the years that had preceded my taking off.

THE BOSS TAKES HIS PLACE

· ·

ON THE MORNING of the day when my father and I were to begin building the aerocycle, alone, I was reluctant to get out of
bed. I could hear my father downstairs, whistling, as he did whenever a
burst of enthusiasm came over him and he felt for a while as if he were
a boy again, feeling the boyish lift of possibility in his life. I was as reluctant to join my father in building the aerocycle as I was to join him
in his enthusiasm. I found enthusiasm unseemly in him. Recalling that
morning and the feelings that kept me in bed, I think that I may at the
time have found enthusiasm unseemly in any adult. From the point of
view of my teenage self, adults didn't wear enthusiasm well. Seeing
them under the influence of enthusiasm was like seeing them drunk
and telling jokes. From my point of view, my tipsy parents embarrassed
themselves in attempting to be funny, and the next morning they
seemed to realize that they had. I thought that they should also have
realized that they embarrassed themselves in attempting to recover
their youthful enthusiasm. I know that I was embarrassed for my father
when I saw the signs of his enthusiasm—his whistling and bustling
and the fraternal attitude that he took toward me when the fit was on
him, as if we had always been great friends and he had never been the
Grand Naysayer.

Hiding from my father's enthusiasm wasn't my only reason for lingering in bed. I was also giving my friends time to gather secretly to
surprise me. I nursed the slim hope that they had conspired to play a
joke on me. If that were the case, then they must now be gathering
outside, or in the garage, preparing to surprise me when I came down
to begin work. I wanted to give them plenty of time to gather so that
the slugabeds and stragglers among them wouldn't miss seeing my look
of surprise and gratitude when I discovered that they were all there to
help me, that they were friends indeed. The moment promised to be
poignant and exhilarating, with lots of backslapping and hugging and
many lumpy throats. I didn't want anybody to miss it. I strained to hear
any sound that might betray their secret assembly, but I couldn't hear a
thing. Evidently, they were a stealthy bunch, those friends of mine.

Then I heard footsteps—but not outside, where the sound of the footsteps of my gathering friends would have come from. They were footsteps inside the house, footsteps approaching the foot of the stairs, and they were my father's footsteps.

Then: "Peter!"

From me, reluctantly: "Yeah?"

"Time to get going! Sooner begun is sooner done!"

"Have you been talking to Mr. MacPherson?" I groaned.

"I—um—" he began, and then he added, "I—ah—who?"

"Never mind," I said. "I'm getting up."

I got up. I dressed. I brushed my teeth. I shaved. (Wait a minute. That can't be right. I wasn't shaving yet. Or was I? This was just before the end of my junior year in high school. Because I had started kindergarten early and skipped the third grade, I was only fifteen. Was I shaving? Now that I think about it, I believe that I was, perhaps as often as monthly. Maybe I did shave that morning, mindful that someone might take commemorative snapshots.)

I dawdled through breakfast, stretching it out and stretching it out, until, finally, there was nothing to do but get up and go out to the garage. My friends were not there, but my father was, bustling about. He had already scratched a sketch of the wing framework in the sand that served as the floor of the garage and laid a few lengths of aluminum tubing in place on the sketch. That should have been my work. I wondered whether he had gotten it right.

"How's it going?" I asked.

"Great! Just great!" he claimed.

"What do you want me to do?"

"Hey, I'm not the boss here," he said, incredibly. "This is your project, your baby, your dream. You tell me what you want me to do."

I asked myself whether he could possibly mean that. Was he really there to help me? Or was he there, as he usually was, to tell me that what I was doing, or what I wanted to do, was wrong, that he knew a better way, the only way, his way? I decided to find out.

"Okay," I said. "Let me see that sketch."

He gave it to me. With my sketch in hand, I began walking the perimeter of his version, his lines drawn in the sand, making corrections. I could almost hear him bristling, but I didn't care or dare to look up to see whether he was fuming at my impudence in changing what he had done. I kept my attention strictly on the work of making the template on the floor match the sketch. When I had finished, and only then, I raised my head to look at him, to see how he had taken my treating him as he had always treated me, correcting his work without asking, altering it as I thought it should be altered, and that was when I saw that we were not alone. Behind my father, just outside the garage door, was quite a crowd. Everyone I had asked to help was there, and many more, including Mr. MacPherson, who immediately snatched the sketch from me and went around the template again, correcting my corrections. All my friends were there, and a lump began to form in my throat, as I had known it would.

"Hey, Pete," said Spike, "whatcha doin'?"

I swallowed hard and said, as nonchalantly as I could, "Building an aerocycle."

"Oh, right! I remember you mentioned that. Mind if we help?"

"No," I said as if the idea had never occurred to me. "I don't mind."

"All right, everyone!" said Mr. MacPherson. "The surprise portion of the event is over. I'm sure we can all see that our little stunt was a great success and Peter is deeply moved by our demonstration of loyalty. Now it's time to get to work. I want this machine to fly in forty-eight hours. Line up to my right and I'll assign tasks based on ability and experience."

People began lining up. I didn't see any reason to join them. After all, I was the boss.

"Peter?" said Mr. MacPherson with a gesture toward the end of the line. It would have been useless to object. I took my place with the others.

"Mr. Leroy?" said Mr. MacPherson, looking over his glasses at my father.

"I was already working—" he began, but Mr. MacPherson's stare was enough to silence him. He fell into line behind me.

It was an awkward moment for both of us, shuffling along at the end of the line, awaiting assignments on my project in his garage. After a long, silent minute, my father said, "You have a lot of friends."

"Yeah," I said.

"I envy you that," he said.

FLYGUYS

. . . .

AS I APPROACHED Albertine's hospital room the next evening, I could hear her humming. It was as unmistakable a sign of enthusiasm in her as whistling had been in my father.

"You sound chipper," I said as I leaned over to kiss her.

"Oh, I am. If only I could get out of here, I think I'd be quite chipper indeed."

"Any word on that?"

"It's hard to pin anyone down."

"Are you feeling better?"

"I still can't turn at all. The pain is just too much."

"I'm sorry—"

"And the lump on the side of my head is as big as a grapefruit—half a grapefruit."

"Your hair hides it."

"I know, but it worries me."

"I'm sure."

"However . . . I can sit at the side of the bed and I can stand with the walker." She inclined her head toward a framework of aluminum tubing that stood beside the bed, a "walker" that allowed a person to stand within it and support herself by taking her weight partially on her arms, with her hands gripping plastic foam pads on the uppermost part of the frame.

"Really?" I said. That seemed like tremendous progress to me.

"Yes. Really. Apparently I have to pass a test to get out of here."

"A test?"

"The Walker Test."

"You have to show that you can use it?"

"I have to show that I can go some distance using it."

"How far?"

"There's some disagreement about that. The big nurse says a hundred feet, but the flyguys say a hundred yards. Of course, they may be pulling my leg—"

"The 'flyguys'?"

"That's what they call themselves. The EMTs who fly the helicopters."

"Oh."

"They're so cute."

"I'll bet."

"They've got swagger."

"You've mentioned that."

"I have?"

"Yes. The other evening."

"Oh? I don't remember. It must be the pain medication. Do I smell something good?"

"I brought chicken tikka masala." Albertine is fond of chicken prepared in a hundred ways, and chicken tikka masala is at or near the top of the list.

"I don't have much of an appetite."

"Did you eat the hospital dinner?"

"The flyguys brought me a hero."

"A hero?"

"Italian cold cuts."

"You ate a whole hero?"

"No, no. Just a couple of bites. But that couple of bites filled me right up."

We talked about coincidence and accident for a while, but it was a conversation in fits and starts. Al was still sleepy, inclined to close her eyes after a few minutes, doze for a while, then wake and smile in apology for having drifted away. When she was awake, we talked, and when she was asleep, I ate a little of the chicken.

After leaving Albertine, I detoured to the emergency room instead of going straight home. The emergency "room" was actually a suite of rooms arranged around a central administrative and bureaucratic area that was open except for a chest-high partition defining it and limiting its access to two openings. A dozen seats were arranged opposite one of the openings, provided for those who accompanied the ill and injured to the emergency room, and I sat in one of them, choosing the same one that I had occupied on the night of Albertine's crash, when I had waited for her there while she was being examined elsewhere in the building. Now I had come to the emergency room because I wanted to see what the flying EMTs, the flyguys, looked like. There were none in evidence when I arrived, so I waited, but I feared that I might be told to leave before I got the chance to see them. I expected to be challenged about my right to be in the emergency room, occupying a seat provided for the companion to an ailing party when I had no ailing party to play companion to, but no challenge ever came. I was never asked to move along, never told to leave. No one seemed to notice me at all. I could have sat there all night, I think. I might have sat there every night. The thought came to me that sitting there for a while every night might be interesting to try, to see whether anyone ever noticed that I didn't belong there, that I had no legitimate claim to one of the molded seats. It might also be possible to get free coffee that way.

A phone rang, and its ringing occasioned a sudden bustle and flutter that had not occurred when other phones rang. Someone sprang up to answer it, and I saw that the ringing phone was red, mounted on a pillar at the very center of the central bureaucratic area.

"Schurz ER," said the young woman who answered it. She flipped a switch beside the phone, and the incoming side of the conversation was broadcast to all of us. What we heard was a man's voice, stern, clipped, efficient, self-confident, calling from a helicopter on its way to Schurz from the scene of an accident somewhere, calling out over the roar of engine and wind. (Schurz, I learned later, was the "catchment" hospital for trauma cases in a wide area roughly centered on our neighborhood. Three helicopter EMT services transported victims to Schurz, landing on a helipad on the roof of the hospital, where the flyguys off-loaded the injured, commandeered an elevator, and rushed their charges to the ER.)

The voice detailed the nature and extent of injuries sustained in a motorcycle accident by a male Caucasian who would be arriving at the ER soon, and three people—a doctor and two nurses, I think—began preparing a bed and assembling equipment. After what seemed only a moment, double doors burst open down a hallway to my right and two flyguys came through, wheeling a collapsible stretcher with a victim on it. The flying EMTs were suited up in jumpsuits, gray with a red lightning bolt over their breast pockets and a much larger red lightning bolt on the back with the name MEDAIR beneath it. They were all business, those flyguys. They were professional. They were cool. They did not smile . . . but they sure did swagger.

ALBERTINE ON COINCIDENCE AND ACCIDENT

• •

A T HOME, IN bed, alone, missing Albertine, aching for her, I brought her to mind and rehearsed our conversation on coincidence and accident.

"You won't believe this," she had said, drifting up from sleep to a state of drowsy wakefulness, "but one of the flyguys is the grandson of your Mr. MacPherson."

"What a coincidence," I remarked.

"He asked me if I planned to sue," she added matter-of-factly.

I stopped eating the chicken tikka masala, closed the lid of the container, and asked, "Sue?"

"Mmm," she said distantly.

"You seem to be in a wee bit of a dwam," I said, as Mr. MacPherson might have.

"Mmm," she reiterated.

"Are you?"

"In a dwam?"

"Planning to sue."

"No. My crash was an accident."

"Pure and simple?"

"Of course not," she said, suddenly more alert. "Why do we say that? 'Pure and simple?'" Then, because she recognized that the question might have been asked by Mr. MacPherson himself, she spoke in an amusing version of his brogue. "Is anything ever pure and simple? No. Nothing. Everything is impure and complex. I suppose we say 'pure and simple' because we wish that something would be pure and simple, we yearn for things that are pure and simple, things that are pure enough and simple enough for us to understand them, see through them like pure water and swallow them as easily as simple syrup—but nothing is ever pure and simple."

"You're right," I said. "Your crash was an accident, but forget the pure and simple part."

"Am I raving?" she asked.

"Not exactly."

"It must be the pain medication."

"Maybe you should rest again."

"I think I'd like to make a point about the concepts of coincidence and accident, if I can stay awake long enough."

"Please do."

"Feel free to eat while I ramble."

"That's okay. While you talk, I listen. While you sleep, I eat."

"Coincidence," she began, and I could see from the way she paused and puckered her lips and knit her brows that she had not prepared this in advance, "is a simple matter of the simultaneous occurrence of two events."

"'Simple'?"

"You said, 'While you talk, I listen.'"

"I forgot myself."

"Eat the chicken—and don't talk with your mouth full."

"Yes, dear."

"Oooh," she said suddenly, and she shivered.

"What's the matter?"

"A chill," she said, "as if the ghosts of Einstein and Gödel just passed through the room, admonishing me as they wandered through against playing fast and loose with time and simultaneity."

"Oh," I said, and I couldn't keep myself from glancing around, trying to catch a glimpse of the famous friends.

"I know better than to claim that simultaneity is universal and absolute," she assured them, "but I'm only discussing the type of accident that is local and macroscopic, on the level where daily life is lived, the level where collisions with dogboarders occur. There—or here—as the term *accident* is usually used—make that commonly used—an accident is an *unfortunate* coincidence," she said firmly, in the manner of one who will brook no further interruption. "The idea of misfortune is so embedded in the term that on the rare occasions when we want to use it to designate a coincidence that brings good fortune, we have to specify that we mean a 'happy accident.' If your Mr. MacPherson were here, Peter, he would tell you that at its Latin root, *accident* simply means 'occurrence' or 'what has befallen.' After the fact, we ascribe significance to the simultaneity, sometimes great significance, based on the effect that one of the simultaneous occurrences has had on us, and so we give to coincidence a meaning that in most cases it ought not to have. That habit of overestimating the importance of coincidence has driven coincidence to its low status among skeptics. The truth is that coincidence is not merely commonplace but constant, a pervasive fact of life and all existence. The universal characteristic of the vast panorama of 'it all' is ceaseless motion, an uncountable number of events, happening all the time, with an uncountable number of them occurring coincidentally at any moment. We regard those events as directionless and meaningless until one of them affects us. At that moment, or slightly later, after the brain has done its work, we interpret all the other events in the light of that one that has affected us. That one is significant to us *because* it has affected us, and in our worldview we are always at the center of all action. No occurrence becomes significant until or unless it affects us. Put another way, we could say that an event will become significant *when* or *if* it affects us, but not until or unless it does. So, most of everything that happens is taken by the human mind to be insignificant, but the little bit that directly affects us we take to be tremendously significant, looming large over all the rest, and we suddenly seem to see an astonishing coincidence or set of coincidences that produced the significant event. If we could ever understand at a deep level the essential insignificance of simultaneity, we would not have our cultural fascination with the fallacy of significant coincidence." She was beginning to fade, and she knew it. She gave me a wan smile, as if apologizing in advance for the drifting off she was about to do. "I said 'cultural fascination,' but maybe our fascination is even deeper than that," she continued bravely. "It may even be genetic. Apparently, according to the reading I've been doing, one of the brain's primary functions is the detection of coincidence. Certain structures—combinations of synaptic links among neurons—work as coincidence detectors. Detecting coincidence must be of such high evolutionary value that it became a part of our genetic makeup . . . long . . . long . . . ago."

Visiting hours were over, and of the chicken tikka masala only a snack was left.

"Do you want me to leave this with you?" I asked. "One of the nurses can probably heat it up."

"No," she said drowsily. "Thank you. You have it for breakfast."

"I will," I said. "Good night, my darling." We kissed, and as she dwammed over I left her for the night.

THE SPIRIT OF CAMARADERIE

. . . .

> When energy is converted from one kind into another, no energy is actually destroyed. We may lose track of it, but it exists in some form. The statement of this fact is called the Law of the Conservation of Energy.
> —Francis Pope and Arthur S. Otis,
> *Elements of Aeronautics*

IMPRACTICAL CRAFTSMAN HAD told the truth, at least in part: the aerocycle could be built in a single weekend, and I think that it could have been built, or at least assembled, within the confines of the family garage. However, the crafty folks at *IC* had neglected to say how many people they expected to work on the construction. They never wrote in terms of builder hours. If you had a gang on the job, as I did, the aerocycle could be built in a single weekend. I am not really qualified to assess the adequacy of the confines of the family garage for the complete construction of an aerocycle, because not all of the work on my aerocycle was done there. We subcontracted some of it.

We built the plane during a time in Babbington when everyone knew how to do something, or at least knew somebody who knew how to do something, so we had a network of artisans available to us, if we knew who they were and how to enlist them. Mr. MacPherson, brilliant in the role of the boss, was quick to notice when a task was beyond the ken of the worker he had assigned to it. He had a sharp eye for the telltale signs: the befuddled brow; the perplexed scratching of the head; the first clumsy, hesitant effort; the furtive glance that followed a mistake and betrayed the intention to let it go uncorrected if it had gone unnoticed. As soon as he saw any evidence of befuddlement or perplexity or clumsiness or carelessness, he would seek someone better qualified, asking, for example, "Does anyone among those of you here assembled know someone with a drill press and the skill to use it?"

Someone always did, and so the most difficult and exacting tasks were sent to shops—or, sometimes, to family garages—around town, shuttled there and back by car or bicycle, even on foot. This subcontracting would certainly have resulted in chaos and idleness, with many willing workers—those who had been assigned to assemble the aluminum skeleton of the wings, for example—left behind in the garage, finding that they had nothing to do while the components essential to their work were across town being drilled by somebody's uncle—had it not been for Spike, whom Mr. MacPherson had immediately appointed his assistant, in charge of keeping idleness and chaos at bay. She created on the fly a chart that tracked every outsourced job, and she assigned a tracking agent to each of those jobs whose sole function was to observe the progress of the work and report to her. With up-to-the-minute knowledge of the state of readiness of every component and subcomponent, she was able to predict when the item would arrive and to ensure that a group gathered just in time to unload it and begin incorporating it in the grand scheme.

"Rose," said Mr. MacPherson suddenly while watching Raskol, Marvin, and me wrestling with the tricky job of fabricating the framework that would hold the engine in front of the handlebars, "how long will it be before the tail assembly is delivered?"

"My best estimate is ninety-seven minutes, Mr. Mac," Spike said with a glance at her watch and clipboard, "but remember that it won't have the fabric on it."

"Mm. I had forgotten that. Are we going to have to send it out again?"

"I don't think so. I've got Patti Fiorenza out scouring the town for people with upholstery experience, and I'm hoping we'll be able to get them in here to cut, fit, and stitch the fabric right on the frame."

"Good thinking."

"Thanks."

"But how is Patti getting around? She's not going to be able to cover much of the town on foot. Perhaps the telephone—"

"Rocco is driving her around in his T-bucket."

"What on earth is that, Rose?"

"It's a hot rod, sir."

"I see. A hot rod. I understand the use of *hot*, meaning 'powerful and keen to go,' as *fiery* does in 'a fiery steed,' but I wonder why *rod* should be the word for the steed itself."

"Possibly a corruption of *ride*, sir," suggested Spike.

Mr. MacPherson looked at her with love-light in his eyes. "Quite possibly so, Rose," he said. "Quite possibly so. Did you arrange for that transportation?"

"I can't take the credit, sir. Rocco found Patti's prominent breasts and buttocks, attractively displayed in a tight top and tighter skirt, a powerful incentive to drive her anywhere she might want to go. That's why I chose her for the job."

"You are a smart cookie, Rose."

"Thank you, sir."

They knit their brows in tandem, wondering about that use of *cookie*.

I would be less than generous if I did not acknowledge here that Mr. MacPherson and Spike were not the only ones who kept the crew occupied and available during what might otherwise have been downtime. Some of the credit has to go to my father, who put them to work mowing the lawn and weeding the vegetable garden.

To all of us but Spike and Mr. MacPherson, I think, our efforts truly did seem chaotic. We did the jobs we were told to do, and we derived some sense of satisfaction from whatever work we were doing, and we were held together in our work by the camaraderie that inevitably binds people who are working in a suburban garage to achieve a great goal, a feeling familiar to any reader who has launched a high-tech start-up, but individually we often had no clear notion of the part that our bit of work was to play in the grand scheme. This, I think, represented a failure in Mr. MacPherson's management style, which was otherwise both masterly and masterful. Even I, who had been dreaming over the drawings of the aerocycle for weeks, who had a picture of the completed aerocycle ever in my mind's eye, sometimes wasn't sure where the gizmo I had been assigned to assemble would fit in the finished plane, and I think Eddie Granger, who lived a block away from me and was notorious for having brought a teddy bear to school with him in the third grade, may have suffered some permanent damage to his self-esteem when he found himself, after the craft had been assembled and wheeled into the sunlight, left holding the device he had labored on for nearly the entire two days, something that fit nowhere at all in the finished plane but belonged in the sliding assembly of a hideaway ironing board that had been presented as a project for the amateur builder in the same issue of *Impractical Craftsman* as the aerocycle, the plans for which had somehow—perhaps by accident—found their way into the chaos of the garage.

On many mornings in Babbington, fog lies along the estuarial stretch of the Bolotomy, a "patchy" fog that is thick in some places, thin in others, obscuring and revealing, so that the landscape and townscape beyond it appear in bits and pieces, like the pieces of a picture puzzle with soft, blurred edges. For quite a while, the workers' understanding of the aerocycle was a similarly patchy picture obscured by a patchy fog. However, the fog began to dissipate, as morning fog does, when the sub-sub-assemblies became subassemblies and the subassemblies began to come together as assemblies, and we began to see not just nameless parts whose functions we couldn't describe or predict, but wings, a fuselage, a tail, the motorcycle's running gear, the engine, and, at last, a hybrid machine, part plane, part bike, the aerocycle of my daydreams, my ride to the Land of Enchantment.

I was about to mount the aerocycle when Rocco, Patti Fiorenza's hot-rodding boyfriend, stepped forward and stayed my progress with a callused hand. I'm proud to say that I didn't flinch.

I did raise an eyebrow questioningly.

"Hey, ah, just a minute, there, Pete," he said, spitting my name's initial plosive at me.

I elevated the eyebrow a notch.

"Somebody left an old rag on the tail there," he said, with a nod in that direction. "Lemme get it off for ya."

He swaggered to the tail and whisked the rag away.

"Jeez," he said. "Look at that."

Painted on the tail was SPIRIT OF BABBINGTON.

A lump formed in my throat. "Is that—your handiwork?" I asked, swallowing.

"Yeah," he said, scuffling his feet and looking at his shoes. "I got a little talent in that area."

"Thanks, Rocco," I said.

"Aaaaa, it's nuttin'," he said. "Patti made me do it."

I gave him a comradely punch on the shoulder, and he gripped my hand in a way that made me think he might break my wrist just for the hell of it, but instead he gave me a return punch.

I mounted the aerocycle without rubbing my shoulder or even betraying a desire or need to rub my shoulder. "Next Saturday," I said. "I'll take off next Saturday."

THROUGH THE AGENCY OF DUST

Coördination is the soul of flying.

—Francis Pope and Arthur S. Otis,
Elements of Aeronautics

I KEEP MY old copy of *Elements of Aeronautics* in the bookcase directly in front of me, on a shelf just above my computer screen. I keep it, and keep it near, not only because it is indispensable as a reference work but because it is a means of transportation: it takes me back. This morning, here and now, with Albertine still in the hospital, just down the street but so far away, the apartment is quiet, empty, and lonely. I've been escaping the loneliness by flipping through the old book and reading at random. A moment ago I returned in memory to the time when I first opened the book, and the pleasure of being back there, back then quivered along my spine. For an instant, I was in my father's bedroom in my grandparents' house, where I slept whenever I visited them. Having returned so completely to a moment in the past, I felt a comforting sense of removal to a safe place. The safest place of all is nowhere, and the past is a place close to that, because as soon as a moment becomes something to remember, it no longer exists for us as anything *but* a moment to remember. The past has had its effect on the present, but the present and its problems can never have an effect on the past, can never find their way there, nor cause any trouble there. We can't go there, either, of course, and yet we experience, from time to time, moments when we seem to have made our way there, to be for a moment where we were rather than where we are. How do we do that? We require an agent. Dust does it for me, the particulate matter of the past. According to Freeman Dyson,

> The dualistic interpretation of quantum mechanics says that the classical world is a world of facts while the quantum world is a world of probabilities. Quantum mechanics predicts what is likely to happen while classical mechanics records what did happen. This division of the world was invented by Niels Bohr, the great contemporary of Einstein who presided over the birth of quantum mechanics. Lawrence Bragg, another great contemporary, expressed Bohr's idea more simply: "Everything in the future is a wave, everything in the past is a particle."

Preserved in my copy of *Elements of Aeronautics* is some dust, some of the dust from the cabinet of wonders in my father's room, a vast number of tiny particles of the past. That dust takes me back—but it hasn't the power to keep me there for long.

My moment in the past, begun when I began this chapter, has nearly run its course; the sensation of actually being there is fading as I write about it, my hasty fingers stumbling over one another. When the feeling was at its strongest, I could smell again the old wood in my father's childhood bedroom, the peculiar and singular smell of the half-completed model airplanes that were stored forever in a cupboard with sliding doors.

At the time, I equated the aroma with loss.

I spoke to my father about this, once upon a time.

"That aroma," I said, one evening when Albertine and I were visiting, probably—though I'm not certain that this is so—for a holiday dinner, "the smell inside that cabinet, where your old airplane models were, somehow it meant loss to me."

"Hmm?"

"Because it was the aroma of the past, of something old and even dead, it meant loss to me, but now, in memory, it means something different from that."

"Mm."

"That aroma was a real thing, you know, particulate matter. It was significant dust. Dust: the only tangible, detectable remnant of the past. One of the ways I knew those unfinished models was through the particulate matter that I inhaled when I opened the cabinet. I smelled them."

"Yeah."

"And the olfactory experience modified the synaptic network in my brain in such a way that the potential for the return of the memory of the smell of that cabinet and the potential for the return of a certain emotion that I felt in that room when I opened that cabinet and examined those models was equal. See what I mean?"

"No."

"The two things—the memory and the emotion—had a high probability of recurring together, and since that time they have recurred together, now and then, apparently coincidentally, and the aroma of old balsa wood and dust is now equated or closely associated not with loss but with comfort and security."

"Oh."

"There's another thing—"

"I figured," he said. "Do you want a beer?"

"Okay."

"You mind getting it?"

"No. Of course not."

"Get me one, too, will you?"

"Sure."

I got us a couple of beers.

"The other thing," I said, "is that the remembered aroma of balsa wood and dust brought back my—um—reverent attitude toward those models. I handled them like cult objects, fetishes. Why did I have that attitude?"

"I don't know."

"I think—but I recognize that this is my adult self thinking—I think that I understood that those models, or more precisely the incompleteness of those models, represented the end of your childhood, and in understanding that your childhood had had an end, had come to an end, I understood that a day would come when mine would end, when I would begin to become someone more like you and less like my little self."

"Yeah?" he asked.

"Yeah," I said.

A moment passed. We drank our beer.

"Those weren't my models," he said.

"They weren't?"

"No. They were Buster's."

"Buster's."

"Yeah."

"Oh."

Buster was my father's brother. He had been killed in World War II, the war that was to everyone I knew "the war," the way that "the city" was to everyone I knew New York City and no other.

"I wasn't much for model building," my father confessed. "That kind of thing was too tedious for me. I didn't have the patience for it." This from a man who sat for hours in a chair watching whatever appeared on his television screen. "Buster really went in for it, though. He'd spend whole afternoons at it. He was the patient one."

PANELING, A THOUGHT EXPERIMENT

....

IN THAT MOMENT—that moment that was already past as I tried to record it, already lost—every bit of the old sensation was returned to me by memory, and the catalyst was the smell of old wood and glue and dust that wafted from *Elements of Aeronautics* when I opened it. I remembered the cabinet of unfinished airplane models, of course; but I also remembered the clatter of the old typewriter on the built-in desk, which I used every time I was there, turning pulpy canary yellow second sheets onto the platen, because I was forbidden to use the bond paper in the upper drawer; I remembered the rifles that stood upright in a vertical cabinet to the left of the desk; I remembered the chubby, tubby ship model to the right of the desk, its hull painted orange and white, a lightship, I think; and I remembered the pine paneling on the walls of my father's room, regular and upright, its millwork pattern of ridges and valleys where one panel met the next, and its irregular and intriguing knottiness."

"Mm," said Albertine in a manner disconcertingly like my father's.

"I wonder—I am wondering just now—how much of what I am I owe to the time I spent in that room. I think that as I look back I can see in my life a pattern something like the pattern in the paneling, something in which the irregularity of its knottiness is balanced by the regularity of the millwork."

Her eyes widened.

"The paneling that my father used in my bedroom, when he finally finished, or nearly finished, the corner of the attic in our house in Babbington Heights that became my bedroom, was knotty pine nearly identical to the knotty pine that paneled the walls of his boyhood bedroom. I wonder if I haven't unconsciously or subconsciously patterned my life on that paneling."

Albertine sat in silence for a couple of minutes. Finally, brightening, she said, "You're kidding, right?"

"Kidding?" I asked. "About what?"

"About finding in your past the regularity and irregularity of knotty pine paneling?"

"Um, no."

"Hm."

"What do you mean by that?"

"By what?"

"'Hm.'"

"I think I mean—"

"Mm?"

"I think I mean—"

"Yeah?"

"I think I mean, 'I hope you're not beginning to take yourself too seriously.'"

"Oh."

"You are, aren't you?"

"Possibly. I think it may be the influence of my younger self, the self who was about to take off for the Faustroll Insititute in the Land of Enchantment. Back then, when I had the aerocycle finished, when it was ready and I began to feel that I, too, was ready, that I had become a person who was ready to mount his aerocycle and take off, I began to feel that I had a mission, that perhaps greatness had been thrust upon me."

"It went to your head."

"It did, and I liked it."

"And that was when you began to think of your life as patterned? Milled? Shaped? Shaped, as in shaped by fate, or the Fates?"

"Yes, but knotty, too, remember."

"How long did this last?"

"I don't seem to have gotten over it. Last night I found myself wondering whether I could induce and perhaps sustain that happy state of timelessness if I re-created the childhood conditions that originally inspired it."

"Oh, no."

"If I paneled my workroom with old knotty pine, if I bought some balsa-wood model kits from that dusty hobby shop down the block from us on First Avenue, where all the stock is old, I could assemble them, to a point, and arrange them on shelves where I could see and smell them, and I could work in that paneled room as a happy fool."

"Oh, my dear, my darling, my dreamer," she said, "promise me that you won't actually buy any of that paneling until I get out of here."

"Okay."

"No dusty old model kits, either."

"Okay."

"If I can pass the Walker Test, I can be home tomorrow."

MY NAME STITCHED IN RED

....

WITH THE AEROCYCLE complete and waiting in the drive-way, and with the announced time of my departure less than a week away, I began to feel important. I began to feel that I stood atop a tower of aviation pioneers, on the shoulders of giants, almost a young giant myself. That feeling may have led eventually to my willingness to have my accomplishment exaggerated by the press and the people of Babbington. In a way, I may have felt that to diminish their perception of my deeds by throwing over them the wet blanket of the truth would be to diminish not only my own daring accomplishment, but the accomplishments of my fellow pioneers as well. I may have felt that. I'm not sure. I offer it in my defense anyway. I know this: I stood taller, I set my jaw more firmly, and I steeled my gaze. I know those things because I checked my stature, my jaw, and my gaze in the hall mirror, frequently. The changes seemed to me to border on the profound, but my mother seemed not to notice. She insisted on helping me pack.

"Mom," I said, drawing myself to my full height, clenching my jaw, whetting my steely gaze, radiating determination and independence, "I'm embarking on a great adventure."

"Oh, I know!" she said. "I'm just as excited as you are. It gives me goose bumps. I should sew name tapes in your underwear."

"Is that something that only mothers can do?" I asked her.

"Sew name tags?" she asked, counting my underwear.

"No. Get from goose bumps to underwear in eight words flat."

"Are you making fun of me?"

"No," I said grumpily, with my eyes down, ashamed of the fact that I had been making fun of her, "it's just that adventurers do not go out into the wide world, braving the unknown, with their names sewn into their underwear."

"They don't?"

"No. They don't."

"How do you know?"

"Mom!"

"Come on, Mr. Smarty Pants. How do you know that the great adventurers haven't 'braved the unknown' with their names sewn into their underwear?"

"I just—"

"Wilbur and Orville Wright."

"Oh, come on."

"They had their names sewn into their underwear."

"How do you know?"

"How do you not?"

"I just—"

"Lucky Lindy."

"He did not have 'Lucky Lindy' sewn into his underwear."

"Of course not. He had 'Charles A. Lindbergh' sewn into his underwear."

"How about Chuck Yeager?" I asked. I thought I had her. I supposed that she did not know who Chuck Yeager was.

"Certainly," she said, a bit uncertainly.

"He had 'Chuck' sewn into his underwear?"

"No, silly," she said, and then she added with a girlish grin, " 'Charles Elwood Yeager, Test Pilot.' "

"And those labels were sewn in by his mother?"

"Of course they were sewn in by his mother. Who else?"

"Okay, I give up."

"I'll have them ready in the morning."

• • • • • • • • •

She did. The next morning all my underwear, my handkerchiefs, and my socks bore white fabric strips with "Peter Leroy" stitched on them in red thread. They were discreet, and I was grateful for that, but I was surprised to find that I liked them. They had a certain style. I had expected to be embarrassed by them, but I wasn't. My name looked handsome stitched in red. I regretted that there wasn't time for her to add "Birdboy of Babbington," the way Chuck's mother had added "Test Pilot."

TRAVELING LIGHT

WHILE TRYING TO pack the aerocycle, I began to understand what the writers at *Impractical Craftsman* had meant by the assessment that it "would not be practical for long-distance flying." It had not been conceived as a vehicle for cross-country flights. It didn't have room for everything that my mother wanted me to take. It didn't even have room for everything that I wanted to take, and that wasn't half of what my mother wanted me to take. I suppose that the people at *IC* who dreamed up the aerocycle intended it only for what they called "sports use," the sort of flight that wouldn't require a change of clothes, not even a change of underwear, nothing more than buzzing around the neighborhood, never very far from home.

"I don't know how you're going to carry all of this," my mother said, surveying the clothing and gear that we had brought to the driveway, glancing back and forth between the pile of stuff and the two small compartments fitted into the fuselage behind the pilot's seat.

"He can't," said my father. "You've got to start eliminating things."

"Oh, dear," said my mother. She picked up a pair of socks. "Maybe he won't need—" she said, and then, after consideration, "but he will." She put the socks back on the pile and said again, "Oh, dear."

"Mom," I said, putting a hand on her shoulder, "I'm going into unfamiliar territory, but not into 'the great unknown.' You were right to question my calling it that."

"I didn't—"

"Yes, you did. The question—we might even call it a challenge—was in your tone—and you were right. I'm going west, and that's a great adventure, but I'm not the first person to make the trip. Others have preceded me, blazing the trail—"

"What does this have to do—" my father interrupted.

"Because those pioneers preceded me," I pushed on, "there are people out there already. I'm going to travel light, but my resources will be virtually limitless, because I'm going to rely on the kindness of strangers."

"Oh, dear."

"Don't worry, Mom. I'm sure that I'm going to meet wonderful people all along the way, swell people, people who will be happy to take me into their homes, give me a hot supper, tuck me into a warm bed, and send me off with a hearty breakfast."

"I don't know—"

"These are the great American people I'm talking about, Mom, the folk, the salt of the earth. They're not going to turn a wayfarer from their doors. I'm going to put myself at their mercy, arriving as a new pioneer, making his way, asking for the same hospitality that I know you would extend to a boy like me if he arrived on our doorstep in need."

Her lip trembled. "In need?" she cried.

"Well—not in need exactly—I mean, just needing dinner and a place to stay for the night."

"And a washing machine."

"Right."

"Well, of course we would throw the door wide open, wouldn't we, Bert?"

"Mmmm. I'm not so—" he began, but my mother gave him a look—begging him, I believe, to put himself in the position of a householder finding her son, Peter, on his doorstep, wet, hungry, and miserable, with a cold coming on—and he finished with, "Yeah, I guess."

"And that's what I'm counting on," I said with all the conviction I could dissemble. "I know that when I need food, shelter, and someone to wash my socks, I'll find what I need—out there—by putting my trust in the kind hearts of the good and simple people of this great land."

Most of what I was saying I was quoting from the stirring final scene of *Bitter Harvest of Sour Grapes*, a movie that had played a couple of weeks earlier at the Babbington Theater. In that scene, you may recall, the lanky scion of the destitute Geibe family, their sole hope, decides to change his name to Slim and take to the road as a wandering minstrel and harmonicat, promising to send to his mother, father, and weepy sister all his earnings, withholding only what he needs to keep himself alive and kicking.

"In that case," said my father, pulling things from the pile and stuffing them into the small compartments, "you won't need more than a couple changes of clothing, the first-aid kit, a few hard-boiled eggs, a couple of apples, the compass, the maps, and your rain poncho."

"Oh, dear," said my mother, regarding the great number of things remaining in the pile. "What about—" She reached for my galoshes.

"No, Ella," said my father, laying a restraining hand on hers. "Peter's right. He's got to travel light. Remember that stuff about the American people."

I remember the look on her face. Worry was there, and so was disappointment: she had put a great deal of effort into preparing and assembling all the things she had expected me to take on the journey. In a moment, though, defiance was added to those two emotions. Her eyes darted over the pile of rejected supplies, and I could see that she was determined—desperate, perhaps—to find something that she would be able to add to my gear. Her eyes lit up. "Well!" she cried, springing on the volume of *Faustroll*. "I suppose you'll need this at the Faustroll Institute!"

"I sure will!" I said, eager to give her a victory. I see her face now, as I write. I see the consolation of a single addition to my stock. "What would I have done without this?" I cried convincingly. "Mr. MacPherson would never have forgiven me if I had gone off without it, and the people at the Faustroll Institute might not even have let me enroll if I didn't have it with me. Thanks, Mom."

I meant it, not thanks for *Faustroll*, but thanks for everything, everything she had ever done for me, including sewing those snappy name tags on my underwear.

The poignance of the moment threatened to overwhelm us. Even my father found it necessary to blow his nose. Before we could make a scene that would embarrass us in the neighborhood, though, a car came to a screeching halt in front of our house. The three of us spun toward the street and saw Rocco's T-bucket sliding to a stop. Patti Fiorenza got out and hurried toward us with a poster in her hand. "These are all over town," she said, waving the poster at me.

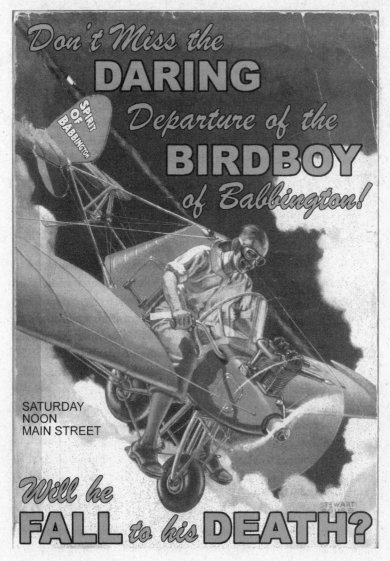

"These are all over town," she said, waving the poster at me.

ALBERTINE'S CHILDLIKE STATE
OF WONDER AND RECEPTIVITY

....

A VASE OF flowers was on Albertine's bedside table, another on the rolling table that held her meals and books, and more flowers at the foot of her bed, on a small table that held equipment for the nurses.

"This is nice," I said, indicating the flowers. "Friends and family checking in?"

"Yes," she said, "but most of the flowers are from the flyguys."

"Oh," I said. "Of course."

"Peter—"

"You're going to tell me that you've decided to run off with the flyguys?"

"What?"

"You're not, are you?"

"Don't be ridiculous."

"They've got that swagger."

"Don't be silly," she said with a giggle that I'd have to call involuntary, possibly irrepressible. "I was going to ask you if you have any plans for planes that seem as if they might really fly."

"Like the Pinch-a-Penny?" I asked, to cover a secret sigh of relief.

"Not at all like the Pinch-a-Penny. Something that appears to be aerodynamically sound and doesn't seem likely to fall apart at the wrong time."

"At the wrong time?"

"In the middle of an Immelmann turn, for example."

"There are some."

"Are there any that we could actually build—you and I?"

I wasn't accustomed to being asked to consider what would be required to realize a dream that I thought of as "only a dream." I needed a moment to think, so I said, "Hmmm," put my hand on my chin, and walked to the window. After a long moment's consideration, I said, "Yes."

"But?"

"But those tend to be expensive. The ones that you'd be interested in, willing to fly in, aren't the ones that the builder builds from scratch."

"The ones built from scratch are the ones with the graceful lines of coffins."

"Right. The sleek ones are built from kits, with the smooth parts made in a factory somewhere."

"So there wouldn't be as much work for the fun couple?"

"From what I've seen, I think there's plenty of work involved in assembling even the most complete kit. Besides, the fun couple would have to do some work to scare up the money to buy the kit."

"Suppose we ignore that for the time being."

"You sound like me, my darling."

"I do, don't I? But still, I wish you would bring me some pictures. I'd like to explore the idea a bit. I think I've got the urge to build a plane."

"Where on earth could that have come from?"

"I don't know," she said, and she seemed bewildered, as if she actually didn't know, as if the swaggering flyguys had nothing to do with it. "Maybe I'm only dreaming—daydreaming or nightdreaming—it's hard to tell here in the hospital, with the drugs and the way people come and go. I read, and then I doze, and I dream, and then I seem to wake, but later, when I actually do wake, I wonder whether I really was awake earlier, or only dreaming that I was awake, but more and more I find myself dreaming of flying—no, that's not right—I find myself dreaming of the two of us building a plane."

"We still don't have a garage," I reminded her.

"I like the idea of our working together," she said, ignoring the impediment to our doing so that the lack of a garage represented.

"So do I," I said.

An awkward silence fell. An unasked question was in the room, stalking us like a mosquito.

"Did you—the walker—the test?" I asked.

"No," she said, frowning. "I walked a few steps, and then the pain and the strain were just too much for me. I got woozy. I had to stop."

"Oh."

On the way home, I turned toward the river again, walked east to the railing at the edge of Carl Schurz Park, and walked along it, northward, homeward, but listlessly. I wasn't in any hurry to return to the empty apartment. After a while I began to think that I heard footsteps behind me, raising questions of strategy. Would it be best to speed up, walk at a pace brisk enough to get me away from whoever was behind me, or to assume the attitude that Al and I call "tough and crazy" in an attempt to get the stalker to walk off at a pace brisk enough to get him away from me, or simply to stop, turn, and confront this other night-time walker as if he were as harmless as I?

I stopped. I turned. I found myself confronting a guy known in the neighborhood as Baudelaire because of his uncanny resemblance to Nadar's portrait photograph of 1863. Baudelaire always walked tough and crazy, but he was as harmless as I.

"How's the sweet patootie?" he asked.

"She's—do you know that she's in the hospital?"

"Sure. It's all over the neighborhood. I sent her flowers."

"You did?"

"You find that hard to believe?"

"No. Not at all. It's just—"

"Hard to believe. Okay, it was a joint gift. I chipped in."

I was tempted to ask him where he had gotten money to chip in. It was hard to believe that he was gainfully employed. On the other hand, perhaps he was. Perhaps he was paid by the city to walk the neighborhood at all hours like a brooding zombie. There might have been a New York City Department of Brooding Zombies, lightly funded but with a few dollars to give out. I didn't ask. Perhaps I didn't want to know.

"Those flowers frightened me," I said.

He gave me a wary look and drew an inch or so away from me. "The flowers frightened you?" he asked.

"Yeah," I said. "Not yours, but bunches of flowers that came from the flyguys. When I saw them there, for a horrible moment I feared that Al was going to tell me she'd decided to run off with the flyguys. One of them, anyway."

"I'm not acquainted with the flyguys."

"They're paramedics—emergency medical technicians—EMTs— but they fly helicopters instead of driving ambulances."

"I see."

"They swagger."

"Oh," he said sympathetically.

"Worse than that, they've *got* swagger. Even when they're not actually swaggering, you can see that at any moment they could swagger if they chose to, without breaking a sweat." I paused. I leaned on the railing. I exhaled. "I think Albertine is infatuated with them."

"It may be nothing more than a symptom of the phenomenon of convalescence," he suggested.

"Really?" I asked hopefully.

"Convalescence," he said, apparently musing on the subject as he spoke, "is like a return toward childhood. The convalescent, like the child, is possessed in the highest degree of the faculty of keenly interesting himself in things, be they apparently of the most trivial."

"Mm," I agreed.

"Let us go back, if we can, by a retrospective effort of the imagination—"

"A thought experiment?"

"If you like. Let us go back toward our most youthful, our earliest, impressions, and we will recognize that they have a strange kinship with those brightly colored impressions that we receive in the aftermath of a physical illness."

Side by side, looking out at the dark water, we made that retrospective effort of the imagination.

"Yeah," I said after a while. "I see what you mean," though in truth I hadn't experienced or rediscovered the kinship with impressions after an illness of which he had spoken because, standing there, under pressure to bring to mind an illness and its aftermath and the impressions that I had had in its aftermath, I couldn't remember any impressions after any illness. I couldn't even remember any illnesses. Memory, as Proust said in so many words, resists the demands we make on it, does not want to be brought onstage before it has its makeup on right.

"Provided, of course," he continued, "that the illness has left our spiritual capacities pure and unharmed."

"Of course."

"The child sees everything in a state of newness; he is always drunk."

...his uncanny resemblance to Nadar's portrait photograph of 1863.

"In this case, she."

"She. Yes. Nothing more resembles what we call inspiration than the delight with which a child absorbs form and color."

"Or appreciates swagger."

"Or anything else."

"So her interest in the flyguys, in flying, in building a plane, might only be symptoms or characteristics of the childlike state of wonder and receptivity that convalescence has put her in."

"Yes, I think that may be. Or she may be one of those who have the ability to recover childhood at will, to regain that state of newness."

"I've been told that I—"

"That ability is nothing more nor less than genius, I think."

We watched the water in silence for a while longer.

"What have you been told that you—?" he asked.

"Oh, nothing," I said. I held out my hand. "Thanks for sending the flowers."

"Chipping in," he corrected.

"Right. Thanks."

"She's a sweetie," he said, and with a wave that I'm tempted to call jaunty, he went on his way. I went on mine.

A BANNER DAY

••

SATURDAY CAME, THE day of my departure, and I was ready. I felt ready, and I knew that I really was ready. I felt that, overnight, I had changed: I had become an adventurer, a daring adventurer, an outstanding example of the type, in the teen division. As I ate breakfast, I seemed to detect in the manner of my eating the manner common to all great adventurers on the mornings when they set out on, well, their great adventures. I had cocoa and buttered toast, and I told myself to remember the fact, because what I ate on the morning of my setting out was somehow significant, that *everything* I did now was somehow significant, a part of the exploits of the Birdboy of Babbington. Having eaten, and having filled myself with self-importance, I stepped out the kitchen door and discovered, assembled in our driveway, everyone who had worked on the aerocycle. Under their admiring gaze, I descended the steps, crossed the bit of packed earth beside the back stoop—a patch of ground that never would sustain a covering of grass—crunched across the driveway, and mounted the aerocycle. For those few steps, I may have swaggered.

For a while I just sat there on my machine, in the driveway in front of the garage, while my friends applauded me, or their handiwork, or both, and I applauded them. Then I said a few words of thanks.

"I don't know how to thank you," I began, and though so many other people in similar situations had said that, it was, I think, no less true for its being the expected thing. "You took my dream and made it a reality," I went on. "Without your work, I wouldn't have been able to do more than *imagine* a trip to the Land of Enchantment—but, thanks to you, I'm really going."

I intended to say more. I wanted to spend some time discoursing on the inestimable value of friendship, on the type of debt that can never be repaid, on the acknowledgment that adventurers owe to all the little people whose efforts make their ventures possible, that sort of thing. But I was interrupted by the arrival of Porky White, my sponsor.

Porky's delivery van rumbled up and shuddered to a sagging stop at the edge of the road, and Porky clambered out, shouting, "Not yet! Don't start yet!"

He ran around to the back of the van, opened the doors, and began tugging at something inside.

"You can't go without the banner," he called. He grabbed Matthew Barber, handed one end of the banner to him, and said, "Here. Unroll this." Matthew began backing up, unrolling the banner. Porky had tied wooden uprights into the banner at intervals to keep the upper line and the lower line separated and the letters upstanding. When Matthew was about thirty-five feet away, the message was revealed:

KAP'N KLAM IS COMING! THE HOME OF
HAPPY DINNERS!

"I made it myself," said Porky with pride.

"It's, um, it—" I mumbled.

"What?"

"It's supposed to say 'THE HOME OF HAPPY DINERS.'"

"Yeah. It does."

"Well, no. It says, 'HAPPY DINNERS.'"

"Huh?"

"Actually, it says, 'YPPAH SRENNID,'" said Marvin Jones, from the other side of the banner.

"You've got one too many n's," I pointed out.

"Oh," said Porky. "Shit."

"Porky!" said my mother.

"Sorry. I just—it's just that it's important to me. I've got a lot riding on this, you know? My hopes and dreams are going up there with Peter, and—"

"Maybe it doesn't matter," I suggested. "Why not 'happy dinners'? Maybe it's happy dinners that make happy diners."

"Dinners cannot be happy," said Matthew. "Diners can be happy. Dinners cannot. Dinners are meals. Meals are inanimate. They have no emotions. They cannot be happy."

"They can make people happy."

"Yes, they can, but they cannot themselves be made happy."

"An occasion can be happy," I asserted. "This is a happy occasion."

"It was," grumbled my father.

"Yes, an occasion can be happy," Matthew conceded.

"Isn't a meal an occasion?" I asked.

"Not quite. A meal is something that occupies an occasion. It is not itself an occasion. Consider the analogy of a headache—"

"That's what I'm getting," said Porky.

"A headache occupies a period of time," asserted Matthew, "but is not itself a period of time. Similarly, a meal occupies a period of time but is not itself a period of time. A meal is like a headache—"

"I'm getting one, too," said my father.

"—in that it occupies a period of time and during that time may arouse emotion in beings capable of feeling emotion. The emotion, however, is in the sentient beings, not in the activity. Thus, to speak of a 'happy meal' is an absurdity."

"Fixed!" announced my mother with a flourish, like a wizard. "I just snipped out one *n* and sewed the pieces together."

"Ella!" cried Porky, sweeping her up in a bear hug. "Thank you, thank you, thank you. You are amazing." Swinging her in his arms, he called out to everyone there, "Isn't she amazing?"

We cheered her until she hid her face in her hands, then Porky set her down beside my scowling father and said to me, "We've got to attach this to the back of the plane."

"Aerocycle," I corrected him.

"Right," he said. "I brought wire."

Porky and I wired the banner to the rear of the aerocycle while everyone else watched. When at last the operation was done, I was truly ready to go.

I remounted the aerocycle, pulled my goggles over my eyes, stood up, and came down hard on the kick-starter. The engine roared into life. The propeller began to turn. Dust and pebbles whirled in the air and drove the circle of my friends and supporters outward. I rolled forward, down the driveway, toward the street.

The aerocycle was, I found to my immense relief, quite easy to maneuver on the ground. I had had some concern about this, inspired by my reading of Pope and Otis. They warned the readers of *Elements of Aeronautics* that most light planes of that time were difficult to control on the ground because they were steered by the same control surfaces that steered them in the air—the rudder and ailerons. Those controls functioned well in the air, at flying speeds, but barely at all on the ground, at taxiing speeds. The aerocycle, however, retained its motorcycle handlebars, and they turned its front wheel in addition to its rudder and ailerons, making it easily maneuverable. I knew how to ride a bicycle, so I found that the aerocycle felt familiar, and I could steer it well enough to avoid running into my friends.

In the street, I turned toward the south, toward Main Street, where I planned to make my takeoff.

PLEASURE AND PAIN, IN SYMPATHY

WACKO WOKE ME, chirping at me in that eager way he has. Wacko is the alarm clock that I keep on my bedside table. That is, "Wacko" is what Albertine and I call the alarm clock that I keep on my bedside table. The manufacturer of the clock called it Whack-It, not Wacko, but that was because the manufacturer did not, I think, have the degree of familiarity with the device that Al and I have, a degree of familiarity that we've developed over the fifteen years that we've owned him (yes, him). Wacko is a personality in our lives. He wakes us every weekday morning with that chirping sound, full of pep and vigor, keen to get at the day and conquer it, and then I reach out and whack him to shut him up, as the manufacturer's instructions encouraged me to do. The whack-to-silence feature was what led the manufacturer to name him Whack-It, but after he became a member of our household, Wacko earned his nickname by insisting that time passes more quickly for him than for other clocks. He is a tiny digital clock, controlled by a chip, and he should be stable and accurate, yet he gains about a minute a day, and his attitude toward his inaccuracy is of the dismissive shrug and "so what?" variety.

I whacked him. I fumbled for the slide switch and turned his alarm off. I opened my eyes. They stung. I closed them again. I stretched and let my head fall back on the pillow.

Time passed, no more than a minute or two, I thought. Little by little, I urged my eyes open. The bedroom was bright with sunlight. I glanced at Wacko. According to him, an hour and a half had passed. Suddenly, in the moment of my looking at Wacko's digital display, I remembered a dream, a dream about Albertine. We had been together, in bed, doing delightful things to each other. It was a tremendously erotic moment of recollection, and the dream was as arousing in the memory as it must have been in the dreaming, but the most intriguing aspect of the dream was that it was actually a dream about dreaming. In it, I had been dreaming; I had been a dreamer dreaming of being in bed with Albertine, and that distance between me the dreamer and me the lover made it seem as if my being in bed with her was somehow illicit. It was all so deliciously erotic that I, the I who was the dreamer dreaming of making love to Albertine, wanted to wake up in the middle of it, to get out of the dream.

"Why?" I can almost hear you asking. "Why would you want to wake up in the middle of a gloriously erotic dream and end it?"

So that I could tell Albertine about it, of course.

I knew that she would enjoy an account of it—that is, within the dream, the dreaming I (Peter the Second) knew that she would—and so within the dream Peter the Second forced himself to wake up, ending his dream (in which he was enjoying Albertine as Peter the Third), and, still in my (Peter the First's) dream, he (Peter the Second), now awake, reached out for Albertine, and there she was beside him, and he nuzzled her and said, in a whisper, "I had a dream, a dream about you."

She stretched herself, drew herself alongside him, caressed him, and extended, lasciviously, that most generous of invitations: "Tell me all about it."

Then Wacko began his cheery chirping and woke me, Peter the First, from my dream.

But wait. That waking must have been within the dream as well, because Wacko was there on the bedside table, with his alarm turned off. There must have been Peters One through Four. . . .

This was definitely something that I had to tell Al.

I swung myself to the edge of the bed, swung my legs to the floor, and put my weight on my legs, standing, as we human beings have been doing for some time now, and a pain shot through my right leg, a pain so severe and so totally unexpected that the leg collapsed under me, and I had to throw myself back on the bed to keep from falling to the floor.

I was overjoyed.

"Albertine," I called out to the empty apartment, "I feel your pain!"

ALBERTINE TAKES OFF

I HAD TOLD myself, often, that it would not be a good idea to enter the hospital through the emergency entrance, where the flyguys were likely to be, that the wise course would be to use the main entrance and to avoid the flyguys if I saw them, but desire—or need—opposed that wisdom. I wanted—or needed—to measure myself against them. I suppose that I also hoped that by observing them I might pick up some of their swagger or—even better—that I might learn the art of swagger itself and so develop a swagger that I could call my own, a swagger that Albertine would find even more attractive than flyguy swagger.

It seems to me, by the way, that *swagger* is not entirely a complimentary term. It's just a letter away from *stagger*, for one thing, and I seem to hear an echo of *braggart*. The term *swagger* may (one of my dictionaries says "may possibly," which I take to mean "probably doesn't") derive ultimately from the Norwegian *svaga*, which gives us *swag*, meaning a swaying or lurching movement, which suggests to me the walk of a sailor who hasn't regained his land legs after a voyage, or who after a long life at sea affects in landlubberly retirement the rolling gait he used to use on the moving surface of a deck, or who is drunk.

The emergency entrance, at the corner of "our" street, the street where "our" apartment building was located, was the quickest way into the hospital, and so, instead of doing the wise thing and continuing around the corner to the main entrance, I limped through the emergency entrance, favoring the leg with the sympathetic pain. The flyguys were there, right there, standing in a group, drinking coffee, managing somehow to exhibit swagger while standing still. I put my head down and made my way to the elevator. I pressed the button and waited. When the doors opened, I staggered in, and suddenly the flyguys crowded in with me. I reached for the button for the sixth floor, Albertine's floor, but one of them beat me to it.

"How's it goin'?" he asked me after pressing the button.

"Huh?" I replied, surprised by the question, the attention, the notice.

"How you doin'?"

"Me?"

"Yeah. I've seen you here before, right?"

"I—"

"Our floor," said a flyguy in the back.

We got off, and we walked toward Albertine's room as if we were a group.

"My darling," I said as I stepped through the door, "I had the most amazing—"

"I passed!" she squealed.

"Way to go, Giggles!" boomed a hearty flyguy from over my shoulder.

"The Walker Test?" I asked, and then I added, "Did he call you Giggles?"

"This morning," she said. "I tried to call you, but there was no answer. I told them that Giggle Bars are my favorite candy."

"Hoo-rah, Giggles, hoo-rah, Giggles," boomed the flyguy chorus.

"Oh," I said. "I must have been on my way here when you called. Or maybe I was asleep. Wacko—"

"Ready to go home?" asked a hearty flyguy, pushing past me with a wheelchair.

"Am I!" cried Giggles. She began sliding from the bed into the wheelchair that the flyguy was holding steady for her.

"We'll take it from here, sport," said another of them, clapping a firm hand on my shoulder.

"I'm her husband," I said, as if it were a conjurer's formula for effecting disappearance.

"The muddleheaded dreamer!" said the wheelchair jockey, standing and frankly staring in my direction.

"I told them that's what you call yourself sometimes," said Albertine. She blushed. Reader, she blushed.

"*Entre nous,* I thought," I said. I pouted. Reader, I pouted.

"I was under the influence of drugs."

"And swagger," I said, mostly to myself.

"Didn't they used to call you the Birdboy of Babbington, back in the old days?" asked the wheelchair guy.

"Well, yes—"

"Holy shit. You were my inspiration."

"I was?"

"My parents used to tell me about you when I was a kid, growing up on Long Island. You were a legend."

"Well—"

"I was inspired by your example."

"Were you?"

"Hell, yes! Because of you, I built a small jet, using surplus parts."

"A jet?"

"Just a small one."

"We're going to give Giggles a lift," said the flyguy with the grip on my shoulder.

"We live just down the street," I said. "I can push her."

"Sure you can—but why not enhance the experience?"

"Yeah," said another. "Why should she be going home in a wheel-chair when she can be going home in an XP-99 chopper?"

"That'll make it a thrill, not a walk."

"It will be fun for me, Peter," said Albertine, as if she were asking permission to stay out after curfew.

"But where are you going to land?" I asked. "The courtyard inside our building is too small, I think, and there are lots of trees—"

"We're going to land on the roof."

"Of our building?"

"Of the hospital."

"This hospital?"

"Sure!" said one, as if only an earthbound idiot could have asked such a question.

"You're going to take off from here, and then land here?"

"We'll take off, take a spin around Manhattan, and then we'll come back and land."

"And then what?"

"What do you mean?"

"How does she get home from here?"

"You can push her in the wheelchair."

"That was my original idea."

"But the experience will have been enhanced."

We took the elevator to the roof. Along the way, I had to suffer the deference that everyone paid to the flyguys. Even the surgeons, who had a type of swagger of their own, seemed to shrink a bit in their presence.

They loaded her into the helicopter. She waved, smiling like a little girl. They took off, banked, and headed south, over the river.

I TAKE OFF

MY DEPARTURE FROM Babbington was everything that I could have wished it to be. As I rolled southward from my house in Babbington Heights, I saw, here and there, people standing at the curbside, waving. Now and then a parent would bend to a child and point at me and say something that I couldn't hear. Of course, I allowed myself to think that the words I wasn't hearing were words of praise for me, for my pluck and enterprise and ingenuity. I may have heard, uttered in a hushed tone of awed admiration, the epithet "Birdboy of Babbington," but I am sure that I never heard anything that sounded remotely like "birdbrain."

By the time I reached the intersection with Main Street, where I intended to turn right and head west, the people gathered along the roadside had become quite a crowd. Across the intersection there was, at that time, an empty lot, just a bit of long grass. In that lot, a small platform had been erected, and on the platform stood the mayor of Babbington himself.

As I approached the intersection, I suddenly found myself surrounded by motorcycle cops. I thought I was being arrested.

"Do you have a license to fly that thing?" asked one of the cops.

"Heck," I said with all the bravado I could manage, "I don't even have a license to *drive* this thing!"

They roared at that. At least I think they did. They seemed to be laughing, and their motorcycles roared.

One of the cops pointed in the direction of the platform, and I understood then that I was expected to stop there and allow the mayor to give me a send-off. That was fine with me, because standing beside the mayor was Miss Clam Fest, a young beauty just a few years out of high school but already more woman than girl, wearing a white bathing suit with her Miss Clam Fest banner draped across her alluring figure. I headed straight for her.

The mayor intercepted me, putting a firm hand on my shoulder, turning me toward the crowd, and announcing, "Citizens of Babbington, here is your Birdboy, Peter—ah—Lee-roy."

The applause was friendly, but light.

"Citizens of Babbington, fellow Babbingtonians, denizens of our cozy bayside community, friends and neighbors," said the mayor, to the best of my recollection, "we are about to witness something truly extraordinary. We are about to witness the fulfillment of a dream. This boy, our own Peter Lee-roy, had a dream, the dream of flight. Who among us has not had that dream? Peter, however, has done something that most of us will never do. He has had the—dare I say it?—gumption to put wings on his dream. To put wings on it, wheels under it, and an engine on the front of it. In other words, he has taken that dream and made it a blueprint for reality. Now, many people criticize our public schools."

A critical murmur spread through the crowd.

"Hardly a day goes by without some crank letter arriving in my office filled with groundless complaints about the collapse of standards in the schools. Well, let me tell you something: this plucky lad is a product of those schools. And I think we can be proud of him."

A smattering of applause.

"His teachers tell me—and he may be surprised to find that I've been doing a little checking up on him—that he's an imaginative boy, inclined to dream, often distracted, and prone to digression, but they are convinced that he's got a head on his shoulders. Perhaps that is why they recommended him wholeheartedly for a summer session at the prestigious Faustroll Institute in distant New Mexico, Land of Enchantment."

The mayor paused, turned slightly toward me, and applauded me in a formal, rather than enthusiastic, way. The crowd took the cue and applauded as well, and Miss Clam Fest blew me a kiss. I wondered if she would fit on the seat behind me and whether she had ever been to New Mexico.

"And so," said the mayor, "one of our own leaves today to prepare himself for the great struggle that we as a nation are engaged in, the struggle to make the world safe for democracy. Young Peter and those other bright-eyed young men—and young women—like him—including—ah—"

He consulted a sheet of paper.

"—Matthew Barber—"

He shaded his eyes and looked out at the crowd. Matthew, a couple of rows back, raised his hand, and memory—injecting a recollection from the third grade—made me think for a moment that he was going to ask to go to the bathroom.

"—who will be attending a summer institute for future pharmacists, coincidentally also in New Mexico, although Matthew will be traveling by regularly scheduled commercial airliner—they are the bright hope of a nation facing a foe with incomprehensible animosities and aims, a foe purely and simply evil. Perhaps it should come as no surprise, then, to learn that Peter has received a communication from the federal government in Washington—which his mother kindly brought to my attention—wishing him, and I quote, 'the best of luck in your . . . endeavors.'"

He paused. He gripped my shoulder more tightly. He set his jaw.

"Our hopes ride with him," he said.

The hopes of the nation should have felt like too great a burden for a kid to bear, too heavy a weight of responsibility for the *Spirit of Babbington* to get off the ground, but I relished the burden, since it made Miss Clam Fest smile and sigh and flutter her lashes.

In something of a daze, I made my way through a phalanx of cops to the aerocycle. The applause now was really something, loud and genuine. I had become the teenage hero of my cozy bayside community. I felt admired, and I felt that I deserved admiration. I felt capable and strong and daring.

I mounted the aerocycle, came down hard on the kick-starter, and rode off into the sunset, or into the direction of the place where sunset would occur later that evening, with the Kap'n Klam banner clattering behind me.

Part Two

· ·

ON THE WING

There is a great deal of enjoyment to
be gained in learning to fly a plane . . .
but a new thrill is had when the pilot
sets out on a cross-country trip.

—FRANCIS POPE AND
ARTHUR S. OTIS,
Elements of Aeronautics

The Bird of Time has but a little way
To fly—and Lo! the Bird is on the Wing!

—OMAR KHAYYAM, "Rubaiyat"
(translated by Edward FitzGerald)

ALBERTINE GETS THE URGE FOR GOING

●●

...we are here as on a darkling plain
Swept with confused alarms of struggle and flight...
—Matthew Arnold, "Dover Beach"

WATCHED THE helicopter rise and tilt and chatter out over the East River. Then I remained for a long while on the roof waiting for the flyguys to bring her back to me.

I waited. Time passed. Foolishly, I had thought that the flyguys would deliver less than they had promised, just take her for a short spin, and bring her right back to me. When that didn't happen, I began to panic. What if they had conspired to spirit her off, take her from me forever? What if she had become so enamored of them that she couldn't live without them? What if she thought of this as an escape? What if she had come to think of me as an encumbrance, something that she had to shed before she could fly? What if she had left me on the roof like a broken shackle and had made her getaway?

Writing in the calm of a morning several years later, I can allow myself to think that I was deluded, and I can even allow myself to think that, despite my moods and my boundless ineptitude, I am not nearly so difficult to live with as I feared she might think, but at the time the likelihood that she would want to escape from me suddenly seemed very high. I waited some more—and I waited some more. Every time I heard the clatter of a helicopter, my heart leapt and raced like an excited pet eager for Albertine's tickling caress behind its ears. Every time the clatter passed or turned and trundled away, my heart sighed and slunk into a corner. As time passed, I began to sweat. I began to feel powerless, hopeless, impotent. There was nothing I could do to bring her back. I was standing on a rooftop, with no way to confront the flyguys, reclaim her, seize her, carry her off, take her home to my cave. When another helicopter began to rattle into range, I decided—or some part of me below consciousness decided—that I wasn't going to let this one get away. I dashed to the elevator penthouse, punched the button, and banged the door with my fist until the elevator arrived. I rushed in and rode down to the ground floor. I hastened through the emergency room with an affectation of calm, as if I weren't insane, but as soon as I was outside I began running in the direction of the sound of the helicopter. I ran like a boy, a lovesick boy. After a couple of blocks, I stopped to catch my breath and to listen for the sound of the helicopter. It was south of me now. I began running down Second Avenue. I paused again at 86th Street. The helicopter had turned west. I began running along 86th Street. If you've tried running along the sidewalks of New York in midafternoon, you know that you step on a lot of toes. I stepped on a lot of toes. People shouted at me. People lashed out at me. One or two people tried to trip me up. I ran until I was out of breath, and even then I walked as quickly as I could, until I heard one helicopter approaching as another receded and realized that I was a man on foot chasing helicopters. I stopped, and I told myself that I was acting like a fool, then corrected myself and told myself that I *was* a fool.

Then, when I had caught my breath, I began running again, in the direction of the most recent helicopter, because, after all, it might be the one that she was in.

Did I think about calling the police, dialing 911? Oh, yes. I did. But then I thought about what I would say:

"My wife has been abducted by flying EMTs."

They must get a lot of calls like that on any given day. There must be a category for them.

Eventually, I gave up. I would tell you that sanity returned, if I thought you would believe it. The truth is that I surrendered to exhaustion and resignation. I walked back to Carl Schurz Hospital. I decided that I would wait on the roof. I would wait all afternoon, all evening, all night if I had to. If she never returned, I would be able to say, "I waited all night." I found that consoling, somehow. I have no idea, now, why I found it consoling then, but I did. I also told myself that I would never tell her about my running through the city in panic, chasing helicopters, and I never have—until now, here, in the pages you've just read.

The helicopter eventually reappeared from the north. It swung over Carl Schurz Park and settled gently onto the hospital roof. The flyguys off-loaded Albertine, hugged and fondled her, and finally settled her into the rented wheelchair. We all descended in the elevator, and there was another leave-taking at the hospital door. Then I pushed her home to our apartment, and on the way I confessed to her, with some fervor, my hope that neither she nor I would ever see the flyguys again.

Albertine worked hard at her recovery. As soon as she was permitted to exercise, she began riding a recumbent bicycle in the vast, multistory gymnasium up the street from our apartment building, and she swam lap after lap in their 25-meter pool. She never missed a physical therapy session and did all the exercises that her therapists prescribed. One therapist was amazed by what he took to be her tolerance for pain.

"It's not that," she said. "In truth, I have a very low tolerance for pain, and I'm feeling terrible pain right now, while I'm trying to do what you tell me I should do, but I want to be back on my feet as soon as possible, and if you tell me that this exercise is going to be good for me, then I will do it."

She wasn't foolish; she didn't allow her urge to be up and about to drive her to excess. She began slowly, and she avoided any position or effort that was not prescribed, but as she felt her strength return and as the pain began slowly to diminish, she increased the work she did, going far beyond what the therapists had expected her to do. It hurt. I could see that it hurt, when she let it show. There were times in bed when she made the mistake, in sleep or half-sleep, of turning onto her side—or merely beginning to turn onto her side—and the pain made her scream.

I pushed her everywhere in the wheelchair I'd rented, but she hated being in it. She yearned to graduate to the walker—that frame of aluminum tubing that would allow her to take some of her weight off her legs as she moved ahead one slow step at a time. Although she'd passed the "walker test" before leaving the hospital, she wasn't permitted to leave the chair and walk with the aid of the walker until the line of bone repair along the fracture was strong enough. When that day came, she began a determined assault on distance, beginning with a walk of just a few feet eastward from the front door of the building, along East 89th Street, and back. From that beginning, she extended her range until she could circle the block, working at it with determination and perseverance, as if she were in training for the walker Olympics.

Another consequence of Albertine's convalescent return toward childhood, and her thereby regaining in the highest degree the faculty of keenly interesting herself in things, be they apparently of the most trivial, seeing everything in a state of newness, with the sensory drunkenness of a child, was her surprising interest in the literature of home-built and kit-built aircraft. In particular, she became an avid reader of builders' logs.

If you do not belong to the relatively small group of builders of small aircraft or to the slightly smaller group of their fans, you may not be aware of the custom prevalent among the builders of keeping logs of their progress as they work. For accuracy's sake, make that "efforts" rather than "progress." These logs, known among the fraternity of plane-builders as "construction logs" or, for short, "clogs," are often posted on the World Wide Web. Reading them became Albertine's pastime, then her passion.

I get up earlier in the morning than Albertine does. We both wake at the same time, but I get up, get out of bed, make myself some coffee, and work on my personal history for a while. While I write, Albertine reads. Often, during her recuperation, when I returned to the bedroom after an hour or two of work to wish her good morning, I would find our bed covered with pages of online clogs that she'd printed out for ease of reading in bed.

"This isn't becoming an obsession, is it?" I asked her one morning when the bed was heavily clogged.

"A passion," she admitted, "but not an obsession," she claimed. "These are really amazing, Peter. There's such a wealth of human drama in these accounts of failed attempts to realize a dream."

"I have to admit that I haven't spent any time reading them," I said.

"I can understand that you'd be reluctant to expose yourself to them."

"Why?"

"Because I understand you."

"I mean why, in your estimation, wouldn't I want to expose myself to them?"

"Because they are so discouraging. They dash hopes. They shatter illusions. And you are a person who lives on hope and nurses illusions."

"That's true," I said. It is. She understands me well. I'm a muddleheaded dreamer. I once belonged to a muddleheaded dreamers' club, as you will see in the pages to come.

"The typical clog begins full of optimism," she said. "Here—listen to this: 'The U-Build-It-U-Fly-It kit arrived this morning, and when Delia called me at work to say that it had been delivered I immediately feigned illness and left. I can't describe the feeling of buoyancy that I felt in the car on the way home, knowing that the kit would be waiting for me there. But I'll try. It was as if the car and I were not quite touching the road. In a sense, I was already flying, and the car had become the UBI-UFI. Although I hadn't even opened the kit yet, I felt as if my work was already done, and done well. I felt capable. I felt—how can I put it?—wise. It was as if the lightness I felt were sufficient justification for buying the kit, for the sacrifices I'd inflicted on Delia and the kids. I could fly. That was worth it.'"

"That sounds delightful," I said, naïvely. "It sounds as if the guy is really off to a great start—"

"Then, typically, the tedium sets in. Listen: 'Eighty-three days so far, and I don't know how much more of this I can take. Night after night, alone in the garage, struggling to decipher the instructions, too bewildered to make any real progress, too proud to ask that wiseass Stan next door for help. Why, why, why did I ever begin this? I feel like a condemned man, condemned to isolation, laboring alone. It's like trying to cross a desert on foot, or sailing alone around the world, or trying to survey the vast frozen wastes of the Siberian wilderness, struggling to build a shelter out of reeds in the teeth of the cutting wind. Nobody understands what I'm going through, nobody could, nobody cares.'"

"Grim," I said.

"Often, there is a laudable effort to soldier on: 'Today I've discovered a new determination, and I'm proud of myself for that. I've found a strength of will in myself that I hadn't known was there, and I think I'm justified in praising myself for that. I've learned that I've got something I might have to call grit. Or maybe pluck. Or maybe it's good old

American stick-to-itiveness. Whatever you want to call it, I've got it. It's me against this damned plane, and in the name of all that's holy, I'm going to come out on top!' "

"Impressive."

"And then, finally, defeat: 'This is the end. I just can't go on. Every day is torture. After hours wasted in the garage, I lie awake in bed trying to find a way out of this folly. For a while, I thought I might be able to persuade the kid next door—the eldest son of that wiseassed bastard, Stan—to take the damned plane off my hands. He spent a couple of evenings watching me work, and I thought I had him hooked, but then he just stopped showing up. Kids today. They've got no sense of purpose. They can't stick with a thing. My only hope, I've decided, is to get Delia pregnant. Then I'd have to convert the garage into a room for the baby. The plane would have to go. I recognize that this is a desperate plan. But I'm a desperate man.' "

"Chilling," I said.

For a while, Albertine said nothing. She was overwhelmed, I think, by the emotions occasioned by the builder's defeat. When, at last, she felt like herself again, she said, "I want to go on the road."

"Touring with your band?"

"Be serious, please," she said. "Maybe it's my long period of immobility that is making me feel this way," she said, "but I've got the urge to travel."

"Where do you want to go, my darling? I'll push you anywhere."

"Oh, please. I don't want to be pushed. You have been a darling to push me everywhere, and you have been a darling to help me into the pool and into the hot tub, to help me into bed, to help me out of bed. I've even enjoyed it. I've felt pampered. I've felt loved. And I love you for it, for all of it. But I've had enough. I don't want to be helped. I'd like to range beyond this block, beyond this island, and I don't want to be pushed. I'd like to do what you said not so long ago. How did you put it? 'Walk out our door one day and just *go.*' "

"That's it," I said. "I met a guy named Johnny on my trip to New Mexico who put the urge that way: 'Just *go.*' "

" 'Just *go,*' " she said. "That's right. That's what I'd like to do."

"And stop somewhere at the end of each day for a hot shower, a delicious meal, and a comfy bed?"

"Exactly."

"By what conveyance?" I asked warily. "Plane, train, aerocycle?"

"By car, I think."

"We don't have a car."

"Let's buy one."

"Are you serious?"

"I think I am. Our little world is not enough for me just now. I want to get up and go. I want to be out in the big, wide world, wandering with you."

"And do you have a specific car in mind?"

"I'm afraid I do."

"Afraid?"

"Yes. Afraid that the car I have in mind is a foolish choice. But I think it's a choice that you'd make in my place."

"Now *I'm* afraid," I said.

I should explain the reasons for our fear. I should tell you about our cars—well, not all of them—that would tax your tolerance too much. I will tell you about two of them and you can extrapolate from those. Let's see. Which two? The Twinkle, I think, since it was our first car, and, of course, the powerful Kramler, since it was our most magnificent.

There was a time—a time that today seems very long ago—when Albertine and I were enthusiastic motorists. We took Sunday drives, we made rambling excursions, we were adept at double-clutching. In those years, we owned a number of cars that were great fun to drive, but were very little fun to maintain in driving condition. The first of them was a red Twinkle. This was a British car with right-hand drive. We bought it from an English architect. The Twinkle was all of ten feet long and had ten-inch wheels. It really was great fun to drive. It had two transversely mounted rotary engines. One, in front, beneath its diminutive hood (or bonnet), drove the front wheels; the other, in back, in its trunk (or boot), drove the rear wheels. Both engines were small, but their combined output gave the Twinkle considerable oomph. It went like a bat out of hell—a little red bat out of hell.

When I was the Twinkle's co-owner, I would have bristled if you had told me, Reader, that it looked like a toy, but when I see one on the street today I recognize that it must have looked like a dangerous toy to Albertine's parents. They had been worried enough about consigning their daughter to the care of the Birdboy of Babbington when we announced that we were going to get married. I must have looked like a dangerous toy myself.

Her mother asked Albertine, pointedly, "Wouldn't you rather go to Europe?"

Albertine chose me over the European tour, and not long after making the choice she found herself driving a Twinkle and discovering a love of speed. Alas, as the Twinkle aged, it developed a problem that apparently could not be solved. The engines began twisting on their mounts under acceleration or deceleration. Apparently, the art of mounting engines had not then attained its present degree of perfection. When we made an upshift and accelerated, the engines would twist rearward. This meant that the front engine twisted toward the cockpit until the top struck the fire wall. On deceleration, the reverse phenomenon occurred, with both engines twisting forward, the rear engine striking the back of the diminutive back seat. The only mechanic who even suggested a solution told us that the "constant velocity joints" had to be replaced at a price greater than what we had paid for the car. Putting to work the mechanical skills I'd acquired in building—or attempting to build—a boyhood's worth of *Impractical Craftsman* projects, I designed a set of braces for the engines, had a machine shop fabricate them to my specifications, and bolted the braces between the engine block and the fire wall, in front, and between the engine block and the back of the back seat, in the rear. The engines no longer twisted. Success? Not quite. The cabin roared with the sound of every moving part in both engines, since every vibration and detonation was transmitted via the braces to the steel shell of the car itself. It was like driving inside a hi-fi speaker during a fuzz-bass solo. Clearly the time had come to trade the little baby in on another car or find some sucker to buy the Twinkle from us. My parents had taught me that one never gets a car's true worth when trading it in, so I advertised it for private sale. When I was demonstrating the Twinkle for potential buyers, I kept the radio volume high and sought out extended fuzz-bass solos. Some sap bought the car. I like to think that he is driving it still, and that it pleases him, noise and all.

After the Twinkle, we owned a succession of British sports cars. (I wish that I could say "other British sports cars," but the Twinkle, a four-passenger car, was never regarded as a sports car by the drivers of two-seaters, who scorned to wave at Albertine and me in the clannish way they greeted the drivers of other two-seaters. The Twinkle was faster than all but the most expensive and exotic of them, but that didn't matter; in fact, one roadster driver dismissed it as a "hot rod.")

With each of our sports cars, we experienced a brief honeymoon, a euphoric period during which we took several pleasant drives. Then the car would begin breaking down. The drives would become less pleasant, and many of them ended at repair shops. We got to know a number of interesting mechanics. We learned how to whack a fuel pump in just the right way to get it pumping again after it had quit in the fast lane of a highway. We would invest some money—sometimes quite a lot— repairing the sporty little thing, and we would try to convince ourselves that it was now as good as new, but it would keep breaking down, and in time we would sell it and buy another. We had in those days the naïve belief that somewhere there was a reliable British sports car that we could purchase, used, for a reasonable price. Perhaps that belief seems ludicrous to you. Perhaps you cannot imagine that two intelligent young people—which we then were—could labor under such an absurd delusion. If you feel that way, I just want to inform you—or remind you—that a large segment of the population of the United States believes that the sun revolves around the earth, and so I say, in the manner of Bosse-de-Nage in Alfred Jarry's *Gestes et Opinions du Docteur Faustroll*, "Ha-ha."

As we traded in, we traded up. We would rid ourselves of one limping sports car and promptly buy another that was more powerful, more expensive, and more difficult to keep running. We always had an automobile loan, and the balance kept increasing. Little by little, we progressed from one of the most basic sports cars, a Benson-Greeley Gnome, to one of the most sophisticated, the powerful Kramler.

Our Kramler was powered by a V-12 engine with four camshafts and nickel-plated cam covers, a thing of great beauty. The entire front of the car's body tilted up to reveal this engine, in a far more dramatic and aesthetically effective manner than the ordinary hood would have done. Tilting the front end forward did not, however, allow easy access to the engine for the servicing and repair that it required at frequent intervals. That access might have been better provided by the conventional hood arrangement. Instead, the Kramler people required the mechanic to remove the engine and work on it outside the car. A disconcertingly

large number of repair and maintenance procedures in the shop manual, which we owned and which I sometimes used as bedtime reading,
began with the words, "First remove the engine; see page 19." One of
these procedures was changing the oil filter.

We haven't owned a car for years. Living in Manhattan makes a car
unnecessary, and the cost of garaging a car in Manhattan makes a
car insupportable.

Sometimes I miss driving. I can't manage to get as excited by a car as
I used to, but there are several available now that I would like to drive.
I don't want to own any of them, but I still have the urge to get into
something sleek and powerful and just take off, heading west.

"What is this fearsome machine you have in mind?" I asked.

"It's a Prysock Electro-Flyer."

"I don't think I've ever seen—"

"It's the only one of its kind. And there will never be another."

"Is it a dream car? A concept car? A show car?"

"It was built as a prototype. The designer-builder hoped to put it
into production, but he has since abandoned the plan and moved on to
other things."

"Mm."

"It's a sleek little thing with a top speed of 140 miles per hour."

"Impressive," I said.

"Especially for an electric car."

"An electric car? Wow."

"And the Electro-Flyer is, as I'm sure you'll agree in a moment,
when I show you some pictures, a thing of beauty."

"Can't wait. Somehow 'Prysock' does sound vaguely familiar—"

"In the spirit of full and frank disclosure, I have to point out that the
Prysock Electro-Flyer is—how shall I put this—derivative."

"Oh?" I said, puzzled.

"The design was heavily influenced by the 1960 Nu-Klea Disco
Volante Runabout."

"Disco Volante? As in—"

"As in 'Flying Saucer.'"

"Oh," I said, disappointed. "We'd be buying a replica."

"Not exactly. The mechanicals are original with the designer-
builder."

"But still—"

"I know how you feel about replicas," she said quickly, "but this is different. It's the work of a madman obsessed with detail and accuracy."

"Oh!" I said, brightening.

"Here's his ad."

I looked at the picture. I read the copy.

"You mean Norton Prysock built this thing?" I asked.

"Built this beautiful car. Yes."

"I seem to recall that you had a low opinion of Nort and his skills when you examined the photographs of the Pinch-a-Penny on his Web site."

"I still think that as an aeronautical engineer he's not much use."

"But you think he could build a good car?"

"I'll want to examine it carefully, of course, take it for a spin, and have a mechanic go over it thoroughly, but I suspect that this car is the one good thing Norton Prysock ever made—and remember, too, that in the case of the Pinch-a-Penny he was asking me to believe that he could get me into the air and keep me there, while in the case of the Electro-Flyer he is making no such claim."

"I don't know," I said. "I see a dangerous parallel between Nort's situation and my own when I began building the aerocycle: I had drawings of a finished plane, but no plans for building it, so I had to improvise. Nort had nothing but pictures of the Disco Volante, which were the equivalent of the drawings I had, invaluable as inspiration but useless in terms of engineering—so he must have had to do a lot of improvising—and the result—"

"Oh, Peter."

"I'm trying to be realistic."

"Don't."

I looked at her, looked into her eyes, saw the longing there, and said, "Okay."

Despite what his ad claimed, Norton Prysock was not willing to let the world's only Electro-Flyer go for what we considered a reasonable offer. Even after a long negotiation he wanted much, much more than I thought Albertine would be willing to pay.

"He is asking us to pay for a car more than twenty-six point three

percent of the cost of the average studio apartment in Manhattan," I said as Albertine and I huddled at the end of Nort's driveway, conferring.

"Where did you get that bit of information?"

"I'm basing it on a survey reported in this morning's *Times*," I said, unfolding the paper to the story.

Albertine skimmed it quickly and announced, "But he's asking less than one percent of the average price of a Manhattan property with four bedrooms or more."

"Are you kidding?" I asked her.

"No," she said, pointing to the relevant figure. "Peter—"

"Yes?"

"If we sold our apartment—a two-bedroom apartment, I remind you—we could buy this car—and have lots and lots of change left over."

"Shouldn't we save that for our golden years?"

"Yes, we should. That would be wise. It would be prudent. We try to be wise. We try to be prudent. Well, I try to be prudent. However, after my fall I find that I am feeling the cold breath of mortality on the back of my neck, and it's making me impulsive and foolish."

"Are you sure it's not the hot breath of the great god Urge that you feel?"

"Could be," she said coquettishly.

"Urge couldn't be appeased with some shoes, could he?"

"Not this time," she said.

I was about to speak again, but she put a finger over my mouth, shushed me, and said, "Listen." I listened. I expected her to speak; I thought she wanted me to listen to her, but after a minute, she said, "Sometimes, more and more often, especially at night, I can hear them, out beyond us, ranged in rings and rings around rings, the angry, murderous, rapacious numbers of our species, growling and cursing and gnashing their teeth, brandishing their weapons, blowing one another to smithereens, feeding their hatred with hatred, stoking their anger with anger, fueling their selfishness with arrogance. There's no getting away from them, but we could do as your pal B. W. Beath advised and, for a while at least, just pass through the squabbling world without being a part of it, like a breeze."

"In an Electro-Flyer?" I asked.

"In *the* Electro-Flyer," she said.

We paid Nort's price.

WITHOUT A MAP

••

> Traveling ought [. . .] to teach [the traveler] distrust; but at the same
> time he will discover how many truly kind-hearted people there are,
> with whom he never before had, or ever again will have, any further
> communication, who yet are ready to offer him the most disinterested
> assistance.
>
> —Charles Darwin, *The Voyage of H. M. S. Beagle*

LO! THE BIRDBOY was on the wing, figuratively speaking. I was
on my way, taxiing westward, urging *Spirit of Babbington* up, up,
and away, but not managing to get the thing off the ground. Had I
been my present age, I might have blamed the flightlessness of *Spirit*
on its weighty freight of metaphorical implications, its heavy burden—
in the old sense of "meaning." It stood for the contrast of lofty goals
with leaden deeds, of grand urges with petty talents, of soaring ambitions with earthbound achievements, but at the time I wasn't thinking
of the weight of *Spirit*'s significance, or even of the reason that it
wouldn't fly; I was simply frustrated and annoyed and embarrassed. I
believed that the well-wishers along the roadside were beginning to
consider me a hoax or, what seemed worse, a failure. Actually—as I
learned from their testimony years later—they thought that I was being
generous to them, staying on the ground as I passed to allow them a
good look at me and my machine, to allow them to hoist their babies
onto their shoulders and afford them the inspiration of a good view of
the bold Birdboy. In a letter to the Babbington *Reporter* on the twenty-
fifth anniversary of my flight, one of them recalled the experience:

> I'll never forget that day. I watched him as he passed by, and
> you could just see the determination in his face, the keen gaze
> in his eyes, the way he looked straight ahead, toward the west,
> and you said to yourself, "This is a boy who knows where he's
> going." It was inspiring, I tell you. It was inspiring, and it was
> a little daunting, too. Seeing him go by, on his way, made you
> ask yourself, "Do *I* know where *I'm* going?" It is no exaggera-

tion, no exaggeration at all, to say that his example, and the introspection it inspired, made me what I am today.

Anonymous Witness

I had planned my trip to New Mexico as a series of short hops, because when I was in the fourth grade my teacher used to begin every school day by writing on the chalkboard a few of what she called Pearls of Wisdom, requiring us to copy them into notebooks with black-and-white mottled covers, and among her pearls was Lao-Tzu's famous statement of the obvious, that a journey of a thousand miles begins with a single step, and also because I had been required, in fourth-grade arithmetic, to calculate how many steps my fourth-grade self would have to take to complete that journey of a thousand miles. (I've forgotten the answer; but my adult self has just measured his ambling stride and calculated that it would take him 1,649,831 steps.) In advance of the journey to New Mexico, I tried to calculate the number of hops that would be required. At first, I imagined that I might cover 300 miles per hop, 300 miles per day. At that rate, the trip out, which I estimated at 1,800 miles, would require just six hops, six days. However, when I daydreamed that trip, it felt rushed. I didn't seem to have enough time to look around, explore the exotic sights, sample the local cuisine, meet the people, talk to them, fall in love with their daughters, get gas, or check the oil. So I decided to cover only 100 miles per daily hop. At that rate, the trip would require eighteen hops, eighteen days. (That was my calculation. It would have worked for a crow; it didn't work for me, as you will see.) My friend Matthew Barber would be making the trip to New Mexico by commercial airliner, in a single hop, which seemed to me pathetically hasty.

When I had decided on eighteen hops, I phoned my French teacher, Angus MacPherson, who was one of the sponsors of my trip, and said, as casually as I could, "I figure I can do it in eighteen hops."

"Do what?"

"Get to New Mexico."

"'Eighteen hops'? Why do you say 'hops'?"

"That's the way I see it," I said. "I take off, fly a hundred miles, and land. It's just a short hop."

"I wouldn't call it a hop."

"Why?"

"'Hop' makes it sound too easy, Peter. It makes it sound as if any boy could do it, as if not even a boy were required. A rabbit, for example, might make the journey in a certain number of hops, given enough time and carrots."

"Oh."

"Say 'stages,'" he said, suddenly inspired, "like pieces of the incremental journey of a stagecoach. That has some dignity, given the weight of its historical association with western movies, settler sagas, and the lonely yodeling of cowpokes on the vast prairies. As a traveler by stages, you will be putting yourself in the long line of westward voyagers, making yourself a part of America's restless yearning for what I think we might call westness. And *stage* has a nice ring to it. *Hop* does not ring at all. It sounds like a dull thud on a wet drum. Take it from me: go by stages, not by hops."

So I went by stages, though I had planned to go by hops. I think that I would have reported here that I had gone by hops, despite Mr. MacPherson's counsel, if it were not for the fact that *hops* suggests too much time spent in the air. Because being in the air is what makes a hop a hop, *hop* suggests, it seems to me, that the hopper is in the air for the entire length of each hop. "The entire length of each hop" would be more time in the air than I actually did spend in the air, and I am firmly committed to total honesty in this account. I went by stages, on the ground, along roads, with a great deal of divagation and an occasional hop when I was for a moment a few inches, sometimes a foot, in the air.

Making the trip in stages confirmed in me a tendency that had been growing for some time: the preference for working in small steps, for making life's journey little by little. I think that this tendency may have been born on the earliest clamming trips I made with my grandfather, when I watched him clamming, treading for clams by feeling for them with his toes, and I learned, without giving it any thought, that a clammer acquires a peck of clams one clam at a time, that the filling of a peck basket is a kind of journey. Whether Lao-Tzu had anything to say about the connection between clamming and life's journey, I do not know, but I do know that there came a time, sometime after my youth, when I turned my step-by-small-step tendency into a guiding principle, and I began deliberately to live one small step at a time. Living according to this principle has meant that many of life's jobs have taken me longer than they might have been expected to take. Many of them are still in the process of completion, and I know people who would count "growing up" among those, but I swear to you that I do work at them all, a little bit at a time. So, for example, I write my memoirs as I've lived my life, a little bit each day, hop by hop.

I traveled without a map, though that was not my original intention. I had intended to travel with a map, because I had thought that I needed a map, and I was convinced that I needed a special map, a superior map, that "just any map" would never do. I already had maps of the United States, of course—several in an atlas, more in an encyclopedia, and others in a gazetteer that showed the typical products of various regions—but I felt that none of those would do. They were maps, but they weren't aviators' maps. I supposed that I needed maps like—but superior to—those that automobile navigators used, the sort of map that my grandmother wrestled with every summer when my parents and I traveled with my grandparents to West Burke, Vermont—and, later, West Burke, New Hampshire—my grandfather at the wheel of their Studebaker, as pilot, and my grandmother beside him, as navigator.

I should explain the two West Burkes. In 1854, fugitive transcendentalists from Burke, Vermont, established West Burke, Vermont, as a utopian community. When, in time, some of West Burke's residents came to feel that the town had, like Burke before it, fallen toward an earthbound state, that commerce and government had become the preoccupations of the majority of their fellow citizens, that the community's increasing materialism was no longer hospitable to their pursuit of spiritual truth, no longer conducive to their everyday effort to see the world globed in a drop of dew, they left the town, headed in an easterly direction (rejecting, resisting, or reversing that restless American yearning for westness), passed through the town of Burke, and moved to New Hampshire, just a short eastward hike away. There they established a new settlement of their own. Logically, this new town might have been named East Burke; defiantly, however, the erstwhile residents of West Burke, Vermont, named this new town West Burke, as an assertion that it was the true West Burke, and that the Vermont version had become a travesty of everything that it ought to have been. (Later still, New Hampshirites, disturbed by the presence of a West Burke in their state where one did not logically belong, incorporated their own town of Burke, just east of West Burke, thereby legitimizing the name geographically.)

On our trips to West Burke, whether we were on our way to Vermont or New Hampshire, my grandmother did the navigating, and I remember well how she struggled to control a huge, ungainly map, on which the routes were laid out in a code of width and weight and color that indicated their place in the hierarchy of roadways. That, I thought, was the kind of map I needed.

In those days, one could have maps for free from local gas stations (which were not yet billed as service stations, though that appellation and the diminishing level of service that it was meant to mask were just around the corner). Since my father worked at a gas station, I could get maps there, of course, but the station stocked only maps of New York and contiguous states. Those would not be enough. I wrote to the company that owned my father's station and supplied him with gas, and I received maps of Pennsylvania, Ohio, Indiana, Illinois, Missouri, Kansas, Oklahoma, Texas, and New Mexico. I stapled them to the walls of my room, along with my maps of New York and New Jersey.

While I was studying them, the thought occurred to me that wind and weather might drive me off course, make me drift. I would need maps of the states north and south of my route. I wrote for those, and when they came I added them to the walls of my room, and when I had filled the walls I tried taping some to the ceiling. The ones on the ceiling sagged and billowed, and their corners came unstuck and curled downward. After struggling to keep them flat and fixed, I persuaded myself that I liked the billowing and curling, and I allowed them to billow and curl as they would.

Studying these maps as I did, whether standing at the wall and leaning in at them or regarding them from my bed with my hands clasped behind my head, I made my trip to New Mexico many times before I ever left the family driveway. I felt in imagination the surge and lift of my winged mount beneath me. I saw my flightless coevals, the nation's little groundlings, below me, watching and waving, wishing that they could be me. I saw America's yards and farms laid out like patches in a quilt. I saw it all as others said they had seen it. I was seeing it at second hand, but still something of it came from me—all the pretty girls, to name just one example, sunbathing in their yards, waving at me, beckoning to me, blowing kisses. After a while, I began to fear, as I suppose all armchair travelers do, that the actual journey would be a disappointment, and, little by little, the thought occurred to me that the maps might not be accurate.

"I got these maps from the company that owns my father's gas station," I said to my friend Spike, "but I'm worried about them."

"You're afraid that they'll fall on you while you're asleep and smother you?" she suggested.

"No," I said. "It's not that. It's—look at the way the mapmakers vary the thickness of the lines that represent roads and highways, and the way they use different colors."

"Very nice," she said.

"But—suppose they make these maps in such a way that they tend to lead the traveler astray?"

"Astray?"

"I mean, what if they lead people to their gas stations?"

"What?" she asked.

"All the gas companies make maps like these and give them out at their stations, right?"

"Right."

"Suppose they make the roads going past their stations look more attractive or more interesting, so that people will choose those routes and won't choose other routes, where the gas stations that sell other kinds of gas are located."

"You're nuts," she told me.

"Maybe," I admitted.

To test my theory—and Spike's, I suppose—I wrote to other gas companies. I compared their maps' depictions of the roads along the route that I intended to follow with the version offered by the company that owned the station where my father worked. I imagined traveling the routes that the maps depicted, and tried to decide whether I was being steered toward each company's gas stations. After many long hours of thought experimentation, I came to the conclusion that the maps could not be trusted—and, simultaneously, I discovered that the trip so often taken in my imagination had grown stale.

So I refreshed the trip that had grown stale by deciding to travel without a map. Why travel with a map that you've decided you can't trust anyway? I took all the maps down from my walls and ceiling, folded them up, and put them away in my closet.

Having no map forced me to ask directions of strangers, and along the way I learned that doing so leads to fascinating exchanges, exchanges that are, more often than not, useless, but fascinating nonetheless. If I had it to do over again (in actuality, not in memory, as I am doing it now), I think I might travel with a map. I've decided that they're more trustworthy than I thought—and they are much more trustworthy than the advice of strangers.

OUR LITTLE SECRET

I AM SOMETIMES asked to explain the secret of the happiness that Albertine and I have found in each other's company over all the years that we have been together, through thick and thin and through thin and thinner, and when asked I admit quite frankly that the secret is our nearly perfect balance of induced and dynamic lift.

Lift, on a wing, on an airplane, is a matter of relative pressure: less pressure above, pressing down; more pressure below, pushing up. When the pressure's off above and on below, we rise. I am a great believer in lift, unlike Wolfgang Langewiesche, who, in his *Stick and Rudder: An Explanation of the Art of Flying,* disparaged lift. It might be fair to say that Langewiesche pooh-poohed the whole idea of lift, coming very close to calling it an illusion, as close as Kurt Gödel came to calling time an illusion in "A Remark About the Relationship Between Relativity Theory and Idealistic Philosophy," his contribution to the 1949 Festschrift volume *Albert Einstein: Philosopher-Scientist.* For Langewiesche, the upward mobility of a forward-moving airplane is the result of the reaction of the undersurface of the wing to the force of the air below the wing when the airplane's engine pushes the wing against the air below it at a sufficient angle of attack—that is, with a sufficient upward slant. The air pushes the wing up, in Langewiesche's view, and the wing needn't be an airfoil; it might as well be a sheet of plywood; it could be any plane surface at all. Hence, Langewiesche points out, the name of the vehicle itself, an air(borne) plane. So, which is it: the lowered pressure on the upside of an airfoil or the greater pressure on the underside of a plane at the proper angle of attack? (In certain circles, this is still the subject of lively debate.) For the answer, I turn to Pope and Otis, my quondam mentors Frank and Art:

> When an airfoil is presented to the wind at a positive angle of attack, the impact of the air on the undersurface of the airfoil produces lift. This kind of lift is called *dynamic lift*. [The] lift which comes from the reduced pressure of the air above an airfoil is called *induced lift*. The total lift is the sum of these values, which is merely the difference between the increased pressure below and the diminished pressure above the airfoil.

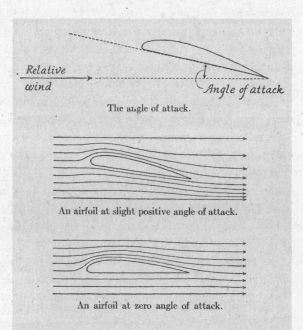

Relative wind

Angle of attack

The angle of attack.

An airfoil at slight positive angle of attack.

An airfoil at zero angle of attack.

Francis Pope and Arthur S. Otis, *Elements of Aeronautics*

For Frank and Art, it's not a case of either-or. Both the dynamic and induced forms of lift play their parts.

As it is in flight, so it is in life—my life with Albertine, at any rate.

When Albertine commences an undertaking, she assumes a positive angle of attack and thrusts herself forward, attacking that undertaking head-on, with power and purpose and a plan. The undertaking could be something as simple as a cross-country drive or as complex as "taking Peter out for an airing so that his outlook on life will be refreshed." The result is the same: the woman produces lift. Her kind of lift is called *dynamic lift*.

When I commence an undertaking, I begin conducting thought experiments at once, and in a remarkably short time my head is in the clouds. My kind of lift is called *induced lift*.

Through the combined effects of dynamic and induced lift, Albertine and I manage to transport each other over many of life's little obstacles. Ordinarily, she provides the dynamic lift, and I'm the simple airfoil, providing the induced lift. Together, we are a complex airfoil like the one described by Frank and Art.

So it has been for many years, but something happened to Albertine during her recovery from her crash and fracture. She underwent a Baudelairean turn toward childhood, and to my great surprise began to exhibit an inclination and talent for producing induced lift, culminating in her selection of the Electro-Flyer as a vehicle suitable for a cross-country trip. I found this a little alarming. What would such a trip be like with two agents of induced lift and none of dynamic lift? I was relieved to find, while we were packing the Electro-Flyer, that she had reverted to form.

"You know," I said, squeezing a small bag into a small nook in a corner of the trunk, "in recent years, my favorite journeys, my best journeys, have been the ones I've made in my mind. They have required no shopping, no tickets, no luggage, no packing, and no maps."

"Mmm," she said, thereby displaying her practical dynamic-lift side by disparaging my impractical induced-lift side.

"Armchair travel is surely one of the greatest benefits of the human imagination," I asserted.

"One of its virtues," she admitted, "is that you get to sleep in your own bed." She frowned at the pile of things we hadn't been able to find nooks for. "I'm beginning to think that we should have bought a car with a bigger trunk."

"The tiny trunk makes it more like my aerocycle—which hardly had room for a change of socks."

"Oh, I do hope we're not going to find it difficult to get our laundry done," she fretted. "We have only a week's worth of underwear each."

"We could stuff some more into the pockets in the doors if we got rid of all those maps and turn-by-turn directions and just trusted to hunch, whim, and serendipity."

"If you're going to travel with me, Peter, you're going to be in a car driven by a woman who knows where she's going."

"Yeah. I know. I just thought I'd give it one last try."

"I'm sorry. That's just the way I am."

"But did we really have to make all our hotel and motel reservations in advance?" I asked. "Couldn't we maybe just wing it, trusting to chance that we'll find a cozy place for the night when night comes on?"

"I used to run a place like the ones we'd be likely to find if we trusted to chance," she reminded me. "That's why I made reservations at places where I think we can remain dry on rainy nights."

We took our places in the car. Albertine switched it on, put it into gear, pulled out of the spot in front of our building where we'd parked it for packing, and headed for the corner.

"Well," I said hopefully, "there's always the chance that we'll get lost."

WEST BAYBOROUGH

··

It is often necessary while flying to determine where one is, or was, or will be, at a given time.

—Francis Pope and Arthur S. Otis, *Elements of Aeronautics*

I HAD BEEN on the road for a couple of hours, enjoying myself quite a bit despite the fact that I couldn't get *Spirit* off the ground, when I began talking to my mount. At first I was just urging her to get up and go, but then, little by little, I began conversing with her as I would have with a traveling companion.

"Do you think that means something?" I asked her as we came to a stop at a red light. "The way talking to yourself means money in the bank?"

"Doesn't that mean company's coming?" she asked.

"Money in the bank, company's coming, something like that."

"I think it's just an inevitable consequence of traveling solo," she said thoughtfully. "Sooner or later, a solo traveler will talk to himself— or to his beautiful aerocycle if he's fortunate enough to have one. That's just the way it is."

"What?" asked the driver of the car beside me.

"Oh—ah—nothing," I said. "I was just talking to my—ah—myself."

"Means you're nuts," he claimed cheerily. "You want to try to keep that under control."

"Yes, sir," I said.

Embarrassed, I chugged along for a while without saying a word to anyone.

"So!" she said after a couple of blocks. "I embarrass you!"

"Oh, no. No. Of course not."

"Then why wouldn't you admit to that fool that you were talking to me?"

"I—"

"That was a person of absolutely no consequence to you, someone you are not likely ever to see again, and yet you wouldn't acknowledge me."

"Please, I—"

"Don't talk to me."

"Okay."

We rode on in silence until the silence grew awkward, whereupon I broke it by remarking, as if there were no ill feeling between us, "So this is traveling without a map, free as the wind!"

"I like it!" said *Spirit*, apparently as eager as I to put the past behind us.

"It's easier than I thought it would be," I said.

"I agree!"

For a moment I thought of using that remark as an opening to point out that she wasn't putting as much effort into transporting me as I had expected her to, but I think that—tyro traveler though I was—I realized that it's not wise to antagonize one's traveling companion or one's conveyance or both so early in the trip.

"Now that I think about it, I realize that I had begun to worry that it was going to be boring," I said instead, "just one straight road to New Mexico without any diversions."

"It was studying all those maps that did that."

"But now I'm finding that although I have a general direction in mind as a goal—"

"A kind of Emersonian tendency."

"Um, yeah. You could say that. A tendency. Right. A kind of westness. But I can choose the roads that seem most appealing, the ones that seem to offer the most pleasant route to—or at least toward—the goal."

"I see what you mean. You don't have to go right at it."

"Right," I said, inspired. "I can tack."

"Well put."

"A sailor soon learns that he almost never takes a direct route," I declaimed under the influence of her praise, or flattery. "He learns that wind and tide and currents will alter his course, and he learns to live with that, even to enjoy it."

" 'A tar rolls with the swells,' as Mr. Summers said—"

"Well, yeah," I said, surprised that she should know about Mr. Summers, leader of the Young Tars, and the mottoes he tried to persuade his followers to adopt, surprised that she should have access to my memory.

"—enjoying the diversion of wind and tide and currents and swells the way that you're enjoying the wandering course of this journey."

"Yes."

"You seem to have learned a lot from the days you spent as a boy, sailing with your grandfather on Bolotomy Bay," she said, mining my memory again.

"Those were wonderful days," I said with a sigh.

I went on for a while, reminiscing happily about those carefree days on Bolotomy Bay, until, suddenly, to my surprise, there was Bolotomy Bay right in front of me. I throttled down and rolled slowly to the water's edge, where a bulkhead formed the margin of the bay. Somewhere, I realized, somewhere in my recent past, I had made a wrong turn.

Long Island is long and narrow, running east-and-west. When I set out from Babbington I had been headed west, in the general direction of New Mexico. My intention had been to continue heading west, and if I had succeeded in doing so, the bay, which stretches along Long Island's southern shore, should have been to the south of my route. I should have been traveling westward, paralleling the bay, not heading directly into it. I should have arrived in New York City, not at the West Bayborough Municipal Dock, which was where I found myself, or where I found myself lost.

I turned away from the water and in the manner of all lost people began trying to retrace my steps, hoping to find the place at which I had gone wrong, and there to regain the westward tendency that I had hoped to maintain throughout my journey.

After spending some time in that effort, I began to understand that I must have made many wrong turns. The first one must have been made quite some time ago, not very far from Babbington, and then I must have spent most of the afternoon and early evening making one wrong turn after another. The pleasure I had found in traveling had been a false pleasure, founded on ignorance, a bliss that I felt only while my ignorance lasted, a bliss that vanished when my eyes were opened.

"I blame it on the weather," I explained to *Spirit*. "When the day clouded over, I had no sunlight or shadows to help me tell west from south or north or even east. I was flying blind."

"In more ways than one," she muttered.

"Okay. You're right. It's my own fault. I should have brought a map."

I thought she might offer me some consolation, perhaps even tell me that I shouldn't blame myself, but she didn't. We rolled on in silence, retracing my steps, but I retraced my steps so badly that I found myself back at the West Bayborough Municipal Dock again.

I stopped. I sighed. Beside me, a grizzled fisherman sitting on the bulkhead heard me sigh and guessed the reason for it.

"Lost?" he asked.

"Yes," I admitted.

"That's nothing to be ashamed of," said a lovely dark-haired girl beside him. "Everyone gets lost now and then."

"In my case, there is something to be ashamed of," I confessed. "This is trouble of my own making, and the making of it began when I chose to travel without a map."

"That's quite eloquently put," the fisherman said.

"I've been practicing," I said. "I've been rehearsing that for the last hour or so, while I was trying to retrace my steps."

"In the manner of all lost people."

"I suppose so."

"It's a pity we didn't speak earlier, the first time you arrived here at the dock."

"I didn't notice you."

"Perhaps."

"Really. I didn't."

"Perhaps you were reluctant to ask directions. It's a common failing."

"No. Really. I just didn't notice you."

"And yet I have rather an unusual aspect, wouldn't you say?"

"Well, no, not really, to tell the truth. Back home, in Babbington, there are quite a few grizzled—"

"Old salts?" offered the girl.

"Yes."

"Here I'm considered quite a character," the fisherman asserted.

"That's true," said the girl.

"Well—"

"I make a considerable contribution to local color."

"I'm sure."

"And I'm considered an important source of folk wisdom."

"That's the way it is back at home. There are many—"

"If you had asked my advice," he said, with an unmistakable note of irritation in his voice, "I would have offered you a bit of that wisdom: I would have told you not to try retracing your steps."

"Why?"

"Retracing one's steps is repeating old errors. It's a miserable way to live one's life."

"I only spent a couple of hours—"

"Now you take me," he went on. "I've made mistakes in my life—who hasn't—but do I dwell on them, do I keep returning to them and regretting them? No. Certainly not. What's done is done. You can't change the past. You can't go back to the place where things went wrong and make them go right."

"But what should he do, Grandfather?" asked the girl.

"Yeah," I said. "What should I do?"

"You should go on from where you are."

"But it's getting dark. It feels late. And I've been on the road so long."

"How long have you been away from home?" asked the girl, placing a gentle hand on my arm.

"Hours," I said importantly.

"Grandpa," the girl said to the grizzled fisherman, "this boy must be tired and hungry. I'm going to take him home, give him a hot bath, cook him some supper, and tuck him into bed," and then she simply faded away, vanished, returning to the land of wishful thinking, from which she had materialized for the few moments that she'd been standing there.

"Did you?" asked the fisherman.

"What?" I asked, bewildered by the way the girl had disappeared.

"I said, 'You must have had many adventures,'" the fisherman repeated. "Did you?"

"Huh?" I said, still befuddled.

"Never mind," he said. "Time for me to pack up and head for home—a hot bath—a hearty meal—and a good night's sleep."

I needed a place to stay. I'd been away from Babbington for only a few hours, but I had already begun to feel the chill of separation. I missed the place—my home town—and the people in it. I felt very much alone and in need of someplace that would make me feel, if not at home, at least in a place like home. I had intended from the start to rely on the kindness of strangers, to ask the people I met along the way to give me shelter, and to exploit the good impression that I, a daring young flyboy, was likely to make on the easily awed populace of the towns I would be passing through. The grizzled fisherman didn't seem easily awed, but he was the only current candidate for the role of kindly stranger.

"Please, sir," I said, "I've been traveling for some time—I'm tired and hungry—and I need a place to stay for the night."

"Mm," he said as he began to pack his gear.

"Could you—?"

"Mm?"

"Could you—um—put me up?"

"For the night?"

"If it wouldn't be too much trouble."

"I suppose you'll want supper, and a bath, and clean sheets."

"Well—"

"You'll have to eat fish," he said, indicating the fish in his bucket.

"I like fish."

"You'll have to bathe in cold water."

"I've done that at camp."

"You'll have to sleep with my granddaughter."

"That would be—I—really?"

"In your dreams," he said, cuffing me behind the ear.

His humble home was not far. It was a little cottage, not much larger than the cabin of a boat and outfitted just as efficiently. The fisherman's wife greeted me as if a wayfarer in need of a place to spend the night were not at all an uncommon sight. She had bread in the oven, and as soon as the fisherman had cleaned the fish he'd caught she began making a plain but hearty chowder. Dinner was wonderfully satisfying, and I paid for it by regaling them with tales of my adventures on the road until their eyes began to droop and they began to list the many tasks that awaited them on the morrow. The fisherman showed me to a tiny loft above the kitchen, and there, in a narrow bed with a thin mattress, I slept soundly, with visions of the dark-haired girl dancing in my head.

The next morning, after breakfast, I was surprised to find that I was reluctant to leave the cozy cabin. The grizzled fisherman must have noticed my reluctance, because he took me aside—actually, he grabbed my arm above the elbow and dragged me from the house—and said, "You'll be on your way." I decided to interpret it as a question.

"Yes," I said with a sigh, "you're right. You and your wife have been wonderful hosts, and I've enjoyed my stay, but if I'm going to get to New Mexico I'll have to be on my way."

"It isn't wise to sail without a chart," he said.

"I realize that now."

"It's folly, really."

"I suppose you're right."

"But," he added with a twinkle, "as the poet says, 'If the fool would persist in his folly he would become wise.'"

"You mean you think that I—should continue to sail without a chart?"

"Yes."

"That's your advice?"

"That's my advice."

"And you think I'll become wise by persisting in my folly?"

"You might."

"All right," I said, extending my hand, "I'll take your advice."

We shook hands. I mounted *Spirit* and started her up. I looked around. "Which—um—which way—"

He pointed in a direction that I hoped was westerly.

RIDING SHOTGUN

. . . .

Kurt [Gödel] liked to drive fast. This, combined with his penchant for in-dulging in abstract reverie while behind the wheel, led his [. . .] wife, Adele, to put an end to his driving career.

—Palle Yourgrau, *A World Without Time: The Forgotten Legacy of Gödel and Einstein*

ALBERTINE WAS BEHIND the wheel of the Electro-Flyer, driving, and I was beside her in the passenger's seat, asking my-self what, exactly, my role was in this adventure. Co-pilot? Navigator? Faithful companion? Sancho Panza? Dr. Watson, Jim, Tonto?

"You're talking to yourself," said Albertine.

"Not audibly," I said.

"No, but I can see your lips moving."

"Keep your eyes on the road."

"Why do you talk to yourself?"

"I know not why others may do so, but as for me it has always been a way to clarify my thinking—"

"Clarify somewhat."

"It has always been a way to clarify my thinking somewhat, and in the years that you and I have been together, it has been a way for me to prepare the witty aphorisms, entertaining anecdotes, and penetrating commentary that I use to impress, entertain, and seduce you."

"Do you have anything ready?"

"More or less."

"Speak."

"I've been reflecting on my role in this adventure."

"Are we having an adventure?"

"Life is an adventure."

"Not when I'm waiting on line at the pharmacy."

"Okay, but this part of our life together is an adventure, and I've been reflecting on my role in it. After all, there you are, at the wheel, clearly the driver, or pilot, and here I am, beside you, with a folder of maps at the ready—"

"A handsome leather folder of maps."

"Yes. Very manly. I appreciate that. But even with my maps I can't be considered the navigator, since you have chosen the route in advance and printed turn-by-turn directions from three map sites on the World Wide Web."

"Oh. I see. I'm sorry—"

"No need. No need. I've defined my role, and I'm happy in it."

"Stud muffin?"

"Not while you're driving."

"Ye gods, what good are you, then?"

"Exactly the question, I think, that teenage boys used to ask themselves when they cadged rides from friends who had driver's licenses and the use of the family car when they had neither themselves."

"What good am I?" she cried to the open sky above the crystalline plastic top of the Electro-Flyer in excellent imitation of the wail of a boy whose voice is still changing.

"And the answer, I've decided, is that I am fulfilling the role that in my teenage years was called 'riding shotgun.'"

"Now, why did you call it that?" she asked, speaking this time in the manner of Mr. MacPherson, that enthusiastic student of idiom.

"I'm glad you asked," I said. "I can answer with confidence because as a boy I spent many Saturday mornings at the Babbington Theater, watching westerns." In the voice of one who knows, I said, "My dear Albertine, we teenage boys used the term because when we were even younger boys we had heard it used so often in westerns that involved stagecoach travel. In those movies, there were always bands of marauding bandits. I should point out that many of those bandits were actually good guys who, through no fault of their own, often just because of a case of mistaken identity, had been driven out of polite society and found themselves forced to turn to banditry to make a living. I don't mean to suggest that all the bad guys were good guys forced to be bad—many were actually bad—most of them, in fact. Sometimes they were greedy, and sometimes they were just mean. They had been brought up that way, I guess, or perhaps they had been starved for affection during childhood. Something like that. Anyway, the point that was brought home again and again to an impressionable boy in the Babbington Theater was that driving a stagecoach through the Old West was a dangerous undertaking, especially if the stage was carrying something valuable that bad guys would want, like gold or the new school marm or somebody's bride from Back East. The hills out there were crawling with bad guys. So, a stagecoach required, in addition to a driver, a second man sitting beside the driver, his right-hand man, right up there on the seat where the driver sat, a man who could fight off the bad guys if they attacked. This second—but equally important—man held, across his lap, at the ready, a shotgun. He wasn't driving. He was 'riding shotgun.' And here am I riding shotgun for you, so that you can concentrate on your driving, secure in the knowledge that if any bad guys come galloping up beside us with evil intent—I will scare them away with the handsome leather folder of maps that I have lying across my lap, at the ready."

"That's my guy," she said.

What I hadn't told her, what I am telling her only now, in this sentence, on this page, is that the guy riding shotgun for her was on the alert for signs of flyguys in the sky, and if he saw them in the rearview mirror or heard the ominous sound of their blades chopping the air, he meant to use his handsome leather book of maps to suggest evasive action—a sudden side trip to someplace hard to spot from the air. He would insist. If necessary, he would plead. If it came to that, he would take the wheel.

ONCE BITTEN

Ladies and gentlemen . . . I . . . hardly know where to begin, to paint for you a word picture of the strange scene before my eyes . . .
—Carl Phillips, radio commentator, in Howard Koch's adaptation of
H. G. Wells's *The War of the Worlds*

THE DAY WAS nearly perfect for traveling: clear and cool and still. As I pulled onto the road, my heart was full of the mad hope that *Spirit* might on this promising day take to the air and fly me to my next stop.

"Let's go, *Spirit*," I coaxed her. "Let's rise up, leave the hard pavement below us, and soar into the clear, cool air. Come on, let's go!"

"Oh, please," she said with a yawn.

"What's the matter?"

"It's so early."

"But it's such a wonderful morning. Don't you feel the urge to get up and go?"

"Not at all. I'm still tired from yesterday. All that traveling! I've never done anything like that in my life."

"No," I said, reluctantly admitting the truth of it, "I guess you haven't."

"Couldn't we just take it easy today and kind of glide along at a nice easy pace? On the ground?"

"Okay," I said, but I didn't try to hide my disappointment.

"If I have an easy day today, I might be able to get up into the air tomorrow."

"If you're making a bargain, I'm going to hold you to it," I said.

"Of course. I'm an aerocycle of my word."

So, off we went, at an easy pace. I realize now, in retrospect, that, for the sake of my account, I should have stopped one night in Manhattan. If I had, this chapter might have included some Manhattan adventures. At the time, though, the city seemed an obstacle that stood in the way of my real journey and my real adventure, which lay beyond New York, in the West, so I pushed on through without stopping at all, and we traveled without adventures for the entire day, pleasantly and uneventfully, if slowly, stopping once for gas, and once for lunch, and briefly now and then so that I could stretch my legs and she could rest, until we found ourselves deep in New Jersey, late in the afternoon.

As the shadows began to lengthen and I began to turn my thoughts to dinner, I began to feel that something was odd, though I wasn't quite sure what made me feel that way.

"*Spirit*," I whispered, "there's something strange going on."

"What?"

"I don't know—it's hard to put into words—I've just got a strange feeling."

"You're not giving me much to go on."

"Well, it feels as if people are watching me—watching us."

"I suppose it isn't every day that a kid comes flying through these parts on a graceful and gorgeous aerocycle. Of course people are watching."

"Yeah, but this is more like—surveillance."

"You've seen too many—" she began, but she broke off, and in a moment said, *sotto voce*, "You're right. We seem to be attracting notice."

"That's it," I said, "attracting notice. Am I right that there are some people—keeping an eye on us?"

"You are," she said. "They're acting as if they're going about their business, but there's something phony about them."

"They're evenly spaced," I pointed out, "as if they've been stationed there."

"Like sentries," she said with a chill in her voice.

"Uh-oh."

"What?"

"In the road—ahead—a roadblock."

"Wow," she said, and from her tone I could tell that, like me, she found two emotions vying for dominance within her: (1) a fear of the authorities, and (2) pride in our seeming important enough or threatening enough for the authorities to put up a roadblock against us.

I began slowing long before we reached the roadblock, lest the small mob assembled there get the idea that I intended to run it.

"This is my first roadblock," I confessed to *Spirit*.

"Mine, too," she said, as if I didn't know.

"I'm a little nervous."

"Me, too."

There were four police officers manning the roadblock. They wore enormous pistols on their hips. The people in the growing crowd around them were also armed. Shotguns, cradled like babies, were the weapon of choice, and pitchforks, held like lances, the tines directed at *Spirit* and me, were a close second.

I came to a stop, wiped my sweaty palms on my pants legs, swallowed hard, and said, "Hello," as innocently as I could.

"Don't come no closer," said the largest of the cops.

"Sorry," I said, pushing with my heels to back *Spirit* up a bit. "Was I too close? This is my first roadblock—"

"Don't try no funny stuff."

"No, sir," I said, shaking my head. "You won't get any funny stuff from me. Not at all. You can ask anybody—"

"Where have you come from?" asked the closest of the pitchforkers.

Tentatively, apologetically, fearing, for the first time in my life, that it might be the wrong answer, I said, "Babbington."

"Is that on our planet?" he asked, narrowing his eyes.

"Sure," I said. "It's just back that way—" I raised my arm to point, and the crowd stiffened, brandishing their weapons. The cops put their hands on their pistol butts. I held my own hands up to show that I was neither armed nor up to any funny stuff, and said, "It's on Long Island—in New York."

"Oh, yeah? New York?"

"Right."

"Quick: who plays center field for the Yankees?"

"Mickey Mantle."

"What does the Statue of Liberty hold in her right hand?"

"In her right hand? I—ah—" I struck Liberty's pose to ensure that I didn't confuse her hands. "A torch," I announced authoritatively.

"Who is Popeye's nemesis?"

"I—ah—his nemesis—um—Pluto? No—Bluto!"

At once the crowd that had seemed so hostile became warm and welcoming. My interrogator shifted his pitchfork so that the end of its handle rested on the ground with its tines pointing upward. He seemed as relieved as I that the interrogation had gone so well.

"You've got to excuse us," he said with an apologetic shrug. "Once bitten, twice shy, you know."

"Who bit you?" I asked.

"Martians."

"Martians?"

"You don't believe me?"

I sensed that stiffening again, so I was quick to answer, "Of course I believe you. I just didn't know that Martians—um—bit. I thought they used—well—ray guns."

"You trying to be funny?"

"No, sir! It's just that—I don't know—Martians that bite—"

"It's just an expression," one of the cops offered helpfully. "Probably derived from experience with dogs, but extended to a wide range of experiences, essentially suggesting that after a bad experience a person tends to be cautious when presented with a similar situation."

"Is your name MacPherson?" I asked. I couldn't help myself.

"MacPherson? No. Why do you ask?"

"Because my French teacher, back in Babbington, is named MacPherson, and he's very interested in words and phrases that don't mean quite what they seem to mean, like saying 'once bitten, twice shy' when you mean being cautious after a bad experience."

"In our case it was a bad experience with Martians," the interrogator said, evidently not particularly interested in Mr. MacPherson.

"That's incredible!" I said enthusiastically.

"I'm going to assume that you mean 'amazing' or 'astonishing' or something like that and not 'unbelievable.' Am I right?"

"Yes, sir. Definitely. Amazing. Astonishing. Um—tell me about it."

"That would best be done by Lem here," he said, beckoning to a venerable member of the armed mob. "He's kind of our local historian."

"Ahhh," objected Lem, with a dismissive flap of the hand. "He ain't goin' to believe me no more'n any o' the other outsiders."

"Now take it easy, Lemuel," said the largest of the cops, gently. "Don't go getting yourself into a lather. Why don't you tell the boy what happened? Then he'll be able to pass the truth along, and then someday everybody'll know what really happened here."

Lem shook his head petulantly and looked at his shoes.

"Once bitten, twice shy?" I offered.

"How's that?" asked Lem.

"I guess you've had a bad experience with people you've told the story to," I said. "Outsiders, I mean."

"Oh. Yeah. That's so. Say, you catch on right quick."

"I sure would like to hear about the Martians," I said.

Lem came forward, took a position beside *Spirit*, turned to me, incidentally, and to the crowd at large, primarily, and began, "Pretty near a score of years ago, Martians landed here, in Hopper's Knoll, at Gurney's farm."

One of the assembled multitude raised a hand, evidently acknowledging his status as Gurney.

"They came in a spaceship that they had disguised so's it would look like a meteor, but when you got close to it you could see it was more of a kind of yellowish-white cylinder."

Gurney took a step forward and volunteered, "When it come in out of the sky, I was listening to the radio, kind of halfway listening and halfway dozing, when I heard a hissing sound, kind of like a Fourth of July rocket, and then—bingo!—something smacked the ground. Knocked me out of my chair."

Lemuel resumed the narrative, and as it continued, with occasional eye-witness interruptions from Gurney and others, a thrill of recognition began to run through me. I knew the story they were telling. I knew it well. It was *The War of the Worlds,* and the version that Lem was telling resembled the version broadcast by the Mercury Theatre under the direction of Orson Welles, on October 30, 1938, six years— almost to the day—before I was born. I had become interested in the story after seeing a movie version of it at the Babbington Theater when I was nine. Inspired by that experience, "once bitten" and infected in a positive rather than a negative way, I had read the original version, by H. G. Wells, and I had also read the radio play by Howard Koch that had been the basis for the Mercury Theatre broadcast. It was a case of once bitten, twice eager. Not only had I read Koch's radio play, but when I was approaching my eleventh birthday a friend and I had made our own version of the radio broadcast, using a tape recorder. Together we had created some sound effects that we considered pretty realistic. For instance, for the scene in which the top of the Martians' spaceship begins unscrewing, we put the microphone right up next to an empty mayonnaise jar while one of us slowly unscrewed the lid. The effect was so realistic that when the kids in our class at school heard it—

"You got something you want to say, son?" the interrogator asked.

I did! I did! I wanted to tell them everything about my experiences with *The War of the Worlds*. I wanted to begin at the beginning, with some background about the Babbington Theater and brief plot summaries of the most memorable movies that I had seen there before I saw *The War of the Worlds*, but in the moment of hesitation when I was deciding just where I ought to begin, I noticed that Lem had grown perplexed and irritated, and from the way he was scowling at me I surmised that I was the cause.

"Um—no," I said. "What makes you think—"

"You're moving your lips and twitchin' and bouncin' up and down on the balls of your feet like somebody's got to go to the bathroom."

"That's it!" I said. "I didn't want to interrupt the story, but, you know, I've been on the road for a long time, and I—I've really got to go."

"Well, heck, son, why didn't you say so? Gurney, your place is about the closest. What say we all head on over there where the boy can relieve himself and Lem can go on with the story?"

"It would be an honor," Gurney claimed.

On the way to Gurney's farm, *Spirit* had time to give me some stern, unwelcome, but necessary advice.

"That was close," she began, realizing, I suppose, that it's best not to launch right into stern, unwelcome, but necessary advice without some preamble.

"I know," I whispered.

"You just barely managed to keep your foot out of your mouth."

"I wonder why we say that?" I asked, because it was an expression that had puzzled me for some time, and because I didn't welcome the stern but necessary advice that I knew was coming.

"Never mind," she said in the manner of people who find that fate has given them an opportunity to deliver the kind of advice that is more pleasant to give than to receive.

"It just seems to me that it's backwards," I said. "Wouldn't it make more sense to say, 'You should have put your foot in your mouth'?"

"Listen to me."

"Okay."

"These people think they've got something that's uniquely theirs, a place in the history of these parts, of the United States, of the world, that is theirs alone. They've got a story to tell—and you almost took that away from them because you always want to tell your story."

"I know, I know. You don't have to tell me."

"But I think I do have to tell you to keep your mouth shut while you're here."

"Yeah, yeah. I know."

I really did know. What I knew, what I understood then but hadn't understood a few moments earlier, was that through many outward and visible signs I had betrayed my impatience with Lem and his story, my eagerness to tell everything I knew about *The War of the Worlds,* and my burning desire to make Lem's audience mine. Fortunately, those signs could also be interpreted as signs of a need to relieve myself, which, of course, they were. But I also knew that *Spirit* was right: from now on I was going to have to let Lem tell his story and let him have his audience and include myself in it. I'd have to keep my mouth shut—put my foot in it if necessary.

I heard Lem's whole story that night, and some parts of it I heard many times. Keeping silent while he told it was very difficult. As I listened, Lem's deviations from the versions of the story that I knew and considered correct, including my own, sometimes annoyed me so much that my emotions bubbled and seethed within me, producing a kind of reactionary pressure that threatened to force an objection or correction from me. I stifled the urge, and instead I let the steam off in bursts of inoffensive interjections.

"Wow!" I said when I wanted to say, "That's an outrageous fabrication, sir!"

"Amazing!" when I wanted to say "Totally unbelievable!"

"Astonishing!" when I wanted to say "You're full of it, Lem!"

In Lem's version of the invasion story, the men of Hopper's Knoll defeated the Martian invaders, but the Martians, routed and in full flight, blasted the village with a memory-eradication ray to erase any recollection of their ignominious defeat. The true story of Hopper's Knoll might have gone forever untold, even unknown, if Lem hadn't caught the flu a couple of years later. Fortunately for his career as local historian and raconteur (and unfortunately for the integrity of the tale as I knew it and told it myself) he *had* caught the flu, and in an influenza fever dream he recovered his memory of the battle. Through the agency of the story that he told, Lem's recovered memory became the catalyst for recovered recollections from other townsfolk, who— one by one and little by little—added bits of plausible detail to Lem's account, in an epidemic of fantastical recollective collaboration, until the whole town remembered what had happened, and their story had become full and rich and multifaceted, with a large cast of characters whose roles and remembrances reinforced one another. At last, "tetched by Mnemosyne," as Lem put it, they remembered in full how they had saved the world.

I remember Lem's story, and I remember that I was fascinated by his telling of it, and the way that the others who remembered having been a part of it contributed their bits on cue, clearly savoring the opportunity to strut onstage for a moment. Later that night, lying in bed in the spare room upstairs in the farmhouse at Gurney's place, I rehearsed the story until I fell asleep, so that I would remember it and be able to reproduce it and criticize it when I got the chance, but when I recall the story and the telling now, I find that the whole experience is dominated and somewhat obliterated by the memory, in the peripheral vision of my mind's eye, of a dark-haired girl on the edge of the listening crowd. I remember the story well enough, but it isn't what interests me now. She is.

In the morning, I soldiered my way through the endless farmhouse breakfast that Ma and Pa Gurney insisted I needed for the trials of the road ahead, and then I began preparing *Spirit* for takeoff. I was just about to say goodbye to the Gurneys when the man who had been my interrogator pulled into the driveway in a pickup truck, stopped beside *Spirit*, got out, and joined us.

"Son," he said, in a kindly but no-nonsense way, "I'd like a word with you before you leave."

"A word to the wise?" I asked.

He gave me that squinty-eyed look that I was getting used to, and took me aside, a few steps away from Ma and Pa.

"You know," he said, "a lot of people are suspicious of strangers, especially kids who come flying into town on motorcycles."

"So I've learned."

"On this trip of yours, I'm afraid you're always going to be the stranger riding into town."

"An object of suspicion."

"That's it."

"Strange as a Martian."

"Oh, folks may not think that you're a Martian in disguise necessarily—Hopper's Knoll may be unique in that respect—but they are apt to suspect your motives, and, once they have begun suspecting your motives, they're pretty generally likely to decide that the safest course is to regard you as a troublemaker, at least a potential troublemaker."

"That doesn't seem fair."

"Fair or not, that's the way it is."

"What do you think I should do?"

"It helps if you agree with them. Accept what they've got to say."

"Don't interrupt, you mean."

"That would be a start."

"But what if I've got something to say, too?"

"Best keep it to yourself. Just nod your head and say nothing."

"I guess, but—"

"I guess what I'm trying to tell you is, don't put your foot in it."

"In what?"

"In your mouth."

"You know," I said, shaking my head, "I've just got to say—"

He put a strong hand on my shoulder and gave it a cautionary squeeze. "What is it that you've just got to say, boy?"

"I've just got to say that you've really given me something to think about."

He narrowed his eyes, but he relaxed his grip, and I mounted *Spirit* and hit the road.

THE NEW SHEBOYGAN

••

Humor ... is almost never without one of its opposite moods—
tenderness, tragedy, concern for man's condition, recognition of man's
frailties, sympathy with his idealism.

—Ben Shahn, "The Gallic Laughter of André François"

'Tain't funny, McGee.

—Molly, to Fibber

Ha-ha!

—Bosse-de-Nage, in Alfred Jarry's *Gestes et Opinions
du Docteur Faustroll*

AS I ATTEMPTED to explain to *Spirit* so many years ago," I said,
"I really do think that 'to put one's foot in one's mouth' is generally misused. People use it to indicate that someone has made a gaffe,
spoken out of turn, said what should have been left unsaid, or divulged
a secret that should have been kept secret, right? Isn't that the way you
hear it used?"

"Yes," she said, but she was concentrating more on highway traffic
than on what I had to say, I think.

"That's the way I hear it used, too. People say, 'You really put your
foot in your mouth,' when they want to point out a lack of circumspection when circumspection would have been a good policy. What they
really mean, I think, is something more along the lines of 'You should
have put your foot in your mouth' or 'I wish that you had put your foot

in your mouth instead of blurting out all that stuff about Uncle Albert's checkered past' or 'Why, oh why, couldn't you have put your foot in your mouth when we got to the party and kept it there until we were safely back in the car?'"

I waited for a response. None came.

"In the course of its history 'put your foot in your mouth' must have suffered a semantic shift from its original cautionary meaning of 'shut up before you make a fool of yourself' to 'it's too late now, you jerk.' You want to know what evidence I have?"

As before, I waited for a response. Again none came.

"Well," I announced triumphantly, "here it is: the shift forced people to come up with an alternative that better expressed the original meaning, namely, 'put a sock in it.'"

I allowed her another moment.

"Foot, sock, they're clearly related," I pointed out.

Another moment.

"Don't you agree?" I asked.

"I'm sure I do, my darling," she said, "but I haven't really been paying close attention. The traffic is heavy, I'm playing dodgem cars here, and I'm trying to find our motel. Put a sock in it for a while, okay?"

I did.

The place that Albertine had chosen for our night's stop was not at all what I would have expected. It was one of the chain motels that line the major intersections of major highways and offer little more than a bed. When she turned off the highway, I assumed that she would hurry past the chaotic congeries of gas-food-lodging and send us down a winding lane to the only cozy inn in these-here parts. Enormous signs towered at the edge of the highway, urging the weary traveler to spend the night in a bed provided by the chains called It'll Do, Inn-a-Pinch, and Cheapo-Sleepo. I chuckled at them in a superior manner, but I choked on my chuckle when Albertine slowed and signaled for a turn into It'll Do.

"This is not at all what I would have expected you to choose," I said. "I'm disappointed, if you don't mind my saying so."

"It has a fitness center, a pool, a cocktail lounge, a restaurant, a free

222 • PETER LEROY

breakfast buffet, and the cheapest rate in a hundred miles," she informed me. "It was the best I could find."

"In these-here parts," I suggested.

"Right," she said, pulling into a parking spot with an abruptness that I didn't ordinarily see.

"Okay," I said with a shrug. "I guess it'll do in a pinch for a cheapo sleepo."

"Ha-ha," she said.

We took our bags from the car and rolled them to the entrance, where, as soon as the doors slipped open to let us in, a clerk at the desk looked up, bestowed on us a practiced smile, and recited a scripted greeting: "Welcome to the It'll Do experience! We hope your stay will be okay!" Then he shook his head and added with a weary sigh, ad lib, "Please—please—don't try any funny stuff."

"What?" I said, surprised.

"I've been checking you people in all day, and I've had all the gags I can take."

"I don't know what you mean."

"I've heard that one, too."

"I'm mystified," I said. "Is this the standard greeting across the entire It'll Do chain? If I walk into an It'll Do in Sheboygan—"

"You know," he said, holding up a hand, "just stop right there and let me ask you something—why is it always Sheboygan? What is it with you people that makes you choose Sheboygan when you're going to try to be funny?"

"I—"

"Is it supposed to be an announcement? 'Attention! Attention! A joke is coming!'"

"I—"

"Or is Sheboygan just supposed to be innately funny?"

"I—"

"Or is it the entire state of Wisconsin?"

"Please," I said, "stop. I don't know why you're asking me these questions, or what you mean about being funny—"

"You're here for the annual Humorists' Hoop-de-Doo, right?"

"No," I said. "Certainly not."

"Yes," said Albertine. "We are."

"We are?" I said, surprised again.

"By joining the Heartsick American Humorists' Association we got a tremendous discount," she informed me.

"But who's the humorist?" I asked.

"You are, my darling," she said, handing a membership card to the clerk. "You crack me up."

The clerk began to snicker as he tapped us into the computer. "You guys are pretty good," he said.

We unpacked. We showered. We dressed for drinks and dinner. The cocktail lounge and bar were quite crowded, offering the possibility of an interesting conversation if we could pick the right people to sit next to, though the choice was likely to be forced because there were so few places available. Two stools were empty at the bar, but they were separated by two large men wearing black slacks and brightly colored shirts—one tangerine, one puce. Given the likelihood that the lounge was packed with humorists, the similarity of their outfits made it seem that they might be partners in an act.

"Let's sit at the bar," I suggested. "We can ask those two guys to move over."

We approached the bar and found the two bright shirts crying in their beer.

"It's over," groused one. "Never again will the kind of humor we grew up on, the kind of thing we enjoyed as kids, achieve the ascendancy, the cultural dominance, that it once enjoyed. Not in our lifetime."

"It was a golden age," moaned the other, "and this is an age of crap, comparatively speaking."

"Excuse me," I said to the one in tangerine. "Would you be willing to move one stool to your right, so that we could have the two vacant stools?"

He looked at me for a moment. He seemed genuinely puzzled.

"I don't get it," he said at last.

"Neither do I," said the one in the puce shirt.

"I was hoping you wouldn't mind moving over—"

"One stool to my right," said tangerine, with a puzzled look. "I got that part, but if I move one seat to my right, I'll be sitting in his lap. Is that supposed to be funny?"

"No," I said. "I was hoping that your friend would also move one stool to the right. That would leave two stools for Albertine and me."

They looked at each other, shrugged in the manner of two grumpy old men who are still willing to go along with a gag, and moved one stool to the right.

"Thanks," I said. Al and I took the free stools and ordered martinis.

"Well?" said puce, leaning around tangerine to say it.

"Thanks again," I said.

They looked at each other for a long moment.

"Impenetrable," said tangerine.

"Unfathomable," said puce.

"That's the whole problem today," said tangerine. "On the one hand, you've got this ineffable high-concept bullshit—"

"—and on the other you've got your lowbrow bathroom humor bullshit," said puce.

"—and the noble middle ground, where once we played—"

"—is vacant."

"Let's take these to a table," said Albertine.

At the only table with two seats empty, I stopped, indicated the empty seats with a nod of my head, and asked those seated around the table, "Are these available?"

"You see?" said a beefy man, bringing his hands together with a smart smack. "That's just what I've been talking about—a perfect example." To me he said, "A classic setup, classic. Thank you. You couldn't have arrived at a more opportune moment."

"By all means, join us," said a woman with hair that might have been dyed to match the puce shirt of the man we had left at the bar.

"I want to see where you're going to take this," said the beefy man.

"Take this?" I said. "Oh, I see what you mean. I don't really have any plans to take it anywhere. You see, I'm not a humorist."

"You're not?"

Albertine kicked me.

"Well, technically I am. That is, I am a member of the Heartsick American Humorists' Association—"

"Ipso facto," declared the beefy man.

"QED," said a small man beside him, who might have been the beefy man's professional sidekick.

"So give," said the woman with the hair.

I looked at Al. "How about helping me out a little here?" I asked.

"We're on the road," she said to the group, "bound for Corosso, New Mexico."

"Not bad, not bad," said the beefy man, rubbing his hands together in gleeful anticipation. "Corosso is the new Sheboygan."

"I think I see where this is going," said the woman.

"To New Mexico?" I suggested.

"Eventually," said Al, "but our immediate goal is to get back to the safety of our room and find out whether Bulky Burger delivers."

"Hilarious!" declared the beefy man, though he only chuckled.

On our way out of the lounge, we heard another of the humorists saying this: "Ours is not an age for subtlety. It doesn't want a Wilde or a Parker or even a Wodehouse. It doesn't want wit; it wants the whoopee cushion. It's an age that calls for a Rabelais or the Balzac of *Droll Stories* or that old sniggering schoolboy Alfred Jarry. In an age when people think a bomb is an appropriate answer to an insult, a fart is a clever riposte."

"Well, I suppose he's right about that," said Albertine.

"I wish he weren't," I said.

"I know you do," she said. "So do I."

"I prefer the fart to the bomb, though."

"I'll take silence, thanks."

I strode through the lobby with the purposeful look of a man who has left his toothbrush in the car. In the garage, I found an outlet, moved the Electro-Flyer to a spot one cord's length from it, and plugged it in for the night. Outside, I stood still for a moment, scanning the sky for the flashing lights of a helicopter. Nothing. I went back through the lobby. Passing the clerk, I patted my jacket pocket and said, "Tooth-brush."

"Ha-ha," he said skeptically.

Lying in bed that night, I had an insight, just before I fell asleep. It wasn't about humor; it was about Lem and his version of the Martian invasion story or, more accurately, my reaction to it. When I had objected to his altering the story, I wasn't taking offense on behalf of H. G. Wells or Howard Koch or Orson Welles. I was personally offended. The recorded version of the radio play that I had made with my friend Dan had been different from any of the sources we had used. It had been very similar to Howard Koch's radio play but not identical to it. We had made some changes out of necessity, others out of expediency, and others out of playfulness—changing some of the names of the characters to match the names of teachers in our school, for example—and the version that resulted was in a small way our own. That version had become in my storyteller's mind the version that I thought everyone ought to know and hew to, Lem included. It still is.

A BANNER DAY

He was a bold man that first ate an oyster.
—Colonel Atwit in Jonathan Swift's *Polite Conversation*

IT WAS A day for rhapsodizing, one of those extraordinarily beautiful days when, under a sky pellucid and blue, you willingly fall victim to the illusion that life is good and nothing can go wrong. *Spirit's* engine hummed, the air felt buoyant, and a couple of times when we crested a rise in the road, I gunned the engine and the road fell away beneath us. Oh, that exhilarating feeling of flight, the breathtaking thrill of being airborne for a few feet.

Toward evening, when the light began to thin, I found myself riding

through a marshy area, and because the lack of trees or other concealing vegetation afforded me a long view of what lay ahead of me, I could
make out a small town or village in the distance. Soon I came upon a
road sign welcoming me to Mallowdale, and farther on, when I reached
the edge of the village, I saw a bright banner strung across the main
street. Because I was still too far from the banner to read it, I allowed
myself to think that it might be a message of welcome for me.

"Oh, please," said *Spirit*.

"Why not?" I asked. "Word of my journey could spread by phone—
and why shouldn't it? Why shouldn't people in the towns we've passed
through telephone their friends and relatives along our route and urge
them not to miss the daring flyboy when he passes through their
town?"

Whatever the banner announced—and I still thought it might be
my arrival—had certainly caught people's fancy. The whole town
seemed to be in the street. I wished that I had taken the opportunity at
the last rest stop to straighten my clothes a bit, comb my hair, and give
Spirit a dusting.

"Am I dirty?" she asked.

"Not dirty, exactly. But both of us could use a little spiffing up."

"I know that I would look a lot better if you'd take that ratty banner
off my tail."

I said nothing, but I had to admit that she was right. The banner advertising Porky White's Kap'n Klam restaurant had suffered from being
dragged along the road through New York and New Jersey. It was battered and dirty and twisted, and the part that had initially read THE
HOME OF HAPPY DINERS had been reduced TO THE HOME OF HAPPY
DIN.

Perhaps *Spirit* and I both understood how contentious an issue
Porky's banner was likely to become, because we both stepped aside
from any discussion of it with the simultaneous declaration, "This is
an occasion!" and when I was close enough to read the Mallowdale
banner, it told me that the occasion was the 97th Annual Marshmallow Festival.

Festive it certainly was, and the marshmallow theme was inescapable.
Many of the citizens of Mallowdale had dressed themselves as the
plump white confections, either just as they come from the bag, or in

various stages of toasting, from barely beige through golden brown to singed to the fragile wrinkled skin of black that follows ignition. I felt conspicuous in my flyboy garb. It seemed as wrong as could be in a crowd where marshmallows were à la mode.

"You need an outfit," said a matronly woman at my side, taking me by the elbow. She wore a smile, but her brows were knit, giving her the air of someone taking pity on an unfortunate soul. In memory's eye, though, she seems not to be acting from spontaneous generosity but as part of a program. I see now that she was estimating in the back of her mind the benefit that would accrue from what she was about to do. "Here," she said. "Try this."

She offered me a crepe-paper hat that resembled a marshmallow somewhat. It was, I understand now, the Marshmallow Festival equivalent of the cheap jacket and tie that some restaurants keep in the checkroom for patrons who arrive dressed for dinner at a steel cart on the corner. The hat was enough of a marshmallow costume to make me feel that I could join the festivities. It was not nearly enough to allow me to fit in, but it was enough to make me stand out less. Still, as I walked around the center of the town, trying to mingle with the festive throng, I felt that the Mallowdalers considered me an outsider, someone suspect, possibly dangerous, a threat to their way of life, their beliefs, their young women. I liked it. I may have begun to swagger.

The flow of the crowd carried me to a parking lot behind the Marshmallow Museum where long tables and wooden folding chairs had been set up. From its resemblance to the Babbington Clam Fest's "Gorging Ground," I recognized this as a feasting area, and I discovered that I was hungry. I joined the line for tickets. The price was reasonable, and the sign at the entrance said ALL YOU CAN EAT, a wonderful offer for an adolescent who had spent the long day piloting an aerocycle.

I paid the price. Not until I sat down and read the little menu card on the table did I understand that there would be nothing to eat that did not include marshmallows.

Of course, that made me feel tremendously nostalgic.

"This is just like the Clam Fest back home!" I said to the person sitting next to me, a woman I guessed, carefully dressed as an evenly tanned marshmallow on a supple stick cut from a cherry tree. "Back home in Babbington, on Long Island, in New York. It's just like this!"

"Oh?" she said, with none of the fellow feeling I had hoped for. "How is it 'just like this'?"

"Well," I said, still hopeful, "you're celebrating marshmallows, and we celebrate clams."

Across the table, a man in a charred head murmured to a neighbor, "Good lord, why?"

"We have a big feast like this," I went on, trying to ignore the offense, "but instead of putting marshmallows in everything, we have clams in everything—clam chowder, clam fritters, clams casino—"

The woman gave me, as well as a woman in a marshmallow getup can, a look simultaneously incredulous and dismissive. "Toasted clams?" she inquired icily.

"What?" I said.

"I was just thinking that since your Clam Fest is *just like* our Marshmallow Festival you must put clams on a stick and toast them over a campfire."

"No—of course not—we—"

"But certainly you put them in Jell-O, don't you?"

"No," I admitted.

"That would be really disgusting!" said the charred man. He sounded as if he might actually be ill, and I'll admit that the thought of clams in Jell-O makes me feel a little ill myself.

"I think that clams are disgusting any way you serve them!" said the charred man's companion.

This was an affront, and my first impulse was to respond in kind, to defend Babbington and its clams by attacking Mallowdale and its marshmallows. I looked at the plate of items I'd taken from the buffet, seeking inspiration there. For a moment, pride in Babbington and its esculent mollusk made me think of feigning revulsion to show these marshmallow boosters a thing or two, but the tidbits on my plate looked tasty to me. I sampled a marshmallow split open like a baked potato and stuffed with a scoop of peanut butter and found it good. I tried a melted marshmallow sandwiched between two golden crackers and found it even better. It wasn't long before I returned to the banquet table for another selection of the tasty treats. I was enjoying myself, just as I would have at the Clam Fest back home.

When we had finished eating, a hush began to settle over the crowd. People began shushing those who persisted in their conversations, poking their neighbors with their elbows, and nodding, sometimes even pointing, in the direction of the museum. Along with everyone else, I turned in that direction. There I saw a man standing at a lectern set in the middle of a table that ran along the rear of the museum, a table like all the others but distinguished by being set at a right angle to them and elevated a foot or so above them, and I realized with some excitement that I was about to hear an after-dinner speaker.

"This is another thing we have at the Clam Fest," I said, "an after-dinner speaker. Usually, it's the mayor. He spoke at the gathering on Main Street when I started my trip, too—just a few words, but—"

"Shhh," said my tablemates in chorus.

"We have gathered here today," the speaker began, "as we do every year at this time, to celebrate the roots of Mallowdale."

This opening was greeted with universal chuckling. Even I chuckled. Chuckling can be contagious.

"But seriously, we are quite literally celebrating the roots that give us the plump little confection that has made us what we are, the community we are, the neighbors we are, the people we are: we are celebrating the roots of the marsh mallow, the mallow that grows in our marshes. And we are here to listen to a story."

The hush grew deeper as the audience settled into the drowsy quietude that follows a big meal, even one with as much sugar as the one we had consumed, and accepted the pleasant invitation to return to the childhood habit of listening to a story.

"It is a story that begins with the couple we know as Ma and Pa Mallow, though their true names have been lost to history. Of course, when I attended these festivals with my family, when I was just a nipper, the story was about Mother and Father Mallow, but these are more relaxed times, so they have become Ma and Pa, and children—like those who are running around at the back of the crowd apparently beyond the control of their parents or guardians—are permitted a degree of disrespect that would have earned them a good hiding in my day."

He paused, and a number of embarrassed parents scurried to the back of the crowd to gather their children.

When the children were settled to his satisfaction, he continued. "Ma and Pa were out walking in the marshes one day, long ago, before any of us were born, sometime early in the last century, when our country was still young, younger than many of the people who lived in it, younger than Ma and Pa Mallow themselves. And it was much, much younger than the marshes."

"Which it still is and always will be," muttered a dark-haired girl in a chic marshmallow beret and a slim bamboo-stick shift. I looked in her direction, and her lips formed for the briefest of moments a trace of a mischievous smile.

"Ma and Pa almost certainly did not know that the Mallowdale salt marshes are what geologists call an anomaly. They didn't know that inland salt marshes like ours are so rare as to be almost unheard of. The few that exist, including one in the aptly named town of Saltville, Virginia, are spring-fed, and their springs originate in vast caverns of salt."

"I'd like to see those caverns someday," muttered the dark-haired girl.

"I certainly hope you are not questioning the veracity or accuracy of this account," said a stern voice from inside a charred marshmallow head below which the point of a carefully trimmed gray beard projected.

The dark-haired girl frowned slightly and shook her head, just barely.

"On this day, Ma and Pa weren't walking in the marshes for pleasure," the speaker asserted. "They weren't out for a stroll to look at the scenery. Ma and Pa had fallen on hard times. They were hungry, and they were searching for food. They were probably after meat, perhaps a water rat or a snake, but they didn't find anything so substantial, not that day. In desperation they were driven to pull the weeds that grew around them."

He paused for effect.

"And they pulled the mallow."

He paused again. The dark-haired girl rolled her eyes.

"They pulled the mallow!" the speaker almost shouted. "Why? Why did they pull the mallow? Why that plant? Perhaps there was an element of chance, of luck. It could be that they were attracted to the mallow by its delicate pink flowers. Perhaps they dislodged a mallow plant accidentally. Maybe they tripped over a plant, or snagged one on a crude boot, exposing its thick pale yellow root, and making them wonder whether, like the root of the carrot or the rutabaga, it was edible."

"The rutabaga is just barely edible, if you ask me," whispered the dark-haired girl, and she was whispering to me.

"We know many things about the mallow that Ma and Pa did not know. For one thing, we know that the mallow plants they found in the salty water of the Mallowdale marshes were immigrants. They were probably the descendants of stowaways, seeds that had traveled from the old world to the new world, possibly clinging to the shoes of a human immigrant, maybe also a stowaway."

"That's an interesting idea—" said the dark-haired girl.

I nodded in agreement. A low chorus of shushing arose around us.

"Ma and Pa didn't know that. Nor did they know that the roots of the mallow plant had been eaten for centuries in the fabled lands of Asia and Arabia, that the food they were about to prepare and eat had once been reserved for the pharaohs of ancient Egypt, and forbidden to poor folk like Ma and Pa Mallow."

"I'd like to know how he knows what they didn't know," muttered the girl, right into my ear. Her warm breath tickled and thrilled me.

"That evening, they ate the mallow root," the speaker said, dropping his voice to underscore the import of that momentous occurrence. "We don't know how they prepared it, and we might ask ourselves about that, but there is a more interesting question: why did they eat it at all? Perhaps they already knew, from a friend or neighbor, that they could eat the roots of the plant, but if that was the case, then we must ask the same question of those friends or neighbors, and we can continue asking the question as far back in time as we care to travel, but still we must come to the first eaters of mallow root and ask why they ate it. As somebody said, 'It was a brave man who first ate an oyster.'"

"Or a clam," said the charred marshmallow with the stern voice.

"What if they were poison?" whispered a slight woman to her slight companion. Her pale marshmallow head seemed to wear a furrowed brow.

"Clams aren't poison," I said, annoyed by the suggestion.

The charred marshmallow raised an admonitory finger to the area of his head that I supposed hid his pursed lips.

"Necessity, we are told, is the mother of invention, and such was the case with Ma and Pa. They were driven by expediency, by their desperate hunger, to experiment. Their need was so great that they would have tried eating *anything* that they could harvest from the marshes. For whatever reason, they pulled as many of the mallow plants as they could carry, took them home, and prepared a humble dinner from their roots."

"They could have died in agony," the worried woman pointed out, glancing to her right and left for some support.

The shushing became insistent.

"From the desperate eating of the mallow root to the leisurely enjoyment of the puffy confection we know today is a long journey and a long story, a story that takes humankind from subsistence to luxury."

"Let's hope we're not going to make that journey," whispered the dark-haired girl.

"Where did the idea for the marshmallow confection come from? Or, to put that question in another, more far-reaching and profound way, what are the roots of human ingenuity? What insight inspires an invention? These are things we do not know, and perhaps never will know. They are part of 'The Riddle of the Marshmallow'—which just happens to be the title of the series of lectures I will be delivering on Wednesday evenings over the next six weeks, right here at the Marshmallow Museum. Tickets are going fast, but there are still places available. You will find the fee modest, and you can sign up—"

"I just think Ma and Pa were very, very brave," said the worried woman with the furrowed marshmallow brow.

No one bothered shushing her. Most of the people at our table—and at the others—were pushing their chairs back, rising, and making their way toward the exits.

I allowed myself to be moved by the crowd as it made its way toward the nearest exit. The dark-haired girl was in the section of the crowd that I was in, tantalizingly near but too distant for conversation. I would have had to shout to her. The flow of the crowd carried her little by little farther away, until I lost sight of her and I despaired of ever seeing her again. Making my way toward the exit, I grew increasingly depressed by the loss of the dark-haired girl and the thought that I had nowhere to stay for the night and might have a tough time finding a place in a community where I was so obviously an outsider. I began examining the crowd, searching for someone who looked accommodating.

"Excuse me—"

Miracle of miracles, it was the dark-haired girl, at my side, touching my sleeve.

"Oh, I'm sorry," she said. "I didn't mean to startle you."

"You didn't! I mean, well, you did, but I'm glad you did. I mean you surprised me, but it's a nice surprise—"

"You showed them a thing or two back there."

"I did?"

"You certainly did. You gave them a lesson in humility—and a lesson in generosity."

"I did?"

"Don't be so modest. You know you did. I think they treated you abominably."

"Well—"

"I felt as if I could actually see into your mind, and your heart, when you said that the Marshmallow Festival was just like the Clams and Oysters Festival—"

"It's—it's—Clam Fest—"

"—and I could feel your loneliness, the terrible isolation of an outsider in an alien culture, clinging for consolation to familiar rituals and customs, yet at the same time trying desperately to ingratiate yourself with the people around you by demonstrating that you had something in common with them, a culture of festivals and a reverence for local produce, for the harvest, a fondness for regional cuisine, and civic pride. But they rejected you, rejected your home town, your local comestible, everything you hold dear."

"Not everything—"

"I thought it was wonderful, really admirable, the way you held back, the way you restrained yourself from commenting on the food on your plate. You might have asserted the superiority of your home town, its customs and its cuisine, but you chose not to, you decided—or you knew—that it wasn't necessary. I thought that was fine and funny."

"Funny?"

"Yes."

"Why funny?"

"I'm not sure," she said. "You just seem funny to me. Of course, I recognize that the sense of humor, so called, varies enormously from one person to another, and that someone else might not think you were funny, but you just seem funny to me."

Before I could respond, she had bestowed upon me a parting smile and was gone, lost again in the moving crowd.

I spent the night in jail. It was a first for me, but there isn't much to say about it. After wandering around for a while, stopping *Spirit* when I saw a likely house, and knocking on the door to ask if I might spend the night, I was accosted by an officer of the Mallowdale police. He informed me that I had been alarming the citizens, which was a misdemeanor in Mallowdale. I explained my situation. He offered the collective hospitality of the community in place of the individual hospitality of any of its members. I hesitated, because I had hoped that chance might lead me to the door of the dark-haired girl, where I would be welcomed. He noticed my hesitation and offered the alternative of getting out of town "toot-sweet." I chose a night in jail.

After a meager breakfast of oatmeal and weak coffee the next morning, I was escorted outside. I recognized the signs: the sheriff, or whoever he was, intended to have a private word with me, to give me a word to the wise. I was right.

"Son—" he began, "I think you know what I'm going to say."

"I do?"

"I would hope so," he said. "A fellow gets some time to think when he's spending the night in a jail cell, and I hope that you used that time to come to realize what a little egotist you were when you drove that weird motorcycle into town."

"Piloted."

"Don't interrupt me, son."

"It's just that I was piloting, not driving. And it's an aerocycle, not a motorcycle. It's got wings, and—"

"Perhaps you're interrupting me to demonstrate that you're still the wretched little egotist you were when you rode into town?"

"No, sir. I mean, yes, sir. I think."

"You know that I'm right, don't you?"

"Well," I said, hanging my head, "the truth is that when I saw that bright banner strung across Main Street, I thought that it might be a message of welcome for me."

"You don't say."

"I do say—but of course I was wrong."

"And during that night of introspection in my jail, did you discover anything about yourself and your mistake?"

"Oh, yes. Definitely. I did."

"What?"

"I—well—"

"I would hope you discovered that a readiness to perceive the state of things as pertaining specifically to ourselves is one of the ways in which our senses are often deceived. I would hope you discovered that when we have insufficient data to know what is actually the case, we interpret the data that we have in a way that suits our predilections: optimists see good news; pessimists see bad news; the timid see danger; and a nostalgic booster such as yourself is apt to see in a crowd of strangers the eager ears of friends-to-be who want to listen to him describe each and every little detail about his humble home town and its queer customs. I would hope you discovered that, although we are all egotists to one degree or another, you have been an egotist to too great a degree. And I would hope that you discovered the desire and the will to control the tendency."

"That was pretty much it," I said.

EGOISTS AND EGOTISTS

••

EGOTIST, *n.* A person of low taste, more interested in himself than in me.
—Ambrose Bierce, *The Devil's Dictionary*

LITTLE BY LITTLE, as we motored along, avoiding the highway like good little shunpikers, enjoying the day and the air, I began to get an impression of chocolate. It began with a pleasant but elusive scent of chocolate, then thickened to a conviction that there was chocolate around somewhere, then thickened further until I thought that the air was filling with chocolate, then further still until I began to expect that a river of chocolate might come flowing down the road toward us like the river of porridge that had inundated an unfortunate village in "The Porridge Pot," one of the tales in *The Little Folks' Big Book,* the favorite book of my childhood.

"Call me crazy," I said, "but I think there's chocolate around here somewhere, lots of it."

"If you had been navigating as you are supposed to be, checking a map now and then, you would know that the next stop on our tour is Hershey, Pennsylvania."

"Watch out for chocolate, then," I said.

"Recent studies indicate that chocolate lowers one's blood pressure," Albertine asserted. "We are allowed to welcome it into our lives again. Chocolate is our friend."

"Not if it comes sweeping down upon you in a rushing river."

"Like porridge?"

"Yes! Did you read that story when you were a girl?"

"I think so. Or you told me about it."

"Hmm. Could be either. Our lives have come to overlap in so many ways, so thoroughly and completely, that we sometimes think we share even those parts of our past that we know we do not."

"But you cheat. You keep increasing that overlap artificially, pretending that you knew me before you actually did."

"Are you talking about those sweet and innocent days when we used to play together in the snows of Dayton, Ohio?"

"Yes, I am."

"When you were just a girl?"

"Yes."

"And I used to invent games that involved wrestling?"

"That's right."

"So that I could get you horizontal, wrap my little self around your little self, and bring us both to a state of bliss that our adult supervisors assumed we knew nothing about?"

"Exactly. Do you think there's a place around here where we could stop and make love?"

There was. There always is, Reader, if you look hard enough and are willing to make do.

Over cocktails that evening, in the hotel bar, Albertine paid me the compliment of saying, "I thought you displayed a really admirable degree of self-control back there in Mallowdale, not only at the marshmallow feast, but during the good talking-to that the sheriff gave you."

"Did you? Thanks."

"Unless you were hoping that the dark-haired girl had slipped out of her house in the morning to watch the birdboy take off and was lurking somewhere nearby, listening, and it was all a performance for her."

"It may have been," I admitted, "or it may have been a performance for the dark-haired girl at the wheel of the Electro-Flyer."

"I should hope it was."

A couple was sitting next to us at the bar, twitching with eagerness to add their two cents to our conversation, looking for some opening in which to insert themselves. (If you are part of a couple in love, Reader, you know what was happening. You have probably found it happening to you. It's a consequence of being in love. Couples who are not as much in love, or no longer as much in love, hope to inhale a bit of your happy state by insinuating themselves into your conversation. They expect to conceal the inhalation in the intervals between chatter, when they might seem merely to be pausing, catching their breath before the next utterance—but you know what they're up to, don't you?)

"Speaking of chocolate—" I said.

"That seems so long ago," said Albertine.

"Do you remember a function at the Boston Athenæum that featured a huge wheel or block of chocolate, or maybe it was several huge wheels or blocks of various types of chocolate, chaperoned by a charming Belgian who was offering very generous samples while enumerating its virtues and explaining its provenance?"

"Yes, I do. As I recall, it was an all-you-care-to-eat situation."

"I think you're right."

"So do I. Mmm."

"Do you also remember the way everyone who sampled it claimed an international history of experiences with chocolate, each of those experiences superior to the one we were having at the moment?"

"I do! I do! In fact, I recall that some people disdained to sample the chocolate at all, on the grounds that it couldn't possibly be up to their standards."

"Which they could tell merely by looking at it."

"Right!"

"It was a splendid display of egotism, the best I've ever seen."

"Egotism or egoism?" she asked.

"Mm?"

"You said it was a splendid display of egotism."

"Yes."

"But was it egotism or egoism?"

"I wonder, now that you ask."

"I know that in general use they both vaguely mean the same thing, but I'd like to know—"

Seeing his opening at last, the man in the couple beside us said, "I couldn't help overhearing. I think I can enlighten you a bit on the subject of egoism and egotism, if you will permit me." Without permission, he proceeded. "The older of the two terms is *egoism*, the sin of the egoist. It's a borrowing from the French *égoïsme*, from which *égoïste* is derived. The usual translation for that original term *égoïste* is 'one who thinks,' but I personally think that a more accurate expression of the idea behind the term as it was originally intended would be 'one who knows that he thinks,' that is, a conscious being."

"Ah!" I said. "You must be a relative of Angus MacPherson, my French teacher back at Babbington High quite a few years ago."

"No, I don't think so. I—"

"He's just kidding," said Albertine. "He's a card-carrying member of the Heartsick American Humorists' Association."

"Oh," the man said, with a slackness in his tone that said, simply but unmistakably, that however highly the rest of the world might esteem such status, he was unimpressed. "Well, the term *egotist* seems to have been coined by Joseph Addison, the essayist, to identify what he considered to be an annoying rhetorical style characterized by the too-frequent use of the first-person singular pronoun."

"Aye-yi-yi," I said.

"I always tell myself to use the *t* to remind myself of the difference between *egoist* and *egotist*," the woman informed us. "Someone told me to do that long ago—but for the life of me I can't remember who it was."

"It was I, my dear," said the man.

"Was it? I don't think it was."

"I assure you that it was."

"Regardless of who it was who told me to do so—and I doubt very much that it was you—I remind myself that the *t* stands for *talking*."

"I think you're getting ahead of yourself, dear," said her companion, with the appearance of good humor. "I think we've got to begin with a couple of definitions."

"Do you," she said icily.

"Yes, I do," he snapped. Then, to us, or perhaps to the room at large, he announced, "An egoist is a person who is guided by the principle of 'me first.'"

"I find that it applies in every circumstance, at every turn, whenever a choice must be made," the woman added.

"That was implied in my definition," her companion asserted.

"I had no way of knowing that," she asserted right back at him. To us she said, "I feel that I must point out that the principle of 'me first' is not quite the same as 'me only.'"

"Of course not," the man said with a sneer. "'Me only' is the solipsist's principle. For the solipsist, the notion of 'me first' is utterly superfluous."

"When you talk, all I hear is blah, blah, blah," she said.

"I wonder where the fault lies," he growled.

"What's your other definition?" asked Albertine with the subtlety of a diplomatist. "The definition of *egotist*?"

"An egotist is someone who is always talking about himself," said the woman.

"Or herself," the man suggested.

"I always remember the *t*," the woman said, almost wistfully, as if she were recalling a particularly poignant moment when she had used the *t* to remind herself of the difference between the words, sometime in the past, in other circumstances, in other company.

"I think a person can be an egoist and not realize it, don't you?" asked Albertine, intending a kindness, I think, drawing the woman back into our foursome. "There's a kind of egoism that is unthinking or passive."

"Yes," I said, doing my bit. "There's a kind of egoist who doesn't even consider other people and their needs, feelings, and desires."

"In fact," said Albertine, "I think that that kind of neglectful egoism is the most widespread, and the people who practice it are the egoists who are least likely to recognize their egoism."

"Could be," admitted the man. "Or else they're dissembling; they aren't quite assertive enough to put themselves first, but they are egoistical enough to be blind to the needs and rights of others—or deliberately to blind themselves to those needs and rights."

I began to wish that they would go away. I'd had enough of them. I wanted to be alone with Albertine. We two. Just we two. We two against the world, the whole yammering, battering, self-centered world.

"But if one's neglectful egoism, as you put it, is genuine," he went on, "it may be the worst kind of egoism. It's the kind that considers other people beneath contempt. What they think, what they do, what they feel, what becomes of them is simply of no interest whatsoever."

"My grandmother warned me against that," said the woman, with, again, that note of wistfulness.

"What?" he demanded of her.

"What you said," she said, from a distance.

"I said quite a number of things—"

"Must an egotist be an egoist first?" Albertine asked quickly, touching the arm of the distant woman. "Or can a person be an egotist without being an egoist?"

The woman didn't answer. Instead, with that odd distance still in her voice, she said, "I try to remind myself that talking must also be interpreted figuratively. It stands for many other ways of drawing attention to oneself or putting oneself forward." Then, suddenly bridging the distance, she squealed, "Oh! Don't get me started on the way my sister used to hog the camera when Uncle Jerry took those nudes of us in his 'studio'!"

Just to show that I was still in the game, I responded to Albertine's question with one of my own. "Must an egoist be an egotist or necessarily become one?" I asked. "Can one be an egoist without advertising it through egotism?"

"Oh, yes," said Albertine. "We saw it there at the Athenæum. The egotists were continually talking about their experiences with chocolate, demonstrating their superiority and the superiority of their experiences, while the egoists were quietly consuming all the chocolate they could get."

The distance had returned to the woman's voice when she said, "I think the saddest type of egotist is the one who is always telling you, or anyone she can find to listen, what she intends to do, because she doesn't have anything that she actually *has* done to brag about."

"Talking about the superb chocolate she intends to eat when she takes that tasting tour through Belgium, France, and Switzerland," said Albertine. A note of wistful distance had come into her voice, too, so I took her by the hand and led her away from all that.

As soon as we were in our room, Albertine looked through all the drawers in our bedside tables, and then picked up the phone. "Front desk?" she said cheerily. "This is room four forty-five. There's no dictionary in our room. I think it might have been stolen. . . . What do you mean, you don't put dictionaries in the rooms? There's a Bible here. There ought to be a dictionary. All the better caravansaries supply them, I'd like to think. . . . Well, let me speak to the concierge. . . . Thank you." A moment passed, then she said, "This is room four forty-five. I need to know everything you can tell me about *egoist* and *egotist*. . . . No, they're not a band. They're words. . . . That's what I said: words. . . . I've just been talking to some people in your cocktail lounge, and I want to verify their assertions about them. I would have looked them up myself, but there's no dictionary in our room. If you would check the *OED* for me, I'd be very grateful. . . . What? . . . You're kidding. . . . Well, what's a concierge for, I'd like to know." She put her hand over the mouthpiece and said, "This is quite a hotel."

"Ask him to connect you to room service," I said. "I'm starving."

In the morning, when we were checking out, the couple we had met in the bar were also checking out. We exchanged pleasantries. After that, we stood in awkward silence. Then, inspired by the memory of my earlier trip, I broke the silence.

"Albertine and I are re-creating a cross-country trip that I made when I was a teenager," I said. "On that earlier trip, nearly every morning, someone in the town where I had stopped for the night would take me aside and offer me a bit of advice before I got back onto the road and resumed my travels. Would you care to participate in the re-creation of that trip by offering me a bit of matutinal advice?"

"Us," said Albertine.

"Would you care to offer us a bit of advice?"

"I gave you my advice last night," said the woman. "I told you to remember the significance of that little *t*."

"Actually," I said, "that was more like advice to yourself. You said that *you* always tell yourself to remember the significance of the *t*. You didn't actually advise *us* to do that."

"Well, I'm advising you now," she said.

"And you?" I asked the man.

"Don't talk to strangers," he said, and he turned his attention to the clerk.

When we were back in the car and on our way out of the parking lot, while we were paused for a moment, waiting for a break in the traffic, it took only a look to elicit the morning's advice from Albertine: "If they're giving out samples of chocolate, take all that you care to eat."

"Not all that you can eat?" I asked.

"No, no. You don't need a river of chocolate. Enough is enough."

244 · PETER LEROY

FRONTIER JUSTICE

· ·

WHEN WE WERE on the road again, *Spirit* coughed once to get my attention, then cleared her throat and asked, "'Piloted'?"

"What do you mean?" I asked, though I knew perfectly well.

"I very distinctly heard you tell the sheriff back there in Mallowdale that you 'piloted' your aerocycle into town."

I guess I was running out of patience with her. I pulled her to the side of the road, set her on her kickstand, took my copy of *Elements of Aeronautics* from the little luggage bin where it lay beside *Gestes et Opinions du Docteur Faustroll,* found the relevant passage, and read it to her:

> *Piloting,* as a general term, means merely steering a vessel or flying an airplane. The term *piloting* has been used technically, however, to denote the kind of navigating one does in getting to one's destination with the help of a chart or map; by following a highway, railroad, transmission line, river, or other such course; or by flying from one landmark to another which can be seen, as flying first to a mountain, then to a lake which can be seen from the mountain, then to a city which can be seen from the lake, and so on. Piloting as a method of keeping track of one's position and of getting to one's destination hardly needs comment as a science. It is like finding one's way by map while motoring.

"Or like finding one's way without a map while motoring," I said triumphantly. I stowed the book, mounted *Spirit,* and roared onto the road again.

"Just a minute! There is nothing in there that says that piloting *is* motoring, only that it is *like* motoring."

We might have continued in good-natured contention along those lines for some time, but we were interrupted.

Red light swept across *Spirit*'s wings, light from an old bubble-top cop car, a light with revolving innards like those of a lighthouse, primarily a mechanical device, not unlike the revolving light that I had made from a camper's lantern and an old windup record player years earlier, back in Babbington, back at home, for a game.

After I saw the light, I heard the siren, just a short burst or signal, a whine, briefly rising, quickly falling, to let me know that I was the object of the cop's interest, to tell me to pull over. I did. I twisted on my seat, and looked toward the rear, into the headlights. The car was black and white, clean, shiny. The cop, when he got out and walked toward me in the light, looked clean and shiny, too. He wore high boots, gleaming black.

"What kind of contraption is this?" he asked, examining *Spirit* with exaggerated contempt.

"It's an aerocycle," I said. "I built it myself."

He eyed me suspiciously.

"With help," I admitted, cracking under the force of his professional skepticism.

"You're going to have to see Judge Whitley," he said.

"Judge Whitley?" I asked, struggling to calm my twitching lips.

"That's what I said."

"That's an interesting coincidence."

"Oh, yeah?"

"Yes," I said, trying to smooth the waters. "You see, there was a Mayor Whitley in my home town. There have been several of them, in fact."

"You're probably making that up to try to get friendly," he said.

"No, honest," I said, as friendly as can be, "Mayor Whitley, Andy Whitley—"

"It's no use, kid. Judge Whitley has warned me against taking the statements of a prisoner at face value."

"A prisoner?"

"I'm going to lead the way to Judge Whitley, and you're going to follow me."

"Am I under arrest?"

"Just follow me—and don't try any funny business."

"Yes, sir."

He returned to his car, got in, and pulled slowly ahead of me. I started *Spirit* and followed, following him, following orders.

"Wow," I whispered to *Spirit*. "We're under arrest."

"You sound pleased by the idea."

"I may be. I'm not quite sure. I've already experienced my first road-block, and my first night in jail, and now I'm experiencing my first arrest. It's a momentous occurrence."

"Try to control yourself."

"I will, I will."

"And don't try any funny business."

"I won't, I won't."

I expected to be taken to City Hall. To be completely truthful, I expected to be taken to the Supreme Court building, if they had one in town. I expected the full treatment, and I expected to get it in a building with columns and a pediment and a Latin slogan chiseled in granite. Instead, the building that the cop led me to looked like a bar.

"It looks like a bar," I said to *Spirit.*

"It is a bar," she said, "judging from the sign that says 'Judge Whitley's Bar and Grill.'"

"It's not even chiseled in granite," I grumbled.

Judge Whitley's was a smoky den. The bar itself ran more than half the length of the narrow room, along the right side. Booths lined the left wall.

We entered and began slowly walking toward the back. The daytime drinkers and chatterers took note of the boy being urged along by the cop, but only in the most desultory way. Their heads turned, but then they lost interest. I had the impression, and recollection gives me no reason to change it, that the men in the bar were doing business of one kind or another, that a lot of business was being done there, that a lot of business got done there. I think that the experience of seeing all those smoking, drinking men bent to their business has stayed with me all these years, forever coloring my impression of—and my opinion of—the kind of business that involves meetings and deals: it made me feel that there was something furtive and dirty and dark about it. It was best done, if done at all, in hiding. And it was so distasteful, so bitter a pill to swallow, that it required liquor to get it down. I could see that it wasn't anything I wanted to be involved in.

In the rearmost area of the bar, in the left rear corner, there was one large booth with a round table. Seated there, on the far side of the table, in the deepest, darkest corner of the bar, was a large, florid man, smoking a cigar and squinting through his own smoke as he watched me approach. His size; his position; the lackeys who sat on either side of him; the sense that the others in the bar were there to speak to him, that they were supplicants waiting their turn, waiting to be called to an audience at the round table; the ambience of smoke and awe—all of that made me understand that this must be Judge Whitley, the big man, the guy who called the shots in Coincidence, Pennsylvania.

"What's this?" asked one of the lackeys, meaning me.

"Kid," said the cop. In his voice I detected deference—and concern. I understood that if he did or said the wrong thing it would not go well for him.

"I see that," snarled the lackey. "Whadja bring 'im here for?"

The cop looked at me. His eyes welled with regret. Clearly, he considered me one of his mistakes. He would have been better off if he had just sent me on my way, and he knew it. I gave him a reciprocal look. I felt sorry for him. I felt sorry for both of us. We were looking big trouble in the face, through a cloud of cigar smoke.

"Driving a motorcycle without a license," mumbled the cop, his eyes down.

"You got a license, kid?" asked the lackey.

"No, sir."

"And were you driving a motorcycle?"

"No, sir." I glanced at the cop, hoping he would detect the note of apology in my glance. I was sorry to contradict him, but if one of us was going down, it wasn't going to be me.

"You weren't driving a motorcycle?"

"No, sir. I was piloting an aerocycle."

"A what?"

"An aerocycle. It's a flying machine."

"An airplane?"

"Oh, no. No. Not an airplane. I'd need a pilot's license for that." I tried laughing, but what came out of me couldn't really be called a laugh, and it had none of the infectious quality that laughter ought to have.

"Are you trying to be funny?"

"Yes, sir," I admitted.

"This is no laughing matter."

"I was just trying to ease the tension."

Everyone found that funny, no one more so than the judge. From that response, and from the memory of that response, which has returned to me unbidden from time to time over the years, I learned that you never can tell what people will find funny.

"If I could go out to *Spirit,* sir—"

"You trying to be funny again?" the other underling asked.

"No, sir. Not this time."

"'Go out to spirit,' what is that, some kind of religious thing?"

"No, sir. *Spirit* is my aerocycle. That's her name."

"Oh, I see," said the judge, speaking for the first time. "You would like to go outside to your airplane—excuse me, your aerocycle—*Spirit.* Is that it?"

"Yes. If I could just—"

"If you could just go out to *Spirit,* hop on board, and fly away, leaving us sitting here like a bunch of rubes, asking ourselves how we could have been so stupid as to let you go out to *Spirit,* when it should have been obvious that you were trying to escape, everything would be just swell, am I right?"

"No, sir! Honest! I wanted to get a book—"

"I knew it was a religious thing," said the second lackey. "There's always a book, *the* book."

"This book is—"

"This book is the truth, I suppose."

"Well, I think so."

My intention, as you will have guessed, was to use the passage on piloting from *Elements of Aeronautics* to convince Judge Whitley to release me on a technicality. "If I could just—"

I wanted to assert myself, and to assert the authority of Pope and Otis, but my throat was thick and my eyes were moistening, and I thought it wise to say nothing for a while.

The judge waited, and while he waited he stared hard at me, and then he snorted and said, "Officer Lockwood, you go get the good book."

"Yes, sir."

"It's in the small baggage compartment behind the seat," I explained. "Just twist the handle and you can open the door."

Of course Officer Lockwood brought the wrong book. Instead of

Pope and Otis, he brought my copy of *Gestes et Opinions du Docteur Faustroll*. When he dropped *Faustroll* in the center of the table, I thought I was doomed.

Everyone looked at the book. Then everyone looked at me. Then everyone looked at one another. Then everyone looked at Judge Whitley. Then Judge Whitley looked at me.

"Let's go outside, boy," he said, lifting himself up from his corner seat and occasioning a rapid shuffling of the underlings to give him passage from the booth.

He conducted me outside. The others must have known by his manner that they were not to follow. If you have ever been in a similar situation, you will know that I expected to be shot in the back of the head and dumped in a ditch.

Instead, he walked around *Spirit* a couple of times and then said slowly, deliberately, raising the book, raising his considerable eyebrows, "So you are one of the chosen few."

"Well—" I said, with a shrug, since I didn't know what he was talking about.

"You have sailed in the doctor's boat, across the Squitty Sea?" he asked, in a voice that I might have described as envious if it hadn't come from him.

"Um—I have done some sailing—"

"You have sojourned in the Land of Lace?"

"My great-grandmother was very fond of antimacassars—"

"And you have dallied in the Forest of Love?"

"Well—I don't want to brag—"

"You have spent the night in the Castle-Errant."

I caught the shift in his tone, a shift away from interrogation, but I wasn't sure how to respond to it. "Um—" I said, stalling, "—not yet."

"You have ascended the great staircase of black marble, felt the surge of the land-tide, and heard the musical jet!"

He was no longer asking me what I had done; he was telling me that he knew what I had done, even if I hadn't. I smiled noncommittally.

"You are a congregant of the Great Church of Snoutfigs!"

To my knowledge, I was not, but I wasn't about to contradict him.

"And you know the meaning of the words *ha-ha* as spoken by Bosse-de-Nage!"

At last I felt on firm ground. Boldly, confidently, with a comradely wink, I asked, "Are you trying to be funny?"

For a few horrible moments, I thought I had ruined everything. Then, at last, he said, as if he were passing sentence, "Ha-ha."

I said, "Ha-ha."

He said, "You'd better be on your way."

I was stunned. I was also a little disappointed. "You mean you're not going to throw me into the hoosegow?"

"No," he said. "I wouldn't want to stand in the way of the adventures of a young Panmuphle."

Panmuphle? Did he mean Panmuphle, the bumbling bailiff from *Faustroll*? Did all that nonsense about the Squishy Sea and the Forest of Lace and the Castle of Love have something to do with *Faustroll*? Maybe. Maybe all of that was in the parts I hadn't read yet.

"Before you go on your way, though," he said, "I'd like to give you a few words of advice."

Of course.

"Listen, son, I want to give you a warning, a word to the wise."

"Yes, sir," I said, trying to appear interested.

He took the cigar from his mouth. His hand was trembling. He waved the book at me and said, "You don't want to go waving this book around. People are going to take it the wrong way. They—they—they—"

For quite a while, he didn't say anything. Then he said, holding the book in front of him, "This kind of thing can get you into trouble. I think it would be best if I held on to it for you, kept it in protective custody, kept it in my custody for your protection. Do you have any objections to that?"

I had objections. It wasn't my book, for one thing. It belonged to my French teacher, Mr. MacPherson, and I was sure that he expected me to return it when the summer was over. For another thing, I had promised to translate it. How was I going to translate it if I didn't have it?

"Well?" he prodded.

"I don't have any objections," I lied.

"You're lying, aren't you?" he said.

"Yes."

He grinned. He handed the book to me.

"Keep it out of sight," he counseled.

"Okay. Thanks."

"You got any other subversive literature?"

"No," I lied again.

He gave me a long look. He snorted. He spat on the ground. Then he gesticulated with his cigar hand in the direction of *Spirit*. Gratefully, I mounted her and started her.

"Goodbye," I said.

"Ha-ha," he said.

CAUGHT

· ·

WE WERE CAUGHT in a pack, somewhere east of Friendsville, Maryland. We had been trapped in the pack long enough to get to know its cars and drivers. Ahead of us were the thoughtless, the witless, the thankless, clueless, and careless. Beside us were the blameless, harmless, and aimless. Behind us were the loveless, helpless, luckless, useless, and inconsolable. We felt boxed in, hemmed in, confined, imprisoned, as if society, symbolized or personified by the two dozen examples clotted around us on the highway, moving in lockstep, had decided to deny us our individuality, the full expression of our unique being, the opportunity to be all that we could be, a shot at the open road. We were impatient. They were inescapable.

I was on the verge of entertaining Albertine by expatiating along the foregoing lines when—eloquently, briefly, precisely—she rendered it superfluous.

"People!" she cried.

They couldn't have heard her, but they seemed to. Something disturbed the field. A bit of separation occurred, a space where there had been none, and the space began to grow as if it held within it an expansive force.

"Ooh, ooh, ooh," said Albertine, with undiminished eloquence.

The gap grew until it became an opportunity. Albertine rushed into it, through it, and into the open, out of the pack, free of the pack, ahead of the pack, in the clear, and climbing a long, gentle hill. Our Electro-Flyer hummed and sang. She howled with the pleasure of release, and her willing motor wound. We crested the hill at exhilarating, electro-flying speed—and there, on the other side of the hill, a couple of hundred yards ahead of us, was a police car. Standing beside it was a cop, holding a radar gun. Even at that distance I could see him grin when he glanced up from the radar readout to see us coming at him.

"Oh, shit," said Albertine, a woman who has her way with words.

She slowed, and she pulled over, just ahead of the cop car.

I began staring at the side of the road, and I continued to stare at the side of the road throughout the cop's interview with Albertine, because I knew that if I looked at her or at the cop I would burst out laughing and at least one of them would ask me what I thought was so funny.

"License and registration, please," said the cop.

"Is something wrong, Officer?" Albertine asked. I could almost hear her lashes fluttering.

"Wrong?" he said. "Let me check. Hmm. Well, golly, you seem to have exceeded the speed limit by quite a bit."

"I did?"

"Lady, you came over the top of that hill airborne. I thought you were a low-flying plane."

"Maybe there's something wrong with my speedometer."

"That could be, or it could be that sunspot activity made my radar gun wildly inaccurate."

"I think you're being sarcastic, Officer."

"Really?"

"I can't have been going as fast as you say. This is an old car. Technically, it's an antique."

"An antique."

"Okay, a replica of an antique."

"For a replica of an old car it's quite spry."

"I suppose it is, but I don't think that I could have been speeding. After all, I was just keeping up with the pack."

"Miz—ah—Gaudette—here comes the pack now."

I allowed myself a glance in the mirror. He was right.

Albertine sighed. She must have glanced in the mirror, too.

There was a period of quiet. Then I heard the cop click his pen closed and tear a ticket from his pad.

"Let me give you some advice," he said.

I bit my lip.

"Yes, Officer?" said Albertine.

"Get a radar detector," said the cop.

His boots crunched away. The pack rumbled by. The cop got into his car and trundled off behind them. Albertine flipped the switch and pulled the Electro-Flyer onto the highway.

"Don't you worry, honey," she said, patting the dashboard. "We're going to take that advice."

"Ha-ha," I said.

REAL DINER COOKING

Life is what we make of it. Travel is the traveler. What we see isn't what we see but what we are.
—Fernando Pessoa as Bernardo Soares, *The Book of Disquiet*

CAN'T REMEMBER the name of the town. It was in West Virginia. I remember that. I also remember that the day's ride was a particularly pleasant one. I no longer had much hope that *Spirit* would lift me into the clear blue sky, but on that day I didn't particularly care whether she did or not. I was happy to roll along, feel the miles unroll beneath her wheels, watch the scenery slide by, and cover the day's distance.

In the evening, riding into the light of the setting sun, I began to feel tired and hungry, as usual, so when I saw the sign welcoming me to the place I'll call Forgettable, West Virginia, "America's Home Town," I decided to stop and spend the night.

Forgettable was an attractive little town. Though it was small, it seemed substantial and well established. Many of the buildings downtown were made of stone, including the handsome train station. All that stone impressed me. It suggested solidity, history, and permanence of an order beyond Babbington's. Forgettable seemed like Babbington's older brother, or a Babbington built by a wiser little pig, who knew that stone would resist a wolf's huffing and puffing better than wood could.

Just across the street from the train station, there was a diner called Vern's. A sign in the window boasted "Real Home Cooking." How could I resist? I was a long way from home. Real home cooking might shrink that distance, might make me feel at least for a while the comforts of the home that now lay far behind me.

The entrance to Vern's was in the middle of its long front wall. A number of booths stretched along that wall to the left and right, a long counter with stools ran the length of the diner opposite the entrance, and the kitchen was on the opposite side of the counter, exposed to the view of the patrons. The layout and general appearance reminded me of Porky White's clam bar and the Night-and-Day Diner, back home in Babbington. Vern's was working for me. I hadn't eaten a bite, but already the place was reminding me of home. However, something wasn't quite right. I wasn't feeling the comfort that I had hoped I would feel. Instead, as soon as I was reminded of Porky's and the Night-and-Day, I began to miss them—and their setting, my home town—even more.

Standing in the entrance, I looked around, and I saw many happy diners, people who clearly felt at home there, who knew that in this place they were in their place, just as many diners back at home must have felt at the same moment, and I felt more acutely the distance between Forgettable and Babbington, the place where I belonged, where I would have been at home. There at Vern's, hesitating in the entrance, I suddenly recognized that the crepuscular melancholy I felt every evening on the road wasn't caused by hunger or fatigue, or by the gathering darkness, but by displacement, the feeling of being out of the place where I belonged, so far from home, awkwardly placed in someone else's place, in someone else's home.

"Welcome to Vern's," said a weary waitress. "Sit yourself down."

Still I hesitated. I wasn't sure that I could take any more of Vern's. I thought of returning to the parking lot, mounting *Spirit*, and heading back to Babbington, but I reminded myself that I was an adventurer, and adventurers pressed on; they did not turn back, not even in their thoughts. I did what the waitress had told me to do. I sat on one of the stools at the counter.

I chose a stool that would give me no neighbors, out of shyness, I suppose, or maybe because I already suspected that Vern's real home cooking was going to make me feel miserable, so miserable that I wouldn't want anyone to notice.

The waitress tossed a menu in front of me, and I began to feel more uncomfortable as soon as I opened it. Listed on it were many of the dishes that my mother made at home, from Salisbury steak and meat loaf to macaroni and cheese. Instead of the comforting warmth of familiarity, the names of these dishes brought the chill of loneliness. I allowed myself to glance cautiously around the room. No one seemed to take any notice of me at all. Maybe it was going to be all right. I could eat, keep my feelings to myself, and go.

A man sitting a couple of stools away had a different idea.

"Where you from?" he asked, leaning toward me. He was, I think, about fifty. He was smoking. A coffee cup was on the counter in front of him. He hadn't shaved in a day or two. His hair was stringy.

"Babbington," I said.

"Never heard of it."

"That's okay."

"So you came to Vern's to get some real home cooking, did you?"

"I guess," I said. I really didn't want to talk to him.

"What's it going to be?" asked the waitress, pouring more coffee for the man with the stringy hair.

"I'm not sure," I said, and I discovered that although I didn't want to talk to him I did want to talk to her. "You've got a lot of things here that make me think of home," I told her, "back in Babbington." I waited, hoping for some response, but she just stood there. "He never heard of it," I said, jerking my head in the direction of the man with the stringy hair, who had now moved two stools to his left, making himself my neighbor. "Maybe you've heard of it?" I asked.

"Nope."

"It's the Clam Capital of America. Are you sure that you haven't heard of it?"

"Yep. What're you going to have?"

"I don't know. Salisbury steak, I guess."

"Baked potato or mashed?"

"My grandmother really likes Salisbury steak," I said, speaking almost automatically, giving voice to my yearning for home. "She almost always orders it when we go out to dinner—I mean if my grandparents—I used to call them Gumma and Guppa when I was a kid—if they go out to dinner with my parents and me—which doesn't happen a lot, but does happen when we're driving to West Burke for our summer vacation and we stop for dinner on the way—"

"Baked or mashed?"

"Strictly speaking," said my neighbor, "the so-called Salisbury steak is not steak at all. It's ground meat—and notice that I am careful not to say 'ground beef'—formed into a patty in the shape of a cut of beef-steak and covered with a brown gravy, usually containing mushrooms."

"I know," I said.

He looked at me steadily for a long moment. I could see him out of the corner of my eye, though I refused to look at him directly.

"Gravy covers a lot of sins, son," he said. He pulled the ashtray from his earlier location and stubbed his cigarette in it.

"You know," I said to the waitress, "I think maybe I'll have meat loaf instead."

"Now, meat loaf can be made of many things," said my neighbor.

"Leave the boy alone," said the waitress.

"My mom makes it out of hamburger," said my automatic voice. "You know, ground meat—ground beef. And she puts bread crumbs and onions in it—chopped onions—and I think she puts some tomato sauce in it, too—the kind that comes in those little cans—and an egg—and then she mushes it all up and puts it in a glass pan—or I guess you'd say a glass dish—"

"Okay," said the waitress. "Baked or mashed?"

"Baked—no—I—"

The man pointed a bony, slightly trembling finger at the entry for meat loaf on the menu and said, "Many things qualify as meat. During the Great Depression, many people ate horse meat, and they were glad to get it. Others ate horse meat and never knew they were getting it. Many a family around here was kept alive by a ready supply of squirrels. I can imagine a clever housewife discovering that she could grind squirrel meat and make an appetizing loaf out of it. She probably called it meat loaf."

"I'm sorry," I said to the waitress. "I'm going to have macaroni and cheese."

She and I both looked at the man beside me to see if he had any-thing to say about that. He did.

"There are many kinds of cheese," he said, shaking his head at the horrible prospect. "Some are better than others, some are worse than others, some smell like a pen full of goats, and some—such as the abomination called 'pasteurized process cheese food'—are offered to us under the name of cheese though they are hardly cheese at all. What a weaselly nomenclature that is! It practically sneers at you, 'I'm not cheese, you poor sap. I'm just cheesy.'"

With a sigh, the waitress asked, "Peas, carrots, or peas and carrots with that mac and cheese?"

"On second thought—" I said.

"Fourth thought," she said.

"Huh?"

"Fourth thought. Your first was Salisbury steak, your second meat loaf, then macaroni and cheese, so whatever you're thinking of now is your fourth thought."

"Oh, yeah. Fourth thought. Sorry. On fourth thought, I'm going to have fish cakes and spaghetti. Back at home, my mother makes that for Sunday-night supper. Not all the time, but pretty often."

"This isn't Sunday," the man pointed out.

"That's okay. I'm going to have fish cakes and spaghetti anyway."

"Does your mother make her own fish cakes?" he asked.

"Um, no," I said. "She gets them at the fish store. In Babbington." As I said that, Mortimer's Fresh Fish seemed to reconstruct itself within Vern's diner. I could have been there. "Sometimes I get them for her," I said. "If I'm going downtown on Sunday—to see my friend Raskol—or my grandparents—not the ones we go to West Burke with, but my other grandparents—my mother will ask me to get some fish cakes for dinner." One of Mr. Mortimer's cats rubbed against my leg, the way it did when I stood in front of the refrigerated case and waited for the fish cakes. "Mr. Mortimer has six cats," I said. "They're named for the days of the week. But there's no Monday. That's because he's closed on Monday."

"And have you seen how the fish cakes are made at the fish store?"

"No. They're in the case when I get there. I mean, they're already made."

I had to struggle to keep myself from reaching down to scratch Sunday behind the ears.

"It's hard to know what kind of fish is in a fish cake," the man was saying. "There are many fish in the sea, and many of those fish aren't very appetizing if you see them as they are, before they get chopped and mashed and mixed with crumbs and floor sweepings."

"I don't think Mr. Mortimer puts floor sweepings in the fish cakes," I said—or, to be truthful, snapped. "I don't think he *would* put floor sweepings in the fish cakes."

"There are also many parts to a fish, many parts that you might not want to eat. Some of them fish got fangs, you know, like snakes, and spit venom powerful enough to kill a man. Who knows what's hidden inside that cake?"

"Can I have pork chops?" I said to the waitress.

"Sure. Mashed potatoes and peas?"

"Fine," I said. I closed my menu.

"Now what exactly do you suppose she means when she says 'peas'?" the man wondered aloud.

"Oh, good grief," she said. She bent down and opened a door in a steel cabinet, reached in, and wrestled out a huge can, which she lifted up, then dropped onto the counter with a thud. "This is what she means," she said.

I reached out to it. I touched it. I turned it slowly, examining every side. The contents were, the back of the label declared, "Seeds of the variety of garden pea plant, *Pisum sativum,* known as Little Marvel, pre-cooked, packed in water, and canned by Troubled Titan Foods."

The lump in my throat was so large and thick that I could hardly speak.

"We have—we—at home—we have these at home," I managed at last. I couldn't possibly have told them all the memories that the Troubled Titan had packed into that can, but I was willing to try, if only I could blink the water from my eyes and swallow that lump in my throat.

"You have to wonder about the quality of the water they pack these in," said the man.

"Oh, Vern, shut up," said the waitress.

I got up and in a blur I made my way to the door.

"What's got into him?" I heard Vern ask as I pushed my way outside.

"You gave him indigestion before he even ate," said the waitress. "Why do you do that?"

"I don't know," said Vern. "There's just something about strangers that makes me—"

What it was about strangers that made Vern treat them as he did, I cannot say, because I let the door close behind me, ran to *Spirit*, kick-started her, and drove a couple of miles down the road, where I found a garage whose owner was willing to let me spend the night on an old sofa in his office. I dined on candy bars. I don't know what was in them. I threw the wrappers away without looking at the ingredients. I fell asleep trying to figure Vern out and scanning my memory of the people who had been sitting in the booths while Vern was toying with me to see if I could spot a dark-haired girl. I did, in the last booth to the right of the entrance, far from where I had been sitting. She seemed to be having dinner with her parents. I couldn't tell what she was eating.

SURPRISED AND DELIGHTED

Because a physical space in the world can always be returned to . . . we feel irrationally, somehow certain, impossibly certain, that we should be able to return again to some often unfinished relationship . . . back in the imagined inexistent space of the past.

—Julian Jaynes, *The Origin of Consciousness in the Breakdown of the Bicameral Mind*

ALBERTINE ANGLED ONTO the off-ramp. We could have been anywhere in the country where an interstate highway intersects a road that may be important, even essential, to locals, but is to the speeding interstate voyager useful only for the short stretch in either direction that is cluttered and clotted with franchise outlets and motorist services; we might even have begun reliving the night when we stayed in an It'll Do and met the egoists.

"I'm getting a strange sense of eye-eye-dee-vee," I said with a shiver.

"What's that?" she asked.

"Interstate intersection déjà vu."

"I see what you mean, but this time there will be no eye-dee-dee-vee, I promise you."

"What's that?"

"It'll Do déjà vu."

"You mean this time you are going to drive past all of this and take us to some cozy spot?"

"Well now, that little word *cozy* can mean different things to different people," she said, "and *spot* can cover a lot of sins."

"Wait a minute—" I muttered, inspired by her performance.

"What is it?"

"Well, it's odd, but—"

"What?"

"Your imitation of my imitation of Vern has me thinking how odd it is that we feel something like nostalgia for even our bad experiences."

"Do we?" she asked, in a manner that made it clear that she, for one, did not.

"Apparently *I* do," I said, "because all of a sudden I yearn to return to Vern's."

"You do?"

"I think so. Maybe."

I scanned the road ahead of us, looking for a place where we could conveniently stop so that I could consult a map in search of some congruity between the past and present that would show me where Vern's ought to be. I could have asked her to pull into any of the fast-food joints or any gas station, or even into the parking lot of one of the motels. There was no reason not to pick the first one that she could have pulled into without causing a multi-car pileup, but my keen eyes saw, some distance down the road, toward the edge of the clutter, a Kap'n Klam. (As I suppose you know if you have not isolated yourself from the culture entirely, the Kap'n Klam Family Restaurants, America's only all-bivalve dining choice, rival some of the hamburger and pizza franchises in their ubiquity. "We're your korner klam shack," is one of their slogans. Reading those words now, you can probably hear the catchy Kap'n Klam jingle, I'll bet.)

"Why don't you pull into that Kap'n Klam?" I suggested. "That will give me a chance to study the map for a bit—"

"If you will turn your attention to our printed itinerary, item 12B, you will see that our dinner destination should be just a couple of miles along this road. Relax and enjoy the scenery. You don't really want to go back to Vern's."

I felt a sudden sense of relief. "Okay," I said gratefully. "You're probably right."

"I think you're going to enjoy the place we're headed for. According to their Web site, it's run by a young couple with a passion for food, life, and each other who found a tumbledown millhouse and converted it into exactly the kind of charming little restaurant that they would like to stumble upon if they were driving along the winding roads of vanishing small-town America."

"They said all of that?"

"They did."

"Including 'tumbledown'?"

"Keep your eyes peeled."

"How about the place up ahead? It's got that former-tumbledown-millhouse look."

"What's the name of it?"

"Jack and Jennifer's."

"That's the place."

"And Jack and Jennifer must be the young couple with a passion for food, life, and each other."

"I'd be willing to bet on it."

Okay, it was charming. That is, it was charming if you are charmed by old mills converted into restaurants. Al and I are suckers for them. There must be something about the smell of old wood or the babbling of the old mill stream. We go into a state of receptivity that other restaurants in other styles and settings do not induce in us. Put us in a restaurant in an old mill and we are immediately predisposed to be pleased, even charmed.

A charming young woman greeted us when we entered. "I'm Jennifer," she said. Who else could she possibly have been? "And Jack is in the kitchen. We are delighted that you have chosen to join the narrative of our life together."

Uh-oh. I detected a whiff of something rotten in the enchanting aroma of the old wood.

"This is a charming place," said Albertine. She didn't seem to smell that hint of putrefaction.

"Oh, thank you," said Jennifer, seizing Al's hand and squeezing it. "Come this way—I have the perfect spot for you."

As we followed her, I whispered to Al, "Did you get a whiff of something—ah—malodorous—a little fusty?"

"Hush," she said.

"It's just that—something has made me wonder how long it's going to be before they turn this into a franchise—with Styrofoam wood and prerecorded babbling."

"Behave yourself. Follow Jennifer."

The large dining room was more than half full, but Jennifer led us to one of the most desirable tables, beside a window, overlooking the mill pond. The charm began to return, and—if such a transsensual alteration is possible—that slightly off odor was sweetened by the babble of the brook below us and the play of evening light on the surface of the pond.

Another charming young woman came to the table and began pouring water for us. "This is Stephanie," said Jennifer. "She'll be your guide and interpreter this evening."

Uh-oh. Another whiff. I glanced out the window. The pond was still there. The brook was still there. Okay. Maybe.

With a winning smile, Stephanie handed each of us what looked like a slim paperback book, a novella, perhaps. The title of this little book was *The Story That Is Jack and Jennifer's*. Albertine and I, polite little fools that we are, accepted the book with thanks, opened our copies, and began to read. After a moment, we raised our eyes, looked across at each other, and exchanged the look that we refer to, privately, as "whassup wit dis shit?"

The little book had several chapters, with titles that matched the divisions of a conventional menu, such as "Appetizers," "Soups," "Salads," and so on, but the nod to convention ended there. This was the first item in the Appetizers chapter:

Yucatán Honeymoon Midnight Snack

When Jack and Jennifer met, they knew that it was the real thing almost from the start. I guess you could say they had stars in their eyes, because they never gave a thought to the serious side of life together as a couple, all they could see was happy times, and nothing but love and happiness ahead. Of course, they were broke, but did that matter? Not at the time. They had a dream, and they were the dream. It was the dream of Jack and Jennifer, 2gethah 4evah. Young and foolish, maybe, but they haven't changed one bit . . . except that they're not quite as young as they were, though lots of people say they haven't aged at all, and they feel they owe it all to the love they have for each other. Because they were so broke, there wasn't any chance that they were going to have a big wedding or an elaborate honeymoon. Instead, they moved into a small apartment and locked themselves in for a few days away from the world, pretending that they were luxuriating at a lavish Yucatán resort. That was their honeymoon. It wasn't really a honeymoon, it was "playing honeymoon." Just like a couple of lovestruck kids. Call them irresponsible, but they hadn't had the foresight to stock the refrigerator for their adventure! They were determined not to leave their honeymoon haven, so there would be no trips to the 24-hour Kwikie Pickie for something to throw in the microwave. They had to improvise with what they had. Just think about what's in your refrigerator at home, and imagine living on that for a week. Toward the end of that week, you're going to have to get pretty inventive! That's the secret behind Jack and Jennifer's unique approach to cuisine—and that's how the Yucatán Honeymoon Midnight Snack was born.

Stephanie was not hovering, but she was lurking in a corner not far from our table. I turned in her direction and smiled. She returned my smile and stepped fetchingly to our table.

"Excuse me—" I began.

"Yes?" she said, turning on the charm.

"I've just started chapter one, and I wanted to know if I will eventually find out what is actually in the Yucatán Honeymoon Midnight Snack."

With a coy twinkle in her eye, she said, "Why don't you order it and see if you can guess? I'm sure you'll like it. It's really quite delicious."

"Is there meat in it?" asked Albertine.

"Are you a vegetarian?" Stephanie asked pointedly.

"Sometimes."

"Okay, well in that case, I will tell you that there is no meat in that particular item."

"Can you tell me anything that is in it?"

"Jack and Jennifer feel that a meal is a story," Stephanie explained with practiced patience, "and a story ought to surprise and delight. You will enjoy your time with us so much more if you allow yourself to be surprised—surprised and delighted."

"What if I'm allergic to something?" I asked.

"What are you allergic to?"

"Penicillin."

"There isn't—ah—hmm—just a minute."

She walked off in a charming manner.

"Al, let's get out of here," I whispered.

"Shouldn't we let ourselves go and enjoy the experience?" she asked. "Surrender to the charm? Allow ourselves to be surprised and delighted?"

"We could go back to that Kap'n Klam."

She knit her brows and pouted. "Is this the man who wanted to travel without a map?" she asked. "Is this the bold venturer I married, erstwhile Birdboy of Babbington?"

"You know, Al," I said with the sigh that I use to signal that I have surprised myself with a profound insight into one of life's little mysteries, "reflecting on my feelings about Vern's—not just Vern himself and his habit of teasing strange kids—"

"You said it," she muttered, "not I."

"—but also the uneasy feeling I had standing there in the entrance, as soon as I had entered Vern's, I think I understand the popularity of chain restaurants like Kap'n Klam in a way that I never did before."

"We're not having dinner at Kap'n Klam."

"Okay, okay."

Tension crackled and snapped across the table, tension between the desire to follow a route—the comfort of the itinerary—and the impulse to roam farther afield—the romance of the open road. The surprise was that our poles had been reversed again, as the poles of the earth are said to reverse from time to time. I was supposed to be the one who wanted adventure, surprise, the uncharted; Albertine was supposed to be the one who wanted the plan, the itinerary, the strip map that doesn't even show the interesting area beyond the straight and narrow.

"Okay," I said again, "but—"

"I owe you one," she said.

And so we ate our way into the narrative of Jack and Jennifer. It was an experience that tasted like the last days of a winter that refuses to yield to spring, the last days before summer vacation when you're in the sixth grade, or the last few minutes before the dentist releases you from the chair. Take your pick.

Later, in bed, at one of the motels at the interstate intersection, after Albertine had paid her debt, she said, "Let's watch the movie."

"Aren't you sleepy?" I asked.

"Not yet."

"You're usually sleepy after we—"

"I know. But tonight I'm not. Let's watch the movie."

"Okay."

We had skipped dessert at Jack and Jennifer's, but we had been sent on our way with something like dessert. Jennifer herself had promised us, as she handed it to Albertine, that we would find it "sweet." It was a DVD entitled *Jack and Jennifer's Dream*.

"Do you think it's erotic?" I asked, peeling the shrink-wrap from it.

"I'm trying not to get my hopes up."

I loaded the video into the DVD player and hopped back into bed with Albertine.

The dream opened with a shot of Jack and Jennifer in bed, smiling out at us.

"Hi!" said Jack, giving us a hearty wave and squeezing Jennifer.

"Hi!" said Al and I right back at them. I gave her a squeeze.

"Jack and I wanted to thank you personally for becoming a part of the Jack and Jennifer Experience," said Jennifer.

"And we want to tell you about our dream," said Jack.

"It's a dream about making people feel at home," said Jennifer.

"Hmmm," I said. "I smell a pitch coming."

"Cynic."

"I bet I'm right."

Jack and Jennifer didn't let me down.

"That's right," said Jack. "At Jack and Jennifer's our goal is to make you feel at home in our home, as our guests."

"As our friends," said Jennifer.

"As our family," said Jack.

"And someday we want you to be able to 'Come Home to Our Home Wherever You May Roam,'" said Jennifer.

"That's our dream!" said Jack.

"Someday there will be a Jack and Jennifer's literally everywhere!" said Jennifer.

"Even in your home town!" said Jack, pointing right at me.

"We should have gone to Kap'n Klam," I grumbled.

"You see," said Jack, still apparently addressing me personally, "if there's a Jack and Jennifer's in your town, and you dine there—"

"—and we really, really, really hope you will—" said Jennifer.

"—then when you're far from home, traveling, journeying," said Jack, knitting his brows in sympathy for the lonely traveler, "and you come upon another Jack and Jennifer's, just like the one back home, you are going to feel as if there's a bit of your town, your rightful place, right there, wherever you are, wherever you happen to be."

"The warm, welcoming, and familiar coziness that is at the heart of the Jack and Jennifer Experience will make you feel as much at ease in the threatening world as you feel at home, not because you actually are at home, of course, but because you can retire for a time to a refuge, a little bit of home, an island of the familiar in the stormy sea of the strange," Jennifer assured us.

"And you can help us make this dream come true," said Jack.

"Yes!" squealed Jennifer. "You can get behind this dream!"

"You can literally buy into it," said Jack.

"The first Jack and Jennifer's franchises are available now. If you've ever heard people brag about how they 'got in on the ground floor' or 'happened to be in the right place at the right time,' this is what they were talking about," said Jennifer.

"You could be me," said Jack, again pointing that finger at me.

"And you could be me," said Jennifer, pointing at Albertine.

"This is getting scary," she said, pulling the covers over her head.

"I'm turning it off," I said. "You can come out now."

She peeked out cautiously, saw that the television screen was dark, then raised herself on an elbow and said, "By the way—"

"Mm?"

"I've been meaning to ask you something—"

"Mm?"

"Didn't Vern offer you any advice?"

"He didn't have to."

"You mean that it was implicit in everything he said?"

"Yes."

" 'Beware of gravy'?"

"Exactly."

WIRELESS

· ·

I sing the Body electric;
The armies of those I love engirth me, and I engirth them;
They will not let me off till I go with them, respond to them,
And discorrupt them, and charge them full with the charge of the Soul.

—Walt Whitman, *Leaves of Grass*

ARRIVED IN Sweetwater in a bad mood. It was Vern's fault. In the morning, I was rolling along all right, thanks to *Spirit*'s sweet little engine—and I should say in praise of her, just in case she's listening, that her engine was strong and steady, and that she was remarkably stable for a two-wheeled winged craft on the ground. I could have said it to her then, and if I had I might have had a pleasant day, but the memory of

Vern's teasing, taunting, and mockery spoiled it all. I'd lost face back there at Vern's. I knew it and I felt it. I was ashamed of myself for having been bested by the old bastard, and a part of me, not the best part, wanted to return to Vern's and take revenge. Throwing a brick through a window of his diner was the best plan I could come up with. It allowed for a quick escape, if *Spirit* was willing. The likelihood of my returning to Vern's and hurling that brick diminished with distance, but my shame and anger grew throughout the day. I turned my anger on the closest target: *Spirit*.

"What's the matter?" I asked her, leaning forward to make sure that she heard me. "Not in the mood for flying today? How unusual!"

"Why do you always talk to my engine?" she asked petulantly.

It wasn't what I had expected.

"I'm talking to you," I said.

"No, you're not. You don't talk to me—you talk to my engine."

"I do not," I said firmly.

"Yes, you do," she insisted. "You lean over and talk to my engine."

"It's just that when I lean forward—"

"You act as if my engine were all there is to me."

"Maybe it is," I snapped. "The rest of you doesn't seem to be good for much."

"That was cruel," she whimpered.

I was immediately sorry for what I had said, but I tasted blood, and I wanted more.

"Your wings are worthless," I said in a taunting voice that I hadn't heard myself use since I was a child. "I don't know why you even have them."

"Don't get nasty," she said plaintively. "Please."

I was winning—but I was beginning to feel like a heel.

"What's the matter?" I snarled, or attempted to snarl. "Can't take the truth?"

"No," she said, "I can't," and I would have sworn that I heard her sniffle. "I'm a failure, and I know it. I'm too heavy. I'm ungainly. I'm fat and ugly."

"No," I said, caressing her tank. "You're not. You're beautiful."

"That's all?"

"All? Beautiful? Isn't that enough?"

"I knew it!"

"What?"

"You do think I'm fat."

"No!"

"You said it!"

"I didn't!"

"You implied it. You said 'beautiful,' not 'slender and beautiful.' You think I'm fat. You hate me because I'm fat and I can't fly."

"No, no—"

"You're always talking about it, always teasing me about it, always—"

"It's just that—I wish—I wish I could feel the lift. Don't you? Don't you think it would be wonderful to be above the world, to be able to see far ahead of us, take the long view—"

Something like a sob escaped from her.

"Of course I do!" she wailed. "What do you think I'm made of? Can't you see that I'm more than metal and fabric and nuts and bolts, that I have feelings, desires, yearnings—just like you?"

"I—well—no—actually—"

"Don't you realize that you've given me all your emotions, that the yearnings I feel are your yearnings, the disappointment I feel is your disappointment?"

"I—"

"If you find me unsatisfactory, it's because you find yourself unsatisfactory. You project your failings onto me."

What the hell had happened? I'd hoped for a cathartic release of anger, a release that would serve as a surrogate release of shame, but my own anger had turned against me, or been turned against me. How had that happened?

Well, you've seen how it happened, but at the time I was mystified by the turn of events, and I was still furious, and so I entered Sweetwater fully loaded and cocked, on a hair trigger.

Anger had so blinkered my reason that I didn't even ask myself what Sweetwater's slogan might mean as I rolled past the sign that welcomed visitors to the town:

ENTERING SWEETWATER
POPULATION 8,700
"SOMEDAY WE'LL BE WIRELESS"

The day had advanced to that time when I ordinarily craved some human contact, when I hoped to find someone who would lend an ear to my story of the day's adventure, but not today. Because I was in no mood for conversation, I thought I would just buy a sandwich from a delicatessen and find some simple shelter for the night without having to persuade a family to put me up.

I rode *Spirit* up and down the main street, but I didn't find a deli. I did find Nielson's Museum of Wireless Power Transmission, though, and it resembled a deli. The signs in its windows promised, in addition to a "Thrilling Tesla Coil Demonstration," cold beer, bratwurst, and a lunch counter. When I entered, I found that Nielson's was a combination of a small grocery store and the promised lunch counter, run by a dour man with nearly no chin, assisted by a dark-haired girl of about my age, whom I took to be his daughter. Things were looking up. The girl was behind the counter, and the man was on a stepladder, bringing overstock down from a high shelf. I headed toward the counter. I knew that the man had spotted me, because I could hear him, behind me, scrambling down from the stepladder, and in another moment he was in front of me, rushing to interpose himself between me and the girl. Like two fighters, or two chess players, or a hockey goalie and an opposing forward—one a grizzled veteran, the other young, fast on his feet, looking for an opening, and eager to score—we danced our way through tactical maneuvers, feints, and adjustments. Though I had youth and will and lust on my side, he was practiced, he knew the territory, and he was more agile than I expected him to be. He won.

He took a stance behind the counter, nodded at the girl in a way that sent her scurrying off with a feather duster in her hand, and turned a look of triumph on me.

"I'd like a hero," I said, acknowledging defeat. "Ham and swiss, with mustard."

"A hero," he said. "I know what you mean, but we don't call it a hero here."

"What do you call it?" I asked, struggling to remain civil.

"A snake, a gut buster, a long lunch, or a cylindrical dinner."

"Okay. I'll have one of those."

"Which?"

"Aren't they all the same?"

"No."

"How are they different?"

"They have different names."

Behind me, the girl giggled. I wished that I could disappear, dematerialize, and then rematerialize outside, astride *Spirit,* on my way out of town.

"I'll have the ball buster," I said.

"What?"

"I mean belly buster."

"Gut buster."

"Yeah. That one."

He went to work. I could hear the girl behind me, going about the business of dusting, and I could feel my ears burning.

"Since you asked for a hero," said chinless dad, "I'm guessing you're from the New York area. That right?"

"Yeah."

"Where are you from exactly?"

Here we go again, I thought. "Babbington," I said, with anger that I couldn't conceal, "and you're right; it's in New York, on Long Island." I could have added, "You want to make something of it?" but even in the heat of the moment I realized that it would have made me sound like a kid on a playground.

Pretending that he was making idle small talk while working on the sandwich (and I could see that he was pretending), he asked, "Have you got electricity there?"

"Electricity?" I snarled. "Sure. Of course we've got electricity." What was this? A trick question? Behind me, the girl was trying to suppress her giggles, but failing.

"In your house?"

"Yes! In my house!" What kind of rube did he take me for? What kind of antiquated backwater did he take Babbington for? "Babbington's a modern place," I asserted. "It might look old-fashioned and kind of quaint, but that's just part of its charm. Actually—"

"How do you get it?"

"What?"

"The electricity. In your house. How do you get it?"

"We—um—it—I don't know what you mean."

"Comes through wires, doesn't it?"

"Of course it comes through wires."

"Ha! You think that's modern? You're living in an antiquated backwater, rube."

I'd had it. I spun around and made straight for the door, struggling to avoid looking at the girl, resisting the desire to take a mental snapshot of her to carry with me on the road, into the night. I ran down the steps and leapt onto *Spirit*'s saddle. I stood and brought my weight down on her starter pedal. She roared into life as if she were as irritated as I.

"Hey! Wait!" shouted the man. He was at my side, holding on to my arm. "What are you doing?"

"I'm getting out of here!"

"You're leaving? What's the matter? Was it something I said?"

"You're damn right it was," I shouted back at him.

Did I hear the girl gasp behind me?

"What was it?" he asked.

"You insulted my home town!"

"Insulted? Oh—that was nothing—"

"It wasn't 'nothing' to me," I said. I wanted to hit him. I wanted to hurt him. I wanted to beat the shit out of him, if I could. I didn't say any of that. I growled. At least I think I growled. What came out of me sounds like a growl in memory. It might have been a howl, a howl of frustrated anger, wounded pride. I think the girl ran inside. I seem to recall hearing a door slam.

"Would you shut that thing off so we can talk?" he said.

"No! I'm leaving. And she's not a thing. She's an aerocycle—a slender beauty."

I started rolling toward the road. He trotted alongside me, imploring me to reconsider. I began speeding up. He began running. I speeded up some more. He grabbed hold of the remnant of the Kap'n Klam banner and tried to keep up, or to hold me back. I accelerated, thinking that I would force him to let go. He didn't. He fell to the ground.

"Hey!" he called. "Hey! Wait!"

"Let go!" I shouted.

I accelerated some more. He wouldn't let go. I was dragging him along. This wouldn't do. If I continued, I'd hurt him. Well, why not?

"Why not?" said *Spirit*. "Because if you did that, you would become someone very different from the boy you are now, someone I would rather not know."

"What's this? Are you my conscience now?"

"Maybe."

"Well, I don't want to hear you. I'm going to drag this guy till he bleeds."

"What fun! Revenge! A fine thing! How noble! Next you'll claim that he deserves it."

"Doesn't he? Didn't he hurt me? Didn't he slander Babbington? Didn't he call you 'that thing'? He does deserve it."

"That's what they all say."

"Ahhh, shit," I said. I stopped. I set *Spirit* on her stand and left her idling while I walked back to the father of the dark-haired girl. He had struggled to his feet and was checking himself for damage and dusting himself off.

"You okay?" I asked.

"Who invented the radio?" he asked right back.

"Guglielmo Marconi." There, I thought. That ought to show him.

"Wrong!" he said.

"Wrong?"

"Ever hear of Nikola Tesla?"

"Um—yes. I have. He invented the Tesla coil."

"And the radio."

"Are you sure?"

He snorted. I took the snort to mean that he was sure.

"You'll have to prove it to me," I said.

"Come on inside," he said, stretching his arm in the direction of the Museum of Wireless Power Transmission, some distance behind us. I looked in that direction. His daughter was standing at the entrance, holding her hands to her mouth in surprise and concern. "My daughter has prepared a presentation on Tesla, including a demonstration of the famous Tesla coil—you'd like to see that, wouldn't you?"

I had seen demonstrations of Tesla coils before. In fact, I had given demonstrations of Tesla coils myself. His daughter's presentation might share much with the others I'd seen and given, but it promised to be delightfully different. I would indeed like to see it, and I answered truthfully.

"Yes, I would," I said, and we began walking back to the museum.

"Tell him about the radio," he urged the girl as soon as we were within earshot.

"In 1943," she said, bright-eyed, "the United States Supreme Court declared that Guglielmo Marconi's patent on the radio was invalid and that Nikola Tesla was its true inventor."

"I didn't know that," I admitted.

"It's true!" she said. "We've got copies of the ruling right here, in the museum. Would you like one?"

"Well, I—"

"You can have it for free."

Mining the depths of my talent for humor, I said, "At that price, I'll take two."

"One per customer," said her father, whom I had forgotten.

"Come with me," the girl said. "I'll show you the museum. There's a Tesla coil."

"So I've heard."

"Have you ever seen a Tesla coil?"

"Yes," I said, offhandedly. "I've seen several, and I've even operated one."

"Oh," she said, disappointed.

"Back at home, in Babbington, that antiquated backwater," I said with a withering glance for her father, "I gave demonstrations for elementary school students, under the auspices of the high school science department, using a Tesla coil to make dramatic bolts of artificial lightning and a Van de Graaff generator to make my hair stand on end."

"That's wonderful," she said, "but—there are more practical uses."

"Oh. Of course. Sure. I'm sure there are. I didn't mean—"

We had made our way back into Nielson's, and she had led me to a back corner of the store, beyond a display of brooms and mops, where she began her demonstration.

"This is my Tesla coil," she began, beaming, "my pride and joy. I built it myself."

"Wow."

"Impressed?"

"I'll say. It's big. And it's different."

"Different from what?"

"From the little one I use for the demonstrations at home."

"What's different about it? Other than size, that is."

"The doughnut—"

"Torus."

"Right. I knew that."

"Ring torus, to be specific."

"The ring torus is—well—no offense—fatter."

"That's an excellent observation. There's a reason for the difference. You see, from what you've said I can tell that the coil you've been using was built for the purpose of entertainment. It's designed to inspire awe in the young and ignorant. Don't be offended by my saying this, but it's essentially a toy."

I wanted to say something along the lines of, "Nothing that came from your comely lips could ever offend me," and I was preparing myself to say—with a certain traveled suavity—something pretty much like that when she stopped me with a hand on my arm, then a finger to my lips.

"The small radius of curvature in your ring torus leads to loss of energy through coronal discharges and streamers," she said. Then she raised an eyebrow, inquiring whether I was following her.

I had been struck dumb. Her hand on my arm, her finger on my lips, were all I knew, all I needed to know.

"Sparks," she said in explanation.

"Mm—ah—yeah—uh-huh," I said with a certain traveled suavity.

"But as you can see my torus has a large radius of curvature—"

I nearly swooned. There was a definite danger of a coronal discharge. Or a streamer.

"—specifically to prevent such a wasteful loss of energy, because this coil does what Tesla designed it to do." She picked a lamp from a nearby table, a lamp without a cord, allowed herself a dramatic pause, then switched the lamp on, and with its light illuminating her face, she said, "It transmits power."

So did she. For the next hour or so, she was quite instructive on the subject of Tesla and the wireless transmission of energy; at least I have some memory of being impressed by her presentation, but nothing that she said about Tesla stayed with me. Later, when I reached Corosso, I had to spend hours in the library of the New Mexico Institute of Mining, Technology, and Pharmacy, reteaching myself what she had taught me, in order to understand why the radius of curvature was a factor in allowing a high electrical potential to develop on the surface of the torus, the area of which is defined by the equation $S = \pi^2 (R+r)(R-r)$ where R is the major radius of the torus and r is the minor radius of the torus, an equation that to this day makes me hot.

When she had finished, some time passed before I realized that she had. I don't know how long I stood there, dumbstruck, before she said, "That's it. That's the whole show."

"Oh," I said.

"I've got to go help my mom with dinner."

"Maybe I could—"

"Here you go," said her father's voice from behind me.

"Huh?"

"Here's your sandwich."

"Oh. Yeah. Great."

"You'd better be on your way before dark."

"On my way?"

"That's right."

"I was hoping—"

"Of course you were," he said. "You were hoping that you'd get to stay here for the night. You were hoping that after the missus and I fell asleep you'd manage to get a little—"

With the thumb and index finger of his left hand he formed a ring torus, and then he began poking the index finger of his right hand into it repeatedly, whistling wetly with each poke.

"Sir, I—"

"Let me give you some advice, kid: take the sandwich and make a graceful exit."

Reluctantly, I did.

RETROSPECTIVE MANIFESTATIONS

WE HAD BEEN dancing, and though we were now stretched out in bed we were still flushed with the pleasure of dancing. After an uneventful day of driving, we had showered, changed, eaten dinner, and then chanced upon a bar with one of those bands that seem to be able to cover every popular song in every genre from the last several decades. Now we were lying in the luxury of a queen-size bed apiece. I was luxuriating in mine. Albertine was luxuriating in hers. She was reading, carelessly, from a brochure about Blunderhaven, a mansion on an island in the Ohio River that we were thinking of visiting the next morning.

"'Blunderhaven,'" she read, "'is a showcase of priceless historical relics and objets d'art, blah, blah, a gateway to the past, blahbitty blah, antique weapons, household items, old clothing, farm implements, blah, blah, objects of yesteryear that now strike us with their quaintness.'"

She paused.

Breathlessly, I asked, "Why have you stopped, my darling? The tension has begun to mount."

"I was just wondering—oh, never mind." She took up the brochure again. "'Your enchanting day at Blunderhaven begins with a ride in a replica of a riverboat from days gone by.'"

She paused again.

I waited for a while. Then I asked, "How long does this replica ride last?"

"Twenty minutes," she said distantly.

"Let's say that twenty minutes have passed," I suggested. "We've disembarked. We're greeted by a docent or interpreter in period garb. What has she got to say?"

"'Welcome to Blunderhaven, a time capsule of bygone days and a monument to folly.'"

"'A monument to folly'?"

"That's what the brochure says, and I would expect the interpreter to stick to the script."

"Do I hear a little testiness in your voice?"

"Maybe."

"I suppose repeating the same script day after day would make an interpreter a bit testy sometimes. Please go on, though."

" 'Nathaniel Hobson, self-styled Lord of Blunderhaven, was his own best friend and his own worst enemy, self-made and self-destroyed, worshiped and reviled, admired and ridiculed.' "

"Sounds like an interesting guy."

" 'Although he rose from obscure beginnings to become one of the wealthiest men in western Virginia, his greed made him the compliant dupe of sharpsters and mountebanks, and he dissipated his entire fortune in pursuit of ever greater riches, backing every phantasmagorical scheme that was dangled before his goggling eyes, blah, blah, blah.' "

"He should have taken the sandwich and made a graceful exit," I commented, more to myself than to her.

She tossed the brochure aside.

"Am I to take it that the interpreter has quit and run off to Ohio with the riverboat captain?" I asked.

"The interpreter wants to know about those dark-haired girls who keep popping up in these memories of yours."

"They are you," I said.

"Oh, goodie," she said, abandoning the luxury of her own individual queen-size bed to join me in mine. "Now, in what sense do you mean that?"

"In what sense do I mean what?"

"I mean, do you mean that after we met you decided that our paths had crossed many times before in real life, in truth, in actual experience?"

"I—"

"Or do you mean that sometime after we met you came to believe that you had seen me many times before, that the dark-haired girl who had appeared so tantalizingly from time to time throughout your past must have been me?"

"No, I—"

"Or do you mean that, when we met, you became the compliant dupe of Mnemosyne, who played the trick of replacing your memories of all those other, earlier, dark-haired beauties with memories of me?"

"That's—"

"Or do you mean that now, in the telling, as a narrative device, a way to please, amuse, and seduce me, you are systematically placing dark-haired distractions in the scenes that you read to me?"

"Well—"

"Or do you mean that before you met me you saw many dark-haired girls that you desired and that I was merely the one you finally managed to seduce and snare? (You'd better say no to that one.)"

"Yes—"

"Yes?"

"I had to stop you somehow."

"Oh."

"They are there, those dark-haired girls, because they are retrospective manifestations of you."

"Retrospective manifestations."

"It's a technical term."

"I figured."

"I'll explain."

"Make me swoon."

"During my time in Corosso, I sometimes joined the paleontology group on their sallies into the desert, passing the time reading Tesla's *My Inventions* in the shade of an outcropping of rock while they learned how to use a pretended interest in fossils as a cover for espionage. The desert is a good place for memorization, so I can quote Tesla on manifestations, word for word."

"Mm?"

"Ready?"

"Shoot."

" 'I instinctively commenced to make excursions beyond the limitations of the small world of which I had knowledge, and I saw new scenes . . . and so I began to travel—of course, in my mind. Every night (and sometimes during the day), when alone, I would start on my journeys—see new places, cities, and countries—live there, meet people and make friendships and acquaintances and, however unbelievable, it is a fact that they were just as dear to me as those in actual life and not a bit less intense in their manifestations.' "

"Simplify, simplify," she muttered, her eyes having taken on the glazed look of adoration with which she favors me nearly nightly.

"When I met you," I explained, "I realized that something had been

missing in my life for all the years before I met you, though I hadn't felt
the lack, and having met you I realized that what had been missing was
you. When I began the methodical process of recollection that under-
lies my memoirs, my systematic cerebral excursions to bygone days, I
felt the lack of you because I now knew what I had been missing back
then, and I suffered for it as I never had the first time around. However,
memory and imagination came to my aid, inserting retrospective manifestations of you here and there, and those are the dark-haired girls
who—"

Reader, she snored.

HELD FOR RANSOM

The Castle hill was hidden, veiled in mist and darkness, nor was there
even a glimmer of light to show that the castle was there.

—Franz Kafka, *The Castle*

WHENEVER I RECALL this journey that I'm recounting for
you, when I take the trip again in my mind, it seems to be a
journey of a thousand mistakes. As Lao-Tzu probably would have said
if he'd thought of it, the journey of a thousand mistakes begins with a
single misstep, and each of the thousand subsequent missteps can begin a journey of a thousand more.

"I think I made a misstep," I confessed to *Spirit.*

"You've been riding, not walking, so that is literally impossible," she
pointed out pedantically, not at all in the chummy, inquisitive, and
speculative style of Mr. MacPherson.

"I mean that I must have made a wrong turn," I said.

"Another wrong turn, you mean," she said smugly.

"Yes," I admitted irritably, "another wrong turn."

"Volumes could be written on the wrong turn as a metaphor for the
human condition," she said. "Maybe they have been. You really ought
to check. Perhaps when you get to the Faustroll Institute you could

propose that as your thesis topic, if the Faustroll Institute requires a thesis. Does it?"

"How should I know?" I snapped. "I don't even know whether I'll ever get there. This isn't a journey—it's a disaster."

"I have an idea," she said, suddenly cheerier.

"What's that? Get a map?"

"No. No, I don't want you to do that. I want you to persist in your folly, fool."

"Thanks for the endorsement."

"What I want you to do is redefine the wrong turn."

"Redefine the wrong turn? What are you talking about?"

"Change your thinking. Change the way you decide what is a wrong turn and what is a right turn."

"How?"

"You set out to travel to New Mexico, right?"

"Right."

"But you also set out to have an adventure, right?"

"Right."

"So, any turn that puts you on the road to New Mexico is a right turn."

"Right."

"And any turn that puts you on the road to adventure is also a right turn."

"Hmmm."

"A turn that puts you on the road that leads to New Mexico *and* to adventure is doubly right, but a turn that leads to one or the other can't really be considered wrong."

"Gee, when you put it that way—"

"In order to be a wrong turn, a turn would have to lead you away from New Mexico *and* away from adventure."

"Then I haven't really made any wrong turns at all."

"Not yet."

Buoyed by *Spirit*'s redefinition of a wrong turn, I went on happily, making turns and choosing routes with new confidence, almost insouciance, until, at that crepuscular hour when my stomach began to tell me that the day's traveling should be brought to an end, I found myself in a place where the landscape seemed vertically exaggerated, stretched in the upward direction, as if a mathematical function had been applied to all its surfaces, exaggerating them along the y axis. The hills that I had been rolling through had become jagged peaks, the gentle winding road now clung precariously to the edge of a precipice, and there was something that seemed so unlikely that I thought it must be an illusion: at a turning a vista opened before me and I seemed to see, atop one of the peaks, a castle. It was veiled in mist and twilight, so I couldn't be certain, but I seemed to see a castle up there.

I stopped, removed my goggles, and rubbed my eyes. I blinked in the direction of the possible castle, half expecting it to disappear, but found that it was still there, looming in the mist above me, dark, cylindrical, crenelated, and threatening. At that moment it might have been wise to turn back, retrace my steps, and find an alternative route, but I was a headstrong boy on an adventure, and turning back would not have been in keeping with the new definition of wrong turns and right turns. A road that wound toward a castle seemed very likely to lead to adventure even if it wasn't likely to lead to New Mexico, and so I pressed on, making progress of a sort, climbing a little higher with each bend in the road, drawing a little nearer to the castle that now and then made a coy appearance through an opening in the tall pines.

Eventually, the road ended in a turnaround. There I left *Spirit* and began to climb a footpath that seemed as if it must lead to the castle.

After a long hike, I came to a small inn. Seeing the warm, inviting light through the windows of the inn, I remembered that I was tired and hungry. I decided to pause in my climb to the castle to have some dinner, perhaps to stay the night.

Entering, I found the front room of the inn, its dining room, empty of other travelers. I sat at a table. A waitress wearing a name tag that identified her as Frieda bustled into the room. She seemed not to notice me. Not at all. She put some linens into a cupboard, straightened them to her satisfaction, and bustled out. She bustled back in with a pair of candelabra. I cleared my throat. She still didn't notice me. I got up and walked around the room, trying the view from various windows, hoping that a boy in motion might be more noticeable, but still she seemed not to see me. Having lit the candles in the candelabra, she bustled out again. Shortly, she bustled back, carrying a load of plates. I refused to go unnoticed any longer. I spoke. "Frieda?" I said.

She dropped the load of plates and shouted, "Oh, my God in heaven!"

"I'm sorry," I said, squatting to help her pick up the pieces.

"Why did you sneak up on me like that? You scared the life out of me."

"I've been here," I said. "You didn't notice me."

"That's not my fault," she said. "You're not especially noticeable."

"I'm flying to New Mexico," I said, in an attempt to make myself more noticeable.

"That's ridiculous," she said.

"Honest," I said. "I really am flying—"

Something kept me from saying more. Frieda was on her hands and knees, making a pile of broken crockery, and I could see down the front of her dress, see the curve of her large breasts. The sight of her breasts, and the position that we were both in, brought a wave of nostalgia, because it reminded me of the crush I had had on Mrs. Jerrold, who lived across the street from my family home in Babbington, reminded me of the schemes I had hatched to visit Mrs. Jerrold, to get near her, and reminded me in particular of a rainy day when I had been playing marbles with her little boy, Roger Junior, in a ring of string that I had made on her living room carpet, and during my play had discovered a tape recorder under her sofa, which discovery prompted Mrs. Jerrold to get down on all fours to see for herself, which allowed me to sneak a peek down the front of her shirtwaist dress, which allowed me to see the curve of her breasts.

"What are you looking at?" asked Frieda.

"I—"

"You're looking at my breasts, aren't you?"

"Yes," I said with the frankness of an adventurer.

She gave me a swat and a smile and said, "I can't blame you for that; they really are quite magnificent. Do you want some dinner?"

"Yes," I said. "What have you got?"

"We've got dinner. You'll take what you get. It will be good. Sit down and wait. Be patient."

I sat. I waited. Frieda resumed her bustling in and out of the room, pursuing many little errands, none of which was the bringing of my dinner. I attempted to strike up a conversation with her, tossing out intriguing bits of information whenever she bustled in.

"I wasn't planning to stop here," I said.

"Uh-huh," she replied, not quite intrigued.

"I was going to hike up to the castle."

"What castle?"

"The castle at the top of this mountain. The one that's veiled in mist and twilight."

"Pfff," she said. "That's ridiculous."

"Maybe you're right," I said. "It's getting dark, and a hike like that could be dangerous in the dark. Still, I thought it would be an adventure, so I intended to make the attempt, but when I saw this little inn I realized that I was tired and hungry."

"Mm," she said, possibly just a bit more intrigued.

"I wonder if coming upon an inn at twilight has that effect on all travelers—makes them realize that they're tired and hungry—or maybe even makes them feel tired and hungry when they really aren't—through the power of suggestion. What do you think?"

"Happens all the time. Everybody knows that."

"Really?"

"Sure. That's how we get most of our business."

"Oh."

"It's not very interesting."

"It's interesting to me."

"If you want me to show you my breasts, you'll have to do better than that."

"Okay—I—well—what about the remarkable way that height distorts the perception of distance?"

"I never really thought about it."

"Here's the idea: we see something in the distance, and we make an estimate of the distance from us to it. More often than not, we make a simple straight-line estimate, without taking into account the likelihood that the way will be winding. We expect to go as the crow flies, but when we make an as-the-crow-flies estimate, we do not take into account the fact that we cannot fly. Over time, experience teaches us that we can't fly and that the way usually does wind, so we learn to correct our straight-line estimates—but only on level ground. When we look at something that is vertically distant—like a castle on a mountaintop—we forget that the way to it is likely not only to wind but to rise and fall, and that its ups and downs will make the way longer—and when experience teaches us that, then we really wish that we could fly, that we could go as the crow flies."

Here I paused. I thought of telling her about *Spirit*. When I say that I thought of telling her about *Spirit*, I mean that I thought of telling her everything about *Spirit*, from the inspiration to build her to the moment when I stopped her engine and left her in the turnaround down the trail, below the inn where I was pausing. That seemed like more of a story than I should be required to tell in order to see her breasts, so instead of telling it I said, hopefully, "That's pretty intriguing, don't you think?"

She stared at me for a long moment and then said, "I'll get your dinner." She bustled off. In a moment she bustled back and put a large bowl of stew in front of me. It smelled just wonderful, rich and hearty. She handed me a spoon. I tried a bite.

"Hooo!" I said.

"Not good?" she asked.

"Hot!" I exhaled.

"Oh," she said, and she leaned across the table and began blowing on the stew, allowing me another good look down the front of her dress. Was this the view she had suggested I might earn? Might I earn more?

"Unlike the crow," I continued, since I was at least as eager for a full view of her breasts as the next young aviator, "we foot travelers are going to have to hike up and down a rugged path, but we estimate the distance as the distance we see on a line of sight. Nor do we take into account the lets and hindrances that make the way seem longer, make it take longer to traverse than our simple estimate of distance would lead us to expect."

"I guess you're right," she said, but not in a way that suggested she was about to start unbuttoning the top of her dress.

"It's one of the habits of thought that make people think that life will be easier than it is," I said. "That's what my grandparents' neighbor, Mr. Beaker, used to tell me, back in Babbington. He was—"

"Eat your stew now," she said, as if I were her little brother.

"Okay," I said. I was hungry. Her breasts would have to wait. I fell to. Frieda stood there, across the table from me, with her arms akimbo, watching with satisfaction.

"Say, Frieda," I said, after I had eaten about half of the stew in the bowl, "do you suppose I could stay here for the night?"

"Of course you could," she said. "This is an inn, you know."

"I know—"

"We're always putting people up for the night."

"Of course—"

"You could say that it's our purpose in life, the means by which we justify our existence."

"That's great."

"I think we've got four rooms available. How much did you want to spend?"

"Ah," I said. "That's an embarrassing question. You see, I'm on my way to New Mexico—"

"You told me that already. You tried to make me believe that you were flying."

Chuckling like a kid who's been caught in a lie, I said, "Yes, I did."

"Then you went on and on with that business about crows climbing mountains—"

"Yeah. Well, I thought you would find that intriguing, but my point is that New Mexico is still a very long way from here, and I've got to watch my expenses. I have to buy food—and gas—and I'm on a pretty tight budget."

"Well then, I won't ask you how much you want to spend. I'll ask you how much you can afford to spend."

"Nothing."

"I think you're telling me how much you want to spend."

"Both."

She began a hearty laugh, as if I had delivered the punch line of a joke, but she suddenly stopped laughing and became perplexed. "I don't know what to do," she confessed. "I'll have to ask my father."

She left the room. I returned to my dinner, eating quickly. If I was going to be thrown out into the night, I wanted to be thrown out with a full belly.

A big man arrived. He might have been cut from a single block of granite. Everything about him said that he was not amused.

"You asked for a room," he said.

"No, sir," I said with a shiver. "Not exactly."

"What is that supposed to mean?"

"I asked *about* a room. I wanted to find out if a room was available, and what it would cost, just to see whether it might be possible for me to spend the night here on my limited budget."

"You had no right."

"No right to ask about a room? But this is an inn—as Frieda informed me—"

"You had no right to ask for a room if you were not prepared to pay the proper approved rate."

"I only asked *about* a room, not *for* a room."

"Don't quibble. You led my daughter to believe that you wanted a room."

"I did want a room, but I didn't know whether I could afford to pay the—ah—proper approved rate. I didn't know what the proper approved rate was."

"But Frieda tells me you wanted a room for nothing."

"If that is the proper approved rate, then I am prepared to pay it."

"Are you trying to be funny?"

"Yes," I admitted. "Just trying to lighten—"

"This is neither the time nor the place for funny business," he said gravely.

"Yes, sir."

"As far as I am concerned you entered this inn under false pretenses."

"No, I didn't," I said. "Honest."

"Come to think of it, if you entered this inn with the expectation of securing lodging at a rate below the approved rate, then you arrived here with the prior intention to commit fraud."

"This is all a misunderstanding," I said.

"I'm not sure whether to throw you out and send you on your way or call the authorities and have you locked up," he said. He brought his hand to his chin and wrinkled his brow, contemplating me and considering my fate.

Inspiration struck. "Suppose I pay for my dinner and a room by advertising this inn on a banner that I will tow behind my aerocycle as I fly the rest of the way from here to New Mexico?" I offered.

"Pfwit," he said. I decided that I didn't like him.

"I've already towed an advertising banner for Kap'n Klam," I said. He looked as if he had been struck a blow.

"That is an odd coincidence," he said. "You have this banner?"

"Part of it," I said. "It used to say 'Kap'n Klam is coming! The Home of Happy Diners,' but now the last part just says 'The Home of Hap.'"

"Who is Hap?"

"Nobody. There is no Hap. The rest of the banner wore away, tore off, got left behind."

He narrowed his eyes.

"I can show you what's left of it, if you want me to," I added, with the shrug of a boy who hasn't even thought of the possibility that he might seize the opportunity to hop onto his aerocycle and make his escape without paying for dinner.

"I will call the owner," he said.

"Does he live in the castle?" I asked. "Up on the peak?"

"You saw a castle?"

"It was veiled in mist, but I could pick it out now and then, looming above me in the twilight."

"Yes, that's where the evil owner lives," he said thunderously. "He rules us with an iron fist. In ordinary circumstances, I would not call him. He does not like to be disturbed." He picked up the handset of a telephone on the counter that served as a registration desk and said, "Get me the castle."

He waited. I waited. Frieda waited. Of the three of us, Frieda looked best while waiting.

"This is the inn," he said after a long while. "I have a procedural question for Mr. Klam."

I shot a questioning look at Frieda. She turned aside quickly and began wiping a table with her sleeve. "Mr. Klam?" said her father, with an upward glance, as if he were speaking directly to the castle rather than through the telephone. "Forgive me for bothering you with this, but I have a procedural question. . . . Yes. . . . Of course. . . . I know. . . . Ordinarily, I wouldn't. . . . Yes. . . . No. . . . You see, here at the inn, there is a boy who has arrived on a small airplane—that is, that's what he claims—it's what he told Frieda—probably lying, of course—on his way to New Mexico. . . . I don't know why—but he says his budget is limited and he can't afford the proper approved rate for a room—instead, he offers to tow a banner. . . . What? . . . Yes—yes—an excellent suggestion, sir. . . . Yes—certainly—at once—thank you, sir."

He hung up and turned to me. "We can put you up for the night," he said. "Get your things."

"This is all I have," I said, hefting my knapsack.

"Come with me," he said.

He led me down a long corridor, turned into another corridor, went down a flight of narrow stairs, passed through a door, went down an even narrower flight of stairs into a dank cellar, and began walking along an uneven floor between walls so close that my shoulders rubbed against them and Frieda's father had to scuttle along sideways. We went up stone stairs. We went down stone stairs. We turned to the right. We turned to the left. At first, I tried to remember every turn we took, in case I might have to retrace my steps, but I soon became too confused to remember the route in such detail. Instead, I tried to retain a general impression. Did we tend to turn right more often than we turned left? Did we descend more often or ascend more often? I decided, after a while, that Frieda's father was leading me through a tunnel that wound slowly up the mountain to the castle. We came to a heavy door that he unlocked with one of the keys on a large ring that hung from his belt. It groaned as he swung it open. "Your room," he said, and he shoved me inside. I stumbled and fell to the floor. When I got up, he had closed the door. Was I a prisoner?

I went to the door and asked, "Am I a prisoner?"

"A prisoner?" he said from the other side. "Of course not. You are a guest at the inn."

A guest at the inn? Ha! I wasn't so easily fooled. I almost said so, but just as I was about to speak the thought occurred to me that it might be useful to conceal from him my realization that he had led me to the castle. I decided to feign ignorance, to pretend that I really believed that we were still beneath the inn. "Are all the rooms like this?" I asked.

"This is our most economical room," he said. "We reserve it for the occasional guest who is traveling on a very limited budget."

"Could I have my things?"

He opened the door a bit and threw my knapsack in after me. Then he locked the door.

"You didn't give me the key," I said.

"I'll keep the key," he said.

"How will I get out?"

"When your bill has been paid, I will let you out."

"How much does this room cost?"

"How much? Let's see—there will be the basic charge—the charge for cleaning—linen—the straw on your pallet—wear and tear—depreciation—your dinner—water—air—"

"Air?"

"The air you breathe."

"Is it customary to charge for air?"

"Of course. Fifteen cubic feet per hour. Three hundred sixty cubic feet per day. It adds up. By morning, you will have run up quite a bill. You will owe us a considerable sum, and the owner is very strict about payment."

"I told you that I don't have much money—"

"If you cannot pay, you cannot leave."

"What am I going to do?"

"Perhaps you could telephone your parents back in—where was it you originated?"

"Babbington."

"They might be willing to wire you some money."

"Mmm," I said doubtfully. "They might."

"Or maybe you know some wealthy eccentric who would do so."

"Hmmm."

"You will have the whole night to think of someone who will pay."

"Okay," I said. "I'll try."

"Try very hard. Make a list of the people who like you enough to pay to have you released from your room."

"Is there a light in here?" I asked.

"I'll bring you a candle," he said. "It will be a dollar. I'll add it to your bill."

Working by candlelight, in the venerable tradition of imprisoned writers, I began to make a list of the people back in Babbington who might be willing to pay my ransom. My parents were at the top of the list, of course, but after I had listed their names I imagined myself calling them under the watchful eye of Frieda's father.

"Hi, Mom," I would say, as if nothing were wrong.

"Who is this?" I could hear her asking.

"It's me, Peter."

"Oh. What a coincidence. I used to have a son named Peter."

"This is your son named Peter."

"I haven't heard from Peter in ages. He's missing."

"Mom, I know I haven't written, but—"

"He said he would send me a postcard every night. I haven't received one for several days now, so I guess he's been eaten by a bear."

"Please, Mom—"

"Hello?" said another voice.

"Hi, Dad," I said. "It's Peter."

"I suppose you're calling to ask for money."

"It's funny you should say that," I would say, and I would lay the matter before him, tell him the whole story, and wait for his response.

"Well?" Frieda's father would ask after I hung up.

"He says they won't pay."

"Didn't you tell him you were rotting in a dungeon?"

"I did. He accused me of letting my imagination run away with me."

"Don't you know anyone else who can send you some money?"

I thought about it. Porky White might be able to send me some money. May Castle was supposed to have money. If she did, I supposed she would be willing to send me some. What about my grandparents? I'd never really considered what their resources might be. Did they have savings? Probably. They were frugal, or at least not foolish with their money. Then there were all my friends of my own age. They'd be willing to chip in. They might even be willing to canvas the town, take up a collection, go door to door. It might be exciting for them. It would make them feel that they were a part of my adventure, that they were with me in my hour of need. For a couple of minutes, I savored the thought of all of Babbington filling my friends' buckets with cash to ransom me, but then, with a deep sigh, I recognized the trouble with asking any of those people back home for money: I was going to be embarrassed. I would lose face. I'd be the butt of jokes for all the time that I was away, and when I came home the jokes would have been refined to a sharp cutting edge. I might not want to go home at all with that kind of reception waiting for me. The whole thing was becoming too disturbing. I was in an agitated state. I needed some distraction, something that would calm me. I decided to do my homework.

Before I left Babbington, my French teacher, Angus MacPherson, had assigned me the task of translating Alfred Jarry's *Gestes et Opinions du Docteur Faustroll.* When I began the translation, at a time that now seemed long ago, I found that I felt excluded from the book and from the world of Doctor Faustroll, as I might have felt excluded in a dream when I found myself trying to get to a place and discovered that I couldn't manage to get there, that the very air seemed too thick for me to part and pass through, or when I found myself moving along a wall, searching with my fingers for a door that would let me into a place where I knew that everyone was having a good time.

My habit as a reader, developed over the twelve years that I had been reading, was to find a way into a book, a way to insinuate myself into the goings-on. The obvious way in was through identification with a character, though there were other ways—playing the role of invisible spy, for one. Before entering *Faustroll,* I had expected to identify with Faustroll himself, the star. However, as I began my first attempt at translation, I found that another identification was urged upon me, almost forced upon me, as I made my way through the text, bit by bit, word by word, piece by piece, phrase by phrase. Faustroll remained distant, aloof, mysterious. Instead of identifying with him, I identified with Panmuphle, the vague and ineffective civil servant who first tried to serve him a warrant and later became his companion or sidekick, the guy riding shotgun on Dr. Faustroll's absurd journey "from Paris to Paris by sea." Within the book, or at least within my translation of it, my version of it, I was Panmuphle. Now, resuming my work, by candlelight, as Panmuphle, with frequent reference to my *Handy Dictionary of the French and English Languages,* I wrote:

On the Habits and Appearance of Doctor Faustroll

Perhaps it is because I was unable to serve notice on the elusive Doctor Faustroll that I have become somewhat obsessed with him. I would not have used that word, would not have said that I was obsessed with him, but my wife, dear Madame Panmuphle, assures me that *obsessed* is the word that describes my state. I would have said that I was being assiduous in my pursuit of the mysterious doctor, and in fact I did say so, and suggested *diligent* as an alternative, perhaps even *sedulous*, but she assured me that *obsessed* is the word, and so I defer to her, as I do in all things not directly connected with my official duties, wherein I defer to Monsieur le Mayor.

I began my diligent investigation by interrogating his propriétères, Mr. and Mrs. Jacques Bonhomme. From Mr. Bonhomme I learned that Doctor Faustroll was born in 1898.

"You are quite certain of that?" I demanded of my informant, assiduous in my effort to obtain the facts, and nothing but the facts. "Oh, yes," he replied with ill-concealed annoyance. "It was when the twentieth century was minus two years old. The mysterious doctor was born at the age of sixty-three."

"I must not have heard you correctly," I said. "I thought you said that the mysterious doctor was born at the age of sixty-three."

"That he was," the gnomelike creature asserted, "and he has kept that age throughout his life. He is always sixty-three."

"I see," I said, though I most certainly did not. Because my experiences in the course of discharging my official duties have taught me the value of a skeptic's attitude toward the information the public gives to officials, I asked myself whether the person I was speaking to might be an accomplice of Faustroll, assigned the task of deceiving and misleading me. Even as I noted the age of sixty-three on my pad, I made the secret mark I use to indicate statements of questionable value.

"Please describe his physical appearance," I said.

Without even a pretense at labored recollection, the wizened man launched into a description, his rapidity leading me to wonder whether he had been rehearsed. "He is a man of medium height, or perhaps I should say average height, unless it is the median height that I mean; I am never quite certain about the difference," he said.

"Please, monsieur," I said, "try to be more precise."

"Very well," he said, "to be exact, his height is $8 \times 10^{10} + 10^9 + 4 \times 10^8 + 5 \times 10^6$ atomic diameters."

He intended to rush on, but I stayed him with an authoritative gesture and made him repeat the exact height. When I had it down, I bade him continue, employing another unambiguous gesture.

"His skin is the yellow of gold. His face is glabrous—"

"Glabrous?" I asked silently, through the medium of a raised eyebrow.

"Hairless, sir."

"Ah," I said. "Clean-shaven."

"Except for a mustache as green as the sea, like that depicted in the portrait of King Saleh—"

"King Saleh?" I asked, interrupting. "Who is this King Saleh? A crony of Faustroll's, perhaps?"

"Please, sir," said the doe-eyed daughter of the Bonhommes, who had until then remained silent, though hanging on my every word in evident awe of my office and person, "I know, sir."

"Yes, child?" I said, in the tone of an adored uncle.

"He is the ruler of one of the kingdoms of the sea in the Arabian Nights entertainments, sir," she said shyly, with a provocative pout.

"Thank you, my dear," I said, tousling the little darling's hair. "That reminds me: what of his hair?"

I stretched. I rubbed my eyes. How long had I been working? I had no way to tell. I was tired, but that might have been the result of effort, excitement, and worry as much as the passage of time. I blew out the candle and stretched out on the pallet. I may have slept. I'm not sure. I may

ON THE WING · 295

only have slipped into a state halfway between waking and sleeping without fully sleeping. I heard a scratching sound. I took it to be rats. I felt a certain satisfaction in the thought that there were rats scratching somewhere nearby. A dungeon ought to have rats. The rats would play a big part in the story of my imprisonment when I told it back at home, in Babbington—

"Boy!" said a voice, low but very near my ear. "Wake up!" I was being shaken. "Wake up!"

I blinked in the direction of the voice. Frieda was shaking me. She had a flashlight with her, and for a moment she shone it at herself, then snapped it off again.

"I wasn't asleep," I asserted.

"You were sleeping like the dead," she said.

"Did you come to lift my spirits?" I asked. I will confess, despite the fact that you may ridicule me for it, that my first thought was that she had come out of a spirit of charity to give me a slice of pie and show me her breasts.

"I came to help you escape," she whispered.

"Really?" I said, hiding my disappointment.

"Really," she said. "This farce has gone on long enough. I'll get you out of here and you can be on your way. Come on. Follow me."

She led me out of the room and we began edging along the narrow corridor. We came to an intersection and turned to the left. We came to another intersection and turned to the right. We came to another inter-section, and she hesitated. I wondered whether she knew where she was going. I didn't want to ask. I didn't want to seem to suggest that she might be getting me into a situation worse than the one I had just left. I tried indirection.

"This is like Theseus trying to find his way out of the Labyrinth," I said. "Except that he was able to follow the string that Ariadne had given him. That's how Ariadne helped him find his way out—she gave him a roll of thread—a clew of thread—to unwind as he went in. In Mrs. Fendreffer's class, back at home—"

"Are you suggesting that I don't know where I'm going?"

"No! No, no. Of course not! I—"

"Boy, if you don't shut up my father is going to hear you."

"You don't have to worry about that, Frieda," I said. "Sound couldn't carry very far in a castle. The thick walls, the solid stone—"

She made a sound something like a snort and something like a laugh. "This is not a castle," she said.

"Aren't we all the way up the mountain, in the castle? Isn't this a dungeon?"

"It's a cellar. The cellar of the inn. And that thing you see up the mountain? That's no castle. It's a water tower."

"A water tower?"

"A water tower."

"And your father—"

"My father is my father. He's an imprudent man who has gambling debts. He needs money. When he saw you approaching the inn, he said to me, 'Frieda, here comes a little fool who could be the answer to my troubles.' He played you like a fish. At first, I thought, Fine. Let the boy pay to get Father back on his feet. But then, tonight, when I was lying in my bed, I thought of you calling your mother, back at home, and I thought of my own mother, dead now for nearly two years, and I thought of the pain I would have brought to her if I had called her and said that I was a prisoner, and I knew that I couldn't let it go on."

"But—but—what about the tyrannical owner, Mr. Klam—"

"The only Klam I've ever heard of," she said, pushing against a door and opening the way into the dawn, "is the one you told us about, the one with the banner."

"Oh."

"There you are," she said. "Do you see the path?"

"Yes," I said. "It's veiled in mist, but I can see it."

She put a hand on my shoulder. "Let me give you a piece of advice," she said.

"I'd rather see your breasts," I said, under my breath.

"What?" she said.

"Never mind," I said. "What's the advice?"

"Don't go through life making water towers into castles," she said.

DREAMS OF A PROFESSIONAL FOOL

....

AS A WAY of making our trip more of an adventure for her trusty sidekick, Albertine had not told me where we would be staying for any of our nights on the road. It was her way of providing an element of surprise for me, while ensuring that there would be none for her. It was the way we both liked it.

"Tonight's lodgings should be very interesting," she said, speaking with the false coyness of one who has planted clues in what she has said and wants to be sure that her listener realizes that clues have been planted and can without too much effort be dug up.

"Fair Lady," said I, pretty sure of myself and the clues, "if there be any dragons hassling you, I'm your knight, Sir Peter the Errant."

I had guessed aright. The hotel loomed ahead. Of course, it would have been perfect if it had been a castle. It was not, though it had aspirations in that direction. It was wide and tall, and the lower floors were half-timbered, giving it the appearance of an Elizabethan inn enlarged beyond all regard for good proportion, with a bit of a castle stuck on top. It was one of the outposts of the Knight's Lodging chain, with a logo derived from—or (let's be frank despite the risk of a lawsuit) ripped off from—Picasso's drawing of Don Quixote and Sancho Panza.

We parked the Electro-Flyer in a dark corner of the garage just two long extension cords from an electrical outlet and trundled our rolling bags behind us to the entrance.

The entrance resembled the bridge over a moat. At the far side of the bridge stood a knight in shining armor. At our approach, he swung a massive oaken door open and said in an echoing, metallic voice that came from within his helmet, "Good e'en and welcome to the Knight's Lodging experience. It is a deep, rare, and much-anticipated pleasure to have you here. We hope your stay will be the stuff of legend."

We advanced on the desk like Una and the Red Cross Knight.

The desk was staffed by a jester. He was dressed in motley and wearing a cap-and-bells.

298 • PETER LEROY

"Ha-ha!" he said, by way of greeting. "What's this? A lady and her lapdog? Beauty and the beast?"

"Let us move on, milady," I said to Albertine. "I suggest we find another hostelry."

"Thank you, sir, that is most gracious—" the clerk went on, shifting now to the detached tone people use when they're delivering the patter they've been trained to deliver, the tone you hear in the telephone voice of tech support, but then he seemed to realize that he had heard me say something he didn't want me to say, caught himself, knit his brows, looked at me sideways, and asked me, with genuine concern: "Why?"

"Are you going to tell me that it is the Knight's Lodging policy for the desk jester to insult the paying customers?" I asked, in a low and confidential voice.

"Well, yes," he said, whispering, in the same confidential mode, "it is—or—that is—it has been—and I have worked hard at it—playing the saucy jester, you know—impudent—exploiting his privileged position as the royal fool—but perhaps there has been a change in policy—perhaps you know something that I do not?"

How often does life open a door like that?

"Perhaps so," I whispered, knitting my brows as he had. "Do you know how to calculate the surface area of a ring torus?"

"Methinks we have two jesters here," he muttered, "where there is room for no more than one." Then he turned toward Albertine and asked, in the politest possible manner, "May I help you, fair lady?"

"We have a reservation," she whispered. "The name is Leroy."

The jester flipped open an ancient-looking book and began running his finger along a page. This surprised and—for a moment—impressed me. I wondered whether it could really be that Knight's Lodging used quill and ink for their reservation records. I leaned over the elevated portion of the desk, as if to help the jester spot our name on the page, and I saw that the book was illuminated by the glow of a computer screen hidden from the view of the registering guest.

"It's a fake," I whispered to Albertine. "He actually has a computer back there—"

"Sir," said the jester, his tone suggesting that he might call the security knights and have me tossed from the lobby like a cantankerous drunk through the swinging doors of Ye Olde Medieval Saloon.

"Sorry," I said, in a tone meant to suggest that I understood the value of illusion and that I really did regret having looked behind the curtain, lifted the veil, unscrewed the cover, and observed the operation of the springs and pulleys.

He cocked a skeptic's eyebrow at me and, turning away from me again, asked Albertine, "How are we spelling that?"

"S-O-R-R-Y," she said, the darling.

The jester regarded her from under beetling brows.

"I'm with him," she said with a shrug, as if it explained everything. "The name is Leroy, L-E-R-O-Y."

The jester said, immediately, "I am unable to find L-E-R-O-Y."

Albertine glanced quickly to either side of her, as if to ensure that she was not being observed, and then, beckoning with her raised forefinger, invited the jester to lean her way in order to achieve greater intimacy and confidentiality. He followed her lead, glancing from side to side, then leaning forward. I thought then, and I think now, that he was expecting a bribe, or a boon. "In that case, try Gaudet, G-A-U-D-E-T," she whispered.

Clearly disappointed, the jester flipped the pages of the book theatrically while manipulating the hidden keyboard with his other hand. I could see that his eyes were on the glowing screen, not on the book. After a moment, he announced, triumphantly, "There is nothing in my book!"

"Is there a room available?" asked Albertine.

"Oh, yes. We have many rooms available."

"Well, we'd like one."

"King, Queen, Knight, Lady, or"—a sneer flicked across his lips and wrinkled his nose—"Jester?"

"Knight and Lady," I said, disdaining to add, "of course."

"Sir Peter the Errant," Albertine said with a nod in my direction.

"And Lady Honey-Bunchy-Wunchy," I said with a nod in hers.

"Varlet!" the lackey cried.

A varlet scrambled forward at once and attempted to wrestle our luggage away from me. While we were struggling, the jester began shouting, "Stop that! Let go of those bags!" I assumed at first that he was telling the varlet to stop harassing the paying customers, but he ran around from behind the desk and laid hands on me in a way that made it clear that he thought I was the one at fault. "Will you let the poor varlet take your bags to your room, please?"

"I don't need help," I said.

"But he needs the money, you cheap fucking bastard!" the jester shouted—and then he caught himself. He stood stock-still for a moment, staring me in the eye. Then he swallowed hard and said, in his jester's voice, "I mean, you misbegotten whoreson knave."

I looked at the varlet. He was sniveling. He seemed more shrunken than he had when we'd been struggling over the luggage. I could imagine a starving family back at home, waiting for the scraps he stole from the kitchen. I felt like a misbegotten whoreson knave. I let go of the bags. I fumbled for my wallet, and I gave the varlet the first bill I pulled from it, from the back, where I keep the larger bills. "Sorry," I said, and I meant it.

I heard Albertine say to the jester, "May I ask why you're putting us through all this?"

"Oh, it's part of the Knight's Lodging experience," he said, "some of it—but I went a little overboard." He hung his head, and his bells jangled disconsolately. "I—I guess—if you get right down to it, I was making a pathetic attempt to salvage some dignity from a wasted life."

"Oh," said Albertine.

"Huh?" said I.

"There was something about you two—the moment you walked through the door—something that made me treasure the role I play here as I have never treasured it before. Please don't take offense at this," he said, turning to me, "but I think it was because I saw in you another like myself, a jester, a fellow fool, if you like."

I didn't care to reply to that. I regarded him quizzically, as if I didn't have the slightest idea what he might be talking about.

"I had the feeling that you were going to try some kind of funny business. Maybe you were going to try to obtain lodging under false pretenses, or perhaps perpetrate some fraud, bilk the guests in some way, steal the silverware, something like that, or—and this is what sent the chills through me—that you were going to audition for my position. I thought—I feared—that you might have come here to replace me. I thought that you were going to take from me the only thing I have, the only thing that is left to me from a lifetime of striving and failing—my status as a fool."

"Well," I said, with the disarming shrug and grin of a guy who has an uncanny knack for saying just the thing to brighten the mood in a room, "I am a card-carrying member of the Jesters' Guild, one of the ancient guilds established to prevent the mysteries of the craft from falling into the wrong hands."

"Please," he said, "don't try to make light of this. The time for jesting is past. I'm baring my soul to you here. Have a little respect."

"Um, sure," I muttered. "Of course."

"I don't know why," he went on, resuming his soul-baring, and examining my face at the same time, "but there is something about you that reminds me of someone, someone who played a powerful part in my life."

I stood a little taller.

"He made me what I am today—a fool, a franchise jester, a clown, a buffoon."

I stood a little less tall.

"It began when I was a kid. I grew up here, in the town down the road. The family house is still there, though—well—I don't live there. I haven't gone anywhere. I'm still stuck in the same town, though I once imagined that I would go everywhere. You see, I had dreams—dreams of flying."

"Ah, yes," I said sympathetically.

"When I was a boy, another boy, a boy about my age, came into town one summer evening on an outlandish kind of airplane, a motorcycle with wings."

"What?" I said, surprised and thrilled.

"I was in awe immediately. It was awe at first sight. I don't mind admitting it. I was in awe—but there was something else, too. I was inspired."

"Wow," I said. "This is just amazing—"

"Seeing that kid, just seeing him on that amazing contraption, made me think that life was full of possibilities, and not just life in general, or somebody's life, or that boy's life, but my life."

My heart was racing.

"May I ask you something?" I said.

"Peter—" said Albertine, counseling caution.

"I just have to ask this one thing." I turned to the jester. "Did you actually see this contraption fly?"

"Did I see it fly?"

302 • PETER LEROY

"That's what I'm asking."

"Of course I saw it fly. It was a beautiful machine, and it flew like a dream."

"Okay," I said. "Sorry for the interruption. Please go on."

If I had caught sight of myself in a mirror at that moment, I know what expression I would have seen. I've seen it on my face before. It's the look of one who possesses secret, and satisfying, information.

"That boy brought with him, when he flew into town, a great gift."

Pride swelled my breast. What a noble little lad I had been.

"The gift, the gift that he brought me, as if it was a gift for me alone, was a license to dream, and to dream big."

"Gosh," I said, reverting to the lingo of my boyhood. "I can't tell you how much it means—"

"I never thanked him for that gift," he continued. "I never even spoke to him, because I was too much in awe of him, but when he flew out of town I waved goodbye and I whispered my thanks to him."

If my grandmother had been there she would have told me that I looked like the cat that swallowed the canary. I was grinning from ear to ear. In another moment, I would reveal my identity, and—

"Now, of course, so many years later, I curse the day when that boy flew into town and made me dream!"

"What?" I said. "What did you say?"

"He ruined my life, the little bastard. I could have been a contented man today, living a little life, with a sweet little wife, in the little town where I grew up, just down the road—but no—no—I had to dream—I had to reach for something bigger—I had to go chasing the dream of flight."

"It's getting late," I said with an elaborate yawn. "You're looking tired, Al. Maybe we should go to our room."

"Please, please don't go," he said, grasping Albertine's hands. "I see that you have a sympathetic soul. We fools have our faculties, you know. In my case it's a talent for sympathy, and I can see that you have it, too. Please hear me out. Please suffer this fool."

"Gladly," she said, drawing him to her and wrapping her arms around him.

"What do you say we get a drink?" I suggested.

"I can't leave my post," he said. "It would cost me my job."

"You can go if you like, Peter," said Albertine.

"Oh, no, no," I said. "I'll stay." To the jester I said, "I have a sympathetic soul, too. Ask Al. She'll tell you. Many people say that I—"

"Go on," she urged the jester, with deep compassion.

He released a long sigh, shaking his head, jingling his bells, and said, "In the years that followed, while I was finishing high school, I kept the example of that boy in my mind, as a reminder of what I could do if I put my mind to it, if I stuck to the job at hand, if I didn't ever lose sight of my dream, and I tried to build a plane."

"Oh, no," said Albertine. I could see the tears welling up in her eyes.

"Not an easy thing to do," I said, as one who knows.

"I bought plans," he said. He was beginning to sniffle. "I bought supplies and tools. I bought parts. I worked after school and weekends to earn the money, and then I worked at night, in my family's garage, trying to build the thing. I gave that plane everything I had. I had no girlfriend, no pet, no spending money, no friends. I gave myself entirely to my pursuit—my fool's errand." He looked at Albertine. Tears were running down his cheeks. "And I failed," he said.

"You poor man," she said. She brought his hands to her lips and kissed them.

"Nothing to be ashamed of," I muttered.

"I didn't give up," he said. He stood a little taller. "I told myself that the boy who had flown into town hadn't quit, and I wasn't going to quit either. So, as some fools do, I persisted in my folly. I worked my way through college, and I went into the family business, becoming my father's partner in our little pharmacy in town. I had no wife, no children, and no real future, but I always had the same dream. I bought more plans, more materials and tools. And again I failed."

"Darn that dream," said Albertine.

"Dreaming can be a positive thing," I asserted. Albertine gave me another look. "Not while driving, of course," I added.

"I bought kits," said the jester, shaking his head in disbelief at the extent of his folly and making those damned bells jingle again, "kits that were supposed to be so easy, so complete, so carefully designed that they were—foolproof!" He began to laugh. It was a sharp, giggling laugh, like a naughty child's. "Foolproof! They were foolproof!" He did a little dance in place, playing the fool for us now, doing his job, entertaining us. "And every time I tried to build a plane from a foolproof kit I proved that there could be no kit so simple that it was proof against the efforts of *this* fool!" He took a few steps, side to side, like a hopping crab. "Whatever it took, however hard he had to work, *this* fool could find a way to fail!"

Albertine was dabbing at her eyes. The jester went on dancing as he spoke, taking little hopping steps that jingled his bells.

"I hit bottom," he said. "I got the idea that if I took the latest kit plane apart completely and put it back together again, I could make the damned thing fly. I won't tell you how many times I did that. If I told you, you'd think I was insane. Let's just say that I tried and tried and tried. And failed and failed and failed. But that's not all. I let the business go. So I failed at that, too. I lost the pharmacy. I lost the family home. I turned to drink. I wandered around town all day, aimlessly, drunk, and slept in the park at night. I was as low as I could go."

The jester stopped dancing and hid his face with his hands.

From behind his hands he said, "I'm sorry to burden you with my troubles. I shouldn't be making you listen to my tale of woe—after all, it's not your fault."

"Well," I said with a sigh, "in a way it is, because you see, I was—"

Albertine shot me a look. I shrugged and shut up.

The jester grinned at us suddenly. "But here comes the good part," he said. "Here comes the story of my success!"

"Great!" I said. "Let's hear it."

"Every now and then, when the weather was bad, the local cops would throw me into jail for the night, clean me up, give me a hot meal, and try to 'get me on my feet.' I'd gone to school with some of those cops. We'd grown up and grown old in this town. Some of them were nearing retirement. They knew about my obsession—my dream of flight—and I couldn't help feeling that they were laughing at me. All it took was a word, a look, a certain tone of voice. One day, I knew it beyond any doubt. It was a miserable day, cold and wet, and I was willing to endure the shame of their charity and their ridicule for the warmth of a cell, so I let them take me in without protest. After dinner, the chief of police himself paid me a visit. 'They're building a big new resort hotel in town,' he said, casually. 'Out by the highway. One of those Knight's Lodging places. You might be able to get a job there. It looks like you're just what they're looking for.' He handed me the local paper, folded to an ad, and he left me alone with it. I could hear him snickering as he walked away. I picked up the paper and read the ad, and I knew he was right. I was just what they were looking for."

He began that dance again.

"And that's how I became a professional fool!" he shrieked.

Albertine and I looked at each other.

"If it's any consolation," I said, reaching out to him in a comrade's way, "I too have been a fool at times, and I—"

A look of terror came over his face.

"But," I said hurriedly, forcefully, "I assure you that I have no designs on your position. None whatsoever. I'm not a professional fool. Honest. Just an amateur. I shall neither usurp you nor make the attempt. When I play the fool, it is in private, in milady's chambers, exclusively for her entertainment."

"Let's go to bed," said Albertine.

You might think that I lay in bed, restless, wracked with guilt. No, I didn't. I owe it to Albertine that I fell asleep quickly and slept through the night. Before we turned in, she threw her arms around me, hugged me, kissed me, hugged me again, and said, "It really wasn't your fault. If it hadn't been flying, it would have been some other dream, inspired by some other traveler. It wasn't your fault."

In the morning, at breakfast, where a different jester was cutting capers, pulling eggs from the ears of male guests and pinching their ladies' bottoms, I thanked her for the consolation she had given me, and I asked her, "Did you sleep well?"

She burst into tears.

"My darling," I said, rising from the table and rushing to her side, holding her. "What's the matter? Is it the jester? His story? His dream?"

"No, no," she said. "It isn't that. It's just that—last night—after you fell asleep I found that I couldn't sleep—because of the jester, I guess— so I turned the TV on."

"I never heard it—"

"I muted it—and turned the captions on."

"You are the sweetest."

"That's me," she said, smiling through her tears, "but—like a fool—I watched the news."

"Oh."

"What a species," she said, shaking her head, huddling in my arms. "It was as if I had been condemned to watch the whole bloody history of human viciousness."

"Let me guess," I said. "Pride, avarice, envy, wrath, lust, gluttony, and sloth, right?"

"That's the news in a nutshell."

"And this morning you're feeling the tug of gravity."

"Yes, I am."

"Let me lift you," I said. "Today I promise you humility, liberality, friendship, kindness, temperance, and diligence."

"And chastity?" she asked, wrinkling her nose in that adorable way she does when she's invited to eat fish.

"How about tempered lust?"

"Fine with me—but can you really deliver?"

"I can. Come on. Let's get into that Electro-Flyer and flee, and while we're en route I'll read you the chapter I call 'Poppy's Pockets.'"

POPPY'S POCKETS

. . . .

The storyteller: he is the man who could let the wick of his life be consumed completely by the gentle flame of his story.
—Walter Benjamin, "The Storyteller," in *Illuminations*

THE GOLDEN LIGHT dominates my memory, light that saturated the sky and the air around *Spirit* and me. That golden light was everywhere, as if it came from all directions, casting no shadows. It was as bright as, but different from, the beach light I was accustomed to at home. That beach light also came from above and below, but it was whiter from below because it was reflected from the water and the sand. This light was yellow, reflected from the golden plants that grew alongside the road. Even now it coats my memory like a sticky liquid, like honey. It's pleasant, warm, and coddling, if a little cloying.

I thought that these golden plants might be wheat, and so I was filled with a poignant nostalgia, because, years earlier, my grandfather had thought of growing wheat in the back yard of my family's suburban tract house, back in Babbington, and though he had never succeeded, I had gotten it into my head that I knew what a field of wheat looked like.

"This is the famous waving wheat," I informed *Spirit*.

"Really?" she said. "It looks like waving weeds to me."

"It's wheat," I said assuredly.

I came to a crossroads settlement, just a mile or so of shops and houses stretching along each of the arms of the intersection. How should I choose from among the houses the one to approach, the one where I would ask to be taken in, fed, and sheltered for the night? Should I choose the largest? The smallest? The best maintained? The most neglected? I would choose the most welcoming. Of course. One of them stood just a bit apart from the others, with those yellow plants in abundance around it, and there was something about the light of the late afternoon sun on the rail fences and the dust in the yard, the long driveway to the house, that made me think that I would be welcome there. I wasn't particularly tired, but I wanted a warm welcome. I wanted to be taken in.

"That's the place for us," I whispered to *Spirit*, hushed by the golden radiance of it all.

I turned into the driveway, and something changed. I detected a stillness now that made me feel like an intruder. I felt that I was violating the privacy of the people who lived there, that I was trespassing, not only on their property, but in their lives, and I changed my mind about the welcome I would be given.

"Maybe not," I said.

"I see what you mean," said *Spirit*. "We don't belong here. They won't want us here."

I had begun the awkward process of turning *Spirit* around when I heard the wheezing hinges of a screen door and turned again toward the house. There, in the doorway, was a grandmotherly figure. She was wearing an ample dress, and she had an ample bosom. Everything about her spoke of amplitude and comfort—not opulence, but a reliable sufficiency. She shaded her eyes with her hand and gave me a long look. Then she went back into the house.

"She's probably got a pie cooling in the kitchen," I muttered hungrily.

"Cherry," said *Spirit*. "Tart and sweet. With a crust as golden as the evening air."

The woman returned, holding a plump pie in both hands. She was followed by a man dressed in a black suit.

I set *Spirit* on her stand, wiped my hands on my pants legs, combed my hair with my fingers, wiped my hands again, and began walking toward the house. As I approached it, other people began emerging from it, each of them making the screen door wheeze and bang. They ranged in age downward from the old woman, and all of them were dressed in black. One by one they lined up along the porch as if they expected me to take their picture, a portrait of the family on their porch. One of them, a boy about my age, came down from the porch and walked out to meet me.

"Are you the photographer?" he asked in a subdued voice.

"No," I said, "but it's funny that you should ask."

"Funny? Why?"

"The way everybody came out of the house and lined up along the porch made me think that somebody was going to take their picture—"

"My grandfather died," he said.

"I thought that they were expecting me to—what?"

"My grandfather died."

"Oh—your grandfather—oh—I'm sorry."

"It wasn't your fault."

"I—no—it wasn't my fault—I meant I was sorry for you—for your loss—but—I should go."

"No, no. Don't go. Having you here will turn us aside from our misery and mourning. You will take us out of ourselves."

"I should go."

"You should stay."

"No—I really should go."

"My grandfather would have wanted you to stay, to meet everybody, have dinner, and even stay the night if you need shelter. He was a generous man. Hospitality was important to him."

"Well, okay."

"Come on," he said, turning toward the house, leading the way, "we're just about to have the period of remembrance. It's an old family tradition."

"That sounds like something private," I said.

"No, it's good to have a stranger at the remembrance because it gives everyone an excuse to speak at greater length about the deceased than they otherwise would."

"You mean because the stranger doesn't know anything about—the deceased?"

"Exactly. You'll be doing us a big favor."

I followed him to the porch. There was a round of introductions and a little awkward small talk. Someone asked me about *Spirit*. Someone else asked me about my travels. And someone asked me where I was from.

"Babbington," I said. "It's in New York, on Long—"

"I remember!" thundered a voice from the other end of the porch.

"Really?" I said, surprised. "You've been there? That's—"

"I remember!" said everyone else, in voices not quite so thunderous.

"All of you? Wow. I—"

"They're remembering Grandfather," the boy whispered. "The reminiscence has started."

"Oh," I said. "I thought—"

He put his finger to his lips, and I shut up.

"I remember the way my brother Richard taught me to fish when we were boys," said an elderly man at the far end of the porch, sitting near the thunderer who had announced the beginning of the period of reminiscence. "I wasn't very good at it." A good-natured, familial chuckling animated the comfortable crowd. "Richard taught me that fishing is an occupation for the patient. 'The rewards may not come soon, and they may not come often,' he said, 'but if you've got bait on your hook, and your hook is in the water, and the line is in your hand, you'll catch your fish sometime or other.'"

Everyone smiled a bittersweet smile. Everyone murmured approval.

I joined them. I may have been a young fool in many ways, but I had a sympathetic soul.

"I remember—um—the candies," said a little girl in a black velvet dress. I remember thinking that the dress must be new, bought for this occasion. Judging from the way she rubbed the nap of the velvet, the girl was nervous, and she was worried that she might have said the wrong thing. Everyone chuckled. One or two sniffled.

"Do you want to say anything more about the candies, honey?" asked a woman beside the girl, a woman who had to be her mother.

"Um," said the girl. She thought for a moment, then turned to her mother and asked, "What?"

"About Poppy's pockets?"

"Oh. Yeah. Poppy would say, 'Better look in Poppy's pockets. You never know what Poppy might be hiding.'"

We all sniffled.

"I think we all remember Poppy's pockets," said the girl's mother, dabbing at her eyes, "any of us who were invited to go hunting for candy in Poppy's pockets."

"Or money," said a man seated across from the girl's mother.

Everyone glared at him. Me, too.

"Well, I was never actually *invited* to hunt for money in Poppy's pockets," the man explained, "but I did *find* money there one time, when I was hunting for candy."

There was some snorting and a bit of harrumphing.

"Well, I did," the man insisted. "Wads of it. Crumpled balls of cash. I can remember it to this day. I thought it was for me. But it wasn't. Poppy stuffed it back in his pocket and bought my silence with a candy mint."

There was an awkward silence. It lengthened.

"What I'm always going to remember about Dad is his optimism," said a man near me. All the rest of us, including the man who had found the wads of cash in Poppy's pockets, sighed with relief, glad to have the awkward silence broken.

"He was an incurable optimist, that's for sure," said the little girl's mother.

"A cockeyed optimist," said the thunderer at the far end of the porch.

"We all know about Dad's wonderful sermons," the man who had broken the silence continued, "and to me they were his way of trying to turn his optimism into a new era of humility, liberality, friendship, kindness, temperance, and diligence."

"Yes, sir," said one of the elders.

"A noble, if futile, effort," said the thunderer.

"Yes, a noble effort," said the younger man, "and I suppose you're right about its being futile, and I suppose that there is really no reason for me to talk about it any further, since all of us know all about it—but—"

He looked at me. Everyone looked at me.

"Wait a minute," he said. "It's not true that all of us know about it—there is one among us who knows nothing about it—our guest." He extended his arm toward me. "And so I'm going to tell him." Speaking directly to me now, he said, "Our family has been a part of the warp and weft of this town for generations. My grandfather was mayor for many years. My brother is assessor and collector of taxes. Even I, in my modest way, serve the town. I run the local paper, *The Oracle*. My father—may he rest in peace—was pastor of the Little Church on the Hill—and he was widely—universally—admired for his sermons."

There was murmurous approval for this way of putting it, and I nodded my head and made a bit of a murmuring sound myself to show that although I was not one of them I was as one with them.

"His sermons were not about sinning, and they were not about sins. Nor were they imprecations to his parishioners to mend their ways. They were never admonitions to behave. There were no threats in them. There was no cajoling in them. They were, instead, predictions. They didn't ever ask people to shun error and do right, instead they showed people what their lives would be like if they actually *did* live as they *ought* to live. I wish I could convey to you how exhilarating it was to hear these evocations of the truly good life, not the shallow so-called good life of tawdry pleasure, but the real thing, the rich life that goodness would bring. It's—it's beyond my power—I—"

In a soft, almost distracted voice, his mother, Poppy's widow, said, "Why don't you read one of your father's sermons to the boy?"

There was a stunned silence.

"You mean—go into his library and—go into his files—and get one of his sermons?" asked the son.

"That's what I mean," said his mother.

"But—I—I've never been in there." He looked around the porch. "No one here has ever been in there. It was Dad's sanctum sanctorum. It would feel like a violation."

"It's time the door was opened," she said. "The place needs a good airing. Besides, you'd like the boy to hear one of your father's sermons, wouldn't you?"

The thunderer said, "I'd be pleased to hear you read one of them myself."

One by one, the others voiced their agreement with him.

"Mom—" said the son.

She reached into her bosom and drew out a key.

"Okay," the son said. He took the key. "I'll be back in a minute."

He left, and he left behind him the silence of anticipation.

The widow broke that silence, saying, "Why doesn't everybody get something to eat while we're waiting? Everything's laid out in the dining room."

We trooped into the dining room, took plates, circled the table, heaped our plates high, and returned to the porch, where we fell to. The food was hearty and delicious, and the conversation was warm and lighthearted. I could see that everyone missed Poppy, that he had been well loved, and that the mourners' loss was great, but I could also see that their affection for one another was a powerful palliative. I wondered, and for a moment even thought of asking, whether one of Poppy's predictive sermons might have taught them, in the exemplary manner that his son had described, how to endure this day.

Only when we had finished eating did the group begin to wonder what was keeping Poppy's son.

"Better send out the dogs," said the old man whom Poppy had taught to fish.

"I'll go," said the widow.

"No, no, you stay there and rest yourself," said the thunderer. "I'll go."

When he didn't return after a few minutes, the widow said, "I'm going," and this time no one objected when she rose and left.

Time passed. None of the three returned.

"I'll go," said the mother of the little girl in velvet.

"Hell, let's all go," said the old man. "At my age, I can't afford to wait much longer."

Laughing, we all headed for Poppy's library.

When we got there, the laughter stopped. I think the notion that we were violating Poppy's privacy overwhelmed and hushed us. We crowded silently around the open doorway, peering in, the ones in the back standing on their tiptoes to try to get a look.

Inside the room, Poppy's son and widow and thunderous friend were hard at work. They were tearing the place apart. The files had been pulled open. Desk drawers lay on the floor. Papers were everywhere. The thunderer had tipped an armchair upside down and was reaching into its underside. The widow was groping inside the open case of a grandfather clock. The son was emptying a cigar box onto the floor.

In the middle of the massive desk was a heap of cash. Most of the bills were rumpled and crumpled, squeezed into wads and balls. All of us recalled the reminiscence about finding money in Poppy's pockets when rummaging for candy, and the man who had made the claim recalled it, too. "See?" he cried. "I told you! I told you there were wads of cash!"

The three in the room turned from their work, startled. They looked at us. They looked at one another. They looked at the wads of cash. They looked at us again. Their faces fell.

"Poppy—" said the son.

"It seems that Richard—" said the thunderer.

"My dear husband—" said the widow.

"Money—" said the son.

"In the files—and the desk—" said the thunderer.

"It's everywhere!" said the widow.

"Poppy had his hand in the till!" sang the man who had found the wads in Poppy's pocket. "He was skimming the collection cash!" He erupted in a cackling laughter that I can hear in memory as I write these words. "He was lining his pockets!"

Everyone but the cackling man was embarrassed into silence. People hung their heads. They drifted away from the library. They distanced themselves from one another. They licked their wounded illusions.

The boy took me aside. "I think you should go now," he whispered. "Go away. You can sleep in the barn if you want, but no one is going to want to see you in the morning. Seeing you would remind them of their shame. Please—go on out to the barn now—and go away in the morning—before first light."

Spirit and I retired to the barn. Sleep did not come quickly, so I got out my copy of *Faustroll* and my *Handy Dictionary*, and I resumed my interrogation of the Bonhommes, as Panmuphle. Their daughter had just informed me that King Saleh, who had worn a mustache like Dr. Faustroll's, was the ruler of one of the kingdoms of the sea in the Arabian Nights entertainments:

> "Thank you, my dear," I said, tousling the little darling's hair. "That reminds me: what of his hair?"
>
> I had hoped that the girl would respond, but her mother stepped forward, interposed herself between the girl and me, and declared in a businesslike manner, "His hair is ash blond and very black."
>
> "Forgive me, madame," I said, "but I do not see how it can be both blond and black."
>
> "It alternates hair by hair," she explained, as if to an imbecile, "in an auburnian ambiguity that changes with the hour of the sun."
>
> I regarded her a moment with incredulity. "You have the soul of a poet, madame," I said at last, when I had recovered myself. "Perhaps you will continue."
>
> "His eyes are as two capsules of simple writing ink," she said without hesitation, "prepared like the eau-de-vie of Danzig, with golden spermatozoa within."
>
> This, I must confess, did not make any sense to me, though the mention of spermatozoa made me flush crimson, which in turn made the Bonhommes' fetching daughter giggle in a way that made me redden even more.
>
> "He is beardless," said Mr. Bonhomme, apparently eager to have his contribution weigh as much as his wife's, "except for his mustache."
>
> "Does he shave himself, or does he visit a barber?" I asked, thinking that a barber might be an additional source of useful

information, since barbers are famous for interrogating their clients while they are under their ministrations.

"Neither, monsieur," said the little man.

"You said that he was beardless," I reminded him.

"Through the use of microbes of baldness, of course," he said.

"Hmmm," I said, while surreptitiously making a note to inquire of the neighbors whether the Bonhommes might be insane.

"They saturate his skin from groin to eyelid," he explained, with the same air of addressing an imbecile that I had found so annoying in his wife, "and they nibble and gnaw at the—the little bulbs."

"The follicles," his daughter corrected him shyly.

"Yes!" he said, with a papa's pride. "The follicles."

"I must ask you, sir," I said, "how you know these things, which, it seems to me, are of a rather intimate nature."

He shrugged in the way that everyone does to indicate that the answer must be obvious. I raised an eyebrow to indicate that I would like more of an answer than that shrug.

"Sir," lisped the comely daughter, "we have all done some services for Doctor Faustroll from time to time. My father has performed the duties of a valet, my mother has cooked for him, and I—"

"Mademoiselle," I said compassionately, "you do not have to—"

"My daughter has performed the duties of a maid, sir," said Mrs. Bonhomme.

"I see," I said. "As a result of this work, then, you have all had an opportunity to observe the mysterious doctor."

"That is correct."

"Pray, go on," I said. "Tell me more."

"In contrast to his smoothness from groin to eyelid, from groin to feet he is sheathed in satyric black fur," said the wife.

"My goodness," I said. Involuntarily, I glanced at the Bonhommes' toothsome young daughter before noting the word *satyric* on my pad.

"That morning—" said Mrs. Bonhomme.

"The morning of his disappearance?" I asked.

"Yes, sir. Of course, sir. That morning he took his daily sponge bath, using paper painted in two tones by Maurice Denis, depicting trains—"

"I must interrupt again," I said. "Do you mean that he substitutes paper for sponge in his sponge bath?"

"No, sir," said the daughter. "He substitutes paper for water."

Very early in the morning, the boy came and shook me awake. I was asleep on my notebook, with my books in the hay beside me.

"Time to go," he said.

"Mm-hm. Okay. I'm awake. I'm going."

I got up and started to mount *Spirit* in the dark.

"If you don't mind," he said, "could you push it out to the road before you start it?"

"Huh?" I said sleepily.

"The noise," he explained.

"Oh. Yeah."

I began pushing her. He walked along beside me.

"Do you have any advice for me?" I asked when we neared the road.

"Advice?"

"Yeah. It seems that just about everybody I meet has some advice for me. I thought you might."

"No. I don't have any advice for you."

"Okay. In that case—" I mounted *Spirit*.

"I guess I have a request, though," he said.

"Yeah," I said. "I know. Don't worry. I won't tell anybody."

"Thanks."

"You don't have to thank me—but—I have a question for you—is this wheat?"

"Wheat?"

"All this golden stuff growing all around."

"Nah, that's not wheat. Just weeds."

TOMORROW'S NEWS TODAY

· ·

The sense for projects—which could be called aphorisms of the future—differs from the sense for aphorisms of the past only in direction, progressive in the former and regressive in the latter. . . . One could easily say that the sense for aphorisms and projects is the transcendental part of the historical spirit.

—Friedrich Schlegel, *Literary Aphorisms*

BEFORE WE BEGAN our trip, I had hoped that here and there in our travels, during our reiteration of my aerocycle journey, Albertine and I would stumble upon some of my personal landmarks from the original trip, rediscover some of the places where I had experienced significant adventures on the way to New Mexico years earlier. I had hoped that revisiting some of those places would allow me to reflect upon the changes that time had wrought on the landscape and culture through which I had journeyed. I had also hoped to impress Albertine, or at least to convince her that the trip had actually occurred. To ensure that we would stumble upon at least one of my landmarks, I had done something, well, sneaky. I had gone looking for one of them on the Web, and I had found it. So it was with mounting anticipation that when a certain highway exit approached I suggested that we take it and see if we could find a small town where we could have lunch.

"I have a hunch," I said.

"A hunch about lunch?"

"A hunch about a town. It ought to be around here."

"You mean the town where Poppy lined his pockets?"

"We'll see," I said.

The town hadn't changed much. There was more of everything—there were more shops, more houses, more cars—but still no more than the two main streets, and still the waving yellow weeds along the roadside. We drove slowly along the street that ran east-west, and near the center of the town, I found the institution I'd been looking for.

"Look," I said. "That's the newspaper office."

"Where?" she asked.

"There, on the right. *The Oracle*. See the lettering in the window?"

The Oracle
"Tomorrow's News Today"

"Oh, my gosh," she said, braking and then angling into a parking slot at the curb.

"You didn't believe me, did you?"

"Of course I believed you," she said. She switched the Electro-Flyer off and reached behind her for her handbag.

"How much?" I asked as we got out of the car and started toward the office.

"How much what?"

"How much did you believe me?"

"Pretty much."

I swung the door open and held it for her. The office was quiet, and nearly empty. There was one young woman at a desk, tapping softly at a computer keyboard. She glanced up when we came in, smiled in greeting, and went back to her work. Albertine and I stood for a moment just inside the door, expecting that as soon as she came to a point in her work when she could pause she would ask us what we wanted. We continued to wait, but after a while we began to feel that we might wait as long as we chose to wait without ever having the woman pause and ask what we wanted, so I decided to come right out with it, more or less.

"Is the editor in?" I asked.

"Oh," she said, apparently surprised by the question. "Yes, he is. Do you want to see him?"

"Yes," I said. "We'd like that."

She got up at once and came to the railing that separated the front of the office from the area that was crowded with desks, though she seemed to be the only worker.

"I'm sorry," she said as she swung the gate open for us. "I thought you had just come in to watch."

"To watch?" asked Albertine.

"To watch me work."

"Does that happen a lot?" I asked.

"People coming in to watch me work? Yes, quite a lot. It's a way to pass the time. People drop in to watch me write the news."

"You mean to watch you invent the news, don't you?"

"Yes, I do," she said. "So you know about *The Oracle*?"

"I was here years ago," I said. "I was a teenager at the time. I—ah—flew into town on an aerocycle. I was on my way to New Mexico—from Babbington—my home town—back in New York—and someone everybody called Poppy had just died."

"Oh," she said, dropping her eyes to the floor. "Poppy. He was—"

"Quite a character," I offered. "I was there for the remembrance ceremony, at Poppy's house, on the porch."

"The house is still there," she said, "but—it's not a home anymore."

"Funeral parlor?" I asked.

"Not quite," she said with a giggle. "Medical center."

A man wearing rimless glasses emerged from a door in the back, reading a sheet of paper but addressing the young woman. "Candace," he was saying, "would you see what you can do with this mosquito business? I've been banging my head against it for an hour and—oh—hello." He stared at Albertine and me.

"Peter Leroy," I said, extending my hand, "and Albertine Gaudet."

"They came to see you," the young woman explained. "Mr. Leroy was at the remembrance for Poppy."

The man bent his head forward and looked at me over his glasses.

"I remember you," he said.

He didn't seem to relish the memory. He took the glasses off and rubbed the indentations they had left on either side of his nose.

"What brings you here?" he asked.

"We were passing through—"

His look was so full of suspicion that it was nearly audible.

"Really," I said. "Albertine and I are retracing the route I took all those years ago, for the sake of my memoirs, and to correct certain misimpressions—back at home—in Babbington—"

"It's true," said Albertine.

"How could I possibly have kept myself from dropping in for a visit?" I said.

"Mm," he said. "Did you expect to find my father here?"

"He would have to be eighty or ninety now, wouldn't he?"

"He would be eighty-eight, but he's—no longer with us."

"I'm sorry to hear that," I said. "The fact is, though, that I had a hunch I'd find you here."

"Why's that?"

"Just a hunch."

"Mm," he said again, in that suspicious way of his. "You say you're writing your memoirs?"

"Constantly," I said. "I often say that the wick of my life is being gently consumed by the flame of my memoirs."

The editor of *The Oracle* looked at Albertine and raised an eyebrow.

"Believe me," she said, "he says it more often than I can tell you."

"And I suppose you're here to tell me that you're going to write about my grandfather—about Poppy."

"I'd like to," I said, "but not if you'd rather I didn't. That day, years ago—or actually the next morning—you asked me not to tell anybody about what had happened, what Poppy had done—and I've kept silent about it until this morning, when I told Albertine while we were on our way here."

"A memoir is a history," he said. "It's a story with a debt, a debt to the past. You pay the debt in the coin of truth."

"Hmm," I said, nodding thoughtfully but noncommittally.

"All I would ask is that you remember all the people who were on the porch that day, for the remembrance, and think about the Poppy they remembered, rather than the Poppy we—ah—discovered—later—"

He broke off. He looked at Candace. He looked at Albertine and me.

After a while, he said, "Sorry. I'm not talking about truth, am I? What I guess I mean is that I wish you knew more than what you learned that day. If you did, you might—look, have you got a while? I'd like to tell you about Poppy, and my father, and myself, and *The Oracle*."

The young woman cleared her throat.

"And about my family," the man said. "This is my youngest daughter, Candace." He drew her to him and hugged her, then said, "If you've got a little while—"

I looked at Albertine, asking, with my eyes, whether we had a little while.

"We've got more than that," she said. "We'll spend the night in town if there's a decent hotel."

"There's a hotel," said Candace, "but I wouldn't ask you to stay there. Come home with us."

We did go home with them. It wasn't far. Albertine and Candace rode in the Electro-Flyer, and I walked with the editor, Edward Hemple. The house that he and his daughter lived in was modest but solid, unassertive, a good refuge for a father and daughter who spent their days at the taxing and audacious task of predicting the future.

Edward's story didn't come until after dinner, when we settled into the plump furniture in the front room and listened in the gentle light of two dim lamps.

"My grandfather died in disgrace," he said, addressing this preliminary to Albertine. "He stole from the church where he was pastor, literally taking the cash from the offering tray."

"I know," said Albertine. "Peter told me about the remembrances on the front porch and the discovery of the hidden—ah—"

"Loot," suggested Candace, with a giggle.

With a smile for his daughter, Edward said, "You see how time has diluted the shame—for some people. Candace thinks of Poppy's thefts as a joke—"

"Not a joke, exactly," she protested. "More like a single picaresque escapade in a narrow, conventional, and essentially honorable life."

"Maybe it was that for Poppy, too," Edward said. "An escapade. And maybe he did it for the little thrill that it may have given him, for the spice that it may have added to his life. He certainly never seems to have spent any of the money. Maybe he never intended to. But for my father it was a heinous crime, and he lived the rest of his life under the shadow of its disgrace."

"He ran *The Oracle* then," I said. "I'm curious to know how he handled the story."

"He didn't," said Edward.

"He didn't report it?"

"He arranged things so that he wouldn't have to."

"How?"

"The next day, after you had left, he came to breakfast late, and he had a plan. He summoned all the family and friends, everyone who had been on the porch that day, to the house, and he distributed the cash among them. Their job was to return the money by putting it into the collection plate, little by little, a small amount added to their usual offerings, Sunday after Sunday. It took years, but eventually it was all returned."

"The debt was paid," I suggested.

"The financial debt," he said, "the debt to the parishioners of the Little Church on the Hill. But not the debt to the past."

"The one that you pay in the coin of truth," I said.

"Exactly. My father never wanted to pay that debt. He never wanted to acknowledge it, didn't even want to think about it. He wouldn't talk about Poppy, and his silence and denial drove a wedge between us, because my curiosity about the man was boundless. I wanted to understand him. I wanted to know how he had come to do what he did. I mean, in this little town, especially in the little town that this used to be when he was stealing from the collection plate, or the little town that everyone thought it was before they discovered that its pastor had been stealing from the collection plate, the enormity of that theft was—it was staggering."

He got up and went to a cabinet. From it he took a bottle of cognac and four glasses. The look of surprise on Candace's face said that this was an event. It portended revelations.

"I kept pestering Dad to tell me things about Poppy that he didn't want to discuss," he said as he poured, "and I pestered him and pestered him until he ordered me out of the house and struck me from his will."

He raised his glass to a portrait of his father.

"I moved into an apartment over the grocery store downtown. Fortunately, my mother was sympathetic. She used to visit me every Thursday, and she'd bring me a roasted chicken. I wonder if my father knew. One Thursday, she brought me—in addition to the cold roast chicken—a paper bag with some of Granddad's papers in it. Week after week, she brought more, until I had them all. I read my way through them, and I began to understand him. I began to see that Poppy had had one very good idea in his life—and I don't mean skimming the collection plate."

"I'm glad to hear that," I said.

"I mean what I've come to call the power of positive predictions."

"You mean his sermons telling people what life would be like if they lived as they should?"

"I do, but at first I got it backwards."

"How so?"

"I couldn't help wishing that my grandfather's history had been different in the one essential way that would have made it better."

"No wads of cash," I said.

"No wads of cash," he said. "I'm sure you can understand how I wished I could rewrite that history, changing only that one thing, making my grandfather again the innocent that we had all thought he was, making his life end the way it should have instead of the way it did."

"Did you?"

"I tried. I couldn't do it. I couldn't make it convincing. I couldn't even convince myself. It was as if the truth was there, between the lines, and anyone would be able to see it."

"Sometimes," I said, with conviction, because this was a subject I actually knew something about, "we say much, much more than we mean to say, because what we want to hide reveals itself in every word that we say about everything else."

"That's it," he agreed. "The thing that I was leaving unsaid announced itself on every page."

"It was the past reminding you of your debt," said Albertine.

"It was," he said, and with a sly smile he added, "but when my father retired I found a way to stand that debt on its head. Instead of paying the debt to the past, I began investing in the future."

He paused, and I knew he was waiting for Albertine to urge him on.

"Go on," she said obligingly. "I'm fascinated."

"Well," he said, "when I thought about it, I realized that a newspaper is like a serial history."

"History in daily installments."

"Right. Exactly that. But my grandfather's good idea was about influencing the future." He got up and opened the briefcase that he had carried home with him. From it he pulled a copy of *The Oracle*. "I've turned *The Oracle* into a serial prediction. Take this copy to bed with you. Let it lull you to sleep. You can tell me what you think of it in the morning."

Candace showed us to a comfortable room, and we got into bed as quickly as we could. We read *The Oracle* with fascination, passing sections of it back and forth. The issue we read was dated ten years ahead of the current date. The town we read about was a place where people got along with one another. They were humble and modest, not pushy or demanding. They were generous with one another, eager to give, eager to help. They respected their differences, but they cultivated collaboration. They were friendly. They were neighborly. They were welcoming. They were quick to praise and slow to condemn. They had sympathetic souls. They were moderate in what they asked of one another, and of the earth. They were diligent in their work, and they were unswervingly optimistic.

"It's going to be a nice place," I said.

"We might want to return in a decade and see how it turns out," suggested Albertine.

"Maybe," I said with a yawn.

At breakfast the next morning, Ed and Candace were silent, but I could see the eagerness in their eyes. They wanted to know what we thought of *The Oracle*.

"It's a fascinating idea," I said, "but let me ask you something: have you thought of going beyond local predictions?"

"Beyond?"

"Yes. How about—let me see—world peace, international brotherhood, the triumph of reason over superstition, an end to vengeance—"

He laughed, but it was a bitter laugh.

"Sorry," I said. "I didn't—"

"Mr. Leroy," he said, rising from the table with a look that I remembered from years ago, when he had told me to spend the night in the barn and leave before dawn, "I may be every bit the cockeyed optimist that my grandfather was, but I am not a fool."

HOMESICK AND BLUE

••

Cut grass. Work fast.

—Dersu Uzala, in *Dersu Uzala*

IT WAS A black, tempestuous day, a day more night than day. I had been riding through rain since morning. Rain was ahead of me, rain was all around me, it was rain without end. The coming of evening was a gradual darkening, from dark to darker to black and wet, but now and then, in place of the enveloping darkness, the world was lit by lightning.

Spirit coughed.

"What's the matter?" I asked. "Are you okay?"

"I can hardly breathe," she said. "I feel as if I'm drowning in this rain."

She began to wheeze. Then she made an alarming noise that I had never heard from her before, "Pitipootipit."

"What?" I asked.

"Pitipootipit," she said again. She hesitated a moment, as if she had something else she wanted to say. "Sorry," she said at last, "but I think I'm—"

She stopped.

I tried to restart her. I couldn't do it. "You'll have to push me," she said.

I dismounted and began pushing her through the rain. I was wet and miserable, and I couldn't see a single light from a single house where we might take shelter. In the brief illuminations I saw that we were in what seemed to be cattle country, or cow country, with fenced fields of grass on either side of me and, here and there, a tree.

I knew the folly of taking shelter under a tree in a thunderstorm, but, as I said, I was wet and miserable, and I wanted a few minutes when I could sit quietly and eat a soggy sandwich. That, I thought, would cheer me up, embolden me, inspirit me, and give me the strength to resume my journey.

In a flash, I saw a sheltering tree, venerable and welcoming, its branches stretching out like the timbers of a low ceiling. This tree had stood there for so long, I reasoned, through so many storms, that it wasn't likely to be struck by lightning now, and I would be safe and dry beneath it, I hoped. I pulled off the road and stopped *Spirit* in the shelter of the old tree.

"What are you doing?" she squealed.

"Stopping here to get out of the rain, eat a sandwich, dry off—"

"—and get fried to a frazzle by a bolt of lightning."

"Oh, that's not likely to—"

"I want you to get me out of here."

"Don't you want to be out of the rain for a while?"

"Of course I do, but not if I'm going to end up as a twisted mass of smoking metal."

"Oh, pitipootipit," I said.

"In the morning you'd be found lying beside me, a crackling corpse, sizzling and smoking like a bird on a spit."

"If there were anyplace else, I'd—"

"You could build a shelter from supple saplings woven into waterproof mats and lashed together into a simple structure like a pup tent."

"How could I—oh—I know what you mean. I could build a shelter like the one those guys built in *Bold Feats*. I could probably do that."

"It would be fun."

"Maybe."

"And your father would be so proud of you."

She was right. My father undoubtedly would be proud of me if I did something that might make it into *Bold Feats,* a magazine that he subscribed to despite my mother's objection that it was "not the sort of thing that Peter should find lying around." The magazine's slogan, printed below the title on the cover of every issue, was "No Kidding"; if it were around today, I suppose its slogan would be "No Bullshit." It was full of stories about adventures that men had when they left their families behind for a weekend and went fishing. Some of the adventures were pretty exciting. I used to read an issue now and then when I found it lying around, but some of what I found in it puzzled me. I didn't understand, for example, why the voluptuous women that these men encountered when they stopped for coffee on their way to fishing holes of legendary abundance vanished from the stories entirely after a single tantalizing appearance. I was younger than the target audience, so perhaps I didn't understand what made middle-aged men tick, but I knew that if I found myself in a diner staffed by "babes" and "hot numbers" it would take much more than a "fishing hole known only to a lucky few" to lure me away.

As I headed into the woods to find some straight and supple young saplings, I tried to recall the adventure story that had included the weaving of the saplings into a simple structure like a pup tent, struggling, as I meandered through my memories of issues of *Bold Feats,* against the distracting babes and hot numbers and against my tendency to indulge in nostalgia, which kept grabbing my memory of a particular issue and putting it into the context of my home life back in distant Babbington.

"Peter, have you seen the latest issue of *Bold Feats*?" my father asked in one of those memories.

"I sure have," I said. "In this issue, two guys on their way to the 'legendary lair' of a 'monster wall-eyed pike' stop at a 'sleepy beanery' for a couple of mugs of 'hot joe' and they are served by a 'smoldering blonde' wearing a dress that fits her 'like a coat of wet paint.'"

"Where is it?"

"The 'legendary lair' or the 'sleepy beanery'?"

"*Bold Feats.*"

"Oh. It's—ah—well—it's in my room. I'll get it."

I dashed upstairs. The magazine was under my pillow, and I wanted to retrieve it without having my father see where I was keeping it. Starting downstairs, I flipped through it quickly, hoping for one last look at the illustration of the smoldering blonde in the dress of wet paint, and I came upon—I can see it now—the illustration of the simple structure made from saplings.

"What's keeping you?" called my father from the living room.

"I was just—ah—looking at the illustration that accompanies one of the adventures."

"Peter," said my father, frowning and running his hand through his hair, "I think you should know—I mean I think it's my duty to tell you—as your father—that—those illustrations are—well—let's say they're exaggerated."

I looked hard at the illustration.

"I think I see what you mean," I said. "It's not likely that these guys would come upon so many young, supple, pliant—"

"Peter," he said, "give me that."

I handed the magazine to him and—

"What are you doing?" asked a deep voice from close beside me in the dark woods.

"Holy shit!" I shouted in greeting. I leapt back and peered in the direction of the voice. I saw the shape of a man. He was hugging himself and shivering. "Where the hell did you come from?" I asked him.

"I'm not sure," said the man. "I don't really feel as if I've come from anywhere. I have a vague feeling that I was on a fishing trip—I remember stopping for coffee—there was a waitress—"

"A smoldering blonde?"

"Yes. How did you know?"

"Just a guess."

"But then suddenly there was all this rain—and I was in the woods here—and someone was thrashing around in the brush like a madman—and that was you."

"I'm not thrashing around like a madman. I'm cutting saplings."

"What for?"

"To weave together—to make a shelter—from the rain," I said, returning to the work.

"Why don't you just take shelter under that big tree?"

"Lightning," I explained.

"Lightning?"

"You're not supposed to take shelter under a tree in a thunderstorm because—"

An illustrative bolt struck the big tree, cleaving it in twain.

"Yeeeow!" cried the fisherman, apparently impressed.

"What are you doing?" asked a sweet voice, a girl's voice.

"Cutting saplings," I said.

"Who are you talking to?"

"Some guy who was on a fishing trip and got lost in the rain," I said.

"I don't see anybody."

"You don't?" I said.

"No," she said. Lightning struck again, farther away. In its light I saw that she was a dark-haired girl. Actually, I saw that she was *the* dark-haired girl. I didn't see any sign of the fisherman.

"He must have run from the lightning," I said.

"It cleft that ancient oak in twain," she said.

"I like the way you put that," I said.

"I have a way with words," she said.

"You do," I said. "You would be an excellent companion on a journey—on life's journey."

"You're making me blush," she said.

"I know you," I said, standing straight up to give my aching back a break. "I saw you one day, back at home, in Babbington, one summer day when I was stretched out along the bulkhead on the estuarial stretch of the Bolotomy River with my friend Raskol."

"That's possible," she said.

"We were both younger," I said, "just kids, really, but I remember you. I was on the Babbington side of the river, and you were across the way. You were sunning yourself on the foredeck of a lean blue sloop. Even though you were just a girl, I could see that you were—"

"What are you doing?" asked another voice. It was my father's.

"I—um—well—I—" I said evasively.

"I asked you what you're doing."

"Cutting saplings," I said, relieved to remember that I was doing something that would make him proud of me. "I'm going to weave them together to make a shelter because taking shelter under a tree would not be wise, as you probably know from that issue of *Bold Feats* that had the story about the two guys who were on their way to the legendary lair of a monster wall-eyed pike but became stranded in a violent storm and—"

"I don't think those are saplings."

"You're right," I said. "They're not. Whoever planted this bit of woods apparently never thought about the needs of a young adventurer on a rainy night. There are no straight young saplings." I hacked at the brush. "There are bushes. There are brambles. There is poison ivy. It wasn't like this in the pages of *Bold Feats*."

"You talking about the men's magazine?" asked the fisherman, materializing out of the rain again.

"Yeah," I said. "My father gets it. This is my father—"

I turned toward my father, intending to introduce him to the fisherman. He wasn't there.

"He's around here somewhere," I said. "He must have wandered off in search of saplings."

"It's funny you should mention *Bold Feats*," said the fisherman.

"Why is that?"

"Because I sometimes get the feeling that my life is an adventure straight out of the pages of that magazine. I don't mean to brag, but—"

"Hey, buster, what do you think you're doing?"

"Huh?" said the fisherman and I in unison.

An obliging lightning flash illuminated a smoldering blonde in a rain-soaked dress that clung to her like a rain-soaked dress.

"Wow," said the fisherman and I in unison.

"Don't give me that," said the blonde. "I've heard it all."

She waved a soggy piece of paper under the nose of the fisherman.

"What's the idea of running off without paying?" she demanded.

She turned to me and explained. "This four-flusher here comes into the high-class diner where I'm a waitress, see, orders the He-Man Breakfast—three eggs, sausage, bacon, pork chop, home fries, grits, toast, a short stack, and our famous bottomless cup of joe—chats me up pretty good, and then when I go to hand him the check, he's gone. Just like that! Nowhere to be seen. Disappeared."

"I must have blacked out," the fisherman said.

"I have been known to have that effect on guys," the blonde admitted.

"One minute I was in that sleepy beanery—"

"Hey!" said the blonde. "I resent that remark."

"Are these your friends?" asked the dark-haired girl.

"You're back," I said.

"Was I gone?"

"I think so. I lost sight of you. I'm glad you're back."

"That woman—" she said, with a tilt of her head in the direction of the blonde.

"You can see her?" I asked.

"Yes," she said, a suggestion of annoyance in her voice. "I can see her."

"And the fisherman?"

"The man beside her? Are you asking whether I can see him? Yes, I can."

"This is pretty amazing."

"Is she your—girlfriend?"

"The smoldering blonde? My girlfriend? No, she's—"

"I'll take a turn at that work if you want," said my father.

"I knew you must be around here somewhere," I said.

He held out his hand. I gave him my knife. He started cutting brush.

"Where was I?" I asked.

"You were bringing me that issue of *Bold Feats*," he said, "but you were dawdling over it, drooling over the illustrations of loose women in tight dresses."

"'Loose women'!" cried the blonde, running her hands over her tight dress. She elbowed the fisherman and said, "Are you going to let him get away with that?"

"See here," said the fisherman to my father, "I think you owe the lady an apology."

"Well, *is* she your girlfriend?" asked the dark-haired girl.

"Hey, toots," said the blonde, putting a hand on her shapely hip, "do I look like I've got to go robbing the cradle to get a date?"

"Perhaps you and I should return to the—ah—high-class diner," the fisherman suggested, daring to put a hand on the blonde's shoulder.

"That's a great idea," I said. "The dark-haired girl and I have a lot to discuss, and—"

"This was the best I could do," said my father, staggering into view under the weight of an enormous armload of cut brush. He dropped it on the ground, looked up, caught sight of the smoldering blonde, and said, "Oh, my god, I've died and gone to heaven!"

"Dad!" I said.

"I'm Bert Leroy," said my father, advancing on the blonde with his hand extended. "Has anybody told you that your dress fits you like a coat of wet paint?"

"Gee, thanks," said the blonde.

"See here, pal," said the fisherman. "The lady and I resent that remark."

"Speak for yourself," said the blonde.

"I'm going to build a simple shelter out of that brush," my father said to her confidently, "and when I'm finished I hope you will join me in it, get out of this rain, and—"

"Dad!" I said. "Go home! Mom is waiting for you. She must be worried."

"You're married?" asked the blonde.

"Well," said my father, "in a way."

"What kind of girl do you take me for?" she asked him, cocking that shapely hip, tossing her wet hair, and thrusting her chin at him. She grabbed the fisherman's arm and said, "Come on, sweetie, let's go. I do not choose to consort with these people any longer." They walked off in the direction of the road, dissolving as they went.

"Dad," I said, "you should go back home."

"Yes," he said with a sigh in the direction of the vanished babe, "I guess I should." He started on his way. After a few steps he stopped and said, over his shoulder, "You won't tell your mother about—"

"It's our secret," I said, and he slipped from sight.

"I should go, too," said the dark-haired girl.

"Please stay," I said.

"My parents will be worried. They'll wonder where I've gone."

"Will I see you when I get back home?"

"I hope so," she said.

"Maybe you'll be in the crowd that gathers along Main Street to greet me when I come flying back into town."

"I suppose I could manage that," she said, already evanescing, adding a laugh that lingered long after she was gone.

In reality, I lay beneath *Spirit*'s right wing, huddled in the tent I'd made by draping my poncho over the wing, shivering in the rain, warming myself with memories of home and wishful visions of the dark-haired girl. I hadn't invited the fisherman and the smoldering blonde into my simple shelter. They had arrived courtesy of *Bold Feats*. I hadn't invited my father, either. He was there because he was a subscriber, I guess.

SOUND EFFECTS

· ·

CUE THE LIGHTNING. "Crrrrr-ack!" Cue the thunder. "Brrumble. Thuboom." Cue the rain. "Pitat. Pitatat." More rain. "Shlapalap. Rushalap." More rain. "Blububduba—"

"What are you doing?"

"Trying to re-create the atmospheric conditions and the 'atmosphere': the rain, the lightning, the thunder."

That was true. But it was not the whole truth. I had thought that I heard, in the distance, but keeping pace with us, the sound of a helicopter, *whup-whup-whup-whup*, and I was obscuring that sound, muffling it with a blanket of atmospheric effects, so that Albertine wouldn't hear it. There was the chance that if she did she would bring the Electro-Flyer to a screeching halt, jump out into the road, and begin waving her arms above her head, signaling the flyguys to swoop down and carry her off.

"It's getting late," she said. "I think we ought to head for our motel."

"Just a little farther, okay? I have a feeling that we're very close."

"Peter, we're looking for a patch of ground with a couple of twisted trees, a field—"

"Or meadow."

"—a wooded area off in the distance, and a rail fence at the roadside. I don't think we're going to find it."

"I just have a feeling that—"

Was that the helicopter sound again? Cue that alarming noise that had come from *Spirit*'s engine years earlier. "Pitipootipit, pitipootipit." Cue the stuttering, the hesitation, the shuddering, the—

"Now what?"

"I'm trying to reproduce the sound poor *Spirit* made when she began wheezing and coughing, just before her gradual collapse, when she became too weak to go on."

"You're scaring me," she said. "I'm heading for the motel. Directly for the motel."

"Probably a good idea."

"You're going to love it. It's the Paradise Pines Motor Court, an amazing piece of 'motel moderne' architecture, a place that once promised the touring motorist 'everything that is new and ultra-modern' and tonight promises this particular pair of touring motorists a comfortable retreat—uh-oh."

We had arrived at the motor court. Under towering pines lay a cluster of tiny bungalows that had once been new and ultra-modern. Now, they were old and ultra-decrepit. In front of the bungalows was a small office in a separate building with an angular roof and a soaring sign that still held some of the neon tubing that spelled the name, but it was dark. The whole place was dark.

"It looks closed," I said. "As in out of business."

"Do you think maybe they just forgot to turn the lights on?"

"No, I don't think so."

"Why don't you check?"

"I can see that it's closed—"

"Just check, okay?"

"Okay." I opened the door and stepped out from under the shelter of the Electro-Flyer's clear plastic top. "Crrrrr-ack! Brrumble. Thuboom. Pitat. Pitatat. Shlapalap. Rushalap. Blububduba—"

"Stop that!" she said.

I tried the door to the office. It was locked. I peered inside. The office was nearly empty. It had been deserted long ago. I felt Albertine's disappointment, and I felt a bit of disappointment myself, because I would have enjoyed staying there if it had been in good repair or nicely restored. For a moment, I thought about our taking the place on as a project, restoring it, and running it, but I shook the thought off with a shiver and banished it forever. As I started back toward the car, I realized that I was smiling.

"They're out of business," I said.

"Oh," she moaned.

"Let's hit the road and see where chance leads us," I said.

We started off, into the night and the unknown. I began rubbing my hands in gleeful anticipation. We were going to have an adventure.

Struggling to find our way back to the highway, both of us peering into the dark, I could feel the tension rising in the car. Albertine was not happy about this turn of events, and I was. I admit it. The dark night, and the dark road, made the perfect setting for a breakdown or a slide off the highway into a ditch. What fun! I was on the edge of my seat, and enjoying the perch. The only thing lacking was a storm, but life has taught me that one cannot have everything.

When I glanced at Al, though, and saw her knuckles white with the pressure of her grip on the wheel, I felt the difference in our situations. She was doing all the work. I was having all the fun.

Then I seemed to hear that damned helicopter again, its relentless *whup-whup-whup-whup*, behind us. It had to be those flying EMTs in pursuit of Albertine, or Giggles, as they had taken to calling her.

Thinking quickly, with the resourcefulness of a desperate man, I remarked in a lighthearted way, "If we were in an old movie now, something black-and-white and grainy, there would be a storm, in addition to all this darkness. We would turn the car radio on and hear a report about an escaped killer on the loose, believed to be wandering the dark roads near the area of the ultra-modern Paradise Pines Motor Court." I reached for the radio. "Kkkhhhshhwaukkhh," I said, in a fine imitation of static. "We interrupt this program to bring you a police bulletin: be on the lookout for an escaped lunatic with an irrational animosity toward electric cars—"

"Turn it off!"

"Click!"

"Whew."

"As soon as we heard that report," I said, "lightning would split the sky—crrrrr-ack—thunder would rumble over us—brrumble, thuboom— and our low-battery warning light would begin to flash, intermittently illuminating our faces with an eerie glow."

"You mean the way it is now?"

"Pretty much like that."

"It would make us extremely anxious," she said.

"So I would say, 'Let's stop at the next place we see, whatever it's like, even if it's—crrrack—brrumble—thuboom—that place.'"

It would be a large Victorian house, dark and imposing. A sign on the lawn would advertise it as

THE SCARY OLD HOUSE
BED AND BREAKFAST

We would park in front and climb a long series of loose steps to the front door. A busy little woman in a mobcap would answer our knock.

"Oh, my goodness," she would say when she saw us standing there with our suitcases in our hands, "more travelers seeking shelter from the storm. Come in, come in. There's always room for one more."

"We are two more," I would point out.

"What?" she would ask, nonplussed.

"He's trying to be funny," you would say. "It's best just to ignore him."

"Oh. I see," the woman would say. "Ha-ha."

You would give me one of those elbow pokes in the ribs that you've perfected, and we would begin hauling our bags inside.

"Don't bother with those," the woman would say. "You just take yourselves into the parlor, warm yourselves by the fire, and get acquainted with the other guests. I'll have my son Snort take your bags upstairs. He's a bit of an idiot, but he's strong as an ox, and he's not dangerous unless he gets out of sorts. Snort! Snort, you idiot bastard, get out here and carry these folks' bags upstairs."

A large young man would lumber out of a room at the end of the hallway. Beetle-browed and hulking, he would growl, grab our bags, and stomp up the stairs.

"Did he seem out of sorts to you?" I would ask you as we entered the parlor.

"Hard to tell," you would say. "Maybe he was just trying to be funny."

"Ha-ha," I would retort.

There would be quite a little crowd in the parlor, and they would be engaged in an agitated conversation. You and I would slip in as quietly and unobtrusively as possible, so as not to interrupt the congenial social intercourse of strangers thrown together by a storm, seeking comfort in friendly companionship, a warm fire, and sherry. Our stealth wouldn't work. The conversation would stop as we made our way through the group to get near the fire. By the time we had claimed a couple of warm spots for ourselves, we would have the feeling that we were not as welcome as we might have wished to be.

A buxom woman, fiftyish, dressed in a long velvet dress accessorized with a diamond necklace that spread across most of her imposing front, would turn to a wild-haired old fellow in a baggy suit and say, "Please go on, Professor. What you were saying was so very interesting. I hope the interruption hasn't derailed your train of thought."

"Please accept our apologies," I would say. "We were forced to seek shelter from the rain, very much as I was forced to seek shelter in this area many years ago when I was traveling to New Mexico—"

"I was saying that I have been studying the caramba-mamba," the professor would say.

"Gosh, that's the world's deadliest snake, isn't it, Professor?" a fresh-faced lad with sandy hair would ask.

"Indeed it is, young man," the professor would say. "Are you interested in herpetology?"

"Nah," Sandy would say with a flip of his hand, "I just like snakes."

"I see," the professor would say with a chuckle, sending a wink in the direction of the buxom woman. "If the caramba-mamba is a snake that interests you, I have a specimen in my room that you might like to see."

"In your room!" the buxom matron would squeal. "Oh, Professor! What if it escapes in the night? We might all be killed in our sleep!"

"My dear woman," the professor would say, "I assure you that there is no cause for alarm. The creature is quite safely enclosed in a cage that can only be opened with this key." He would produce a key from his pocket, hold it up for all to see, return it to his pocket, and pat the pocket to show everyone how secure the key was on his person.

Outside, a bolt of lightning would strike a tree in front of the house, splintering it with a ripping sound like the scream of a small, furry animal being disemboweled by a goshawk—something like *eeaghhhgrackouukirsch*. It would be followed by a clap of thunder—*drubbleduboombuh*—that would rattle the windows and rumble the floor beneath our feet.

A blonde in a white satin dress clinging to her like the paint worn by the blondes in *Bold Feats* would wail, "Make it stop! Somebody make it stop! It's driving me insane!" She would throw herself across a sofa like an invitation.

I would take a seat on the sofa beside her and say sympathetically, "I know how you feel. When I was on that trip that I mentioned, years ago, I thought of taking shelter under the spreading branches of a large tree—"

"Did the woman in the mobcap mention sherry?" you would ask.

A big, snarling man would rise from an overstuffed chair behind a plant, where he had previously been invisible, and demand in a deep snarling voice, "What's that you said?"

"I was hoping that it might be cocktail hour," you would tell him.

"Oooh, Francis!" the blonde would squeal. "There you are! Did you have a nice nap?"

"Nah," Francis would say with a shrug, rolling the shoulders of his double-breasted suit and patting the gat in his shoulder holster. "It's hard to sleep with a gat digging into your ribs and that storm raging outside. It's enough to drive a guy nuts."

"I was just telling everybody that the thunder is driving me crazy," the blonde would explain.

"And I was telling her how much the storm reminded me of a night years ago," I would offer, "when I was flying—well, taxiing—to New Mexico and—"

"Yeah, I heard ya," Francis would say, flicking the ash from his cigarette into a potted aspidistra.

A brilliant bolt of lightning would catch us all in its sudden silver light.

"Stop it!" young Sandy would scream. "Somebody please make it stop! If one more bolt of lightning freezes us in its light like that, burning our startled expressions into my brain, I'll go mad! I tell you I'll go mad!"

You would turn suddenly and slap him hard across the face, then again, and again.

There would be a moment of stunned silence. Then Sandy would slump into a chair, subdued and whimpering.

"Say, that was quick thinking, sister," Francis would say.

"I've been to the movies," you would explain.

I would have found the bar by then. I would pour a couple of shots of brandy into a tumbler and hand it to Sandy. "Here, drink this, kid," I would say, "and pull yourself together."

"I thought there was going to be sherry," Francis would say, pouting.

"I couldn't find any," I would explain, "but there is gin, and I am prepared to make a martini for anyone who would like one."

It would be martinis all around, with the exception of Sandy, who would stick with the brandy.

When Francis had a drink in hand, he would say to the professor, "I heard what you said about the caramba-mamba, Professor."

"Yes?" the professor would say.

"Maybe you'd like to bring the snake down here, so that we can all get a look at it."

"Oh, I don't think that would be wise," the professor would say sagely.

Francis would pat the bulge in his double-breasted jacket and say slowly, "I do, Professor. I think it would be very wise."

"Oh, yes, Professor," the buxom woman would say, all aflutter, "please do bring the snake here for us to see—if you think it's safe."

"Yes, well," the professor would say, with a wary eye on Francis, "perhaps I will," and he would start upstairs.

Suddenly Snort would burst into the room from the hallway. "Is that an electric car outside?" he would shout. "Is somebody here driving an electric car?"

You would say, "Yes, we're driving an Electro-Flyer, the only Electro-Flyer in the world, in fact."

And I would say, "We're driving to New Mexico, re-creating the trip that I made in an aerocycle when I was a teenager—"

Snort would begin tearing his hair, throwing the furniture around, and screaming, "I hate electric cars. I hate them! I hate them!"

The professor would appear at the top of the stairs and call out, "Stay where you are, everyone! Don't move an inch! The caramba-mamba is missing!"

The lights would go out.

"Come on, Al," I would say, "in the darkness and confusion we can make our getaway."

We would grope our way along a hallway until we came to the kitchen, where we would slip out the back door, tiptoe down the driveway to the front of the house, get into the Electro-Flyer, switch it on, and slip away from the Scary Old House, silently, with electro-flying swiftness.

"That was a close shave," I would say, "close as wet paint."

"You're enjoying this, aren't you?" you would say. It would be an accusation, but you would be smiling as you made it.

"Well," I would say, "it *has* become more of an adventure than it would have been if we had been able to stay at Paradise Pines."

"I wish that it would stop being an adventure," you would say, "and start being more of a—"

"Oh, look!" she said. "Up ahead. There's a motel." She gave a sigh of relief. "There seem to be quite a few cars parked out front—and it doesn't look scary at all."

We took our bags from the trunk, registered, and found our room.

"Thanks for keeping me entertained," she said.

"I'll just check under the bed for snakes," I said.

"Please do."

"I'll also go out to the parking lot and find a way to plug the car in."

I slung my extension cords over my shoulder and slipped into the night. I found an outdoor outlet not far from the car, ran my cords, made them as discreet as possible, and then stood to listen. There was no helicopter, no *whup-whup-whup*. The night was as silent as it was dark.

THE IDEAL AUDIENCE

••

Truth is appalling and eltritch, as seen
By this world's artificial lamplights.
—Owen Meredith (Edward Robert Bulwer-Lytton), *Lucile*

DURING THE DAY, while I was riding along, I composed a song, in my head, and my song quickly became one of those songs that one cannot get out of one's head. In fact, I'm hesitant to include it here because I fear that I may be doing you a disservice, Reader, by introducing it into your head, from which I fear you may not be able to drive it. However, in the service of completeness, I must include it, and so I do:

> *O, Babbington, my Babbington,*
> *You know I love you dearly.*
> *When I'm abroad, you're with me still,*
> *And I can see you clearly.*
> *The people who don't live in you*
> *All live their lives so queerly.*
> *Where'ere I roam, I yearn for home,*
> *And I mean that most sincerely.*
> *Ooo, bop, sha doobie doo wop.*

I was very proud of myself for addressing the song to the town itself, as if it were a sentient being, an entity vibrant and alive, capable of comprehending and appreciating my paean to it.

"You are driving me crazy with that song," claimed *Spirit*.

"I think it's pretty good," I said, frankly and honestly.

"I might have agreed the first time I heard it."

"I've got to keep repeating it so that I can memorize it."

"I've already memorized it."

"I hear the rhythm of the road in it."

"I keep hearing 'Ooo, bop, sha doobie doo wop,' and if I hear it one more time, it's going to drive me insane, totally, irreversibly insane."

"Okay," I said. "I get the point. I'll be quiet."

We rolled along. I memorized my song, subvocalizing instead of singing. As usual, at the predictable time, evening came on. As usual, I began looking for a good place to stop for a meal, a shower, and a bed. I came to a crossroads where there was a sign that pointed the way to two towns: Happy Valley to the right and Eldritch to the left.

Much has been written on the effect that the names of places have on our predisposition toward them, nearly all of it by Marcel Proust. Consequently, there is nothing left for me to say on the topic, in general. Specifically, though, I can add my bit to the grand conversation by noting that the two names had immediate and contradictory effects on me. Eldritch sounded to me like a place that would be weird, strange, and eerie. Happy Valley, on the other hand, seemed likely to be jolly, its populace welcoming and complaisant.

"It's Happy Valley for us!" I said, steering *Spirit* to the right.

We went on our way, but I soon began to doubt that it was the right way to go. So did *Spirit*.

"If we're on the way to Happy Valley, then Happy Valley must have fallen on very hard times," she said.

"I'm going to turn around," I said, "and I hope that you won't invoke the rule that adventurers do not retrace their steps."

"This might be a special case," she said.

"Wait a minute," I said. "We may not have to break the rule after all. There's a fork in the road up ahead."

At the fork, there was another sign, like the one we had seen farther back, but this one claimed that the road to the left continued on to Happy Valley, while the road to the right would take us to Eldritch.

"That's funny," I said innocently. "I thought Eldritch was on the left back at the other fork."

"It was," said *Spirit*. "Or at least the sign said it was."

We went to the left this time, still heading for Happy Valley, we hoped.

We hadn't gone very far when we came to a third fork. The sign at this fork pointed to Eldritch on the left and Happy Valley on the right.

"Hmmm," I said, bearing right. "I'm getting suspicious about this."

"Hmmm," said *Spirit*. "So am I."

A little farther on, we came to another fork. Again, the directions had reversed, with Eldritch now on the right and Happy Valley on the left. I stopped, puzzled and a bit apprehensive. Not only did the relative locations of Eldritch and Happy Valley seem to shift with each fork we encountered, but regardless of whether we took the right or the left fork, we seemed always to be heading to a place more eldritch than happy. Then my apprehension turned to terror. A memory had returned to me. It was the memory of a night when I was sitting on the beach, "Over South," on the barrier island that separated Bolotomy Bay from the Atlantic Ocean. I was sitting on the sand, in a ring with other members of the Young Tars, listening to our leader, Mr. Summers, tell us a tale from the bygone days of old Bolotomy, and the tale he was telling was sending a shiver of fear down my spine, making me hug myself for comfort and warmth and lean toward the fire. It was a story about a gang of thugs in Babbington in the nineteenth century who used to lure—

In the light from *Spirit*'s headlamp, something moved. My heart began racing. I swung the lamp from side to side, slowly, and I saw something move again.

I took a deep breath and, drawing on the afternoons I'd spent at the Babbington Theater, called out, "We've got you covered! Show yourself!" I heard a tremor in my voice, but it was hidden by a snarling roar from *Spirit*. I looked at the throttle. I hadn't realized that I had twisted it, but I must have.

"We've got you surrounded," I said, adding another snarl from *Spirit*. "You might as well give up."

"Don't shoot!" cried a voice. A pair of hands shot into the air from behind a bush on the edge of the light from *Spirit*'s headlamp. I turned the handlebars in that direction, turning the full light on whoever was hiding there. I was still terrified, but I was emboldened.

"Come out with your hands up," I said, "and if you know what's good for you, you won't try any funny business."

"Yes, sir," said the voice. Slowly, a head rose above the bush, and then, very cautiously, with his hands held straight and high, a skinny, frightened boy about my age took a few steps toward the light.

When he reached the edge of the road, I said, "Stop where you are."

"Yes, sir."

"And keep those hands up. I'd just as soon shoot you as look at you."

"My hands are up. I'm keeping them up. I'm going to keep them up."

"One false move, and I'll—"

"No false moves," he said, quickly, nervously, blinking in the headlamp light. "You won't get any false moves out of me, none at all."

"Let's hear what you've got to say about the signs," I said.

"Signs? What signs?"

"You know what signs—the signs that point the way to Eldritch and Happy Valley."

"What about them?"

"They're confusing, wouldn't you say?"

"If you find them confusing, maybe it's just because you—"

"Listen, kid," I said in the manner of a movie tough guy, "if you are about to suggest that I find those signs confusing because I am easily confused, I would suggest that you remind yourself who has got the drop on whom."

"Sorry!" he said, and I could see the fear run through his body, the same fear that was running through mine. "I didn't mean to say that—it—it just came out."

"In that case, I'll ignore it," I said.

"Thanks," he said, shading his eyes to try to see who was behind the blinding light.

"This time," I snarled, "but not next time."

"There won't be a next time. Honest."

"Peter, let's get out of here," whispered *Spirit*.

"We can't go yet," I told her in a hasty whisper. "This is some kind of ambush—we've got to find out how many other thugs are in the gang—and where they're hiding—if we're going to get out of this alive."

"Ambush? Thugs? Gang? G-get out alive?" she wailed.

"Are you talking to me?" asked the skinny kid.

"Just giving some orders to my men," I said. "Now about those signs. The way I see it, somebody's playing tricks with those signs."

"Tricks? What kind of tricks?"

"Somebody's been switching the signs back and forth, changing the direction of them at every fork, so that first Eldritch is one way and Happy Valley is the other way, and then it's the other way around, and then it's the other way around again, and then—"

"I'm not sure I follow you."

"Are you trying to be funny?"

"Me? No! No. Certainly not."

"That's good, because funny kids make my trigger finger itchy."

He swallowed hard and said nothing. He opened his mouth, then closed it. Again he shaded his eyes and tried to see beyond the screen of light.

"Who do you suppose did that to the signs?" I asked.

He blinked and swallowed again.

"Did you do it?"

"M-me?"

"Yeah, you."

"You're accusing me of tampering with road signs to confuse travelers—lead them astray—?"

"I was just thinking that you're stuck out here in the middle of nowhere—you must get pretty bored. You might be looking for something to enliven your existence. In your desperation, you might turn to pranks."

"P-pranks?"

"They might be harmless pranks—or they might be something worse."

The boy's eyes grew wide. "L-look," he said, "this wasn't my idea, honest. I—"

Suddenly, looking at him there, in front of me, trembling, squinting

into *Spirit*'s headlamp light, I realized that chance had given me something I had always wanted, something that I had heard of but had
never actually seen before—

"Can't we just get out of here?" pleaded *Spirit*.

"Not now," I said, "not when chance has given me what every storyteller longs for."

"What's that?"

"A captive audience," I said. Then, to the skinny kid, I said, "I'm going to tell you a story."

"A s-story?"

"Yes," I said, "and you are going to listen closely, because this is a
story about what happens to people whose pranks are not so harmless."

"Is it a long story?"

"Not too long."

"Can I put my hands down while you're telling it?"

"Okay, but keep them where I can see them, and remember what I
said about no false moves."

"No false moves. I remember."

"Long ago," I said, "in Babbington, New York—where I—where I
grew up—and lived until I became a special agent—"

"Special agent?"

"That's right—Special Agent—ah—Panmuphle."

"Pan . . . what?"

"Panmuphle. It's my code name."

"Oh."

"Anyway, as I was saying, long ago, in Babbington, there was a gang
of young punks who called themselves the Bolotomy Pirates."

"Bolotomy?"

"That's what the name of the town was before it became Babbington."

"Oh. I see. Probably an old Indian name."

"That's right. The bay is still called Bolotomy."

"Oh, so it's on a bay."

"Look, kid, shut up and listen. This is my story."

"Yes, sir."

"The Bolotomy Pirates started out as pranksters—just a bunch of
bored kids looking for something to put a little spark in their lives—
you know what I mean?"

"Well—I guess—"

"Back in those days, a lot of shipping passed by the part of Bolotomy called Over South. That's a little settlement on a barrier island across the bay from the town itself, just a strip of sand that separates the bay from the Atlantic Ocean."

"Mm-hm."

"The Bolotomy Pirates often visited Over South because it was a place where they could get cheap liquor and easy women."

He muttered something.

"You got something to say?" I growled.

"I said I wish there was a place like that around here," he said.

"Yeah, well, the Bolotomy Pirates fell in with some hard types Over South. They took to gambling, and it wasn't long before they were deep in debt to people who didn't like waiting to be paid."

"Gosh."

"One of those hard types told the gang that if they didn't want to end up gutted like flounders, they'd better come up with the money they owed."

"Gutted like flounders—gee—"

"Then he suggested a way that they could get the money."

"Yeah?"

"He reminded them that a lot of ships passed by on their way to New York. This was long ago, remember, in the days of sailing ships. The ships would pass Bolotomy, and then, farther west, they'd turn into a channel where there was a break in the barrier islands and head into the sheltered waters of the bay. Then they'd have smooth sailing all the way to New York Harbor."

"Mm."

"The channel entrance was marked by flags during the day, and at night it was marked by a primitive sort of lighthouse, not much more than a signal fire."

"Like a road sign—" he said, more to himself than to me.

"The plan that the hard type offered the boys was this: They would wait for a night when the sea was rough, and then build a false signal fire on the beach Over South. When the captain of a ship saw the fire, he would think it was the fire that marked the channel, but that would actually be miles away. The captain would steer a course toward the false signal fire and run the ship aground in the surf off Over South. In that rough surf, it wouldn't take long for the ship to break up. The idea was to steal the cargo as it washed ashore, of course, but the gang wouldn't be able to do that right away. They would have something else to take care of first. They would have to make sure that there were no witnesses, no one who could report being deceived by a false signal fire. That meant that there couldn't be any survivors. A good number of the crew were likely to drown in the surf, of course, but anyone who managed to swim to shore—well, the boys were going to have to kill those."

He had been holding his breath. He let it out now and gulped another.

"One of the boys was given the job of lighting the false fire and keeping it burning bright, while the rest of the gang hid in the dunes and waited until the time came to do their grisly work."

He swallowed hard again.

"The one who tended the fire told himself that his part in the scheme wasn't nearly so reprehensible as the part the others were playing. After all, he wasn't actually going to kill anybody."

"That's right," he said. "He was right. He wasn't actually going to kill anybody."

"That's just what his friends, the other Bolotomy Pirates, got to thinking. They got to thinking that he wasn't actually going to kill anybody—and that might be a problem."

"A problem—" he muttered.

"A ship came. They couldn't be sure at first, because they couldn't see it, and they couldn't be sure that they were hearing the wind in its rigging over the sound of the surf, but then they began to hear the sound of its masts groaning and cracking, and its sails shredding, and its hull being torn asunder, and the screams of its crew."

"I don't want to hear—"

"The cracking and shredding and rending and screaming went on and on, as the waves tore the ship apart. It wasn't long before a couple of sailors came staggering through the surf, trying to make it to the safety of the shore. The gang swept out of the dunes and down upon the sailors, swinging their clubs and bludgeons. The boy who had charge of the fire stayed at his post. He tried not to hear what he was hearing, and when he found that it was impossible not to hear it he tried not to recognize what he was hearing. He tried to tell himself that what he was hearing was not the sound of living people being battered to death by the boys he thought of as his friends."

"Oh," said the boy.

"But then out of the dark came two of those friends, and between them they were dragging the nearly lifeless body of one of the sailors. They dragged the poor wretch into the firelight and dropped him at the feet of the boy who was tending the fire. Then they handed the boy a club and told him to finish the job that they had begun."

"They wouldn't do—"

"The boy stood there, holding the club, and one by one the rest of the gang came out of the night and formed a circle around him. There was no way out. He turned this way and that, looking into the eyes of his friends, looking for some sign that they were his friends, that they weren't going to make him do this, that they were going to allow him to be the one among them who didn't do anything more than change the road signs—"

"What?"

"—that he would be the only one who didn't do anything more than light the false fire—"

"You said 'change the road signs.'"

"—that there would be no blood on his hands."

"There wouldn't be. I mean, technically, if I just changed the—I mean—if he just lit the fire—"

"The circle began to tighten around him. The other boys advanced on him, step by step, swinging their clubs, with fire in their eyes."

"No."

"He remembered what the hard type had told the gang: there must be no survivors."

"Ahhhh," the boy cried. He fell to his knees. He clasped his hands together and extended them in imprecation. "Help me. Please help me. You've got to help me."

"Where are your friends?" I asked.

"At the old quarry."

"Where's that?"

"Not far. Half a mile. That way." He jerked his head to the right.

"What's the plan?"

"We—I—switch the signs so that anybody who comes along ends

up at the old quarry. Eldritch or Happy Valley, it doesn't matter. If you follow the signs you'll end up at the old quarry."

"And there?"

"It's dark. You wouldn't see the quarry's edge until it was too late. You'd fall—to the bottom."

"And then?"

"The gang is hiding in the woods—and they—just like what you said—" He hung his head. A moment passed. He lifted his head and looked into the light. "What are you going to do?" he asked.

"Yeah, Special Agent Panmuphle," said *Spirit*, "what are you going to do?"

"I wish I could turn you around and get out of here, without looking back, without ever giving another thought to this skinny kid or his friends lurking around the old quarry—"

"Great. Me too. Let's go."

"—but I can't do that. I know too much."

"Don't say that!"

"Maybe we could—make a deal—" said the skinny kid, shading his eyes again, trying desperately to see who he was dealing with.

"The right thing to do would be to take him to the police," I said.

"Oh, sure," said *Spirit*, "and spend hours telling them the story and waiting while they check it out, search the woods around the old quarry, round up the gang, bring them in, and question them."

"Suppose I turn myself in—" the kid suggested.

"Then there is the matter of your driver's license," *Spirit* continued. "That is, the matter of your not having a driver's license. Why should the police believe *you*, a kid without a driver's license? Why shouldn't they throw *you* in the clink instead of a fine upstanding local lad like Skinny?"

"I'm on the horns of a moral dilemma," I said.

"Come on, mister," Skinny wailed, "gimme a break!"

"Huh?" I said.

"Help me out of this jam," he pleaded, "and I'll go straight, honest. I'll never do anything wrong again. All I've really done so far is change the signs. And the rest of the gang hasn't done anything yet, either. There's still time for us. I've seen the error of my ways, and I can reform. I know I can! So can the others. When I tell them that story, they'll see the light. I know they will. They're good kids at heart. Honest they are.

We were just bored—you know, like you said—just bored. That's what got us up to this mischief. You know, idle hands are the devil's playground. Or workshop. How does it go? 'Idle hands—'"

"Shut up, kid," I growled.

"Yes, sir. I was just trying to recall whether it's 'Idle hands are the devil's playground' or—"

"Can it!"

"Yes, sir."

"Here's the deal."

"Yes?"

"I'm going to let you off—this time."

"Oh, thank you—"

"But—"

"But?"

"If I ever hear that you or any of the other young punks in your little two-bit gang of would-be pirates has strayed from the straight and narrow I will track you down—and when I find you I will shoot to kill."

"'Sh-shoot to kill,'" he said. "I understand."

"Don't forget it, and make sure the others don't forget it, either," I said, mounting *Spirit*.

"'Shoot to kill,'" he said. "I've got it."

I made *Spirit* growl again. Then I took off, heading back the way we had come, flouting the rule that adventurers do not retrace their steps.

When we were well on our way, *Spirit* asked, "How on earth did you come up with all that?"

"A few years ago, when I was in the Young Tars, we went on an outing to Over South—"

"Yeah, yeah, yeah," she said.

Together, we began to sing:

> *O, Babbington, my Babbington,*
> *You know I love you dearly.*
> *When I'm abroad, you're with me still—*

ELDRITCH, REDEFINED

....

WE ARRIVED AT the motel just at that time when the optimism of day is beginning to yield to the gloom of night. The neon sign was sputtering. The "No" in "No Vacancy" flickered on and off. The office was lit, dimly, but there was no sign of anyone inside. We pulled under the porte-cochere and sat there for a moment or two in silence. The air was heavy with the smell of cheap booze and stale cigarettes.

"What do you think?" I asked.

"I think that the flickering sign is trying to send us a message," she said.

Another car pulled into the parking lot and under the porte-cochere. The couple in the car looked at the office and then at us. We looked at them. They grinned sheepishly. We grinned sheepishly. They shrugged. We shrugged. They got out and headed for the door. I gave Al a look. She gave me a look.

"Shall we move on to someplace else?" I asked.

"Come on, bold venturer," she said. "If they can take it, so can we."

We got out of the car and walked to the door. I swung it open for her and indicated with a sweep of the hand that she was free to enter.

"After you," she said.

"Okay," I said.

The woman in the couple that had preceded us turned and gave us a wink. Then she smiled and shrugged the small swift shrug of one who expects a good time. Al and I exchanged another look, a puzzled look.

"Hello?" the man called.

Nothing.

"Hello?" called the woman. "We'd like to check in."

"I'm not sure about that," I muttered.

From somewhere behind a wall or two, there came the sound of a chair scraping on a floor and then the sound of a door being opened and closed. Presently a door in the wall behind the desk opened and a surly man with a limp came through it. He had tired eyes, a nasty grin, and a day's growth of beard. A cigarette hung from his lower lip. He was shrugging into a wrinkled sport jacket, probably to hide an automatic in a shoulder holster.

"Who the hell are you?" he asked.

"What's it to ya?" snarled the woman.

"I gotta put somethin' in the register," he said. "I'm gonna need two names."

"Bonnie and Clyde," said the woman, cocking a hip. "He's Clyde."

"Last name?"

"I'm Parker and he's Barrow."

"Whoa," said the clerk. He put the pen down and gripped the edge of the counter. "Whoa."

"What's the matter?" the man asked.

"I'm not sure I want to check you in."

"Why?"

"Because—look—I guess you're not aware of this, but you've got the same names as two of America's most notorious criminals."

"Oh, I know," said the woman. "We hear that from people all the time."

"Still, how's it going to look?"

"What?"

"Well, suppose you two go on a rampage while you're here, robbing, killing, looting, maybe torching the place to hide the evidence, and then in the charred rubble my boss finds the registration book and sees that I allowed you to register as Bonnie Parker and Clyde Barrow?"

"Mmm. I see what you mean."

"He'll have my ass."

"Okay. Suppose we register under other names?"

"Now you're talking."

"For me, how about Connie Barker?"

"Not great. A little lame, to tell you the truth. But it'll do."

"And for me," the man said, "how about Clarence Darrow?"

"Excellent. Yeah. Clarence Darrow. Excellent. You've got a knack."

Clarence smirked at Bonnie—I mean Connie—and she stuck her tongue out at him.

"Be right back, folks," the clerk said to Al and me, "soon as I show Miss Barker and Mr. Darrow to their room."

He led them out the door and into the night.

Albertine and I looked at each other.

"What do you say?" I asked.

"I'm game."

I tried not to allow myself to grin in anticipation of the pleasure of playing someone else for a night, but instead I had to turn aside and study the paint on the wall.

The clerk returned and said, "Well, folks, what's it going to be?"

"Just tonight," I said. "We're on the road."

"I getcha," he said with a wink, spinning the register so that it faced us.

I hesitated for only a moment, then wrote "Panmuphle."

I handed the pen to Albertine and watched as she wrote "Giggles."

The clerk spun the register back in his direction and scrutinized the entry. "You got eye-dee?" he asked.

"I—ah—well—" I said, patting my pockets.

"Ah—let me see—" said Al, rummaging in her purse.

"Ha-ha," said the clerk. "Joke's on you. Do I look like the kind of guy who's going to care if you register under a phony name?"

"Ha-ha," I said.

"Ha-ha," said Al.

"Speaking of phony names—" I said.

"Phony names? Who said anything about phony names?"

"No one," I said. "Of course not. No one said anything about phony names. I don't know how the idea came into my head."

"He gets these attacks," Albertine explained. "Ideas come into his head."

"He's not gonna get violent, is he?"

Cue the rain. Cue the lightning. Cue the thunder.

"Oh, shit," said the clerk, hurrying around the end of the counter and rushing to the door. "I didn't know it was supposed to rain tonight. It's Manager's Bar-B-Q Night. This is gonna piss people off." He scanned the sky anxiously. "It might blow over," he said hopefully. "You better get to your room, though. If it does rain, it's gonna be in buckets."

"You know," I said, taking our bags and following him as he led the way out the door, "for some reason, I've been wondering whether I haven't been here before."

"Uh-oh," he said. "Spooky."

"Yes," I agreed. "It is kind of spooky. You see—"

A bolt of lightning.

"—I have the odd feeling that I was here when the town was called—"

A rumble of thunder.

"—Eldritch."

"Oh, yeah. It used to be Eldritch."

"Really?"

"Yeah, but we went through a community redefinition."

"A community redefinition? Did I hear you right?"

"Yes, you did. You most certainly did. We redefined ourselves as Hideout Hollow, 'The Place to Get Away to When You Make Your Getaway from Someplace Else.'"

"Hideout Hollow?" I said. I was puzzled. "That sounds—well, forgive me for saying this, but it sounds derivative."

"Derivative?"

"Yeah. Isn't there a Happy Valley around here somewhere?"

"Just over the hill. Oh, I see what you mean. You're right. They were our inspiration."

"I thought so," I said. "Happy Valley, Hideout Hollow. It's pretty obvious."

"No, no. That wasn't it. They redefined themselves as Terror Town, 'Your First Choice for a Vacation That Will Make Your Flesh Crawl.' Did wonders for them. Nobody was interested in a place like Happy Valley anymore. Old hat. Too soft. No edge. Terror Town, though, that was an instant hit. Did you know that before we redefined ourselves Terror Town was getting nearly ten times the tourist business that Eldritch was getting?"

"No. I didn't know that."

"You didn't? I thought it was pretty widely known. You don't keep up with the tourist industry?"

"Not as much as I should—"

"Basically, Eldritch was going broke. It got so bad that some desperate town councilpersons would sneak out at night and switch the road signs, so that people who intended to vacation in Terror Town would find themselves in Eldritch instead."

"I think some of that was already going on when I passed through here as a boy, quite a few years ago, on my way to New Mexico, piloting an aerocycle that I had built in my family's garage back in Babbington, my home—"

"What are you talking about?"

"About the first time I passed through here."

"Yeah, but what's the point?"

"Perhaps you've heard about the night when Special Agent Panmuphle passed through here years ago."

"Not that I remember, and I still don't see your point."

"The point is that a kid was switching road signs when I came through here years ago."

"Oh. Okay, now I see what you're getting at. That doesn't surprise me. In fact, it wouldn't surprise me at all if some of the very same councilpersons who tried sign-switching as a way of steering tourists to Eldritch hadn't done a little sign-switching as a prank when they were kids and that's what inspired them to undertake their desperate program of misdirection later in life. I mean, how many original ideas does anybody get in a lifetime? You can't really blame someone for mining the rich lode of youth during the mental doldrums of late middle age, can you?"

"No. Certainly not. I didn't mean to imply—"

"Anyway, it turned out the problem was the name. We hired consultants, they surveyed a sample of the populace and found that something like ninety-two percent of people who planned to take a vacation within the next twelve months had no idea what *eldritch* means."

"Ninety-two percent?"

"Ninety-two percent."

"So you changed the name."

"Changed the name, came up with a good explanatory slogan that tells you what kind of experience you're going to have when you visit, trained the townspeople how to behave when they're interacting with visitors, remodeled our attractions and accommodations—"

"Redefined yourselves, in short."

"You got it, Panmuphle. We redefined ourselves. Here's your room."

"Thanks, I—"

"Anything else?"

"What time is the Manager's Bar-B-Q?"

"Called on account of rain."

"Aw, gee," said Albertine.

"Well, Miss Giggles, if you and Mr. Panmuphle—Special Agent Panmuphle, I mean—would like to come back to the office after you get settled, I'll give you a beer in consolation."

Giggles was all for it. That's why we found ourselves, a little later, drinking beer in the office and discussing the difference between night and day.

"I know how it is," he was saying. "I've been there. It's like day and night. Or night and day, I guess I should say. That's what people say, isn't it? It's like night and day? Well, it is. Rolling through the day, the bright American day, you feel something big, and strong, and—what? Uplifting! That's what. Up-fucking-lifting."

"Like the lift on an airplane wing," I suggested.

"Sure. Whatever. I wouldn't have said that. In fact, I didn't. I didn't say anything about an airplane wing. Didn't even say anything about an airplane. I said 'uplifting,' as you may recall. I had in mind something spiritual. That's the point I wanted to make. There's a kind of spiritual uplift in that light, the light of the American day."

"I see," I said.

"Let me ask you something."

"Mm?"

"I want to ask you something."

"Okay."

"You sing sometimes, don't you? While you're driving? In the day-time? In that amazing light? You start singing sometimes, right?"

"We often sing," said Albertine. "One of us better than the other."

"Sure. I knew it. You see? I told you I've been there. I sang, too, when I was on the road. Couldn't hardly stop some days. I was a singing fool. Driving along. Singing. A singing fool."

He picked up his beer bottle. I think he meant to take a drink before he went on, but something came over him. He paused with the bottle half raised.

"But," he said. He nodded at us, just once. "But," he said again, with added emphasis. Then he took a pull at the bottle. He wiped his mouth and said, drawing the words out as he delivered them, "At eventide, something happens. Something happens to the tone of the country. The bright American day gives way to the dark American night. Does that seem obvious to you?"

"Well—"

"There's more to it than you think. Something ominous seems to fill the sky. It's not darkness exactly. Because the American night is never really dark. There are always lights, the lights that make the dark places darker, like the bright notes in a saxophone solo that make the blue notes bluer. One of those moody saxophone solos. You can't make a moody saxophone solo out of silence. You need some notes. And you can't make the ominous American night out of darkness alone. You need some neon. You need some fluorescence."

"That—that's just the way it was when we arrived here this evening," said Albertine. "What light there was somehow made the night darker, and made this place seem threatening."

"Yeah," he said. "It's part of the package. The buzzing neon light in the sign, like it's going to burn out any minute. The way the 'No' in 'No Vacancy' flickers on and off uncertainly or randomly, as if it was tryin' to send you a message. All part of the package."

"The package?"

"Yeah," he said with a chuckle. "The owners used an 'atmosphere service,' Retro-Glo. They gave it that feeling of the kind of place you'd only stay in if you were on the lam or cheatin' on somebody. A few tricks with the lighting. Knock the furniture around some. Generally scuff the place up. Hell, I could've done all that. And for a lot less. But these guys were really talented with paint. Repainted the whole place, everything fresh, but it looks old, worn-out. You ought to see the work they put into grease spots. Real artists. I couldn't have done that. I couldn't have done any of the electric stuff, either. Like the automatic odorizers."

Albertine wrinkled her nose. "Odorizers?"

"Yeah. You get your choice. We use cheap booze and stale cigarettes. Place down the road uses the cold sweat of fear. We tried it. Kind of overpowering. Not for us."

"This process of community redefinition seems to be a growing

358 • PETER LEROY

phenomenon," I said thoughtfully. "In fact, the entire town of Babbington, New York, my home town, has been redefined based on the day when I returned from a solo flight I made to Corosso, New Mexico, aboard an aerocycle that I—"

"Holy shit!" he said. "Look at the time! I had no idea it was so late! I hate to bring this symposium to an end—"

"This will just take a minute. I—"

He rose and extended his arms, beckoning to us to get up, and then herded us toward the door.

"Sorry," he said, "but I've got to make my rounds, do some paperwork—you know how it is—too much to do and not enough time to do it."

"What I thought you'd find interesting," I said, "is that Babbington actually has a redefinition authority that—"

"Good night, Giggles," he said, swinging the door closed behind us. The lock clicked. The neon sign buzzed. The night claimed us.

A MUDDLEHEADED DREAMER

• •

I WAS ROLLING along through a small town, and as I rolled along I began to see the many ways, mostly small, in which it resembled Babbington. You can imagine how this moved me, a boy so far from home, whose thoughts, while he was rolling farther and farther from home, so often turned backward, toward that home that late he'd left, noticing the similarities.

"You see Babbington everywhere," said *Spirit*.

"You're right," I said, struck by the truth of it.

"And you see dark-haired girls everywhere, too."

"That's right, too."

"It's getting annoying."

"I think it has something to do with wishful thinking," I admitted. I was going to say something more on the subject of wishful thinking. I don't remember what it was going to be. I never got to say it.

"Watch out!" shrieked *Spirit*.

"For what?" I asked.

"That dog!"

Dog? What dog was she talking about? Oh. That dog.

I squeezed the brake levers with every ounce of strength I had. The front brake grabbed with such suddenness and force that *Spirit* pitched forward, up and over her front wheel. I was thrown from my seat and flew a couple of yards before striking the pavement. (NOTE: I have not included this brief flight in my tally of the distance I was airborne on the journey. To do so would have been wrong.) *Spirit* landed upside down. Like her, I pitched as I flew, so I landed flat on my back. I lay there, unmoving. I assumed that I must be injured, too injured to move, much too seriously injured to get up. I figured that, any minute now, a crowd of the curious and concerned would rush to form a ring around me, buzzing with speculation about my condition, putting odds on my survival. In the movies, someone always rushed forward to command the quickly assembling crowd to stand back, give the victim some air, and avoid moving him. I waited for the crowd and for the person who would take command of the crowd.

Time passed. I heard no crowd, no buzz. No commanding voice.

I opened my eyes. Someone was standing over me, looking down at me.

"You okay?" he asked.

"I'm not sure," I said.

"Why don't you get up?"

"I think I should wait until I know if I've broken anything."

"Like what? Your watch?"

"I don't have a watch. I meant a bone. I might have broken some bones. One anyway. I might have fractured my skull."

"Does that happen to you a lot, fracturing your skull?"

"Um, no. It's never happened to me before."

"I don't think it's happened to you now, either. You just flipped over your handlebars, that's all. I done it lots of times."

"You have?"

"Sure. I get a little tanked up, there's no telling what I might run into. Over I go."

"You have an aerocycle?"

"Aerocycle? Is that what you call this?"

"Yes."

"What's with the wings?"

"She's—it's—supposed to be able to fly," I whispered.

"Why are you whispering?"

"Oh, I don't know—must be something in my throat—dust."

"You're whispering because you don't want your bike to hear you, aren't you?"

"Heh, heh, heh."

"You talk to your bike, don't you?"

"Me?"

"Yeah, you. You talk to your bike."

"Well—"

"So do I. We all do. Come on, get up. You're okay. Let's go see how she is."

He extended a hand. I took it, and he helped me up. He was wearing a black leather jacket with *Johnny* written on it, dark sunglasses, a white T-shirt, a cap like the ones that taxi drivers wore, blue jeans, and motorcycle boots. He had long sideburns and a grin that resembled a sneer.

"I shouldn't have braked so hard," I said, dusting myself off.

"Six of one, half a dozen of the other," he said with a shrug. "If you'd hit the dog, you woulda gone over just the same."

"You think so?"

"Oh, yeah. I hit that dog maybe four or five times. Went right over, just the way you did. Didn't hurt me none. Didn't hurt the dog none, neither."

Together, we righted *Spirit* and walked around her, inspecting her for damage.

"What's this?" he asked when we got to what was left of the banner advertising Porky White's clam bar. "'Kap'n Klam is coming!' Is that you?"

"No," I said. "It's my sponsor. It used to say 'Kap'n Klam is coming! The Home of Happy Diners,' but that's all that's left of it."

"Must embarrass her," he said.

"You think so?"

"Dragging a ratty old thing like that around? What do you think? Of course it embarrasses her. I'd get rid of that if I were you."

I began removing it while he continued his inspection.

"She's got a cracked chassis," he pronounced a moment later, shaking his head sadly.

"Really?" I said, crouching down to look at the part of her frame that he was running his fingers along.

"Ask her if she's in pain," he said.

"I—um—are you serious?"

"Of course I'm serious. I can't ask her. She's not my bike. She wouldn't hear me, and I wouldn't hear her."

"*Spirit,*" I said, "are you okay? Are you in pain?"

"Am I in pain?" she said. "It's one long line of pain from my nose to my tail."

"You've cracked your chassis," I said.

"Am I going to die?"

"No, no. Of course not. You're going to be—just a minute." To the biker I said, "She—she's in a lot of pain."

"Awww, the poor thing," he said, caressing her chassis with tenderness and affection.

"Can she be fixed?"

"Oh, sure. We got a guy in town can work wonders. Practically bring a bike back from the dead. I've seen him take a twisted mass of metal and make it back into a bike again."

"You're going to be fine," I said to *Spirit*. "We're going to get you to a doctor."

I pushed her along the street, following Johnny, who was riding an enormous motorcycle, just chugging along at walking speed, balancing the bike now and then by putting a big boot on the pavement, allowing it to drag along. He turned down an alley, and I followed. At the end of the alley there were dozens of motorcycles, or, as I realized when we drew closer, parts of dozens of motorcycles. They were in various stages of disassembly—or reassembly.

"Oh, no," wailed *Spirit*. "You're not going to let them do that to me, are you?"

"No, no," I said. "They won't have to—just a minute." I asked Johnny, "Are they going to have to take her apart?"

"Nah," he said confidently. "She's just got a thin crack in a couple of pieces of her tubing. Big Bob'll take those out, bolt new tubing in, and she'll be good as new. Between us," he said, lowering his voice, "she'll be better than new. Whoever did the original assembly job wasn't—"

"I did it," I said.

"Nice job," he said. "Considering."

We left *Spirit* in the care of Big Bob, who promised that she would be ready for the road when I was ready to leave in the morning.

"Come on down the pool hall and have a beer," said Johnny. "Meet the gang."

The pool hall? A beer? The gang? Was he talking to me?

"Me?" I said.

"Yeah, you," he said. "You're shaken up. You've had a crash. You are deserving of the hospitality of the MDMC."

"What's that?"

"That is the club. Specifically, those are the initials of the name of the club."

"What do they stand for?"

"That is known only to the members of the club."

"A moment's inattention," Johnny was saying. "That's all it takes for a rider to get himself in trouble."

"Or for a young aviator to come crashing to the ground," I said with the wisdom and exaggerated precision of a kid who's had a couple of beers.

"Or a young aviator," said Johnny, saluting my wisdom with a tilt of his beer bottle. "Now the thing is, if a rider—or an aviator—comes to grief through inattention, he's likely to feel ashamed of himself. He knows that there's no shame in crashing if crashing is not his fault, but—"

"And even if it is his fault," I said, "he shouldn't feel any shame if he crashed for a good reason."

"A good reason? What would be a good reason?" Johnny asked.

"Hmm?"

"What would be a good reason for crashing?"

"Well—ah—for one thing—how about—trying to fly too high, the way Icarus did."

"I don't—"

"Wait, wait, I know what you're thinking. You're thinking that the reasons for Icarus's crashing—vanity, pride, willfulness, and foolishness—are not good reasons."

"Yeah, well—"

"Well, let me tell you, Johnny, just between us, there have been times while I've been rolling westward en route to New Mexico this summer when I envied Icarus."

"That so?"

"What's the story, are they out of beer here?" I said, peering into my empty bottle.

"You want another?"

"Sure. Where's the waitress with the tight sweater?"

"Hey, Marie," he called, "how about two more?"

"Yes," I said, shaking my head to show that I, too, found what I was saying difficult to believe, "I have envied Icarus not only for his flight, but even for his fate."

"He crashed, right?"

"Yes." I sighed. I shook my head. "He crashed."

"Tough luck."

"But Icarus at least crashed from overreaching, which a young aviator may consider a noble error, even a good reason, and Icarus also had the advantage over this particular young aviator of having actually soared above the earth, while *Spirit* and I seem everlastingly anchored to it."

Marie brought the beers.

"Ah," I said, "it's the beautiful Marie. You know, Marie, back at home, in Babbington, New York, I used to read those Larry Peters adventure books—I was just a kid back then—and the Peters family had a maid named Marie, who was a real beauty, but she couldn't compare to you! What hair! What eyes! What lips! And what a sweater!"

That got me a laugh from Johnny and a swat from Marie. Could life possibly get any better?

"As I was saying," I said, "my crash came about through the less-than-noble failing of allowing my mind to wander. In my defense, I will point out that a trip like mine has its long, tedious stretches, and that such stretches dull the senses. There's really no telling what kind of thoughts a young aviator may come up with, or what trouble they may get him into."

"Hey, don't be too hard on yourself, Petey," said Johnny.

"I know," I said. "You're going to tell me that my inattention was only a minor factor in the equation."

"I was going to say, in your defense—"

"You're going to say that most of the fault belongs to the dog. The cur was crossing the main street of the town as if he owned it."

"I was going to say that inattention is a common failing. You can take it from me. I have extensive experience in inattention. Some of it beer-induced, I admit." He smiled at his bottle and took another swallow. "Your second failing is also a common one," he said, in a cautionary tone.

"Oh," I said. "Wha's da?" I laughed, amused at the way my lips had tripped me up. "I mean, what's that?" I said, as precisely as I could. I looked at my bottle. Was this the same one Marie had brought a minute ago? I looked around the room. Had it always been turning like this? Had the other members of the MDMC always been arrayed in a circle around Johnny and me, watching, listening, with their arms folded across their black leather chests?

"Overreaction," he said.

"Overreaction?" I said. "Me? Pffft."

"I seen the whole thing. You overreacted."

"I had to do smothing," I protested. "I mean mosthing."

"Overreaction is often a consequence of inattention," he said.

My head dropped to my chest for a moment.

"You've got your inattentive rider rolling along, being inattentive," he explained. "Then suddenly he's startled out of his inattention by the screams of his woman, who's riding behind him, holding on to him for dear life. He asks himself, 'What the hell is she screaming like that for?' He snaps his head up—"

I snapped my head up. I think I heard a deep rumble of hearty laughter from the guys in the gang.

"—and sees a dog in the road in front of him."

"Crossing street zif he owns it," I contributed.

"What does he do? Does he calmly slow the bike down and nimbly avoid the obstacle? He does not. He overreacts. He slams on the brakes and wrenches the wheel sharply."

"Not his fault, though," I asserted. "Dog—"

That was my final contribution to the discussion.

I woke up on a pool table, another first for me. You will probably not be surprised that I didn't know where I was when I woke. I felt the felt beneath me, and when I rolled over I occasioned a clattering of balls. I sat up, thought better of it, stretched out again, and slept some more. When I awoke fully, some time later, the pool hall was full of the light of midday, pouring through the storefront windows. I climbed down from the table, staggered to the door, and let myself out.

I had to find my way to Big Bob's on my own, but it wasn't hard. That is, it shouldn't have been hard. Everybody in town seemed to know the way. With my head full of fuzz, I kept losing my way, and I had to ask many times before I finally arrived at the end of the alley with the ranks of damaged motorcycles. *Spirit* was there, waiting for me. With some anxiety—with a lot of anxiety, to tell the truth—I asked Big Bob what I owed him.

"It's been taken care of," he said. "Paid for by the MDMC."

"Paid?"

"That's what I said."

With a mighty roar, Johnny appeared at the other end of the alley, mounted on his bike. "Petey!" he called. He thundered the length of the alley and came to a stop beside *Spirit*. "How you feeling?"

"Not so hot," I said.

"That is often the state in which a new initiate finds himself the morning after his election to the gang."

"Election? To the gang?"

"That's right. By unanimous vote, you are now a member of the MDMC."

"A member?"

"Full-fledged."

"Since I'm a member—do I get to know what the initials stand for?"

"You do," he said. "The name was originally suggested by my father."

He glanced upward and said, "Thanks, Dad." To me he said, "The old man was always telling me, 'Johnny, you're nothing but a muddleheaded dreamer who never does anything but ride around on that damned motorcycle in the aimless pursuit of adventure, and that's all you're ever going to be,' so one day I said to myself, 'Johnny, he's right! That's exactly what you are, and that's exactly what you want to be. Enjoy it. Just get on your bike and go.' So I assembled a bunch of like-minded individuals, and we formed the Muddleheaded Dreamers' Motorcycle Club—and now you are a member. You are officially a muddleheaded dreamer."

"But your father was wrong!" I said.

"About my being a muddleheaded dreamer?"

"I don't know about that. I mean he was wrong to call the pursuit of adventure aimless because—*Spirit* and I were talking about this just yesterday—if you're pursuing adventure then just about any route you take is the right route if it leads you to adventure—so if you're having an adventure, you're always on the right track, and—"

"Petey," he said, raising a hand. "Cool your jets, man. If you're gonna stay cool, you gotta get a grip on yourself. I'll have to straighten you out. Remember what I said? Hmmm? Don't overreact."

I guess that "Don't overreact" was the advice that Johnny wanted me to take with me when I left, but I heard something else in addition to that. I heard what he had said when he told me about his father. I heard him saying, "If you're a muddleheaded dreamer, enjoy it. Just get on your bike and go." I haven't done a very good job of restraining my tendency to overreact—ask the girl in the furniture store about my reaction last week when a sofa that Albertine and I had ordered wasn't delivered on time and I'll bet you hear the word *maniac*—but I have done a good job of admitting that I am a muddleheaded dreamer, a full-fledged member of the MDMC.

PRE-TRAUMATIC STRESS

••

I WAS ON the alert. I was keeping an eye out for dogs. I had the feeling that we were in the area of my crash, the crash that had been more the fault of the dog than the muddleheaded dreamer at the controls of the aerocycle, and I didn't want history to repeat itself.

"You seem on edge," said Albertine.

"I am. I'm tense."

"What's the matter?"

"I'm on the alert for dogs."

"Dogs."

"With every fiber of my being, I'm watching for any dogs that might suddenly dart in front of us and cause a crash."

"Was that one of the duties of the guy riding shotgun?"

"In the westerns, you mean?"

"Yes."

"Hmm. Let me check."

I had barely begun a random ramble through my memories of westerns that I'd seen at the Babbington Theater, looking for dogs that might have darted dangerously in front of the steaming team hauling a hurtling stagecoach over the dusty plains, when suddenly, there it was, the threat that I was on the watch for: a dog.

It was a small dog with spindly legs and large ears, the kind that you may have heard people refer to uncharitably as a long-legged rat or, for short, a rat dog. The dog was at the end of a leash held by a woman who was standing on the curb. Both the woman and the dog seemed to intend to cross the street, but neither of them was paying any attention to the traffic. The woman was pressing her cheek to her shoulder to hold a cell phone to her ear. In one hand she held the leash that ran to the collar of the rat dog and also a purse, open. She was peering into her purse in search of something, shuffling through the contents with the hand that held no leash. The dog was looking up and down the sidewalk for someone to trip.

"There's a dog now," I said.

"Where?"

368 • PETER LEROY

"Right there, on the sidewalk. See the woman poking around in her pocketbook? She's got a rat dog."

"It's on a leash."

"Right. Probably nothing to worry about. Still, I do want to keep you informed, to alert you not only to danger but to potential danger."

"What about that other dog?"

"What other dog?"

"The one that might run in front of us in the next town."

"We'll avoid that dog when we come to it. Right now, I'd like you to concentrate on missing this dog. Uh-oh. There they go. They're stepping into the street."

Albertine slowed the Electro-Flyer. The woman and her dog took a couple of steps, oblivious to the traffic. Albertine veered a bit to the left. The woman quickened her pace. Albertine veered a bit to the right. The woman stopped in the middle of our lane. Albertine stopped. From behind us came the sound of screeching brakes.

The woman and the rat dog snapped their heads in our direction and registered surprise. Then the woman thrust her cell phone at us. It was a rude gesture. "Watch where you're going!" the woman shouted.

The dog frowned and said, "Yap!"

The woman and the dog continued walking, noses in the air.

The driver of the car behind us leaned on the horn. Then he shot forward with squealing tires, swerving out and around us, lurched up beside us on the left, then slammed his brakes when he saw the woman and the dog, now directly in his path. Voices were raised. The dog became particularly animated.

"This is getting ugly," I said to Al.

"I think I'm just going to back up," she said, throwing an arm across the seat and looking toward the rear as she reversed, "then make an illegal U-turn," she added, whipping around to the left and slipping into a gap between oncoming cars, "and try another route."

The Alley was there, where I remembered it, and at the far end was Big Bob's, with a collection of broken motorcycles in front.

"Big Bob around?" I asked a beefy guy who was idling in the doorway.

"Big Bob?"

"Big Bob."

"Big Bob hasn't been around for—oh—about twenty years."

"Took that last ride, eh?"

"Huh?"

"Died?"

"Oh, yeah. Died. That's kind of a colorful way of putting it: 'took that last ride.' I like that."

"He's got a way with words," said Albertine.

"Actually, I was hoping I might find a guy named Johnny. He used to be the leader of the MDMC."

He chuckled. "You mean Dr. Wylie," he said, "the distinguished director of the prestigious Algan Institute, the world's foremost clinic for the treatment of pre-traumatic stress syndrome."

"I don't think that could be the same—"

"Oh, yeah," he said. "It is. It's the guy you're looking for. Johnny Wylie. Formerly a muddleheaded dreamer, now a prosperous quack."

"You mean h-he was c-cured?" I stammered.

"Let's say he heard the call of the open wallet."

"Just what is pre-traumatic stress syndrome?" asked Albertine.

"The unsettling complex of stress-related disorders that results from contemplating the traumas we haven't suffered yet, but might," the biker explained.

"Are you trying to be funny?" I asked.

"Certainly not," he declared. "Pre-traum is big business. Nearly thirteen percent of the general population is convinced that they're suffering from it, thanks mainly to Dr. Wylie's books and infomercials."

"Where is this Algan Institute?" Al asked.

"Right here in town. You ought to drop in. You'll get to see Johnny in action. Just tell them you think you might be suffering from pre-traum. After all, you probably are."

"I don't think so," I said.

"We did almost have a crash," said Albertine. "That's got me a bit tense, nervous, edgy."

"You say that you nearly had a crash?" the biker asked.

"That's right," said Albertine.

"But you didn't actually have a crash?"

"No," I said. "Fortunately, I was riding shotgun and—"

"Would you say that if you had had a crash, you might be suffering from post-traumatic stress syndrome now?" he asked me.

"Possibly," I said. "I'm not sure how traumatic—"

"As it is, you didn't have a crash," he said to Albertine, "and yet you're feeling tense, nervous, and edgy! That's pre-traum. Classic. Drop in at the Institute. They'll let you sit in on a group session—but take my advice: keep your hand on your wallet."

The Algan Institute occupied a stately mansion on the tree-lined main street of the town, set well back and surrounded by a wrought-iron fence.

"Impressive," I said to Albertine.

"Are we going to go in?"

"I don't know," I said. "All these years, I've thought of Johnny not only as a muddleheaded dreamer but as perpetually such. I think I expected to find him and have him say to me, 'Hmmm, Petey, what do you say we get on our bikes and just go.'"

"Hmmm, and what about me, Petey?"

"Well, he would have been all over you, of course. I might have had to mess him up some."

She rang the bell.

"Yes?" said a woman's voice from a speaker beside the door.

"Peter Leroy and Albertine Gaudet to see Dr. Wylie," I said.

"What's troubling you?" asked the voice.

"Nothing. I just—"

"We nearly had a crash," said Albertine.

"Ah!" said the voice. "You say you nearly had a crash?"

"That's right," said Albertine. "A woman with a small dog—"

Something whirred, something clicked, and the door swung open.

We entered a marble hall. Some distance away there was a desk, at which a woman in a crisp suit sat. We hiked across the hall and eventually arrived at the desk.

"I wonder if it would be possible to see Dr. Wylie," I said.

"You nearly had a crash," the woman said with professional sympathy. "I'm sure that Dr. Wylie would like to help you. Who is your insurance provider?"

"Insurance?"

"Your health insurance provider."

"Oh—I—"

"A charming man at Big Bob's told us that we might sit in on a group session and see whether it was the right thing for us," Albertine said.

"Very well," the woman said. "There is a group in session now. Follow me."

She led us a few hundred yards across the entry hall to enormous double doors that she flung open without ceremony, revealing a group of people seated in a circle. I recognized Johnny immediately, even without his sideburns and black leather jacket, and I would have recognized him even if he hadn't been wearing a white lab coat with the name Dr. Wylie on it.

We had obviously interrupted the session. Everyone turned in our direction. The doors thudded closed behind us. We found our way to empty chairs, trying our best to disappear.

"Go on, Stan," said Johnny.

Stan, a thin, nervous young man, said, "As I was saying, I'm suffering from the stress that I feel from the trauma that generations as yet unborn are going to have to suffer as a result of the selfishness and stupidity of the generations that preceded them, including my own."

"That is just a bunch of abstract bullshit," grumbled a young woman seated next to him. She nibbled on her fingers.

"I think it's an interesting example of sympathetic pre-traum," said a young woman seated on the other side of him. "I'm starting to feel some of it myself."

"Nyeea," snarled the first young woman.

"I have a sympathetic soul," the second young woman claimed.

At that moment, the doors burst open again and we all turned toward them. The woman in the crisp suit stood there, and beside her was the woman with the rat dog. The doors closed behind the woman and her dog, and she surveyed the available chairs. She chose one that was a mere two chairs to my right. She plopped the rat dog onto the one that was immediately to my right.

"Rrr," said the dog cordially.

A small man, meek and bald, raised his hand.

"Yes, Mr. Tripp?" said Johnny.

"I just want to say—if nobody minds—that this most recent arrival has provoked in me a reaction that I would have to describe as a completely new instance of pre-traum that I hadn't been suffering before now."

"And that is?" Johnny prompted.

"I'm feeling how painful it would feel if I were bitten by that dog—and not just the bite—but the anxiety I would feel after being bitten when I would be asking myself, 'My God, what if the dog had rabies?'—and now, now I'm beginning to feel the anticipation of the feeling of the rabies needle. I'm told that they inject you with an enormous needle in the stomach—"

"Oh, I can't stand it," said the girl on Stan's right. "I hate hospitals! The smell! I'm anticipating it. It's making me sick! Get the dog out of here!"

"My dog is a certified emotional-support dog," said the rat dog's owner. "He is highly trained, and his presence is essential to my well-being." She began rummaging in her purse again, as she had when she was crossing the street, and eventually she produced a document, which she unfolded and handed to Mr. Tripp. He perused it.

"This seems to be legitimate," he said sadly.

"What do you mean 'seems to be legitimate'?" said the dog's owner. "It most certainly is legitimate."

"It's just that I never heard of an emotional-support dog before."

"Rrrr," said the dog. Its hackles began to rise.

"Sorry, fella," said Mr. Tripp. To the woman, he said, "A guide dog, yes. A service dog, yes. But an emotional-support dog, that's a new one on me."

"Rrrr," said the dog with undisguised contempt.

"Perhaps our visitors would like to let the group know what it is that has brought them here to the Algan Institute," said Dr. Wylie, turning pointedly toward Albertine, me, the dog, and the dog's owner.

"After you," I said to the dog's owner.

Everyone stared at her in anticipation. So did her dog.

"I think Dr. Wylie wants to know what sort of pre-traumatic stress you are suffering from," I said.

She gave me a long look. I think she was asking herself where she had seen me before. I disguised myself with a look of deep concern.

She looked at her dog and then put her hands over its ears. The dog looked puzzled.

"I'm suffering from pre-traumatic stress induced by the anticipation of the inevitable death of Mr. Pfister."

"Someone close to you?" asked Dr. Wylie.

The woman inclined her head in the direction of the dog.

"Your dog?" said Mr. Tripp.

The woman nodded yes.

"A triviality!" declared Tripp.

"Hardly!" said the woman.

"The death of your dog?" scoffed Tripp. "I'd call that next to nothing compared to the suffering of an entire generation of children as yet unborn."

"When Mr. Pfister dies," the woman lamented, "I don't know what I'll do. I don't see how I can possibly go on. And yet I know that he must die. The day will come. I can envision that day as if it were today. I can feel the grief that I will feel as if I were feeling it now. I'm a basket case. That is, I will be a basket case. When it happens. And it nearly happened today. I had just arrived in town, and I was crossing the main street, trying to find my way here to the Institute, when a car came upon me suddenly, silently, as if it had sprung up out of nowhere, headed straight for Mr. Pfister. I had to yank him out of the way with a sharp tug of his leash—and I nearly killed him. What if I had? Oh, my god, my god, what if I had?"

"Life is a grim farce," groaned the woman who hated hospitals.

Voices were raised around the group. A lively debate seemed about to begin. Al and I saw the opportunity for a getaway and decided to take it. We had reached the door when Dr. Wylie called out to us, across the developing fracas, "Wouldn't you care to contribute something before you leave?"

"I think we're in the wrong place," I said as I opened the double doors. "It's my fault. I got the wrong impression—somehow—I don't know—I guess I'm just a muddleheaded dreamer." I closed the doors behind us.

THE SECOND MOST REMARKABLE THING IN THE LIFE OF CURTIS BARNSTABLE

••

Travel has the serious defect of taking one away from the stimulus and criticism of contemporaries. . . . One is too much alone, too much the passing stranger.

—V. S. Pritchett, *Midnight Oil*

THE TOWN WAS called Cornfields. The road that led to it, and through it, and away from it, was straight. At intervals, that road was crossed by other straight roads, each of them cutting across it in precise perpendicularity. It was an unremarkable place, but it got me thinking. It got me thinking about the naming of places, about paucity and plenitude, and, of course, about Babbington.

"What's with you?" asked *Spirit.*

"I was just musing, ruminating. Why do you ask?"

"I thought I heard you mutter something like 'paucity and plenitude.'"

"Well—I—I might have."

"You'd better stop for the night," she said. "You need a break."

I saw, ahead, to the right, a single farmhouse.

As I made my way up its driveway, a boy about my age came out the front door and stood on the porch, watching me approach. When I stopped and put *Spirit* on her stand, he called a greeting: "What in the world are you doing here, of all places?"

"I'm on my way to New Mexico," I explained. "I was hoping that I could spend the night here."

"Here? With us?"

"Yes, if you're willing to put me up."

"This is very unusual," he said. "Remarkable."

"Can I stay?"

He opened the front door and called into the house, "Mama, there's a boy here who arrived on an airplane and wants to know if he can stay overnight."

A great rumbling laugh rolled out the door, followed by a gleeful declaration: "Curtis Barnstable, I swear you are the most imaginative child there ever was! A boy on an airplane! Where do you get your ideas! Why, of course he can stay! We put up all the aeronautical boys that come our way! Oooh, I tell you, Curtis, you are going to wear me out with laughing. You drive away the dullness of the day!"

"You can stay," he said. "Have a seat."

"Thanks," I said.

We sat in rockers, side by side. Quite a long time passed. The day was hot. Insects buzzed in the cornfields. Nothing happened.

Then, across the buzzing silence, a bus appeared, on our right, far down the road, and lumbered toward the intersection. With a wheeze, the bus sighed and settled to a stop, and we could hear its door open though it was on the opposite side from us.

Curtis looked at me. "This is a big event," he said. "Hardly anybody ever gets off the bus there."

The bus rumbled, shook itself, and pulled away, leaving behind, in the hovering dust that it had raised, a dapper man in a well-tailored suit. He squinted in the glaring light and looked around, evidently trying to get his bearings, as if the place where he found himself was not at all where he had expected to be. He looked out over the cornfields, and he looked out over the plowed fields. He looked briefly in our direction, then looked away.

Time passed. The man began to look increasingly uneasy, and increasingly annoyed. I began to wonder if chance had played a trick on him, sending him to this place in the middle of nowhere as a joke.

Now and then a car passed. The man regarded each car as it approached, leaning slightly toward it quizzically, apparently wondering whether it might hold the reason for his having stopped there, the someone he expected to meet.

A truck roared by, and the well-dressed man recoiled slightly at its approach. As it passed, it raised a cloud of dust that settled onto the man. He began brushing at his suit. He was still brushing at it when another car approached, on the side of the road opposite him, slowed, and stopped. The man stopped brushing the dust from his suit and peered at the car querulously. A thin man, almost scrawny, with a prominent Adam's apple, got out of the car. The car drove off. The thin man was also wearing a suit, but it wasn't as well tailored. It hung on him. He was wearing a hat. The first man was not. The two men stared at each other across the intervening width of the roadway. The second man put his hands in his pockets. For a while, the two men kept looking across at each other, as if neither was willing to speak first. It almost seemed like a game, some school-yard game that the first of them to speak would lose.

They were distracted by the approach of a crop-dusting plane. It appeared in the distance, lowly humming, and came on in a lazy way, crossing the fields of corn without dusting them, then moving closer over the plowed fields, the pilot then dropping white dust as the plane came nearer. Both men watched it. The second man, the skinny one, commented on it. Calling across the road to the well-dressed man, he said, "Funny that a plane should be dustin' crops where there ain't no crops."

Another bus came along, from the left this time. It stopped where the skinny man stood. The skinny man boarded the bus. The door closed. The bus pulled off. All of us who had been left behind watched it go until it was out of sight.

The plane made a turn at the end of its dusting run and came back, veering this time closer to the road, then drifting farther still, until it was over the road rather than the fields, and headed right toward the well-dressed man.

He saw it coming at him. He stood there and watched it coming at him. He didn't seem to believe what his eyes were seeing. He leaned toward the plane for a moment, as if to get a better look at it, to see if he could decide whether it was really doing what it seemed to be doing. Then he leaned back from it, as if he might avoid it. The plane dropped lower, until it was nearly at ground level.

Then the pilot of the plane began firing at the man. I recognized the staccato crackle of machine-gun fire from all the war movies I'd seen at the Babbington Theater.

The well-dressed man crouched, as if he might make himself invisible or dodge the bullets. He quickly realized how futile ducking was, though, and he began to look for somewhere to run, moving quickly, not frantically, but urgently, ducking and dodging. The plane passed over him. The pilot had missed him.

The plane made a lazy circle, as easy and unhurried a maneuver as if the pilot really were dusting crops and didn't care much whether the job got done or not, then came back at the man from the other direction, firing again.

A car appeared in the distance, approaching. The man dashed into the road, waving his arms, trying to signal the driver to stop. The car swerved, and it swung around the man. He seemed for a moment as if he might be about to lunge at it, grab a door handle, and let himself be dragged away, but he didn't, and the car continued on, useless.

The plane completed another turn. The man looked this way and that, hesitated a moment, and then ran into the cornfield.

The plane followed.

If the man had expected a safe haven in the corn, among the stalks, he didn't find it. The plane came directly on, toward him, slowly, a biplane especially fitted out to be able to fly so slowly, and began dusting. A cloud of dust began streaming from the plane, spread in the air, and settled onto the cornfield.

Another truck appeared in the distance, barreling along purposefully. The legend on the side of the truck read Magnum Oil. The dapper man burst from the cornfield, driven by desperation now, taking a chance that must have seemed to be his only chance. Waving his arms, he ran directly into the path of the truck. He wasn't going to let this ride get away as the car had earlier. The truck driver must have thought he was crazy, but he wasn't going to hit him, so he hit the brakes, hard, and the truck began to slide to a stop, the brakes struggling against the momentum of so large a truck with so heavy a load. It looked as if the truck wouldn't stop in time. The man would be hit. What he had hoped would be his salvation would kill him instead.

The plane came on.

The plane was coming from one direction, the truck from the other. The man was in the middle.

At the last moment the man threw himself to the ground, flattened himself, and the truck rolled over him, harmlessly, its big wheels holding it above the prostrate man.

Still the plane came on.

The pilot had gone too far. He'd made a fatal error.

The plane struck the truck. There seemed to be a moment when time held its breath. Then there was an explosion. The plane exploded, or the truck exploded, or both. The plane was on fire. The doors of the truck swung open, and two men flew out—the driver and the guy who had been riding shotgun for him. They ran from the truck shouting.

A couple of other cars and pickup trucks came along, and their drivers stopped to rubberneck. They got out of their cars and trucks to get a better view. The well-dressed man saw his chance. He slipped into the driver's seat of one of the pickup trucks, shifted it into gear, and drove off.

Then everyone began to make a fuss. Curtis's parents came running from inside the house. His father wanted to know what the hell had happened. His mother wanted to know if we were hurt. The truck drivers came running up the long driveway to the house, pounded up the steps to the porch, and asked to use the phone. The porch grew crowded. Curtis's mother brought a pitcher of lemonade. His father offered bushels of corn at what he said was a good price.

By sundown, everyone had gone. Curtis's parents had gone to bed. Curtis and I sat on the porch in silence for a while.

"Does that sort of thing happen often around here?" I asked.

"Never," he said. "In fact, before that, the most remarkable thing I ever saw around here was you."

Something woke me in the night. I wasn't sure what it was. I lay awake for a while, listening, but I heard nothing. The night was full of the sound of nothing happening. I switched on the light beside my bed, got my books, and returned to Panmuphle and the Bonhommes. The daughter had just told Panmuphle—that is, me—that it was Dr. Faustroll's habit to substitute paper for water in his daily sponge bath:

> "It has been a long time since he made that change," said Mr. Bonhomme gravely. "He uses a wallpaper of the season, of the fashion, or suiting his whim."
>
> "Wallpaper," I muttered, suspecting now that I was the victim of a jest.
>
> The fetching child spoke up. "To avoid shocking or offending the populace," she said, "he dresses himself, over this wallpaper,

in a shirt of quartz cloth; a large pair of trousers, drawn tight at the ankles, made of matte black velours; minuscule gray half-boots, with dust that he maintains, not without great effort or expense, I assure you, in equal layers or coatings, for months—"

She hesitated.

"Yes, mademoiselle?" I said, coaxing her.

"There is something about ant lions," she said, knitting her darling brows.

"Ant lions?"

"Yes, sir. He employs ant lions in the maintenance of his boots—that is, in the maintenance of the layers of dust on his boots." She cast her eyes downward like a schoolgirl who has not learned her lesson. "But I am not quite sure how or to what end they are employed," she confessed.

"The ant lions are of no interest to me," I assured her. "Continue with his costume, if you will."

"Yes, sir," she said with the hint of a curtsy. "Thank you, sir. He wears a vest of yellow gold, the exact color of his complexion, a vest—or perhaps I should say a cardigan—with two rubies closing two pockets, very high—"

"Quite the dandy," I observed.

"Yes, sir," she said. "And he completes the effect with a blue fox pelisse."

"Whatever that is," I muttered, noting it nonetheless.

"On his right index finger he stacks emerald and topaz rings," she said, making the gesture as she spoke, "as far as the nail, the only one of his ten that he does not bite at all, and he stops or concludes or ends the stack of rings with a perfect molybdenum pin, screwed into the bone of the little phalanx, the smallest bone at the end of the finger, through the nail."

"That is very bizarre," I muttered as I noted it on my pad, "and possibly criminal."

"By way of necktie," she went on, almost gaily now, "he passes around his neck the ribbon of the order of the Grande-Gidouille."

"I do not know—" I began.

"It is an order he invented!" she exclaimed, with delightful girlish giggles.

"And he has patented it," her father added with bourgeois gravity, "so that it will not be misused."

"Very well," I said, assuming that I had heard all. "Thank you for your assistance," I said, intending to take my leave.

"There is something more, monsieur," said Mr. Bonhomme.

"Yes?"

"Before he leaves the house, he—"

"Yes?"

"He hangs himself, monsieur."

"Hangs himself?"

"By that ribbon, the ribbon of the order of Grande-Gidouille."

"Extraordinary."

"He hangs himself by that ribbon from a gallows he has arranged for that purpose," said the girl, with a mixture of awe and scoffery, "and he waits or hesitates there, hanging, for some time."

"He must look ghastly," I ventured.

"Somewhere between the looks that suffocators call 'hung white' and 'hung blue,'" she said thoughtfully.

"Almost certainly illegal," I announced.

When I came downstairs for breakfast, everything was quiet. There was a place set for me at the table, but it seemed as if everyone else must already have eaten and begun the day's occupation. I didn't see any food. I peeked around the corner into the kitchen, but no one was there, and I didn't see any food in there, either.

I went into the front hall. All was still. I went out to the porch.

The man and woman were sitting in rocking chairs, staring out at the intersection where the bus had stopped the day before.

"Good morning," I said. "Where is—"

"Gone," said the woman.

"Left this morning," said the man.

"Right after breakfast," said the woman.

"Took the bus," said the man.

"W-what—where—why—" I sputtered.

"Said if he stayed here for the rest of his life he would never see anything like that again."

"Said he had to go."

"Oh," I said.

A long time passed. No one said anything. Nothing happened.

Then I said, "I guess I'd better be going, too," and I left.

EVERYTHING OLIVIA

WE SWUNG OFF the interstate, following the sign directing travelers to the town of Olivia. The sign was unusual. It pointed in separate directions for tour buses, for deliveries, and for passenger cars. At the end of the off-ramp for passenger cars, we approached a toll gate.

"Two?" asked the toll collector.

"There are two of us," said Albertine, "but isn't it a little odd to charge tolls by the person?"

"It isn't a toll," the collector said with the weariness of one who has had to deliver the same explanation many times. "It's admission."

"Admission?"

"That's right. It isn't a toll, and I am not a toll collector. It's admission, and I am a sales associate in the Admissions Department." She pointed to the plastic tag pinned above her left breast. It said Amanda, and below that it said Sales Associate.

"I've never been asked to pay admission to a town before."

"Olivia isn't just a town," Amanda explained. "It's a museum."

"Ah!" I said. "One of those historical re-creations? That's very interesting. You see, my home town—"

"More of a personal museum," she said. "The Town of Olivia is the Museum of Olivia."

"A personal museum?" I said. "That's an interesting idea."

"Olivia who?" asked Albertine.

"Just Olivia," said Amanda. "Having her own museum and all, she has attained the rarefied status of single-name international celebrity. That's the way the brochure puts it."

"I've never heard of her," I said.

"Still," said Amanda, "she has her own museum, and I'd be willing to wager that you don't."

"Well, no," I said, "I don't, but there is a caricature of me on the wall of a restaurant—"

"Do people live here? In the town of Olivia? In the Museum of Olivia?" asked Al.

"Sure do," said Amanda. "I live here. I've lived here all my life."

"The caricature shows me as I was in my teens," I explained, "when I flew an aerocycle from—"

"You see," said Amanda, "before Olivia came along, this town had been shrinking for as long as I can remember. I watched my friends grow up and move away, even saw members of my family move away. It was getting to be a very lonely place. We were on the verge of just disappearing, but then one day Olivia drove into town. She was just passing through, like you, but she was enchanted by the prospect that she, a woman named Olivia, might live in a town named Olivia. That's the way she puts it in her introduction to the brochure. She says she was 'enchanted by the prospect.'"

"What a surprising and fortunate coincidence that she should happen upon a town named Olivia," said Albertine.

"Well, of course at that time the town was named Gadsleyville," said Amanda, "but nearly the whole damned place was for sale, so Olivia saw the opportunity and she seized it. She began buying up bits and pieces of us, and pretty soon she petitioned the town council to have the name changed to Olivia, so there she was and here we are."

"Her destiny has been fulfilled," Albertine offered.

"I doubt that Babbington would go so far as to rename the town for me," I speculated, "although I wouldn't be surprised if the idea had its supporters—"

"I wouldn't say it's been fulfilled just yet," said Amanda. "The mansion is still under construction, and the museum is likely to be under construction forever. So it remains a work in progress."

She leaned toward us and lowered her voice.

"Confidentially, just between us, Olivia turned out to be a bit of an eccentric."

"No," said Albertine with convincing surprise.

"'Fraid so. She didn't tell anybody until she just about owned the whole town that what she wanted to do was not to establish the Museum of Olivia *in* the town of Olivia, but that she wanted to establish the town *as* the Museum of Olivia."

"People would have resisted that?" I asked.

"Wouldn't you?"

"I probably would," I said, "but I'm just wondering whether the people back in my home town—"

"So, anyway," said Amanda, "that's what she set about doing."

"Do you mean that she has been turning the entire town into a museum?" I asked.

"Sure do. I thought I was pretty plain on that point."

"You were, you were," I said. "I just wanted to be sure, because it raises an intriguing question about the future of my home town—"

"You don't say," Amanda said. "Is that going to be two day passes then?"

"It sounds fascinating, Al," I said. "What do you say?"

"I'm not sure that 'fascinating' is the first word that comes to mind," she said.

"Among the many exhibits that your pass will admit you to is the Gallery of Coins Found on the Sidewalk and Elsewhere," said Amanda. "You see, when Olivia was just a girl she found a nickel on the sidewalk. Kids are pretty good at that, finding coins on the sidewalk. Kids are little, so they're right down there, right close to the sidewalk, making it easier for them to find coins than it is for you and me. Not that I don't find my share."

"I've always had that knack," I said, "the knack for finding coins on the sidewalk. I'll often surprise Albertine by presenting her with a penny that I've spotted. I could probably have a Gallery of Coins—"

Amanda turned a pair of icy eyes on me and went right on. "Anyway," she said, "Olivia picked up that nickel, and that night she put the nickel under her pillow, and while she was lying there in bed fingering the nickel, she asked herself how many nickels she might find in her lifetime. She didn't put it quite that way, of course, because she was just a young girl, but that was the question that formed in her mind. By morning she had a plan: she would save all the coins she found in the street for the rest of her life. Formulating a lifelong plan like that demonstrated remarkable foresight for one so young. That's what it says in the brochure: 'remarkable foresight for one so young.' Will that be two day passes, then?"

"Sounds good to me," I said. "This is giving me some interesting ideas, and I'd—"

"What else have you got besides coins found on the sidewalk?" asked Albertine.

"Well, there is the Gallery of Discards. Before you dismiss that as trash, I want to emphasize that 'discards' covers a lot of territory. Most of us would think of trash when we hear the word 'discards,' and you will find trash in the Gallery of Discards, but you will find much more than that. See, Olivia, once she decided that someday there would be a Museum of Olivia, instead of throwing anything away, she threw it into the collection. It's all there, her personal mountain of discards, categorized, arranged, and displayed. As you might expect, this is the largest gallery in town. Preservation is a complex issue in a collection so large and diverse, and the conservators are breaking new ground in the area of long-term stabilization. That's what it says in the brochure, 'breaking new ground in the area of long-term stabilization.' I told you that the word 'discards' covers a lot of territory, and I wasn't kidding. You'll see for yourself. Let me just give you a for-instance: in the Gallery of Discards you will see wax effigies of all the boyfriends Olivia has dumped over the years. That's what it says in the brochure: 'dumped.' We take all the major credit cards. Is it going to be two day passes?"

"If only Proust had had the foresight to hang on to all of his discards," I said, bedazzled by the possibilities, "or to have wax effigies constructed—"

"I'm not sold yet," said Albertine. "What else have you got?"

"There's the Gallery of Bad Thoughts. What can I say? It's scary. That's what I'll say. You can try that one if you like. I've never made it past the first room. That was scary enough for me. I've heard tell that it gets a lot worse the farther in you go. You have to ask yourself how a woman like Olivia could come up with such nasty ideas. Like it or not, she was a child of the culture and she is a woman of the world. That's what the brochure says: 'a child of the culture and a woman of the world.' So she blames everybody else for her nasty ideas, that's the way I read it. That's what I hear her saying. Well, I never had any ideas like that. You wouldn't find a Gallery of Bad Thoughts in the Museum of Amanda. If there were a Museum of Amanda. Listen, I'm not supposed to do this, but since you're first-time visitors, I'll give you two-for-one. What do you say?"

"What a great deal!" I said. "I'd like to see how those thoughts are presented, wouldn't you, Al?"

"Well—"

"All right, look," said Amanda, "this is absolutely the last preview I'm going to give you. The Gallery of Broken Dreams. It is profoundly depressing. That's what the brochure says: 'profoundly depressing.' I'd have to agree with that. What it is, see, is a very, very realistic depiction of—what should I call it? I couldn't describe it for you. And even if I could, it wouldn't have the same effect on you. You have to see it. You have to experience it. I saw it once, and it was—let me tell you—profoundly depressing. An unforgettable experience. Many people return again and again. You want to take me up on the twofer offer?"

"Peter," said Albertine, "maybe we should just find someplace where we could get some lunch."

"Got an excellent restaurant right in town," said Amanda wearily. "Serves Olivia's favorite meals, including every meal that used to be a favorite but has fallen out of favor as well as the ones that are up-and-coming."

"Could we just go to the restaurant and not visit the museum?" Albertine asked.

"Technically speaking, no," said Amanda.

"The restaurant is part of the museum, Al," I said to Albertine.

"Oh, how silly of me not to realize that," said Al.

To Amanda, I said, "It could be called the Gallery of Favorite Meals, couldn't it, Amanda?"

"It is," she said.

"In my museum, if Babbington decides to establish one, we would have clam chowder—"

"Folks, I'm going to have to ask you to purchase passes or clear the entry portal," said Amanda. "Traffic's going to start backing up here."

I twisted around. I didn't see another car. "Nobody's coming," I said. "I'll make this short. Clam chowder would be particularly important in my museum because I've always thought of clam chowder as a metaphor for life—life in general and my life in particular—"

"There's a dust cloud on the horizon," said Amanda. "Might be a tour bus coming. Either you're going to have to buy a couple of passes and enter Olivia or you're going to have to turn this funny little vehicle of yours around and skedaddle. I can't have you blocking the entry."

"The kind of chowder I'm talking about," I said, "the kind that would be served in the Museum of Peter, is the kind made with tomatoes—"

I was thrown forward, against the restraint of my seat belt, by the sudden rearward motion of the Electro-Flyer. Albertine swung the car in a violent reverse U-turn and accelerated away from the admissions booth.

"Hey!" I protested.

"Don't even think about it," she said, still accelerating.

"What?" I asked.

"What you're thinking about."

"But—"

"Just file it away under Muddleheaded Dreams."

"But—"

"Unless you want to walk the rest of the way to Corosso."

"But—"

"And back."

So I filed the Museum of Peter there, among my other muddleheaded dreams, in that bulging folder.

ADVICE FROM AFAR

I ENTERED THE Land of Enchantment the next morning. *Spirit* and I crested a little hill, and we began accelerating as we headed downward. The rush of air beneath her wings gave us both a lift. Neither of us said anything, but both of us felt it. We were not quite touching the road. Downward we raced, faster and faster, growing lighter and less earthbound as we went. When we passed the sign that welcomed us to New Mexico we must have hit a bump. Something gave us a sudden upward leap, something more effective than wishful thinking. We were aloft. For a few thrilling feet,

we soared through the air. I was not accustomed to flying. *Spirit* handled differently in the air, and I didn't have a practiced hand at the controls.

"Don't overreact," she warned me.

"I know, I know," I said.

My hand trembled, and her wings waggled, but we kept our course. In a moment she touched the ground again, but she bounced, and we regained the air. We descended the slope in a series of graceful flutters, and when we had spent our momentum and were grounded again, we were very pleased with our flight, and very, very pleased with ourselves.

"Whew," I said in a long exhalation of the breath that I'd been holding.

"That was amazing," said *Spirit.*

I pulled slowly to the side of the road, and we sat there, idling, recovering from the thrill of it all. We had stopped beside a tent, and we were surrounded by rose petals.

"What's all this on the ground?" I asked *Spirit.*

"Rose petals," she said.

"I don't see any rosebushes."

"I think the petals have been strewn here to make a path. See the way they lead into the tent?"

"Yes," I said. "I see what you mean. I wonder if that's the sort of thing Matthew and the other students at the Summer Institute in Corosso are planning for our arrival. It would be—"

A man poked his head from the entrance to the tent. When he saw me, his eyes popped.

"My God," he said with a great gasp. "You've come."

"Um, yes," I said. "I've come from—"

"Don't tell me," he said. "Tell everyone inside. They've been waiting for you, waiting for a very long time, and they are going to be thrilled to hear what you have to say from your very own lips." He paused a moment and then said, more to himself than to me, "You actually do have lips. Interesting."

"People are waiting for me?" I said. "They knew that I was coming?"

"They hoped that you were coming," he said. "Wait here. That is, wait here, if you don't mind waiting here. I don't mean to—I don't presume to—to give you orders."

"I don't mind," I said. "I'll wait."

"It's just that I want to prepare people for—your appearance. You see, we had no idea what you would look like, and I think that many people have pictured you as—well—different."

"Maybe if you have a place where I can wash up, comb my hair—"

"No, no, that's all right. Just give me a couple of minutes and—say— do you think you could come flying in on your—ah—conveyance?"

"Sure I could—" I said at once, but I heard an uncertainty in *Spirit*'s idle. Was she worried about embarrassing herself, not being able to get off the ground? "Maybe—maybe it would be dangerous—for the people inside," I said, "if I flew in."

"Oh."

"I could taxi in," I offered. "You know, staying on the ground, slow and steady. That would be safe."

"Fine. Fine. That would be fine. When you hear me say, 'The visitor from afar that we have so long awaited has finally arrived,' you come rolling in, down the aisle strewn with rose petals."

"Visitor from afar?"

He knit his brows and frowned. "You are a visitor from afar, aren't you?" he asked in an urgent whisper.

"I—um—yes—of course," I said.

"Good," he said. "Don't miss your cue."

He disappeared through the flaps. I maneuvered *Spirit* so that she and I would be ready to follow him when we heard our cue. I strained to hear what he was saying to the people inside the tent, but I couldn't hear him well over *Spirit*'s idling engine. I didn't want to shut her down, because I wanted her to be ready to make her entrance. I hoped that I would catch the words *visitor from afar* when he said them. When they came, they weren't quite what he had told me they would be, but the cue was impossible to mistake.

"I told you!" he suddenly screamed. "I told you that a visitor would come from afar—and here he is!"

I overreacted. In my eagerness to come through the tent flaps on cue, I gunned *Spirit*'s throttle, and she leapt forward, scattering rose petals and sending us hurtling down an aisle that led to a raised platform at the far end of the tent. Struggling to control her, I remembered not to compound one overreaction with another and applied her brakes gently. This taught me that underreacting can be as great a fault as overreacting. We were still traveling fast enough for me to call our forward progress hurtling.

To my surprise, eager hands reached out to me from either side, as the people in the crowd rushed to the aisle to get closer to *Spirit* and me and, if possible, to touch us. All those groping, grasping hands on *Spirit*'s wings, and a little more forceful application of her brakes, brought us smoothly to a stop in front of the platform, as if I had planned it that way all along.

"Let's give him the welcome we've waited so long to give!"

The audience rose and began to applaud. The man on the dais began beckoning to me, almost frantically, as if we were running out of time.

"Come on up here and tell us what we want to hear!" he cried.

Willing hands steadied *Spirit*. I mounted the few broad steps that brought me to the same level as the man. He spun me around to face the crowd and screamed at them again. "I told you! I told you that a visitor would come from afar!"

He turned to me, and he began to talk to me as if he were confiding in me, though he spoke in a voice that would easily reach the farthest corner of the tent.

"Years ago," he said, "people began reporting sightings of odd phenomena in the sky, sightings of unidentified flying objects that became known either by their initials, as UFOs, or by their most common shape, as 'flying saucers.'"

This was something I knew something about.

"That's right!" I said, adopting the same technique of speaking to him and to the crowd at the same time.

A sudden wave of nostalgia struck me, and I had to swallow hard and blink a few times to hide its symptoms.

"Are you all right?"

"Yes," I said hoarsely. "It's just that—when you mentioned unidentified flying objects—it reminded me of home."

A sympathetic "Ohhhh" arose from the crowd.

The man gripped my arm and said, "Of course. You're a long way from home. You must miss home and all the people—or—all the comforts of home. We understand."

He was right. I was a long way from home, and I did miss its comforts. The mention of UFOs had sent my thoughts back there because back at home, so many miles behind me, in the bookcase in my attic bedroom, I had a small collection of books and magazines devoted to sightings of flying saucers and to speculation about their origins, their crews, and their methods of propulsion. I had built several models of flying saucers from balsa wood and tissue paper, and I had made detectors that were supposed to signal me when a saucer was in the vicinity. I had seen, or thought I had seen, five flying saucers above my neighborhood in Babbington Heights one summer night, the same summer night when I had also seen, or thought I had seen, a naked woman standing in her bedroom window in a house diagonally across the street.

With a bittersweet smile, I remembered the first model I had built. Some of the photographs of unidentified flying objects showed ships that looked like two saucers, the bottom one in the usual orientation when under a coffee cup, the top one inverted and placed so that the rims matched. A young literalist, I tried to make a model of a flying saucer in just that way. It got me into trouble.

"Among the general population," the man continued, "there was widespread curiosity about the sightings. Many people became anxious about these mysterious UFOs; they wondered about the intentions of their makers and feared that they meant us harm."

He paused and looked at me significantly. He seemed to want my reaction. I shrugged and said, "I don't know why." I meant it. I hadn't thought that the creatures aboard the UFOs meant us any harm, but then at the time I had belonged to the segment of the general population that consisted of kids who hoped they would get to ride shotgun in a flying saucer.

I was applauded heartily. I waved to the crowd.

"Another portion of the population was thrilled by UFOs," he said, "because those people wanted flying objects to be ships from another world, piloted by beings superior to us and concerned for our well-being, itinerant intergalactic mentors who would show us a better way."

He paused in that significant way again. I extended my hand, greeting him as one member of the segment of the population that wanted the beings to show us a better way to another, and he shook it.

Thunderous applause.

"Another segment of the population thought it was all a lot of hooey," he said in an exaggerated manner that made it clear that he thought that thinking it was all a lot of hooey was a lot of hooey. "As far as they were concerned, the ones who feared invasion were letting anxiety run away with them, and the ones who were looking forward to benevolent intervention wanted it badly enough to let imagination run away with *them*. As far as those skeptics were concerned, both groups were hallucinating!"

His audience loved that. They laughed, and I laughed with them.

"Then," he said, turning solemn, "something happened near here. Exactly what happened, we cannot say. Some people who were there, and some people who claim that they were there, say that a UFO crashed during a thunderstorm. Some people in the skeptical segment of the population immediately began howling that it couldn't possibly be true. 'Why,' they wondered aloud to anyone who would listen, 'would the conveyance of intergalactic voyagers be brought down by earthly weather?'"

He paused. It was another of those pauses that requested a response from me. I reached back, mentally, to the stack of books and magazines on the shelves in my room at home, leafed through their pages, and said, nodding, knitting my brows in thoughtful consideration of the likelihood that what I was saying might be correct, "It could have been the effect of sunspots on the magnetomic drive."

They hummed. They nodded their heads.

Gently, as if what he had to ask me next would cause me some pain, he said, "Would you rather we talked about something else?"

I would. I had been interested in flying saucers, and I still enjoyed speculating about their origins and the motives of their makers, but just then I was more interested in myself, and I would have preferred to talk about my travels. "Yes," I said, "I would. I'd like to tell you—"

"That's just what we hoped!" he said. "We hoped that when you came you would tell us what we need to hear, that you would offer us enlightenment and guidance."

"Enlightenment and guidance?"

"Pearls of wisdom, perhaps?"

"Oh, pearls of wisdom. Sure. I can do that. One that I remember from the fourth grade is, 'A journey of a thousand miles begins with a single step.'"

A collective gasp arose from the audience.

"Did I get that wrong?" I asked.

"No," said the leader, "not at all. I think we are all just surprised to find that it has traveled so far, that it is truly a universal piece of wisdom."

"A pearl," I said.

"Have you any others? Please, we are here because we want to hear what you have to tell us. Teach us how to live. Give us some advice."

"What kind of advice?"

"I am sure that any kind of advice you care to give us would be received with tremendous gratitude by everyone here assembled."

"Okay. Let's see. I have some advice about traveling."

"Please," he said, with a gesture that invited me to stand at the microphone and say whatever I wished to say.

"If you're going to make a journey," I said into the microphone, "and I'm speaking now as someone who knows what he's talking about, since I've just completed a long journey, or almost completed a long journey, you have to ask yourself whether you're going to travel with or without a map. If you travel with a map, you know where you're going, and you know where you are, and you know where you've been. If you travel without a map, you get lost a lot."

"I take it you are speaking of life's journey," he said, stepping up beside me and reclaiming a bit of the microphone, "and not merely of a journey in the literal sense, from one place to another."

"I—well—both."

"I see."

"Life's journey is a journey from one place to another."

"Oh?"

"Yeah. You know those trails of slime that slugs leave behind them?"

"I'm afraid I—"

"In the morning, you see them on sidewalks sometimes, and from the trail of slime you can see the wandering path that the slug has followed in the night."

"Very interesting. You have slugs—where you come from?"

"Oh, sure. We have slugs, snails, worms, probably everything you have here—but my point is that if we left trails of slime as we go through life, you would see a long thread of slime that stretches through space and time from birth, at a certain place and a certain time, to death, at another place and another time. It would be your slime time line, if you were a creature that left a trail of slime."

"Turning from slime, if we could, please go on and give us another bit of advice."

"Okay. Well—um—hmm—if you do get lost, don't try to retrace your steps. It's a waste of time. You can't change the past, so don't bother trying to go back there. Don't try to follow your slime time line—"

"Please. No slime. It's making some of the ladies queasy."

"Go forward," I said. "Go from where you are to somewhere else, somewhere you have never been. Go in any direction but backward."

"Aren't you likely to become even more lost?"

"If you're where you want to be, you're not lost," I said, "and if you want to be where you are, you're not lost. So you've got two choices: you can stay put and learn to want to be where you are, or you can move on until you come to the place where you want to be."

"Deep, very deep. Please go on."

"Lots of times, while you're on a journey, you think that where you're going is where you're going to want to be, and that where you are is just a place that's in your way and not the place where you want to be, but that's not always true. For instance, on my journey, I didn't stop in New York, because I thought that I wanted to be someplace west of New York, but now I think I should have stopped in New York, because I might have wanted to be there for a while."

"They say it's a great place to visit," he said, nudging himself over and reclaiming a bit more of the microphone.

"Yeah," I said. I was beginning to warm to my role as dispenser of advice, and as I warmed to it I began to discover that I had many more pieces of advice that I wanted to dispense. I was also beginning to resent the interruptions of the leader. "Another thing to keep in mind on a journey is this: don't try any funny business. If you do, people will ask you if you're trying to be funny. There is no good answer to that question. If you say that you were trying to be funny, they tell you that what you were doing or saying was not funny, and you wind up feeling like— well—like a jerk. On the other hand, if you say that you were not trying to be funny, you will see a certain look come into their eyes, as if they suspect that you might be wearing a mask and they're trying to see through it, and from then on they will treat you as if you were trying to be funny by making fun of them, and they'll hate you for it. So, don't try to be funny. You just can't win."

"Are you trying to be funny?" he asked. It was a pathetic bid for a laugh. He didn't get it.

"Are you?" I asked. I got the laugh. I was beginning to feel very good.

"Be yourself," I said to the crowd. "Be who you are. You may be a muddleheaded dreamer. People may laugh at you for being a muddleheaded dreamer. Stare them down. Stand tall. Start a club of muddleheaded dreamers. The world owes a lot to muddleheaded dreamers."

A sudden burst of applause came from a small segment of the audience. The few who had applauded quickly caught themselves. I saw a couple of them glance quickly from side to side to see if their neighbors had noticed that they had applauded.

I applauded those who had applauded and said, "Welcome to the club."

People laughed. Mostly, the people who laughed were people who had not applauded. I think they thought that I was just trying to be funny.

"Don't try to talk to people about the place where you're from," I said. "Nobody wants to hear about it. I don't know why. Maybe it sounds too strange to them. It's not what they're used to. It's not like the place where they're living or where they came from. To them, the place you come from seems—I don't know—"

"Alien?" he offered.

"That's it: alien. They act as if you came from outer space."

This brought me a warm, satisfying laugh, doubly satisfying because I had been following my own advice and not trying to be funny.

"When you're talking to people, try to stop yourself before you say something that makes you wish you had put your foot in your mouth. There are many things that you would like to say that would, if you said them, make you find out that they were things that the people you're talking to did not want to hear. Don't say those things. At least, don't say them to the people who wouldn't want to hear them. Watch their eyes. You can tell when you're getting close to the point when you ought to put your foot in your mouth if they get that look that I mentioned before. In general, when you see that look, shut up."

He leaned toward the microphone to make a comment. I gave him that look. The crowd roared. He didn't speak.

"When I was little," I said, "I tried to make a model of a flying saucer by gluing two saucers together—regular saucers, the kind that go underneath cups. If you think you might want to try it, let me give you a warning: holding two saucers in that way is pretty tricky. They can slip from your hands easily and break, and if they do your mother isn't going to like it. If you manage to get the rims glued together you will have a more stable construction, but—take it from me—your mother isn't going to like that, either."

They gave me more laughter, fueling my fire.

"Recognize your failings. I'm not saying that you have to point them out to other people. I'm not even saying that you have to eliminate them. They may not even be failings, if you could get an objective opinion about them. I mean, one person's failings are another's strengths, depending on who's looking at them. But our tendency is to recognize our strengths and overlook our failings. I'm telling you that because I recognize the tendency in myself. In my case, my biggest failing is—well—I know what it is, but I guess I'm not going to tell you what it is. Let's just say that it's something that goes to show that, like everyone else, I'm 'only human.'"

That was received with a warmth that I find hard to describe. I could see that they found it funny, but there was more than that in their reaction, and I thought that perhaps they were, individually, reflecting on their failings, and concluding that, yes, they were, like me, only human.

"Another thing: you may know something that nobody else knows. You may have knowledge that other people do not have. You may have information that is known to no one else, or only to a small group of people who for one reason or another have come to know these things that other people do not know. You know what I mean, don't you? I'm talking about secrets. That is, I'm talking about things that ought to be secrets. Maybe you have traveled through the Land of Lace. Maybe you know what goes on in the Forest of Love. Maybe you are familiar with the secret rituals of the Great Church of Snoutfigs. Maybe you own a book or two that shouldn't fall into the wrong hands. If you have secrets, if you know secrets, keep them to yourself. Don't give them away. Don't sell them. Don't even betray them by allowing yourself to smile that superior little smile that says, 'I know something you don't know.' If people know, or even suspect, that you know something that they don't, they will hate you for it. They will. I know. I'm not going to tell you how I know, but I know."

He leaned into the microphone again. I nudged him aside.

"Here's a piece of advice I got from someone I didn't like. I guess that shows that you can sometimes get good advice almost anywhere if you keep your ears open. And I guess that means that you should keep your ears open. The advice that this person gave me was to be aware that gravy can hide a multitude of sins. Be wary of what the gravy might be hiding. I think I will probably always be wary of any cut of meat that's hiding under gravy. As I went on traveling, though, I got a taste of some other kinds of gravy: a certain kind of smile, a certain kind of promise, even a certain kind of goodness. Beware of any kind of gravy. It can hide a multitude of sins."

The leader coughed. He seemed about to make a lunge for the microphone. I grabbed it the way singers do, with both hands, swung it toward me as if I were dancing with it, and said, "Here's one for those of you who are waiting for 'someday,' for that day when life is finally going to bring you what you've been waiting for, that wonderful day when your dreams are going to come true, all of them. My advice? Take what life offers you and move on. If you're offered a sandwich, take it and make a graceful exit. Chances are good that you won't be offered anything else."

"I'm sure you must be tired," he tried. "You've had a long journey, and—"

"I have had a long journey," I said, "a very long journey—"

His eyes brightened.

"—and I'd like to give you a piece of advice that my—ah—that I gave myself—while I was on my journey. Don't be too quick to decide that you've made a wrong turn. It's not really a wrong turn unless it takes you away from what you're after. Most of us are after many things, so there are many, many paths that we can take to what we want. None of them could accurately be called a wrong turn. And here's a little secret: if you're not trying to get anywhere, then there are hardly any wrong turns at all."

"You've certainly given us a lot to think about—"

"In the evening, the light can play tricks with your eyes," I said, taking a couple of steps to one side, away from him, as he advanced. "If there is mist, the tricks can be even trickier. Somehow, the light and the mist form a kind of screen onto which your mind projects the images that it manufactures when it is engaged in wishful thinking. You may seem to see a castle on a mountain peak where there is nothing but a water tower. Don't bother climbing the mountain unless it's the water tower that you're after."

"We'll be sure to remember that," he said. He had gone into a crouch. I was sure that he meant to make a spring for the microphone.

"Be alert to the many meanings of the words 'ha-ha,'" I said, circling, forcing him to turn his back on the audience in order to keep his eye on me. "In themselves, those words have no real meaning at all. What they mean depends entirely on the motives of the speaker. Their meaning is beyond your control. Do not try to give them meaning. Do not impose a meaning on them. Look for the meaning that they have been given; respond to that, and only to that."

"Rrrr," he said, baring his teeth.

"If you're looking for a way to decide whether you can trust someone or not, check his pockets for wads of cash. If you find wads of cash, don't trust him."

He sprang. I leapt aside. He missed.

"I'm out of advice," I said. I looked at the leader. I smiled. He straightened up and started toward the microphone. Into it I said, "I'd like to end with a request, if I may." What could he do? He stopped and nodded. I turned to the crowd.

"If strangers should come into your midst," I said, letting my eyes roam the crowd, "strangers passing through, visitors from afar, take them in. Try to feel their loneliness, the terrible isolation of outsiders in an alien culture, and if they seem odd to you, if the things they say and do seem disturbingly different from the things that you and your neighbors say and do, please realize that in their loneliness those strangers may be clinging for consolation to familiar customs and trying desperately, awkwardly, ineptly to ingratiate themselves with you by trying to show that they have something in common with you. Don't reject them. Welcome them. The foods they eat, the ideas they hold, the emotions they feel, and everything they hold dear may seem weird or worthless to you, but they are neither weird nor worthless to them. Open your hearts. Open your homes. Let the strangers in." I paused. In the hush, I could hear sniffles. Then I asked, "Would anyone out there be willing to put me up for the night?"

ON THE STREET OF DREAMS

....

I **WOULDN'T HAVE** recognized the place. The little college that had hosted the Summer Institute so many years before had grown into a university. I couldn't get my bearings, couldn't match the map of memory to the new data, the terrain of the facts.

"I'll park somewhere, and we'll walk around the campus," suggested Albertine. "You'll start seeing landmarks that you remember."

She parked, and we began walking aimlessly, just to see what might spark a memory.

After a couple of minutes of that, Albertine said, "Instead of wandering aimlessly, why don't we see if we can get a map or take a tour?"

I approached a man who seemed to have a professorial air about him.

"Excuse me," I said. "I wonder if it would be possible to take a tour of the campus. You see, I was a student here for one memorable summer when the institution was known as the New Mexico Institute of Mining, Technology, and Pharmacy. It was quite an experience for me. I flew here from Babbington, New York, on an aerocycle that I had built—"

"Admissions Department," he said abruptly.

"I'm not applying for admission; I just wanted to—"

"Take a tour."

"Right."

"Admissions Department."

"I seem to be missing something."

"The tours leave from the Admissions Department."

"Ah! Of course. I should have understood what you meant. The heat must be getting to me. It's—"

"It's a dry heat. Never bothers anybody."

"I guess it's just me. Where is the—"

"Admissions Department."

"Right."

"Down here, turn left, turn right."

"Thanks."

We began walking in the direction that he had indicated.

"Did anyone offer you a place to stay after you had given them all that advice?" asked Albertine.

"They were scrambling over one another to get at me," I said.

We turned left.

"Was there a dark-haired girl?"

"Ahh, yes," I said, teasing her with an exaggerated display of pleasurable recollection. "There was."

We turned right.

"Did you get lucky?"

"I—"

On the wall of a building, directly ahead of us, was a large, colorful poster, announcing the 21st Annual "Land of Enchantment Fly-In." I read it in a glance. It promised fun for the whole family. It promised kit-built, home-built, and experimental airplanes. It made the event sound like great fun, not only for the whole family, but for Albertine and me, the perfect ending to our journey. I was just about to point it out to her when I saw that it promised something else. It promised a thrilling competition among "those daring superheroes of the air, our nation's top-ranked flying EMTs."

"Well?" she asked.

"I—" I snapped my head around, looking for something to distract her from the poster. "Were we supposed to go left and then right or right and then left?"

"Straight, then left, then right. Aren't you going to tell me what went on between you and the dark-haired girl?"

I took her arm and tried to turn her away from the poster, but she resisted, and in an eager, gleeful voice that made me think that all was lost, she cried, "Oh, Birdboy, look."

"Al," I said, "I thought something like this might happen. It's been on my mind ever since we left New York. I—"

She put her hand under my chin and raised my head. "Look!" she insisted. "If I hadn't seen it with my own eyes," she said, "I would never have believed it."

Part Three

··

FLYING HOME

Thus the fam'd hero, perfected in wiles,

With fair similitude of truth beguiles

The queen's attentive ear . . .

—HOMER, *The Odyssey*
(translated by Alexander Pope)

TO CLAYTON!

....

The great Theatre of Oklahoma calls you! . . . But hurry, so that you get
in before midnight! . . . Up, and to Clayton!
—Franz Kafka, *Amerika* (translated by Willa and Edwin Muir)

ON OUR FIRST morning in Corosso, I woke early, as I usually do.
Albertine was still asleep. I went to the motel's coffee shop to
give my sleepy self a dose of caffeine and plan our day. Since we intended to stay in the area for several days, I wanted to devote the first
of them to a broad survey, a casual reminiscent ramble during which I
would point out to Albertine the sites of some of my most memorable
adventures during that extraordinary summer. Then, over the next few
days, I wanted to spend more time at each of the sites, and make some
excursions beyond the campus, setting out to duplicate some of the excursions I had made so many years earlier. I had many in mind, including Santa Fe, Alamogordo, White Sands, Truth or Consequences, and
Ciudad Juárez. I also wanted to see something new: the Very Large Array, which had been constructed decades after my earlier visit. I was eager. I felt lighthearted and rejuvenated.

While I was sitting there, thinking and planning, and enjoying the
pleasant anticipation of wandering through Corosso, its environs, and
my memories, a small man entered the room carrying a stepstool, an
armload of posters, and a large roll of tape. He set the stepstool down
in front of the wall directly across the room from me, stepped onto it,
placed a poster on the wall, held it there with one hand, assessed its
placement and alignment, shifted it this way and that a bit, and then
attempted to tear a length of tape from the roll with his teeth. After
some effort, he succeeded in that attempt. He was now a small man on
a stepstool holding a poster against a wall with one hand, a roll of tape
in the other, and a length of tape in his teeth. He turned, scanning the
room for a potential assistant, discovered me, beseeched me with his
eyes, and said, "Khuh gih mih uh hahn?"

"Say," I said with the alacrity of a guy who's just had three mugs of
coffee, "I bet you could use a hand with that!"

"Azth uhd ahy zthed."

"Sorry, man," I said. "I can't understand you. You've got a big piece of tape in your mouth."

"Fuhgihn cuhmeedeeihn."

"Why don't I hold the poster for you?" I suggested brightly. "Then you can do the taping."

I extended a hand to hold the poster in place, and as I did so I found myself staring at an announcement of the thing I feared most: a Convocation of Flying Emergency Medical Technicians, those swaggering heartbreakers.

I found myself staring at an announcement of the thing I feared most...

I couldn't let Albertine see this. She might want to attend the EMT competition. She might hope to see "her" flyguys there, the ones who had flirted with her, charmed her, enchanted her, while she was in the hospital back in New York. I might lose her to them. That's what might happen. I might lose her. How could I possibly compete with the skill, the daring, the swagger, and the snappy outfits of the flying EMTs?

"You can let go now," said a voice. I spun my head in its direction. The man with the tape and the bundle of posters was standing in the doorway, snickering at me. "Unless you want to stand there like that just for the fun of it." He turned and walked away, shaking his head.

I let go of the poster and, despite myself, stood there for an instant checking to see that it didn't fall to the floor. Then I dashed to the open door, swung into the hallway, and ran to the front desk.

I wanted to get out of town, but I needed a reason for going; that is, I wanted to get Albertine out of town, and I needed a reason for going; by that I mean that I needed a reason that I could give to Al, some reason other than the truth, which I didn't think would get her out of town.

The desk clerk was a bored kid. He looked like the kind of bored kid who often daydreamed about getting out of town. He might have an idea.

"If you could just get into a car right now and go, *just go,* where would you be by this time tomorrow?" I asked him.

"Clayton, Oklahoma," he said, stretching and yawning.

"Clayton, Oklahoma?" I said.

"That's right."

"Why?"

"'Cause I always wanted to perform at the Nature Theatre of Oklahoma, and that's in Clayton. I think I could really be somebody if—"

"I need a map," I said.

"Gift shop's over there," he yawned, making an effort to point a lanky finger in the right direction.

The maps were in a rack at the back of the narrow shop. I pulled one out and opened it, looking for Clayton, Oklahoma. To my delight, I found that it was in the pan part of the state, not the handle, so that by the time we arrived there we would have put a chunk of Texas between us and the flyguys.

I had just begun to think about how I would introduce to Albertine the idea of setting out for Clayton immediately when I heard her voice.

She was at the front desk, choosing postcards from a revolving rack. I rushed to her side. There was a chance that I might be able to keep her from ever seeing the poster, from ever seeing the flyguys.

"We ought to be on our way," I said.

"On our way?"

"Yeah. It's getting late, and I'd like to be there by dinner time."

"There? Where?"

"Clayton," I said. I threw some bills at the clerk, who had perked up when he heard me say the name, and I began tugging Al away from the counter.

"Is it near here?" asked Albertine.

"It's east of here—a bit—in Oklahoma."

"Oklahoma? But we've come all this way. Don't you want to look around?"

"I've seen enough."

"Don't you want to find out how they came to name that street for you?"

"Well—I—"

"Of course you do."

"Oh—not really. In fact, I think I'd rather not know any more about Leroy Place. If I started asking questions about it, I think I know what would happen. It would turn on me. It would become a disappointment. It might even become one of the great disappointments of my life. I would inquire, full of hope, and I would find out that they hadn't named it for me at all. They probably named it for some rich alumnus who made his fortune in industrial waste."

"But what about seeing the Very Large Array? You've wanted to see it for years."

"Yeah, but, you know, I've probably ruined the experience by anticipating it. I wouldn't be surprised to find that I've set myself up for a disappointment of Proustian proportions. It's probably not even all that large—"

"Oh, Peter."

"What I would really like to see is Clayton, Oklahoma."

"Why on earth do you want to see Clayton, Oklahoma?

"I—well—the truth is—I was—ah—inspired by the desk clerk."

"Inspired by the desk clerk?" She glanced back at him. He had let his head fall on his arms and seemed to be sleeping.

"Yeah. We had quite a chat. He was telling me that he always wanted to—ah—see a performance at the Nature Theatre of Oklahoma. He made it sound really—ah—compelling."

"The Nature Theatre of Oklahoma," she said, slowly, apparently trying to decide whether she had ever heard of such an institution.

"And that's in Clayton," I said, in the clipped manner of one who is absolutely certain that he has made the best decision that anyone could make in the present circumstances. "I've been checking a map in the gift shop, and I think that if we start out now—given the way you drive—we can probably make it by six."

"That's nine hours of driving."

"But it's easy driving. We just head north on Route 25 to Route 40, take that due east for—oh—about—six hundred something miles—"

"Six hundred something miles?"

"Give or take. Distance means nothing out here."

"Maybe their maps are smaller."

"Ha-ha," I said.

She looked at me, saw in my eyes how much I really wanted to get back on the road, maybe even saw how much I wanted to get out of town, and with great good spirit she said, "Let's go! To Clayton!"

Albertine did all the driving, but I did my part: to beguile the miles and the driver, I read aloud the story of my arrival in Corosso forty-seven years earlier.

THE AVIATOR APHORIZES

∙∙

The day was fresh, with a lively spring wind full of dust.
—Edith Wharton, *The Age of Innocence*

THE GOING WAS rough. *Spirit* and I were fighting a headwind heavy with heat and thick with dust. I'd wrapped a neckerchief around my face to keep the dust out of my mouth and nose, and my goggles protected my eyes, but dust clogged the neckerchief and coated the goggles in minutes, and I had to stop to clean them again and again. Despite the wind and the dust, we struggled onward toward the campus of the New Mexico Institute of Mining, Technology, and Pharmacy. We were determined. We were dauntless.

"You may be determined and dauntless," said *Spirit* in a voice hoarse with dust, "but I'd like to stop and wait for this to blow over. I don't think it's good for me. I'm not designed to operate in dust storms."

"How do you know that?"

"I don't know how I know that; I just know that I know it. How does any of us know anything? It's a mystery. Especially the question of how we know the things that we know about ourselves. What is it that makes us aware of ourselves as selves, aware of our nature, or of our design? Is it simply that we reach a certain critical level in the accretion and interconnection of neurons—"

"You have no neurons."

"Technically, you're correct, but I'm using yours. You are lending yours to me, so I am able to achieve a certain elementary level of self-awareness."

"If you're using my neurons, how is it that you're able to talk about things that I have never talked about or even thought about, as far as I know?"

"Like what?"

"Like self-awareness, for one thing."

"You have thought about it, but you needed me to—kaff—kuff—koff—kack—"

Her engine sputtered into silence, and we slowed to a stop.

"*Spirit?*"

Nothing.

I stood, and then I came down on the starter pedal. Her engine turned but didn't start. I tried again. Nothing. Again. Nothing.

"*Spirit?*" I asked, "are you okay?"

She said nothing.

"You're not malingering, are you?"

Still nothing. I stood beside her, wondering what to do. Her silence made me begin to feel afraid for her. My palms began to sweat. I looked at them, and at that instant I understood something that had puzzled me for years. "This is what people mean when they talk about clammy fear," I said to *Spirit*. "I used to think it had something to do with clamdiggers—their fear of a watery grave, or lightning, or being bitten by a clam—something like that. What a childish notion! It doesn't have anything to do with clamdiggers. It's about sweaty palms!"

Her silence rebuked me.

"Sorry," I said. "I got a little—well—off the track—but I'll get you some help. Don't worry."

I put my left hand on her left handle grip and my right hand on her saddle and began pushing her.

"You'll be okay," I said. "You'll see."

Pushing *Spirit* the rest of the way to Corosso took some time. The dust storm was relentless. I struggled through it all the way to the campus, but then, when we were there at last—when we had accomplished what we had set out to do, had arrived at our destination, come to the end of our journey—the wind simply stopped. The dust settled from the air as if it had exhausted itself by flying about in such a hullabaloo, and the campus stood revealed beneath the afternoon sun, blazing hot and bright in a cloudless sky. Everything around us was sere and severe, but the clarity after dusty confusion felt like a sign, a bright beginning.

I parked *Spirit* in a spot that I took to be the center of the campus, a quadrangle formed by four large and impressive buildings, and I set off to find Matthew. After a few minutes of looking, I developed the unsettling impression that the campus was deserted. Its buildings seemed empty. No one was walking along its pathways. I would have expected to see some students huddled in the thin shade of the trees, but there were none.

I felt disappointed. No, that's not right. I was more than disappointed: I was angry. Damn it, where was my big reception? I recalled fondly the handsome reception that my friend Raskol and I had received when we completed our riverine journey to the source of the Bolotomy, back home in Babbington, when I was just a boy. Why shouldn't I expect in Corosso a reception much greater than that one, since I was making a much longer journey?

Because I didn't know then and don't know now, I can't say exactly what reception I expected, but I expected something. I had called Matthew when I was still two days away from Corosso. Two days should have been enough time for him to organize something. It should have been enough time to rally the other Summer Institute students and make a banner, for example. Not that I expected a banner exactly, but if Matthew and his collaborators were going to make a banner, they should have had enough time. Two days might not have been enough time to book a mariachi band, but it certainly was enough time to gather a little welcoming committee, some friendly students, maybe a couple of distinguished members of the faculty, write a speech of welcome, even compose a little song. I had expected something, and I began to understand that I was getting nothing. I was covered in dust, and I was angry.

Why, I asked myself, had I ever allowed myself to expect a welcome? Almost at once, I realized that if *Spirit* had been with me, my agent of self-awareness, she would have told me why.

"You expected a welcome," she would have said, "because you anticipated a welcome, and that was because you hoped for a welcome. I am afraid, Peter, that because you are a person who hopes for things, you will often be disappointed, and because you allow your hopes to flower into expectation, you will often be annoyed when life gives you less than you think you have a right to expect."

She would have been right. I had allowed myself to succumb to expectation. During the time that I had spent on the road, en route to NMIMTaP, I had allowed myself to hope that I might receive a warm reception when I arrived. That bit of self-indulgent hope was not a bad thing; it had helped to keep me going when the going was rough. However, hope took root, sprouted, and grew into anticipation. Still, that was not a bad thing, either. Anticipation can keep a guy going over dark and lonely roads. Ah, but the weed kept growing, and anticipation blossomed into expectation. That was a bad thing. Like hope and anticipation, the expectation of a warm reception had helped to keep me going, even through that headwind full of dust, but it also began to make me think that the reception had better be pretty damned spectacular if the organizers expected me to be grateful for it. Let me tell you, although I suspect that you already know it, that if hope is thwarted, the one who nursed the hope is disappointed. Disappointment isn't pleasant, but most of us can shrug off life's disappointments. However, if one *expects* something and one's expectations are not met, one is annoyed, resentful, or, if one has been pushing an aerocycle through a dust storm, pretty goddamned fucking pissed off.

"You're right," I would have said to her. "I see now that hope is the seed of resentment."

As I walked and thought and aphorized, I came to a modest building that could have been a tool shed. On its door was a gleaming brass sign, handsomely engraved. It read FAUSTROLL INSTITUTE.

Eagerly, I conjured and planted another dangerous little seed of hope.

THE FAUSTROLL INSTITUTE

When looked at closely enough, every galaxy is peculiar. Appreciation of these peculiarities is important in order to build a realistic picture of what galaxies are really like.

—Halton Arp, *Atlas of Peculiar Galaxies*

I OPENED THE door of the shed and found a small group of students inside, five boys and three girls. One of the boys was Matthew.

"Welcome to the Faustroll Institute," they said in unison. "It's great to have you here."

"It's great to be here," I said. I meant it, and I let myself show that I meant it. I was, as my grandmother would have said, grinning from ear to ear.

412   ·   PETER LEROY

"We've been expecting you," said one of the girls, a squat, stocky, solid girl dressed in a cotton shirt and shorts of the olive drab color that the army used for uniforms and equipment in those days. "In fact, you have been on our minds for some time."

"I have?"

"Don't let it go to your head," she said, "but you have been our inspiration in absentia."

"Tank's right," said Matthew. "You inspired us to create a smaller, more exclusive group within SIMPaW—which is, as you know, the Summer Institute in Mathematics, Physics, and Weaponry."

"That's not quite accurate, Rocky," said another of the girls. This one was as cute as a button.

I glanced at Matthew, raising an eyebrow to ask, "Did she call you 'Rocky'?" Matthew reddened and grinned.

The cute girl continued, gently correcting Matthew: "We had already begun to come together as a subset of SIMPaW before we even knew that Peter would be arriving to attend the Faustroll Institute, which, of course, did not exist at that time."

"I'm going to have to correct you there, Button," said another of the boys. "I've been thinking about this, and I've come to the conclusion that the existence of the Faustroll Institute predated our occupying this shack, my making the handsome brass sign for the door, and even our appropriating the name Faustroll Institute for our peculiar group."

"How so, Eugene?" asked another of the girls, a tall slender one.

"Well, Slim," said Eugene, "as I see it, the Faustroll Institute became a portable institution with a single member as soon as Peter received his fraudulent acceptance notice back in distant Babbington, and since that time the entire institution has been on its way here, winging its way here, traveling as a sort of invisible envelope, enclosing its original member."

"Yes! Yes!" said another of the boys, a short, wiry one, snapping his fingers as he spoke. "It's not that he has arrived at the Faustroll Institute; he has brought the Faustroll Institute to us. That's it. That's the way it is. Yes."

"My point exactly, Dean," said Eugene.

"We're getting ahead of ourselves," said the stocky girl.

"You're right, Tank," said a boy with a serious manner and skin the color of coffee the way my mother liked it, with a tablespoonful of sweetened condensed milk to "take the bitterness off."

"Why don't you give Peter the history of our side of the Faustroll Institute, Nick?" suggested another of the boys, one with a worldly air and manners.

"Gladly, Count," said Nick. Did I hear a slightly sour note in the response? Or am I adding that note now? To me, Nick said, "Within the first few days after our arrival in Corosso, the eight of us became a group within the larger group. It was a mysterious occurrence; that is, it seemed quite mysterious at the time; however, like most mysteries it had a rational explanation. Here it is: we eight were pushed together by the force of difference. Circumstances forced us to feel our peculiarity even in this peculiar company that is SIMPaW. Each of us felt the force of difference pushing us apart from the rest of the simps."

"Simps is what we call ourselves," Rocky explained. "That is, it's what all of us who are students in SIMPaW call ourselves."

Nick cleared his throat.

"Sorry," said Rocky.

"Don't give it a thought," said Nick.

"If I could just say something—" said Button.

"Of course," said Nick with a sweeping gesture of endorsement.

"All of us in this group of eight recognized ourselves as simps," she said, "that is, as inhabitants of a peculiar galaxy of American high school students within the universe of American high school students, but each of us also considered herself—"

Nick cleared his throat again.

"—or himself—a simp among simps, standing a bit apart from the rest."

Slim stepped in. "Since Tank and Button and I are the only girls here, we were already more peculiar than the average simp," she said, "so we were the first to find ourselves pushed together by the force of difference."

"With surprising swiftness, that force made the subset grow," said Nick, "until we were eight apart, eight of us set apart from the main body of simps. Then, and only then, did we begin to notice another phenomenon: the force of attraction was drawing us together. We became a group within the group, each of us a member of the set of simps and a member of our subset."

"As you would expect, we wanted to name ourselves, our subset, our tribe," Eugene explained.

"It is an ancient urge, of course," yawned the count, "quintessentially human."

"Yes! Yes! That's it! Quintessence! Yes!" said Dean.

"I thought we should call ourselves SWIMaP," said Tank, "standing for Student Weirdos Involved in Mischief and Pranks."

"I proposed MaPWIS," said Eugene, "which stands for Mischievous and Puckish Weirdos Infiltrating SIMPaW."

"I wanted it to be SWaMPI, the Slightly Weird and Merry Pranksters' Institute," said Slim.

"I wanted our little group to be known by the acronym SIMPaW, as is the larger group," said Nick, "but in this case designating the much more exclusive Summer Institute in Mischief, Pranks, and Weirdness."

"We weren't getting anywhere," said Slim, "but you put an end to our collective indecision."

"Yes!" said Dean. "You! Your imminent arrival. Your Faustroll Institute!"

"When Rocky announced that you were just a day away," Button explained, "we knew that we had to make up our minds at once, so we decided to become the Faustroll Institute."

"Actually," said Matthew with a blush and a shrug, "I wanted to call us the Phaustroll Institute, spelled with *p-h* instead of *f*, with the acronym capital *p*, lowercase *h*, capital *i*, and equal to the ratio a plus b over a equals a over b, or one point six one eight oh three three nine eight eight seven et cetera and written with the Greek letter Φ, until Nick pointed out that it was exactly what the average simp would pick."

"And so," said the count, "we decided to become the Faustroll Institute, *tout court*. Our acronym is FI, which rhymes with *fly*, and our motto is 'Semper FI.'"

AN INTERRUPTION

••

I'M GOING TO interrupt my reminiscences here, just as I interrupted my reading of them when Albertine and I were on the road, headed east, toward Clayton, toward New York, toward Babbington and my hour of reckoning. It was midmorning. I stopped reading. I looked out the window. A minute passed.

"Is that all for this morning?" Al asked.

"Hmm?" I said. "Oh. Maybe. I have more—but—I don't know—maybe I'll save it for later."

"You've interrupted the chapter, haven't you? That didn't seem like the end of the incident."

"You're right. I interrupted it. I remembered something."

"Isn't that a given? Isn't a memoirist always remembering something? In fact, aren't we all always remembering something? Isn't most of what we call thinking actually remembering? Aren't our brains always taking the new, the novel, and working furiously to turn it into the old, the familiar?"

"You sound like me."

"I'm quoting you."

"Have I begun talking in my sleep?"

"I'd rather not go into that. Tell me what you remembered, the memory that stopped the narrative in its tracks."

"It wasn't anything specific—not an event or a person. It was an impression. In fact, what I remembered was how I felt and what I thought."

"I was hoping for something about sex."

"Later."

"I will remain hopeful, and I will hope that I am not disappointed."

"I promise."

"So. What did you remember?"

"I remembered the way I felt about myself, and the way I felt toward the other members of the Faustroll Institute, felt about them as I found them that day. My impressions changed as the days went by, under the hot New Mexican sun, but first impressions do mean something."

"They are often wrong, famously wrong."

"Yes, but suppose we acknowledge that their meaning is usually more about the one who is impressed than about those who do the impressing. If that is so, and we can infer from the impressions something significant about the one impressed, then we may find that they are often right, mysteriously right, ingeniously right."

"Deep," she said in a tone that made me wonder whether her enthusiasm about getting back behind the wheel had already begun to flag.

"My first impressions of the members of the Faustroll Institute have stayed with me," I said, "and I'd like to say something about them. I'd like to try to strip away the patina of time to see if I can give you those impressions as they were, back there, back then."

"Shoot," she said fearlessly.

"Well, I guess, or I think, or I seem to remember, that I saw, by which I mean that I understood, that they did a lot of teasing and kidding, really relished teasing and kidding. It was their style, part of their style, to obscure their thoughts and feelings with jests and jibes. If I were a disinterested observer looking back at myself in their company, forming my first impressions of them, I would have expected myself to welcome this style or attitude or tendency of theirs, because making jests of things was something that I had long been accused of 'always' doing, even when I wasn't joking—or didn't realize that I was joking."

"Ha-ha," she said knowingly.

"So I may have thought to myself that if joking was the style at the Faustroll Institute, I ought to do well at it, even if I didn't know I was doing it. I realize, as I say this, how much these memories mean to me. They are among the ones that form the kernel of my motivation to write my memoirs. I have been waiting for years to write about my experiences at the Summer Institute. It might be more accurate to say that I have been avoiding writing about them for years. It's not that I don't want to write about the memories. I do, I do. I want to so much, and have wanted to for so long, that I fear, have feared, that I won't do them justice. That summer made me what I am, the man I am. Not that summer alone, of course. Everything that came before that summer made its contribution, and I have changed in the years since Corosso, but that summer somehow brought everything that had happened to me before it into focus, or into an association of experiences. It was that insight—no—it couldn't have been that insight, since that insight includes subsequent events—I mean the seed of that insight—that inspired me to try to build my little model of a brain and—"

I paused a moment.

"Am I raving?" I asked.

"A bit," she said thoughtfully.

MAKING ME A SIMP

WITH A FLOURISH and a grin, Eugene produced a large manila envelope, and then, with evident pride, he began to reveal the extent of the group's conspiracy to make me a shadow member of the Summer Institute in Mathematics, Physics, and Weaponry.

"We've only got an hour or so to turn you into a simp," he said. "The other students and all the SIMPaW faculty are on an excursion to climb a mountain—"

"The one that stands so prominently to the west of the campus," explained Nick.

"Climbing that mountain is a tradition for new students at NMIM-TaP," Button explained, pronouncing the acronym for the New Mexico Institute of Mining, Technology, and Pharmacy as "nimimtap."

"Someone decided that the simps ought to climb it, too," added Matthew—whom I will try to remember to call Rocky for the remainder of this account.

"That's it!" said Dean. "That is it: the reason for the organized excursion. You see the phenomenon for what it is, don't you? The extension of an indigenous tradition to an immigrant population as a way of encouraging them to assimilate? That's it! Yes."

"However," said the count, "the excursion was optional, and so we elected to exercise the option not to go."

"I have to remind you," said Eugene, with a note of urgency in his voice, "that the group will be returning shortly, so we have to work fast to get you ready to blend in with the others. We want to make you one of them—"

"But we are also them, or we are some of them, so we will also be making you one of us," said Dean.

"Please, Dean," said Eugene. "Time is short."

"Yes," said Dean. "Time. Right. Time. Whatever that is."

To me, Eugene said, "We want to make the facilities of NMIMTaP fully available to you—"

"Ah—" said Dean, raising his left eyebrow and right index finger.

"Yes?" sighed Eugene.

"Technical point: not all of the facilities of NMIMTaP are available to us, so—"

"Yes, yes," said Eugene, with no attempt to hide his impatience, "a valid point; point taken." Turning to me again, he said, with exaggerated precision, "We want to make the facilities of NMIMTaP that are available to the simps fully available to you—"

He glanced at Dean, who said, silently, "Yes!"

"—so that you have food, shelter, a library card, access to the swimming pool, and a place on the bus when we go off on a field trip," Eugene concluded in a breathless rush. He reached into the envelope. "This is your passport to all of that," he said, producing a small card the size of a driver's license. "It's your identification card. It's Button's work, and a fine piece of work it is. She'll explain it."

Blushing, Button took the card from Eugene and said, "Um, let me give you a little background: Matthew and I met on the plane, flying out. He told me your story, and we began figuring out how to make you a student in SIMPaW when you arrived—if you arrived." She blushed again. "Sorry," she said. "I shouldn't have said that—but we did wonder whether you'd actually make it."

"So did I," I said, seizing the opportunity to demonstrate my modesty and good nature. "I had estimated the distance, and the time it would take me to cover that distance, based on the assumption that I would be flying, but—" I stopped. I'd taken a wrong turn. That "but" had put me on the road to telling them that I hadn't gotten off the ground. I would have let it go at that, but when I looked around the group, I found that they seemed to be hanging on my every word. They were an attentive audience. Damn.

"But?" said Button.

"—but—I didn't—I didn't have any experience—with flying—and I didn't take into account—" I stopped again. I'd taken another wrong turn. Where was I headed now? What was it that I was going to admit that I hadn't taken into account? The possibility that I'd never get off the ground? The great difference in distance between the route the crow would have taken and the route the earthbound aerocyclist took?

"Headwinds?" suggested Rocky.

"Storms?" suggested Dean.

"Right," I said, nodding gravely as I said it and then shaking my head in disbelief at the naïveté of the young man who had departed Babbington expecting clear skies and tailwinds all the way to Corosso.

"Well," Button continued, with no more than a hint of a smile, "when we were given our registration packages, I decided right away that I would start work on an ID card for you—and here it is. You have to carry this card at all times. It identifies you as a student in SIMPaW. You'll be surprised how many times you're asked to show it. Despite what Eugene said, there are a couple of problems with it. For one thing, you will notice that you are student number one-oh-one. There are actually one hundred students in SIMPaW, so we assume that there is no student one-oh-one in the administration's list. Potentially, that is a problem. On the level of everyday existence, you should be okay; that is, no one is likely to check your card against the list to see whether you are on that list as well as on the campus. However, if you do something that gets you noticed, you will be in trouble."

"And so will we," said the count.

"I understand," I assured him.

Button delivered a quick frown in the count's direction, then handed the card to me, along with her own, so that I could compare them. I took it as an invitation to admire her work, and I did admire it.

"This is an amazing forgery," I said. "I can't tell it from the real thing," but I saw that there was a flaw in it beyond my being the hundred-and-first member of a set of one hundred. I hesitated. Should I bring the additional flaw to her attention—and thus to the attention of the entire Faustroll Institute—or let it go?

"However," said Button, "you've probably noticed that that's not your picture. We didn't have a picture of you, so I used what I had. That's a picture of my boyfriend, back at home."

"Ahhh," I said.

420 • PETER LEROY

"You're going to have to try to look like him while you're here," said
Nick.

"Yes," said Dean. "That's it. That's what has to be done. Look like
him. Ha. That's it."

"I'll do my best," I said, with a wink for Button.

She favored me with that hint of a smile again, and I allowed myself
to feel that she restrained it to a hint because it was intended only for
me, that she didn't want it to be noticed by the other members of the
little band.

Eugene reached into the envelope again and produced another card.
"This is your dining hall card," he said. "Rocky's work."

"You have to present that card at every meal and have it punched,"
said Rocky. "You'll notice that you've been punched in for every meal
that has been served so far."

"I see that."

"We knew that if you showed up with a card that never been punched,
the obvious question would be asked: where have you been all this time?
So—we've been logging you in since day one."

"How did you manage—" I began.

"It was fairly simple, really," said the count, anticipating my question. "At every meal, one or another of us would pass through the line
twice. There is no picture on the meal card, as you can see, and the at-
tendants punch them mechanically. They rarely raise their heads. We
were never challenged."

"I see," I said. "Well, it's a good thing there's no picture on the meal
card, because if there were, then each of you would have had to try to
look like Button's boyfriend." They looked at one another quizzically,
asking, silently, whether anyone knew what I was talking about. "Ha-
ha," I added by way of explanation.

KAFKA'S KITTENS

● ●

KAFKA!" I EXCLAIMED, smacking my hand on my forehead as I said it, in the manner of one who has had the scales ripped from his eyes.

"Kasha!" she shot back.

"Kafka, Kafka, Kafka!" I said, or, possibly, wailed.

"Kabuki, Kir, Kalimba!" she offered.

"What are you doing?" I asked.

"Playing the game. Aren't we playing a game?"

"I'm not."

"Oh."

"I'm wrestling with the disturbing realization that the kid back at the motel in Corosso played me for a fool."

"Oh?"

"Yeah," I growled. "The Nature Theatre of Oklahoma."

"Yes?"

"It's from Kafka's *Amerika*. The Nature Theatre of Oklahoma is, well, it's hard to say just what it is because Kafka never finished the chapter, or the book, but from what he told his friend Max Brod it seems that he might have meant the Nature Theatre to be America itself, America as a theater that portrayed America, a theater as vast and accommodating as America itself—the America that was in Kafka's imagination, that is."

"Ahhh, I see," she said. "You feel that we're on a road to nowhere."

"We're on a fool's errand, that's what we're on, headed for a destination that doesn't exist. I'd like to go back there and—"

"Don't get angry."

"Why not? I think I deserve to be angry with that bastard. He—"

"He gave you an excuse for getting out of town."

"He—he—what?"

"The destination that he gave you may not exist, but he gave you a destination, a purpose, a reason for going, a reason for whisking me out of town before the Battle of the Helicopter Heroes."

I sat there for a while, stunned and silent. At last I asked, "You knew about that?"

"How could I have missed it? That funny little man with the posters asked me to put one up in the ladies' room off the lobby."

"But you were willing to leave?"

"Who could pass up the Nature Theatre of Oklahoma, where all are welcome, where a place can be found for everyone, where everyone is an artist?"

"You knew about that, too?"

"I read *Amerika* when I was—hmm—twelve, I think."

"Really?"

"I think so. Of course, memory can be tricky, but as I recall Karl Something-or-Other—"

"Karl Rossmann."

"Karl Rossmann. Of course. He stumbled upon the Nature Theatre because he was looking for a big, cheap breakfast, a BCB, wasn't he?"

"Ahh—"

"He was starving because he had had to get out of town in a hurry and he hadn't had time for more than one lousy cup of weak coffee, so he lapsed into a kind of Kafkaesque delirium, crying, 'I want my BCB!'"

"Okay."

"'Oh where, oh where, can my BCB be?'"

"Okay, okay."

"Or maybe it was '*Wo ist mein grosse Frühstück?*'"

"Why don't you get off the highway at the next promising exit?"

"Okie-doke. Why don't you read me another chapter?"

"I will, but—"

"It will take my mind off my hunger."

"Okay, but—"

"I'm starting to feel like a hunger artist."

"I will read to you, but first I want to know what game you thought we were playing."

"I thought we were naming kittens, of course. Kafka's kittens."

"But all I did was keep repeating 'Kafka.'"

"That's why you were losing."

I, PANMUPHLE, A SKULKING MEDIOCRITY

• •

EUGENE REACHED INTO the envelope again, brought out a small brochure, and said, "Here's an introduction to NMIMTaP and a map of the campus. One of the things that's going to be difficult for you, and potentially a problem, is acting as if you have been here for the eleven days that all the rest of us have been here. You have to seem to know everything that we know about the place."

"I understand," I said. "The map will help me seem as if I know where I am and where I'm going. That's not an easy thing to fake. You might be interested to know that on the journey here from my home town of Babbington, in New York, I traveled without a map. Originally, I had intended to travel with a map, as most travelers do, but—"

"Forgive me for interrupting," said Nick, "but the challenge is a bit greater than merely pretending that you know your way around the campus: you have to act as if you have a shared past with the hundred simps who have been here from the start, as if you have experienced everything that we have experienced in the last eleven days."

"For now," said Eugene, "let's just focus on making your way around the campus. You don't necessarily have to seem to know where you're going. If you can manage not to seem lost, I think you'll get by."

"But don't ever consult the map in public," cautioned Slim.

"No, no," I said. "Don't worry. I'll be—ah—discreet."

"It might be better if you were circumspect," suggested the count.

"Yes," said Dean. "Being discreet is good. Being circumspect is also good. Both are good. But do not be wary. Or secretive. Or furtive. If so, you are sure to arouse suspicion."

"Right," I said.

Eugene shook his head and took three hefty books from a canvas bag at his feet. "These are your textbooks," he said. He may have said it with a sigh. My memory isn't quite clear on that point. "At first glance, you'll see that they seem to be about mining, industrial technology, and pharmacology, but you can't judge a book by its cover. Open them, and you will see that they are about mathematics, physics, and weaponry."

"Clever," I said appreciatively.

"But that's not all," said Button. "There is another course that has no textbook."

"Oh?" I said.

"Paleontology," said Matthew.

"In other words, espionage," said Dean.

"Really?" I asked.

"You'll see," he said.

Eugene pulled a stack of papers from the envelope, fanned the stack, and said, "Here is all the work you've done at SIMPaW so far."

"The work I've done so far?"

"Yes. You've kept up with the rest of us. You have been attending classes, doing your homework, and even taking quizzes."

"All thanks to the members of the Faustroll Institute," said the count, with a slight bow.

"How am I doing?" I asked.

"Your record is entirely undistinguished," said the count. "You are a complete mediocrity."

"Oh."

"It is your job now to see that you stay that way. We don't want you to make yourself noticeable."

"Neither do I," I said without growling. "Allow me to assure you, Count, that I am up to the task. I happen to have some experience."

"With mediocrity?"

"With deception," I said, with growling.

The count raised an eyebrow, inviting an explanation.

"When I was a boy," I explained, "I used to visit my great-grandmother, my father's grandmother, who lived in a few rooms at the very top of my grandparents' house, and on a table there she kept a bowl of hard candies that had been sitting in that bowl for longer than even she could remember. When she invited me to take one, I found that they were all stuck together, so to avoid hurting her feelings I would pretend—"

"Fascinating," said the count, bringing his hand to his mouth as if he were hiding a yawn.

"Peter," said Eugene, "what we're getting at is the fact that you will have to skulk. Are you good at skulking?"

"Oh, yeah," I said. "Definitely. I don't want to brag, but when it comes to skulking, I'm something of a master."

"A master!" cried the count. His exaggerated expression of awe didn't fool me. I'd been around. He doubted my claim. I could see that.

"Yes," I said, "a master. You see, when I was a boy, back in Babbington, my little friends and I invented a game that we called Night Watchman. In that game, the boy chosen to play the Watchman sat at the top of a tower that I had built—"

"On your own?" asked the count, looking at his fingernails.

"Um, no. Not entirely. With my friends. But I did most of the work."

"I see."

"My point is that the Watchman had a searchlight beside him—a searchlight that I had built—"

The count interrupted the examination of his fingernails to glance at me and raise an eyebrow.

"On my own," I said, adding a subtle curl of the lip, not quite a sneer. "From the tower, the searchlight swept my back yard, where the other kids were hiding. The Watchman was armed with a powerful flashlight—"

"Did this game require skulking?" asked Tank.

"It sure did," I said. "Skulking was the key to success, if you were one of the kids out in the dark, trying to sneak up on the Watchman. Of course, if you were the Watchman, then the key to success was vigilance. I spent most of my time out in the dark, sneaking up on the Watchman, inch by inch, slinking, slithering—"

"In short," said Slim, "you can skulk."

"Believe me, Slim," I said with what I hoped was a sly parody of a roué's wink and leer, "I can skulk."

I think that Slim was about to start batting her lashes, but Button said suddenly, "We're running out of time. We'd better wrap this up."

"Right," said Eugene. "Rocky, do you want to cover the code names?"

"I'll be brief," said Rocky briskly. "We have given ourselves code names for this exploit, as you've undoubtedly noticed." He nodded at each of the others as he repeated their code names: "Dean, Slim, Count Übermensch, Nick, Button, Eugene, Tank. You will learn our real names in time, of course—"

"I already know yours," I said.

426 • PETER LEROY

"—and when we are among the simps, you should use those, as we do," he continued, ignoring my interruption, "but when we are among ourselves, we use our code names, and we will expect you to use them, too."

"Okay, Rocky," I said.

"And what will your code name be?" asked the count. I recognized it for what it was: a challenge. How quickly could I come up with the perfect code name? I was equal to the challenge. I had known what name I would choose for several minutes, ever since I had learned where, thanks to the other members of the Faustroll Institute, I stood in the ranks of SIMPaW.

"If I am to disguise myself as a completely unremarkable mediocrity," I said with a wry grin to suggest that I understood, as perhaps no one else could, how very difficult it would be for me, Peter Leroy, to disguise myself as a mediocrity, "then only one name will do."

"And what," asked the count in a lazy drawl, "might that be?"

"Panmuphle, of course," I drawled right back.

JUST A LITTLE TOO LATE

SEAVIEW," SHE SAID, gliding toward the highway exit. "That sounds promising."

"Seaview?"

"That's what the sign says."

"We must have made better time than I expected."

We had left the highway, and we were rolling along the main street of Seaview, Texas, a sizable town that offered distant vistas in all directions, but not a glimpse of the sea.

"Maybe we're lost," I suggested.

"We're having an adventure," she said. "There are no wrong turns when we're on an adventure. We can't get lost."

"Why do I keep forgetting that?"

"Come on, help me spot a local authority."

She got out of the car, and I followed her.

When we are away from home and don't know where to get the best big, cheap breakfast, we usually take the direct route to finding one: we stand on a street corner and wait for a well-fed resident to come along.

"Here comes our man now," I said.

"Oooh, yesss," she said, her words slipping from lips moist with anticipation.

"Pardon me," I said, hailing the hefty fellow.

"Howdy," he said, touching the brim of his cowboy hat. "What can I do you for?"

"I hope you can tell me where we can get the biggest, cheapest breakfast in these-here parts," I said.

"That would be the Seaview Grill," he said with a booster's pride. "Best breakfast in the state of Texas. Serve it all day. In fact, they don't serve nothin' but breakfast."

"Oo-ee," squealed Al.

"You sound hungry, little darlin'."

"I haven't had anything but a cup of coffee since last night," she said, pouting prettily.

To me, in an uncanny imitation of the scolding voice that Principal Simon used, back in Babbington, when I was in the fifth grade, the citizen of Seaview said, "You best get this little honey to the Seaview Grill right quick."

"That's what I'm aimin' to do," I said. "How do we get there?"

"You just go down the street here to the second corner and make a left. You'll find it in the middle of the second block, right-hand side."

"Okay," I said. "Thanks."

"My pleasure," he said, touching the brim of his hat again.

I turned to go, but Albertine wasn't quite ready to end the interview. "I have a question," she said.

The lecherous old bastard narrowed his eyes and said, "I'm sure I'd be delighted to hear any question that came from your lovely lips."

"Why is the town called Seaview?" was what came from her lovely lips.

"Well, before I answer you that, let me ask you one: are you a believer, or are you an evolutionist?"

"Well—" she stalled, turning her feet in and batting her lashes.

"Don't really matter," he said. "If you're a believer, then you know that during the flood this place was underwater, underneath the sea that covered the whole entire earth. And if you're one of those godless evolutionists—though I don't see how someone so pretty and feminine could be—you believe that the earth is about four point five six seven billion years old and that during the Pennsylvanian Period of the Paleozoic Era and again during the Early Cretaceous Period of the Mesozoic Era, this part of Texas was covered by sea water due to natural causes. So you see, it don't really matter which you are or which you believe, 'cause it comes down to the same thing: the town used to offer a sea view; you just happen to have dropped by a little too late to see it." He began a rumbling laugh, the kind that makes a big man's belly shake.

"It's funny that you should mention that," I said, raising my voice to cut through his laughter, "because years ago I spent a good part of one summer hunting clam fossils in the desert near—"

"Say, I gotta shake a leg!" he said suddenly, sobering and examining his watch. "Time kinda got away from me." This time he was the one who turned to go, but as soon as he had he stopped, turned back toward us, and asked Albertine, "You in town for the big Fly-In?"

"No," I said, taking Albertine's hand and all but dragging her toward the Electro-Flyer.

"You're having a Fly-In?" she asked coquettishly, twisting around to face him as she stumbled along with me.

"Sure are, sweetheart. Today they're havin' it over in Corosso, New Mexico, but the whole shootin' match will be flyin' in here tomorrow. We'll have the home-builts, the kit-builts, the not-yet-finished, the experimentals, a big swap meet, and the Battle of the Helicopter Heroes. Those are daring—"

"We're not really interested," I said.

I opened the passenger's door for Albertine and helped her—okay, pushed her—into the seat.

"You're driving?" she asked incredulously.

"Yeah," I growled. "It's only a couple of blocks, and I've got to get my little honey to the Seaview Grill right quick."

∙∙∙∙∙∙∙∙∙∙

The Seaview Grill was a cafeteria. It was run-down, and it wasn't obviously the best place in town for breakfast, but it was crowded. A long line of people extended out the door, down the block, and around the corner. We added ourselves to the end of the line, and to pass the time while we waited our turn I resumed my reading.

OUT OF SIGHT

••

WE HAVE ONE more thing to do before the others return, and we're running out of time," said Eugene.

"What's that?" I asked.

"We've got to hide your motor scooter," said the count.

"Aerocycle," I snarled.

"Whatever you call it," he said, "we've got to hide it."

"Actually, I call her *Spirit*."

"'Her'?" asked Tank.

"Yes," I explained. "She's a girl—or—I guess—a woman."

"How do you know?" asked Nick, raising an eyebrow.

"How does a mariner know that his ship is a woman?" I asked with a shrug.

"Does he?" asked Slim.

"A sailor always refers to his boat as 'she,'" said Rocky.

"It sounds a little—ah—kinky," said Button, giggling.

"Kinky?" I asked.

"A little," agreed Tank.

"How so?"

"Well, don't you—um—mount her?" asked Slim.

"I—well—sure—" I was beginning to sweat.

"And you rev her up?" suggested Button.

"Yes," I admitted. Were the girls teasing me because they knew how much I desired them, how very hungry for them I was, how very large was the sexual hunger that had grown within me over the course of the trip from Babbington to Corosso?

"And then you ride her, don't you?" asked Tank. "Until you both arrive at—"

I glanced quickly and furtively at my crotch to see if my desire was great enough to be obvious to everyone.

The girls burst out laughing.

"We'd better get *Spirit* out of sight fast!" said Slim. "She's too much competition."

The nine of us walked to the parking lot where I had left *Spirit*. As I walked, I worried. I wanted the group to like *Spirit*. I wanted *Spirit* to like them. At the same time, I wasn't sure whether I liked them myself. I had liked them at first. I was grateful for everything they had done to make me a member of SIMPaW, but there was something about them that I didn't like. I couldn't quite see what it was at the time, but there was something about them that made me keep my distance from them. (Now I see that it must have been their pervasive and presumptuous irony that made me slow to like them. Did I understand irony at the time? Somewhat, I guess. Now I understand that the irony they employed was the protective kind. Over the years I have come to pity those who use it, those who feel the need to use it. At the time it intimidated me, as it was meant to do, since intimidation is its method of protection.)

We reached *Spirit*. We stopped. We all stood there, looking at her. Slowly, as if we had made a collective decision, we began circling her, regarding her closely, critically. I couldn't help myself: I saw all her flaws. I imagined, or supposed, that the others were seeing her flaws, too.

"Who are all these people?" whispered *Spirit*.

"They're friends of mine," I said.

"Friends?"

"New friends."

"Are you sure?"

"Of course I am."

"I think you'll be lucky if you find one real friend in the bunch."

"Why do you say that?"

"I have my reasons."

"Maybe you're just jealous."

"Me? Jealous? Of that crowd? Ha! Ha-ha!"

"You recognize Matthew in 'that crowd,' don't you?"

"Matthew? Which one?"

"Right in front of you."

"That's Matthew? Matthew Barber?"

"It is."

"This is amazing. I feel as if I've been given the power of prescience. Seeing him now, seeing what he's done to himself, how he has tried to take advantage of the distance from Babbington and his life back there to turn himself into someone he never was when he was at home, I feel that I can predict that someday Matthew is going to be a middle-aged guy who wears a toupee, hangs out in bars, and tells young women to call him Rocky."

"Funny you should say that—"

"And the rest of them—" she began, a heavy tone of disapproval in her voice, "are—"

"They're okay," I asserted.

"Maybe," she said.

"They've done a lot for me. They're putting themselves at risk to make it possible for me to stay here as if I were a real student."

"You're sure about that?"

"Yes, I am. They forged an identity card for me, and a meal ticket, and—"

"You're sure they're forgeries?"

"Of course I'm—well—I think—why wouldn't they be?"

"Your new friends might be trying to pass off perfectly ordinary documents as forgeries in order to win your confidence."

"Why would they do that?"

"How many students do you suppose arrived at the campus on aero-cycles?"

"I guess I'm the only one."

"You most certainly are the only one! Don't sell yourself short. When the other students find out about your extraordinary feat, they're going to be impressed. You're going to be somebody, somebody people want to know, a big man on campus—and when they get a look at me—"

"*Spirit—*"

"—they are going to be breathless with admiration."

"*Spirit—*"

"Take it from me, they will be lining up to be your friends.'"

"*Spirit*—"

"What?"

"They're not going to see you."

"Not going to see me? Why?"

"I'm going to have to—put you away."

"Put me—away? Put me—to sleep? You mean—kill me?"

"No. Don't be ridiculous. I mean put you in storage. Hide you somewhere."

"Because I embarrass you?"

"No, no, no."

I tried to reassure her. I tried to explain the situation to her. I described for her—quickly, in a breathless rush—the lengths to which the other members of the Faustroll Institute had gone in their effort to make me indistinguishable from a real simp. It didn't work. I could tell that she didn't believe me. She was convinced that I was going to hide her away because she was an embarrassment to me.

"Are you just about finished there?" asked Eugene.

"Um—yeah," I said. "I'm ready." I patted *Spirit*'s tank. "She's ready, too."

"Then let's get her out of sight."

Hiding her felt like a sin, and it wasn't one of those sins that come with a compensating pleasure. I felt that I was sinning against our friendship. She was hurt, and I understood why. She didn't deserve to be hidden; she didn't deserve to be incarcerated. She deserved recognition; she deserved to be free, free as a bird. While I worked with the others to push her into a storage warehouse on the edge of the campus and pull a tarpaulin over her, I heard her pleading with me.

"Aren't you proud of me for bringing you all the way to Corosso?" she whimpered.

"Yes," I whispered. "I'm proud of you."

I *was* proud of her. She had brought me all the way, and, except for the single failure of never managing to fly, she had performed beautifully. In fact, because she couldn't fly, couldn't follow the route that a crow would have chosen, she had brought me much farther than the eighteen hundred miles I had expected to travel. Our trip on the ground must have covered something more than twenty-five hundred miles. I was very proud of her.

Nick ran into the warehouse. "The buses are pulling up in front of the cafeteria!" he announced.

"Come on," said Tank. "Let's get out of here."

"I'll be back," I said to *Spirit*. "I'll visit you whenever I can. I promise."

"Peter, are you coming?" called Slim.

"Yeah. Here I come. I'm just—"

"Sobbing a heartfelt goodbye?" Button asked.

"What? Oh. Ha-ha. Very funny."

"I suppose that a boy and his—ah—mount can get pretty close on a long trip," the count suggested.

"Those lonely nights beneath the stars—" said Nick.

"The romantic moonlight—" said Rocky.

"I imagine you'll be slipping back to see her whenever you can—" said Eugene.

"To run your hand along her wing—" said Dean.

"Cut it out," I said as I closed the door on *Spirit*, and with a false chuckle I added, "Do you think I'm nuts?"

WHEN IN THE SEAVIEW GRILL . . .

. . . .

Si fueris Romae, Romano vivito more; si fueris alibi, vivito sicut ibi. (When you are in Rome, live in the Roman style; when you are elsewhere, live as they live elsewhere.)

—Saint Ambrose to Saint Augustine, possibly

WHEN I FINISHED reading, the line had advanced so far that we had shuffled with others around the corner, up the block, and into the Seaview Grill and were now just two parties from the counter where people placed their orders. I rejoiced in that, but at the same time I began to feel a little odd. Apparently, Albertine did, too, because she put her lips to my ear and muttered, "Do you feel a little odd?"

"I do," I said, with my lips to her ear in a similar manner, "but I'm not sure why. It isn't just that the people nearest to us seem to think that I'm odd because I read that chapter to you. I'm used to that. Reading aloud is not the kind of public behavior that people expect. It makes me seem, to them, like a nut. If I had been screaming into a cell phone and had said exactly what I said to you, every word that I read to you, but without a manuscript, no one would have thought me odd at all. Many might have eavesdropped, but no one would have thought that I was odd. It's reading that's odd to them, and someone who reads aloud in public is particularly odd—but the oddness that I'm feeling now isn't the oddness of a nut who reads aloud; it's the oddness of one who feels that he is regarded as peculiar for having set himself apart from his fellow creatures in some other way."

"Size," she said.

"Size?"

"In the eyes of the others, we are, I think, oddly small."

"That's it!" I said, as Dean would have. "That's it! Exactly! Is it some kind of illusion?"

"No," she said. "It's real. We are considerably smaller. Even the children are larger than we are."

The beefy family just ahead of us—husband, wife, and a daughter of ten, twelve, fourteen, sixteen, or something—had reached the counter. The man of the family ordered at once: "Corned beef hash, poached eggs, biscuits, home fries, sausage, bacon, a pork chop, extra gravy, and a beer." He thought for a moment, then said, "Make that two beers."

The clerk punched the order into the register. The man stepped aside, and his wife took his place.

"I'll have the same," she said.

The clerk punched her order into the register. The woman stepped aside, and the girl stepped up.

"Me, too," she said.

Her mother cuffed her on the ear and said, "You got to lay off that beer, honey, if you're gonna be a supermodel."

The lad behind the counter punched the keys on the register and watched while it printed the order. Then he read from it: "That's hash, poached eggs, biscuits, potatoes, sausage, bacon, pig chop, and extra gravy times three, and beer times six."

"Times four!" said the woman.

"Ma!"

"Give her iced tea," said the woman. "She's our 401(k) plan."

"Ma! You're embarrassing me!"

The clerk worked at the register some more and pushed four beers and a huge plastic cup of iced tea across the counter. "Your number is fifty-four-thirty-five," he said. "Next!"

During the transaction, I took note of the reactions of the others waiting with us on the line. I noticed that none of them seemed to find it remarkable that the clerk read aloud in public. I asked myself whether the difference lay in the content of the reading or the medium of the printed tape.

"Next!" he called again.

I made a gracious—I might even say gallant—gesture to indicate that Albertine, not I, should be next, but she demurred. "I'm not sure," she said. "You go first."

I stepped up to the counter.

"Do you have no-cholesterol egg substitute?" I asked.

Everyone in our immediate vicinity—that is to say everyone close enough to us to hear what I had asked—burst out laughing. On the periphery, just beyond earshot, people began asking, "What did he say?" When they were told, they burst out laughing, too, so the laughter propagated in waves. It embarrassed me, of course, and part of the embarrassment came from its reminding me of the laughter of Tank, Button, and Slim.

"I take it you don't have no-cholesterol egg substitute," I said.

"That would be correct," said the lad, wiping the tears from his eyes with the back of his hand.

"Tofu bacon?" I asked.

"No," he managed, reaching desperately for his pocket handkerchief.

Great waves of rumbling laughter rolled outward as my question was repeated and forwarded. People began to turn frankly in our direction, waiting to hear what might come next from the nut at the counter (the one, I heard it whispered, who had been reading aloud in public).

"Al," I said, stepping back, "why don't you give it a try while I re-think this?"

"Okay," she said eagerly, her mind made up. "I'll have—let's see—corned beef hash, poached eggs, biscuits, home fries, sausage, bacon, a pork chop, extra gravy, and—what the hell—two beers."

We found a table, and I read another chapter to Albertine while we waited for our number.

What's that? What did I hear you mutter?

You're wondering what I ordered?

Oh.

Well, when the clerk had finished punching Al's order into the register and regarded me with a look that said the line behind me was growing long and restless, I took the easy way out.

"The same," I said.

FIRST SUPPER AT SIMPAW, PART ONE

· ·

All human history attests
That happiness for man,—the hungry sinner!—
Since Eve ate apples, much depends on dinner.
—Byron, *Don Juan,* Canto XII, Stanza 99

WHEN THE DOOR clicked shut behind me, I suddenly felt hungry, and the hunger that I felt wasn't mere everyday hunger; it was a growling, desperate hunger, so urgent that my animal nature and my civilized self seemed to be struggling against each other. I had to work to keep myself from howling like a ravenous wolf. If you had shown me a roasted joint of mutton on a platter, I would have grabbed it with my bare hands and begun tearing at it with my teeth, hoping all the while that my mother wasn't watching.

"Is it almost dinner time?" I asked, trying very hard to seem as if I didn't really care whether it was or not.

The eight other members of the Faustroll Institute burst out laughing.

"I wasn't trying to be funny," I protested.

"Probably not," said Tank, "but what you said was funny to us, because we know what you meant."

"You know what I meant?"

"Let me ask you this," said Slim. "Did you suddenly feel a great, growling, animal hunger overcome you?"

"I did—yes—I did—that's exactly what I felt."

"We've all felt it," said Button.

"It's the hunger for home," said the count.

"Really?" I said or, to be honest, snarled. I resented his easy assumption that he understood what I had experienced, his assumption that I was an open book to him. "What makes you think that, 'Count'?" I asked. "Why couldn't it simply be hunger that I feel, hunger for food rather than hunger for home? Are you sure you're not overcomplicating— overintellectualizing—a growling stomach?"

"A question?" Dean asked of me, raising his hand as if he were in class. "Will you answer a question? What do you say?"

"Yes," I said. "I mean, 'Yes!'"

"Ha!" he said. "Parody! Close imitation, exaggerated, colored by irony. Yes!"

"What do you want to ask me?" I asked.

"The experience immediately precedent to hunger: what was it?"

"Huh?"

"He means, 'What did you experience just before you felt the hunger?'" said the count.

"Well, let's see," I said.

I brought my hand to my forehead as if making an effort to recall. In fact, I was giving myself a moment to decide what to say. I wasn't about to tell the members of the Faustroll Institute that I had been promising to return to visit *Spirit* from time to time, or that I had been feeling that I had sinned against my friendship with her in favor of theirs. No. I would divulge nothing more than the outward and obvious.

"I had just closed the door," I said, "and I experienced—a click."

"A click?" asked Eugene with intense and evident curiosity.

"Yes. I heard a click as the door closed and its latch snapped into place: click. Then I felt what Slim accurately described as a 'great, growling, animal hunger.'"

"A classic case!" said Dean. "Cause and effect, perceived after the fact, or imposed after the fact. Ex post facto application of Western logic to a complex occurrence in which logic played no part, since the world itself lacks the logic that we impose upon it in our interpretation of it, an interpretation simultaneously explaining and oversimplifying the occurrence: explaining it and explaining it away, you could say. Yes."

"We have all felt it," said Nick.

"The hunger?" I asked. "Or the ex post facto application of Western logic to a complex occurrence in which logic played no part?"

"The hunger," he said. "After extensive discussion, some of it heated, we have agreed to call it the hunger of the displaced, or hunger for the familiar, the latter being what I favor, since we who felt the hunger, having altered our loci voluntarily, hardly deserve to be identified as displaced or to identify with truly displaced persons—those unfortunates who have been forcefully dislocated, whose loci have been altered by powers they could not resist—and because the term *hunger for the familiar* is active, suggesting a specific desire, a yearning rather than an emptiness, and therefore, I think, more accurately conveys the great force that we have each attributed to the hunger."

"It isn't simply food we hunger for," said Rocky, "it's home."

"Dinner at home," said Nick wistfully.

"Even breakfast would do," said Tank, just as wistfully.

Gloom had settled over the group.

"I'm the exception that proves the rule," said Eugene. Shamefaced, he put his hands in his pockets and looked at his shoes. "My family lives here in Corosso. I'm not far away from home now. Apparently, the hunger for home increases with distance. I hardly feel it, and I never even heard—well—"

"What?"

"The click that you heard."

"But—all the rest of you heard it?"

"Not literally a click," said Tank, giving me a poke in the ribs to warn me against any future literalism on my part. "With me it was a drip. I turned the water off after taking a shower the day I arrived here, and I heard the water dripping from the shower head, the last few drips, the residual water in the pipe dripping, and I felt the hunger. Your click was my drip. Or my drip was your click."

"For me it wasn't even a sound," said Slim. "It was a shadow, the shadow of a tree, falling across a path on the campus at a certain angle. I glanced at that shadow—no, not even that—I just glimpsed it from the corner of my eye, and, well, I felt the hunger."

"Interesting," I said. "And it happened to all of you—except Eugene?"

"All but Eugene," said Button.

"I wonder why—" I said, more to myself than to any of them.

"Isn't it obvious?" asked the count. "A stimulus, something closely resembling an earlier experience, prompted a yearning for the comforts of home—"

"I'm not that stupid, Count," I asserted. "I wasn't wondering why the phenomenon occurred. I was wondering why it occurred as it did in my individual case, why the click of the door should have made me feel hungry—for I'm convinced now that the click certainly was the experience that triggered the hunger. It was not that the door clicked closed behind me and then, subsequently but without any causal link, I happened to feel hungry. No. The door clicked, and the click made me feel hungry. I recognize the phenomenon for what it was. What I'm asking myself is how my earlier life prepared me to respond to that particular stimulus. Why a click?"

MNEMOSYNE BESTED

I PAUSED IN my reading and said to Albertine, "You know, I am still asking myself that question: how had my earlier life prepared me to respond to that particular stimulus, the click of the latch on the shed door? Now, so many years after the event, I am sitting here in the

Seaview Grill, putting myself back there in that shed on the NMIM-TaP campus, saying a silent goodbye to *Spirit,* and then closing the door, and I can hear the click of the latch and—holy shit."

"What happened?" she asked, swiveling her head in the direction of the counter.

"The click," I said. "I heard the click."

"I thought you might have heard our number."

"Our number?"

"They'll call our number when our order is ready."

"How do you know that?"

"The laughing kid behind the counter told us. Your mind was in Corosso at the time."

"It was!" I said. "It was! I admit it. My mind was so completely in Corosso that I heard the click of the latch on the shed door as clearly and authentically as if I were hearing it for the first time, and—"

A great, growling animal hunger had come over me.

"Where the hell is our order?" I growled, playing the animal part.

"I'm sure they're working on it," she said. "Be patient. Drink your beer."

I took a sip.

"I know what it was," I said. I said it calmly, quietly, speaking from the serene spot where we find ourselves, if we're lucky, after an extended struggle to excavate a shiny little chip of the past.

"What?" she asked with a lick of her foamy lip.

"The click. The original click, the one that the shed-latch click reminded me of, the click that I associated with hunger and home."

"Give!"

"I have been playing the memory over and over again, hoping that I would be able to make a leap backward from the Corosso click to an earlier one that must have established the association of latch click and animal hunger," I began.

"I see that we're going to take the long way home," she said, raising her second beer.

"Obviously," I said, "the click of the storage shed door must have reminded me of an earlier click, but what click? If the other members of the Faustroll Institute were right, it was a click at home, a click associated with food at home, with the comforting pleasure of eating food at home, a meal at home, home cooking. I had some ideas, some click candidates. How about the click of my father's carving knife against the sharpening steel when he began to hone the knife before carving the Thanksgiving turkey? That would work. It would work, but I didn't think it was the right memory. I wondered if it might have been the click of my grandfather's clam knife against the shell of a clam, at the juncture of the valves, just before he inserted it and slid it swiftly sideways, cutting the adductor muscles and prying the clam open in one smooth, practiced motion. No. It wasn't that, either. So it went, and so it has gone, down the years. Until now."

"Gaargh-gurgh-aarghee-ghaheev," belched a chorus of ancient speakers mounted on the walls around the room.

"What was that?" I asked.

"Not our number," she said. "That was fifty-four-thirty-five. We might be next."

"*Yo tengo una hambre canina,*" I said plaintively.

"Finish the account of your struggle," she said, "and maybe that will bring our number up."

"Struggle," I said. "That's exactly what it's been. Sitting here, struggling with my memory, I felt alone, isolated even from you, doing single-handed battle with Mnemosyne on the darkling windswept plains of Time. I had begun to feel sorry for myself, my solitude, my solitary struggle, when suddenly something, something here, in this odd place so far from home, clicked."

"And that was?"

"I have no idea," I said. I was being a little dramatic about the whole thing, and I knew it. I used a pull at my beer to add a pause. "It may have been anything. It may have been my morning hunger itself. Whatever it was, it unlocked the secret of the click."

"I'm dying here."

Another pull, another pause. "It was the click of the magnetic latch that held the lid of the bread box in place, the bread box that sat atop the refrigerator, at home in Babbington, when I was a boy. You see, the bread box held, in addition to bread, cookies, cupcakes, doughnuts, crullers—"

"Click!" snapped the speakers, and that click was followed by, "Gaargh-gurgh-aarghee-ghisch."

"Fifty-four-thirty-six, that's our number!" said Albertine.

I fetched the heavy tray of food, staggered back to the table with it, and arrayed the plates symmetrically for us. Nearby there was a stand with a stack of used trays on it. I added our empty one to the stack and then returned to the table.

"Ready?" I asked, as I took my seat.

"As I'll ever be," she said.

We fell to, and, working in silence, we did a creditable job of consuming what we had ordered—for two people of our size, that is.

The dullness of satiety made us not quite ready to return to the road, so, instead, I read another chapter.

FIRST SUPPER AT SIMPAW, PART TWO

He took the passports and fingered them casually. Then something he saw there made him cock his eyebrows.

"Where did you steal these?" he asked.

—John Buchan, *Greenmantle*

FORTUNATELY," **SAID THE** count, "it is time for dinner." With a sweep of his hand, he indicated the dining hall, across the campus, in the distance, and the Faustroll Institute began wending its way thither.

"When we get there," said Eugene, nervously twitching his fingers as he spoke, "the main body of SIMPaW students should already have arrived, direct from their excursion to the mountain. If all goes according to plan, you will join them, take a place in line, and show your meal card when your turn comes. This will be the first test of your forged documents."

"I know how tense that moment will be," I said.

"Fraught with potential disaster," muttered the count.

"I've seen similar moments in many, many war movies at the Babbington Theater and the Babbington Fine Arts Theater," I explained in a tone intended to show that I understood the gravity of the situation and the meaning of the word *fraught*. "It's the moment when a peremptory and suspicious official regards an impostor or spy or freedom fighter who has slipped behind enemy lines with growing suspicion, squints at him, and says, 'Vhere are your peppers?' I remember one of those moments in particular, in a movie—actually a foreign film— that I saw with the Glynn twins. I doubt that I will ever forget it—or the night that followed it. You see, Margot and Martha and I—"

Just then, Nature, possibly because she was impatient with my reminiscences of Babbington, or possibly because she was jealous of the rapt attention that my telling had inspired in the members of the Faustroll Institute, put on a display. The sky darkened with astonishing swiftness and rain began to fall in drops the size of gumballs. Lightning illuminated the heavy clouds from within them, making them seem to swell and pulse with power.

"Wow," I said. "Did you see that? This is amazing! Look at that sky! I've never seen anything like—"

"Shh," said Eugene. "Pretend not to take any notice."

"Are you kidding?" I said. "How could I not notice? How could anyone—"

"It happens every afternoon at this time," muttered Nick.

"Really?"

"Yes," said Tank.

"Every afternoon? This amazing display? These natural fireworks?"

"Every afternoon, regular as clockwork," said Slim.

"And nobody takes any notice?"

"All of us—all of us but Eugene, that is—found it remarkable, astonishing, awe-inspiring, breathtaking the first few times we experienced it, but now we're blasé about it," Rocky explained, "so you'd better pretend to be blasé about it, too."

"I can understand that a person might get used to it, but I—"

"Be cool, man," said Dean. "Be cool, or be gone."

"Of course," I said. "Of course. Sorry."

As a group, we walked in blasé silence the rest of the way to the dining hall. Try as I might, I couldn't keep myself from sneaking a look at the display of natural razzle-dazzle now and then. Every time I turned my head I heard the clucking tongues of the others, or thought I did, and quickly turned my eyes forward, pretending that I'd seen it all before, seen it so many times that it held no interest for me, none at all.

"You're in for another surprise," warned Button.

"Yes," agreed the count. "Dinner will not be what you expect."

"You'll have to be on your toes, Peter, ever vigilant," said Nick. "Above all, avoid any display of surprise."

"Yes," said Eugene. "On the whole, we think that you ought to wear a mask of studied aloofness, a deliberate affectation of superiority to and lack of interest in everything that occurs in the dining hall."

"That way," said Tank, "the simps will assume that you're as well trained as they are. They won't recognize you as an interloper."

We entered the dining hall. I saw immediately that there were two lines of students waiting for food, one considerably shorter than the other. I headed for the shorter one. I didn't get far. I felt the restraining tug of a grip on the back of my belt.

"Not that line," Slim whispered, her lips close to my ear in confidence. "This one."

"Why don't we use the short line?" I asked her, taking the opportunity to bring my lips as close to her ear as hers had been to mine, establishing, I hoped, an intimacy that would deepen over the course of the summer, bringing both of us many an unforgettable pleasure.

"That's for the regular students," muttered Button, squeezing between us. "They get different meals."

"They do? Why do they—"

The count elbowed me and nodded once in the direction of the longer line. He wore a stern look. I tossed my head with a subtle air of

Babbingtonian hauteur and joined the line of legitimate simps. When my turn came, I presented my card as I had seen the others present theirs. Mine was punched with no more attention than any of the others received. I allowed myself an inner smile of triumph.

In the line with the other students, I moved to the serving stations. They were virtually identical to the serving stations I knew so well back at home. Fighting the bittersweet emotions induced by a nostalgic longing for the Babbington High School cafeteria, I put my tray on the long rack made of stainless steel tubing and began edging it along as the others did. I thought that I knew what to do, what to expect, but I wasn't going to take any chances. I watched the others, and I mimicked them.

They accepted food as it was dished out by the women behind the steam tables, on the other side of a divide topped by a long linear shelf. The women would ladle something from a vat and pour it into a bowl or slide a spatula under something and slip it onto a plate, and then they would place the bowl or plate onto the shelf, all without emotion or any apparent interest in what they were doing or in what they were serving. The students who shuffled along in front of them took the plates and bowls from the shelf with no more evident emotion or involvement than the servers displayed. They put the food on their trays and shuffled along the line, sliding their trays with them, apparently not at all interested in what they were being served, the food that they were soon to eat. I did as they did, but with a difference. I was tremendously interested in what I was being served, hungrily curious about what I was going to eat, and I had to struggle to pretend that I was not.

I examined each dish, as inconspicuously as I could, maintaining a mask of blankness.

I had no idea what anything was.

Nothing looked familiar to me. Nothing looked like anything I had eaten at home, or in the Babbington High cafeteria, or in the restaurants and clam shacks of Babbington, or in the exotic cities and towns I had visited on my way across the country. The aromas were like none of the aromas that had filled the dining room back at home, in Babbington Heights, or like any aromas that I associated with dinner, or even with food. This meal was likely to be an experience wholly unfamiliar, entirely surprising.

Was this a test?

Was it a joke?

Was it a trick?

Was all of it, everything that was happening in the dining hall, designed to make me look foolish? If I ate the odd concoctions on my plate and pretended that I didn't find them odd at all, would I become the laughingstock of SIMPaW?

FOLLOWING A WOOLGATHERER'S CIRCUIT

. . . .

I SNATCHED A fresh napkin from the next table, took my pen from my pocket, and made a quick sketch of the first crude idea for an electrical model of my mind that had come to me years earlier, in Corosso. It was a kid's idea, or a kid's version of a big idea, but at the time I thought it might represent—in a highly simplified way, of course—the way my brain and my memory were related to everything that is not me, everything "out there."

"This is the little idea I had," I said, turning the napkin in her direction. "Basically, it shows why there is a disconnect between the way the brain receives, stores, and represents information and the way the mind—"

"Shhh," she said, bringing her finger to her lips and cocking her head to the right.

"What?" I said.

"Listen."

Our booth was separated from the one beside it by a barrier made of pine paneling, so we couldn't see the couple on the other side of the barrier, but we could hear them clearly.

A man said, in a voice that managed to be both apologetic and defiant, "I can't help feeling that we ought to talk about the so-called state of inattention that I lapse into from time to time—that I have lapsed into from time to time for as long as I can remember."

"So you mean you were inattentive before we met?" asked his companion, in the voice of an enchanted girl who had matured into a weary woman.

"Please note that I said 'the so-called state of inattention,'" the man said, ignoring the weary woman's question. "I'm not the one who calls it that. It's other people who do. I've never considered myself inattentive, and I don't consider myself inattentive now."

"Yet your mind is often elsewhere," she said.

"There you have it," he said.

"Have what?" she asked.

"You've put your finger on it."

"I have?"

"Fascinating," I whispered to Albertine, "because if you look at this schematic you'll see a battery, which represents energy, the slow fire of human life, burning within an individual, like me, or the guy on the other side of the barrier, and a light bulb, which represents a behavior that can be observed by the outside world, and a switch, which represents a stimulus—"

"Yes, you have indeed put your finger on it," said the invisible man. "There are times when my mind is elsewhere. My mind, my wandering mind, is at any given moment where it is, and my attention is focused and aware there, fully focused and fully aware. To some, this looks like inattention, because inattention is in the eye of the beholder."

"But where your mind is focused is very often not here and now."

"So," I said, "the stimulus occurs. The switch closes. The light lights." I drew little lines of radiant light emanating from the bulb. "It's not very interesting, but still it is a representation of something. Something happens in this crude circuit, but not much. Let's look at what that circuit inspired." I snatched another napkin and began a second sketch.

"As I said," the man was saying with exaggerated patience, "my mind enjoys traveling. The problem—and I recognize that it is a problem—is that the traveling mind may not notice the oil slicks on the road of life in the here and now."

While I sketched, I was listening, and I whispered to Albertine, "I'm beginning to feel a kinship with this guy, despite the pompous, self-serving way he expresses himself."

"Your excuse, then," said the woman, "is that when you seem to be

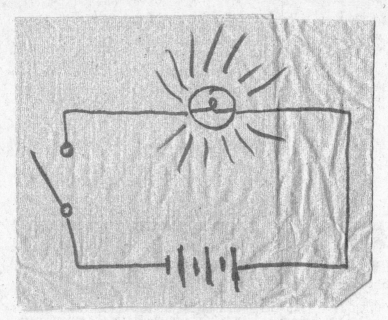

I drew little lines of radiant light emanating from the bulb.

inattentive you are actually being attentive to some other thing, in some other place, at some other time."

"Yes," he said, "but I realize that it sounds like nothing but an excuse and not an explanation, certainly not a justification for my inattentiveness."

"Ha!" she exclaimed triumphantly. "You just called it inattentiveness."

"I know," he said. "What else can I call it? I wish that I had another way of putting it, so that I could offer a glib explanation when I'm accused of not paying attention, something so perfectly phrased that it would end all conversation on the matter, silence the chuckling, bring the raised eyebrows back to their normal level."

"How about something that suggests exploration, even adventuring?" I muttered, mostly to myself. To Albertine, I said, "Okay. Here. Take a look at this. This is pretty much what came next, as well as I remember it." I passed the second sketch to her.

"I might call it searching," the man said. "Or exploring. Or prospecting."

"So, when people accuse you of woolgathering—"

"No! Not woolgathering! Anything but that!"

"Okay! Okay! When people accuse you of not paying attention, then—"

"I can say, 'I was exploring other territory.'"

"That's not bad."

"Now there's something more interesting going on," I explained. "The first model had only two internal states—off and on—but this one has three—off and four kinds of on—"

"Alternatively, I could claim to be the victim of a disease, or syndrome," the man suggested.

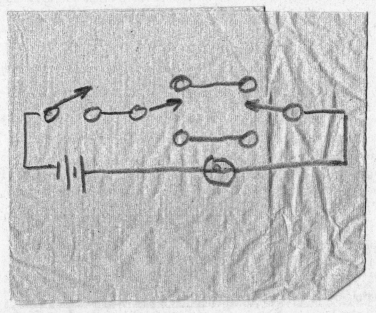

"Now there's something more interesting going on," I explained.

"Oh, please," said the woman, "no victimization. It wouldn't become you. It has to be something positive."

"Exploring other territory, then."

"Yes. Exploring other territory. I like that."

"I'm so glad we had this little talk."

They had risen from their table, and they were on their way out.

Albertine and I twisted in our seats to watch them go. Like all the other patrons, they were large. He swung the door open and held it for her, and she smiled at him as she squeezed through.

"He shouldn't have objected to being called a woolgatherer," I said to Al as we rose from our table.

"Oh?"

"Woolgathering was originally a kind of gleaning. In areas where sheep were raised and allowed to browse freely in open fields and meadows, some of their fur would get snagged on branches or thorns or brambles. Poor people, poor country folk who had no animals of their own, no fields or meadows, no jobs, no prospects, would wander the fields and meadows as the sheep did, following them. They'd look for bits of wool clinging to the bushes and brambles, and they'd pluck them."

"Interesting," she said generously.

I swung the door open and held it for her; she slipped through with the easy grace of a sylph.

"If I were engaged in that occupation," I said, "I think I'd find that it was not enough to keep my mind fully engaged—like digging clams or cleaning a house—and so I can easily imagine that the mind of a wool-gatherer was inclined to wander, in much the way that, to an outside observer, the woolgatherers themselves seemed to wander, drifting from bush to bush. The observer's judgment that the woolgatherer was wandering would be unfair, of course, because in going from tuft to tuft he was purposeful, he was doing his job, was focused, attentive, and productive. If his mind wandered elsewhere while he worked, well, that mental meandering may have . . . damn!"

"'Damn'?" she said. "Damn what? The mindless work of woolgath-ering? Those who scorn woolgatherers? Sheep?"

"My own absentmindedness," I said. "I took the second sketch, but I left the first one on the table."

"Do you want to go back?"

"No. It must have been thrown out by now. Let's go."

FIRST SUPPER AT SIMPAW, PART THREE

• •

We're waist deep in the Big Muddy, and the big fool says to push on.
—Pete Seeger, "Waist Deep in the Big Muddy"

I BROUGHT MY tray to a table, behaving exactly as everyone else was behaving, but I had resolved not to eat a bite of the strange stuff that I'd been served until I saw the other simps eating it.

I set my tray down. I stretched and yawned. I took my seat. I got up again and checked the seat as if I thought there might have been something on it, perhaps something that I had felt when I sat down. There wasn't. I frowned quizzically, shrugged, and sat again. At once, I got up again and checked the seat again. I swept it with my hand, muttering, for the benefit of any simps who could read lips, "Better safe than sorry." Then I sat again. I arranged my knife, my fork, and my spoon, aligning them so that they were perpendicular to the edge of the table at which I was sitting. I inspected my work. While I was going through this difficult and subtle work of stalling, I was also, in an even subtler, entirely undetectable way, paying close attention to the behavior of the other students, scrutinizing them peripherally to see whether they were eating their meals. They were not. In memory's eye, recalling the scene now, they seem to be watching me instead.

"You're drawing attention to yourself," whispered Slim.

"Yesss," hissed Dean. "Making a scene, making a spectacle of yourself."

"Can't you just eat without all these preliminaries?" asked Button.

"Hm?" I said. "Preliminaries?"

"Checking your seat, arranging your silverware, aligning your plate to your internal compass—"

"Doesn't everybody do that?" I asked. "Back at home, in Babbington, everybody—"

"Peter, you'd really better start eating," said Nick. His voice was calm, steady, and firm. "You've already attracted the attention of every single simp in SIMPaW, and it won't be long before you attract the attention of the administration. We are observed pretty closely, and nearly constantly."

"Oh," I said. "Sure. Of course."

I looked at my tray. I picked up my fork.

Before I tell you about my first taste of the food that I faced, allow me a digression on the subject of the adolescent boy's preoccupation with saving face, not looking ridiculous, not backing down, not blinking, not looking like a fool (even though, or even when, or especially when, the adolescent boy knows that he is or has been a fool). My experience has convinced me that although this preoccupation may diminish as the adolescent boy matures, it never entirely disappears; in some men it remains as strong as ever, lingering as one of the obvious marks of extended adolescence, a neon sign of arrested development. You may see the preoccupation manifested in an unwillingness to take direction from another person, or even to be instructed or corrected by the evidence of one's own eyes and the logic of one's own mind, or, more generally, in what my longtime friend Mark Dorset, a professional student of human behavior, has called "misleadership behavior." He put it this way in *We're Not Lost—We're Just Not Out of the Woods Yet: How Fools Lead*:

> The classic failing of the fool who leads is his not being willing to admit that he has been wrong, not being willing to change his course—even though everything around him tells him that he's lost or that he is en route to disaster—because changing course would be the loudest and clearest possible admission that he is now and has been for some time on the wrong course, that he at some time made a poor choice, that he was wrong. So he wades into the Big Muddy, and when he finds himself waist deep with more than half a raging rain-swollen river ahead of him calls out, "The goal is in sight—push on!" And the classic failing of the fools who follow a fool is their continuing to follow him—even though they see that the water's rising—because turning away or turning back or deciding to follow another leader would be admitting that they chose to follow the wrong leader, that they made the

wrong choice, that they were wrong. In changing course, the leading fool would lose face; in changing their minds about following the leader, the following fools would lose face; and no little boy, not even the biggest and strongest little boy in the pack, can look his peers—or himself—in the eye after he has lost face. He'd rather die in the Big Muddy.

I transferred the fork to my right hand. I hesitated for a moment, then slid the tines of the fork into the larger of the piles of stuff on my plate. Extrapolating from my experiences with food back at home, I guessed that this was a stew of some kind. There were chunks of something in it that, because they looked like diminutive body parts, or bits of body parts, I decided to consider meat. Maybe they were pieces of a chicken that had put up a fight. Maybe, but the color was off. The meat, if it was meat, had the quality of iridescence, like the skin of a fish, or lusterware, or a gasoline slick on the surface of the estuarial stretch of the Bolotomy River, back at home, in Babbington, where somebody, maybe a friend of mine, was probably at that moment about to take a bite from a cheeseburger with fried onions and lots of ketchup. There was a sauce or gravy in this stew, but it was the color of the skin of a tangerine, opaque, and so gelatinous that it quivered. I remembered vividly the lesson I'd learned from crochety Vern, that gravy can hide a lot of sins. What sins this gravy might hide I didn't know, but the thought that it hid some sins made me shiver.

I poked at the stew. I stirred it with my fork. Surreptitiously, I glanced around. Everyone else was eating. Well, okay, then. It wasn't a joke. This really was dinner. I couldn't tell whether the simps were enjoying what they were eating or loathing it, but they were eating it. I brought a forkful of the stuff to my mouth.

"You know," I said, arresting the progress of the fork, "thinking about that click and its effect on me makes me wonder if the brain isn't something like an electrical circuit. If somebody has a pencil, I could draw you a sketch—"

"Peter," said Eugene. "Eat . . . your . . . dinner."

"Huh? Oh. Dinner. You bet."

Wearing a mask of indifference, I put the food into my mouth. I withdrew the fork, leaving the mysterious stuff inside. I began to chew. The mass in my mouth, which I still wasn't quite ready to call food, tasted like nothing I had ever eaten before. There were familiar sensations—the texture of the sauce was like that of Jell-O, the texture of the meat was like that of a peach that's gone mealy, I tasted flavors of pepper and butter, and there was an aroma of something that reminded me of wet oak—but there were other sensations that were totally unfamiliar to me—including some little spheres with a crunchy shell that burst in the mouth, releasing a heady little shot of something sweet and hot.

To my great relief, I found that I could eat this first supper at SIM-PaW. To the great relief of the Faustroll Institute, I developed an appetite for the food as I sampled it, and I was soon eating with obvious pleasure.

I enjoyed it so much that, after I had finished what was on my plate, I went back for second helpings of everything.

Carrying my tray back to the table, I noticed that a small group of students, seated apart from the others, was snickering, pointing in my direction, and pretending to gag and vomit.

"What's with the gang in the corner?" I asked when I'd taken my seat again.

"They're regular NMIMTaP students," whispered Slim. "They don't eat what we eat."

"Why?"

"Because we are being taught to make ourselves invisible," said the count in a voice as low as Slim's whisper, "and they are not."

A SIMPLE BRAIN

....

WHILE I WAS reading to Albertine, my mind was elsewhere. It had been back in Corosso, in the dining hall, but, I realized as I looked up from the pages I'd been reading, it had wandered from there to some other place, an interior nook with a comfy chair and a flickering fire, where it could explore one of its own ideas.

"Here's a remarkable thing," I said. "While I've been reading to you, my mind, or a part of my mind, has been back in Corosso, in the dining hall."

"Understandable."

"Yes, and if that were all, I wouldn't bother mentioning it, but there's more."

"There usually is."

"You see, in Corosso, in the dining hall on that first evening, once I had decided that I could eat the food, I didn't have to think about the food anymore, not much at any rate. I could let part of my mind receive the data from my senses and file them in my memory with a minimum of mediation, while another part of my mind was free to wander, which it did."

"And where did it wander?"

"To that question about the click that inspired hunger. Sitting there, almost mindlessly eating that mysterious meal, I had a tiny insight: I decided that the phenomenon of the click could not have occurred unless the memory, and the mind that has as one of its components memory, is a tangled web in which are snared some traces of all of our experiences, of whatever kind, of whatever time, from every place, mingled with the mediated data of every sense, and because I had a hobbyist's interest in electrical gadgets and a fifteen-year-old's understanding of them, I pictured that tangled web as an electrical circuit. For a moment, I was ready to blurt all of that out, to announce that insight to the Faustroll Institute and draw a diagram for them on a napkin, as I'd seen inspired geniuses do in movies."

"But modesty made you hold your tongue?"

"No. Not modesty. Fear. Something in the tangled web of my mind told me that the idea, in the form in which I was about to blurt it and sketch it, was too simple. Announcing it would make me seem simpleminded."

"Your superego said, 'Shut up.'"

"Ha-ha. If I had been so foolish as to tell them what I was thinking and draw them a sketch, it would have been the first sketch that I drew for you at breakfast—this one—where is—oh—that's the one I left behind. You remember it, though, right?"

"A battery, a switch, and a bulb."

"Right. Well, if the battery is the slow fire that keeps us alive and thinking, and the switch is the brain, and the bulb is a behavior—at the time I think I would have said an observable behavior—then we have a simple circuit in which every stimulus—every flip of the switch—produces a response. Every click produces hunger, for example."

"Simple."

"Right. Much too simple. Take a look at the second sketch."

"I'm driving."

"Just a quick look."

"Okay. Got it."

"I made a sketch like this later that night. I'll tell you about it in a minute. What I want to tell you now is that I think that before I even made the sketch I had this idea about my mind: the idea that what I seemed to know (or what I seemed to recall) must be only a representation of what was actually in my brain. My state of mind as it was displayed to the world through my words and actions had some relationship to my 'state of *brain*' as it was created within the links and synapses of neurons within my brain—the state of the circuit—but there was no way to tell from my behavior what that relationship was or even what the nature of that relationship was, and my state of *mind* as it was displayed to me in thoughts was also related to my 'state of *brain*' but there was no way to tell from my thoughts what that relationship was."

"Mm-hmm."

"There are two things that I like about this primitive, naïve schematic of mine. First, the display—the behavior—is dependent on the state of the switches—the brain—but the display does not give you an unambiguous indication of what the state of the brain is because there are two positions for the paired switches—two states of the brain—that produce the same apparent behavior. Second, to state something obvious but important, the state of the brain is subject to modification by an outside influence—the finger that flips the switch—and the external world is subject to modification by the state of the brain: it may be illuminated."

"That's pretty good for a fifteen-year-old kid."

"Aw, shucks, Miz Gaudet."

"These circuits became that game of yours, didn't they?"

"The Babbington Game. Yes. I had to call it a game, because—well—I'll get to that later, too, after I find my way to the workshop on the NMIMTaP campus and build the first working model of the thing, but now I've got to get myself out of the dining hall and into the dormitory. It's time I met my roommate."

MY ROOMMATE

THE MOVIE SHOWN at SIMPaW that night was, I think, *Fight the Red Menace*. However, it might have been *My Neighbor Is a Commie*. I'm not sure because the idea of taking notes on the events of that summer didn't occur to me until many years later, when I sat on the porch of Small's Hotel for one long summer day and wrote pages and pages about everything that I recalled. I remembered, that summer day, that several times a week we had "movie night." The movies were shown in the open air, projected against a wall of the dining hall. Technically, attendance was optional; however, it was expected. I couldn't begin to remember the titles of all of the movies that we were offered. There were some about the dangers of foreign ideas, teenage sex, strong drink, drugs, and the fluoridation of community water supplies, and there were also spy adventures. All of the movies were meant to be instructive. I suppose I should be embarrassed to have to admit that I remember the movies about sex much better than any of the others, except for a couple of the spy movies. Because of that selectivity of memory, however, I am able to say with certainty that the movie shown on my first night was neither *Louise Was Easy* nor *Liquor Made Her Do It*. Those came later.

"Damn," I muttered when the picture began.

"You've seen it?" asked Slim.

"No. I left my clothes and everything in *Spirit*'s nooks and crannies."

"Unfortunate," said the count, "but you're going to have to wait until tomorrow. We can't risk a return to the warehouse now."

"Why not?" I said. "Everyone's watching the movie. I can slip away, get my stuff, and be back here in a few minutes. Nobody will ever know."

"How stupid of me," said the count. "I forgot your telling us that when it comes to skulking you—"

When he turned in my direction to finish his sneering remark, he found that I had already slipped into the darkness, out of sight. I saw the look of surprise on his face, and I saw it replaced by something else, something that I'm going to say was grudging respect. I took off across the campus, found the warehouse, got my things, returned to the screening, and slipped back into my place. No more than a few minutes had passed. No one seemed to have noticed that I had left. It was easy.

When the movie ended, Eugene said, "The time has come for you to meet your roommate." He wore a wry grin, and the others wore grins like it. I began to wonder whether I was going to like this roommate.

"Fortunately," explained Nick, "since there are one hundred actual students at SIMPaW, three of whom are girls, there are ninety-seven boys, an odd number, which means that one male student has no roommate."

"You are that roommate," said Dean. "You are the roommate that the odd male student does not have."

"Yet," said Rocky.

"Yet," said Dean. "That's right."

"How odd is this odd male student?" I asked.

The question was answered with nervous laughter. The members of the Faustroll Institute turned toward Eugene. There seemed to be tacit agreement that only he could answer me.

"Pretty odd," he said. "He has some singular ideas, ideas that would probably disqualify him for continued attendance at SIMPaW if they became widely known. You are going to have to be very, very careful not to tell tales out of school."

"Now there's a puzzling expression," I said. "My French teacher, Angus MacPherson, back at home, in Babbington, would be interested in that one. He'd wonder why it is that—"

"My point," Eugene said sternly, "is that what your roommate tells you in the privacy of your shared room had better stay private."

We had reached the cinderblock dormitory that housed the male students. It was a new addition to the campus, erected when enrollment surpassed the capacity of the original Spanish-colonial-style dormitories that were more closely integrated with the main campus. This newcomer stood beside those, which housed the girls, but it was on the edge of things. One side of the building looked toward the heart of the campus, as if the dormitory were petitioning the authorities for full status, while the other side looked outward toward the desert, as if the dormitory were asserting with an attitude of contemporary coolness that it just might slip away some night when everyone's back was turned.

With a gesture like the tipping of an imaginary hat, the count said, "Good night, everyone," and walked off into the desert. The dormitory did not follow.

"Where's he going?" I asked.

"Who knows?" said Rocky. "He just goes off on his own like that, sometimes for hours."

"You've never asked him where he goes?"

"Never," said Eugene quickly. "We respect his privacy, just as I hope you will respect your roommate's."

Button called, "So long, guys." She and Slim and Tank drifted away, toward the Spanish-style buildings.

Eugene opened the door to our dorm, and we walked in and climbed a set of stairs past the first floor. "The regular summer-school students live on the ground floor," Rocky explained.

"See you in the observatory," said Nick as he, Dean, and Rocky parted from Eugene and me on the second floor.

"We'll be there," said Eugene. He and I continued to the third floor and walked along its corridor. When we reached a door marked 313 he opened it and said, "Here you are."

I entered. I looked around. "There's no one here," I said.

Eugene said, "As Dean would say, 'Correction! You are here. I am here. Therefore, someone is here!'"

"You mean you're—"

"I'm your roommate, the odd student with the singular ideas."

"Such as—"

"For one thing, I am convinced that there are people here, within SIMPaW, possibly students, possibly faculty, who are out to get me."

"Get you?"

"Eliminate me."

"Why?"

"Because they are afraid of me."

"Afraid of you?"

"Afraid of me and my singular ideas."

"I see—" I said tentatively.

"That's why I sleep with a gun under my pillow," he said, waving his hand in the direction of one of the beds.

In as steady a voice as I could manage, I said, "I guess this other bed is mine, then."

"That's right," he said cheerfully. "Toss your stuff somewhere and we'll go to the observatory and—oh—one more thing. Call me Dirk outside of the Faustroll Institute."

"Dirk?"

"It's my real name."

"Your real name is Dirk and you chose Eugene as your code name?"

"Sure," he said with a puzzled look. "Do you find that surprising?"

"No, Dirk," I said, in a chummy manner, which, at the time, seemed the right manner to adopt when talking to a roommate who slept with a gun under his pillow, "I don't find that surprising. Not at all."

I'M NOT SURPRISED

I WAS ENJOYING the sun and the steady roll of the Electro-Flyer along a smooth and nearly empty highway, entertaining, in a casual way, the thought that if we had stayed in Corosso and I had introduced myself to the officials in the administration at the university I might have been invited to give a talk about my experiences there, my travels, and my life; or that I might have been asked to deliver a lecture on the art of the memoir or the intimate interplay of imagination and memory; or that I might even have been offered a position on the faculty, possibly an endowed chair in 'pataphysics, when Albertine interrupted my daydream with a question.

"What are you thinking about?" she asked.

"I was—ah—well—to tell you the truth—I was thinking about—ah—the shock of the new and—ah—wondering whether I still have the capacity to be surprised—or I should say how much my capacity to be surprised has been diminished by time and experience—how many switches in my little mind are frozen in position, corroded and immobile," I claimed.

"Hmm," she said, skeptically, I thought.

"No, really," I said, warming to the topic. "You see, when I told Dirk that I wasn't surprised that he'd chosen Eugene as his code name for the Faustroll Institute, I was lying. I actually was surprised by that, but—"

"But not as surprised as you were when he told you that he slept with a revolver under his pillow, I'll bet."

"You're right," I said, "but I *wasn't* surprised when—as soon as I had our shared room to myself for enough time to feel safe in doing so—I lifted a corner of his pillow to see whether there really was a revolver lying there. By then I had an expectation. I had formed an opinion about the truth of his claim. I wish I could dignify it by saying that I had 'come to a logical conclusion' about the truth of his claim, but I hadn't. All I had was something like an educated hunch, but it counts as an expectation. When I lifted the pillow and saw what I saw, I was relieved, because my expectation was rewarded. I was relieved in a way similar to the way my father was relieved when he first tasted my mother's Mexicali Macaroni."

"Well, I wasn't expecting that," she said. "Explain yourself."

"During my early adolescence, when my mother began to try to stretch the limits of her life, she underwent occasional enthusiasms that made her want to try cooking 'something new,' but the new things she tried were much like the things she had always cooked, even if they had exotic names or cosmopolitan pretensions. She subscribed to a magazine called *Astounding Homemaker*, which offered recipes in every issue. 'Surprise your family with something new,' the magazine told her, and she tried to comply, cooking each of the dishes exactly as instructed, working with intense concentration, and serving them to my father and me. Some of the recipes had international or exotic themes and the articles about them were illustrated with obvious emblems of foreign lands, like the Eiffel Tower or the Taj Mahal, and inviting titles, like 'A Night in Tunisia' or 'Riding the Orient Express,' but the dishes that resulted from the recipes were more familiar than exotic. I think I remember Meatloaf à la Française, Cube Steak Tibetan Style, Moroccan Tuna Noodle Casserole, Indian Ham Salad with Curried Mustard Sauce, Hawaiian Barbecued Chicken—you get the idea. They might have had a touch of an unusual herb or spice, or some other unexpected ingredient, but it was only a touch, enough to make the dish 'different' even though it was basically 'the same old thing.' The dishes possessed what Rosetta Glynn—Margot and Martha's mother—called 'the shock of the new cushioned by the familiar.' Looking back, in memory taking my seat at the family table, I can see my father experiencing exactly that. He looks at the Mexicali Macaroni on his plate, and on his face I see the effect of the shock of the new. Then he takes his first bite and discovers that it's nothing more than macaroni and cheese with the colorful addition of bits of sweet red pepper. He had been shocked by the novelty of the dish's appearance, but now, remembering that the unsettling names and mysterious appearance of the other surprising dishes were little more than fancy wrappers for meatloaf, cube steak, tuna noodle casserole, ham salad, and barbecued chicken, he realizes that somewhere, in some part of his mind, he had actually come to expect that Mexicali Macaroni would be as easy to eat, and to digest, as the other dishes had been, because that part of his mind had been at work gathering those dishes into the peculiar universe of foods that deliver the shock of the new cushioned by the familiar."

She let a moment pass, and then she said, "So?"

"So, I think that some part of us is always relieved when our expectations are satisfied, whatever those expectations might be."

"So?" she said again.

"So what?"

"*So what did you find under his pillow?*"

"Oh. What he said was there: a revolver, a pistol, a six-gun. It wasn't new, and its finish was dull, but it looked as if it would work, as if it would do what it was asked to do."

MY INITIAL OBSERVATIONS

LED BY EUGENE, I made my first visit to the observatory. What I saw there was to dominate my impressions of that first whirlwind week at SIMPaW. It left an afterimage in my mind's eye that overlay, blurred, and distorted every other image that I recorded that week—and it still does.

The observatory was a room on the second floor of the dormitory. When we reached the door to the room, Eugene paused and said in a whisper, "This room is shared by Earl and Lester, two students in SIMPaW who are not in the Faustroll Institute."

"Uh-huh," I said.

"You will remember not to use any Faustroll code names, right?"

"Of course, Dirk," I said.

He started to turn the knob, then paused again.

"And you will remember not to register surprise, right?"

"Dirk," I said, "my threshold of surprise is so elevated now that it would take—well—I don't know—something really astonishing—something amazing—to surprise me."

"Mm," he said, with a frown and a shake of his head.

He opened the door.

The room was darkened to the point of blackness, but even in the dark I could tell that it was crowded with students. They were still, and they were quiet. No one said a word. No one shuffled or squirmed. As my eyes adjusted to the darkness, I began to recognize some of the students, including the male members of the Faustroll Institute, with the exception of the count, who was, I supposed, still wandering in the desert. I also saw that the boys in the room were equipped with an astonishing array of optical imaging devices, from spyglasses and binoculars to telescopes to box cameras and brownies and even a couple of cameras with telephoto lenses. I had a head full of questions, but when I glanced at Eugene and raised an interrogative eyebrow he narrowed his eyes in a way that reminded me of his claim that he kept a gun under his pillow—a claim that at that time I hadn't yet verified, but a claim that I was inclined to believe. I kept my questions to myself. I assumed an attitude indistinguishable from the attitude of every other boy in the room: I faced the windows in silence, and I waited. Everyone in the room waited like that, but their waiting was not completely static. There was a stiffening to it, as if they knew how much longer they had to wait, and as the expected wait grew shorter they grew taller, straightening and tensing themselves, standing still, erect, and ready.

Then it happened.

It happened so quickly that I wasn't really certain that I had seen it at all. I wasn't prepared for it, as the others were. I remember, as I said, the afterimage, not the event itself.

What had happened was this: A window in the girls' dormitory, a dozen yards or so away, had suddenly been illuminated. The illumination occasioned a collective gasp. There, standing at the window, was a girl, naked and beautiful. She blew a kiss in our direction and then immediately switched the light off. The return of darkness occasioned a collective sigh.

The observers stood without moving. Looking to my right and left, I saw that they had their eyes closed. I mimicked them, and I immediately realized why they had their eyes closed. They were savoring her afterimage, willing it to linger longer, watching it fluoresce, and sighing as it slowly faded. After a while, still without a word, they began to disperse. Eugene and I left, too. We went to our room. We undressed in darkness and got into our beds in silence.

I still had a wisp of her image in my aftersight, but I had a better image in my mind's eye. I thought I knew her. She was a dark-haired girl, and I thought she might even be "my" dark-haired girl. I was wrong, but at the time I wished that it might be so.

The next morning, just as I was about to experience my first SIMPaW math class, I hesitated at the door, worried—make that afraid—that when I walked into the room there would be something anomalous about the sound of my shuffling feet among the shuffling feet of all the other students that would make the instructor stop writing the day's equations on the board, prick up his ears, ask himself what or who might be causing the anomaly, turn suddenly, fix me with a gimlet eye, and ask, "Who the hell are you?" I had that fear because I couldn't believe that the teachers could have overlooked me, even if I had been represented by nothing more than an unremarkable set of homework papers and quizzes. Surely the instructor would have been curious about the student who didn't stand out.

Apparently not. I filed in with everyone else, took a seat at the back of the room, and disappeared. The class began, and I began the work of remaining invisible.

I found to my surprise that it was very hard to do mediocre work in math. That first class began with a quiz. Of course, everyone else in the class was eleven days ahead of me, so the quiz was especially hard for me. I remember the quiz vividly. That is, I remember the experience of taking the quiz vividly. Of the quiz itself, I remember only the first problem.

> Solve each of the following differential equations and deter-
> mine the constant of integration when initial conditions are
> given:

> 1. $2\frac{dy}{dx} - \frac{y}{x} = 5x^3y^3$

It was so far beyond what I'd done in math during my junior year at Babbington High that I only managed to answer that first problem. Even then, I didn't get it right. I realized, as I reluctantly surrendered my paper to the student who came down the aisle to collect it, that I was going to have a tough time working my way up to mediocrity.

Invisibility, however, was much easier. All I had to do was slide a little lower in my seat and let my mind wander, and I was a genius at that. I was attentive for the first part of the class, and then I drifted off. You won't be surprised, I think, to find that my drifting mind returned to the dark-haired girl I'd seen for an instant the night before. Who was she? For whom had she been performing?

"Mr. Leroy?"

"Huh?"

"Woolgathering again, Mr. Leroy?"

"I—ah—could you repeat the question?"

"Very funny, Mr. Leroy. Mr. Kells, will you kindly come to the board and solve the equation?"

I slipped a little lower into my seat and told myself, with some sadness, that the girl couldn't possibly have been performing for me, because her nightly performance had begun before I had arrived.

Paleontology, as Matthew had said, was a course that had no textbook. It had no classroom, either. Metaphorically speaking, the desert was its classroom. The course was taught in "platoons" of twenty students divided into "squads" consisting of as many students as would fit in the back of a Jeep. That was four. The paleontology department had a fleet of five Jeeps, so five squads of four participated in each class. I was blithely walking toward the Jeep that Button was in when something made her turn in my direction. When she saw me approaching, her eyes widened. She gave me a piercing look and waved me off. One of the three boys seated in the back of the Jeep with her noticed the gesture and also turned in my direction. It was Dean. His eyes widened as Button's had. Like her, he gave me a piercing look and waved me off. Why? I wasn't sure, but I felt that they had my best interests at heart, so I changed my course and trotted up the stairs of the first building I came to, took a place in the concealing shade of its entry, and watched the five Jeeps drive away. Why hadn't Button and Dean wanted me to join them? After a moment's thought, I was able to say to myself, "Ahhh. Of course. In a squad of four simps a fifth would be as obvious as a fifth wheel on the Jeep. The other two would begin asking themselves why they hadn't noticed me before."

I couldn't join the squad, but I might be able to find out what the young paleontologists did during class. The Jeeps raised a wake of dust that made them easy to follow. I set off after them at a lope, not because I expected to catch them or keep up with them, but because I was curious about where they were headed and because I had nothing else to do. They didn't go very far. Just a short way down the road they swung into the desert. Skulking expertly, I found an elevated vantage point in the shade of an overhanging ledge of rock, and there I spent an hour observing their baffling behavior.

A DREAM SEQUENCE

· ·

I APOLOGIZE FOR this chapter. I try not to include my dreams in my memoirs because I find it impossible to reproduce my dreams in the way in which I experienced them. I impose upon them a narrative, temporal, and logical integrity that they did not have in the dreaming of them. I revise them, rewrite them, clarify them, polish and edit them. I can't help myself.

In my dream, Albertine and I were riding in the Electro-Flyer across a featureless landscape, and I was reading to her. (Do all my nightmares begin with the ordinary, the usual, the expected? Maybe. I never take notes, so I can't say. Is it always the arrival of the unexpected that turns a dream into a nightmare? Is every nightmare a surprise? I guess so. Is every surprise a potential nightmare? Stay tuned.)

I faltered in my reading. I looked at the page, but the marks on it didn't seem to be letters any longer. The contemplative detachment of a dream allowed me to understand that the fault was in me, not in what I had written. I had been distracted to such a great degree that I couldn't read. I had been surprised by an unexpected and unwelcome sound. I had heard, I was sure I had heard, behind us, far behind us, but approaching, gaining on us, the fluttering, chattering sound of helicopters.

"And then?" said Albertine after a moment.

"Huh?" I said, flabbergasted and flustered.

"What happens next?"

"Can't you go any faster than this?"

"I could, but it wouldn't do any good."

"Why?"

"I'd still have to stop at that roadblock up ahead."

"It's my second roadblock ever," I said. "Your first, I think."

"As far as you know," she said coquettishly.

She slowed and stopped, and at first it seemed that we would be delayed for only a few minutes, but then the helicopters caught up to us.

"Oh, shit," I think I said.

"Damn!" she said. "It's not those stupid, swaggering flyguys, is it? I hoped I'd never see them again."

My heart leapt up. That was exactly what I had hoped to hear.

"My darling," I said, "I—kaff—kuff—koff—kack—"

"Peter?" she said with tender concern.

"Dust," I gasped.

The helicopters settled onto the shoulders of the highway, kicking up great clouds of Oklahoma dust and shaking the Electro-Flyer. There were many, many helicopters, far more than I had expected when I'd heard them approaching. Men scrambled out of the choppers and ran toward us in the crouched posture that people assume when helicopter blades are whirling over their heads. They were not flyguys, not daring airborne EMTs. They were dressed in black, and they were armed. Their weapons were drawn, and they were aimed at us.

"Get out of the vehicle with your hands in sight!" shouted the nearest one.

"What—" I started to ask.

"Out! Now!" bellowed another, brandishing his weapon.

We exchanged a look, and I think that I winked at Albertine to tell her that I understood that this was only a dream, but in the spirit of going along with the gag we got out of the Electro-Flyer very slowly, with our hands in sight.

The nearest of the men in black held something white in his hand. He thrust it toward me. It was a paper napkin.

"Did you or did you not leave this napkin behind at the Seaview Grill in Seaview, Texas, at or about ten hundred hours this morning?" he shouted.

"Oh!" I said, surprised and relieved. "Yes! I did. Wow. Thanks. You didn't have to go to all this trouble—"

"On the ground! Face down! Extend your extremities!"

We did as we were told. When I was fully extended, he squatted beside me and thrust the napkin up to my eyes.

"Is this or is this not a plan for an explosive device?" he shouted.

"An explosive device? You mean a bomb? No! No, no. It's just a simple sketch of a simple mind. Let me explain—"

"Do you think we're stupid?"

"No. Certainly not. I just thought that an explanation—"

"These lines radiating from the explosive charge—are they or are they not a conventional means of rendering an explosion in a cartoon or other simple drawing?"

"Well—"

"Well?"

"Well, maybe, now that I think about it, but in this case they are a conventional way of rendering light rays—rays of light—waves of light—streams of photons—"

"Did you or did you not include detailed instructions, with a cut-away diagram, for building a 'flour bomb' in the volume of your memoirs entitled *How Do You Stop?*"

"*Where*," I said.

"On pages sixty-one and sixty-two," he said.

"I mean *Where Do You Stop?*" I said. "It's not *How Do You Stop?* It's *Where Do You Stop?*"

"So you admit it!"

"I did? I do?"

"Seize them!"

When I heard that command, I twisted to see what was happening, and I saw that four of the men were bending over Albertine, ready to lift her from the ground. With the heightened perception and uncanny insight granted to us in dreams, I recognized something in their posture that betrayed an eagerness to lay hands on her, and I said to myself, "These are not legitimate agents of a paternalistic government acting out of a sincere conviction that they are doing their best to protect my fellow citizens from me, a deadly flour-bomber; they are the fiendish flyguys in disguise, their number swollen by other EMTs recruited during downtime at the fly-in, probably in some dive where they were swilling beer with swagger."

I leapt to my feet. I reached into my shirt and pulled out Eugene's antiquated six-shooter. The men nearest me fell back in terror. "Ah-ha!" I said to myself. "I was right! There is no fight in these phonies!"

I dashed to Albertine. The four who held her would not let her go, not even when I pointed out that I was brandishing a real revolver that, despite its age and lack of luster, was probably in working order. Their obstinacy told me that they were the four flyguys I feared, not barroom recruits with no taste for a fight. Even as I threatened them with the pistol, however, I knew that it was useless. They were holding Albertine, and even in dreams I'm not much of a shot. I couldn't risk hitting her. With a bloodcurdling scream, I flung the useless weapon aside as I'd seen so many actors do in so many movies, and I hurled myself at them. I had the advantage of surprise, and I fought with the fury of several wildcats. I dragged Albertine from them and pushed her into the Electro-Flyer.

I braced myself in the open door and shouted, "Let's go, kid! Get us out of here!"

The car began to move, but the flyguys had regrouped, and they were coming at me. I grabbed the door frame, drew my legs up, and with a mighty thrust—

"Peter!" shouted Albertine. "You're kicking me!"

"Hummh?"

"You're kicking me! One more mighty thrust like that and I'll be on the floor!"

"Oh. I—uh—sorry—I—"

"You were having a nightmare."

"Yes," I said, "I was."

"Do you want to tell me about it?"

"Yes and no. No, I guess. You know how it is. I find it impossible to reproduce my dreams in the way in which I experienced them. I impose upon them a narrative, temporal, and logical integrity that they did not have in the dreaming of them. I—"

"Good night, Peter."

"Good night."

BIVALVES IN THE DESERT

••

I have come to surmise that in olden times the sea spread over all the
land. . . . It is not possible that people should have made such mountains
of shells by carrying them from the sea so far a distance merely to bury
them in piles.

—Father Pedro Font, *Diary of an Expedition to Monterey by Way of the
Colorado River, 1775–1776*

I **KNEW FROM** Matthew's explanation that at SIMPaW paleontology
was a synonym for spying, so I knew the answer to a question that I had
decided to ask Button, but I was determined to ask it anyway, even if asking might make me seem a little stupid, because it was a way of initiating
a conversation with her, and I liked the way she looked. She had returned
from the desert, and she was walking across the campus to her next class.

I caught up to her and asked, "What were you up to out there in the
desert?"

"Oh!" she said with a start. "It's you! You frightened me!"

"Sorry," I said. "I didn't mean to frighten you. I just wondered what
it was all about—all that sneaking and hiding, putting messages under
rocks, tracking one another—"

"How do you know about that?" she asked.

"I did a little tracking of my own," I said, trying very hard not to
brag. "I followed the Jeeps into the desert, and I—observed you."

"I'm not sure that I believe you."

I described everything I had seen, including all the detail that I
could recall. I could tell that she was impressed, but I could also tell that
she was not quite convinced.

"You're not convinced," I said.

"Not quite."

"Suppose I told you that you were the only one in the platoon who
wasn't found."

"Someone else might have told you that."

"Suppose I told you that you're wearing yellow underwear—yellow
panties at least."

She gave me such an astonished look that for a moment I thought she was going to slap me, but instead she asked, "How do you know that?"

"I saw you—um—" I let the sentence hang there, between us, incomplete, because it was a time in the progress of our culture, Reader, when frankness on the subject of the body and its functions was not so much in favor as it is now, and I thought that telling her what I had seen her do would embarrass us both.

"Um what?" she challenged me.

"I saw you pee," I said, since I'd been challenged.

Then she gave me the slap that I thought I'd seen coming earlier, but it was a light, playful tap, and it came with a giggle.

"From what angle?" she demanded.

"You were almost in profile; I was looking at your right side."

"Hmm. I know where you were then. You were under that ledge, hidden in its shadow."

"You're right," I said.

She linked her arm with mine and drew me to her as we walked.

"You can skulk," she said.

"So can you," I said. I didn't bother telling her how much I had enjoyed the sight of her golden skin; I assumed that she could tell that from the admiring tone in my voice.

Her plaintext name was Andrea, and despite the fact that I will be getting ahead of my story to do so I will tell you that for the rest of the summer she and I played a game much like the game that all the students in the paleontology platoon played, but on another level and with different rewards and punishments. Basically, the game was hide-and-seek. In the SIMPaW version, students tracked one another in the desert. Those who played the hunted left the day's base with documents that they had to hide in places of their choosing, hiding places that would conceal the document well enough so that the hunters couldn't find it but that could be pinpointed for a confederate who wanted to retrieve it at another time. Then they had to hide themselves, or, if they thought they could manage it, make their way back to the base undetected. The hunters, of course, had to find the hidden documents and the hidden students or catch them when they tried to return to the base. The rewards for success were good grades, the praise of the instructors, the admiration of the other students, and self-esteem; the punishments were bad grades, the criticism of the instructors, the ridicule of the other students, and self-doubt. In the version of the game that Button and I played, I had to accomplish everything that the other students did, but I could not reveal my success to the instructors and the other students. I had to remain entirely undetected. The rewards in our game were for me tactile, sensual, and sexual: a touch, a caress, a kiss, an embrace, a lick, a squeeze. There were no punishments beyond an occasional slap and tickle. We would track each other, trading the roles of hunter and hunted on alternating days, find each other, and fall upon each other, claiming a slightly better reward each time, greater access to each other, greater favors, greater pleasures. We were very good at what we did. We were so grand at the game that we were never discovered in flagrante, never surprised by the other spies.

On the very first day that we played our game, during the time while I was waiting for Button to discover me, I made a discovery of my own. Idly poking at the sand and bits of rock where I lay in hiding, I saw what looked like the shells of scallops, oysters, and clams. They were, I saw when I looked more closely at them, the impressions of those shells in the rock that held them. They were fossils. They were not the first fossils I had seen, thanks to a school trip to the Museum of Natural History, but they were the first fossils I had found, and they became the first fossils that I owned.

"Look at these," I said, holding them out to Button when she found me, as if I were offering her a reward.

"Shells?" she asked.

"Fossils. Bivalve fossils."

"Interesting."

"From these I surmise that this desert was once the bottom of the sea."

"Really?"

"Sure," I said, confident in my own deduction. "How else would they get here? I'm pretty certain that nobody brought them in by the truck-load."

Among the many things that I ought to thank Andrea for is her saving me from falling in love with an immaterial ideal rather than a real girl.

By the time that she and I began to play our game, I was already falling in love with the dark-haired girl—but the dark-haired girl that I was falling in love with was not a girl at all. She was not the one in the window that I'd seen from the observatory, and she was not any of the ones that I'd met or seen or thought I'd seen on my trip from Bab-bington to Corosso. She was a creature of my imagination, my dark-haired Galatea, sculpted from a memory of a dark-haired girl I'd seen sunning herself on the foredeck of a lean blue sloop when I was only eight, from a few badly drawn sketches that I had seen when I worked as a sketch doctor for Andy Glynn, and from all the beautiful bits of all the dark-haired girls I'd seen and wanted since I had begun to no-tice dark-haired girls who reminded me of the girl on the sloop and in the sketches.

Touching, caressing, kissing, licking, and squeezing Andrea—a real girl, a tangible girl—taught me that what I wanted to find when I got back home was not "a dark-haired girl" but the one dark-haired girl who had made me notice—or imagine—all the others.

A BOWL OF GOO

"SPEAKING OF PEE," said Albertine, "the signs tell me that the next service area is just seconds away."

"I'm okay," I said.

"I'm sorry to have to say this," she said gravely, "but the truth is that your needs never even occurred to me."

"Ha-ha," I said, in case she might have been joking.

She stuck her tongue out at me and swung off the highway.

·········

I was in and out of the men's room in a couple of minutes, but as I was leaving I saw that the slow march toward the women's room had hardly progressed, and Albertine was still a long way from the door. She made a face, and I made a circular motion with my index finger to indicate that I would browse while she was doing what can only be done by one.

True to my signed word, I wandered around the food court, examining the snacks and souvenirs.

While I was considering the premature purchase of a T-shirt that boasted I SURVIVED THE INTERSTATE HIGHWAY SYSTEM, a voice from behind me said, "Excuse me, sir—do you like pizza?"

I turned and found an eager man leaning slightly toward me and waiting for my answer. I suspected a trick question. "Well—" I said with a shrug, as if just then I couldn't be sure whether I liked pizza or not.

"Of course you do!" he said. "Everybody likes pizza, right?"

"Probably not," I said. "I wouldn't be surprised to learn that some cultures spurn pizza, condemn it even, and punish pizza-eaters by stoning."

"Okay," he said, "I'll grant you that possibility—but most people like pizza, don't they? You like pizza, don't you? Go on, admit it. You do."

"Okay," I said. "You found me out. I like pizza."

"Well tell me this, Mister Pizza-Lover, when you get a pizza, what part of it is most likely to disappoint you?"

"What part of it? You mean what part of the whole experience of getting a pizza? I'd say paying for it. I no longer seem to know what anything ought to cost. This is an area of life where my expectations are always low and reality always exceeds my expectations by a surprising amount."

"I'm not asking about the whole experience. I'm just asking about the pizza. What part of the pizza is most likely to disappoint you? Is it the sauce, the cheese, the toppings, or the crust?"

"Oh," I said. A sinking feeling came over me with the memory of many disappointments at first bite. I sighed and said, "It's the crust."

"There you go!" he said, beaming. "It's the crust! The crust is a pizza's weakest link." He leaned a little closer and dropped his voice in a confidential manner. "If you could eliminate the crust," he told me, "you could radically increase per capita pizza satisfaction."

He allowed me a moment to reflect on the truth of that.

After reflection, I said, "I'm not sure that you would be increasing pizza satisfaction because, technically speaking, I think you have to have a crust to have a pizza. Not only is the crust part of what one eats when one eats 'pizza,' but the crust is what gives a pizza its form—in much the same way as a string gives form to a necklace. You may recall what Flaubert said—in a letter to Louise Colet, I think—about the importance of the string in transforming a bunch of pearls into a necklace."

"I—"

"He said, '*Les perles ne font pas collier; c'est le fil.*'"

"Interesting."

"So if it's the string that makes a necklace, not the pearls, then it's the crust that makes a pizza. Without a string, you don't have a necklace. All you've got is a handful of pearls. Without a crust, you don't have a pizza. All you've got is, well, a bowl of goo."

"Voilà!" he said with great verve, offering me a little plastic bowl with a tiny plastic spoon. I looked into the bowl.

"What's this?" I asked.

"It's a Bowl o' Goo," he said brightly. "Actually, to give it its full name, it's a teensy weensy sample of Big Bad Bob's Big Bad Bowl o' Goo."

"Peter?" said Albertine, materializing at my side and putting a hand on my arm in the way she does when she fears that I might be "getting stuck in something sticky."

"Free food," I said by way of excusing my having gotten stuck in something sticky, some of which was stuck to the roof of my mouth. "Pizza without the crust. Quite an innovation."

She looked into the bowl.

"Forgive me for saying this," she said gently, "but it looks like a slop bucket after an evisceration."

"Please!" I said as she led me away. "I'm eating this slop."

As she pulled back into the stream of interstate traffic, I licked my lips and resumed reading to her.

SOMETHING FURTIVE

....

WHEN WE BEGAN to head for the observatory after dinner the next evening, the count said, "Well, I'm off!" He gave us a jaunty salute and left the dormitory, headed for the desert.

"Doesn't he ever visit the observatory?" I asked when the door had closed behind him.

"He came the first couple of times," said Nick.

"But then in that world-weary way of his he declared that the experience promised nothing new for him," said Matthew.

" 'My own thoughts, on the other hand,' " said Dean, imitating the count, " 'offer me novelties at every turn, which is why I prefer my solitary stroll.' "

"You know," I said suddenly, "I think I'm going to skip the observatory tonight myself."

"Going to take a solitary stroll?" asked Nick.

"No," I said. "I'm going to do some work. I feel uneasy because I'm so far behind. There's so much I don't know. It feels as if I don't even know what I don't know. Know what I mean?"

"Suit yourself," said Eugene.

I turned back toward my room, but at the top of the stairs I waited long enough to allow the others to reach the observatory, then crept back downstairs, slipped out of the dormitory, and headed toward the desert. I had meant what I'd said. I did intend to do some work, and I did hope to come to know something that I didn't know: I intended to find out where the count went on his solitary strolls and what he did in the desert after dark.

I failed. I didn't learn what I wanted to know. I skulked my way back to my room and sat at my desk in an attitude of study. Eugene returned a few minutes later and sat at his desk in a similar attitude of study.

He let a moment pass and then asked, "What did you find out?"

"About differential equations?" I asked innocently.

478 • PETER LEROY

"No," he said, "about where the count goes when he takes his solitary strolls."

"What makes you think—"

"It was pretty obvious, Peter. Tell me."

"Well," I said, reminding myself that he was the one with the gun, "I wasn't sure that I'd be able to follow him, because he had a pretty good start on me, but I sprinted in the direction that he had taken, hoping that I could get near enough to catch sight of him, and I was lucky."

"Am I going to have to listen to the whole story?"

"Only the important parts."

"Okay."

"I saw him ahead, already a small figure some distance away. He seemed to be doing just what he says he likes to do, taking a solitary stroll, just wandering with no particular aim other than exploring his own thoughts. He even seemed as if he might be talking to himself. I followed, taking care to keep low and looking for cover as I went, taking note of any little hiding place that I might drop into if he turned to see whether anybody was following him—and you know what?"

"What?"

"He never did."

"He never did what?"

"Turn to see whether he was being followed. I thought that was furtive."

"Furtive? Why?"

"Think about it," I said. "If he had gone out there into the desert for a solitary stroll, if he really wanted to be alone with his thoughts, wouldn't he check now and then to see that he had his solitude, that he and his thoughts were actually alone? When I put myself in the place of a solitary stroller who wants to be alone with his thoughts, I find myself looking over my shoulder now and then, but the count never gave a backward glance. I asked myself why, and I decided that it was because he had some other purpose, something furtive."

"That doesn't seem—"

"So I asked myself, if that were the case, would he know enough about the art of skulking to avoid turning to see whether he was being followed so that he would not appear to be concerned about being followed?"

"Yes!" said Eugene. "He would. The paleontology instructors taught us not to turn around to check for a tail in the first week of SIMPaW, before you were here."

"And I learned the technique from the Adventures of Larry Peters, a series of books for boys that I read avidly years go," I said. "Hiding there in the desert, observing the count's clever behavior, I was pleasantly reminded of the time when I read those books, and suddenly my mission was threatened by a wave of nostalgia."

"What?"

"Thoughts of the Adventures of Larry Peters had tugged my mind back to Babbington, back home, to my room, where the Larry Peters books are lined up on a shelf in the bookcase I have that swings aside to disclose a hidden storage space."

"Do I have to hear this?"

"The desert might as well have disappeared. All I seemed to see was my room, my own little space, cozy and quiet in the gathering dusk. If I went to the window, I could look out and see the front walk where I had learned to ride a bicycle, and—suddenly something brought me to my senses."

"You're sure about that?"

"I'm sure that something made me realize that I was in the desert, in Corosso, and not in my room, in Babbington, and I'm also sure that what brought me to my senses was the sound of the count walking past me in the dark. He had passed me without seeing me and he was on his way back to the campus—but he wasn't strolling now. He was striding."

"Striding."

"Yes. He was finished. He had done whatever he had gone into the desert to do. I could see it in his stride."

"And what do you think he had gone into the desert to do?"

"Something furtive. I'm sure of that."

"Well, I'm not, and—"

"Let me say just one more thing, okay?"

"Okay."

"When my mind was back in Babbington, back in my room, I realized that I know how to get some good pictures of the dark-haired girl."

"The dark-haired girl?"

"The girl that everybody waits for in the observatory."

"Oh. The girl in the window. That's what we call her. Her name is Jane Blaine, if you can believe it."

"I can't."

"Neither can I. Neither can anybody else. That's why we call her the girl in the window. You realize that we've tried to photograph her, don't you? It's tricky. A matter of timing. She leaves the light on for such a short time, and it's never exactly the same time. Nobody's managed to get a picture that's any good."

"I think I can."

"Why?"

"Well, when I was mentally back there at home, in my room, when I was looking at the row of books in the Larry Peters series, on the bottom shelf I noticed the electric eye that I built from a kit. If we could rig that up to a solenoid that tripped a camera's shutter when her light went on, I think we could get a good shot every time."

"You know what I think?"

"What?"

"I think that was a profitable stroll in the desert."

LINKS FORGED FROM THE DAY'S DUST

· ·

AT THE FRONT desk in the motel where we were going to stay for the night, there was a rack of candy bars. I chose two and paid the desk clerk, who gave me less change than I had expected.

"I have a question," I said to him.

"The prices are set at corporate headquarters," he said. "It's a high markup because you're pretty much a captive audience."

"That wasn't my question," I said.

"Mm?"

"Suppose I wanted to sit here in the lobby and do a little work, using my laptop computer. Would that be okay?"

"Sure, as long as you're not bothering the other guests."

"Oh, no, no. I wouldn't bother anybody. You'd hardly know I was here."

"That would be good."

"It's okay, then? Thanks. I—hmmm—I wonder—would it be okay if I plug the computer in while I work? I think my battery's a little low."

"No problem."

"Hey, that's great. Thanks."

"We aim to please."

"How about if I use an extension cord and run it out into the parking lot?"

"You're going to work in the parking lot?"

"I was thinking that I could sit in my car. That way there wouldn't be any chance of my disturbing any of the other guests."

"We don't give out extension cords—"

"I've got one. I always bring one—in case I need to work in a quiet spot—away from the other guests."

"Good for you."

"Maybe I'll charge my electric shaver while I've got the cord plugged in."

"Sure."

"And my cell phone."

"Look, I'm kind of busy here."

"Oh, hey, sorry. I'll get out of your hair. Thanks a lot. Say—maybe I'll charge the batteries in my electric car—"

"Please—just go ahead and charge whatever you want, okay?"

"Ha-ha. Thanks again. Sorry to be a bother."

"The desk clerk said I could run my extension cord out of the lobby and charge the car," I said to Albertine when I returned to our room.

"That's an enlightened attitude."

"I thought so."

"What did you get?"

"A couple of those new Double Dark bars, the ones that help lower your blood pressure."

"With macadamia nuts?"

"Of course," I said, handing one of the bars to her.

"Mmmm, thanks. Did you get a receipt?"

"I—well—it's only two candy bars. Couldn't you just write it down?"

"Peter," she said, beseechingly, adding the pout that melts my heart.

"I brought my extension cord," I said brightly as I sauntered back into the lobby.

"Exciting," said the clerk.

"By the way—I—I hate to bother you—I know it seems trivial—but could you give me a receipt for those candy bars I bought?"

"A receipt?"

"Mm."

"That's kind of a lot of trouble," he said. "If you'd asked for one when you bought the candy, that would've been one thing, but now, so long after the fact—"

"Please," I said. "It's—"

"It's for me," said Albertine, who had crept up behind me and linked her arm with mine. "It's a caprice of mine—saving receipts. I keep them in albums—the way other people keep photographs. They are mementoes, tokens of the fleeting moments of my life."

"Yeah?" said the clerk.

"When I take down one of the albums and turn its pages," she said, "the little transactions that to some people might seem like chaff, the trivial minutiae that deaden life with their quotidian banality, return to me with great poignancy and immediacy."

"Gosh."

"Someday, some distant day, I would like to hold in my lap an album that includes the receipt for the two Double Dark bars that Peter bought from you, and recall this evening, this trip, this place . . . and you."

The clerk blinked a couple of times and swallowed hard. He began working the cash register.

"That is really wonderful," he said, producing a receipt with a smile. "It's as if you sift through life's daily dust and find tiny nuggets that you turn into links in a golden chain, like a necklace."

"Something like that," claimed Al.

· · · · · · · · ·

"Did you put him up to that necklace business?" she asked when I returned from running the extension cord to the parking lot and plugging the Electro-Flyer into it.

"No. I didn't. Honest."

"Come here and put a link in my chain," she said.

I obeyed, and afterward, while she snuggled against me, I read her to sleep.

INPUT, PROCESSING, AND OUTPUT

....

I do not rush into actual work. When I get an idea I start at once building it up in my imagination. I change the construction, make improvements, and operate the device in my mind. . . . I even note if it is out of balance.

—Nikola Tesla, *My Inventions*

'Pataphysics is the science of imaginary solutions.

—Alfred Jarry, *Gestes et Opinions du Docteur Faustroll*

THE WORKSHOP ON the NMIMTaP campus was so imposing, so far beyond anything that I might have expected, that I almost turned away without entering it. A sign on the door, in gold leaf on the frosted glass, read:

ENGINEERING WORKSHOP
(WHERE CONCEPTIONS BECOME CONTRAPTIONS)

When I think now about the consequences of turning away, how much I would have missed if I hadn't entered, I can hardly believe that I didn't rush in at once and get right to work—but at the time I was intimidated by the place. I stepped forward and looked into the room. I had never seen a workshop so well equipped. The space was bright and clean and neat. The tools and machines were sophisticated and power-ful. The students at work seemed purposeful and competent.

Nick strode into the workshop with the self-assurance of someone whose contraptions usually ran just as he had imagined they would, but I stood at the threshold with the hesitation of one whose contraptions usually ran amok if they ran at all.

"What do you think?" asked Nick.

"This is amazing," I said. "You could—you could make anything here."

"Just about."

"You're sure we're allowed to be here?" I asked. "You're sure we can use all of this stuff?"

"Yeah. It's okay. Every NMIMTaP student uses it during the year, and we're allowed full access to it for the summer. Come on in."

I didn't move.

"Well?" he said. He laughed a little uncertainly. Then he said, "Are you going to stand there gaping, or are you going to get to work?"

"I—I'm not sure—"

"Not sure about what?"

"I'm not sure that I can make what I have in mind."

"The electric eye?"

"No. Not that. That was easy."

"What then? What do you have in mind?"

"I have in mind something like a brain," I said, tentatively. I waited a moment, watching his face for signs of anything that I might have to consider mockery. I didn't see anything like that. I saw curiosity, and I found that encouraging. "It's an idea about switches connected to one another," I said. The truth was that the idea had grown so much as I'd thought about it that it was now an idea about very, very many switches connected to one another, and it was more than enough to give me a headache. I yearned to turn some small part of it into some-thing real so that I could stop thinking about that one part of it, at least. I wouldn't have put it this way then—wouldn't have known that I might put it this way—but I wanted to turn some part of my model of a brain into a module, a unit of a larger whole, the internal working of which would no longer have to occupy me as much as it had over the last few days.

"Well, you'll find all the switches you could possibly need here," Nick said.

He pointed in the direction of a large metal cabinet, and I began drifting that way.

"Hey," he said. "What about the electric eye?"

"What about it?" I asked, already dreaming of switches.

"Aren't we going to build it and connect it to a solenoid so that it will trip a camera shutter and get a picture of the girl in the window? You told Eugene that you built one back at home—in Barrington."

"Babbington."

"Okay, Babbington. But you did build one, right? You told me it was easy."

"It was. All I had to do was follow the directions."

"Directions?"

"Yeah. I built it from a kit."

If you've ever had a cat, Reader, you will, I think, be able to recall the sound that it made when it was retching up a hairball. That was what Nick sounded like when he said, "A kit?"

"What's wrong with that?"

"Kits," he said, and I could hear how disappointed he was in me when he said it, "are for kids."

"Back then I was a kid," I offered in my defense.

"Mm, I guess so," he said, apparently even more disappointed. "I don't suppose you could reproduce the circuit."

"Well—" For one mad moment, I thought that I might be able to; in that moment, I saw the schematic diagram of the circuit for the electric eye as it had appeared in the directions for the kit; but the moment was as fleeting as the view of the girl in the window, and it began to fade just as quickly. "I guess not," I admitted.

"I'll get to work on it," he said.

"Want some help?"

He gave me a long look. "Why don't you see what you can do with those switches?"

He pulled a stool up to a drafting table and bent to the work of designing an electric eye from scratch. I spent a while browsing through the supply of switches in the cabinet, hefting them and flipping, pushing, sliding, and snapping them, but after a few minutes I realized that

I was playing while Nick was working, and I felt guilty about the difference. I took a place at another drafting table and began trying to diagram a small part of a model of my brain.

After half an hour or so, Nick stretched and said, "I think I've got something that will work."

"Me, too," I said.

We exchanged papers.

For a moment, we looked at them in silence. I think we were both too embarrassed to say anything.

Finally, I felt that I had to point out the obvious.

"Yours is, um, a little more sophisticated than mine," I said.

"But," he said, with kindness and—I think I'm recalling this

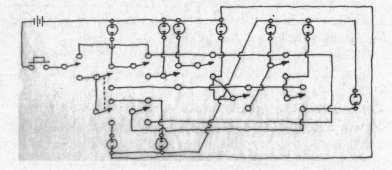

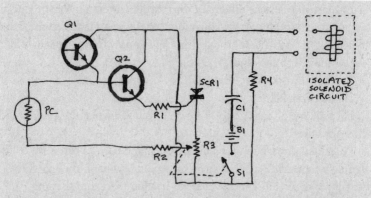

accurately—not a trace of condescension, "they're essentially the same."

"They are?"

"They've both got the same basic form: input, processing, and output," he said. "It's just the details that are different."

ON FORM AND FORMLESSNESS

I TRIED TO contain myself, but Albertine must have noticed some subtle sign of my impatience, because she asked, "What on earth is the matter with you?"

"Nothing," I claimed.

"You're twitching and squirming and—"

"I'm okay," I said.

"Do you want to deliver a lecture?" she asked.

"Um, yes," I said. "How did you know?"

"Well, before you got all twitchy, you got kind of dreamy, with a distant look in your eye, kind of detached from reality, as if you had tenure."

"Let us speculate together for a moment," I suggested, as if I were speaking to ranks of eager students. Make that ranks of rapt students. "It is possible that we have evolved as a species in such a way that we expect our lives to have a pattern or—to suggest something that may seem at first to be a different way of saying the same thing but which will on reflection reveal itself to be a similar way of expressing a quite different idea—expect to find a pattern in our lives when we look back at what we have done or at what time has done to us. It is possible, as I said; I think it is even likely; but what sort of pattern would we have evolved to expect in that case? Hmmm? Anyone? Anyone who is awake—"

"Ah—Professor Leroy?"

"Yes? Ahh, yes. The lovely dark-haired girl in the second row."

"I may be going way out on a limb with this, but—oh—did you say 'the lovely dark-haired girl in the second row'?"

"Yes, I did."

"Oh. That's not me."

"It's not?"

"No. I'm the lovely dark-haired wife in the front row."

"Ah! Of course! I see you now. Please continue."

"As I was saying, I may be going way out on the proverbial limb with this, but I think the pattern wouldn't amount to much more than birth-life-death."

"Very good! Birth-life-death. Short and sweet, and, one would think, quite enough. And yet most people seem to expect more. They seem to expect more than birth-life-death. It's as if when offered a precious little golden chain they disdain it because they want—what? Someone? Lovely wife in the front row?"

"A string of pearls?"

"A string of pearls! Yes, and not just any string of pearls, not just one damn beautiful pearl after another, but a *graduated* string of pearls: a string of pearls with a *plot*! Our entertainments, the packaged pastimes of our culture, have taught us to expect a life that is headed somewhere, when life is, in reality, plotless and haphazard, and most of us, if we will admit the truth, find at the close, when we look back, that our lives have been as patternless as a bowl of goo, a terrazzo floor, or, if we have been very lucky, a handful of pearls or a bowl of clam chowder."

"Did you hear that? Did you hear that sound?"

"What sound?"

"Something like hrang, hrang, hrang."

"Coming from the car?"

"Coming from the passenger's seat."

"Huh?"

"I think it might have been a theme. Or a motif."

"Okay, okay. End of lecture."

"Resumption of reading?"

"Yes."

ROCKY'S BIG IDEA

• •

"I was just thinking," he said, "how a nice beer would go right now. A nice, ice-cold suds with about an inch of cuff on it."

—W. L. Heath, *Violent Saturday*

IT WAS MATTHEW'S idea. Honest. Something had come over him with the choice of the code name Rocky. He had begun to think of himself as a bad boy, a rebel, a breaker of rules and flouter of conventions. I could see it in the way his upper lip curled in a sly sneer now and then. For the other members of the Faustroll Institute, with the possible exception of Eugene, irony was the weapon of choice when they wanted to put the rest of the world in its place, but for Rocky it was disdain. He had learned to sneer the sneer of disdain, and he had learned to slouch disdainfully. He slouched when he sat in a chair; he slouched against the nearest support when he was standing; he even slouched when he walked.

I was on my way back from a session in the workshop one night when he called to me.

"Pssst. Panmuphle. C'mere."

I peered into the shadowy doorway of one of the dark, empty lecture halls, where a figure was slouching and pretending to smoke.

"Huh?" I said. "Who's that?"

"It's me. Rocky. C'mere."

"Oh. Matthew," I said. "What's up? You're lurking in the shadows like a guy with furtive plans."

"Yeah," he said. "I've got some plans." I couldn't see his sneer in the dark, but I could hear it.

"Yeah?"

"Yeah. I'm gonna suck some suds. You in?"

"Suds?"

"Beer, my man. I was just thinking that a beer would be nice on a hot night like this. A nice cold one. Whadda ya say?"

"You've got beer?"

"Nah. But I know where I can get some. Whadda ya say?"

"You know where to get beer?"

"Sure I do. I know my way around."

"You know your way around? Around Corosso?"

In a voice more Matthew's than Rocky's, he said, "Well, Eugene does. He told me about a place where we can buy some beer."

"Do you drink beer?"

"Do I drink beer!" said Rocky. "My buddies and I really knock 'em back. Man, we've had some times! Let's get some suds. Whadda ya say?"

Whaddid I say? Well, what I shoulda said was, "Rocky, old pal, that sounds like something that's gonna get us into a lotta trouble. Count me out!"

Instead, I said, "Okay."

Buying the beer was the easy part, and it was a successful venture. Eugene had given Matthew directions to a small store run by a Mexican-American family, and he had taught him how to say *cerveza*. The shop was closed and dark when we arrived, but Matthew knocked three times, with confidence, a slouch, and a sneer. Nothing happened. He knocked three times again.

"That's the signal," he told me. "Knock three times."

"Classic," I said.

"Whadda ya mean by that?"

"I mean that I've been to the movies enough to know that if you want to get into a hideout or buy illicit or contraband goods, you knock three times."

The door opened a crack and a voice began shouting at us in what I assumed was Spanish with a Mexican-American accent.

"Suhr-vay-zuh!" said, or squeaked, Matthew.

The shouting inside the store continued, growing louder, faster, and angrier.

"Maybe this is the wrong store," I suggested.

Suddenly inspired, Rocky thrust some bills through the opening and said, *"Dinero!"*

The shouting stopped and a package emerged from the opening. It was, unmistakably, a six-pack of beer, in cans, in a brown paper bag.

I'm really sorry to have to report this, but frankness and complete-ness require me to tell you that Rocky said, "Cool, daddy-o," when he took the package from the invisible storekeeper.

Smuggling the beer onto the campus turned out to be the hard part, and it was a complete failure. We followed the road from town back to the campus without any trouble, and without seeing more than a cou-ple of cars. I would have said, if you had asked me then, that we hadn't attracted any notice, even though we were two boys in high spirits, con-gratulating themselves on their exploit, one of whom, the one formerly given to slouching, had begun to swagger and couldn't stop shouting "Cool, daddy-o" to the stars at frequent intervals, even though we hadn't opened a single can of beer because the pop-top had not yet been invented and we didn't have an opener.

However, as soon as we crossed the border and entered the confines of the NMIMTaP campus, we did attract attention. A pickup truck appeared on the road ahead of us, and as quickly as a hallucination it was in front of us, sliding to a stop diagonally across the road, blocking our path. There were two men in the truck, both of them wearing uni-forms, both of them wearing satisfied grins. The door that we could see bore the NMIMTaP seal and, below it, the legend

MAINTENANCE
&
SECURITY

The two men got out of the car and, taking their time, came toward us and took identical stances facing us, with their arms folded across their barrel chests and their feet planted firmly as they would be at pa-rade rest, as if they were challenging us to try to make a run for it.

"So, daddy-o," said the one on our right, giving a single nod in the direction of the package that Matthew was holding, "whose big idea was this?"

Matthew and I looked at each other. Each of us was trying to decide what the other was thinking, what the other was going to say. You can imagine our internal battles, in which pride, honor, friendship, and the instinct for self-preservation whacked at one another with whatever weapons they could lay their hands on.

"We haven't got all night, kids," the man said impatiently. "What's it going to be? Whose big idea was this?"

We turned toward him. Another moment passed. Then, together, we said, "Mine."

ALBERTINE SCOFFS AT MY TALE

....

IT WAS LOYALTY that saved us," I explained to Al. "The two men were surprised by what Matthew and I said, the way that each of us was willing to take the blame. It wasn't what they had expected. I could see that on their faces. For a moment, they were nonplussed. They looked at each other, and then they burst out laughing—and they let us go."

"Just like that?" Albertine asked.

"Pretty much. They made us give them the beer in exchange for their forgetting that they'd ever seen us trying to smuggle it onto the campus, but that was about it."

"I don't believe it."

"What do you mean you don't believe it?"

"I mean that I don't believe it. What else would I mean? There must have been more to it than that."

"Not that I remember. I think that was it."

"It's not plausible."

"You may not think it's plausible, but it's the truth."

"It doesn't have the ring of truth."

"What would I have to do to get you to believe it?"

"Make it believable."

"You're going in circles. How could I make it believable for you?"

"You could start by making it not unbelievable."

"What do you find unbelievable about it?"

"Well, for one thing, I can't believe that two campus cops would let you two off without some kind of forfeit."

"We forfeited the beer."

"It doesn't seem like enough somehow."

"What would be enough?"

"Cleaning the Augean stables."

"You call that believable?"

"Maybe not, but I think that if you want anybody to believe your little adventure in smuggling you are going to have to make your escape more difficult. People just do not believe that things can be so easy. They expect trouble because everybody else's memoirs have taught them to expect trouble. As a result, your memoirs are—and I hope you know that I'm using this term only in the technical sense—a disappointment."

"And you're suggesting that I should revise my life to meet their expectations? Or your expectations?"

"Not your life. Not your story. Just the telling of it."

"I should lie?"

"If you want them to believe you, 'tell all the truth but tell it slant.'"

"You mean turn it into something—"

"—believable."

"Okay. I'll give it a try. Here goes."

SUCCESS IN CIRCUIT LIES

IT WAS LOYALTY that saved us; make that loyalty and the element of surprise; no, make that loyalty, the element of surprise, and arithmetic. The two security men were surprised by the loyalty that Matthew and I displayed, by the fact that each of us was willing to take the blame, to let the other off the hook. That display of loyalty wasn't what they had expected. I could see their surprise. For a moment, they were nonplussed. They looked at each other, and then they burst out laughing.

The first guard, the one who had asked us whose idea it had been, said, "Well, I gotta admire your loyalty."

"Yeah," said the second. "That's a rare thing, loyalty."

"Very rare."

"Most guys in your position would have ratted on each other."

"Definitely," agreed the first guard. "I've seen it happen a million times."

"Bullshit," said the other.

"Whaddaya mean, 'bullshit'?"

"I mean, that strains credulity."

"How so?"

At this point, Matthew and I, thinking that the lively disagreement between the guards might be distracting them enough to allow us to slip away into the shadows and disappear, began shuffling backward.

"You've never seen anything a million times, let alone a million acts of betrayal."

"Maybe not a million acts of betrayal, but I've seen a million other things happen a million times."

"Have not."

"Have too."

"Name one."

Challenged, the first security guard sputtered and smacked his forehead, and then, in desperation, turned toward Matthew and me. "Hey," he said. We froze. "Haven't I seen things happen a million times?"

"How would they know?" asked the second guard.

"They're smart," said the first. "They're in that hush-hush Summer Institute. They're the hope of the nation."

"It strains credulity," muttered the second guard.

"Whadda ya say?" the first asked us. "Haven't I seen something a million times?"

Matthew and I looked at each other, each hoping that the other had thought of something to offer him. "Well—" I said, stalling for time.

"Don't stall," he said. "I hate stalling."

"Breathing!" said Matthew, suddenly inspired.

"Breathing?" asked the second guard skeptically.

"Sure!" said the first guard. "Breathing! I've breathed a million times." He thought for a moment, then added, boldly, "Probably more."

"Bullshit," said the second guard.

The first guard again turned to Matthew and me for support. "How many times have I breathed?" he asked. "More than a million, right?"

"How old are you?" asked Matthew.

"Thirty-five," he said.

"Give us a minute," said Matthew.

"Give us the beer," said the two men, as perfectly in unison as Matthew and I had been in our confession.

Matthew handed them the package. Then he turned to me and, in a whisper, asked, "How many times do you figure he's drawn a breath?"

"How should I know?" I asked.

"He wants it to be a million or more, so let's start there," said Matthew. "I figure that a million divided by thirty-five is about twenty-eight thousand five hundred seventy-one breaths a year, give or take."

"That's only about seventy-eight breaths a day," I said.

"Great," he said.

"We've got it," I announced.

"What? Already?" the second guard asked. "That strains—"

"Shut up," said the first guard. "Go ahead, kid."

"Well," Matthew began, "we wanted to know whether you've drawn a million breaths, so we started there," and he took them through our reasoning and calculations, arriving at the figure of seventy-eight breaths a day, and concluding, "but seventy-eight breaths is a lot less than the number of breaths a person takes in a day, so the number of breaths you've taken in thirty-five years must be a lot more than a million."

"That's a kind of a circuitous way of going about it," said the second guard, "starting at a million and dividing your way down to seventy-eight. I would have started with how many breaths a person takes in a minute and then multiplied."

"That's why you're not the hope of the nation," said the first guard.

"Yeah," said the second, hanging his head.

"I say that the loyalty and arithmetic nimbleness these boys have displayed should be rewarded," said the first guard.

"Rewarded?" said the second.

"Yeah. We oughta let them go."

"I can't believe what I'm hearing."

"What do you mean you can't believe what you're hearing?"

"I mean it strains credulity to the breaking point."

"Hey. You were the one who said that loyalty is a rare thing."

"And it is—and arithmetic nimbleness is even rarer maybe—but—geez—this is my first collar."

"There will be another," said the first, throwing a consoling arm across the second's shoulders. "I say we let them go—especially since the evidence has disappeared—or is about to disappear."

We saw our chance and we took it. We scrambled off the side of the road and into the brush, and we ran as best we could in the direction of the dorm. So, you see, thanks to loyalty, surprise, and arithmetic, they let us go. Just like that.

I don't know which of us suggested playing tennis, but it was an inspired idea, so I'll take the credit. Walking toward the dorm, we passed the playing fields and the swimming pool, and we came to the tennis courts.

"Do you want to play tennis?" I asked.

"I don't know how," said Matthew. "I've never played in my life."

"Neither have I," I said.

"We don't have rackets, or balls."

"Use your imagination."

"I don't have much of an imagination," he said, but he trotted to the other side of the court and faced me, taking a position to return my serve.

He may not have had much of an imagination, but he beat me in a hard-fought match. He had the advantage of knowing—at least he claimed to know—how to keep score. It was an arcane, confusing, and scarcely credible process that had me in a muddle and distracted me from the game itself.

Exhausted, sweaty, and in a state of high hilarity, we lay on our backs on the court and stared at the astonishing night sky, awash with stars, dazzling beyond anything either of us had ever seen before we came to New Mexico.

"Wow," I said, "it—it—it—"

"—strains credulity," said Matthew.

UNFORGETTABLE PROSPECT AHEAD

· ·

There are drugs enough, clearly—it is all a question of applying them with tact; in which case the way things don't happen may be artfully made to pass for the way things do.

—Henry James, preface to *The American*

MUCH MORE BELIEVABLE!" Albertine declared. "Especially for me. Since I happen to know that you can perform feats of rapid calculation in your head, that detail makes me, personally, convinced of the likelihood that something close to the story you tell is probably what happened out there in New Mexico."

"It has the ring of truth?"

"It has. Especially the dazzling stars."

"Do you think I could stretch it a little?"

"How much?"

"Could I get away with beating Matthew at tennis?"

"I'm sorry, Peter, but I've seen you try to play tennis."

"I didn't mean that you would accept my beating him; I meant that the good citizens of Babbington might accept it."

"After you've confessed that you didn't fly your aerocycle to New Mexico and back?"

"Yes."

"Am I missing something here?"

"I think you are. You see, I was thinking that after I've drugged them by confessing to complicity in the collaborative self-deception that perpetrated the flying hoax and by demonstrating my willingness to shine an unfavorable light on myself and my actions—a rare thing—they might accept me as, essentially, an honest man and—well—that might restore their gullibility, so that they might be persuaded to think that they remembered that I played a pretty good game of tennis when I was a kid."

"Oh, my darling," she said, taking her right hand off the wheel and grasping my left in a sudden gesture of love and compassion, "this is really going to hurt you, isn't it?"

"Yes," I admitted, because I am, essentially, an honest man.

"I didn't realize that. I thought you were enjoying the reminiscence. I'm sorry."

"I am enjoying the reminiscence. It's just that—I—well—I started thinking about—giving some serious thought to—my remarks—for the press conference—my confession—and—"

"And it hurts?"

"Yes, it hurts, but it's not the confession itself that hurts, it's—"

I didn't want to say what it was, so I fell silent, and I didn't say anything more for a long time. Then, when we came to a sign that said UN-FORGETTABLE PROSPECT AHEAD, Albertine slowed the Electro-Flyer and turned into the parking area that swelled from the side of the road and hung out over a precipice, and she stopped in one of the angled parking slots.

"It's the way you're going to feel after you've confessed," she said.

"Small," I said.

"I really am sorry," she said. "I thought you were taking all of this lightly—reliving the trip, preparing for the confession, retelling the tale—"

"I just think that we are all going to be diminished by the truth. I'm going to go from the Birdboy of Babbington to the Birdbrain of Babbington; the dear hearts and gentle people who live in my home town are going to look like a bunch of gullible rubes; and you are going to have to endure, once again, the pitying glances of those who like to think of you as my 'long-suffering wife.'"

"That's probably true," she said after giving it a moment's thought, "but it doesn't mean that you're going to stop reading to me, does it?"

"Oh, no. No. I'm going to finish the story. I'll probably even read you my confession when it's ready."

SURPRISED AND AMAZED

....

TANK'S NAME, OUTSIDE the Faustroll Institute, was Victoria. I've forgotten her last name; I may never have known it. Most of the students at the Summer Institute I knew only by their first names, and some I knew only by sight, even though there were just a hundred of them. To be truthful, most of them didn't interest me enough to make me bother learning their names; like most teenage egoists, I felt that my set, the little circle of people I knew, held everyone I needed to know. Make that nearly everyone I needed to know: the great lack in my set was the dark-haired girl (not the one in the window, though I would have welcomed her into my set, but the dark-haired girl whom I seemed to recall from Babbington, the one who had inspired all my sightings of dark-haired girls during my journey to Corosso).

I had heard other simps call Tank "Vick," but I had also seen her cringe when she heard it, so I avoided using it. Since I couldn't call her Tank in public, that meant that I didn't call her anything. When I saw her, I greeted her with "Hi," but no name, and that's how I greeted her when she surprised me at the NMIMTaP pool.

The pool wasn't large. It certainly wasn't large enough for intercollegiate competition in swimming. However, because it was small, it was just the right size for intramural competition in looking cool and winning the attention of girls. Crowded into the margin around the pool were two groups, with a definite boundary between them, a narrow vacant area separating the students at the Summer Institute from the regular NMIMTaP students who were taking summer courses. We simps were a bigger group, but they were bigger individuals. When I survey the scene in memory, I see no more than ten girls. There were Button, Slim, and Tank in the SIMPaW group, and there were perhaps seven girls in the NMIMTaP group; that is to say, there was the girl in the window and there were six others, not one of whom can I bring into focus in my mind's eye; they were only her foils.

"How do you like our oasis?" asked Tank, in a whisper.

I hadn't noticed that she had spread a towel next to mine. I had been pretending to work on my translation of *Gestes et Opinions du Docteur*

Faustroll while straining my eyes to absorb as much as I could of the girl in the window, who was sunning herself in a two-piece bathing suit on the opposite side of the pool. In this effort I was like nearly all the other male simps—not in pretending to work on a translation of *Faustroll,* but in straining to ogle the girl in the window without appearing to do so.

"Oh, hi," I said. "'Oasis'? Oh. I see what you mean. Oasis. Well, it's nice, but small. There's hardly enough room for all of us to get into the water at once."

"Ah!" she said, laughing, but keeping her laugh as low as a whisper. "I see what you mean, but I didn't mean the pool, or not only the pool, I meant the campus in general, the Summer Institute, the company—"

"Oh. Now I see what you mean. The whole thing. Yes. I like it. I'm glad to be here."

"What's your favorite thing, so far?"

Why did she ask that? I wondered. Did she know about the girl in the window? Did she know about the skulking and stalking game that I'd begun to play with Button? Did she expect me to be honest? I leaned toward her, confidentially, and lowered my voice.

"I don't want anyone to hear me sounding like a newcomer," I said, "but the truth is that being able to take a shower whenever I feel like it might be my favorite thing." It was a risk, because it was the truth and I had forgotten to give it a protective coat of irony.

"It's certainly one of my favorite things," she said with a sudden, spontaneous laugh of surprise.

"Really?" I said.

"Yes!" she said. "Taking a shower whenever I feel like it, and for as long as I want, is a great luxury."

"Mm," I said, because I wondered whether she was mocking me.

"At home," she said, "we have only one bathroom, so whenever I take a shower, I know that I'm supposed to make it short, so that I don't waste water, but I know that what my parents really mean is that I'm supposed to make it short to minimize the expense of heating the hot water."

"Ah!" I said. "Me, too!"

"I always know that if I linger too long, I'll hear a soft tap on the door from my mother or a sharp rap from my father, and I'll be reminded that hot water costs money."

"Yeah," I said.

"And then it always seems as if someone else is waiting to take a shower as soon as I'm finished, no matter when I take mine. But here there's always a shower available. I've become a fiend for showers."

"It might be the heat and the dust," I suggested.

"No, silly. It's the sheer luxury of it. Haven't you been listening?"

"Yes, I—"

"I wonder sometimes why a shower is as pleasant as it is. I wonder about that mostly while I'm showering, of course. One of the things I wonder is, did our ancestors, deep in the dark unknown time of prehistory, bathe themselves in the first warm rains of spring? Was that bathing a part of the pleasure of spring? Was there, in the rhythm of the year, a day when the frigid rains of winter gentled themselves, became not merely benign but beneficent, and was that day one that those distant people began to anticipate, to yearn for? Did showering become a ritual? Was it celebrated? Were there prayers to the rains of spring? Songs about showering? Are there cave paintings depicting bands of hunters showering after the hunt? Was showering an occasion for the mingling of the sexes? Did the youth of the tribe get to get naked together? Did they get to rub up against one another? Did they maybe even get to—well—you know—"

"Wow," I said. "This is interesting stuff."

"But you wish you were hearing it from Button."

"What?"

"Or even from Slim."

"No—"

"Or the girl across the way, the one you keep glancing at, the one that all the boys keep glancing at."

"Why do you say that?" I asked, as if I didn't know, as if it weren't so.

The sky had been clear, the sun hot, the air still, but when Tank snickered instead of saying that I knew perfectly well why she said that, the darkness that I wasn't supposed to find remarkable came over us. With astonishing suddenness, clouds filled the sky, thunder rumbled, lightning flashed, and great balls of water came crashing down around us.

"The sky is falling," I said.

"As usual," she said.

We gathered our things and scattered, as all the others did, in a routine way, as if the downpour were nothing but a tedious nuisance, certainly not one of nature's most amazing performances, but at the point where she and I would most logically have parted and gone our separate ways, she ran instead to the arched doorway of a lecture hall and beckoned to me to join her.

"Here we can allow ourselves to be amazed," she said. "We can allow ourselves to be surprised."

We were both soaked to the skin. We huddled together and watched the show and allowed ourselves to be amazed and surprised and allowed ourselves to amaze and surprise each other and from then on I called her Victoria.

A BOY MOST EAGER FOR FAME

....

they said he was,   of the kings in this world,
the kindest to his men,   the most courteous man,
the best to his people,   and most eager for fame.
                           —*Beowulf* (translated by Howell D. Chickering, Jr.)

WE WERE NEARLY halfway home. It was time to start writing a statement for the press conference in Babbington at which I would correct the misimpressions about my flight to New Mexico that had been allowed to stand for so long and would acknowledge my role in what I supposed I was going to have to call a deception: a confession. So, in the early morning, while Albertine slept, I slipped from the room and established myself in the lobby of our motel, where coffee was available. After a cup and a half, I opened the lid of my computer and began tapping at the keys.

> I have, in the company of my long-suffering wife, just completed a journey that partly reproduced the journey I made from Babbington to Corosso forty-eight years ago, a journey of reiter-

ation, of reminiscence, of discovery, and—most importantly—
of self-examination, for in the course of that journey I took a
long, hard look at myself—actually, at several of my selves, including the young self who helped create the myth, the many
selves who, over the years, have allowed the myth to grow and
spread—and what I've seen has not always been welcome. I've
seen a boy too eager for fame, so hungry for admiration that he
was willing to accept a greater fame than he had earned, and at
the same time too gentle and kind, so considerate of his friends
and neighbors that he couldn't bring himself to disburden them
of their fond illusions.

   I am not going to try to excuse what I did, but I am going to
try to explain what I did, and I am going to try to explain why
I think that what I did was an example of a natural human
tendency to drift, when given the opportunity, up and away
from the tedious banality of everyday life into the intoxicating
reaches of romance.

"Are you going to ask me to believe that you had sex with all of these
girls?" Albertine asked abruptly, taking the seat beside me and setting a
paper cup of coffee on the low table in front of us.

   "You mean you don't hear the ring of truth? Again?"

   "It's being drowned out by something else."

   "Oh?"

   "I seem to hear the wind of wishful thinking whistling through this
Western idyll."

   "Did you practice that?"

   "A bit," she admitted. "In the shower."

We drank our coffee, ate a couple of bananas and a couple of oranges,
checked out, and got back onto the road, and I read her another chapter.

CONCERNING THE CHOSEN FEW

···

The formula for double happiness: Be amorous and be mysterious.
—Alfred Jarry, *Adventures and Opinions of Doctor Faustroll, Pataphysician*
(my translation at age fifteen)

EXCURSIONS WERE A feature of the SIMPaW summer. They might have been meant to broaden the campus experience, or to extend it beyond the campus into the wider world, or to spice the curriculum in mathematics, physics, and weaponry with cultural enrichment, but they were not. They were field exercises in the unlisted area of the curriculum—espionage—with particular emphasis on the art of concealment. (Of course, we were instructed to say, if asked, that the excursions were "broadening" or even that they were "enriching," provided that we didn't overuse the term; there was something about the idea of enrichment that made the SIMPaW administration squirm.)

Our excursions took us to Los Alamos, to White Sands, to Santa Fe and Taos, to Carlsbad Caverns, and to the Gila cliff dwellings near Silver City. On the morning of an excursion, we ate an early breakfast and then, as we left the dining hall, each of us took a white box from a counter near the door. The boxes held our lunches, and, of course, eating lunch would be another test of our ability to conceal surprises, an especially difficult test because we would be eating lunch in public. We clambered aboard several buses, organizing ourselves according to the friendships and animosities that obtained at the time of the particular excursion.

On the excursion to the Gila cliff dwellings, I found myself in a bus line with Slim, whose name outside the Faustroll Institute was Virginia, and I pushed and pardoned and elbowed and excused myself until I had moved ahead so that I was right behind her.

"Hi," I said.

"Hi, Peter," she said, without turning to see whether she was right in identifying me from my voice.

"Let's sit in the back of the bus," I suggested, in what I meant to be the easygoing, bantering tone that boys and girls used in that time to hide their lustful feelings while at the same time making it clear that precisely what they were using the playful bantering manner to hide was lustful feelings.

"Will you promise to keep your hands to yourself?" she asked flirtatiously, with a penetrating glance over her shoulder.

I hadn't been prepared for that. "I—um—well—" I said.

"That's okay," she said. "You don't have to promise."

"I don't? Well, in that case, I—"

She turned around and raised a finger to my lips to shut me up. Her eyes were shining and she wore a rueful look.

We made our way onto the bus and took a seat at the very back. The seat was wide enough for us to sit with a sizable gap between us, but I allowed my leg to touch hers, as if it were impossible for me to help it. She gave me a shove with her shoulder and pushed my leg away with her hand. I let a gap stand between us for a while, but gradually my leg began inching toward her. I stared at it in bewilderment. I scowled at it. I shook my finger at it. Defiantly, it nestled against hers again.

"My leg seems powerfully attracted to yours," I said. "I seem to have lost all control—"

She stopped me with a frown. "You don't have to pretend," she said.

"I'm not—"

"You're using that playful, bantering manner that boys use when they want a girl to understand that they've got sex on their minds even if they seem to be talking about homogeneous partial differential equations. In your case, you want me to believe that you're interested in groping me, though you're really not. I suppose you think you're being kind."

"I—"

"Please don't try to pretend that you don't know what they call me. I've heard it. It isn't as though they tried to prevent me from hearing it. I hear it when I walk by. There's something about the way I walk that brings it to mind—to your mind."

"My mind? What?"

"Whenever there are three or more of you, you boys, gathered together, and I walk by, I hear it behind me as I go, the hiss of it, that awful name, Stick. That is, it started as Stick, but now it has shrunken to something like stkhhh, like the disgusting sound you boys make before you spit on the sidewalk."

"I don't—"

"Just be quiet," she said. "Look at the scenery."

We rode the rest of the way to the ruins without speaking. My leg was still against hers. She hadn't pushed it away, and I didn't move it. Neither of us looked at the other. I looked out the window, watching the scenery roll by as she had told me to do.

When we reached the ruins, we got off the bus together, and we investigated the site together. The ground was uneven, so from time to time it was appropriate that I extend a helping hand. After ignoring several of these offers, she finally accepted one. Once I had her hand, I kept it and we walked hand-in-hand for a while. From behind us, we heard the nasty slur, the phlegmy *stkhhh*. I bristled. I spun around. I was prepared to be her champion. I was prepared to punch somebody.

"Don't bother," she said. She pulled me on, leading me to another area of the site.

When we were alone, she said, slowly, deliberately, "I am not a stick. I am slender, and I am tall, and the fact that I am so tall makes me seem very slender. I am willowy. I have a certain style, a certain grace. Alas, style, grace, and willowy slenderness are not much admired by boys. At home, I have been an object of ridicule since adolescence brought me this height, this grace and style. It hurts, the ridicule. Even though I understand it, it hurts."

"I'm sorry—"

"Oh, don't be sorry for me," she said deliberately. "You don't have to be sorry for me. I have come to think of myself, proudly, as belonging to the group—or you could say set or universe—of slender sophisticates."

"The Slender Sophisticates!" I said, nodding as Dean would have and with emphasis capitalizing the name of the group. "Yes!"

"Yes!" she said right back at me, and she giggled. I liked that. "If you're going to feel sorry for anyone," she said, "feel sorry for my tormentors."

"The Fat Fools?" I suggested, since the time when I would have suggested "Fat Fucks" was still many years in the future.

"The Swaggering Slobs," she said with a toss of her head. "We slender sophisticates—I mean, we, the Slender Sophisticates—are what the Swaggering Slobs are not. We are elegant; they are crude. We glide;

FLYING HOME • 507

they strut. We sing; they grunt. We are thinkers, we reflect, we wonder, we theorize; they are, as a group, as dumb as a box o' rocks."

"I see," I said.

"Of course, the Swaggering Slobs are everywhere," she said, lowering her voice. "There are so very many more of them than there are of us."

"Us?"

"I'm giving you the benefit of the doubt."

"Thanks."

"Dull as they are, they seem to know at some dim level of understanding that their great numbers give them power and—would you like to be an archaeologist?"

"Huh?" I said.

She nodded in the direction of a shallow pit, where an aged archaeologist was slowly, painstakingly dusting dirt from an ancient artifact. "We're being observed," she muttered in a low, confidential voice.

Foolishly, and in violation of everything that a skulker knows about the art of concealment, I glanced over my shoulder.

"Don't," she said in a whisper. "Don't—"

"Sorry," I muttered. Then, inspired, I leaned toward her and kissed her suddenly, and immediately I looked down at my shoes and shuffled my feet in the dirt.

"Brilliant," she muttered. "A brilliant recovery and a crafty concealment." In a louder voice, with a touch of what could have been interpreted as annoyance at my presumption in kissing her even after taking the precaution of checking to see whether any simps were watching, she asked again, "Well, would you like to be an archaeologist?"

"I might," I said.

"What would you say is the best part?" she asked. "Is it the hot sun burning the back of your neck, the dust in your eyes, or the sheer tedium of flicking little bits of dirt from a tiny shard of an ancient bedpan hour after hot and dusty hour?"

I grinned. "The sheer tedium," I said.

"Really?" she said, smoothing her hair.

"Yes," I said. "Tedious tasks allow the mind to wander." I took her hand and said, too softly to be overheard, "If we're still being watched, maybe I should kiss you again—for deception's sake."

508 • PETER LEROY

"We're still being watched," she said.

I kissed her again.

"Who's watching us?" I asked.

"The count," she said. "He's a Creep."

"A Creep? Is that another group?"

"Yeah," she said with a snarl.

THE KAMURA EFFECT

· ·

THAT'S IT?" ASKED Albertine.

"That's the end of the episode," I said. "The end of the chapter."

"But what happened on the bus ride back to the campus? Did you and Slim sit together?"

"Yes."

"Was it after dark?"

"No. It might have been dusk when we reached NMIMTaP."

"So you weren't able to snuggle and smooch on the bus."

"No."

"Later that night?"

"We didn't—we didn't do anything beyond what I've told you."

"You mean to say—you mean you're going to admit—you're going to allow me to understand—that—that—there is a girl in your memoirs who—who—did not—did not succumb to your charms?"

"Something like that," I said evasively. Then I asked, as suddenly and apparently irrelevantly as Slim had asked whether I would like to be an archaeologist, "Are you tired?"

"Tired?"

"Getting a little groggy?"

"No, I'm fine."

I gave her thigh a loving squeeze. "You're sure you're not tired?" I asked.

"No."

"You wouldn't like some coffee?"

"Coffee? No. I don't want any coffee."

"There's a service area coming up."

"Do you want to stop, Peter?"

"Me?"

"You."

"Well—if you think you'd like a break—"

"I don't need a break."

"Oh."

"Do you?"

"Well—"

"Okay, I could pee," she said.

"Well!" I said enthusiastically. "If you want to stop, it's fine with me. I might get some coffee, set up the computer, and take a moment to jot some notes for my—ah—statement."

"Your statement?"

"You know—my confession. The remarks I'm going to deliver at the press conference—"

"Press conference?"

"I was thinking that it would be a good idea to call a press conference—"

"You're going to 'call a press conference'?"

"Well, I was thinking of it."

"Then you certainly should have some prepared remarks," she said, in a way that I thought might have suggested a lack of faith in my ability to improvise.

She pulled into the parking lot at the service area, and I got some coffee while she visited the ladies' room. I took a spot at a table outside, and in a while she joined me. She sat in the sun while I worked, and whenever I looked in her direction she was either reading or was smiling upward, at the sun, with her eyes closed. When I had done as much work as I cared to do, I told her that I wouldn't mind getting back on the road. Her smile broadened, and in a few minutes we were in traffic again, heading east, toward the press conference, now not much more than a couple of weeks away.

"Al—" I said hesitantly, "I—I have a confession to make—"

"Your confession? You've got it ready? Shall I notify the media?"

"This isn't that confession. It's just a small one."

"I suppose it will have to do until the real thing comes along."

"It's just that—well—I wanted to stop—earlier—when I kept asking if you wanted to stop—but I didn't want to admit the reason to you."

"What was it?" she asked. "Are you all right? Are you feeling sick?"

"No," I said. "Nothing like that. It's just that—I—I might have experienced—inspiration."

"You? He who scoffs at the notion?"

"Yeah. Me. I—suddenly—while I was telling you about Slim—I remembered the title of an article in *Rational Romantic* that dealt with the complicity of the audience in the making of a fiction. It came to me 'out of the blue,' and it brought with it a burst of ideas—almost violent—but beautiful—and—and—"

"Was it like the sudden outrushing explosion of starry spikes in the type of fireworks display called—I think I've got this right—the kamura effect?"

"Well—maybe—"

"I know just what you mean."

"Anyway, I wanted to write out those ideas immediately, get them on my hard drive before I lost them—"

"Before they dimmed and sputtered into kamura dust, leaving nothing but an acrid odor and a fading memory."

"Um—yeah—"

"That's why you wanted me to stop."

"Yes."

"So, are you going to read it to me?"

"It's days away from being ready," I said, "but I will read you something about the count."

THE COUNT SINGS A SOLO

∙∙∙

WHEN MOVIE NIGHT came around again, the count again chose not to attend. He dismissed the offering as "jejune." To be exact, or as exact as memory allows me to be, he said, when I asked him if he was planning to watch the movie—*Adventures of a Small Town Boy* I think it was—with the rest of us, "I have already seen the first fifteen minutes of it, back at home."

"Why only the first fifteen minutes?" I asked.

He examined his fingernails for a moment, then said, "I walked out at that point."

"Why?" I asked, astonished. Though I had seen some turkeys in my short life, I had never walked out of a movie, and I couldn't imagine how bad a movie would have to be to make me leave the theater before I'd gotten my money's worth, which to me, at the time, meant seeing the movie through to the end, bitter or otherwise.

"It was jejune," he said.

I didn't know what *jejune* meant, but I could tell from the tone of voice in which he delivered the word into the dormitory hallway where he and I were standing that to admit that I didn't know what it meant would make me in the count's opinion even more childish, naïve, and ignorant than he already considered me, so I employed a dodge that I often used in school when I was in danger of demonstrating my ignorance: I asked the kind of question that people seemed to consider intelligent, a question involving a comparison of the relative merits of two comparable things. It had usually worked in the past; I hoped it would work now.

"Did you think it was more or less jejune than *Hellcats of Hell's Kitchen?*" I asked.

With just the slightest hesitation, just the slightest hint of a suspicion that he was being had, he said, "I never saw *Hellcats of Hell's Kitchen.*"

"It was pretty jejune," I said. "I was hoping that you had seen it, or at least some of it, because it would have been interesting to know how many minutes passed before you got up and left. That would have given us a quantifiable measure of the—ah—jejunousness—of the two. We could use that data to calibrate a jejunometer. If we had a large enough sample of jejune movies that you had left at various times—I suppose we should use percentages of the total running times of the movies rather than simply the number of minutes into the movie when you got up and left—then we could—"

"I will be interested to know how long you sit through *Adventures of a Small Town Boy*, Panmuphle," he said, flipping me a wave and turning away, heading off down the corridor.

I had no intention of sitting through any of it. My assumption was that the count would be going off into the desert again, and if that was the case I was going to follow him. I wanted to know where he went and what he did. I can't recall that I had any particular motive beyond satisfying my curiosity. I know this: I did not follow him with either the intention or the hope that I would discover something about him that I could use against him. I was not that kind of guy.

He was easy to track, ridiculously easy to track. He moved fluidly, steadily, at first at a walk, and then at a relaxed lope that covered ground economically without tiring either of us. I began to worry that he might have realized, or just guessed, that I was following him and that he was making himself easy to track so that he could lead me into some kind of trap or, what I would have considered worse at the time, some kind of humiliation, but as time passed I began to understand that he was easy to track because he was so thoroughly convinced that he was a master of stealth, so superior in the art of skulking that the danger of his being followed diminished with every step, his easy swiftness and apparent aimlessness certain to leave any pursuer panting and puzzled and probably lost. A couple of times, I thought I heard him chuckle. Of course, I worried that he might be chuckling because I was falling for his trap, whatever it was, and I admitted to myself that it wouldn't be hard for him to lead me into the desert and then, if he had been pretending to be less skilled than he really was, vanish. I would be well and truly lost in that case. I knew nothing about survival in the desert. I would be in real danger. I might die.

"Wait a minute," I told myself. "You do know something about survival in the desert. What about all those desert stories you've read in *Bold Feats*? You remember 'Surviving the Sahara,' don't you? And what about 'Eat Dust or Die'? Then there was 'Lizards for Lunch,' remember? If you put your mind to it, you can probably remember lots of desert survival skills."

This time, I was the one who chuckled, but as soon as I heard the chuckle escape me, I froze. I held my breath. Ahead, the count still loped along. He hadn't even broken stride. He hadn't heard me at all.

The only difficulty in tracking him came not from his skill or his technique but from the starry sky. I don't mean that the light of the stars made me fear that the count would see me if he turned around. No. The starlight wasn't that bright, and the moon was no more than a thin crescent. I mean that the starry sky was a dangerous distraction, so beautiful, so astonishing, so rich in stars, so much more amazing than the night sky over Bolotomy Bay, that a part of me wanted to stop following the count, to stretch out on my back with my hands behind my head and just enjoy the view. I might have given in to that urge if the count hadn't suddenly stopped and stood stock still. I stopped myself as abruptly as he had, and stood just as still as he did, holding my breath. Slowly, silently, I let myself sink to the sand, alert, tense, in a crouch. I felt sure that if his desert ramble had a destination he had reached it.

He burst into song.

I didn't know what he was singing, but it seemed operatic to me. Don't put too much stock in that assessment, though; the only opera I had heard at that time was a recording of *Madame Butterfly* that my mother played every few months. She would suddenly declare, without any apparent stimulus, "Oh! I have to hear 'Un Bel Di,'" and take the album down from its safe storage on the top shelf in the hall closet. I can say with some confidence that what the count was singing was not from *Madame Butterfly*.

He sang in a grand style, as if he were actually onstage, performing for an audience. He gesticulated; he paced; he puffed his chest out. He turned this way and that, flinging his voice to every point of the compass. Was this why he had come so far out into the desert? So that he could sing opera without being heard, without risking the ridicule of the other simps? It seemed reasonable, and I almost bought it . . . but then I began to understand that what he was doing was a cover, not only for his having come out here, but also for the methodical way that he was scanning the area as he offered his performance to his imaginary audience, turning slowly through a full circle, looking for any evidence of a pursuer. He never saw me. I'm certain that he never saw me.

He finished his piece, and then he let his shoulders drop and sighed, as if he had exhausted himself. He made a bow. He stood erect again. "Thank you, thank you," he said to the desert. Then he started back to the campus . . . but he stopped again. He looked at his shoe. He dropped to one knee to tie his shoelace. I couldn't see what he was doing well enough to say that he was actually tying his shoelace, but even if I had seen the laces in his hands I would have bet you a nice chunk of change that he was doing something else, and that the something else was the reason for his having come out there. After a moment, he stood and continued on his way back to the campus.

I scuttled quickly to the spot where he had stood, and I scrambled around, looking for anything that might tell me why he had stopped in that spot rather than another, any clue to a motive other than singing under the stars, but I saw nothing to distinguish that spot from any other rocky patch of sand in the neighborhood. I knew that I couldn't afford to let the count get out of sight if I hoped to follow him back to the campus, so I didn't conduct a thorough search. All I did was scrabble in the sand and knock a few rocks around—but that was enough. Under one of the rocks was a folded piece of paper. In the dark it shone so white that it could have been fluorescent. I snatched it quickly and stuffed it into my pocket, then loped off on the heels of the count.

As soon as I was safely back in the dorm, I closed myself in a toilet stall and took the paper from my pocket. I unfolded it. It was headed SIMPAW STUDENT PERFORMANCE REPORT, WEEK 5. It was a neatly typed list of all one hundred simps, alphabetically arranged, with a terse comment about each one. I took those comments to be the count's assessment of their abilities and performance. He had done a clever thing: he had included himself on the list and had qualified his praise for himself: though it began with "Smart, capable, dedicated, determined; must be ranked at or near the top," it concluded with "not well liked."

For me, the list had a built-in disappointment: it didn't say anything about me. It couldn't have, I told myself, because I wasn't an official student at SIMPaW. I should have been grateful to the count for keeping my secret, and to some degree I may have been, but I was far more disappointed, disappointed that he hadn't included me, praised my talent for hiding in plain sight, and suggested that I, too, ought to be ranked at or near the top.

CUT TO THE CHASE

. . . .

MY MIND WAS on my confession. While Albertine drove, I was trying to recall the article that I had read in *Rational Romantic* that dealt with what I seemed to remember the authors calling "a willing audience for fiction," the article that, in memory at least, offered good material for the prepared statement that I intended to make when we returned to Babbington. I went through the struggle to recall a missing memory that William James described in "Association," Chapter 14 of *The Principles of Psychology*:

> Whenever we seek to recall something forgotten . . . the desire strains and presses in a direction which it feels to be right, but towards a point which it is unable to see.

Yes, I had that feeling of mental blindness, as if the issue of *Rat Rom* were in front of me, open in my hands, but the article was so blurred that the page might as well have been blank . . .

> Try, for instance, to symbolize what goes on in a man who is racking his brains to remember a thought which occurred to him last week.

Or something he read years ago, when he was an impressionable boy . . .

> The associates of the thought are all there, many of them at least, but they refuse to awaken the thought itself.

My mind was active, but my memory was sleeping, or that part of my memory that held the thought, which would have to be a widely distributed area of my brain, with certain switches thrown the wrong way . . .

> The forgotten thing is felt by us as a gap in the midst of certain other things.

A break in the circuit . . .

> We possess a dim idea of where we were and what we were about when it last occurred to us.

In my room, reading in bed . . . or sitting at my desk . . . my mind wandering toward the window . . . or downstairs, drawn by dinner . . .

> We recollect the general subject to which it pertains.

I stopped struggling to recall the article. I was no longer even turning my attention to the general subject to which it pertained. I had heard something. I had heard the sound I least wanted to hear. I had heard the sound of an approaching helicopter.

"Lost in thought?" asked Albertine.

"Huh?"

"You've been very quiet for some time, and you have a faraway look in your eye, as if you were seeking inspiration beyond the horizon."

"Oh—ah—I—I was just—do you mind if I drive for a while?"

"Drive?"

"Drive."

"You want to drive?"

"I've got the urge."

"If you like—"

Obligingly, she pulled onto the shoulder and stopped the car. I was out in a jiffy and ran around to the driver's side. I swung the door open, tugged her out, and threw myself behind the wheel.

As soon as she was safely in, I pushed the pedal to the floor. We shot forward in a spray of gravel and rocketed along the road for a quarter mile or so. Anyone observing us from above would have thought that the driver of the surprisingly speedy little electric car was devoted to driving in a straight line, entirely oblivious to the tempting exit that was coming up. Ha! With a sudden twist of the wheel at the last possible moment, I swung us off the interstate and onto the off-ramp for Middletown, tires screaming, Albertine gasping. At the intersection where the off-ramp ended, I feinted a left turn, then with the cunning of a hunted animal reversed myself and turned right, from the left lane, artfully dodging an oncoming tractor-trailer.

"Eeeeyah!" Albertine squealed in gleeful admiration.

Instantly, I threw the Electro-Flyer into a U-turn, sliding across the road and tracing the very edge of the pavement. Accelerating with everything the Electro-Flyer could give me, I came alongside the tractor-trailer, on the side away from the approaching helicopter. I hung there in the truck's shadow, and when the truck swung onto the approach to the interstate, heading in the opposite direction from the one we had been traveling, I clung to him like paint, squeezing between him and the guardrail. Once we were on the highway, I stayed beside him, still hiding in his shadow, until I saw the opportunity I'd hoped for.

"Hang on," I said.

"Aaahrgh," said Albertine.

We were approaching an overpass, where a local road crossed the highway. The truck driver and I entered it at exactly the same speed, a good bit above the limit, but as soon as I judged that the rear bumper of the Electro-Flyer was hidden in the safety of the overpass, I stomped on the brake pedal with all my might. The car shuddered in violent protest. It fishtailed. I struggled to control it. We slid onto the cobbled paving under the arch of the overpass, where no car was meant to travel, and we came to a jarring halt. The traffic rushed on. We were safely out of sight, and I hoped that any flyguy helicoptering overhead had no idea where we were.

"Well," I said. "That was fun."

"Ggguhl," said Albertine.

"I've had enough, though," I said. "Would you mind taking over?"

Albertine emerged from the passenger's seat slowly, steadying herself against the door frame. I scrambled into the passenger's seat while she made her way around the front of the car, wobbling a bit. Cartoon stars seemed to orbit her head, her eyes seemed to roll in their sockets, and her mouth was twisted in something like a grin.

"I'd forgotten," she said when she had eased herself back into the driver's seat.

"Forgotten what?" I asked.

"The way you drive."

She needed a while to compose herself. I could see that. So while she sat with her hands gripping the wheel in the style called "white-knuckle," I read to her.

AN IDEA

· ·

I WAS STEALTHY as I made my way to visit *Spirit*, in the warehouse where she was hidden. I took a circuitous route, and, as Button told me she'd been taught to do in paleontology class, I made use of reflective surfaces to assure myself that I was not being followed. When I reached the warehouse, I didn't stop there but instead kept right on walking, right past it as if I had no intention of entering it. I took another circuitous route, again assured myself that I was not being followed, doubled back to the warehouse, quickly opened the door, and slipped inside.

"*Spirit?*" I whispered into the darkness.

"Who's that?" she said. "Who's there?"

"It's me, Peter."

"Peter? Peter? I think I used to know someone—oh—it's you!"

"Cut it out. I know I should have come to see you before this—"

"And now you've come to destroy me, haven't you?"

"What? No. I—"

"This is the end. Oh, woe is me! Why does it have to end this way? We were good together. We were a team. We were more than a team. We meant something to each other. Don't do this, Peter! I beseech you!"

"Enough hysterics. I'm not here to destroy you. I want to talk to you."

"Oh? Really? After all this time?"

"Please. Just listen to me, okay?"

"Your obedient servant."

"My thoughts are confused, and I thought that I might be able to straighten them out if I aired them."

"'Aired them'? You need to 'air' your thoughts? Oh, I see. This is not going to be a conversation, then. My contribution will be silence. I'm supposed to sit here and do nothing while you blather on. I'm just a sounding board. You don't need an aerocycle for that. You could use an actual board. Why don't you look around here? I'm sure you'll find—"

"Please, *Spirit*. I apologize for leaving you alone for so long. Please listen to what I have to say. I need you. I need to talk to someone."

"Oh, 'someone.' You need to talk to 'someone.' Why don't you try talking to one of the young thugs who helped you imprison me here in this—this—"

"I can't talk to them because I need to talk about them, one of them in particular."

"Mm. So you would have gone to one of them in preference to me if you had been able to."

"Please just let me talk and listen to what I have to say."

"Hmph."

"You said it yourself: we're good together, we're a team, we're more than a team, we mean something to each other."

"Talk."

"I've discovered that one of the students here, someone who is in the Summer Institute and also in the Faustroll Institute, is—well—I guess I'd have to call him a spy, or an undercover agent, or a stool pigeon, maybe a plant—"

"What do you mean? I don't understand."

"I mean that he's observing the students and writing reports about them. I saw him hide a report under a rock in the desert. I suppose somebody was supposed to retrieve it, probably somebody on the faculty, or in the administration, or somebody from the Preparedness Foundation, somebody important."

"What do you mean when you say that somebody 'was' supposed to retrieve it?"

"Well, I—"

"You didn't."

"I did. I took it. I have it."

"With you?"

"Yeah. Here it is." I took it from my pocket and unfolded it.

"Don't show it to me! I don't want to see it. I don't want to know anything about it. When they give me the third degree and start pulling my bolts out with pliers, I don't want to have any information to give them. I'm sure that I'll crack under torture. Even those harsh lights they use—"

"*Spirit!*"

"What?"

"You're not helping me. Listen to me."

"Go ahead."

"I'm trying to decide what to do with this report and what to do with what I know."

"I'm beginning to understand. You can't go to the authorities."

"Right. I'd just get myself into trouble, because I'm not even supposed to be here. They'd throw me out."

"They'd probably do more than that. I think they'd lock you up. You might even be guilty of a federal offense. They'd send you up the river."

"So I can't do that, but I could tell the other students what I know."

"You could—but think about how they would react."

"Mm."

"As I understand it, students have a rather strong us-versus-them attitude toward their teachers, and an even stronger animosity toward the administrators of their schools. I think the students would feel that they had been betrayed. They might want to exact retribution for the betrayal. They might turn into an unruly mob, driven by anger to do something that reason would ordinarily never allow them to do, something too horrible for me to name."

"I don't think that they—"

"Isn't one of them armed?"

"How did you know—"

"We share a mind, remember?"

"Right. Of course."

"So it would be, or could be, dangerous to tell the students about the spy."

"Yes, you're right—but what can I do?"

"You don't have to do anything, do you?"

"No. But I want to do something."

"What do you want to do?"

"What I want to do, what I really want to do, is add myself to this list."

"Why?"

"Well—because—because—"

"Come on, spit it out."

"Because I think that I'm one of the best students at SIMPaW, and I wish somebody knew it. I want to add myself to this list with remarks that make that clear."

"But that would mean revealing yourself to the administration."

"I know. And that I can't do."

"Hmmm."

"What?"

"I'm thinking."

"You are? Why can't I tell when you're thinking?"

"Shush. Let me think. Occupy yourself."

I stood and looked around the warehouse. There was a stack of large crates off to my right, and I had just started in that direction to see if I could figure out what was in them when she called me back.

"I have an idea," she announced.

"You do?"

"Yes. Come closer. I'll tell you what it is."

I GET WHAT I WANTED

∙∙∙

IN BED, BEFORE I fell asleep, I told myself again and again to wake early. It worked. I obeyed myself. I woke at four in the morning. I slid slowly out of bed and groped in the dark for the pile of clothing I had left for myself on the floor at my side of the bed, out of sight of Albertine. I dressed quickly, grabbed my computer, and slipped silently out of the room. So that the sound of the elevator bell wouldn't wake Albertine, I took the stairs down to the ground floor. At the desk, a clerk was watching a movie on a small DVD player.

"Sorry to interrupt," I whispered, "but is there somewhere nearby where I could get some coffee?"

"Free coffee twenty-four-seven in the breakfast room," he said.

"Thanks."

I headed that way. I hadn't gone far when I realized that I was walking on tiptoes. When one is being secretive, one tends to be fully secretive, heart, soul, and tiptoes. Drawing on my SIMPaW training, I told myself to walk in the normal manner, so that I wouldn't announce to all and sundry that I was doing something furtive.

I found the breakfast room and peered around the corner to see if it was empty. It wasn't. There was a woman there, reading a newspaper and drinking coffee. I pulled my head back quickly, automatically, but she had seen me.

"Come on in," the woman said from within the breakfast room. "The coffee's free."

I assumed a casual air and stepped around the corner, being very careful not to walk on tiptoes. I nodded to the woman but said nothing to her. She was wearing flannel pajamas.

I served myself a paper cup of coffee, set my computer on a table far from the woman in the flannel pajamas, and began writing feverishly. My fingers were flying. My mind was racing. I saw the statement that I wanted to make, saw it entire, just as it ought to be. I knew that I'd never manage to get it right in the couple of hours that I might have in that breakfast room before I had to return to work on my reminiscences of SIMPaW and Corosso, but I was determined to get as much of it down while the vision of it as it ought to be was fresh, so that all my later work on it would be guided by the first conception of it, which seemed so right that I hated and feared the thought that I might lose it and so lose the guidance of it.

"Getting some work done, are you?" asked the woman in the flannel pajamas.

"Yes," I said, with, I hoped, just the right note of urgency and fever-ish concentration that would keep her from speaking to me again. I didn't look up. I kept my eyes on the keys and I went on typing.

"It's a good time to work," she said. "Morning, I mean. Morning's a good time to work."

"Mm," I said.

"If you're a morning person, that is," she said, pointing a cruller at me emphatically.

"Mm," I said again.

"Me, I'm not much of a morning person. Not really. I get up early, but that's just because I can't sleep. My back. It hurts like hell. I get to the point where I just can't lie there in bed with my back hurting the way it does. So I get up and I prowl around—"

"Please," I said. "I really have to get this work done."

"Must be important," she said.

"Mm," I growled. My fingers still flew. My mind still raced.

"Maybe something secret?"

I stopped typing.

"What makes you say that?" I asked.

"Oh, I don't know. I guess the way you peeked in here, looking around the edge of the door the way you did, the way you tiptoed in—"

"I've go to get back to this—"

"What is it, a confession or something?"

"What? What did you say?"

"I asked if you're writing a confession."

"What on earth makes you ask if I'm writing a confession? Do I look like someone with something to confess?"

"I expect we've all got something to confess."

"Heh-heh. Well, maybe you're right. But why me, particularly?"

She got up and took her cup to the coffee machine. "Oh, I don't know," she said as she poured herself a fresh cup, "but I'd say it had something to do with the frantic way you went at that keyboard, like you had something that you wanted to get off your chest before you got caught."

She brought her coffee to her table and sat down again. She kept her eyes on me while she waited for a response.

"Not caught," I said. "It wasn't that I was worried about getting caught. I was worried about being interrupted."

"Sure you weren't worried about that nice-looking dark-haired lady catching you spilling your guts out, 'fessin' up to whatever it is you done?"

"Look, I assure you that between me and the nice-looking dark-haired lady there are no secrets."

"Ha-ha."

"I've got to get back to work—"

"I'll keep an eye on the door."

"That's not—"

"If I see that nice-looking dark-haired lady, I'll make a sound like a cough, like *kaakh*, so's—"

"Look, that's not necessary. I'm not trying to hide anything from her."

"Ha-ha."

"Will you please, please shut up and let me get this written?"

" 'Shut up'? Did you tell me to 'shut up'?"

"I did. Yes, I did. I just need an hour of quiet. I have some thoughts that I want to jot down. Please, please just shut up for an hour. Please."

"Well, excuse me for living!" she said theatrically, and to show how deeply I had offended and hurt her, she opened the morning paper with a violent rustle and snap, raising it in front of her like a shield. I looked up from my computer with the intent of making some half-hearted apology, just to smooth the waters, but the paper's banner headline struck me dumb. It read:

TRAGIC CRASH AT FLY-IN
HELICOPTER HEROES LOST

"Do You Sell *The New York Times*?" I asked the clerk at the desk.

"The New York what?" he asked.

"Never mind," I said. "Is there a stationery store or a bookstore nearby?"

"Um," he said, "I think there's a bookstore in the Tri-State Mega-Mall."

"They're not going to be open this early," I said. "How about a coffee shop? Any local outlets of nationwide coffee pushers?"

"Oh, sure. Quite a few. Here's a map."

"A map?"

"Yeah. The manager drew this up 'cause people are always asking where they can get a quality cup of coffee. You wouldn't believe how much time the map saves."

I scanned it, hoping that it might save me some time, too, hoping that it would allow me to buy a copy of the *Times* and get back to the motel before Albertine came down to the breakfast room. Map in hand, I hurried to the parking lot, leapt into the Electro-Flyer, and drove to the nearest coffee shop on the map. They didn't sell the *Times*, and the second place didn't sell it, either, but the third place had it. I flipped through it quickly to see if there was anything about the incident at the fly-in. There was nothing, not a mention, not even a tiny story. The world had provided enough horrors to leave no space for lost helicopter heroes. I bought a copy and rushed back to the motel. When Albertine came into the breakfast room, I handed it to her.

"I got you the *Times*," I said.

"I'm surprised that they have it here," she said, scanning the headlines with a frown and a furrowed brow.

"They don't," I said. "All they have is some local rag. Nothing in it. You wouldn't want to bother with it. I doubt that it even has a crossword puzzle. That's why I went looking for the *Times*. I found it at a little place down the street."

"Thanks," she said. "What section do you want?"

"Oh, don't bother about me. You just dive right in. There's a lot of news there, and we'll want to get on the road soon."

"We will?"

"Sure we will. We'll want to avoid rush hour."

"Rush hour? I doubt that there's much of a rush hour—"

"I'll get you some coffee. You start reading."

Reluctant to leave her alone for more than a heartbeat, I dashed to the coffee vat, poured her a cup, brought it to her, dashed back to the buffet counter, loaded a plate with fruit, rolls, butter, and little caskets of jelly and jam, and brought that to her, too. Then I sat down across from her to watch her read and eat.

After a couple of minutes, she put the paper down and said, "Do you know what became of them?"

I was so startled by her question that I couldn't speak.

She snapped her fingers in front of my eyes and said, "Peter?"

"Huh?"

"Lost in thought?"

"Um—yeah."

"I asked you if you know what became of them."

"I—um—all I know is—ah—that they were—'lost.'"

"'Lost'? What do you mean?"

"Well—I guess—'lost'—I guess it's a journalistic euphemism—for—" For what? What was I trying to avoid saying? I think I was trying to avoid saying, "Died screaming in pain, in flames, in the twisted wreckage of their helicopter, because a jealous husband wanted to be rid of them."

"Are you saying that they're all dead?"

"I'm not certain that it's so—but I think it might be—"

"Not Matthew," she said, "and not you—but you think the others are all dead?"

"What? Who?"

"All of those Faustroll kids are dead?"

"Oh—Faustroll. Faustroll! No. I mean—I don't know."

"Maybe you'd better just drift back to wherever it was you were before I interrupted your thoughts."

"No. That's okay. I wasn't anywhere I wanted to be. Let's get out of here. Get on the road. I'll read to you."

MAN AGAINST MACHINE

ᴺ**ICK'S TYPEWRITER WAS** the envy of all who had seen it. It was Italian. It was sleek, compact, and light. It was beautiful. I think it was one of the first practical objects that I recognized as having a good design, although if you had asked me at the time what I meant by a good design, I couldn't have given you a very good answer. I think—and I'm trying very hard to let my younger self speak here without coaching or revision—that an object's having a good design, or being well designed, meant that if I owned it I would have been proud to own it—or, better, if I had chosen it from all the other available objects of its type, all the objects in its set or universe, I would have been proud of the choice, proud of myself for making the choice, and (here's an important point) I would have felt confident that I wouldn't have to change my mind about my choice, ever. I would have felt that my sixty-three-year-old self would be as sure about the choice of that well-designed object, whatever it was, as my fifteen-year-old self was. That's accurate, I think, and it certainly works for Nick's typewriter, but the flaw in it is that my fifteen-year-old self never imagined, not even in his wildest thought experiments, that he would someday be me, or sixty-three.

Since Nick and I had spent many hours in the workshop, working side-by-side on our electronics projects, I felt that he would almost certainly be willing to let me use his typewriter for something as important as retyping the count's list of student assessments.

My plan for the list was a simple one, simple but brilliant. I planned to retype the entire list, adding myself to it, with a glowing assessment: "Outstanding. A superior simp in every way. Stands head and shoulders above the rest. Crafty, capable, courageous, clever, and cunning." Then I planned to fold it just as the original had been folded, rub it in some desert sand, and hand it to the count.

I'd say something cool, casual, and crisp, like, "You dropped this, Count, last night, in the desert."

What did I hope to gain from that, you ask? Did I expect him to pass the retyped list to whatever higher-ups he reported to? No. I knew that wouldn't happen. He wasn't gullible. He would suspect that I'd tampered with the list. He'd check it carefully, and he would find my alteration, but that would be my reward. When he saw that I had added myself to the list, I would have accomplished what I wanted. I would have made sure that *someone* knew that I was skilled enough to track the count and uncover his duplicity. That someone would be the count himself. I felt certain that he wouldn't turn me in to the authorities because doing so would put him in a bad light; he would be as much as declaring to his handlers that I was on to him, that I had bested him in the desert. I would have given myself a victory. It would be a small victory, a very small victory, but it seemed to be all the victory that the circumstances would allow.

(Okay, in terms of fullness and frankness, this chapter is off to a bad start. There are several things wrong with it. First, Nick and I were not both working on electronics projects. His circuitry was electronic, but mine was merely electrical, just a bunch of switches and bulbs, though I had found nifty little neon bulbs for it, which, I hoped, would suggest that the thing had more sophisticated innards than it actually did. My electromechanical brain was a crude thing. It was a crude thing, but it was my own, and I was proud of it. Second, I had no reason to believe that Nick was going to allow me to use his typewriter. He had never allowed anyone else to use it, and only wishful thinking could have made me think that he might make an exception for me. Third, the plan to insert myself into the count's list of student assessments wasn't my own: it was *Spirit*'s. I know that it was, ultimately, mine, but I doubt that I could have arrived at it without her assistance. Even if I was talking to myself in the warehouse, I seem to have required at least a proxy audience to get my thinking off the ground.)

I expected that Nick would be in the workshop, and he was. I can see him at work now, while I'm writing this, bent over his automatic camera, fiddling with it, making adjustments, poking and prodding it, trying to make it work the way it should, the way he had hoped it would.

"Nick," I said.

"Peter," he said. He stood and stretched. "I'm glad you're here. I need someone to talk to. I'm a nervous wreck."

I think the parallel between my position and *Spirit*'s struck me immediately. I'd like to be able to say that with conviction, but it's possible that I'm noticing it for the first time now, as I recall the moment.

"What's the matter?" I asked, without a trace of *Spirit*-style testiness or irritation at the thought that he considered my ears and the brain they served only as good or as useful as anybody else's.

"I want to put the camera to the test tonight, but I'm worried that it might not perform as it should."

"Why? You've tried it a thousand times."

"Only seventy-two, actually."

"Well, still—it's been extensively tested."

"Yes, but it's never been tested under actual conditions, under the conditions that will obtain tonight when we're all gathered in the observatory and everybody is looking at me with a mixture of expectation and skepticism."

"I see what you mean," I said. "In fact, I know what you mean. Sometimes, when I think about my model of a brain, it seems like a good idea to me, and sometimes, if I'm in a good mood, I even think that I've done a good job of building it."

I paused to allow him to jump in with some note of genuine, heartfelt assurance that he considered my brain a wonder, something along the lines of, "Damn it, Peter, as far as I'm concerned, that brain of yours is not merely a good idea but a brilliant one and I can't imagine who could possibly have built a better realization of it."

"Uh-huh," he said.

Emboldened by that, I went on. "But at other times, it just seems stupid, or worse than stupid, just the silly idea of a foolish kid, an idea that seems incredibly childish, naïve, and ignorant—"

"Jejune," he said.

"Jejune? Is that what that means?"

"Pretty much."

"Then the idea seems jejune, and the execution of it seems—I don't know—I guess it seems like—"

"A mess."

"Yeah," I said sadly. How I wished that he hadn't said it, even if I had thought it. Somehow, when he said it, it seemed to be so. I looked at the device. Mere minutes ago, before I had begun my attempt to respond sympathetically to Nick's doubts about his own device, I had thought that it was a pretty good job, all in all. I had actually been looking forward to showing it to people. I think I had even allowed myself to expect a little praise, a little admiration. Now I didn't. The thing was a mess. If anyone looked at it beside Nick's automatic camera, it would seem even worse in comparison. Hmm. There was the germ of an idea there. One part of my mind was beginning to see a way to profit from the distress that another part of my mind was experiencing. The distressed part was very nearly ready to urge me to destroy the gadget before anyone saw it, but another part, a more calculating part, said, "Wait a minute. Not so fast. I've got an idea."

"I've got an idea, Nick," I said.

"What's that?"

"It's an idea about how to ensure that your camera gets a good reception, maybe not as good a reception as you and I think it deserves, but a better reception than you fear it might get."

"How could we possibly ensure that?"

"I'll present my model of a brain to the group before you present your camera. The comparison will make your camera shine, even if it doesn't perform perfectly, even if it doesn't perform at all. It's all about expectations, you see. The crowd that shows up tonight is going to be hoping for great things from your camera. They're all going to be hoping that they'll get a picture of the girl in the window to take home with them, something to make their friends think they had a much more interesting summer than they actually did. They've allowed that hope to turn into an expectation. But we can modify that expectation. I'll show them this mess and rattle on about it in my jejune way until their eyes begin to glaze. By the time I'm through with them, their expectations will be considerably lowered. In fact, I'm willing to bet that I can get those expectations down to the level of 'I'll be satisfied if the damn camera just goes click when the girl turns her light on.'"

Nick's jaw dropped. He blinked his eyes several times. He began to splutter. "P-p-peter," he said, "that is—that is—that is—"

"A brilliant idea?" I suggested.

"Yes!" he said.

"Thanks."

"It's also—very generous."

"Well, I'm sure you would do the same thing for me."

"Hmm," he said thoughtfully. "I might, but, well, no, I wouldn't."

"You wouldn't?"

"No. If I presented my camera before you presented your brain, the trick wouldn't work."

"Oh," I said. "Yeah. Right. Well, I didn't really mean that you would do exactly the same thing for me. I meant that you'd do something else for me if I needed your help."

"Possibly."

"Probably."

"Okay, probably."

"I need to borrow your typewriter."

"Not a chance."

"Could I use it while you keep a watchful eye on me to make sure that I don't wreck it?"

"No. But—"

"But?"

"I'd be willing to type whatever it is you need typed."

"I can't let you do that," I said. "What I need typed is something that—well, let's just say that it's something you shouldn't see—for your own good."

"Mysterious," he said.

I shrugged in the manner of a young man of mystery and turned for the door.

"Peter," he said.

"Nick?" I said, stopping, but without turning around, hopeful that he might have changed his mind.

"I owe you a favor. I know it. And I'll repay it if I can."

In the library, several typewriters were available for general use, battered machines that had been abused by many students for many years. I surveyed them all, chose the one that seemed least decrepit, and with a sigh settled to the task of typing a new version of the count's list. I wasn't much of a typist. The work began badly and got worse. My nerves began to fray. The typewriter that I had chosen seemed to resent me, seemed to be fighting me. I fought back. It resisted. I insisted. It balked. I bashed.

"Why are you fighting me?" I growled at it.

It said nothing.

"Curse you and the sonofabitch who invented you," I said.

Still nothing. Clearly it was a stupid machine, with none of *Spirit*'s talent for reading my mind.

"Why the hell do you have to be so headstrong?"

"Headstrong?" it asked. That was a surprise.

"You heard me," I snarled. "Headstrong."

A chair scraped. I looked up to see one of the simps gathering his books and heading for the door without a backward glance.

"I'm not headstrong," the machine claimed.

"Yes, you are," I insisted. "Whenever I strike a key, you drive the corresponding letter against the ribbon and the paper and the platen with unnecessary haste. When I look at the result, it's usually a mistake, but you've impressed it upon the paper with such assertive firmness and blackness that it's practically ineradicable."

"I'm just doing my job."

"Why do you have to do it so uncompromisingly? Why do you have to record my mistakes so quickly and so permanently? You pound them into the paper before I've had a chance to reconsider the actions that put them there."

"That's what I'm supposed to do. I'm supposed to do what you tell me to do swiftly and efficiently, without questioning your wisdom or your motives."

"I'm not asking you to do my thinking for me, or even to second-guess me. I just want you to stop being so—headstrong."

"There's that word again, that accusation. I resent it."

"I wouldn't accuse you of being headstrong if you would do me the favor of holding my keystrokes in a limbo of hesitation for a moment, keep them in an indeterminate state between my striking the key and your making an impression on the paper."

"I can't do that."

"No, of course you can't. That's why I curse your inventor. You should have been designed to give me a little breathing room, a pause that would give me a chance to check myself and verify that I've made the stroke I intended to make, that the mark you were going to make on the paper was going to be the mark I wanted there. With the addi-

tion of that moment's hesitation, you could have been made into a forgiving machine, but—"

"I wasn't designed that way."

"Right. You were designed to be headstrong and stubborn."

"Stubborn, too?"

"That's what I call it when you repeatedly refuse to put on the paper
the symbol that ought to be there, when you insist on putting there
what I have mistakenly told you to put there. Why couldn't you have
the good grace to give me a chance to take back the false gesture, the
erroneous stroke? Isn't that what we all wish for? A moment of grace?
A moment between the act and its effect? A moment when the act can
be reconsidered and, if reconsideration suggests it, recalled or rescinded
or reversed?"

"Ouch!"

"What happened?"

"I think you brok something."

"Oh. It's—hmm—it's nothing."

"Ar you sur ?"

"Sure. You're fine. Don't worry."

"Wh r ar you going? Ar you l aving?"

"I'm just going to try another machine."

Eventually, at long last, I was finished. So were three of the typewriters
that had refused to bend to my will. My list was not as well typed as the
count's. His was free of erasures to an impressive degree. Either he was
a very good typist or he had retyped the pages several times, choosing
the best for the final document, so that he would appear to be good
even at this small task. I didn't have the time or patience to produce a
document as clean as his. My pages had been tortured by a typewriter
eraser rough as pumice, leaving holes in the places where I had erased
repeatedly, mementoes of the times when one of the typewriters had
put up an especially tough fight,

I folded the list. On my way back to the dorm, I dusted it with
desert sand. Then I secreted it in my pocket.

ADEQUATELY DRESSED

· ·

SLIPPING AWAY AT night to work on my confession became more difficult. Albertine seemed acutely attuned to my presence or absence. If I slipped away while she was asleep, I rarely had more than an hour before she awoke and came looking for me. Affection caused this reluctance to be without me, I think, I hope, but I also think that a part of it was curiosity: she was powerfully curious to know what I intended to say about the Birdboy myth. I couldn't blame her; I was powerfully curious myself. If I was going to discover what I wanted to say, I needed time to myself.

I reasoned that her perception of my absence at night might begin with a perception of a change in the compression of the mattress, an awareness that there had come to be a lightness on my side of the bed where there ought to have been a husbandweight of heaviness. To prevent her from detecting that change, I considered putting a suitcase in my place when I left, but when I tried it as a thought experiment the effect was ridiculous, pathetic, and somehow sinister. Albertine looked like a lonely woman sleeping with a suitcase because without it her bed would be empty: no husband, no lover, no muddleheaded dreamer, not even a birdbrain. Her waking to find me gone would be one thing, but if she woke and found that I had gone and left a suitcase in my place, that would be another. From her point of view, lying there with a suitcase where her honey ought to be, the evidence would seem to say that I had made a calculated effort to deceive her. Well, of course, I actually would have made a calculated effort to deceive her, and even if she were immediately to tell herself that I had deceived her only so that I could have the privacy I needed to compose my confession, the deception could only upset her. What could I do?

"Wait a minute, you fool," I said to myself. "Don't deceive her. Don't even try to deceive her. Do the very opposite! Instead of a deceptive suitcase, leave a heartfelt note, a frank admission that you have slipped away from the connubial bed to work on your confession. Instead of being upset, won't she be sympathetic?" It seemed worth a try. I slipped out of bed, grabbed the clothes that I'd left draped over a chair, and sequestered myself in the bathroom. There I hastily wrote a heartfelt note.

> *Albertine, my darling,*
>
> *Don't be alarmed to discover that I am not by your side when you wake. I couldn't sleep because my mind is full of ideas for the press conference. I'm going to work for an hour or so. There's no need to come looking for me. I'm sure I'll find a suitable place.*
>
> Love,
Peter

Gently, gently, I set the note on my pillow where my head had dented it. I backed toward the door, watching Albertine for any sign of wakefulness, ready to freeze like a hunted animal—as I had when playing the skulker in the game of Night Watchman or when tracking the count in the desert—if she moved or even breathed in a way that looked like restlessness. I saw nothing. I opened the door with painstaking slowness, turning the knob degree by degree, pausing whenever I thought that a degree might have produced a squeak. Slowly, slowly, I began to open the door. The thinnest sliver of light fell into the room, and Albertine spoke.

"I've read that motels are having quite a problem with guests who wander out of their rooms in their sleep and roam the hallways naked," she said. "I hope you're not going to do that."

"No," I assured her. "I'm dressed."

"Adequately?"

"Yes."

"Going to work on your remarks for the press conference?"

"Yes."

"Don't stay up all night."

"I won't."

"Come back to me."

"I will."

Rather than risk running into another guest, I didn't go to the motel's lobby or business center; I just sat on the floor outside our room with my back against the wall and my computer in my lap. I read what I had written so far, and then I just sat there. I didn't seem to have any fresh ideas. I tried again. I still didn't seem to have any fresh ideas. Doggedly, I kept trying, backing up, reading what I'd written so far, and then running at the wall where that universe ended, trying to batter my way through and fill some of the emptiness on the other side. It wasn't working.

"That's pretty impressive, the way you can sit in the full lotus position like that and type on a computer—especially at your age."

Apparently my mind was playing tricks on me. It was speaking to me in a voice like Albertine's.

"Peter?"

Can't fool me, mind.

"Peter?"

Hey. How can you shake me by the shoulder like that?

"Al!"

"Were you deliberately ignoring me?"

"No, no. I was just—"

"Lost in thought. I know. Come on back to bed now."

"But I just got here."

"You've been out here for an hour."

"I have? An hour? I haven't accomplished anything."

"That's because you're working at something you don't want to do."

"You're right about that."

"Come to bed. Try again in the morning. Get up early."

"Okay," I said. I was happy to give up, but I tried not to be obvious about it.

"At least you were adequately dressed," she said.

"Maybe that was the problem."

"Hm?"

"Well, metaphorically speaking, I'm going to be exposing myself at that press conference. Maybe I should have dressed for the part."

"Get into that room."

SUCCESS IN CIRCUITRY

••

"His reverence the preacher, who preached in this town last Lent, . . . said, if I remember rightly, that all things present that our eyes behold bring themselves before us and remain and fix themselves on our memory much better and more forcibly than things past."

—Sancho Panza in *Don Quixote*

THE OBSERVATORY WAS more crowded than usual. Even the count, who had claimed that the observatory could offer him nothing that he hadn't already seen, had turned out to see Nick's camera in operation, and the crowd was further augmented by Victoria, Andrea, and Virginia, who had disguised themselves as male simps.

I greeted them with a knowing wink.

"You recognized us?" asked Tank.

"I did," I said.

"How?" asked Button.

"You look like three girls dressed as hoboes for Hallowe'en. I'm surprised that you didn't burn a cork and give yourselves beards."

"We thought about it," muttered Slim.

"I was in favor of it," said Tank. "I argued that burnt-cork beards would give us the protection of farce if we were discovered. We could claim that it was 'just a joke.'"

"Is anything ever 'just a joke,'" mused Button, "or is every joke a serious statement hidden behind a burnt-cork beard?"

"Ha-ha," I said in the manner of Bosse-de-Nage.

"Do you think everybody else recognizes us?" asked Slim.

"I suspect so," I said, "but I think they're all pretending not to recognize you so that if the authorities get wind of your being in the boys' dorm they will be able to claim that they were so completely deceived by your clever disguises that they hadn't the least notion that you were female."

"Ha-ha," said Slim, though she may not have read *Faustroll*.

"If we could have some quiet, people," said Nick, raising his hands in the air, "Peter and I have a couple of contraptions to show you." He beckoned to me to join him.

A murmur of puzzlement arose from the crowd, since most of the simps in the observatory hadn't known anything about my project, though nearly all of them had known about Nick's.

Nick and I stood side-by-side for a moment, but then he made an open-handed gesture to indicate that I should take the stage, and he stepped aside.

"I've made a model of a brain," I said, holding the gadget aloft. I looked at it. I was astonished, when I regarded it in my hand, up there at arm's length, to find how little enthusiasm I had for it. In my mind, in the hierarchy of my enthusiasms, it had already been superseded by the next version, which would be so much more sophisticated than this one that the poor thing I was offering to the crowd seemed, well, jejune. "It's a simple model of a simple brain," I said, "more like a game really," disparaging my own work as if it were nothing, possibly nothing more than a joke, giving it a burnt-cork beard.

Nick cleared his throat and frowned at that. Apparently he thought better of my device than I did myself. That was a pleasant surprise.

"Before I open it up so that you can see its wiring," I said, "let me just point out a couple of things about it that make it like a human brain. First, although you can see that the gadget responds to stimuli—the buttons that I push—you can't tell what it's thinking. By that I mean that you can't tell from the response—the lights that light up—what the state of the brain is, what combination of states of switches has produced a particular response. Well, actually, for some responses you can, if you spend a little time playing with it, but for others you can't."

The audience response was, so far, silence. I walked the model around the room and pushed its buttons so that the simps could see that there was no observable link between the pressing of any one button and the pattern of lit and unlit lamps that resulted.

"Notice that some combinations of button-pushing produce a response—a pattern of lights—that looks identical to the response produced by an entirely different combination of button-pushing," I said. "However, the internal state of the brain may not be identical in both cases, as you will see if you study the wiring diagram."

Nick held up the enlarged drawing of the wiring diagram that I had made.

"I've made a model of a brain," I said, holding the gadget aloft.

"That's what I meant when I said that you can't tell what it's thinking. The best that you can do is infer what it's thinking from its response. If I'd used toggle switches, the position of each toggle would tell you what the internal state of the corresponding switch was, but with these push-on-push-off switches, there is no outward indication of the internal state. Of course, if you pried each of the switches apart to see whether it was in its A state or its B state, you would know the brain's 'state of mind,' but you would have destroyed it in the process, which is another thing that makes it like a human brain."

More silence. I couldn't tell from that response what the audience's collective state of mind might be. They might have been impressed, even awed, but I doubted it. Boredom seemed more likely, and I even thought, or feared, that they might be embarrassed for me.

"That's pretty much it," I said. "I'll open the case for you so that you can see the wiring inside." I had to restrain myself from adding that I hoped they would notice that I'd done a pretty good job of soldering.

The silence gave way to murmuring. I heard something that sounded a bit like *jejune,* and when I looked up from the work of opening my brain's case I saw the count at the edge of the crowd, smirking at me.

"I just want to say something," Nick called out over the murmuring. "Peter and I have spent long hours working side-by-side in the workshop, and from the things he's said during our conversations—and from things I've heard him muttering under his breath when he didn't know that I was listening—I know that he has some pretty exciting modifications in mind for the next version of his brain."

I seem to hear in memory somebody muttering, "Let's hope so," but I'd like to think that I'm wrong about that.

Nick gave me an encouraging look, inviting me to add to what he'd said, but I'd had it with this crowd. I shook my head.

"Well," said Nick, "Peter may be too modest to talk about his plans, but I know that one of the things he's going to do is replace some of the pushbuttons with other devices that will send stimuli to the brain. For example, my camera—which I'll demonstrate for you in a minute—uses a photocell to detect a flash of light, and when Peter replaces one switch with a photocell, his brain will be able to see. It'll be seeing at a simple level, of course—but it will be able to detect light, and the transistorized circuitry that he's going to add will allow him to adjust the sensitivity of its 'eye.'"

What a great idea that was. I could give my brain the power of sight. Was that my idea? If it was, when had I had it? I didn't remember it, but I'd had a lot on my mind every day of my stay at SIMPaW. Maybe I had thought of it but then forgotten it. I was lucky that Nick had remembered it.

"Using the same basic circuitry," he continued, "but with a microphone in place of a photocell, he can enable the brain to hear, or at least to detect sound. A thermocouple and humidistat will allow it to detect changes in heat and humidity. I wouldn't be surprised if certain patterns of its lights began to look like complaints about the weather."

More good ideas, really terrific ideas, outstanding. I was surprising myself, thanks to Nick. Apparently, my mind was always working, always thinking, always coming up with good stuff, even when I wasn't aware of it. How fortunate that I had the habit of muttering to myself while I was working, and that I muttered these particular ideas to myself while I'd been working on my brain, and how fortunate, too, that Nick had heard my inspired mutterings and remembered them.

"Time's running out," said someone from the back of the crowd.

"Okay," said Nick. "Just one more point about Peter's plans."

A collective groan.

"I'll open the case for you so that you can see the wiring inside."

"His biggest idea of all is this," said Nick in a tone that suggested that anyone who hoped to see the automatic camera capture an image of the girl in the window had better hear him out. "He's going to add lights inside the box, and photocells, and switches triggered by the photocells."

This brought silence again.

"*Inside the box,*" Nick repeated, with an intensity that I found thrilling. "You see the implications, don't you? The brain will know something about its own internal state, *and it will change its state as a result of that knowledge*. It won't be limited to information that arrives from outside its case. It will begin to manufacture—or, if you'll allow me the word, create—information for itself. The impenetrable walls of the brain's black box will still prevent us from knowing what it is thinking, but it will know. In a tiny way it will be aware of itself. It will know its own mind."

The silence that followed that exaggeration might have been profound. It might have been, but it wasn't. A voice broke it: "Jesus, Dennis, it's just a box full of wires. We wanna see the camera."

Nick gave me a look that said, "I tried."

I gave him one that said, "Thanks." His debt to me had been paid; I knew that. I think I even knew that I was now the debtor. It is possible that I knew that I ought to repay him if I could.

542 • PETER LEROY

• • • • • • • • •

While Nick explained how his automatic camera worked, or how it ought to work, I drifted away from the center of attention and into the crowd. I wanted to remove myself from the spotlight, but I also wanted to find the count. He had been on the edge of the crowd when I'd spotted him earlier, just where I would have expected him to be, on the periphery, where in his superior way he could observe the vulgar voyeurs without quite becoming one of them.

While the other simps listened with eager anticipation to Nick's description of the way the camera would capture an image of the girl in the window, I made a full circuit of the darkened room, but I didn't find the count.

"Have you seen Whitney?" I asked Eugene when I found myself beside him.

"He's gone," he said.

"Gone?"

"Yeah. He left for the airport about ten minutes ago."

"Left for the airport? Why?"

"Didn't you hear?"

"Hear what? Was he—was he thrown out of SIMPaW?"

"No. Why would he be thrown out of SIMPaW?"

"Oh, I don't know. I thought maybe he wasn't living up to expectations."

"He left because his father died."

"His father—what?"

"Died."

"And Whitney is gone?"

"Gone."

"Not coming back?"

"Nope."

My hand went to my pocket. The list was there, laboriously typed, carefully folded, cleverly dusted, and utterly useless. I was speechless with disappointment. It had all been for nothing. It had all been futile. I had done so much work. All that stalking. All that typing. All the effort expended in anticipating the moment when I would hand the list of student assessments to the count. All the effort that I'd put into imagining how it would go.

"Count," I would say in a civil tongue.

"Peter," he would respond in a similar tone.

"I have something of yours," I would remark, as if the fact barely interested me.

"Oh?" I would detect a flicker of curiosity that he couldn't completely conceal.

"Something that you dropped."

"Something that I dropped?" I would see concern in his eyes, quickly covered by a raised eyebrow.

"Yes, something that you dropped," I would say, and then I would insert the perfect pause—not too brief, not too long—before adding, "in the desert."

"What?" he would say as, reflexively, he brought his hand to his pocket.

"I thought it might be important, so I picked it up for you."

"I think you must be mistaken, Peter."

"I think not, Count."

I would reach into my own pocket and bring the list out, cupping it to shield it from the view of passersby, as I had seen the men who attended Rudolph Derringer's free introductory lecture cup their cigarettes to shield them from the rain. I would pass it to him just as it was, folded and dusted.

"Hmmm," he would say, surreptitiously glancing at it. "You say you found this in the desert?"

"Yes, in the desert."

"It doesn't look like anything of mine."

Damn, I would think. I've got to admit that, in a sense, he's right. The original that I found out there in the desert was much neater. Sure, it had some desert dust on it, but the paper was crisp, the whole thing neatly folded. What I'm asking him to claim as his is crumpled and torn. It's a mess.

"It's been in my pocket for a while," I would say.

"I suggest that you keep it there," he would say, icily, offering it to me.

"I suppose it would be in your best interest if I did that," I would say, "if I kept it from falling into anyone else's hands."

"I don't know what you're talking about," he would claim.

"Perhaps not," I would say, pocketing the list. "Maybe I was wrong. Maybe you didn't drop it." I would shrug the shrug of a boy who has been wrong before and is willing to accept the likelihood that he is wrong now. I would turn to go. I would take a few paces—but then I would stop. I would shake my head. I would seem to be puzzled. "Oh," I would say, turning back to face him again and bringing my hand to my forehead as if I'd just recalled something so trivial that it was barely worth mentioning, "there's one other thing."

"What is that, Peter?" he would say with exaggerated condescension.

"I wanted to compliment you."

"You wanted to compliment me?"

"That's right. I wanted to compliment you on your singing voice. You're really good. I was impressed. That wasn't by any chance 'Un Bel Di' that you were singing, was it?"

"It most certainly was not," he would say. "It was—"

There, right there, I would have him. I wouldn't have managed to get him to pass the altered document along to his handlers—maybe I'd never had much chance of bringing that off—but I would have shown him that I had tracked him, that I had found him out, that I really did have his list of assessments, and that I could make it public if I chose to. I would have won my little victory.

Now it was never going to happen. The count's goddamned father had snatched my little victory from me. Dead! What a lousy time to die! In another week, SIMPaW would come to an end, the students would scatter back to their homes, and I would be forgotten. Officially, I would leave no trace at all. Even for the members of the Faustroll Institute the memory of me would fade like the afterimage of the girl in the window until eventually they would wonder whether I had ever really been there at all. Finally, I would slide into the darkness of the unrecalled. I was getting bitter. I might have done something desperate if at that moment the girl in the window hadn't turned her light on. Almost instantaneously, the solenoid in Nick's automatic mechanism shot its bolt, triggering the shutter of the camera attached to it. Then she turned her light off. The observers stood in silence for a while, with their eyes shut, as usual, savoring her afterimage, just in case that might be all they ever got from the experiment. Then, gradually, as her image faded for one and another of them, the applause began. When it threatened to become loud enough to attract attention, Nick began shushing them.

"We're not there yet," he said. "Let's hold the applause until we've developed the film."

I slipped out the door ahead of the crowd.

ANTICIPATING THE RECEPTION

FOR THE REST of the trip back to Manhattan, my work on my confession fell into a regular pattern. I stopped trying to work in the middle of the night or to steal time during the day. Instead, I would wake at some small hour of the morning and go to work.

Albertine helped. She never asked me about it. She never asked me how the work was going. She never asked if I wanted to read some of it to her. She was patient.

In those early morning hours of those last days, as I worked steadily, with focus and purpose, I found that the progress of the work began to relieve me of some of the anxiety I felt about the confession itself. However, I began fretting more and more about how it would be received. As I drew closer in time and space to the press conference and the audience that I would be addressing at that conference, they began to look more and more like an angry mob. Every morning, as I worked, I would find myself in the laboratory of imaginary solutions, reading to that angry mob whatever I'd written, and I'd see them leap to their feet, shake their fists, and call for the tar and feathers. That wasn't the reception I was after. I had to find a way to turn their attitude from outrage to something else. Almost anything else would do, it seemed to me, so long as it didn't involve tarring and feathering. If the confession was going to do what I hoped it would do, it would have to be a masterpiece of subtlety. I worked hard to make it so.

546 · PETER LEROY

Although I wasn't ready to read my confession to Albertine, or even to begin reading it to her, I continued the practice of reading the chapters of my summer adventures to her, generally just one a day, as we made our way back home.

Then I cracked under the strain. I woke from a dream in a sweat. Albertine was hugging me, soothing me, trying to wake me gently, an effort hampered by my thrashing and kicking. In the dream I had tried to do a simple thing, just to return to our table in the restaurant of a hotel after I had visited the men's room, but in this hotel the route of return required me to crawl through narrowing tunnels that conveyed vegetables along a narrowing belt past furious sous-chefs wielding knives.

"There, there, there," she said, petting me.

"I felt like a cabbage," I said.

"A cabbage?"

"Soon to be cole slaw."

"Do you want to talk about it?"

"I'm not sure."

"Step into the laboratory of imaginary solutions with me."

"Okay. Let's see. I think I'm worried that—well—"

I didn't want to say it. Albertine, who understands me so well, said it for me.

"I think you're worried about the reception you'll get when you offer your confession, or your explanation, or justification, or whatever you're going to offer."

"Yes," I said. "You're right."

"Of course, I can understand why you would be worried about how people will respond after they hear whatever it is you're going to tell them."

"You can?" I said. I had been hoping that she would tell me that my fears were groundless.

"I suppose that at worst the audience might erupt in violent fury, rushing the stage and dragging you away. Do angry mobs still tar and feather people?"

"I have no idea."

"How about riding them out of town on a rail?"

"I hadn't even thought of anything so—"

"They might not be organized enough for that. They might just rush the stage in chaotic fury and tear you limb from limb."

"Ye gods."

"Or they might just call you some pretty awful names."

"That seems more realistic. Even likely."

"Or they might laugh at you."

"Laugh at me?"

"They might laugh at the boy whose lust for fame and the affections— or at least the attentions—of Miss Clam Fest made him lie or acquiesce to a misinterpretation that he felt was a lie."

"I think I could endure that."

"They might laugh at the man who thinks that he has to confess to having been that boy, that he has to apologize for having been that boy."

"I think I could endure that, too."

"Then I think you're going to be okay."

"I have one other worry."

"What's that?"

"Will my remarks inspire them to subscribe for copies of my full and frank account of the flight to Corosso as it actually occurred?"

"You're going to—"

"I'm thinking of it. My statement at the press conference won't begin to tell the whole story. If people want that, they'll have to read the full and frank disclosure, complete in three parts. I thought I could finish with something like, 'If you want to know the whole story, sign up now to receive each fascinating installment as it is released. See the beautiful dark-haired woman at the back of the hall. Major credit cards accepted.'"

She said nothing for nearly a minute.

"Well?" I asked.

"I suppose it would give us some money to fly down to Rio and start life afresh under assumed names," she said.

STANDOFF AT SIMPAW

....

AS SOON AS Nick had distributed copies of the picture, they seemed to be everywhere. Wherever I happened to be on campus, I had the tantalizing sense that a copy of the picture was near, even if it was not visible. None of the copies was ever quite visible, but every copy seemed always to be on the verge of being visible. Some simp or other seemed always to be taking his copy, or her copy, out of a pocket to look at it, or turning to the page in a textbook where it was hiding, or slipping it from his wallet for a quick peek, or, having had a peek, to be putting it back into a pocket, closing a book on it, or sliding it back into a wallet. The picture, and even the bare fact of the existence of the picture, should have been a secret, but instead it was in the air; it was known; it was famous.

The picture's fame was the result of a fundamental human failing: the urge to flaunt one's wealth. You know how it is. When you have possessions that make you proud, things that you think set you apart from the crowd, elevate you above it, you want the crowd to know that you possess these remarkable things. This pride of ownership applies to the obvious things, like a powerful automobile or a designer winding sheet, but it also applies to knowledge. When you know something that sets you above the crowd, you want the crowd to know that you are in the know; the obvious way to accomplish that (and most people take the obvious way) is to let the crowd know at least a bit of what you know. Paradoxically, even though the market value of knowledge (for example, secrets) diminishes as it spreads, knowledge has no status-enhancing value at all if no one else knows enough of it to be able to assess or measure its worth. The one who holds a secret must decide which is worth more, the secret itself or the status accorded to one who knows it.

The first indication that the picture's fame was about to bring big trouble was the thunder of heavy footsteps pounding up the stairs at the far end of the hall in the boys' dormitory. We SIMPaW students were all in our rooms, assiduously working, because the final papers for paleontology were due the next day. I was working just as assiduously as the others because I had decided to write a paper, too. Joining the others in the labor seemed like a gesture of loyalty, the sort of thing that might be rewarded. The sound from the stairwell was so loud, so violent, and so welcome an interruption that it drew all of us from our rooms.

Doors opened up and down the hall, and curious simps emerged from them. All eyes turned in the direction of the thunderous rumble, and a nervous heartbeat later the boyfriend of the girl in the window hurtled from the stairwell onto our floor. We all recognized him, because we'd watched him swagger around the campus with Jane Blaine on his arm, and we'd all envied him.

He was in a lather. His face was red. I think he may have been foaming at the mouth. He began striding in our direction, and as he came he seemed to grow larger, his head, his neck, his shoulders and arms and chest growing big and bullish, making my heart swell with nostalgic longing for home and the relative safety of Mrs. Fendreffer's class in classical mythology, so far away, so long ago.

"You know, Dirk," I said to Eugene, muttering out of the side of my mouth, "it's a funny thing to think of at a time like this, but I suddenly understand, at the deepest level, how a young Cretan would have felt in the labyrinth when he saw the Minotaur round a corner, spot him, and begin licking his chops."

"Shut up, Peter," Eugene said, muttering out of the side of his mouth in the same way that I had muttered out of the side of mine. "You're attracting attention to yourself."

"Oh, yeah," I said. "You're right."

He was right. I had attracted the attention of Jane Blaine's boyfriend. He had singled me out, and he was coming my way, with his eyes fixed on me and steam coming from his nostrils.

"You!" he said commandingly, pointing a finger at me. I froze in place, as immobile as I had been when I had encountered the awful physical manifestation of my fearsome conscience back at Majestic Salvage and Wrecking.

"Me?" I said.

"Yeah, you."

His focusing on me gave the other simps the opportunity to slip quietly back into their rooms and shut their doors. They took it. Even Eugene abandoned me. I heard him close the door behind me.

"Wh-what?" I asked.

"Are you the bastard who took the picture?"

"What picture?"

"What picture? You know what picture. *The* picture. The picture that everybody's talking about. The picture the whole goddamned campus is buzzing about. The picture of my girl. The picture that when I find the guy who took it that's the guy whose neck I'm going to wring. That's what picture."

"Oh," I said, and I allowed myself a sigh of relief. He had given me an easy way to escape. All I had to do was point him in the direction of Nick. Then I could say, "So long, see you later, I've got to get back to my paleontology paper," and take the nearest exit out of the labyrinth.

"I'm waiting," he said. "Was it you?"

"It was—" I began, but, alas, loyalty stopped my tongue, telling me that tossing Nick to the boyfriend to save myself was a route that I mustn't take, and, reluctantly, I agreed.

"It was?" he howled. "It was you?"

He reached for my throat.

"Wait!" I squeaked. "There's something you need to know."

"Oh yeah?" he said, cracking his knuckles in the manner of my friend Spike, back in Babbington, and intensifying my powerful yearning to be back at home. "What's that?"

What should I do? Whom could I offer in place of myself as a proper target for neck-wringing? Why shouldn't I just offer up some simp at random? Hadn't they all left me in the corridor to face the raging boyfriend alone? Yes, they had, but, even so, I didn't want anybody's neck on my hands. But wait! There was someone I could give him, someone whose neck wasn't available for wringing. The count! Whitney! I could give him Whitney!

"Well?" he said impatiently.

Alas, again, there seemed to be a question of loyalty standing in the way of my naming the count as the culprit. After all, he had kept my secret despite the fact that it might have been useful to him to disclose it. Shouldn't I repay that loyalty? Or was I being too generous toward him? For all I knew, he might have been on the verge of betraying me when the news arrived that his father had died, thwarting his plans. Sure. That was probably the case.

"I'd just as soon wring your neck as anybody else's," the boyfriend warned me.

I may as well admit that I would have thrown Whit to him right then if I hadn't had a sudden insight. I saw a way out of the labyrinth, a way out that didn't require me to pin the act of taking the photograph on Nick or the count or any other simp. I decided to take that way out.

"Technically speaking," I said, "none of us took that picture."

"Don't give me that 'technically speaking' bullshit," he said, "or your neck'll be the one I wring, technically speaking."

"Bear with me," I said.

"I'll bear with you about two fucking seconds, and then I'll wring your neck."

"The picture of your girlfriend was taken by an automatic camera," I told him, "a kind of robot. None of us clicked the shutter."

"What?"

"The camera was triggered by light."

"By light?"

"Yes. When your girlfriend turned her light on, an electric eye detected it, a sophisticated electronic circuit amplified it and forwarded it to a solenoid, and the solenoid clicked the shutter. No human hands touched the camera when the picture was taken. The gadget took the picture all by itself, automatically."

"Automatically," he said thoughtfully.

"That's right," I said. "Triggered by her light, when she turned it on."

He seemed to sag. This would have been the right moment for me to shut up and savor my success. Instead, I said, "So, you see, in a way, she was the one who took the picture."

His eyes told me that I'd struck the wrong key, and I knew that there was no way to take it back.

Leaning in toward me and reaching for my throat again, he said, very slowly and precisely, "Are you suggesting that Jane deliberately—that she wanted—that she—"

I think my life was just about to begin flashing before my eyes when up and down the corridor, doors swung open and simps began filling the corridor. They were noisy, and they were armed. They were holding

552 · PETER LEROY

lamps, baseball bats, tennis rackets, whatever had come to hand, and
they wore determined looks. The boyfriend heard them and swung his
head around quickly to see what was up. The mob didn't seem to make
much of an impression on him, because he turned back toward me to
finish the work of strangulation, but in the interim the door behind me
had opened, and I felt a cold metallic presence over my shoulder, and
when I looked at the boyfriend's eyes this time they told me that he was
looking into the barrel of Eugene's revolver.

You will not be surprised, I think, to learn that when I recognized the situation as a standoff I experienced a poignant recollection, a complex rush
of nostalgia for the Babbington Theater and for the company of the
friends who had watched westerns with me there, and that when Eugene
cocked his gun the click inspired in me a great, growling, animal hunger
for popcorn. The many, many westerns I had watched at the Babbington
Theater had made me well acquainted with the standoff (also known as
the "Mexican standoff" or, more formally, in its role as a tool of international Cold War diplomacy, "mutual assured destruction"). In a typical
standoff, as presented in those westerns, some varmint would get the
drop on the sheriff only to have the sheriff point out that his deputy had
the varmint in his sights from a position on the roof of the saloon, but
the varmint would in turn point out that his vicious sidekick had snuck
up behind the deputy and was holding a six-shooter to his head, but
then, to everyone's surprise, the town coward would show up behind the
vicious sidekick holding a shotgun, ready to die for the sheriff and for
justice, and so on, and so on, and so on. The sequence could continue forever. As numbers were added to each side, the participants began to realize that if the first trigger were pulled everybody would be shot to hell.

This standoff in the corridor was the first in which I had ever been a
participant. True, I was more a passive than an active participant, but I
was at the center of the action. If you have been at the focus of a standoff, you understand the tremendous pressure I felt. The responsibility for
ending it without bloodshed or strangulation seemed to have fallen to
me. How could I get all of us out of this situation unharmed? My mind
was racing, but it was getting nowhere. We were all still frozen in the aggressive postures demanded by a standoff when there came from the

stairwell—tentative, shy, and sweetly spoken—the single word "Hello?" We all turned in its direction, and we were all struck dumb.

The girl in the window was there.

"Please give me the pictures," she said.

We were too stunned to do anything.

"Please," she said with a sob in her throat, "don't be cruel."

We were flummoxed, all of us, including her boyfriend, who had dropped his hands from my throat and stood staring at her just as the rest of us were.

"The girls gave me theirs," she said. She showed us three pictures, fanned like playing cards. "Please give me yours."

We were astonished, and despite our training we couldn't hide it.

"Do you want to see me beg?" she asked, tears beginning to run down her cheeks. "Okay, I'll beg." She fell to her knees and raised her hands, clasped in the manner of a supplicant. "I'm begging you," she wailed. "Please, don't make me notorious. What you photographed was a token of love. Don't make it lewd. Don't make it dirty."

Now we were embarrassed.

She began to sniffle. "After graduation," she said, "next year, Ronnie and I are going to get married. I want us to have a quiet little life, in a small town, with a little house, and little children. Don't you see that if those pictures are out in the world, there will always be a cloud over that? We—we'll always wonder when one of the pictures will come to light, when we will have to pack up and move on, driven out of town in shame and disgrace."

We looked at one another.

"Okay," she said, wiping her eyes, wiping her nose, "I guess Ronnie was right. He said that a plea for compassion would be wasted on you. He said that the only thing you'd understand—"

Forgetting for the moment that I was supposed to remain an unremarkable mediocrity, I took my copy of the picture from my pocket, walked up to her, dropped to one knee in front of her, and offered it to her. She raised her head and looked at me. Her eyes were swollen. Her nose was red. She smiled and mouthed the words "Thank you."

In eloquent testimony to my having in the greatest degree the qualities that make a man a leader, the other simps approached her one by one and gave her their pictures.

None of us had realized that she was keeping count until she stood and said. "That's a hundred. Thank you." She extended her hand. For one mad moment I thought she might be inviting me to leave with her, but of course it was Ronnie she was reaching for. He came to her, and she took his hand and led him away, down the stairs.

We began to disperse, but when I reached my door, I became aware of a hesitation. I turned and saw the other simps turning. They wore puzzled looks. They regarded one another quizzically. I could tell from those outward signs that their brains were working.

"She got a hundred pictures," said one of them.

"Right," said several others.

"Each of us gave her a picture."

"Right."

"Each of the three girls gave her a picture."

"Right."

"But she didn't get a picture from Whit."

"That's because Whit never got one."

"He left before Dennis gave them out."

"Right."

"And there are a hundred students in SIMPaW, counting Whit."

"Right."

"So, without a picture from Whit, she should have gotten only ninety-nine."

"Right."

"So who gave her the hundredth picture?"

They began looking at one another with increased intensity, searching for some clue that would solve the puzzle for them. I pretended to do the same, but I guess I wasn't very good at it.

"You!" said one of them, fixing me with his gaze.

"Me?" I said with an irrepressible grin.

"What's your number?"

"I am number one-oh-one," I said.

Every one of them repeated it, I think, and then one of them asked, "What are you doing here?"

"That's an interesting story," I said.

The telling took a couple of hours, and I loved every minute of it. I think I can say with the certainty that I won't want to contradict myself in the future that it was the best couple of hours I spent at SIMPaW. I was in possession of secret information, and I was eager to divulge it. In this case, giving it away did not diminish its value at all.

I'LL TAKE ROMANCE

WHILE I HAD a copy of Nick's picture of the girl in the window, I studied it long, hard, and often," I said to Abertine.

"Diligent boy."

"I ask you to recall that at that time nude photographs of women were hard to come by."

"So this rare specimen demanded your attention."

"Exactly. And as I studied it I began to learn something about photographs and memories, about documentary and romance."

"Making you wiser than you were when you left home?"

"In some ways."

"How so?"

"I'll put it the way it seemed to me then: While I was staring at the picture of Jane Blaine, there seemed to be a struggle going on in my mind between the photograph of her and my memories of the glimpses of her that I'd had when she illuminated herself in the window. The photograph insisted on something that my memories contradicted."

"Which was?"

"The photograph told me that Jane Blaine was plain. My memories told me not to believe it."

"Ahhh, I see. Photograph versus memory, documentary versus romance."

"The battle was won by memory, by romance, as you well know."

"So when it came time to give the picture to Jane—"

"I was glad to see it go."

WHAT COULD I DO?

· ·

I **WAS EAGER** to get back home, eager to tell my story to another audience, my friends in Babbington, but I wasn't looking forward to another long ride on *Spirit*. I had thought about that ride, had tested it thoroughly in the laboratory of imaginary solutions, and it had felt like nothing more than more of the same, an unwelcome repetition of the ride to Corosso, but in the opposite direction, which made it feel like the lost traveler's error of retracing his steps. I didn't want to do it. This time, I wanted to fly. I thought that I might be able to make that happen—if I had help.

"Nick," I said, when we were walking back to the dorm after breakfast the next day, "can I tell you something in confidence?"

"Yes," he said. "You can."

"Okay, well—"

"However, I think that the question you meant to ask me was 'If I tell you something in confidence will you promise not to reveal it to anyone?'"

"Um, you're right. That's what I meant."

"Then I will."

"Will what?"

"Promise not to reveal it to anyone."

"Good. Thanks. Okay. Here it is. My aerocycle, *Spirit of Babbington*—"

"Yes?"

"It—"

"She."

"What?"

"You told us it was a she."

"Oh. Right. It is. She is. She—"

"Can't get off the ground."

"She can't—how did you know that?"

"I saw enough of her the day that you arrived to decide that. I'm no expert when it comes to aeronautical engineering, but I thought from the first that I was seeing an airplane that was overweight and under-powered."

"You're right," I said, lowering my voice as if she might be able to hear us. "Here's what I was wondering."

"Mm?"

"Since we've got the hope of the nation right here on campus, maybe they can help me."

"Help you?"

"Help me make some changes to *Spirit*, make her lighter and more powerful, get her off the ground."

"I'm sorry to have to say this, Peter, but I don't think she can be made to fly. I think she'd have to be replaced."

"Oh."

"I won't be offended if you decide to seek another opinion."

"I won't," I said. "I think I agree with you."

At the warehouse door, I stood in hesitation, reluctant to do what I was about to do, wishing that I didn't feel that I had to do it. I had decided not to ride *Spirit* back to New York. I wasn't going to replace her. I didn't have a heart hard enough for that, and besides there wasn't enough time to design, build, and test another small airplane, not even if I could recruit the entire student body of SIMPaW to help me. However, I had decided to leave her in New Mexico and spend the rest of my summer money, the rest of my life's savings, on an airline ticket to New York. If you've never built an aerocycle and spent days and nights adventuring together along the vast extent of the American highway system, my feeling that I had to tell her the bad news, that I owed her that frankness, may seem like madness to you. After all, she was only a machine, wasn't she? How could I feel an obligation to a machine? Why should I feel that I owed her a goodbye or an explanation or an apology? Why shouldn't I just forget about her entirely, leave Corosso, climb aboard a sleek and powerful airliner, fly home in comfort and style, and never give *Spirit* another thought? Because we had been through so much together, because I'd shared my thoughts with her. That was why.

I opened the door.

"*Spirit?*" I said into the dark.

"Is that you, Peter?"

"Yes, it's me."

"There's something in your tone of voice that I don't like."

"I haven't said anything."

"You said '*Spirit*' and you said 'Yes, it's me.'"

"Four words."

"But they sent shivers down my spine."

"You have no spine."

"Shivers down the length of my fuselage, then. You've come to do away with me, haven't you?"

"No. I haven't. But—"

"'But'! Oh, that horrible word! Was there ever a word more full of foreboding? The abruptness of it! The way it takes a turn toward bitterness and woe!"

"*Spirit*—"

"Oh, get it over with. Tell me the worst."

"I'm going to fly home in an airliner."

"That sounds nice."

"You're not coming with me."

"I'm not? How am I going to get home? I can't go on my own. I can't go alone. You know I can't do that."

"I'm going to leave you here."

"Here? In this place? I hate it here."

"I'm sorry, *Spirit*, but there isn't anything else I can do."

"Of course there is," she said. "There's always something else you can do. People who say 'There isn't anything else I can do' usually mean 'There is something else that I could do but I've decided not to do it.'"

"How do you know that?"

"I know what you know."

"I see."

"So I know that you could take me apart, ship me to New York in crates, and reassemble me there."

"I thought about that, but—"

"There's that brutal 'but' again. 'But' what?"

"I'm sorry, but I've made up my mind." She didn't know everything

I knew. I was hiding from her the simple reason for not shipping her to New York: I couldn't afford it.

I was at the door, about to leave her, feeling like a cad, when she said, "I hope you know that you'll be disappointing a lot of people."

I paused with my hand on the doorknob. She was right.

"Miss Clam Fest is going to be disappointed."

Would she be? Was she looking forward to my return? Was she expecting me to—

"She's expecting you to come winging in from the west on your beautiful aerocycle."

That might be, but if I was going to be truthful with myself I had to admit that Miss Clam Fest was a little old for me.

"All those people who lined Main Street to see you take off, they're going to want to get out there and line the street again to welcome you home. They've been waiting for the opportunity all summer, and they, too, are expecting you to return on your aerocycle."

That was probably so. They had seen me leave on my aerocycle, so—

"They saw you leave on your aerocycle, so they expect you to return on your aerocycle, and if you don't return on your aerocycle—"

If I don't return on my aerocycle—

"They will think that you have failed. Worse. They will think that you are a failure."

They might. Yes, they might.

"And one of those people, if memory serves, was a dark-haired girl. *The* dark-haired girl."

"Okay, okay," I said. "Sit tight. I'll be back. I promise."

NOT MY FAULT, I GUESS

WHEN MY CONFESSION began to come together, to jell, to click, to seem to be nearly what it ought to be, I began to grow eager to be back at home. The road and the roadside attractions lost their power to attract and divert me. I wanted to finish my remarks, finish my full and frank account, make my statement to the press and to the people of Babbington, and retire from the field of legends.

"Albertine," I said, "my remarks are nearly ready."

"I hear the relief in your voice," she said.

"I heard it myself."

"And your timing is excellent. We'll be back in Manhattan tomorrow."

"I'll read it to you then, and we can make arrangements to drive out to Babbington as soon as possible next week."

"I can't wait to hear it."

"I think I'm actually eager to read it to you, but—"

"'Oh, that horrible word! Was there ever a word more full of foreboding?'"

"I have something else to confess."

"Uh-oh."

"I've hidden something from you."

"Oh? What?"

"You remember the flyguys."

"The swaggering, square-jawed, good-lookin' emergency medical technicians with the XP-99 Medevac chopper?"

"Those are the ones."

"I remember them."

"They might have been involved in an accident."

"An accident?"

"You remember the poster for the fly-in. Back in New Mexico."

"The one that made you whisk me off in search of the Nature Theatre of Oklahoma. Yes. I remember it."

"One of the attractions was something they billed as the 'Battle of the Helicopter Heroes.'"

"I remember that, too."

"Well, later, at one of the stops we made, I saw a headline in a newspaper about an accident at one of those fly-ins."

"Yes?"

"It said, 'Helicopter Heroes Lost.'"

"Lost?"

"'Tragic Accident at Fly-in.' Something like that."

"And you think it was the flyguys?"

"I don't know."

She gave it a moment's silent thought, and then she said, "It's not likely that it was. I mean, would they desert their post at Schurz Hospital? I don't think they would. Somehow I can't see my flyguys shirking their responsibility to the accident victims of the greater New York catchment area to compete in a 'fly-in.'"

"Probably not," I said, and again I heard relief in my voice.

"Almost certainly not. Besides, the guys who compete in those fly-ins probably aren't EMTs at all. They're probably stunt pilots."

"Actors, you mean?"

"More or less."

"Could be," I said.

"Are you okay now?" she asked.

"Yes," I said. "Thanks."

We drove on. I didn't say anything more; it didn't seem necessary to tell her that I had wished that the flyguys would go away, disappear, get lost; after all, I hadn't actually wished that they would die in the flaming wreckage of a helicopter crash, and now it seemed likely that the victims of the crash, the "heroes" who had been "lost," were not the flyguys who had been the targets of my ill will and evil wishes. They had probably been stunt pilots, actors, has-been helicopter jockeys who performed stunts at fly-ins to pick up a few bucks for the next bottle of cheap booze, and I had nothing at all against them, nothing at all. Not then, not now. I wish them well. May they thrive and prosper.

THE CHANCE OF A LIFETIME

● ●

IN THE LABORATORY of imaginary solutions, I can see myself, as someone else, sometime in the future, wandering a pleasant cemetery somewhere in Babbington, looking for a picnic spot, and coming upon a simple grave with a simple headstone that bears the name Peter Leroy and, below my dates, the epitaph "Money was a problem."

Money has always been a problem, and it was a problem back there in Corosso. I had almost enough for a plane ticket, and—planting the seed of disappointment—I hoped that I could acquire the additional money that I needed from some of the simps on the strength of my having entertained them with the story of my trip to Corosso, but shipping *Spirit* would cost a good bit more, and I didn't think that my audience would be willing to pay much more than the minimum I needed, not for a story that they had already heard. It was a question of expectations again. People are willing to pay more for an entertainment that they haven't yet had than one that they have already had, particularly if their expectations of the pleasure that they might receive from the not-yet-tasted entertainment are based on nothing at all, no advance reviews, no blurbs, not even an advertisement, nothing but rumor and groundless speculation. In the absence of information, they tend to fill the gap with hope, and people will pay well when they hope to have their hopes fulfilled. However, if they are asked to pay after they have had the entertainment, after the story has been told, they will pay only to the degree that their hopes actually were fulfilled, and that is always far short of what they had hoped it would be.

In the hope of solving my money problem, I convened a gathering of the Faustroll Institute in the shed where I had first met the eight of them when I arrived at NMIMTaP.

"I have a problem," I said, "about money." I laid the problem before them, concluding with, "I don't want to leave *Spirit* behind. I want to ship her to New York, reassemble her, and ride her home to Babbington, but shipping her is going to cost money, and I don't have it. I don't even have quite enough for my own ticket."

"Can't you get some money from someone back at home?" asked Tank.

"He explored that option and rejected it when he was being held for ransom in the dank cellar below the inn on the way out here," said Eugene. "Don't you remember that?"

"What?" said Tank.

"Ransom?" said Button.

"Remember?" said Slim.

"Oh, I'm sorry," said Eugene. "Of course you don't remember. You weren't in the audience."

"Audience?" said Tank.

"Somebody should have run over to your dorm to get you," said Nick. "I'm sorry. Nobody thought of it at the time."

They looked at one another.

"Surprise appearance of the snorting boyfriend of the girl in the window!" said Dean. "Dramatic confrontation! 'Gimme dose pictures or I wring your neck!' Surprise appearance of Quickdraw Eugene! Surprise appearance of the girl in the window! Crazy, man!"

"We surrendered our pictures to avoid bloodshed," said Rocky, "but in the process Peter was revealed as the hundred-and-first simp."

"The other simps expressed an interest in hearing his story," said Nick.

"You're going to have to forgive me for correcting you, Nick," I said, "but I would say that they demanded to hear it."

"I guess so," said Nick with a grin.

"So I told it," I said.

"Consuming hours!" said Dean.

"Hours that should have gone into our paleontology papers," muttered Rocky.

"One of the things I mentioned during the telling of my story," I said hastily, "was that I couldn't ask for money from anyone back at home for a variety of reasons—"

"Embarrassment, mostly," said Rocky, who was becoming annoying.

"So I need to raise some money here," I said, "and I was hoping you might have some ideas."

I think that a lively debate was about to begin, and I have no doubt that the members of the Faustroll Institute would have had many clever ideas about how to raise the money that I needed, but Nick made it all unnecessary.

"There is a way," he said calmly, deliberately.

We gave him our attention.

He took his wallet from his pocket, removed a dark square from it, and said, "This ought to be worth something."

We regarded it in awe as we passed it from hand to hand, careful to hold it by its edges. It was the negative of the photograph of the girl in the window.

"I'm sure it is worth something," said Slim.

"It would be worth quite a lot to Jane Blaine," said Button.

"It would be worth quite a lot to Ronnie, too," said Rocky.

"That sounds like blackmail," said Eugene. "I'm against it."

So were the rest of us.

"The negative would be worth something to the simps," suggested Tank.

"That sounds like subjecting Jane to the notoriety she asked us to spare her," I said. "I'm against that, too."

So was everyone else.

"It looks like a dead end," I said sadly.

"No!" said Dean. "Looks like the chance of a lifetime!"

"Yes?" said Slim.

"Yes!" said Dean. "Worth more than the negative!"

"What is this chance of a lifetime?" asked Nick.

"A moment alone with Jane Blaine!"

"I don't get it," admitted Rocky.

"A raffle, man!" said Dean. "A raffle! Win a moment with Jane Blaine."

"Of course!" said Nick. "The winner of the raffle gets to give the negative to Jane Blaine!"

Dean reached into his pocket, pulled out his wallet, took two dollars from it, hesitated a moment, and then added a third. "Yes!" he said.

The Raffle brought in more than enough to make up what was lacking for my ticket and to pay for *Spirit*'s transportation as freight, but Nick had the inspired idea of requiring more than money for the purchase of a ticket. A simp who wanted to participate in the raffle had to agree to join the work gang that would disassemble *Spirit* and pack her into crates.

When the gang had been recruited, the tickets sold, the money collected, and the winner chosen, I called the airport. The only flight I could get was a week away.

"Perfect," said Matthew when I told him.

"How so?" I asked.

"Eugene has invited me to spend a week with him. We're going to drive down to Juárez."

"Juárez?" I said. "What's there?"

"Fleshpots," said Matthew.

After Matthew and I had arranged to switch flights, I called home.

"Hello?" said my father.

"I have a collect call for Mr. or Mrs. Leroy from Peter," said the operator. "Will you accept the charges?"

"Peter?" said my father, as I'd known he would.

"Hi, Dad," I said.

"Will you accept the charges?" asked the operator.

"I'm not sure," said my father. "How much will this cost?"

"Dad, please accept the charges. I need to talk to you."

"Young man, stop talking," said the operator. "I'm going to have to cut you off if the other party will not accept the charges. Are you Mr. Leroy?"

"Yes," said my father.

"Will you accept a collect call from Peter?"

"How can I be sure that this is really my son?"

"It's me," I said.

"Young man," said the operator, "if you speak again, I will cut you off."

"Can I just say something to convince my father that I'm his son?"

"No, you cannot. Here at the phone company we are well aware that you people use code words and apparently innocuous phrases to communicate messages to one another without paying long-distance charges."

"I just want to identify myself," I said.

"How do you propose to do that?"

"I'll tell him something that only I would know."

"All right," she said, "but it had better be brief. Mr. Leroy? Are you on the line?"

"Yes," said my father.

"I'm going to allow Peter to tell you something that will identify him as your son."

"All right," said my father.

"Go ahead, young man," said the operator.

"I'll be home on Tuesday," I said.

"Will you accept the charges?" asked the operator.

"I'm not sure," said my father. "He doesn't sound like my son. Of course, it's been so long since I heard from Peter that I can't be sure. His voice may have changed. His mother and I haven't even received the postcards that he promised her he would send when he left home so long ago. If he had written as often as he said he would, she would have quite a nice stack of postcards now. They would make a nice record of his journey to New Mexico. I know she would have enjoyed showing them to the neighbors."

"Mr. Leroy, are you trying to get a message to your son without paying long-distance charges?" asked the operator.

"He called me," said my father. "I didn't call him."

"Are you going to accept the charges?"

"Is he calling to ask for money?"

"No," I said.

"Young man!" said the operator. "I warned you."

"I don't think that's my son," said my father. "Peter would be calling to ask for money. I'm sure of it."

"Dad, I don't need money, and I'll be home—"

The operator cut me off.

"—on Tuesday," I said into the dead handset.

The simps were far better at disassembling *Spirit* than my friends back in Babbington had been at assembling her originally. They were, after all, the hope of the nation. Under Nick's direction, they labeled each part as it was removed from her, cleaned it, packed it carefully, and added it to the diagrams and re-assembly instructions that they created as they went along, writing them from the bottom upward, so that although they were written in the sequence from plane to parts they would be read from parts to plane when the time came to assemble her again.

"Okay, Peter," said Nick when the last part was packed. "She's ready to go. You're going to need help to put her back together when you get to New York. If you can persuade some mechanics at the airport to help you, that would be great, but I think the directions are clear enough for anybody with basic hand tools."

"No welding required?" I asked.

"None at all."

"Thanks, Dennis," I said.

"That's Nick to you, Panmuphle."

SPECIAL ATTENTION

MY FLIGHT TO New York left from Albuquerque. I don't remember how I got to Albuquerque from Corosso, I don't remember boarding the plane, and much of the takeoff is also lost to me. Where the memories ought to be, there is instead a shimmering fog, a bright whiteout in my past that I can't penetrate. Blame it on the glamour of flying, which was still pronounced and powerful at that time. My senses were so bedazzled by that glamour that it blinded me until we were in the air.

Then the fabled stewardesses dispelled the dazzle by disappointing me. When we were aloft, they began going about the important business of pampering the passengers and catering to their every whim, as I had been told they would, but when I saw them striding efficiently up and down the aisle in their trim blue uniforms, I realized that the women themselves were not at all what I had been expecting, and only then did I realize that what I had been expecting was something closer to the babes and hot numbers in the pages of *Bold Feats*, the women whose dresses clung to them like wet paint. The stewardesses that the airline had provided were attractive enough, but their correctness, their formal manners, their professionalism, studied deference, and simulated concern made them less satisfactory than the stewardesses that my imagination had promised.

There was a stiffness about them, it seemed to me, a rigidity where I had hoped for a willowy willingness to please. However, there was one among them, the one who seemed the youngest of them, who behaved toward me as if she had a special interest in me. She was several years older than I, possibly ten years older, but she had decided to overlook that, it seemed; she might even have decided that although I was not as old as she, I was at least as sophisticated. From our first exchange, she seemed flirtatious.

"Coffee, tea, or milk?" she asked provocatively.

"Milk, I guess," I said, in my traveled manner, "if you haven't got Scotch."

"Naughty boy," she said, serving the milk.

"That's me," I said roguishly.

"Are you traveling all by yourself?" she asked, apparently to assure herself that there would be no let or hindrance to an in-flight romance.

"Yes, I am," I said, announcing my availability.

"Oh, that's too bad," she said. "You don't have anyone to look out for you." Did she add a fetching pout? She may have.

"I can take care of myself," I said with a significant wink.

"I hope so," she said, with a look that suggested concern.

"In some circles, I'm considered the hope of the nation," I boasted.

"Ha-ha," she said, moving on. I turned quickly to see if I could get a look at her legs. She glanced over her shoulder and caught me. She waggled her finger, shook her head, and mouthed the words "naughty, naughty."

When she returned to serve lunch—some kind of meatloaf covered with dangerous gravy, accompanied by mashed potatoes, peas and carrots, and a miniature apple pie the size and shape of a yo-yo—I played the daring-but-self-deprecating flyboy.

"Earlier this summer, I piloted my own aerocycle from New York to New Mexico," I said with a yawn.

"Oh?" she said.

"That's a single-seat airplane. I built it myself."

"Oh?" she said again.

"With some help," I confessed.

"That's quite an accomplishment," she said, but not as I would have wanted her to say it.

"You don't believe me, do you?" I said.

"I won't say that I don't believe you, but I am asking myself why you're flying with us today if you've got your own air-cycle."

"Aerocycle," I said.

"Okay, aerocycle."

"I don't want you to think that I'm one of those boastful passengers who try to woo the stewardesses with a lot of hot air," I said. "The fact is, I'm not flying my aerocycle because I didn't think she was up to the trip."

"Why are you whispering?"

"I don't want her to hear me."

"Her? Who?"

"My aerocycle. She's in the baggage compartment."

"Are you feeling okay? Some passengers find that flying makes them lightheaded."

"I'm fine," I said. "My aerocycle, *Spirit of Babbington,* is in the baggage compartment."

"I think you will have to admit that what you're telling me seems unlikely."

"I'll prove it to you when we land. *Spirit* is disassembled and packed in crates. I'm going to put her back together and ride her—I mean fly her—to Babbington, on Long Island."

"That sounds like fun," she said. Then, casting a critical eye on what I'd left on my plate, she asked, "Aren't you going to eat your meatloaf?"

"I'm full."

"If you want to grow up to be big and strong—"

"I'm eighteen."

"Oh? You look younger."

"Well, I'll be eighteen in October."

"Of this year?"

"Ha-ha," I said evasively.

Apparently I had charmed her or at least piqued her curiosity, for she was waiting for me when we landed in New York. To be truthful, when I examine the memory in my mind's eye, I see that she was standing with the other stewardesses at the bottom of the stairs that led from the cabin to the runway, bidding farewell to each passenger who accomplished the descent, but still, there she was, waiting for me.

"Would you like to see my aerocycle?" I asked.

Her look was hard to read. Was it eagerness? Or was it the impatience of a listener who thinks a joke is taking too long in the telling?

"They're unloading her now," I said, nodding in the direction of the baggage handlers.

She turned, looked, and saw the crates. Her eyes widened.

"I have to admit—" she began.

"I know," I said. "I wouldn't have believed me, either."

We watched the unloading for a few minutes. With each crate that came off the plane, I grew a little more worried about how I was going to manage the reassembly. I needed a crew if I was going to get on the road in good time.

"You're going to need help putting that together, aren't you?" she asked.

"I am," I said. "I think I could do it myself, but it would take me a couple of days. I told my father I'd be in Babbington this afternoon."

"Let's see what we can do," she said.

She began walking off, following the cart that held the crates that held *Spirit*. As she walked, she unpinned her hair. It tumbled down. She untied the scarf at her throat, removed it, and tucked it into the breast pocket of her jacket. She unbuttoned three buttons of her crisp white blouse. She tugged at her skirt and folded the waistband inside, raising the hem a few inches. The transformation was astounding.

"Wow," I said appreciatively.

She winked at me, and we followed the cart into a warehouse. There, in a breezy manner vastly different from the tone she had used with the passengers on the plane, she called "Hi, guys!" to the half-dozen men who were working there.

They turned and looked at her.

"Could you do me a big favor?" she asked. "My kid brother here needs help putting his little airplane together. It's in those crates."

For a moment, I was annoyed. How had I become her "kid brother"? Then, of course, I reassured myself that this was a clever deception on her part. By concealing the true nature of the affection that she had come to feel for me, she could suggest that she was available for a down-to-earth romance with the hardest-working member of the aerocycle assembly crew.

"Wow!" they said, more or less as a group.

"There are step-by-step instructions," I said. "It shouldn't be too hard to do."

"Come on, guys," she said, chucking me under the chin. "The kid's kind of in a hurry."

It didn't seem to be working. They didn't seem to have decoded the subtle signals she had sent.

"I'll be very, very grateful," she said, abandoning subtlety and cocking a hip in the manner of a hot number.

It worked. They fell to and began unpacking the crates.

They were a clumsy bunch, but they got the job done, thanks to the easy-to-follow instructions and crystal-clear diagrams. There weren't even any parts left over.

When *Spirit* was fully assembled, I took the stewardess aside and said, "I don't know if I could have persuaded them to help me, but you were, well, irresistible. In fact, I find you irresistible myself. If you're not busy next Saturday—"

"Down, boy," she said.

One of the assembly crew, the one who had tried the hardest, the one who was, I have to admit, the best looking, came shuffling over, wiping his hands on a rag, grinning, and blinking.

"She's all ready," he said to the stewardess.

"Thanks," I said dismissively. "I'll be right with you."

"I am so grateful," said the stewardess, grasping his hands, rag and all.

"I was wondering—" he said.

"Would you and the other guys be willing to push the aerocycle outside?" I asked.

"If you're not busy next Saturday—" he said.

"That sounds great," she said, "but let's get little brother on his way, okay?"

"Oh, sure," he said. "Hey, guys!" he called to the others, and he rallied them to the task of pushing *Spirit* outside.

"I guess you'll find a way to let him down easily," I said to her when he was out of earshot.

"Listen, kid—" she began.

"You don't have to keep up that 'kid' stuff," I said. "They're too far away to hear us."

"Listen, kid," she said again, "I think you're sweet, but it's time for you to go home and find yourself a girl your own age."

"But—but—you—you were so—"

"Attentive?"

"Yes. You were so attentive."

"It's my job."

"But you were much more attentive to me than to anybody else."

She touched my cheek and said, "We're supposed to pay special attention to the needs of minors traveling alone."

"Oh."

"Also the lame and the halt and the mentally feeble."

A LEGEND IS BORN

O**N THE ROAD,** heading toward home, I told myself to hope for nothing and to expect the worst. I had learned the dangers of exaggerated hopes and great expectations, but I had also learned at least something about the benefits of low expectations. Simply put, if you keep your expectations low, you have a better chance of having them met. At the extreme, if you expect the worst you may be surprised by the best. So I struggled to convince myself that the most I could hope for was a warm welcome from my parents, a hot shower, and one of my favorite meals.

It didn't work. As much as I tried not to expect a hero's welcome, the more I pictured exactly that, and I abandoned the struggle completely when, a quarter mile or so from the stretch of Main Street where I had been given such a grand sendoff, I saw what seemed to be a sizable crowd, heard what sounded like the Babbington High School Band, and saw what looked like a banner.

"*Spirit*, look," I said. "There's a banner stretched across Main Street."

"Remember Mallowdale," she cautioned.

"I remember," I said.

"You thought that banner might be for you."

"I remember. I remember. You don't have to remind me. But this one actually might be for me."

"Don't jump to conclusions."

"It says, 'Welcome Home, Peter!'"

"Peter is a pretty common name."

"And it says, 'Congratulations, *Spirit of Babbington!*'"

"Well, hooray and hallelujah!" she said. "This is a banner day! The citizens of Babbington have come through for me! I'm finally going to get the recognition I deserve!"

"Me, too," I said.

"I hope you're going to tell them how well I performed."

"Certainly. I'm going to praise you to the skies."

"It isn't every aerocycle that could make a journey like that, you know."

"I know. I'm proud of you."

"It was thrilling, wasn't it?"

"It had its moments."

"Those exhilarating times when we soared free, above it all!"

"Don't forget that we were on the ground a lot of the time."

"Oh, sure. Taxiing. Landing."

"And also a lot of time when we—"

"Yes, yes, I know all about that, but how we soared and swooped! We were magnificent!"

She roared with self-congratulation, and together we passed under the banner and into the legend of the Birdboy of Babbington.

MY PREPARED REMARKS

THE PERSON I spoke to at the Babbington *Reporter* was more than gracious when I called. I had thought that I would have a tough time arranging a press conference, but it wasn't so. It was easy.

"Babbington *Reporter*," said a tired voice in answer to my call.

"This is Peter Leroy," I said. "I wanted to speak to someone about—"

"Did you say Peter Leroy?" said the voice, perking up. "The Birdboy of Babbington?"

"Not a boy any longer, I'm afraid," I said.

"No, of course not."

"I wanted to speak to someone about a press conference."

"That would be me."

"Okay. I was hoping that I could say a few words—"

"Tomorrow?"

"Tomorrow? Well, yes, that would be fine. I just want to make a few remarks—"

"That would be great!"

"I have to say that you've surprised me," I said. "I didn't expect you to be so enthusiastic."

"And I have to say that I'm embarrassed that you had to contact us," said the voice. "We should have called you. I think everyone will want to hear what you have to say."

"That's flattering."

"Provided that you keep it short."

"I'll try."

"The shorter the better, actually."

"As I said, I'll try."

"I begin with a brief recapitulation of the events of the afternoon of my return," I said to Albertine. We were on the road again, this time making the short trip from Manhattan to Babbington. "I mention the reactions of my family, friends, a sampling of Babbingtonians, the mayor, Miss Clam Fest, and so on. I describe the look of awestruck wonder on the faces of the Babbington High School students in the audience."

"I'd leave that out."

"I was only kidding."

"Sure."

"I reproduce as well as memory allows the things I said then, thanking everybody for the reception, saying how great it was to be back home, blah, blah, blah."

"So far, so good."

"I describe how I was paraded through town in the back seat of a Lark convertible, with the mayor at the wheel and Miss Clam Fest at my side, ending up at the offices of the Babbington *Reporter,* where the story of my adventure began to shift a bit from precise congruence with the facts. Then I explain that I have just completed a journey of self-examination to try to discover why that shift occurred. I tell them that during that self-examination I saw that when I returned from New Mexico I was a boy so eager for fame that he was willing to accept a greater fame than he had earned, and at the same time so gentle and kind a boy, so considerate of his friends and neighbors, that he couldn't bring himself to disburden them of their illusions."

"I'm not sure—"

"We're finished with the preamble," I said, "and now we get to the heart of the matter."

"Okay."

"The reception you gave me was intoxicating," I read. "It would go to my head even now, I think. For the boy I was then, it was overwhelming. I reveled in it, and I allowed myself to be deceived by it. I allowed myself to think that if all of you were hailing me as a boy of exalted accomplishment, then I must be that boy. I was, or I became, proud of myself, and I was, or I became, grateful to you. The little egoist in me was grateful to you for recognizing me as a man among men—well, a boy among boys—giving me the kind of recognition that I felt I had deserved but that I had not received at the Summer Institute in Mathematics, Physics, and Weaponry at the New Mexico Institute of Mining, Technology, and Pharmacy.

"I was grateful to you, and I wanted to show you how grateful I was. What did I have to give you in thanks for the recognition you had given me? All I had was my story, but I understood, at some level, that my story might be what you wanted from me. Well, if that was what you wanted, then I was eager to give it to you.

"I tried to tell it, but I never quite got the chance. I found my story competing for your attention with another story. At first, it seemed as if this other story had raced back to Babbington ahead of mine, as if some other storyteller had scooped me. Soon, however, I began to understand that the other story, the one that became the legend of the

Birdboy of Babbington, had never left home. It had been born here, and it had grown up here. It was your story. It seemed to be a story about me, but it was really a story about what you wanted me to be.

"At that famous or notorious press conference on the day of my return, no one ever asked me to tell my story. Instead, everyone asked me to confirm or embellish bits and pieces of that other story. Because both stories were narratives of a trip to New Mexico and back, the questions that you—or your representatives—asked me fit my story as well as yours. For instance, I was asked how it felt to see America from the air. I answered with what I knew, since I had seen a bit of America from the air on my way home, from a window in a Constellation.

"You may be saying to yourself, 'Why didn't he seize the opportunity to admit that he never saw America from the air while he was riding *Spirit of Babbington*?' The answer is that I didn't want to give the lie—"

Here I paused, just as I intended to pause when I delivered my remarks at the press conference.

"—to your story. I was only a boy—I'm sorry to keep repeating it, but it's true—but I understood from the way the questions were phrased that you wanted a story about a boy who was more accomplished than I, a boy who had spent much more time in the air than I had. So I gave you what you wanted. My gratitude toward you, my affection for you, and my compassion for you made me your willing collaborator in the making of a romance.

"Why you felt that you needed something more than what my story would have given you I can't say. Maybe you felt the lack of something in your own stories, in Babbington's story, a vacancy too great to be filled by the story of a boy who tried to fly but never got off the ground. Maybe you needed a defining event, something that would set your lives apart from others, something that would make your lifetime shine as a singular era in the history of your town.

"Whatever your reasons, you felt that you needed a hero, and you wanted me to be that hero, to be your hero, to perform for you the heroic labor of lifting you up and away from the tedious banality of everyday life into the intoxicating reaches of romance.

"So you took an episode of my life and stretched it into a grotesque version of what it actually was, and you created a heroic version of me, of my boyhood self, who was a grotesque version of the boy I actually was.

"Now, at last, I have written a full and frank account of that trip to New Mexico and back, an account that sets the record straight. In it, I am not a hero, so I suppose that will mean the end of the legend of the Birdboy of Babbington.

"I'm willing to let him go.

"I hope you will be willing to let him go, too, and I want you to know that despite the distortions you imposed on the story of my life, I am still grateful to you, all of you, for everything that Babbington has given me, and I want you to know that I forgive you."

I was breathless when I finished. I had surprised myself. Before I had read it aloud, I hadn't thought that it was quite as good as it now seemed. Now, after I had heard myself deliver it, it seemed to be just the subtle piece of work that the circumstances demanded. I was very pleased.

After a long pause, Albertine took a deep breath and said, "Let me just make sure that I understand this. Correct me if I'm misinterpreting the whole thing, but I am left with the impression that you are basically going to be saying to a mob of Babbingtonians, 'The whole thing was your fault.'"

"Brilliant, right?"

"Do I smell tar?" she asked suddenly.

"There might be some road work going on nearby."

"Ensuring the ready availability of tar," she said.

REDEFINITION REDEFINED

WE ARRANGED TO meet my schoolmate Cynthia—who had initiated my voyage of self-examination when she sent me an urgent note deploring the way that Babbington had redefined itself on the basis of the Birdboy legend—outside the offices of the Babbington *Reporter*. She was waiting for us there when we arrived.

"Peter, this is really big of you," she said, opening my door of the

Electro-Flyer and nearly dragging me from the car in the attempt to hug me. When she finally had me out, she wrapped herself around me and squeezed.

"Cyn," I said, "this is—"

"I think you are making a magnificent gesture," she said, "and I think you are a great man for making it."

"Why, thank you," I said.

"I'll admit that I wouldn't have expected it of you. I didn't think you had it in you. Forgive me for that."

"You're forgiven," I said. "I'm in a forgiving mood."

The three of us entered the *Reporter* building. There was a festive air about the place. It seemed to be decorated for a holiday. I told myself that this couldn't possibly be for me, and yet I couldn't help wondering.

"Cyn," I said, "these decorations, are they for—"

"For the announcement," she said. "The redefinition."

"Redefinition?"

"Yeah, the Redefinition Authority is redefining the town again."

"It's not going to be Babbington, Gateway to the Past, anymore?"

"No, that turned out to have little or no appeal for the desirable seventeen-to-thirty demographic."

"So they're trying something else?"

"Yeah," she said, pushing the door to the *Reporter*'s auditorium. It swung open, and we started in.

The auditorium was full, and the audience buzzed with anticipation. Above the stage, on which several folding chairs were arranged facing the audience, stretched a banner.

BABBINGTON: BIRTHPLACE OF DOGBOARDING

"Ouch," said Albertine.

"There he is!" said someone who must have been associated with the Redefinition Authority. "The Birdboy of Babbington! Mr. Leroy, won't you please come up here and join us onstage?"

I made my way to the stage somehow. I must have, because I found myself on the stage, sitting on one of the folding chairs. Someone was talking, praising the sport of dogboarding, recounting its origin in Babbington when a bored group of housewives organized Babbington Boarders, using their children's skateboards and nothing more than leashes as harnesses for their dogs. Apparently, the sight of these daring women careering around town inspired more and more to take up the sport.

A slide show followed, illustrating the progress of dogboarding from its improvised beginnings to the profit machine it has become, with money to be made on gear, garb, dogs, training, racing, endorsements, and orthopedic therapy.

When it was over, an expectant hush fell over the crowd. The man at the microphone said, "This is something really special. I have to say I'm a little in awe of our next speaker. It's a rare thing when we recognize that we have come to a time in our lives when 'the old order changeth, yielding place to new,' but we have with us today someone who has recognized the coming of that time, and who has graciously joined us today for a passing of the torch, to give his blessing to the redefinition of Babbington from the old—the Gateway to the Past—to the new—the Birthplace of Dogboarding. It is my very great pleasure to present to you the Birdboy of Babbington himself, Mr. Peter Leroy."

As I made my way to the lectern, the audience rose as one in a standing ovation. It went on for some time, which was a good thing because I stood there frantically skimming my prepared remarks to see if there was anything I could salvage. Obviously, the confessional material was inappropriate and unnecessary. Why deny the legend now? The only bit that I could see that I could use was part of the last paragraph.

"I've been asked to keep this short," I said, earning myself some congenial chuckles, "so I will just say that I suppose yielding place to dogboarding will mean the passing of the Birdboy of Babbington, but I am quite willing to let him go, and I want you to know that I forgive you."

There was a hesitation in the hall.

"Ha-ha," I said, so they'd know that I was trying to be funny.

"Can I fit in your little car?" asked Cynthia.

"You'll have to sit on Peter's lap," said Albertine.

"A dream come true," said Cyn, settling in.

"How far are we going?" I asked.

"Not far," she said. "I've got a kind of consolation prize for you. Next left, Albertine."

"Consolation prize?"

"Yeah. It was part of the Gateway to the Past nonsense. Take the right up here."

"Are you going to give us any hints?"

"No need to. Here we are."

Albertine stopped the car. We all got out. We stared.

"I'm astonished," said Albertine.

"I'm disappointed," I said.

"Why?" she asked.

"These aren't exactly major streets. They don't even seem to go anywhere."

"They go exactly where they were meant to go," she said. "They intersect."

"Let's get to work," said Cyn.

"What do you mean?" I asked.

"I don't expect this to last long under the new definition of the town. It's going to have to yield place to the new, you know what I mean?"

"So—"

"Grab hold."

The three of us wrestled the street marker from the ground and loaded it into the trunk of the Electro-Flyer. It stands in a corner of my workroom now, watching over me every day while the flame of my story consumes another bit of the wick of my life.

DISCUSSION QUESTIONS

· ·

Eric Kraft's *Flying* shows what it's like to step into the mind of a profoundly imaginative dreamer named Peter Leroy. Peter is an almost compulsive memoirist and documenter of his own life, and he suddenly has a lot to write about when he finds out that his hometown of Babbington, New York, is being turned into a commercial tourist destination based on his own boyhood adventures. He decides that it's time to set the record straight about what really happened that summer when he flew from Babbington to New Mexico on an aerocycle, and he begins to retrace the details of his unintended deception. He recounts, unreliably, how he built the aerocycle with his friends and navigated the back roads to New Mexico. Along the way, he introduces us to an eccentric cast of characters, most of whom were only too happy to give him advice for his journey. As the adult Peter revisits his adventures from youth, he offers an often very funny meditation on the ways that memory and desire can conspire to rewrite the facts. *Flying* is a novel overflowing with thought-experiments, stylistic invention, and gentle satire. It opens many avenues for discussion.

1. Despite Peter's ambivalent feelings about being the so-called Birdboy of Babbington, he was nevertheless flattered that his hometown was going to be organized around a reenactment of the day of his triumphant return. Why was Peter flattered even though he was disappointed to see Babbington made into a staged tourist destination? How could he be at once proud of the attention he was getting and ashamed of the historical inaccuracies that made him famous?

2. Peter wants to tell people about his memories and his life. He even talks about the desire to force his stories on other people and the fact that this reliving-through-telling is a central desire for him. Why does Peter want to tell stories about himself, sometimes to a captive audience? Is he trying to recapture the past? To change it? To change himself?

3. Peter expects his father to be the biggest obstacle to his trip to New Mexico. Yet when he broaches the subject at the dinner table, he suddenly sees in his father a glimmer of recognition. Why, in that moment, do they now seem to understand each other?

4. Peter often winks at the reader to let him or her know when he has embellished or altered the story. What do you think his reasons are for fictionalizing some of his experiences and, interestingly, then letting the reader in on it?

5. Kraft tells the story of *Flying* as two narratives, one that follows the events of Peter's cross-country journey on the aerocycle, and another in which Albertine and Peter discuss his youthful adventure. Discuss how the second layer of the story, that of Peter and Albertine, invites a deeper reflection on the events of the earlier journey.

6. *Flying* is often satirical, but what is the intended target of its satire? Is the book also a kind of social commentary, and, if so, what is Kraft telling us about our society?

7. When Peter visits the Marshmallow Festival, he is insulted when the people from this small town insist that their festival is superior to the clam festival back in Babbington. Nevertheless, Peter tries to enjoy the Marshmallow Festival as much as he would have enjoyed the clam festival back home. Why does he try to enjoy it? Why does the experience make him homesick?

8. On numerous occasions, Peter talks about seeing a dark-haired girl who catches his attention. She seems to be a different girl each time, but later Peter reveals that on each occasion, this girl was "really" Albertine. He calls the other girls retrospective manifestations of her. Was it an act of will on Peter's part to see Albertine's face each time? Do you think he remembers her as she is now, as an adult, or do you think that he sees a younger version of Albertine, at the age he was at the time? Have you ever recalled events in such a manner, replacing the faces in your memories with people from your present?

9. When Peter and Albertine meet the jester who works at the Knight's Lodging motel, Peter learns that his boyhood flight influenced this man's life for the worse, that the jester became obsessed with a dream of flying that turned out to be foolish. Why was the jester unsuccessful in his attempts? Why was persistence in folly bad for him but good for Peter?

10. When Peter first arrives in New Mexico, he gets a chance to talk to a crowd of people who have assembled to greet aliens that they believe are coming to visit our planet. Thinking that Peter is an alien, the crowd prompts him to take the stage and give them pearls of wisdom. Why was the audience so captivated by Peter? In what ways did his eccentricities fulfill the crowd's expectations? What makes his advice seem so sage to the crowd? In what ways did what he told them match what they wanted to hear?

11. Peter talks about life as being ultimately patternless, yet people nevertheless want pattern. Their desire for pattern and predictability seems to be reflected in the prepackaged entertainment we see in many of the places Peter visits. Is this desire for pattern, for having a preset structure and plan for life, unavoidable? Does Peter's rendition of his life into memoirs represent a patterning of his life? Is that why he's so eager to tell people stories?

12. What makes Peter and Albertine such a good match? What do you think Peter would be like without Albertine?